# The Short Story in a Polish Context

# The Short Story in a Polish Context

## Classic Short Fiction from the Seventeenth to Twentieth Centuries

Edited and with Commentary by Oscar E. Swan

PIASA BOOKS
New York

Published by PIASA Books
The Polish Institute of Arts and Sciences of America
208 E. 30th Street
New York, NY 10016

http://www.piasa.org/pb.html



ISBN 978-0-940962-17-0

Library of Congress Control Number: 2024931502

Publication of this book has been aided by the University of Pittsburgh

Printed in the United States of America

# CONTENTS

# PREFACE

*The Short Story in a Polish Context* contains stories well worth reading on their own, but whose enjoyment can be enhanced by understanding the specific social, political, or historical context in which they were written. The stories selected are ones judged by the editor to be not only good but also rich in analytical possibility. Stories are listed in roughly chronological order, and to a greater or lesser extent, they chronicle Polish literary-cultural history over the last four centuries as reflected through the medium of shorter prose fiction.

Extensive endnotes following most stories have two aims, the first being to help the reader get a fuller understanding of the stories by pointing out things that otherwise might be missed, if only for a lack of familiarity with the Polish cultural context. A second, aspirational, aim is to help orient student readers in the basic analytic approaches, processes, concepts, and literary terms that come into play when reading, discussing, or writing about a short story in general, whether Polish or otherwise. Readers without such interest may freely skip the commentary, or read it selectively, for even without it they will acquire a good idea of Polish short fiction as it developed from its beginnings through the end of the twentieth century.

I have left out the works of many authors who would be covered in a book whose main concern was documenting what was being written or read in Poland in the realm of the short story at a particular historical moment. Many or most of the stories selected here, having withstood the test of time, belong to what could be called the "Polish short-story canon," and prospective teachers will find more than enough material here for organizing a university course on "The Polish Short Story," possibly supplemented by works of their own choosing. Many will wish to extend coverage into the twenty-first century, where a good many authors are active and deserving of attention. One is fortunate in this regard to look forward to the publication of Antonia Lloyd-Jones's *The Penguin Book of Polish Short Stories,* in which several authors representative of the present century are represented.

*Note on orthography.* Different translators have different approaches to rendering Polish proper names in a way that makes it easier for non-Poles to guess the proper pronunciation, including not doing anything at all. I have not been overly concerned with consistency in this regard but have let individual translators make their own decisions.

Oscar E. Swan<br>*Pittsburgh, 2023*

# The Short Story in a Polish Context

# INTRODUCTION

## What Is a Short Story?

A short story is a brief work of fiction, complete in itself, which typically can be read in a single sitting. Anything fictional that meets that general definition can be called a short story. If a work of fiction exceeds the length that can be comfortably read in a single sitting (but, say, in two or three sittings), it can be called a "long short story" which, at its outer length, transitions into what can better be called a novella, or a short novel.

The brevity of the short-story form means that authors tend to resort to various means of economical expression to save space, one of the most frequent being the technique of starting the narration with the action already in progress. Another is for the author not to spell everything out but to rely on readers' ability to fill in the blanks of a story for themselves, sometimes from the merest of suggestive hints. For that reason, short stories are best read slowly, with attention paid to the significance of each detail. Speed-reading is inimical to the nature of the short story form, and even if a story can be read in a "single sitting," it often takes many careful readings of a well-crafted story for one to begin to appreciate the fullness of the author's talent and intent.

A short story can attempt to evoke nothing more than an atmosphere or appearance of a place; it can sketch a particularly interesting event, person, or character type; or it can present an especially poignant or significant moment in a person's life. More often, however, a short story will be plot- and action-based, possessing a structure depending on a usually small set of characters and a "problem" to be resolved among them. Such a plot will typically involve an initial setting followed by one or more twists and turns in it until, by the end of the story, a resolution is reached. Often the resolution will be nothing more than an ironic twist or a surprise outcome. More often, however, the story will have both a resolution and a Point, Effect, or Moral, reflecting the underlying purpose of the author in writing the story. Most stories in the present collection are of the plot-based variety, and most contain a main point that the author wishes to impart. Another way of putting this is that most short stories here have an underlying agenda that asks to be discovered.

Short narrative forms, including myths, legends, folk tales, fairy tales, and fables, have been around for as long as human civilization. All these subgenres first developed orally and were transmitted that way until the spread of writing.

Particularly important in the development of the modern short story are the *anecdote* and the *tale,* which have been around in published form since the late Middle Ages, well-known authors of tales being Giovanni Bocaccio (1313–1375) in Italy or Geoffrey Chaucer (ca.1340–1400) in England. An anecdote is a short, entertaining, and usually humorous story, best delivered orally and in an informal setting—around the dinner table, say, or by the fireside. A tale is typically longer and usually placed in the past and often in an exotic setting with larger-than-life characters, not infrequently featuring the intervention of magical or supernatural forces. A well-known example would be the collection of Middle Eastern folk tales known under the title "The Arabian Nights." Anecdotes and tales have no "agenda," no greater ambition than to hold readers' or listeners' attention for as long as it takes to tell them.

The short story is a more sophisticated literary form than the anecdote or tale. It is more complex and more carefully constructed, and it has more intellectual heft. It is more ambitious in that, as noted, it usually contains an underlying point that the author wishes to make. Short stories most often involve realistically drawn contemporary characters that one might know or identify with. After it is finished, a short story frequently leaves the reader or listener with something to think about, whereas anecdotes or tales typically do not.

The short story reached maturity as a widely practiced literary form as late as the mid-nineteenth century, its development being closely tied to the rise of mass print media and a corresponding readership. Magazines and newspapers offered a convenient format in which a short story could be featured as a lure to customers, at the same time providing a means by which short-story writers could earn money or, for the better ones, even a livelihood. As the short story gained in popularity, periodicals began to appear devoted exclusively to them. Today, although some magazines do print short stories, many or most short story writers meet their readership in the form of a published book containing compilations of stories by one or more authors.

*Plot-Based Short Stories.* Most short stories are "plot-based," meaning that their structure consists of identifiable points and movements through which the central issue of the story progresses on the way to its eventual resolution. This is especially true of the short story in its "classic," mid-nineteenth-century form. No rule says that a short story must contain every structural part listed here, nor must the pieces occur in the exact order given. Nevertheless, extrapolating from examples of the genre over time, one may identify what one may call the typical parts of a plot-based short story, which are the following:

the *Pre-History*
the *Development*
the *Turning Point*, leading to:
the *Complication* or *Entanglement.*
the *Crisis Point,* initiating:
the *Crisis,* leading to

the *Climax*
the *Aftermath* or *Denouement*
the *Post-History*

Most frequently, the Pre- and Post-History will be omitted and left to the reader's imagination. Accordingly, a short story will usually begin with a *Development* already in place. At some point, a significant turn of events intrudes on the Development in the form of the *Turning Point*, setting the story off in a more clearly focused direction, a stage called the *Complication* or *Entanglement*. The *Crisis Point* amounts to a turning point in the Complication. It sets in motion one or more events, often in rapid succession, leading to a resolution of the story's main issue, the resolution being known as the *Climax*. The *Aftermath* or *Denouement* briefly describes the situation resulting from the climax; it provides an emotional letdown and serves to tie up any loose ends or to resolve any unexplained mysteries.

The traditional parts of a short story may be summarized graphically as follows, where the angle of the arrows on the "*y*-axis" represents an increase in dramatic tension as the story progresses until finally being released in the Climax:

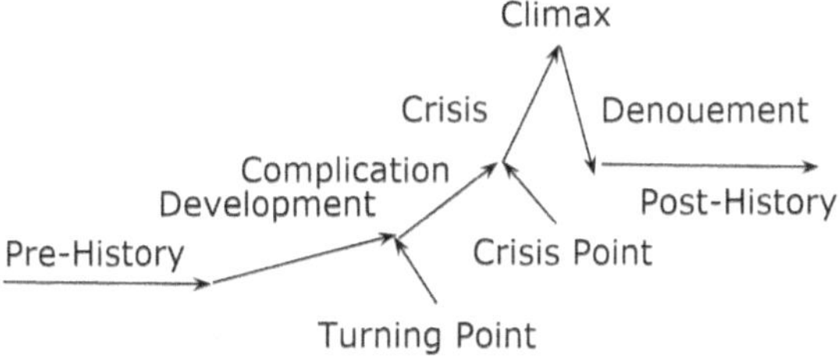


One may easily identify the traditional short-story parts in the following brief work by Wiktor Woroszylski (for more on him, see the section following the story):

## The Watch

I wouldn't say that Mother and Father really disliked Roman, or that they took a dim view of our marriage. On the contrary, they were rather impressed by their educated, well-bred son-in-law, and Father gladly discussed international politics with him.

One thing, however, my parents could never forgive Roman—his failure to share their reverence for "things." A material possession, in our household, meant everything; it was the measure of attained wealth and social standing, the repository of ambitions and dreams, the symbol of a happy family life, the goal and the crowning glory of all efforts. A possession was a moral ideal, character was judged by the quality of a person's possessions, and his attitude toward possessions determined whether or not he could be trusted. We lived simply. Father had no expensive vices; he didn't smoke or drink. But after almost every payday a new object appeared in our room: a silver sugar bowl, a pillow, a lamp. On the thirty-fifth anniversary of his employment at the factory, the workers' committee gave Father a phonograph—and Father was proud to have been worthy of such a splendid gift.

Roman never ridiculed this passion of my parents—he considered it understandable and natural—but he was just a little too quick in taking for granted each new acquisition, or, once in a while, he would absent-mindedly bump into some of the objects arranged around the room. What's more, he sometimes spent money on flowers or theater tickets, and when Mother and Father would begin enumerating all the "lasting" things he could have bought instead, he just shrugged his shoulders.

When, during the First World War, Roman was called up. Father gave him his old watch—a very good watch, foreign-made. Roman thanked him, put the watch in his pocket, and said nothing more about it. But a few weeks later Father spoke up at dinner:

"Mark my words, he's bound to lose it somewhere in the trenches."

More time went by, and then again Father remarked,

"A sloppy fellow, that hubby of yours. I'd bet my boots someone swiped his watch without him knowing a thing about it."

After this, there were long daily discussions—that one didn't really need a watch at the front, and that a reasonable man would have left it at home. And besides, there were watches and watches; one should realize this, but, regrettably, some people didn't seem to. And, surely, there must be something behind the fact that Roman never mentioned in his letters whether the watch was running well, whether perhaps it needed fixing, or even whether he still had it

A year later Roman came home on leave. When asked about the watch, he took it out of his pocket and put it on the table.

"You know," said my father, "we're adults, all of us; we understand what war is. Should, God forbid, anything happen to you …

"Dad!" I exclaimed.

"Father is right," said Roman indifferently. I'll leave the watch at home."

You see!" cried Father, delighted. "Roman is more sensible than you."

Roman went back to the front, and a month later we were notified that he had been killed in action.

I haven't spoken to Mother and Father since. I didn't move out of the house, for I had no place to go, but I ate alone and hated to touch any of their things. Mother cried all the time, and Father, seeing this, would leave the house at once. It was then that he started drinking. The habit developed rapidly, and after a while things began to disappear from the house. Father held on to the watch for a long time—he didn't sell it until after the phonograph, the pillows, and the silver sugar bowl were gone.

—1958. Translated by Barbara Vedder

Born into an assimilated Jewish family, Wiktor Woroszylski (1927–1996) was a prominent post–World War II poet, prose writer, publicist, and translator. Like many writers in this collection, he was born in the *kresy*, or "borderlands"—parts of contemporary Lithuania, Belarus, or Ukraine that belonged to Poland before World War II and were "ceded" to the Soviet Union as one of the war's outcomes. Because of his Jewish ethnicity, Woroszylski survived the war by living on "false" or "Aryan" papers in Grodno, Belarus, working as a cabinetmaker. After the war, his family moved to Łódź in central Poland, where he graduated from the university in Polish literature. He joined the communist party and, loyal to the Russian-installed puppet regime and its ideology, in addition to his literary output, while working as the editor of various literary periodicals he churned out pro-communist anti-western propaganda. He eventually broke with the communist party over the Soviet Union's suppression of the Hungarian uprising of 1956.

*Structural Analysis of "The Watch."* As is frequently the case, the story begins with the Development already in progress. A young newly married woman, the narrator of the story, is living with her husband, Roman, in her parents' home, presumably because they cannot afford separate accommodations. Roman is more educated than his parents-in-law (the father is a relatively well-to-do factory worker), but he does not look down on them, and in general he gets along with them. However, they hold against him that he does not share their reverence for material possessions. Instead, he prefers to spend his money on pleasures and perishable things, like flowers and entertainment.

The Turning Point, introducing the Complication. When World War I breaks out, Roman is called up for service and is sent to the front. As a going-away present his father-in-law gives him his valuable foreign-made pocket watch. While Roman is away, the father constantly expresses more worry about the fate of the watch than he does about Roman.

The Crisis Point. When Roman comes home on leave, the father drops not very subtle hints that Roman should leave the watch behind, because who knows what can happen at the front, and Roman does so without any hesitation. Shortly afterward, Roman returns to the front and the family soon receives word that he has been killed in action (the Climax).

The Aftermath. The family falls apart. The daughter stops talking to her parents. Her mother constantly cries, and the father, who up until then had been sober, takes to drink and slowly sells all of his valuable possessions one by one to support his drinking habit until finally only the watch is left, which in the end he sells too.

The Main Effect of the story is the outcome of an insincerely given gift, the placing of value of material things over human life until it is too late, and the irony of the father's eventual descent from stolid respectability into alcoholism. In its criticism of the bourgeois attachment to "things" as opposed to humanistic experiences and values, the story has a social ideology behind it.

A special feature is the connection between the Turning Point (the leaving behind of the watch) and the Climax (Roman's death). The connection is associative without being literally causal, but it is causal in a poetic sense. Of course, in the back of the reader's mind are stories about how a life has been saved by a bullet striking a watch, cigarette case, or another hard object in one's breast pocket (one knows that this is a pocket watch, because wristwatches did not come into wide use until after World War I).

In its ideology "The Watch" is politically correct within the political ideology of the time at which it was written, without the ideological aspect becoming dominant; the story stands on its own merits and avoids being overtly tendentious. The far-removed setting of World War I (before Poland regained statehood following 130 years of partition under Prussia, Russia, and Austro-Hungary) further serves to universalize the sentiments expressed in the story. One does not even know on what side Roman was fighting in the war, and as far as the story is concerned, it does not matter.

*The Symbol of the Watch.* The watch in the story is used as a fitting symbol of both a material possession and a person's life, both of which have value, but obviously of a different nature. Like people, wind-up watches have a "heartbeat" (they tick), and they have a "lifespan" in that they eventually run down. The plot hinges on the symbolic exchange of one thing of value, the watch, for another, Roman's life, with the father realizing too late that his materialistic values may somehow have been the cause of his son-in-law's death. His daughter certainly holds him responsible for it.

# Precursors

Although the origin of modern Polish short fiction, as in most European countries, goes back to the end of the eighteenth century, as noted in the introduction the short story in its mature form did not appear until the second half of the nineteenth century. Important literary precursors of the Polish short story, interesting in their own right, include anecdotes, tales, sketches, and diary entries, not all of which were originally intended for publication at the time they were written. In Poland as elsewhere, the ghost story, gothic tale, and anecdotes told purely for entertainment, were important paths along which the short story developed, and those strains, of course, continue to the present day in the work of many authors. The following three stories by Pasek, Potocki, and Rzewuski can serve as examples of precursors of the short story as it developed in Poland.

# Jan Pasek

Older Polish literature is full of surviving memoirs and diaries, of which Jan Chrysostom Pasek's (1636–1701) is considered to be one of the best. In fact, it is so colorful that when it appeared in print at the beginning of the nineteenth century, some were convinced it was a literary forgery. A cavalry officer who took part in many of the campaigns in which Poland was involved in its turbulent seventeenth century, in later age Pasek married and settled down to the life of a country squire and, as court records attest, the quarrelsome scourge of his neighbors. Although one of Pasek's motives in committing his memoirs to paper was to justify his own life and to present himself in the best possible light, as the hero of his own narrative, his memoirs have rather the opposite effect, for they reveal the author to be uncouth, given to crude practical jokes, and prone to laughing at other people's misfortunes.

The stories that Pasek's memoirs are populated with, given their lack of sophistication, can be characterized as a kind of literary folk art. Most of them describe military engagements, but the story included here, about Pasek's trained otter, is a relatively tranquil exception. It serves as an example of how a narrative, having been honed in the course of what must have been countless oral retellings before eventually being committed to paper, can begin to take on the outlines of a well-crafted short story.

*Note*: The above portrait is not that of Pasek, for whom no known likeness exists, but that of his close contemporary Wespazjan Kochowski (1633–1700), a prominent poet and historian of Pasek's time, serving here as a stand-in for him.

## The Year of Our Lord 1680 (Robak)

This year also—God be praised!—I began in Olszówka. Right at the start something novel befell us; winter, having already ceased, entirely melted away and so warm did it become, so mild, that the cattle went out to pasture, the buds came out, and the earth pushed forth grass, we plowed and sowed. I hesitated for a long lime with the sowing; but then, seeing others had their crops already half-sown, I too began. While on outings with friends who were courting, or going to weddings, so hot was it that you could not stand your fur gown, only your summer one, as if it were in *Augusto.*

By then nothing was left of winter, only passing showers. That grain sown in

*Ianuario* grew so high before Easter that we even pastured the cattle in it, and so that winter the cattle used little hay, there being excellent feed in the fields.

A gentleman of the court, *Pan* Straszowski, came to me with letters from his Majesty the king, earnestly begging me to make him a present of the trained otter I had, who was such a delight that I would have given away a part of my fortune rather than her whom I loved so. The king first heard from somebody there about this otter with such and such *qualitatibus* that belonged to a squire in the province of Kraków, but my name was not known, nor did they know where to direct these pleas. So then, the crown equerry wrote to *Pan* Bełchacki—who later became vice notary in Krakow—to find out who had such an otter and what his name was.

Well, since this otter was famous throughout the province of Kraków—and, later, all over Poland too—*Pan* Bełchacki found out that she belonged to me and sent back word. The king was overjoyed and took hope, saying, "I have known *Pan* Pasek a long time; I know he will not refuse me." And off he sends *Pan* Straszowski with a letter. The crown equerry also writes—so does *Pan* Adrian Piekarski, a relative of mine and a courtier. They beg me not to deny the king this gift, as his Majesty will reward me with all his favor and esteem. After having read the letter, I wondered who could have spread the news about her there. And I asked, "Lord! What can his Majesty want with her?" The deputy said that his Majesty the king very much desires and requests it. I replied only: "I've no mind to refuse." But I was as pleased as if he had been pulling a curry-comb over my bare skin. Then I sent to the tavern-keeper, a Jew, for a sleeve of otterskin, which, when it had been brought, I laid on the table in front of him, saying, "How's that, Your Excellency, for a speedy delivery!" The man stares: "But his Majesty is asking for a live one, a pet." So then I, having had my joke, was obliged to present her, and since she was not in the house but roaming somewhere about the ponds, we took a quaff of vodka and walked out to the meadows. I started calling her nickname, which was Robak, and she came out wet from the reeds, began fawning upon me, then followed us back to the house. Straszowski was amazed and says: "By God, how could the king help loving so gentle a creature!" I answer: "My Lord, you are seeing only her gentleness and you praise it, but you shall praise even more, once you have viewed her *qualitates*." We walked to the pond's edge, and standing on a mound, I say: "Robak! I need some fish for my guest; into the water!" The otter went; and first she brought out a small white fish; the second time I ordered her in she brought out a small pike; the third time, a pike the size of a platter, just a trifle bruised on the neck. Straszowski clutched his head: "Lord! What am I seeing?" I say then: "So you want her to fetch more? For she'll carry them out as long as I need them, and if it's a tubful she'll bring it, for her net costs her nothing." Straszowski exclaims: "Having seen this; I believe it, but if somebody had told me, I would not have believed him." Straszowski took to her exceedingly *et consensit* [to watch her fetch more] seeing there would not be the least bother and besides, he would be able to tell the king about her *qualitates*.

Up to the time he left, I showed him all of her talents, which were the following: first, she slept with me in my bed, and was so tidy that not only did she never make a mess in the bedclothes but did nothing under the bed; she had one place where a potsherd had been put down for her and she used to go there to relieve herself. Second, she made such a night watch the Lord preserve anyone from setting foot near the bed! She barely let my servant pull off my boots—and then keep clear—for the racket she raised would wake the soundest sleeper. If I was drunk, and someone were to walk by the bed, she would trample on my chest, barking, until I awoke. And during the day she would sleep so, sprawling anywhere, that even if you picked her up, she'd not lift an eyelid, so trusting of man was the beast! Neither raw fish, nor raw meat would she eat; even on Fridays or a fast-day when a chicken or pigeon was stewed for her, but the parsley not added as was customary, she would not eat it. Like a dog, she understood "Stay!" and such things. If somebody tugged at my gown and I said: "Sic'em," she would leap up with a fierce shriek, tear at his clothes, his legs, just like my dog, the only one she was fond of—Kapreol he was called, a long-haired German dog—and from whom she learned this, and other tricks too. This dog alone, being a house pet, was her friend and they went about together. Other dogs she didn't like and if one came into the house, she would cut it down to size at once, be it the tallest greyhound.

Once, *Pan* Stanislaw Ozarowski came to visit me, or rather, we were simply driving together and he stopped by. I was pleased and so was my otter, not having seen me for three days; she came to me and couldn't get enough of being glad and playful. My guest had a handsome greyhound bitch with him and he says to his son: "Samuel, hold on to the greyhound so she won't devour this otter." I say, "Don't trouble yourself. Your Honor, the little creature won't let herself get hurt, though she's small." And he exclaims: "What, Sir? Are you jesting? This greyhound tangles with wolves; a fox has only to yawn once." Having had her fill of being glad to see me, the otter took notice of the hunting dog; she goes up to that greyhound, looks her in the eye, the greyhound looks back; then she circled her, sniffed at her hindleg, backed off, and went away. I think: "She won't do anything now." Well, we had begun to talk about something or other, when the otter gets up again from where she had been lying at my feet, moves quietly under the bench and falls upon the dog's hindquarters again, nipping her in the calf; the greyhound jumps toward the door, the otter after her; then toward the stove, the otter on her tail. Seeing no escape, the dog leaps onto the table, wanting to break through the window, when Ozarowski grabbed her by the leg. She broke two glasses with wine, however; and after they let her out, she did not once show herself to her master, even though he did not leave until the next day after dinner. And so, all the dogs around were afraid of her. Even traveling with me, if a dog but sniffed at her, she would screech fiercely and off the dog ran.

Traveling with her during Lent, a great convenience she was. For things being what they are, especially in our country, you arrive in a little town, you ask: "Is there any fish to buy here?" And they can't even imagine: "Now where would you be getting 'em here! We don't know of any." Then you ride along a river somewhere, or a pond, and with the otter along you need no net. You step out of the cart for a while: "Robak, hup! into the water!" and in she went and brought out whatever fish was to be had, one after the other, until there was enough. On the road, I would not pick and choose [from her catch] as I do at the pond on my estate—no sooner did she bring it, you take it, save for the frog, for she'd bring out those too, since as I've already written she was not particular, she took whatever came her way. Thus, my servants as well as myself fared well, and sometimes we even fed a guest if he was stopping at the same inn, even several guests. And they wondered: "I had them search in this town and that town for fish but they couldn't get any; where did Your Lordship get such excellent fish?" So I told them that I got them in the water. Sometimes even on a meat day, my servants would say: "Oho, Good Sir, the fish are jumping in this pond here; let the otter go." So I went off with her—she not wishing to go with anyone else—and out she carried them; if there was a good fish, like a pike, or a large bass, I would dine on it too, not only my servants; for a good fish I'm prepared to forego the best meat dish. The irksome thing about traveling with my otter was that wherever you went, people were amazed; they mobbed us just as if we were transporting something from India; no meager audience we had, especially in Kraków, so that riding through the streets on my way out of town, I was accompanied by a throng of divers people.

Another time I was at the home of a cousin of mine, *Pan* Szczesny-Chociwski, and a priest. Father Trzebieński, was also there; he sat down beside me at the table. My otter was lying next to me on the bench. She had eaten her fill and was sleeping, sprawled on her back, that being her favorite posture. The priest, upon sitting down, saw the otter, and thinking it a sleeve, catches it up, wanting to have a look at it; the otter, awakened, shrieks mightily, seizes his hand and bites it; the priest fainted away—half from pain, half from fright. They could scarcely revive him.

After Straszowski had seen the *qualitates* of that otter, he also had a look at my other game, such as the aviary I'd had built; it was covered with wire-netting and in it were birds *omnis generis* [of all sorts] to be found in Poland; the birds were making their nests and sitting on them in the trees planted there; not only were there birds from Poland but I had also foreign birds, and from wherever I could acquire them. Straszowski was there when the young were hatching and when they were still in the nest; he saw it all, how the birds obey me; he saw how they let themselves be stroked in their nests; he saw the partridges hatched there, leading their nestlings around, and how they came to my call like chickens at the strewing of grain.

Off to the king went Straszowski and told all he had seen. Hardly had he arrived and given his account, when the king was overcome with an impulse: "Impossible! go there once more and bring her here somehow, no matter how, so long as I have the otter." Again, letters were written, asking me what I wished in recompense for her. The crown equerry and *Pan* Piekarski both wrote, begging me: "For Lord's sake, don't refuse now; but let him have it and save yourself bother, for you'll have no peace so long as the king thinks of nothing, whether walking, sleeping, or eating, save that otter. For her sake, and so that nothing should stand in her way, he has already given away his beloved lynx to the governor of Malbork, and has sent his cassovary bird to Jaworów that the otter might be his sole delight."

Back came Straszowski and delivered the letters, telling me how obliged the king was for my promise of the otter, how eager to have her, and how he entreats me with the words; *"Qtii cito flat, bis dat."* [he who gives promptly gives twice]. There are some mighty fine promises in the letters; Straszowski tells me that the king wanted to send me a contentment in money but *Pan* Piekarski said; "Gracious king, it will be useless to send money there, for it won't be accepted; that gentleman has a gallant nature and for sure would not take it; if anything is sent, let it be something that can be received without embarrassment." Whereupon the king sent to Jaworów for two Turkish horses, very handsome horses they have there—and ordered them presented to me, richly harnessed. I said that neither money nor horses would I take, as I would be ashamed for so humble a gift to accept such *honoraria.*

I despatched my otter then to her new master; she very ungratefully accepting that despatch and her new service; whining so and yelping in her cage as they rode through the village, that I went into the house, not wanting to listen, for it made me sad. On the road, while traveling, whenever they spied some water in a flat place, where she could not hide, they would let her out into the water, several times even, to cool off and content her nature; but as before it did not help; there was squealing aplenty and uproar. Thus, she pined away and was miserable; and they brought her to the king, looking like a puffed owl. He was overjoyed to see her and says; "She has pined away but she'll come around." Whoever is asked to pet her, the otter snaps at his hand. The king says; Marysienka, it's my turn now." The queen tries to coax him out of it, lest he get bitten; but he sits down beside the animal after they had put her on the bed, and stretches his hand out to her slowly; "I'll take it as a good sign if she doesn't bite me, and if she does, what of it, they won't be writing in the newspapers about it." He stroked her then; she was friendly with him. So delighted was the king, he began to pet her all the more, then he ordered something to be brought for her to eat. And so, there he was, feeding her bit by bit, while she ate, but without appetite, lying on that rich samite. When she had been there two days, she moved more and more freely about the rooms, going wherever she pleased. They poured water into some large vessels for her and dropped in fish and crawfish: she was happy, she fetched them out. Says the king to the queen; "Marysieńka, tomorrow I'll eat no fish but what this otter will catch for me; tomorrow, we'll go to Wilanów, God willing, and there we'll try her, to see if she will get acquainted with the fish."

I had written, at the time, a page of instructions on how they were to treat her; and I wrote that she was never to be tied by the collar, but alongside it by the neck, since an otter's neck is thicker than the head and she could slip right out of even the tightest collar. And so she did. They tied her by the collar with the little bells and she got away. She crawled down the stairs during the night and somehow got outside, as she had learned to do at my house when she was bored, going whither she liked, ferreting about to her heart's content among the ponds, the rivers, and coming home according to her habit. There, having gone out on some paths, she got lost, and knew not where to turn. As soon as it was morning, a dragoon spied her and, not knowing whether she was domestic or wild, struck her with his battle-axe and killed her. They get up—no otter. They call, search; dreadful confusion. They send round the city, entreating anyone who finds her to give her up and threatening anyone who dares not, when there arrives a traveling Jew from Pinczów, and a dragoon on his heels, seeking payment for the pelt. "What have you got there, Jew?" asks a gatekeeper. The Jew keeps his hand in his pocket. The gatekeeper peeks under his gown; and what does he see, but a pelt stuffed with straw. Both Jew and dragoon were seized at once and taken to the king.

The king examines the pelt, then claps one hand over his eyes, clutches his hair with the other and begins to shout; "Kill him whoever be righteous! Kill him, whoever believeth in God!" Both were thrown into the tower; it was decreed to shoot the dragoon, and he was ordered to prepare for death. But priest-confessors and bishops came to the king to plead with him and persuade him that the man did not deserve death, having sinned through ignorance. With difficulty, they managed to bring it about so that the man was ordered not to be shot but to run the gauntlet through Gałecki's regiment. The regiment then stood in two rows, as was customary. It was so decreed that he should run through fifteen times, resting, however, at the ends. He ran through twice—1500 men in the regiment and each thrashes him once—the third time he fell half-way through the row, against the rules they flogged him lying on the ground. They carried him off then in a sheet, but later it was said that he never came to. Thus, a keen joy was turned into a great sorrow, for all day long the king neither ate nor spoke with anyone; and the whole court was downcast. And I was deprived of a beloved animal; far from being gladdened, they had even brought themselves chagrin.

For some time my aviary was the admiration of all around. Having started with birds, I always had excellent falcons, hawks, kestrels, hobbies, ravens; they would come to the perch, the partridges would let themselves be seized; they would circle round a hare like a saker [a large falcon]; everyone of these birds carried on his proper activity. I had one hawk, somewhat too large, but so swift he outflew every bird; clutch it he would in those fearsome talons and every bird I always retrieved from him live as could be. Throw him even the largest bird, he'd not be ashamed; he'd pursue geese, ducks, heron, kites, and ravens as well as quail, for he caught several a day. So strong was that hawk that sometimes having to do with an old hare, gripping and choking him, he would then let go, preen himself, and, after a second swoop, fly up with him, lifting him off the ground as if he were a partridge. Eight years I had him, before he died on me.

As for hunting with greyhounds, I had bred a kennel of greyhounds for myself from those of my cousin, *Pan* Stanislaw Pasek of Sochaczew, whose greyhounds were both handsome and strong-bodied and at the same time so swift that never once had you need to let the pack of hounds loose on foxes or hares, only by turns, one greyhound for every hare, a different dog each time, and that hare never got away; whereas, for a wolf there was a levy in mass. And my huntsmen neighbors used to have such a saying; unhappy the beast who meets up with *Pan* Pasek, for he'll escape no more.

I was always particularly fond of training wild animals so that they grew tame;

and these would not only live with the dogs but also, with the dogs, join in the chase after their wild brothers. Somebody would come to visit me and a fox would be in the yard, frolicking with the greyhounds; my guest would enter the house and a hunting dog is lying under the table with a hare seated on him. Should somebody who does not know me meet me riding to the chase, he would look, and here he'd see several handsome greyhounds, several pointers with a fox among them, here a marten, there a badger, an otter; behind my horse gambols a hare with little bells; a hawk is on the hunter's arm, a raven flies above the dogs, sometimes lighting upon a greyhound and so letting itself be borne along; then that man could only cross himself: "For God's sake! This is a wizard: every type of beast is walking there amongst the dogs. What are they seeking? Why are they not going after those in their midst?" Should a hare break into flight, they're all after him; even my trained hare, seeing the dogs dash off, he too bounds after them. But when that hare out there begins to pray, my tame one flees back to the horse, not wanting to watch. My bestiary acquired renown far and wide in Poland and people told of even more things than I have here; however, leaving my animals aside, I return *ad cursum anni* [to the course of the year's events].

This year an unfortunate boundary agreement was made with the Turks concerning Podole. The army was encamped at Mikulenice. I set off for Gdańsk with two barges; nine days later I had reached Gdańsk, the current being swift and the water calm; I sold wheat to his lordship *Pan* Tynf at 160 zlotys. I returned by land, and the barges arrived at the pier six weeks later.

This year on the evening of October 17, the barns in Smogorzów burned down. Prices were also exessively low, and therefore I sold nothing; in Gdańsk rye did not pay either, only wheat. On this account, I suffered a loss of about 20,000 zlotys reckoning lightly. The peasants *ex invidia* [out of spite] put the blame on the overseer, as to how he was to have dropped an ember from his lamp while looking for his hog. I had him put to the rack, having taken him to court; he did not confess for he was not guilty, and those scoundrels through hatred had falsely accused him, and led me into sin, and deprived me of a good steward, for I took an aversion to him for having been in the torturer's hands and I ordered him to leave. But I regretted it later, having found out that something else had caused the damage. The fire started at the blacksmith's; at the time, a fierce wind was blowing straight toward the barn; it's likely the barn caught fire *non ab intra* but *ab extra,* and then it spread to the other barns, the haystacks, the corn ricks and racks. The which is God's will: *Dominus dedit, dominus abstulit* [God gives, God takes away].

—1680. Translated by Catherine Leach.

*Cultural Commentary.* No record of Jan Pasek's marvelous otter Robak is preserved outside Pasek's diary; for that matter, Pasek's own existence is barely attested, in some obscure court records of the time. Nevertheless, there is no reason not to believe this story in its general outline. The value of the story, and its qualification as a "short story" instead of just being a diary entry, depends not on its historical veracity but on the way in which it is told and the "meaning," if any, one may extract from it. "Robak" was clearly written for a potential audience, although there would have been few, if any, outlets available for its publication during Pasek's lifetime.

Through much of the sixteenth and seventeenth centuries, a large part of Poland was Protestant. Pasek was raised during the Counter-Reformation in Poland, when the Roman Catholic Church was reestablishing its authority over the nation's churches and the school system. Pasek would most likely have been trained in a school run by Jesuit priests, where he probably would have received no more than an elementary school education, concentrating on Latin. Graduates of such schools often liked to show off by sprinkling their speech and writing with Latin words, as though no Polish words existed for expressing the same thing. For example, Pasek keeps using the Latin word *qualitates* for "qualities," even though Polish words would have done just as well; and he needlessly uses the Latin names for the months.

Pasek means "belt" or "stripe" in Polish, and it possibly refers to a motif in Pasek's coat of arms. The title *pan* means "sir." Its use in Pasek's time was limited to the nobility. Today the title is more or less the equivalent of "Mr.," and it is used for all men.

Olszówka is the name of Pasek's agricultural estate in the south-central part of Poland, not far from Kraków. Olsza means "alder tree," so the estate's name is something like "The Alders." Pasek's farmland would have been plowed and harvested by tenant farmers, who lived on or near the land, giving most of their produce to the landowner, and putting enough aside for themselves to live on.

The King, Jan III Sobieski. and his wife Marie (affectionately called Marysieńka, or "Molly"), ruled during Pasek's time. She was French, and this was her second marriage. Unlike many royal couples, the king and his wife were reputed to be lovebirds, and while on campaign the king wrote nearly daily love letters to her, which have survived and are still read for their record of the times. The royal castle was in Warsaw, a two- or three-days' trip north from Olszówka. The king's "summer home" mentioned in the story, Wilanów, was and is a grandiose Baroque palace just south of Warsaw, next to the Vistula River (so a good place to bring a pet otter to practice her fishing skills).

Despite Pasek's belittling portrait of him, Sobieski was a popular king and one of Poland's greatest military commanders, including on the international stage. He organized a Christian league of nations to combat the threatened conquest of Europe by the Turks and led a combined European army which defeated the Ottomans and broke the siege of Vienna in 1683, some three years after the events described in "Robak."

Kings in Poland by this time were not hereditary but elected by the nobility, and even minor Polish nobles like Pasek considered themselves to be the king's social equal. Thus, Poland had a kind of nobles' democracy, a very unusual form of government for Europe of the time. From the story it is evident that Polish kings had considerable power, for example, in this story, the power to execute prisoners for petty crimes. However, Pasek's attitude toward the king is worth commenting on. Being a nobleman, he was not obliged to yield his pet otter to the king, but his respect for the king's office leads him to do so. Nevertheless, his story is critical of the king in several ways. The king is depicted as a frivolous monarch who acts on whims, who selfishly wants somebody else's trained otter for himself, who as king does not have anything better to do than to feed a pet otter crayfish, and who, ultimately, does not know how to care for animals or even how to follow simple instructions for their upkeep. He is worried about his wife's opinion and about "what people might say about him in the newspapers," a strange statement, considering that newspapers at the time were virtually nonexistent.

Otters (in Polish *wydra*, etymologically related to English *otter* and the Proto-Indo-European word for water), apparently occurred commonly in Poland in Pasek's time. They are rare in Poland nowadays, occurring mainly in the east of the country. Otters have short, thick, rich fur and strong tails, and they are playful, gregarious, and, like ferrets, are easily tamed. They have a voracious appetite, mainly for fish, and they are territorial and fearless of would-be predators, however large. The otter's nickname "Robak" means the kind of worm that eats carrion. It is a funny nickname, and refers to the squirmy, worm-like appearance and actions of an otter.

A dragoon is a low-ranking, well-armored European light horse-soldier, typically armed with a battle-ax or spontoon, having a blade on top of a pointed spike, good for spearing and for hacking (or for slaying a passing tame otter).

Jews were common in Poland in Pasek's time, many having arrived there in the fifteenth and sixteenth centuries or even earlier to escape the Spanish inquisition, and it would have been natural for a Jewish merchant to be engaged in the fur trade.

*Structural Analysis.* While one may easily make the argument that a story about one's pet otter does not rise to the level of a true short story, the tale of "Robak" exhibits the rudiments of classical plot structure, even if the parts are somewhat disjointed and are hard to see at first. To be sure, its type is chiefly anecdotal, consisting of a chain of anecdotes within an overall anecdote. The Pre-History to this story is short and consists of a description of the unusually warm weather and early crop planting in the year 1680. The Turning Point and Complication occur almost immediately, when we learn that Pasek, the narrator, has a marvelous trained otter, Robak, of which the king has heard and which he desires for himself. The king has sent his emissary, *pan* Straszowski, on his behalf. Next follows the longest part of the story, an interlude in the Complication, devoted to various anecdotes related to the otter, telling of its devotion, cleverness, bravery, and skill. Functionally, this interlude serves as an extended Development, or scene-setting part of the story. The anecdotes are told with a crude kind of humor, which laughs at other people's misfortunes, such as Ozarowski's embarrassment over his greyhound's being so cowardly, and the fainting of Father Trzebieński when he takes Robak for a fur muff and tries to pick him up.

The literary purpose of the interlude is twofold. Having heard that the king wants the otter, we are now delayed from hearing how the matter turns out by listening to the backstories about the otter that might also have come to the king's attention. This narrative delay is an example of *narrative retardation*, a slowing down in the pace of action in order to heighten suspense, a characteristic feature especially of oral narratives. At the same time, the interlude gives Pasek a chance to brag about his animal-training prowess, which he loves to do.

After the narrative interlude, the king's emissary returns, picking up the end of the split Complication. Naively, and against his own self-interest, Pasek cannot help but show off his otter and all his tricks to the king's emissary, Straszowski, thereby unwittingly convincing the king not to change his mind. In the Polish tradition of gift giving, Pasek makes a big point of being offended at the idea of accepting money or an expensive horse and bridle from the king in exchange for Robak. A gift is not a gift if it is not freely given, a principle we have already seen demonstrated in Woroszylski's "The Watch."

The Complication continues, with the description of the otter's sorrow at being parted from her master, but slowly getting used to life in the royal castle and taking crayfish from the king's own hand. The description of Robak's departure to the royal castle and what follows takes place mainly in the narrator's imagination or from hearsay (for example, Pasek could not possibly have been present in the king's private bedchamber.) At this point, we have what could be called a *false lead*, and the prospect of a *happy ending*. After an initial period of distress, the otter settles down in its new home and seems to develop a special fondness for the king, who reciprocates in kind. We see here an intimate domestic picture of king Jan Sobieski and his wife Marie, as they play with the otter in their bedroom. The story could, at this point, end "happily ever after."

However, misfortune (the Crisis point) suddenly strikes. In quick succession, the king fails to tether the otter properly, the otter escapes, gets lost, and is killed by an unwitting dragoon, who takes the unsuspecting tame otter for a wild one. The otter's death comprises the structural Climax of the story, after which follows a strange Aftermath, which tells of a much more tragic outcome than that of the otter. In a fit of pique, the king orders the dragoon to be executed. Pasek sees a crude humor in the fact that the king commutes the dragoon's sentence of death by shooting to the even crueler punishment of being flogged to death by running the gauntlet. The fate of the hapless Jewish merchant who was trying to buy the otter pelt is left hanging, suggesting that Pasek either does not know it or considers it not worth mentioning. One could characterize this omission as a failure to tie up obvious loose ends, as one is supposed to do in the Aftermath of a story.

Pasek narrow-mindedly sees the significance, or "Point," of the story as being that the court was saddened for a day or two, and that he, Pasek, was pointlessly deprived of his otter. Pasek also implies that the king "got his just deserts" for not following the instructions he had left with his pet. The Post-History first continues Pasek's bragging about his skill in training animals and raising exotic birds, followed by a rather gruesome story of barns burning down and an innocent estate manager being unjustly tortured over it. Torturing in Poland usually took the form of pulling a person's hands backwards over his head until the shoulders pulled out of the sockets. Pasek sees no moral problem in his firing the estate manager out of his own sense of embarrassment and regret but, in fact, justifies it.

At one point in his diary Pasek launches into a lengthy rhymed funerary tribute to a favorite horse he had just lost in battle. Similarly, the story of his dead otter in some respects reminds one of a funeral oration, the rhetorical parts of which Pasek would have picked up from his Jesuit schooling. According to the canon of a funerary speech one recounts the dead person's virtues and tells a few uplifting anecdotes from his life, showing him or her in a positive light, and making the sense of our loss over the person's death all the greater.

Pasek is completely unaware of the effect of *estrangement* he creates on the reader throughout his story, arising from the reader's not identifying with him but, on the contrary, feeling a chasm of moral distance from him. The most striking estrangement between narrator and reader probably has to do with the irreconcilable viewpoints as to what the chief tragedy of the story is: the death of the otter or that of the dragoon and the Jew. For Pasek, the latter are treated as purely incidental and not worth mentioning aside from its dubious humorous potential.

# Jan Potocki

Count Jan Potocki (1761–1815) was a colorful figure of the Polish eighteenth-century Enlightenment. Born in Podolia, Ukraine, into a renowned Polish aristocratic family which owned vast estates around Poland, he was educated in Lausanne and Geneva and was reputed to speak French better than Polish. Widely traveled and fluent in eight languages, Potocki was a "renaissance man" with interests and publications in archeology, ethnology, and Slavic pre-history, to name only a few of his fields. Besides the occult, he had a special interest in the Orient, the Levant, Egypt, North Africa, and Spain under Moorish occupation. Qualified as a military engineer, he served twice in this capacity in the Austrian army. In addition, he was an adviser to the Russian government on its relations with China. On top of all that, he was a pioneer balloonist. Outside Poland, Potocki is mainly known as the author of a highly original box-within-a-box novel, *Rękopis znaleziony w Saragossie* (Manuscript Found in Saragossa), which itself had a colorful history. Written in French and published in small editions in Russia in various lengths as the novel developed, French versions of the novel were mostly lost or misplaced, but not before they had been translated into Polish. As a result, today's French versions of the novel are to an extent pieced together from a Polish translation of a no longer extant French text, although a partial French manuscript surfaced a few years ago. The novel was turned into a lengthy cult film in 1965 by Wojciech Jerzy Has.

In the novel from which the following stories are taken, the young hero, Alphonse van Worden, travels on horseback through the Sierra Morena Mountains in Andalusia, Spain, in an attempt to join his regiment of Walloon Guards in Madrid. On his first night, while staying at a tumbedown country inn, Alphonse is visited by two beautiful Moorish sister seductresses who try to get him to convert to Islam so they can marry him, both at once. He falls asleep blissfully in their arms only to awake next morning beneath some gallows next to the rotting corpses of two robber brothers. The recurring sisters and other characters encountered along Alphonse's journey to Madrid tell an elaborate chain of mostly interlocking stories which are constantly being interrupted by other characters who join the stories and begin telling their own stories, and soon the reader becomes hopelessly lost in the resulting narrative labyrinth. Many stories are told only for long enough to whet the reader's interest, to be interrupted by outside events and never completed. The following narrative, at least, consisting of two interlocking stories, those of the notorious libertine Thibaud de la Jacquière and his would-be prey, the gentle maiden Dariolette, adds up to a complete whole.

[As a curious historical aside, the story "Commander de Toralva," also contained in Potocki's novel and written in or around 1805, mysteriously turns up in an openly plagiarized version as Washington Irving's "The Grand Prior of Minorca," published in 1855.]

At the age of fifty-four Potocki, neurasthenic, depressed, and possibly the victim of early-onset dementia, committed suicide, reputedly by carving a bullet from the knob of a silver sugar bowl and inserting it into the barrel of an antique pistol, which exploded upon firing, but still did its job.

## Story of Thibaud La Jacquière

Once upon a time there lived in France, in the city of Lyons on the Rhone, a rich merchant named Jacques de La Jacquière, though he did not take the name of La Jacquière till he had retired from business and had become provost of the city, a post the Lyonnais give only to men who have a great fortune and a spotless reputation. Such, therefore, was the good provost de La Jacquière: charitable towards the poor and liberal to monks and other friars who, according to the Lord, are the truly poor.

But such was not the provost's only son, Messire Thibaud de La Jacquière, standard-bearer of the king's men-at-arms, unscrupulous ruffian and overfond of using his sword, gay deceiver of young girls, thrower of dice, breaker of windows, smasher of lanterns, curser and blasphemer. Many a time he held up a worthy citizen on the street to exchange his old coat for a new one and his worn felt for a better one. So that it was not long before Messire Thibaud was the talk of the town, in Paris as well as at Blois, Fontainebleau and wherever the king was in residence. Now therefore it happened that Francis I, our good sire of holy memory, was finally grieved by the behavior of the young subaltern and sent him back to Lyons to do penance in the house of his father, the good provost de La Jacquière, who was then living at the corner of the Place de Bellecour and the rue Saint-Ramond.

Young Thibaud was received in the paternal mansion with as much joy as if he had arrived laden with all the indulgences of Rome. Not only did they kill the fatted calf for him, but the good provost invited his friends to a banquet that cost more gold *ecus* than there were guests. He did even more. The guests drank the young man's health and each one hoped he would acquire wisdom and repent. Those charitable wishes displeased Thibaud. He snatched a gold cup from the table, filled it with wine and cried:

"Hells bells! In this wine I pledge my body and soul to the devil if ever I become a better man than I am today." At those terrible words the guests shuddered and their hair stood on end. They crossed themselves and some of them rose from the table.

Messire Thibaud rose, too, and went to take the air on the Place de Bellecour, where he found two of his former comrades—lawless ruffians like himself. He embraced them, led them into his house, plied them with bottle after bottle, and ignored his father and the latter's guests.

What Thibaud had done on the day he arrived, he did the next day, and every day after that. With the result that the good provost was cut to the heart. He thought of appealing to his patron. Saint Jacques, and placed a ten-pound candle before the saint's image; but as the provost was about to put the candle on the altar, he dropped it and knocked over the silver lamp that was burning before the saint. The provost had had this candle molded for another purpose, but as his son's conversion was the thing closest to his heart, he was only too glad to make an offering of it. When, however, he saw the candle fall and the lamp upset, he thought it was a bad omen and he returned home sadly.

That same day, Messire Thibaud feasted his friends again. They tossed off many a bottle, and then, as the night was already far advanced and very dark, they went for a stroll on the Place de Bellecour. The three young ruffians linked arms and strutted arrogantly back and forth, like libertines who think they can attract the attention of young girls that way. But this time they had no luck, for not a girl, not a woman, passed and as the night was dark, they could not see them from the windows. Then young Thibaud, swearing his customary oath, cried out in a loud voice: "Hells bells! I pledge myself body and soul to the devil, and if that great, strapping she-devil, his daughter, passed by I would wanton with her, so greatly am I overheated by the wine."

This suggestion displeased Thibaud's two friends, who were not such great libertines as he. And one of them said:

"My friend, don't forget that the devil is the eternal foe of mankind. He does harm enough without inviting him and invoking his name."

At that Thibaud replied:

"I shall do as I said."

In the midst of all this, the three ribald youths saw a young woman, veiled, but with the charming figure of a very young person, come out of a nearby street. A little negro walked behind her. He stumbled, fell on his nose and broke his lantern. The young girl appeared to be greatly alarmed and did not know which way to turn. Then Messire Thibaud went up to her and, in his most courteous manner, offered his arm to lead her to her home. After protesting a little, poor Dariolette accepted. Turning towards his friends, Messire Thibaud said to them in an aside:

"Well, you see, the one I invoked hasn't kept me waiting. So then, I bid you goodnight."

The two friends understood what he wanted and laughing and wishing him joy, they took leave of him.

Thibaud therefore gave his arm to the veiled beauty, and the little negro, whose lantern had gone out, walked ahead of them. The young lady at first seemed so upset she could scarcely stand, but little by little she became reassured and leaned more frankly on the cavalier's arm. Sometimes she even made a false step and clutched at his arm to keep from falling. Then the cavalier, to support her, pressed her arm against his heart, which he did, however, with much discretion in order not to frighten the quarry.

They walked so far, through street after street, that Thibaud began to think they had lost their way. But he was well pleased, for he thought he would make all the shorter work of this beautiful lost lady. First, however, he wished to know with whom he had to deal, and he urged her to rest on a stone bench they could see near a door. She consented and he sat down beside her. Then clasping her hand with a lover-like air, he said to her boldly:

"Beautiful wandering star, since my star has willed that I meet you tonight, be so kind as to tell me who you are and where you live."

At first the young girl hesitated shyly, but then, taking heart, she told him the following story.

## Story of the Gentle Dariolette of the Châtel de Sombre

My name is Orlandine—at least, that is what I am called by the few people who live with me in the Châtel de Sombre in the Pyrenees. The only human beings I saw there were my governess, who was deaf, a servant who stammered so badly she was almost a mute, and an old porter who was blind.

The porter had little to do save open the castle door once a year to a gentleman who came to us only to take me by the chin and speak to my duenna in the Basque tongue, of which I knew not a word. Fortunately I had already learned to talk before I was locked up in the Châtel de Sombre, for I would certainly not have learned from my two companions in that prison. As for the blind porter, I saw him only when he passed our dinner through the bars of our one window. In truth, my deaf governess often shouted in my ears some lesson or other on morals to which I paid as little attention as if I, too, were as deaf as she, for she talked about the duties of marriage and did not explain what a marriage was. She also spoke of many other things she would not explain to me. Often, too, my stammering servant made an effort to tell me some story, which she assured me was very funny, but she never got farther than the second sentence. She had to give it up and would go off stammering excuses that were just as impossible to understand as her story.

I said we had only one window—by that I mean only one overlooking the castle courtyard. The others looked out on another court which, being planted with a few trees, could pass for a garden. The sole exit led to my bedroom. I raised a few flowers in that garden and it was my only pastime. But I am wrong: I had one other pastime, a very innocent one: it was a large mirror in which I used to look at myself as soon as I was up, even the moment I got out of bed. My governess, in scanty attire like mine, would come and look at herself too and it amused me to compare my figure with hers. I indulged in this pastime also on going to bed and after my governess had fallen asleep. Sometimes I imagined I saw in my mirror a companion of my own age who responded to my gestures and shared my emotions. The more I indulged in that illusion the more the game pleased me.

I told you there was a gentleman who came once every year to clasp me by the chin and talk Basque with my governess. One day, instead of taking me by the chin, he took me by the hand and led me to a closed carriage in which he imprisoned me with my governess. "Imprisoned" is really the word, for the only light that penetrated the carriage came from above. There we had to stay for three days, or rather until the third night, for when we emerged it was well along in the evening. A man opened the door and said to us;

"Here you are at the Place de Bellecour, at the entrance to the rue Saint-Ramond, and here is the house of the provost de la Jacquière. Where do you wish to go?"

"Drive under the first porte-cochere after the provost's," said my governess.

At this, young Thibaud was all ears, for he was actually the neighbor of a gentleman called the Sire de Sombre, who was said to have a very jealous disposition. Many a time had the said Sire de Sombre boasted in Thibaud's presence that one of these days he would prove that a man could have a faithful wife. In his little castle, he was bringing up a virgin who would become his wife and would prove his contention. Young Thibaud had not known she was in Lyons and he was delighted to have her in his hands.

However, Orlandine continued as follows:

We therefore drove under a porte-cochere and they led us through vast and beautiful rooms, and from there, by a circular staircase, into a little tower from where it seemed to me one could have seen the whole city of Lyons had it been day. But even by day we could see nothing, for the windows were covered with a heavy green cloth. To make up for that, the tower was lighted by a beautiful crystal chandelier set in enamel. My duenna seated me in a chair, gave me her rosary to amuse me and went out, locking the door behind her with a double and triple turn.

When I was alone, I threw down my rosary and with a pair of scissors at my belt I made an opening in the green cloth that covered the window. I saw another window very close to me and through that window a brightly lighted room in which three young cavaliers were dining with three young girls, handsomer and gayer than anything one can imagine. They sang, they laughed, they drank, they embraced each other. Sometimes they even took each other by the chin, but it was quite different from the gentleman of the Châtel de Sombre who, however, came only for that. Moreover, those cavaliers and those young women were always taking off more and more of their clothes, the way I did at night in front of my large mirror and, in truth, it was most becoming to them and not at all like my old duenna."

Here Messire Thibaud saw clearly that the supper in question was one he had given the evening before to his two friends. He put his arm around Orlandine's round and supple waist and clasped her close against him.

"Yes," she said, "that is exactly what those young cavaliers did. In truth, it seemed to me they all loved each other very much. But then one of those young men said he was a better lover than the others. 'No, I am, I am,' cried the two others. 'He is!' 'No, the other one is,' cried the young women. Then the one who had boasted of being the best lover thought of a curious device to prove what he said."

Here, Thibaud, who remembered what had happened at the supper, almost choked with laughter.

"Well," said he, "lovely Orlandine, what was that device the young man thought up?"

"Ah!" replied Orlandine, "do not laugh, sir. I assure you it was a very beautiful device and I was paying close attention to it when I heard the door open. I quickly picked up my rosary just as my duenna entered.

"Without a word my duenna took me by the hand and made me get into a carriage, which was not closed like the first one, and I could certainly have seen the city in this one. But the night was too dark and all I could see was that we went a long, long way until we came to open country at the farthest end of the town. There we stopped before the last house. From outside it looked like a simple hut and it was even roofed with thatch, but inside it was very pretty, as you will see if the little negro knows the way, for I see he has found a light and is relighting his lantern."

Here Orlandine ended her story. Messire Thibaud kissed her hand and said:

"Beautiful lost lady, pray tell me, do you live alone in that pretty house?"

"All alone," replied the beauty, "with the little negro and my governess. But I do not think she can return tonight. The gentleman who takes me by the chin sent word to me to bring my governess and meet him at his sister's, but he could not send his carriage, for it had gone to fetch a priest. We therefore went there on foot. Someone stopped us to tell me how pretty I was. My duenna, who is deaf, thought he was insulting me and answered back. This attracted a crowd and I began to run. The little negro ran after me. He fell down. His lantern was broken and it was then, my good sir, that to my good fortune I met you."

Charmed with the naiveté of that recital, Messire Thibaud was about to make a pretty speech in reply when the little negro returned with his lighted lantern. As its light fell on Thibaud's face, Orlandine exclaimed:

"What do I see! It's the same cavalier who thought up the fine device."

"The same," said Thibaud, "and I assure you that what I did then is nothing compared to what a charming and respectable young girl could expect from me. For the girls I was with were anything but that."

"You certainly looked as though you loved them—all three," said Orlandine.

"That's because I didn't love any," said Thibaud.

And so well did they pass the time, that walking and chatting of this and that, they came to the end of the town to a solitary hut. Here the negro opened the door with a key he wore at his belt.

There was nothing of a hut, however, about the interior of the house. Instead there were beautiful Flemish tapestries with figures of people so well drawn, so cleverly portrayed, that they seemed to be alive; branch candlesticks in exquisite heavy silver; rich cabinets in ivory and ebony; armchairs covered in Genoese velvet and trimmed with gold fringes, and a bed in Venetian moire. But Messire Thibaud paid no attention to all that. He saw only Orlandine and was eager to come to the end of the adventure.

Then the little negro came in to set the table and Thibaud noticed that he was not a child, as he had thought at first, but an ancient dwarf, all black and with an ugly face. What the little man brought in, however, was not at all ugly: an enamel dish in which four partridges, succulent and well prepared, lay smoking hot and, under his arm, a bottle of hippocras. The moment Thibaud had drunk and eaten, he felt as though liquid fire were flowing through his veins. As for Orlandine, she ate little and looked steadily at her fellow guest, now with a tender and naïve expression, now with eyes so full of malice that the young man was almost embarrassed.

At last the negro came to clear the table. Then Orlandine took Thibaud by the hand and said to him:

"Handsome cavalier, how shall we spend the evening?"

Thibaud did not know what to reply.

"I have an idea," said Orlandine. "Here is a large mirror. Let's pretend as I did at the Châtel de Sombre. I used to amuse myself there by seeing that my governess was not made like me. Now I want to know whether I am like you."

Orlandine placed two chairs in front of the mirror, after which she unlaced Thibaud's ruff and said to him:

"Your neck is almost the same as mine. Your shoulders, too—but your chest! What a difference! Mine was like that last year, but I have put on so much flesh I hardly know myself any more. Take off your belt. Unfasten your doublet. Why all those laces? … "

Unable to control himself any longer, Thibaud carried Orlandine over to the bed of Venetian moire and thought himself the happiest of men …

But he soon changed his mind, for he felt something like claws piercing his back.

"Orlandine, Orlandine," he cried, "what does this mean?"

Orlandine was not there. In her place Thibaud saw only a horrible grouping of strange and hideous forms.

"I am not Orlandine," said the monster in a terrible voice, "I am Beelzebub."

Thibaud tried to invoke the name of Jesus, but Satan, who guessed what he was about, seized the young man's throat in his teeth and prevented him from speaking the sacred name.

The next morning, some peasants on their way to the Lyons market to sell their vegetables, heard groans coming from an abandoned roadside hut that was used as a refuse dump. They went in and found Thibaud lying on a half-rotted carcass. They took him up and laid him on top of their baskets, and thus they carried him home to the provost of Lyons … The unhappy La Jacquière recognized his son.

The young man was put to bed. In a little while he seemed to regain his senses to a certain extent and, in a feeble and almost unintelligible voice, he said:

"Let the holy hermit in, let the holy hermit in."

At first they did not understand him. At last they opened the door and they saw a venerable monk enter, who asked to be left alone with Thibaud. They obeyed him and closed the door on them. For a long time they could hear the hermit's exhortations, to which Thibaud replied in a loud voice:

"Yes, Father, I repent and I trust in divine mercy."

At last, when they heard nothing more, they thought they should go in. The hermit had disappeared and Thibaud was found dead with a crucifix in his hands.

—ca. 1805. Translated from the French by Roger Callois

*Critical Commentary.* In the novel that contains the intertwined stories of Thibaud and Dariolette/Orlandine, they appear in a book of "strange narratives" left out for the hero Alphonse van Worden to read for any light they might shed on the mystery of the two Moorish sisters he had met in the inn at the beginning of the novel. Are they possibly mischievous sprites who can assume various forms, or perhaps vampires in female form, bent on seducing men in order to lead them to perdition? Whether or not it is true that men have a deep-seated fear of the Devil hiding beneath the skin of beautiful seductresses, especially at the point of sexual consummation, this theme appears often enough in literature across time and cultures. Together the two stories add up to a tongue-in-cheek riff on the theme of the consequences of breaking the ancient taboo against speaking the Devil's name lest he appear. Potocki is far from moralizing here, merely using this theme to propel the plot. At points the story appeals to the reader's prurient and voyeuristic interest, but it (just barely) stops short of becoming pornographic. Besides these observations, little by way of ideational analysis is suggested by these or any of the other stories with which Potocki's novel is packed.

The type of stories found in *Manuscript Found in Saragossa,* including the present one, leads to the consideration of whether there is a definable difference between what one would prefer to call a "tale" as opposed to a "short story." Tales usually occur in the past and in far-off places with exotic characters, whereas short stories tend to be realistic and to deal with normal people with whom one can identify, and with life in the present. Figuratively, the difference has been compared to a short story's paddling upstream against a current and encountering odds and obstacles and overcoming them (or not), whereas a tale flows downstream, is carried along with the current without special goal or effort, and usually proceeds in a straight line. Tales are generally simple in plot and are lacking in a thesis, while short stories are more complex in both structure and in the intellectual capital one is asked to invest in them. They typically have an argument or point that the author wishes to make or an identifiable ideology or agenda that is presented along with the story, whereas tales, like these two connected ones here, are largely devoid of points, ideologies, and agendas.

The foregoing considerations aside, the outlines of a traditional plot structure do emerge when Potocki's two tales are arranged side by side. The narration up until the moment Thibaud meets Orlandine can be considered to be the story's Development and, as is usual for a Development, it is the longest part of the narrative.

Toward the end of the Development, possibly overlooked by the less observant reader, a major clue to the story's outcome has been deposited. Namely, under the influence of drink, Thibaud expresses a willingness to take even the Devil's daughter to bed should he encounter her. Soon enough he does, of course, although for the time being Thibaud, and maybe also the reader, may not recognize her appearance. At the story's turning point, Thibaud encounters an enchanting young lady, Orlandine, as she calls herself, who is lost and wandering the dark streets of town with her servant, whose lantern has gone out. Much of Orlandine's story about her early sheltered life and innocence of the world can be considered to be an intensional prolongation of the narrative, in other words, a kind of *narrative retardation,* having the aim not only of further inflaming Thibaud's desire but also of heightening the story's tension by pushing the ending farther into the future. The crisis point comes when Orlandine leads Thibaud to a modest-looking cottage on the outskirts of town. When they enter, the hut turns out to be a luxuriously appointed apartment complete with Flemish tapestries, exquisitely inlaid cabinets, upholstered furniture, a table set for two, and a bed.

As is usual during a story's structural crisis, one event quickly succeeds another on the way to the climax—in the present instance, a ruined one. Following their lavish meal, Orlandine wonders out loud how they should spend the rest of the evening, and she leads Thibaud to a full-length mirror, where she provocatively points out the differences in their anatomies. Continuing to take the initiative, Orlandine starts to help Thibaud out of his clothes and he, by now uncontrollably burning with desire, and scarcely believing his good luck, lifts Orlandine off her feet, carries her to the bed, and pounces on her, expecting to bring his desires to a satisfactory conclusion. Suddenly, instead of Orlandine he sees beneath him a hideous monster and feels its talons digging into his back. The story reaches its climax not as Thibaud had hoped, but as he loses consciousness in Beelzebub's embrace. In the Aftermath, the barely alive Thibaud is transported to his father's house by some passing farmers on their way to market. From his bed he calls for a specific hermit priest, who magically appears and administers confession and last sacraments to the repentant Thibaud just before he dies, a crucifix in his hands.

As the diagram given in the introduction to this book suggests, the classical parts of a short story bear a close resemblance to the stages of sexual encounter as they stairstep their way from arousal, to foreplay, to sex, to an eventual climax, followed by a sense of letdown (in French, *la petite mort*). Whether there is any deeper significance to this similarity is anyone's guess, but one can imagine a Freudian psychiatrist suggesting that a sexual undercurrent underlies much of what we think about, say, or do, and that reading a short story in the classical mode is a subliminal form of sexual pleasure. Whatever the case, if one accepts the analogy, then one sees that the structural parts of the overall plot of Potocki's story as it unfolds overlap with the evolving and ever-increasing degree of sexual involvement of Thibaud with Orlandine, producing a virtual literalization of the structure/sex analogy. The coordination of the structural parts of the story with the stages of Thibaud's rising involvement with Orlandine is possibly not intentional on Potocki's part but comes about naturally, given the ribald nature of the story.

The question remains whether the narrative of Thibaud and Dariolette is, in the end, best considered a "tale" or a "short story." Even though one may spot in this story all the expected points and movements of a classical short story, consideration of the many tale-like features already mentioned, and the fact that in the end there is no "afterlife" to the story in the form of a lingering moral, message, ideology, or "something serious to think about," pushes the scales in favor of this being a tale.

# Henryk Rzewuski

Count Henryk Rzewuski (1791–1866) was a member of an immensely wealthy and powerful family of Ukrainian magnates. His great uncle had been not only a writer of plays and poetry, but the Great Crown Hetman, that is, commander-in-chief of the Polish army. He had been a supporter of the Bar Confederacy mentioned at the beginning of the story to follow, raised to protest the election of the Russian-backed candidate for king. Another Rzewuski relative was a prominent early explorer of the Far East and the Middle East.

Although writing and publishing mainly in the early nineteenth century, in spirit Rzewuski was firmly rooted in the traditions, attitudes, and writing style of earlier centuries, exhibiting a penchant among the nobility for writing memoirs and keeping diaries of their experiences and observations, and for retelling stories they had accumulated over the years. Rzewuski's major work was a would-be real-life memoir entitled *Memoirs of His Grace Seweryn Soplica, Butler to the King* (1839), a prime example of Polish literature of the anecdotal *gawęda* (raconteur) style, imitative of diaries of the seventeenth century like Jan Pasek's, based on a rambling structure and highly colloquial language, with anecdotal interstices told for sheer fun. In this fictionalized memoir, Rzewuski gives a vivid picture of the mindset of the conservative Polish nobility, clinging to a nostalgia for and allegiance to their habits and social privileges of the past and blind to changes taking place in the world around them, threatening both their country and their own social position in it. With Rzewuski, this style went together with a dismissive contempt for the rationalistic ideas of the French Enlightenment that were spreading across Europe at the time. The playful story "I Am Burning" exemplifies this anti-rationalist trend as it delves into the supernatural.

## I Am Burning

Following the dissolution of the Bar Confederacy, which resulted in the confiscation of even the modest patrimony I had inherited from my forebears, I found myself in a desperate situation. The conquered have nothing good to expect from the conquerors, and I would have had to cast myself upon the charity of various noble households had not the bishop of Kraków, Prince Kajetan Sołtyk, to whom I was related on my mother's side, remembered about me. Prince Kajetan, of immortal memory, extended his hand to me, took me under his wing, and favored me for as long as I should live with the gift of a small village, which to this day keeps me fed and clothed.

Prince Kajetan, before accepting the Kraków bishopric, had been bishop of Kiev, and he accordingly had extensive holdings in Ukraine. Upon moving to the Kraków region, he had brought with him a certain Ukrainian nobleman, Mr. Pogorzelski of the Krzywda crest, a virtuous man and so accomplished in agriculture that the bishop entrusted to him the keys to Samsonów, one of his most sizable properties. And even though in Ukraine, so blessed by God with its innate fecundity that crops there almost raise themselves without any outside help, he soon mastered farming in our parts to such an extent that he served as a model for all Krakowian farmers, and out of all his estate managers, Prince Kajetan prized him the most.

We all liked Mr. Pogorzelski very much, for he was not only virtuous and wise in the ways of the world, but also exceedingly polite and obliging, and of a merry disposition. In the opinion of many landowners hereabouts he also had his eccentricities, but I personally never shared that opinion, although it is true that he occasionally told tall tales about himself. For example, he once swore that one day while riding through Polesie he stopped before a tavern to give his horses a rest, but did not alight from the carriage. Some local Polesian approached him with rifle in hand and says,

"Here, my lord, buy this flintlock. You'll find nothing better for hunting."

"And how much do you want for it?"

"Thirty tynfs, sir. Lower than that I cannot go."

"Are you out of your mind? You can see that every part of this piece is taken from a different maker. The lock is tied on with string, the barrel is half eaten away with rust, and the stock is in such a deplorable state that God pity the man who takes it up and tries to fire it."

"All that is true, my lord, but it still has its virtues."

"And what virtues might those be?"

"Well, its main virtue is that when you get ready to aim, even before loading it, you only have to think of an animal for it to appear in your gunsight, and you'd better shoot right away, lest something unfortunate happen."

"Here, show me that rifle. Is it loaded?"

"Loaded it is, sir. Here, give it a try, but I warn you: you'd better fire it, because the moment you set it aside loaded and cocked, it'll go off and shatter in your hands.

"So you see, gentlemen," he continued, "I was so tempted to give this firearm a try that I took it up while thinking about a bear, and what should I see in my sights a dozen paces or so in front of me but a Gypsy leading a bear on a chain. I let loose, and the Gypsy disappears along with his chain in the puff of smoke out of the rifle. All I see is this bear, lying there dead at my feet.

"I paid the man his price, and I would have paid three times as much if he had asked for it. I wouldn't have hesitated to hock my last shirt for it. And so I rode on with the rifle in my lap. Trying it out time and again, I loaded up the carriage with all manner of game, until finally it occurs to me that perhaps an evil spirit is at work here. I began to pray, and after praying I became even more convinced that this was the work of the Devil. I threw all of the animals out of the carriage along with the rifle, but looking back, I see the rifle chasing after me. I ordered the driver to stop. I grabbed the rifle and tied it to a tree with my own hands. I rode on, but still I see the rifle running alongside the carriage. I was frightened beyond measure, but as we were already approaching Uszomierz, I took the rifle up again and ordered the driver to take me straight to the cloister there of the Carmelite fathers. I told the prior all that had happened and handed him the rifle. He ordered it to be burned in my presence right there in the cloister yard, and as it burned an unbearable sulphurous stench arose in the yard, and what is even more amazing, when the fire had died down, not only was the stock gone, but the barrel and the flintlock as well. Not a trace of it remained; all of it had disappeared in the flames: lock, stock, and barrel, as if it had been made of straw.

On another occasion he told how one day, upon leaving his manor house together with his hounds and riding off some distance, an old woman stopped his horse by grabbing its reins. She was begging for alms.

"So I go for my pocketbook," he says, "for it's never right to neglect the poor, but not a copper coin do I find. There was nothing there but a half-zloty piece. This was, you know, when they began issuing złotys, half-złotys, and silver groschen. I felt sorry for the old woman, but even in Ukraine, where you have everything in abundance, a half-zloty or even a silver groschen is still worth something."

"This is what I say to myself, but out loud to the woman I say, 'I could manage a silver groschen, but half a złoty is overdoing it. But if you could give me a silver groschen back in change, I'd gladly give you what I have in my pocket.'

"And she says to me, 'Give it here, then, and here's your silver groschen.'

"And so the exchange was made, and I put her coin into my pocket. And do you know what, gentlemen? I was never able to get rid of that silver groschen. Whoever I'd give it to, it would end up back in my pocket again. For the life of me I couldn't figure out what this meant, until one day I was playing cards with some friends, and when it came time for me to cover my bet, in my enthusiasm I tossed in that silver groschen. I immediately thought the better of it, but then I figured it'd be back soon enough. But it never was. It disappeared like a stone in the ocean, and that very day I swore I'd never lay hands on another card for as long as I live, and as you can see for yourselves, gentlemen, I have kept my word."

All of these things were rather difficult to take on face value, and everyone around here said that since he was a Rusyn, he shared with his compatriots a proclivity for superstition, and so he mixed up in his mind various things he had experienced, but as for me, I knew him to be an honorable person, and I took him at his word. After all, were we to reject from the totality of human knowledge all the accounts of reliable people, that would add up to a very small sum indeed. To be sure, a gullible person is easily fooled, especially if he consorts with any odd sort of person, but if a man relies only on his own intellect, and sweeps aside the testimony of respectable people simply because it seems to him that their God-given intellect is inferior to his own, he will never become truly enlightened.

The Samsonów estate had once been the property of the Zator princes who, though themselves Poles, fell within the German realm. Legend has it that Witibald, the last of the Zator princes, had as an only child a daughter who, in her tenth year, was betrothed to a nephew of the Roman emperor. Witibald's purpose was to preserve the independence of his principality, which, according to law, was to become part of Poland upon the death of the last male heir of the line. That mighty and independent prince erected a defensive castle in Samsonów, and he resided in it from time to time. Witibald was arrogant, cruel, and without fear of God or love for humankind. In any case in her sixteenth year that only daughter of his fell in love with a young Polish knight and allowed herself to be abducted by him on the same day that the Roman emperor's nephew arrived in Zator to take her for his bride. It is easy to imagine the mighty prince's humiliation, and the anger he felt upon being deceived in a way that foiled all his well-laid schemes. He left Zator and settled for good, so he said, in the Samsonów castle. There he seemed to have given himself over to a life of piety, praying daily in his chapel and generously receiving pilgrims and men of the cloth. However, he never forgave his daughter, and he forbade anyone so much as to mention her. In the meantime, the daughter, weighed down by her father's curse, journeyed to Kraków along with her husband to seek the special indulgence of the bishop of Kraków. She begged the bishop to try to obtain her father's forgiveness. The bishop journeyed to Samsonów and was received with all due pomp and circumstance, emboldening the bishop to speak with his pastoral voice. He beseeched the prince that he allow himself to be propitiated in regard to the anger he felt toward his daughter. The prince allowed himself to be propitiated, and he declared that if his daughter, his son-in-law, and the parson in Kielce who had married them would gather together at his castle, he would persuade them of the affection he bore for them. The bishop brought them to Samsonów himself, wanting to be a witness to the festive reconciliation of father and daughter. Everything took place in the bishop's presence, and the prince showed himself to be so kind that the tenderhearted bishop, in taking leave of him, repeated over and over how he considered that day to have been the happiest one in all the days of his pastoral ministry.

Barely had the bishop entered the grove of pine trees that fronted on Samsonów than he was set upon by an armed detachment of soldiers who dragged the bishop out of his carriage and began attacking him with their swords. They no doubt would have hacked him to pieces had it not been for the divine intervention of God in the form of a gallant count from Skałka who, along with several knights and retainers, at just that moment had been heading to Tyniec for a tourney. The count wrenched the bishop from the arms of his assailants, took them all into custody, and transported the prisoners, along with the half-dead bishop, to Kraków. There it transpired that these assailants belonged to the court of the Prince of Zator. They readily admitted that they had been sent by him with instructions to murder the bishop and his entire entourage.

The bishop laid a curse on the prince, and the king commanded that he appear before him in Kraków. The prince haughtily replied that, being a sovereign ruler of another jurisdiction, he recognized no authority save that of the Roman emperor; that he had no intention of standing before any court, whether royal or ecclesiastical; that he was prepared to meet force with force; and that he had no doubt that the emperor of Rome would not stand idly by while his vassal was threatened with violence.

It would no doubt have ended badly were it not for the circumstance that not a trace of the daughter, the son-in-law, or the parson from Kielce could ever be found. It was merely surmised that the prince had had all three of them murdered. The prince himself died shortly thereafter, still under the bishop's curse, without benefit of sacrament, which in any case he had not even requested. It was said that the last words he uttered were a blasphemy, and that his body at death was black as coal.

Upon his death the principality of Zator was incorporated into the Crown Kingdom along with part of its movable possessions. Another part was distributed to the son-in-law's relatives, who had initiated an investigation into his murder, and no less of a part to relatives of the parson from Kielce. The Samsonów property was joined to that of the Kraków bishopric, and with time the entire incident receded into the past and was forgotten.

While under the management of Mr. Pogorzelski, the prince bishop, in the course of inspecting his various properties, paid a visit to Samsonów, where he tarried for several days. I, along with with several other courtiers, comprised his retinue. The prince expressed the desire to see the interior of the castle, where for several centuries the foot of man had not trod. The locals said that during the night something haunted the place, and that as if from somewhere deep within its bowels moans could be heard. Sometimes there were even sounds of a terrible scuffle. With the assistance of several blacksmiths Mr. Pogorzelski had all the castle doors opened, and we, along with the prince, entered it on the following day.

The castle, walled in on all sides according to the ancient fashion, had withstood the centuries intact, although bats, spider webs, and thick dust so disfigured everything inside that one might have thought that all was in ruins. There were the traces of paintings and decorative friezes carved in stone, along with hanging spiders and various implements, but it all looked terrifying as we walked about the enormous halls, overcome by an inexpressible sense of gloom. However, it seemed to have no unpleasant effect on the prince bishop, who, having walked about the entire castle to his heart's content, turned to Mr. Pogorzelski and said,

"My dear Mr. Pogorzelski, this castle is beautiful; a view of the entire surroundings spreads out before one's eyes in all directions. We must make it habitable again. Find yourself a place in the castle to live, and do it as quickly as possible, so that you may oversee the work. As early as next year, God willing, you will welcome us here; for I have a mind to spend several weeks a year here, along with my retinue."

As soon as we had left Mr. Pogorzelski spotted for himself on the right-hand side of the castle a comfortable enough place for himself and another place for an accountant, and he ordered everything to be cleaned up, the stoves to be put in working order, and the windows to be caulked. Shortly afterwards, in accordance with his master's orders, he moved in, and restoration work on the castle began. Already in the reconnoitering stage, during which the castle was inspected from top to bottom, a barrel of Hungarian wine was found in the cellar hanging from its iron hoops, but you could cut the wine with a knife. In the end they managed to extract several bottles-worth of liquid from it, while the prince seasoned the cellar with the dregs.

Mr. Pogorzelski often found himself in Kraków. We had always known him to be of a rather ribald disposition, but of late we had noticed that he had become increasingly morose, to the point that he finally fell into a deep melancholy. At last he went to the bishop and asked to be relieved of his duties, so that he could return to Ukraine. That both surprised and upset the prince bishop, who had an angelic heart and who had become very attached to Mr. Pogorzelski's services.

"Tell me, my dear Pogorzelski, have you suffered any wrong here, that you wish to leave me?"

"Oh no, my most reverend prince. I have never had it better anywhere else than here. Your bread is tasty, and I shed tears at the prospect of leaving such a benevolent master, but I am being pestered and persecuted."

"By whom, my dear sir?"

"By whom? Why, by an evil spirit."

"Get a grip, Pogorzelski, whatever has come over you? You must be sick."

"I know that I will be thought a madman, but I swear on my lord Jesus Christ that from the moment I set foot in this accursed castle, the Devil gives me no peace."

"And what does he do to you?"

"What does he do? Why, he follows me around everywhere and keeps repeating the same thing after everything I do. When I wake up in the morning, I say my prayers, and no sooner have I finished them than I hear the loudly uttered words: 'Mr. Pogorzelski, you are praying, while I am burning!' I cross myself, and the voice repeats, 'Mr. Pogorzelski, you are crossing yourself, and I am burning!' No sooner do I order the horses to be harnessed than I hear the voice: 'Mr. Pogorzelski, you are heading out into the fields, but I am burning!' Whatever I might try to do, the Devil keeps repeating to me, 'Mr. Pogorzelski, I am burning!' I think I can escape by leaving the castle and returning to my former residence, but no! Once having caught the curse, I can't get rid of it. Whether in the castle, going out into the fields, or traveling to Kraków, the Devil's voice follows me. Even today, as I ordered my things to be packed for my trip to Ukraine, I hear the same voice: 'Mr. Pogorzelski, you are heading for Ukraine to get rid of me, but nothing will come of it. You're packing your things, but I am burning!'"

"Tell me, my dear Pogorzelski, does anyone besides yourself hear this voice?"

"Well, it would be hard to swallow if I were the only one to hear it. People would think me a madman and be done with it. But several days ago at night I began to have a headache, and I ordered my servant, a Rusyn just like me, to brew some saffron tea. He rustled it right up and served me a pot of boiling liquid and a teacup on a tray. No sooner had I stretched out my hand for the tea than the voice resounds: 'Mr. Pogorzelski, you want a cup of tea, but I am burning!' My servant Chwedko dropped the tray and its contents right on my lap, scalding me, while he himself ran out of the room screaming at the top of his lungs."

"This is an extraordinary matter indeed," replied the prince bishop, but it will do you no good to leave me, because you yourself say that the voice travels with you. It will catch up with you even as far away as Ukraine."

"I hope that the most holy Lady of Berdyczów will rescue me from that."

"My dear Pogorzelski, the most holy Maiden reigns over us all, both here and in Berdyczów, but it was the Lord Jesus Christ that gave us power over evil spirits. Return to Samsonów, and tomorrow I will visit you in my ecclesiastical role and hold a mass with my travelling altar. Arrange everything with my chaplain."

Next day we rode behind the prince bishop to Samsonów. The prince stopped in at the local manor house, since the castle was not yet ready to receive guests. Only masons, carpenters, and stove-fitters were working there. And Mr. Pogorzelski, keeping to his room, was dealing with the voice. Having spent the night in the manor house, at the break of day the prince asked to be taken to the castle, where we were all waiting for him. Lickety split a proper altar was set up in a hall that had just been tidied up, and in which a goodly number of people were already assembled. We waited behind Mr. Pogorzelski at the entrance to welcome the bishop, and, as we were leading him into the room in which the most holy of secrets were about to be revealed, in passing we all heard the voice: 'Mr. Pogorzelski, you have called in the bishop to deal with me, but I am burning!' This discomfited the bishop a little, but he kept moving forward.

Before the mass began the bishop spent an extraordinarily long time praying; evidently trying to summon up the strength for his mission. All of a sudden, his face began to shine with a marvelous holy radiance. As befits a bishop, the mass was sung responsively, with the clerics and nobility who had accompanied him singing the responses along with the local folk. Mr. Pogorzelski listened to the holy mass while lying on the floor in the shape of a cross. Following the mass the bishop, still at the altar, leaned on his crozier, took a cross in his hands, and intoned at the top of his voice: 'Every spirit praises God!' 'And we too praise him,' everyone responded. Then, and no one could see from where, a solitary voice rang out: "Mr. Pogorzelski, you are praising God, but I am burning!"

You can imagine, gentleman, how we all took fright, even though it was not at night but in broad daylight.

The prince bishop began his exorcism. Villagers still live in Samsonów who remember it, and you can ask them whether I am telling you the truth. After the exorcism was finished, the prince bishop proclaimed:

"Oh Spirit created by God, in the name of that God, who became incarnate in the womb of the Holy Virgin, and from whom I have received my pastorship over this flock, I enjoin you to say who you are and how I may bring you salvation."

Upon which a shrill voice replied:

"For me there is no salvation. I was the prince of Zator, and I caused the death of my daughter, my son-in-law, and the priest who married them. Ever since then, when human footsteps enter this castle I give no peace to the person who manages this castle, until such time as the bodies of my victims be buried in sanctified ground."

"Where are these bodies?"

"In this castle. Bring in your architect, and he will find them."

Forthwith they brought out Bojanowski, the bishop's own architect, and he began to measure the castle. He came upon a double wall, and he ordered that it be penetrated. Inside, a small room was revealed, containing three skeletons, two male and one female. It appeared that the prince had immured them alive and left them there to starve to death.

The prince bishop conducted a sumptuous funeral and funded the construction of a beautiful chapel which one may still visit in Samsonów, and he further established a fund for a chaplain to say three masses per week, one each for the repose of those three souls. And ever since that funeral Mr. Pogorzelski ceased to be pestered by the voice.

—ca. 1850. Translated by Oscar Swan

*Cultural References.* The Bar Confederacy of 1768–1772 was an armed insurrection raised by wealthy Polish magnates in the fortress of Bar in Podolia (now in Ukraine) against the increasing influence of Russia in Polish affairs, and specifically against the installation of Stanisław August Poniatowski as king, at Russia's behest. Its defeat resulted in the first partition of Poland, as the result of which large portions of Polish territory were ceded to Austria, Prussia, and Russia.

Kajetan Sołtyk (1715–1788) was bishop of Kraków from 1759 until his death. Active in politics, Sołtyk, a supporter of the Bar Confederacy, was a fanatic opponent of non-Catholics (meaning Protestants, Orthodox Christians, Muslims, and Jews) and of King Stanisław August.

Polesie is a natural and historical area stretching from the eastern reaches of central Poland into contemporary Ukraine and Belarus.

The tynf was a silver coin, partially made of silver, more or less the equivalent of a złoty, emitted during the 1660s but still in circulation through much of the eighteenth century. There were thirty groschen to a tynf.

The Rusyns are an ethnic and dialect group in Western Ukraine living close to or in the Carpathian Mountains.

Tyniec is a historic village on the Vistula River just south of Kraków, inhabited since prehistoric times. Tyniec is known for its enormous Benedictine abbey, founded in 1044, built on a promontory overlooking the river.

The Polish-Lithuanian Commonwealth consisted of the Crown Kingdom of Poland and the Grand Duchy of Lithuania. The alliance of Poland and Lithuania existed by dynastic union from 1386 and by official union from 1569, and from then until the dissolution of Poland under the partitions in 1795.

Our Lady of Berdyczów was a revered seventeenth-century icon of the Virgin Mary, enshrined in 1756 in the Carmelite Monastery in Berdyczów, a major trading center now in Volhynia, Ukraine. The icon was consumed by fire in 1941 during World War II.

*Critical Commentary.* Some say that the gothic tale, of which "I Am Burning" could be proposed as an example, was a response to and rejection of late eighteenth-century rationalism and its reliance on science and the progressive social thought that characterized the spirit of the European Enlightenment, more or less on the principle of the common interpretation of Hamlet's admonition that "there are more things in heaven and earth, Horatio, than are dreamt of in your philosophy."

The gothic tale is exemplified in world literature by the English novels *The Monk* (1796) by Matthew Gregory Lewis, *Frankenstein* (1815) by Mary Shelley, or *Jane Eyre* (1847) by Charlotte Bronte. In American literature, Washington Irving, with his "Rip van Winkle" and "Legend of Sleepy Hollow" (1820) and other stories, and Edgar Allan Poe, with many or most of his short stories, are good examples of the gothic spirit. A continuant in contemporary American literature is Stephen King (for example, *The Shining*). Classic American television programs like Rod Serling's *The Twilight Zone* or *Alfred Hitchcock Present*s are also largely in the gothic mode and, of course, the television and film series *The Addams Family* parodies the conventions of the genre.

It is an unresolved question whether Rzewuski's "I Am Burning" should be viewed as a legitimate attempt at a "ghost story" or "gothic tale," or instead as an intentional spoof of the genre. Janusz Majewski, a Polish film director who created a 1967 short film based on the story for Polish television, chose to interpret it as a spoof (see discussion further below). A third option is that Rzewuski was just an inveterate spinner of tales for their own sake, and "I Am Burning" gave him the chance to concoct three memorable anecdotes (the rifle, the Devil's coin, and the prince of Zator), all folded into the backbone story of the colorful character of Mr. Pogorzelski.

One of the reasons "I Am Burning" is narratively effective is that, like a Walter Scott novel, it is firmly embedded in the historical reality of the country (here, Poland) in a way that makes the points at which the story diverges from reality difficult to detect. The Bar Confederacy was a real, and in Rzewuski's time, a still-living memory, as was the figure of Kajetan Sołtyk, a prominent bishop of Kraków who, unlike his depiction in the story, was a religious fanatic and a generally disagreeable individual and, at one time, was declared by the Polish Sejm (parliament) to be insane. The figure of Prince Witibald of Zator and the legend surrounding him and his cruelty are wholly confabulated, but the Duchy of Zator did exist, and the fact of its incorporation into the Crown Kingdom of Poland as of a particular date is a historical fact. The castle of Samsonów, supposedly built by the prince and later acquired by the bishop, is a figment of Rzewuski's imagination. One cannot visit either it or the charming chapel devoted to the memory of the murdered daughter and her husband, as Rzewuski encourages his readership to do, but in a land full of the tumbledown remains of medieval castles and ancient cemeteries, along with legends of past deeds and misdeeds of its early rulers, it seems reasonable to suppose that the story could just as easily be true as not, as could the legend of the burial alive of the prince's daughter, son-in-law, and the priest who married them, a well-enough known method of execution both in legend and sometimes in reality. By legend the medieval Catholic church sentenced monks and nuns to immurement and starvation for having broken their vows of chastity.

In its telling, "I Am Burning" ticks off many or most of the commonplaces one expects to find in a gothic tale. There is (a) a gloomy and mysterious setting, and, all the better, it is a medieval castle hanging with spider webs, bats, dank cellars, and rumors of mysterious voices and sounds; (b) a cruel and vengeful prince whose actions go beyond the bounds of moral acceptability, reminding one of the real figure of the sadistic count Dracula of Transylvania. Figures like this abound in eastern and southeastern European legends, and Rzewuski no doubt took inspiration from them, possibly wanting to create a similar legend for Poland; (c) an illicit, or at least an unsanctioned, romance and marriage as a backdrop to and propellant of the action; (d) the well-known themes of implacable revenge and a hereditary curse; (e) the appearance of a ghost and other supernatural occurrences (including the events described by Mr. Pogorzelski in the beginning, that is, the story of the Devil's hunting rifle and the Devil's silver coin; (f) the prominent role of a religious figure and a clash between the powers of the Devil and those of the Church; (g) a naïve and basically kind-hearted central victim who, through no fault of his own, lands in a situation where he finds himself out of his depth when challenged by evil powers. Mr. Pogorzelski has a veritable knack for landing in such predicaments.

Some aspects of "I Am Burning" suggest that this is not really a "serious" gothic tale, but a spoof of one, an intentionally humorous, all-in-fun piece meant to mock the genre, entertaining the reader along the way. At various points one has the feeling that the story is openly not taking itself seriously, undermining the gothic tone that the story otherwise would seem to be trying to maintain. It seems likely that Rzewuski has no serious agenda as a believer in the supernatural or in the hidden mysteries undergirding the world of visible reality but is just using the conventions of literature of the supernatural in order to hold his reader's attention, mocking the conventions of the gothic tale along the way. Here are some further considerations that might be used to support such an interpretation.

Mr. Pogorzelski's last name sounds perfectly plausible in Polish and, in fact, it is listed as a searchable surname on ancestry.com. However, it is based on the Polish word for "fire victim" (*pogorzelec*). Consequently, as soon as the ghost starts haunting him with his repeated chant "I am burning," the Polish-speaking reader begins to suspect that Rzewuski is pulling his leg.

In order to establish the authenticity and veracity of his story, Rzewuski purposely undermines it by presenting it to us through a double-distorting mirror of two first-person subjectivities, allowing the reader to dismiss everything as being the product of (a) the credulousness of the narrator, and (b) an over-active imagination on the part of his acquaintance Mr. Pogorzelski, whose fantastic stories of the magic hunting rifle and the ever-returning coin already predispose one to skepticism regarding anything further he might say.

After introducing himself at the beginning, the narrator disappears into the woodwork, so to speak, only to re-emerge conveniently toward the end on the same plane of action as Mr. Pogorzelski at the exorcism, in order to serve as a corroborative witness to the ghost's voice. However, one must take what this gullible witness says with skepticism. Perhaps Mr. Pogorzelski, who has a reputation as something of a prankster, was somehow playing an elaborate trick on everybody by projecting his voice. Perhaps his servant Chwedko, who, according to Pogorzelski, was also a witness to the voice, was in on the prank. Or maybe the narrator himself was. Or perhaps this was all just an all-for-fun piece of imaginative fiction told for the sheer enjoyment of telling it.

The voice of the ghost of Prince Witibald as he hounds Mr. Pogorzelski with his repeated incantation that "he is burning" becomes increasingly funny with each iteration, until the reader is practically laughing by the time the crucial and supposedly most serious and dramatic part of the action takes place, in which the bishop conducting the exorcism communicates directly with the ghost and asks him to identify himself and to tell him what he needs to do in order to obtain salvation. The seams of the story are partially revealed when the ghost intones that "for me there is no salvation." If that is true, then why is he going out of his way to free the spirit of his three murdered victims? After all, he has never before shown any inclination toward charity toward them.

It is certainly a peculiar way for a ghost to go about haunting someone. He seems more of a poltergeist (a prankster spirit) than a serious ghost. The prince's ghost, supposedly in need of salvation (of which he has just claimed he has no hope of attaining), just barely helps his cause to find the remains of the people he starved to death several centuries earlier by suggesting that they look for the bodies in the castle walls. If he truly wanted to speed up the work, he could have just come out and told them where to look, instead of forcing them to call in an architect to survey the building. For that matter, he could have told the same thing to Mr. Pogorzelski a long time ago, instead of following him around and haunting him to no evident purpose other than to satisfy his perverse need to annoy someone.

Among other unanswered questions is the mystery of just why Kajetan Sołtyk, the bishop of Kraków, was so tender-hearted as to go out of his way to help the prince escape the flames of eternal damnation for his past dastardly deeds, for which the prince's ghost himself gives no particular indication of being repentant. After all, the prince's ghost was operating under the curse of the bishop of several centuries earlier, whom the prince had outright tried to murder, and for which the prince has expressed no contrition. Why would the current bishop let the prince's ghost off so lightly, acting counter to the wishes of his predecessor? And what about his unburied victims who, after all, should have some say in the matter? One would also like to know how the mischievous ghost, if he were really being consumed by flames, would have had the leisure to playfully pursue and mock Mr. Pogorzelski in the first place. Possibly he was just enjoying finally having someone to pester. after waiting several hundred years for the opportunity to do so.

Another question that Rzewuski skillfully slips past the reader is how the story of the evil Prince Witibald of Zator ever became known in the first place since, as the narrator himself says, "with time the entire incident receded into the past and was forgotten." Clearly, an omniscient narrator has at this point sneakily displaced the original narrator, that is, the distant relative of the bishop of Kraków.

Logical questions like this do not occur to the reader during the course of a first reading. The reader becomes so absorbed by the unfolding action that he or she *suspends disbelief* in the interest of finding out what happens next. Only later, when one has had time to look back on the story critically, does one begin to raise questions of this sort. Whatever it is, a ghost story or a spoof of one, on the whole "I Am Burning" succeeds because of the author's skill in spinning a good yarn.

*Cinematic version.* In his 1967 made-for-TV version of this story, director Janusz Majewski takes major liberties with the plot. In it, Mr. Pogorzelski turns up in the dark of night in the study of a contemporary mystery-story writer to whom he wants to tell his story. In Majewski's adaptation of the story, once the bishop of Kraków finds out that the haunting ghost is that of the former owner of the castle, he shuts his exorcism down and tells Mr. Pogorzelski that his hands are tied, since a person has the right to haunt his own castle. There's nothing more he can do in the matter, he says, unless possibly write the Pope in Rome for advice. The Prince of Zator continues haunting Mr. Pogorzelski until his death two years later, and even after that he visits him in the grave, saying, "Mr. Pogorzelski, you are turning over in your grave, but I am burning." Mr. Pogorzelski says his greatest regret is that during his last two years on earth he lived a life of strict virtue, neither drinking nor chasing after young peasant girls, hoping thereby to rid himself of the voice by going to heaven. Instead, if he had lived a life of iniquity and gone to burn in hell, the prince would have been deprived of a logical basis for continuing to haunt him, for then they would both have been burning. The story ends as the writer receives a phone call for Mr. Pogorzelski who, when handed the phone, hears the familiar voice saying "Mr. Pogorzelski, you are telling your story to this mystery-story writer, while I am burning." Mr. Pogorzelski runs from the room to return to wherever he came from.

# The Later Nineteenth Century

The distance in sophistication between the anecdotal stories of Henryk Rzewuski and the mature short-story work of the Polish Positivists, with Bolesław Prus at the forefront, is sizable and made all the wider because Rzewuski places the action of his stories some fifty to seventy years prior to the time in which they were written. Polish literature of the early nineteenth-century Romantic period, was exceedingly rich and of high quality, but it was largely devoted to poetry and drama, not to prose fiction. In order to bridge the gap, as it were, between Rzewuski and the Positivists, we have chosen the following story by the late Romantic writer Cyprian Norwid to represent in this collection that otherwise missing link.

# Cyprian Kamil Norwid

Primarily a poet and essayist, with ambitions as a sculptor and painter, Cyprian Kamil Norwid (1821–1883) was either ignored or downright disparaged by the literary establishment of his day. As a result, he remained practically unpublished and unknown during his lifetime. Specializing in poetry of a national historiosophical nature, often imbued with a Christian sensibility, Norwid was "discovered" in the early 1900s by poets of the neoromantic Young Poland movement, who saw in him an originality well in advance of his time. Today Norwid is considered to be one of Poland's greatest nineteenth-century poets, and a major precursor of modern Polish poetics.

Orphaned at an early age, and quitting his studies before finishing high school, Norwid was a largely self-educated person of considerable erudition, particularly in history and archaeology. He left Poland at the age of twenty-one to study sculpture in Germany and Italy and was destined to live abroad for the rest of his life—for a while in the United States, where he had a chance to experience American baronial capitalism firsthand. Belonging to no literary movement other than his own personal one, Norwid made a meager living primarily from his skill as an illustrator and engraver. He was buried in a pauper's grave in Paris, soil from which was removed in 2001 and returned to Poland to be interred in the "crypt of poets" in Kraków's Wawel Cathedral.

Probably because Norwid wrote increasingly without benefit of a critical audience, much of his writing is idiosyncratic to the point of obscurity. The following work in prose, "Ad leones" (To the Lions), is the best known of a limited number of short stories Norwid left behind. In both style and theme it stands starkly apart from the socially committed literature of Positivism being written by his contemporaries in Poland. Like most of Norwid's work, it requires more than one reading to get close to a sense of the author's intent in writing it.

## Ad leones

His was a talent by no means unpromising, nor was he of an order disinclined to persevere, the red-bearded sculptor who went to the Café Greco almost every evening after working hours, accompanied by his Kirghisian greyhound bitch.

The very choice of such an animal, in whose plainly marked muscles grace and strength were combined, would have led any thoughtful observer to a favorable impression of the spiritual dignity of the man who favored this creature and no other.

General Jomini maintains that it is the horse and not the rider that makes the cavalry. If this is true, then, for reasons more deeply psychological, it should also be proper to maintain that the selection of one species of dog or another provides a telling indication of the mind and sensibility of the chooser. Clearly, the dog in the mind of a butcher would be altogether different from that of a hunter or a noblewoman. Lovely she was, that red-bearded sculptor's dog, pacing slowly before him, with open mouth, her amarant tongue spread over the white fangs like the fresh leaf of some purple flower.

She stepped slowly, with a kind of urbane grace, never brushing against anyone. But if any street urchins sought to annoy her she would glance back once at her master and then, like a perfect spring uncoiled, leap clean over the crowd and continue on her way, while the mischief-makers picked themselves up from the ground, not yet recovered from the shock, completely at a loss as to what had happened.

Likewise, at the café, she would leap over a few tables laden with glasses, disturbing nothing, then resume her slow and natural movements. She expected no applause, as if she deemed each of those sitting at the tables capable of doing the same themselves.

The lovely greyhound was therefore held in the same high regard by all. When we say "by all," we mean by a certain group, and by two Greek choruses, by the chorus of reciters and that of the gesticulators.

The red-bearded sculptor's group took up one of the four corners of the billiard room and consisted principally of the editor of a political and literary gazette, a handsome singer who gave lessons to foreigners, a gifted painter, and a young tourist whom his parents had sent, as he himself expressed it, "to form his opinion on things." The latter was accompanied by a tutor so "inseparable" that one was perpetually seeking the other all over the town, asking everywhere until eventually they met in the evening at the Café Greco.

All this and details more personal—one might have known almost involuntarily. Owing, perhaps to a certain transparency in the moral and social atmosphere and to the clarity with which the characters outlined themselves (two things little familiar to northern towns and people), it could happen that even a stranger who came to the café only once could easily have distinguished who worked at what, was busy with what, concerned with what, and even preoccupied with what at the moment.

A figure like the editor might, in fact, have been known by his public attributes alone, but a stranger would have been assisted in more rapid identification by his alert eyes, his facile courtesy and easy gestures, his reluctant speech and his faded umbrella, something like a cardinal's, and finally by the fact that when he once started speaking his style was that of a writer.

Anyone who has observed revolving glass gimlets kept in motion by a concealed mechanism, imitating to perfection a gushing stream of water, or seen such glasses revolving in the mouths of plaster lions surrounded by flowers and greenery and realized that neither leaf nor flower there has felt the proximity of a drop of water or its coolness and sustenance—will have a perfect picture of the style and eloquence of the editor.

What is his most recent preoccupation? Clearly it must be something exceptional, for he is dressed more carefully than of late and comes to the café at odd hours and for fleeting moments only.

The singer, likewise, with his mantle thrown over his arm or shoulder, humming a tune under his excessively groomed moustache, with a roll of music under his arm, was not at all difficult to decipher.

A less distinct type was the tutor (hunted by the youth entrusted to him), speaking rapidly with a faint lisp and spluttering saliva whenever he was in a fit of enthusiasm. He would, however, have been more amenable and comprehensible had he made less liberal use of the adjective "scientific," to which he was addicted. But he was adept with his pen, for while rolling a cigarette, one of his none too discreet but observant guests had spread his tobacco on a sheet of white paper, and had there observed, a year ago, the first words of a manuscript: "Survey of …" Yesterday, in the same place and under similar circumstances, he could see nothing added to it.

It was however generally known that he was working at the "Survey of …," but what was all the more astonishing in a man so scientifically minded was the fact that, when a billiard ball went off in the wrong direction, he would at once shift the weight of his body in the desired direction, helping to push the ball along with his eyes, seeking with his heel to change the course of the mass … An effort as useless as it is unscientific, contrary as it is to the law of gravity.

Of the red-bearded sculptor in black velvet, who is sitting motionless like an old Venetian taking no part in the trials and toil of the table, it is known that he has had enough already in the course of his daylong labors at his great work, carried on with great zeal; he is not looking for any further recreational effort in the evening.

However, you need not belong to an artist's intimate circle in our honored Rome to have a preconceived idea of his work. The Spanish Square is quite close to the Café Greco—wide steps spreading like two wings rising toward the Monte Pincio like some enormous legendary bird that wishes to soar from the pavement, waiting only for people to gather on its wings.

That square and those stairs are the forum for models, some of them resting, some looking for jobs, one has only to approach one of these sculpturable, paintable and witty groups to learn about every artist's work.

There also it was very well known that the sculptor was working on a colossal group, that the work was to reflect the inner tragedy of mankind, that it was a composition in the mood of Euripides, representing two Christians thrown to the lions at the time of Domitian, and these particulars were so commonly referred to that an intimate friend would not call the sculptor by his name but by "ad leones."

To this the sculptor responded in the right spirit, by slightly raising the wide brim of his hat and accentuating this with a significant movement of his right arm, as if he were adding a handful of clay, which made the greyhound stoop and look up into her master's eyes as it trying to guess what he wanted.

The artists' work, which had barely seen the light of day, which had hardly been born, was becoming some kind of magic symbol. Sitting in a café and reading in the paper of some tragic political event, people would turn to the sculptor and say, meaningfully, "ad leones"—to which he would reply with a conspiratorial and ambiguous wink of his left eye.

The farcical aspect of this custom notwithstanding, it is really remarkable (and quite unheard of in cold and northern countries) how much the good will of the public contributes towards the perfection of a work of art and its introduction into the world.

Indeed, happiness is only for an artist who knows how to understand and coolly accept so hospitable a reception of his work.

It is a custom of many years' standing to use the Greek café as your address and collect your post there. I was slightly astonished, coming one morning at an early hour, to find the editor and the sculptor already there.

I even thought of going past them, thinking them particularly occupied with some important business, but the greyhound which was sent to fetch me compelled me to approach her master and his friend. Having done so, and after receiving a verbal invitation to visit the sculptor in his studio at a set date and hour, I said:

"I'm not quite so profane as to think that you want to show us a work of art which has already been completed! ... But I think that you may have reached that interesting stage at which an artist has already revealed and established his general idea; experts however maintain, and not without reason, that an artist should reserve to the very end the right to alter his composition entirely, and it is in fact this that gives a composition life, motion, and spirit ..."

The editor promptly began to support and develop this theme, and though he was making some pencil notes he continued to take an active part in our conversation. Then, for politeness' sake, they both asked me if I wouldn't like to tell them what I was working on?

"My small part in things artistic does not permit me to make much of myself; but reciprocating your frankness I confess I have lately been working on two heads. When I say two heads, this also implies everything pertaining to their completeness and motion, for the leading idea of the composition is embodied in these two heads alone. The object being that one of the figures should turn her eyes towards heaven and the other either towards the ceiling or towards a hook where a chandelier will be suspended. The eyes of both are turned upwards—I must admit that this task has often proved trying enough!"

The sculptor rested his head on his strong hand in a manner that made the greyhound lying at his feet get up and try to catch her master's eye. The editor was making lines with his pencil on the table and I, politely taking my leave of them, left the place—being stopped for a moment at the door by the young tourist enquiring after his tutor.

A few steps away, I met the tutor on the steps and was informed that my invitation to the studio was no special favor and that all his friends and acquaintances were expected there, to help establish the ultimate and irrevocable spiritual content of the group and the attributes of the individual figures. Moreover, the editor, owing to his connections, had scored a splendid success: the rich correspondent of a big American newspaper was considering commissioning the sculpture, buying it and shipping it to America provided that both the composition and its execution were in accord with his wishes and ideas.

On the day of my visit to the sculptor's studio I found myself among a number of well-known people and in the presence of an interesting sight.

The disorder and the untouched layers of dust in the four corners of the large hall made a fantastic frame. But dust covering exquisite works in plaster highlights them and renders a good sculpture more comprehensible.

The disorder, which can be explained, should not be put down to untidiness, but rather to drama.

In the center of the studio, exposed to the full light, stood a bulky mass of damp clay, representing an unfinished group, from which the sculptor was just moving the last pieces of moist cloth.

This task was accompanied by loud cheers, freely proffered in anticipation: "Bravo, bravo!" they cried, whenever the removal of a rag revealed a well-molded shoulder, a hip, or the main folds of a robe.

The male figure promised a very beautiful torso, the girl's, a dramatic attitude; both figures exalted the pro Christo sign of a cross. The lion which was supposed to be stunned and faltering at their feet was only a lump of clay, resembling some piece of furniture which gave the rest of the group a more finished appearance.

"Ad leones, ad leones!" exclaimed the young tourist.

And rushing to the darkest corner of the room, by the door, from behind a Dionysiac figure he pulled a small boy with a napkin over his shoulder and a basket full of wine, the immediate consumption of which helped to intensify the cheering.

The sculptor himself spoke in an appropriately challenging tone.

The tutor, among some busts standing on the floor, pointed to the nearest and said:

"This surely is Domitian?" "You are not mistaken," retorted the sculptor, and kicked the emperor's nose off, which made the greyhound, who had been lying there like a bronze griffon, rise and sniff the bits of broken plaster, whereupon she resumed her former statuesque and serene posture.

The handsome singer threw his cloak gracefully over one shoulder and began to sing in his superb baritone, first very low, then in a booming voice:

Tyrants, bow down!
Judgment draws nigh.
The people shall strike
As a bolt from on high …
—taramta tata rata …

Tyrants, bow down! …

The painter and the young tourist seconded him:

—ramta tarata tata! …

Tyrants, bow down!

This moment of ecstasy was followed by a psychologically necessary silence, which was interrupted by the painter:

"I also happen recently to have created something which gratifies me, but I have still to ask some well-read person what it represents, what it will finally be … For as it is, it could be Cleopatra … or the Assumption."

When silence reigned supreme and everybody had taken their seats again, the editor, addressing himself primarily to the sculptor but simultaneously to the audience as a whole, spoke as follows:

"No one present here has any other thought, nor will have after careful consideration, than to see the work of our friend and great master gain its rightful place in the future. Considering that investments have already been considerable and will continue to increase … "

Here everyone indicated his affirmation in one way or another before listening to the sequel.

"Well then, a rich correspondent of a big American newspaper might be, or in fact already is, a welcome sponsor. As we do not know what church this gentleman belongs to (and there are scores of them in America) it might I think be wise, and aesthetic, to remove the crosses from the hands of the figure. Why is it necessary to have this lifeless symbol, whose feeling at all events prevails in the work as a whole but whose actual presence might make it impossible for the client (who may be of the Jewish faith) to set the sculpture up in the park in front of his house and might prevent him from acquiring it?

The sculptor remarked that the crosses were breaking the main lines of the composition to advantage but, playing with the box-wood handle of a wide chisel, he looked at everyone attentively, as if he were trying to fathom the general opinion. As I was standing nearest he turned to me with a look.

"I personally think," I said, that the grasping of the cross is one of the most complex problems both of choreography and of sculpture.

THE FINGER TOUCHES THE SYMBOL—this should be neither clever nor elegant, menacing nor meaningless, neither easy, nor exaggerated, neither too simple nor too sophisticated … neither beautiful, nor ugly. I don't know anything more difficult. An artist who can handle that can handle any composition in the world … "

So said I, hardly aware that this remark had the opposite effect to that which I intended, for the sculptor and the editor suddenly exclaimed, "Why, that's one great difficulty less," and the sculptor, repeating the remark once more to himself, ran up the steps leading up to the sculpture, where with two rapid strokes of his box-wood chisel he chopped the cross out of the male figure's grasp, and then stayed his hand above the hand of the female figure, while the tutor exclaimed:

"If anything is to be placed in the woman's hand for the sake of breaking the main lines the scientific approach should be that the Jews and later the Christians had taken over the old Chaldean and Egyptian custom, according to which keys are placed in the hands of persons revealing or predicting important matters. (Traces of this are found in the Evangelists—the keys of St. Peter—and in the Apocalypse)."

The sculptor, whose hand had been at rest during this speech, lowered the tool over the second cross and, with a few deft strokes, indicated the outlines of a key.

This happened almost like magic, the results of a common trend of feelings and ideas and a complete absence of rational protest.

However, when the sculptor descended he turned to the editor, saying:

"But in this way and for these very reasons the whole Christian scene would have to be changed!"

The editor, as though he were taking the tutor for a witness, said with an impatient smile:

"Is this a historical work? Isn't this scene placed in the times of Domitian and not those of Nero? Are these figures portraits of some definite martyrs? Of course not, it isn't the individuals that matter, but the drama.'

To which the tutor added:

"A cursory scientific survey of the sculpture could explain everything—they need not be Christians thrown to the lions at all. They may in fact represent struggle, sacrifice, or in fact merit. They may in fact represent all that the artist was searching for in that work, all that he cultivates, and everything that the public expects."

The slightly drooling speaker wiped his mouth while the sculptor was shaking both their hands.

Meanwhile the singer, the tourist and the painter, who were in the habit of avoiding any discussion (unnecessarily taxing their brains) had withdrawn quietly and politely from the studio.

The silver bark of the greyhound, whose custom it was to accompany departing guests with the usual ceremonial, was suddenly heard from the corridor. The sculptor made a sign to the editor and to all of us that he could guess from the dog's voice what was happening.

Suddenly the door opened, admitting a short gentleman in a flat gray hat and a neat gray suit, with an impeccable white kerchief and waistcoat, under which appeared a thick gold chain, maintaining on his belly a number of keys and seals studded with precious stones. It was the American, correspondent of a big United States newspaper.

He greeted the editor cordially, bowed to the sculptor and, waving politely in our direction, approached the sculpture directly.

For a brief moment he stood looking at the statue with gray, deep-set eyes, his hat pushed back from his brow, stroking his reddish beard—which owing to the lack of moustaches looked all the more bushy.

"I wish to get a detailed explanation of the figures," he said, turning to the editor and to the sculptor, who suddenly withdrew half a step so as not to be the first to speak.

"This is … er … as it has been mentioned before," said the editor, "a pathetic scene taken from life's tragedies … the man represents energy, action, which initiates work … the woman hastens to participate. "And she," interrupted the American, "is, I think, holding a key, because I see below (and here he pointed to the lump of clay intended to become a lion) a coffer …,

"This woman, then, symbolizes thrift … The man's energy promises to become very beautiful and appropriate. In my opinion some agricultural implements and artisans' tools should be sculptured near the coffer. As it is now, the thing looks more like a sleeping animal than a coffer! … "

The sculptor approached the group, and marked out the form of a sickle and the sides of the coffer. The American, having walked once more round the statue, exclaimed:

"Never before have I struck on a more clearly expressed and beautiful thought. The group symbolizes CAPITALIZATION, in a most comprehensive and accessible way … For the moment, while the work is at its present stage, it will suffice if my friend the editor will kindly write on my card …"

He handed his card to the editor, who was obligingly getting ready to write, and continued.

"The following:

"Isaak Edgar Middlebank, Junior, hereby orders from the distinguished Sculptor: a group symbolizing CAPITALIZATION, which is to be executed in spotless and flawless white marble and whose price should not exceed by much the sum of fifteen thousand dollars."

"Will that be satisfactory?" the American asked. The sculptor in turn handed his card to the editor who wrote:

"The Sculptor undertakes to execute a group CAPITALIZATION in white marble, as spotless and flawless as possible, the price of which shall not exceed by much the sum of seventy-five thousand lire according to the order of Isaak Edgar M Junior, Esq., etc., etc."

Whereupon the American scanned the cards carefully through his eyeglass, requested that the date, which had been omitted, be added and when this was done exchanged the cards, saying: "Now everything is all right … I congratulate you on your great talent (here they shook hands) and on your beautiful dog! What an exquisite animal—what breeding! … I'm convinced there isn't another like her in the world." Saying this, he bowed and made for the door.

With one hand the sculptor deftly threw the wet rag over "Capitalization," with the other he caught his hat and hurried after the editor and the tutor, who were complimenting the guest, for whom a modest carriage was waiting to take him elsewhere.

My heart was full and heavy and I felt humiliated … A wind or a moan was dismally whispering in my ear:

And thus everything, in this justly cursed world of ours, has to be sold for six dollars! (30 pieces of silver) …

And although I had promised myself not to say anything, not to add anything nor repeat anything, I could not bear all that moral burden. I told the editor:

"How far remote are faith and the faithful being thrown to the lions from the idea of capitalization! … "

Adjusting his spectacles, drawing something with his umbrella on the pavement and not raising his eyes, he answered:

"A newspaper office is not a telephone. We do the same thing every day with every feeling and every thought … REDACTION IS REDUCTION … "

"Just as conscience is conscience," I replied.

—1881. TRANSLATED BY ILONA RALF SUES

*Cultural Notes.* Antoine-Henri, Baron Jomini (1779–1869) was a French-Swiss officer who served as a general in the French and later in the Russian army, and who was one of the most celebrated writers on the Napoleonic art of war. The Roman Emperor Domitian, AD 51–96, ruled AD 81–96, was a staunch upholder of the traditional Roman Gods.

*Commentary.* Although they are somewhat hidden, one can detect the classical short-story movements in this crotchety story, narrated by someone who depicts himself as an outsider to the main story, a person having a decidedly jaundiced view of the chance acquaintances he has made who, together with him, habituate the Café Greco in Rome, an artist's hangout full of various types of posers, at the center of whom is an up-and-coming sculptor, given to airs and to surrounding himself with the accoutrements appropriate to the artistic persona he tries to project, including his rakish hat and a coterie of admirers who gather around him, and most prominently, the elegant Kirghisian greyhound that accompanies him at work and on his jaunts about town. The sculptor is said to be working on an ambitious sculpture tentatively entitled "Ad leones," depicting two Christian figures, a male and a female, about to be devoured by lions during the time of the tyrant Roman emperor Domitian. The lion is temporarily stunned by the crosses held in the hands of the figures and lies cowering at their feet.

The Turning Point occurs when the sculptor decides it is time to have a showing of his project in its rough stage, with the lion and his victims barely hinted at in the wet plaster model. His admirers suitably ooh and aah over it. The Crisis begins as a wealthy American newspaper publisher, a prospective purchaser of the work when finished, visits the studio. Totally misunderstanding the spirit of the piece in its inchoate form, and with the active encouragement of the editor, the American purchases it in advance with the proviso that certain changes be made to it to suit his taste. Among other changes, the lion becomes transformed into a money-chest, while the cross in the hands of the female victim is exchanged for a set of keys, now representing "thrift." With a few tools and agricultural implements thrown in for good measure, the work, now entitled "capitalization" (a more current translation might be "capitalism") will fit the client's needs and expectations perfectly. The climax occurs as the sales agreement is drawn up, leading to the Aftermath, as the narrator expresses disgust at the corrosive and debasing effect of commerce on art.

In the end, the artist willingly prostitutes his talent and artistic vision for financial gain, and it is "art" that ends up being thrown to the lions of commerce. At least that is a common interpretation of the story.

There is a question as to how committed the sculptor was to his "artistic vision." His red beard (and that of the American newspaper man) is what today would be called a "dog-whistle"; it suggests that both men are Jewish and that, therefore, the Christian theme of the sculpture was chosen only provisionally, not out of any feeling for the subject.

Norwid was a practicing Christian, but there is no suggestion in his other writing of any hostility toward Judaism or Jews (if anything the opposite). The point here is that the sculptor did not necessarily prostitute any artistic vision he may have had, but that he never had one in the first place. He was interested in fame and money all along, and was more than willing to accede to the customer's preferences.

The sculptor is possessed of great skill, as his ability to quickly transform his sculpture from one representation into another amply testifies. The narrator is duly appreciative of the sculptor's talent, at one point conceding the inferiority of his own modest abilities when compared to those of the other man's. Norwid seems to be saying that, no matter how valuable skill is, there is a profound difference between a skilled artisan and an artist.

Norwid's main focus of criticism is on the symbiosis he sees as having developed in his day between "business" and "art." He is especially disparaging of the effect that "new" and "American" money is having on art, money which in the present instance has likely been made by peddling sensational newspaper stories to the masses.

One thing everyone in this story can agree on, ranging from the hangers-on, to the narrator, to the rich American, is that the sculptor's Kirghisian greyhound bitch is of unparalleled natural grace and beauty. All by herself she is able to transcend and cancel out the crassness of the characters and the transactions taking place around her.

# Bolesław Prus

Born Aleksander Głowacki, Bolesław Prus (1847–1912) took his pen name from the name of his family's hereditary coat of arms. He had a day job as a journalist and commentator with a regular column in the pages of an important Warsaw newspaper. Besides writing feuilletons depicting and commenting on everyday Warsaw life, he wrote several important novels and short stories, all of which are still widely read today, especially in schools. His four-volume novel *The Doll*, about a successful department-store owner who unsuccessfully courts a woman above his middle-class station, is widely considered to be Poland's best nineteenth-century novel.

Prus was an example of the type of person he sometimes features in his works: a displaced former nobleman who has moved to the city for economic reasons. As a fifteen-year-old, Prus had participated in, and was badly wounded in, the disastrous 1863 or "January" uprising against Russian occupation in the eastern part of the country. He was imprisoned for a while for his role in the insurrection and was stripped of his official status as a nobleman.

## The Waistcoat

Certain people have a bent for collecting curios of greater or less value, depending on their pocket. I, too, own a collection, though it's a modest one, as is usual at the beginning stages.

It includes the play I wrote back in grammar school, during my Latin classes. 'I'here are a few dried flowers, which will have to be replaced with new ones. There is . . .

I don't believe there is anything else, other than a certain tattered old waistcoat.

Here it is: faded at the front, worn at the back. It's covered in stains, some of the buttons are missing, and there's a hole in the side that was probably made with a cigarette. But the most interesting things are the adjustable straps. The strap with the buckle has been shortened and sewn onto the waistcoat in an unprofessional fashion, while the other has marks from the teeth of the buckle along almost its entire length.

Looking at it, it's easy to guess that the owner of the garment was probably losing weight daily, until he finally got to the stage at which the waistcoat was no longer of any use, but instead he was very much in need of a dress coat from a funeral parlor, fastened up under his chin.

I confess I'd be glad to pass this rag on to someone else; it's creating a bit of a problem for me. I don't have a cupboard for my collection, and 1 don't fancy keeping this wretched item among my own things. And yet there was a time when I bought it for a price greatly exceeding its value, and I would have given even more if the seller had known how to barter. There arc times in life when one likes to surround oneself with objects associated with sorrow.

That sorrow did not dwell in my home but in the flat of my next-door neighbors. Each day I could look from my window into their little room.

Right up till April there were three of them: the gentleman, the lady, and a little maid, who I believe slept on a trunk next to the wardrobe. The wardrobe was of dark cherry wood. In July, if my memory serves me rightly, only two of them were left, the gentleman and the lady, for the maid had gone to work for a family who paid her three rubles a year and who ate a hot dinner every day.

By October, the lady was alone. Or rather, not entirely alone, for the room still contained a lot of furniture: two beds, a table, the wardrobe. However, at the beginning of November the unneeded items were auctioned off, and of all the mementos of the lady's husband, she kept only the waistcoat that is now in my possession.

But one day at the end of November she called a secondhand dealer to the empty flat and sold him her umbrella for two zlotys and her husband's waistcoat for forty groszes. Then she locked up the flat, slowly crossed the courtyard, handed the key to the care-taker, stared for a short while at what used to be her window, on which small snowflakes were falling, and then she walked through the gate and disappeared.

The secondhand dealer remained in the courtyard. He lifted up the great collar of his cloak, thrust the umbrella he had just bought under his arm, and, wrapping the waistcoat around his hands, which were red from the cold, he grunted, "Goods for sale, gentlemen! Goods for sale!"

1 called him to my flat.

"You have something to sell, good sir?" he asked as he came in.

"No, I want to buy something from you."

"No doubt the umbrella you want?" responded the Jew.

He threw the waistcoat on the ground, shook the snow from his collar, and set about strenuously opening the umbrella.

"Nice job!" he said. "Just the thing for this snow. I know that you, sir, maybe have a pure silk umbrella, even two, But they only good in the summer!"

"What do you want for the waistcoat? "I asked.

"What waistcoat?" he replied, surprised, probably thinking I meant his own.

But he quickly realized what I was talking about and picked the item up from the ground.

"For this waistcoat? You asking about this waistcoat, sir?"

And then, as if his suspicions had been aroused, he asked, "What you want with such a waistcoat, good sir?"

"How much do you want for it?"

The yellowish whites of the Jew's eyes flashed, and the tip of his elongated nose turned even redder.

"You have it for one ruble!" he replied, holding the garment out before me to display all its fine qualities.

"I'll give you half a ruble."

"Half a ruble? For such a clothing? That's not possible!" said the dealer.

"Not a penny more."

"I wish you healthy joking, sir!" he said, slapping me on the shoulder. "You can see yourself how much a thing like this is worth. After all, it's not a child clothing, it's for grown-ups."

"Well, if you can't sell it for half a ruble, then off you go. I won't give you any more."

"No need to get angry, sir!" he put in, softening. "By my own conscience, I can't sell for half a ruble, but I trust vour judgment. You say how much it's worth, and I agree. I rather come out at loss, so long things turn out the way you wish,"

"The waistcoat's worth fifty groszes, and I'm giving you a half ruble."

"Half a ruble? All right then, let it be half a ruble," he sighed thrusting the waistcoat into my hands. "Let it be my loss, just so long as I don't break my word. My, that wind!"

And he pointed at the window, outside of which there was a swirling cloud of snow.

As I reached for the money the dealer, evidently remembering something, snatched the waistcoat back and began quickly rummaging through the pockets.

"What are you looking for?"

"Maybe I leave something in the pocket, I don't remember!" he answered in the most natural tone of voice, and as he handed back my new acquisition he added, "Throw in another ten groszes at least, kind sir!"

"Mind how you go!" I said, opening the door.

"Your humble servant! I also have good-quality fur coat at home …"

And even after he had crossed the threshold he poked his head around the door and asked, "Perhaps you like me to bring some sheep's-milk cheeses?"

A minute or two later he was already back in the courtyard and once more was calling, "Goods for sale!" and when I stood in the window he bowed to me with a friendly smile.

The snow began to fall so densely that it was almost like night. I put the waistcoat on the table and began to think about the lady who had walked out of the gate and gone goodness knows where, and about the flat that stood deserted next to mine, and also about the owner of the waistcoat, who was being covered by an ever thicker coat of snow.

It had only been three months before, one fair Septembcr day, that I had heard them talking to each other. In May the lady once even hummed a song, while the gentleman laughed as he read the Sunday newspaper. Whereas today …

They moved into our building at the beginning of April. They got up quite early, drank tea from a tin samovar, and left for town together, she to give lessons, he to his office.

He was a low ranking clerk who looked upon his departmental superiors with the same admiration that a traveler looks upon the high Tatra Mountains. He had to work long hours, for days on end. I would even see him at midnight, bent over the table by the lamp.

His wife usually sat by him and sewed. Sometimes she would look at him, break off from her work, and say reproachfully, "Come on, that's enough now, go to bed."

"When are you going to bed?"

"I'm … just going to finish off a few more stitches."

"Well then. I'll just write a few more lines."

They both lowered their heads and got on with their work. Then once again, after a while, the lady would say, "Go to bed … go to bed … "

Sometimes, in response to her words my clock would strike one o'clock.

They were young and neither good-looking nor ugly; they were quiet people. If I remember correctly, the lady was considerably slimmer than her husband, who was quite heavily built. I would even have said that he was too portly for such a low-ranking clerk.

Every Sunday, around midday, they would go out for a walk arm in arm and would return home late in the evening. They probably ate dinner in town. I once met them at the gate between the Botanical Gardens and Łazienki Park. They had bought themselves two mugs of first-rate mineral water and two large gingerbread cakes, and had assumed the untroubled expressions of townspeople who are in the habit of eating hot ham and horseradish sauce, washed down with tea.

In general, the poor need little to maintain their spiritual equilibrium: some food, a lot of work, and ample good health. The rest seems to take care of itself.

My neighbors, it seems, did not want for food, and certainly were not short of work, but their health was not all that it might have been.

Somehow the gentleman caught a chill in July, though it was not very serious. By a strange coincidence, however, he began to bleed so badly that he lost consciousness.

Night had already fallen. The lady, wrapping her husband in blankets on the bed, called the caretaker's wife into the room and ran off herself to fetch a doctor. She tried five different doctors, but found only one, and that by accident, on the street.

The doctor, looking at her by the flickering light of the streetlamp, concluded that above all she needed to be reassured. And since she stumbled from time to time, probably from exhaustion, and there was no dorozhka to be found on the street, he gave her his arm, and as they walked he explained that bleeding alone meant nothing.

"The bleeding may come from the larynx, the stomach, the nose, it's only rarely that it's from the lungs. Besides, if the person has always been healthy, and has never had a bad cough …"

"Oh, only from time to time," whispered the lady, halting to catch her breath.

"From time to time? That still doesn't signify anything. He may have a slight touch of bronchitis."

"Yes, it's bronchitis!" repeated the lady, aloud this time.

"He's never had pneumonia?"

"Yes, he has," replied the lady.

Her legs shook under her slightly.

"But I expect that was a long time ago."

"Oh, a long, long time ago!" she agreed hurriedly. "Right back in the winter."

"A year and a half ago."

"No … but before the New Year. Such a long time ago!"

"Ah. How dark this street is! Especially as it's rather cloudy tonight," said the doctor.

They entered the building. The lady anxiously asked the caretaker whether anything had happened and heard that nothing had. In the flat the caretaker's wife also said that nothing had changed, and the sick man was dozing.

The doctor woke him gently and examined him, and he also declared that it was nothing.

"I said right from the beginning that it was nothing!" put in the sick man.

"Yes, nothing!" repeated the lady, holding his hands, which were wet from perspiration. "Of course, I know that bleeding can come from the stomach or the nose. With you it's probably from your nose. You're so stout, you need exercise, and you spend all day sitting down. Isn't that right, doctor, that he needs exercise?"

"Yes, indeed! Generally speaking, exercise is necessary, but your husband must rest up for a few days. Is it possible for him to go and stay in the country?"

"I'm afraid it isn't," whispered the lady sadly.

"Well, never mind! He'll stay in Warsaw. I'll be visiting, and in the meantime he should lie in bed and rest. If the bleeding should recur … " added the doctor.

"Then what, doctor?" asked the wife, turning as white as a sheet.

"Well, not to worry. If your husband gets plenty of rest, things will heal up in there."

"In there … in his nose?" said the lady, clasping her hands before the doctor.

"That's right. In his nosc! Of course. You stay calm, ma'am, and entrust the rest to the Lord. Good-night."

The doctor's words reassured the lady so much that, after the anxiety she had suffered for the last few hours, she became almost merry.

"So what's all the fuss about!" she said, laughing and crying at the same time.

She knelt by the sick man's bed and kissed his hands.

"What's the fuss!" the man repeated, and smiled. "Think how much blood a man can lose in a war, and yet afterward he's fine!"

"Don't talk any more now," the lady begged him.

Outside dawn was breaking, for in the summer the nights are very short.

The illness lasted much longer than had been expected. The husband stopped working at the office, This was not such a problem for him because, as a contract worker, he didn't need to take leave and could return to work whenever he wanted and whenever he could find a job. Since he felt better when he stayed at home, the lady took on even more lessons each week and in this way provided for their daily needs.

She usually left for town at eight in the morning. Around one she would come back home for a couple of hours to cook lunch for her husband, and then she would run out again for a time.

The evenings, however, they spent together; though in order not to be idle, the lady took in a little more sewing.

Around the end of August it somehow transpired that the lady met the doctor on the street. For a long while they walked together. Finally, the lady seized the doctor's hand and said imploringly, "But either way, please come and see us. Perhaps God will have mercy! He always calms down so much after your visits."

The doctor promised, and the lady returned home, looking as if she had been crying. The man, through having to stay at home, had become somewhat irritable and despondent. He began to try to persuade his wife that she shouldn't be so concerned, that he would die anyway, and in the end he asked her, "Didn't the doctor tell you that I wouldn't live more than a few months?"

The lady froze.

"What are you talking about?" she said. "Where did you get an idea like that?"

The sick man grew angry.

"Come here to me, here!" he said abruptly, grabbing her by the hands. "Look me straight in the eye and answer me: Didn't the doctor say that to you?"

He fixed his feverish gaze on her. It seemed as if under this scrutiny even a wall would whisper its secrets, if it possessed any.

A strange calm appeared on rhe woman's face. She smiled gently, not flinching from that fierce stare. Her eyes just seemed to glaze over.

"The doctor said," she replied, "that it's nothing, you just need to rest a little."

The husband suddenly let go of her, shivered, laughed, then with a wave of his hand said, "Therc, you sec how edgy I am! I'd gotten it into my head that the doctor had given up hope for me. But … you've convinced me. I feel reassured now!"

And, more and more cheerfully, he laughed at his imaginings.

In fact, such an attack of suspicion never occurred again. His wife's gentle calm was the best indication for the sick man that his condition was not serious.

For why should it be?

He did have a cough, but that was from the bronchitis. Sometimes, from the long periods of sitting, there was bleeding—that came from his nose. And he also had what seemed to be a fever, but really it wasn't a fever, just nerves.

Overall, he felt better and better. He had an overwhelming desire to go on long trips, though he didn't quite have the strength. There even came a time when during the day he didn't want to lie in bed, but instead would sit in the armchair, fully dressed, ready to go out if only this temporary weakness would pass.

There was only one detail that worried him.

One day, as he was putting on his waistcoat, he felt that it was somehow very loose.

"Can I really have lost so much weight?" he whispered.

"Of course, it's natural that you must have become a bit thinner," answered his wife. "But we mustn't exaggerate."

Her husband looked at her intently. She didn't even lift her eyes from her work. No, that calm couldn't be dissembled! His wife knew from the doctor that he was not so very sick really, and so there was no reason to worry.

At the beginning of September the nervous attack, which resembled a fever, occurred more acutely, lasting almost all day.

"It's nothing serious!" the sick man said. "When summer is turning to autumn even the healthiest person can be off color, everyone feels out of sorts. The only thing that surprises me is that my waistcoat feels looser and looser. I must have lost an awful lot of weight, and I won't get better until I put some back on."

His wife listened carefully and had to agree that her husband was right.

The sick man got up every day and dressed, even though without his wife's help he was unable to put on any of his clothes. The only thing she managed to persuade him to do was to wear an overcoat instead of a frock coat.

"It's hardly surprising," he would often say, gazing in the mirror, "it's hardly surprising that 1 have no strength. Just see how I look!"

"Well, it's always the face that changes the most," put in his wife.

"That's true, but I'm losing weight all over."

"Arc you quite sure you're not imagining it?" asked his wife, with an expression of great doubt.

He fell to thinking.

"I think maybe you're right. For even … the last couple of days I've had the impression that … my waistcoat … is a bit … "

"Oh, come on!" interrupted his wife. "You're not trying to tell me that you've put on weight!"

"Who knows." From what I can tell from my waistcoat, it … "

"In that case you should be getting your strength back."

"Oh yes, you want it to happen all at once, first of all I have to put at least a little weight back on. And even then, you know, I won't get my strength back straight away. What are you doing behind the wardrobe?" he suddenly asked.

"Nothing. I'm looking for a towel in the trunk, but I'm not sure … whether it's clean."

"Don't strain so much, even your voice is different. That trunk is heavy."

The trunk must indeed have been heavy, for it had brought a flush to the lady's cheeks, but she was calm.

From then on, the sick man paid more and more attention to his waistcoat. And every few days he would call his wife and say, "There, just look at that. See for yourself: yesterday I could get my finger in here, right here, and today I can't, 1 really am beginning to put on weight!"

But one day the sick man's joy knew no bounds. When his wife returned from her lessons, he greeted her with shining eyes and said excitedly, "Listen, I'll tell you a secret. You know, 1 was cheating a bit with that waistcoat. In order to keep you from worrying, each day I shortened the strap, and that was why the waistcoat was tight. Yesterday, I pulled the strap right to the end, I was beginning to worry that my secret would be out, but today … Do you know, today, I give you my solemn word, instead of tightening the strap, I had to loosen it a little! It really was genuinely too tight for me, even though yesterday it was a little loose.

"So now I too believe that I'll get better. I do! The doctor can think what he wants."

This long speech cost him such an effort that he had to go across to the bed. There, however, as a man who without tightening any straps, was beginning to put on weight, he didn't lie down, but as he sat in the armchair he leaned on his wife while she put her arms around him.

"Well, well!" he whispered. "Who would have thought it? For two weeks I deceived my wife by saying that the waistcoat was too tight, and today it really *is* too tight! Well, well!"

And they spent the whole evening in each other's arms.

The sick man was affected as never before.

"Dear Lord!" he whispered, kissing his wife's hands. "And I thought that I would just go on losing weight like that till … the end. This is the first time in the last two months that I've believed I can get better again."

For everyone lies to a sick man, most of all his wife. But a waistcoat—that will never lie!

Today, looking at the old waistcoat, I can see that two people had been at work on the straps. The gentleman moved the buckle along each day to set his wife's mind at rest, while each day the lady shortened the strap to raise her husband's spirits.

"Will they ever meet again, to tell each other the whole truth about the waistcoat?" I wondered, staring at the sky.

It could scarcely be seen anymore above the earth. There was only snow falling, so dense and cold that even human ashes froze in their graves.

And yet who will say that beyond those clouds there is no sunlight?

—1882. Translated by Bill Johnston

*Literary Positivism.* "The Waistcoat" is an example of "positivist" literature, which takes its name from a philosophical movement founded in France by Auguste Comte (1798–1857), who aimed to turn it into what amounted to a secular religion. Polish Positivism is a socially engaged literature, usually expressed in prose, that reflects a generally positive attitude toward people and believes in their basic goodness and in improving society not by introducing radical or revolutionary change but through methodical grassroots hard work. Positivism reflects a rational, "curative" approach to society's imbalances through recognizing problems and curing them through the spread of education, scientific inquiry, economic development, benevolent government, volunteerism, self-help, and a kindly and helpful attitude toward the less fortunate. It is realistically indulgent of human foibles and frailties and how they can sometimes stand in the way of making social progress.

Social equality for all, regardless of ethnicity, background, sex, or belief were major components of the Positivist agenda. Positivism came into vogue in Poland at more or less the same time as the trend toward realism in literature. Realism aimed at the accurate depiction of ordinary people and their lives, and it often dealt with the typical stress of life in a big city. Despite people being closely packed together, life in a large modern city tends toward the impersonal and leaves many people feeling marginalized. Because of its social engagement, and its conveying a more-or-less overt "message," positivist literature creates a different impression from most literature one usually thinks of as "realistic." One can think of it as realism with an upbeat message.

In Poland, Positivism became the dominant literary trend following the defeat of the 1863 uprising against Russian occupation (in which Prus himself had participated as a fifteen-year-old boy). That tragic event resulted in many casualties, the expropriation of people's land, imprisonment, the exiling of many Poles to Siberia, and other harsh measures, leading to a reassessment of the usefulness of staging a revolt against a much larger power. Writers and intellectuals began to recommend working within the system and waiting for the system to evolve slowly and organically into something better.

*Cultural Notes,* As noted, being packed together with other people in apartment houses can leave people feeling deprived of normal human contact. Traditional apartment houses in Poland were generally on the French model: four or five stories high, usually with no elevator, built around a central inner courtyard. Entry to apartments was from the courtyard by various entryways and stairwells, and entry into the courtyard itself was by way of a central gate, closed at night, and guarded by a caretaker who would take a modest tip for letting in latecomers at night.

Apartment-house arrangements resulted in placing people of different walks of life in close proximity to one another. They might know a good deal about each other even while never officially meeting. In Prus's short stories "The Waistcoat" and "The Barrel Organ" the unfolding of the plot relies on the literary device of looking out one's window facing the courtyard and peering into other people's lives through their windows.

The man in "The Waistcoat" is a copyist, and his waistcoat (a kind of vest worn as an outer garment by office workers) is his "uniform." He copies documents all day long and into the night, long before the days of photocopying. Such work is repetitive and mindless, and it is badly paid. The copyist in the story has no job security; he is not on salary but works as a private contractor. When he becomes sick there is no social safety net or health insurance for him to fall back on.

Signs in the story indicate that the man and his wife may have come down in life. Recall the man's initially portly physique; their attempt at maintaining certain niceties; their Sunday "soda-water-and-gingerbread" strolls; the cherrywood wardrobe in their apartment; and the fact that the woman gives lessons, hence must have had some kind of schooling.

The man falls ill with tuberculosis, an infectious disease which was one of the major killers in the nineteenth century and well into the twentieth. It was also called "consumption," because a period of weakness and weight loss preceded death. Especially rampant in cities, tuberculosis is spread due to poor hygiene, close living conditions, and a harsh climate. No cure for the disease was available until the discovery of penicillin by Scottish scientist Alexander Fleming in the late 1920s and its broader availability after World War II, but life could be prolonged by moving to a warmer, drier climate, which of course the clerk in the story cannot afford to do.

Currency in Warsaw at the time of "The Waistcoat" was mostly Russian; there were 100 kopecks to a ruble. The author also makes reference to groszes, a Polish coin with 100 groszes to a Polish zloty, worth at the time much less than a ruble.

The stereotyped image of the Jewish rag merchant may be forgiven in view of the passage of time, just as one may forgive Shakespeare for his depiction of the conniving Jew in *The Merchant of Venice*. Given that one of the aims of Positivism in Poland was to better integrate the Jewish population into the country's mainstream cultural life, there is little doubt that in Prus's times the man corresponded to a colorful type encountered on the streets of Warsaw and did not reflect anti-semitism on the author's part, even if the description sounds jarring today.

*Narrative Technique.* The narrative structure of "The Waistcoat" is roughly symmetrical. The story is told by an uninvolved first-person observer, who dissolves imperceptibly into third-person objective narration. Prus's typical narrative perspective is similar to that of a motion picture camera (which, of course, had not been invented yet). The dominant point of view in the central part of the story is objective, but alternately close up or at a distance. To be sure, at times the narration crosses the line of what an "eye" could see and becomes omniscient: for example, in the comment that the couple ate cake and soda water in a way that suggests they were more used to eating ham with horseradish; or where the way the man looked in awe on his superiors at work is described.

Often Prus's narrative eye does not merely register what it sees but also expresses an ironic attitude toward it. This technique allows him to inject certain subtle comments and observations into his narrative. Prus's gentle irony depends on understatement and often becomes apparent only on second or third reading. He indirectly comments on such things as the uselessless of Latin classes; the odd habit of pressing flowers to remind one of past sentimental experiences; or the difficulty of getting and keeping good household help (the maid leaves for a place where she won't have to cook so much and will be better paid). Note also the ironic way in which Prus tells of the man's death at the beginning of the story: a look at the waistcoat suggests that its owner had probably more need of a frockcoat from a burial parlor than of a waistcoat.

Prus similarly ironically comments on the lack of job security: the man's illness is no problem, since he is not employed steadily for anyone anyway. The narrator is also self-ironic: he is someone who has no life of his own but lives vicariously through observing the lives of others around him through his window. Apparently retired, his experiences, summed up in some old dried pressed flowers, are no longer fragrant; they have become "albumized."

The narrator *lays bare the device* of introducing the story with his tiny box of "treasures": they are so few and pathetic that it is an obvious narrative ruse. This device helps the reader to *suspend disbelief* and enter into the spirit of the story without asking pesky questions about the logic of the narrative perspective when it shifts from the initial first-person objective perspective to something else. The narrator could not possibly have heard the conversations between the husband and wife, much less the street conversation between the wife and the doctor. He likewise would have had no way of knowing for how much the wife sold the waistcoat; and so on.

*Plot Analysis.* The plot is classical, with an introduction and an ending that serve as a frame to the central story. The Pre-History, which, from the chronological point of view, could also be considered a Post-History, introduces the mystery of the waistcoat and tells in advance of the man's death, leaving that question not in doubt from the beginning. A long vignette describes the narrator's haggling with the Jewish used-clothing dealer over the waistcoat after its owner's death. It is humorous, and the narrator is clearly proud of having out-haggled the rag merchant.

The Development consists of the picture of the narrator's two neighbors, a man and his wife as they go about their everyday routine. In the Turning Point, leading into the Complication, the man falls ill, and the doctor gives him and his wife false hope that the husband merely has bronchitis and will get better with rest. The Crisis, leading to the Climax, occurs when the man notices he is losing weight and starts fiddling with his waistcoat's adjustment strap to make up for it. The wife does the same on the other strap, and both work in secret from the other. The man works clumsily on one side, while the wife, an experienced seamstress, shortens the strap, but professionally and invisibly, on the other side. As a result of the wife's deceit, the husband thinks that his waistcoat has become tighter, so he falsely takes heart that he is gaining weight. As the story reaches its Climax, the man, now convinced he is getting better, confesses his deceit to his wife, while she keeps her secret to herself, and the husband and wife attain bliss in each other's arms just before the man dies, possibly that same night. Note that the Climax is more the moment of tenderness between the husband and wife than it is the man's death, which has been foretold in the Pre-History. The story's aftermath presents almost a literalization of the idea of a denouement, which in French means "unravelling." It reveals the wife's behind-the-scenes work on the adjustment strap, thereby explaining the appearance of the waistcoat as we saw it at the beginning of the story. The Denouement thus ties in a circle back to the introduction, which also dealt with the waistcoat, structurally closing the story.

In lieu of an unnecessary Post-History, the story ends with a lyrical query as to whether husband and wife will ever meet again to share their story of mutual tender deceit. The Main Effect or Point of the story seems to be that death can often be tragic and unfair, but that people can be kind to one another along the way.

Among the story's many ironies are that the supposedly "weak" wife turns out to be both biologically more robust than her husband, but also more devious than either her husband or the doctor. A web of deceit is created, with the wife on both the inside and outside of the web, helping to create the central irony:

WIFE (DOCTOR (HUSBAND ( WIFE )))

→→→→→→→→deceives→→→→→→→

In other words, the doctor thinks he deceives husband and wife, and the husband thinks he deceives his wife who, however, successfully deceives both of the men.

*Social Criticisms.* Prus's story contains several relatively hidden social criticisms, most importantly the lack of a social safety net (medical care, job security), and the failure of society to provide meaningful ways for educated and hard-working people to contribute to society by productive and meaningful labor. The author has no programmatic solutions to these dilemmas other than to work slowly toward correcting society's injustices and inequities. There is no strong criticism of the medical profession, even though the doctor's role is merely to prescribe rest and to counsel the couple not to worry. In the end, he is a positive type. He knows from the beginning that the man is sick with tuberculosis, which is fatal, but there is nothing he can do about it, and he sees no point in upsetting the couple needlessly. In a way, the doctor, who is emblematic of Positivism's whole "curative" agenda, symbolizes the plight of the Positivist predicament: sometimes there is nothing one can do but be kind.

*The Symbol of the Waistcoat.* The titular waistcoat is a cleverly constructed emblem of the man and his life, a record of his body type, his habits, his status as a low-ranking clerk, his seeming smoking habit, his illness, his own and his wife's way of dealing with it (showing their devotion to one another), and, at last, the man's death. In the end, the garment symbolizes, or rather serves as a kind of record of and testimony to, the love of the husband and wife for each other. In these respects it is like an archaeological or forensic artefact whose clues can be interpreted or "read," lending to the story an element of a Sherlock Holmes mystery story.

## The Barrel Organ

Every day around noon, on Miodowa Street you could meet a middle-aged gentleman who was on his way from Krasińskich Square to Senatorska Street. In the summertime he wore an elegant dark blue overcoat, gray trousers from a first-rate tailor, shoes that shone like mirrors, and a slightly discolored top hat …

This gentleman had a ruddy face, graying side-whiskers, and mild gray eyes. He walked with a stoop, his hands in his pockets. In good weather he had a cane under his arm; on cloudy days he carried an English silk umbrella.

He was always deep in thought and moved along slowly. As he reached the Capuchin church he would touch the brim of his hat religiously, then cross to the other side of the street to check the barometer and thermometer at Pik's. Then he would return to the right-hand sidewalk, stop in front of Mieczkowski's display, look at the photographs of Modrzejewska, and walk on.

As he walked he gave way to everyone, and when someone bumped into him he would smile benevolently.

If he saw a beautiful woman, he would put on his pince-nez to take a good look. But since he did this in a phlegmatic sort of way, he usually met with disappointment.

Thc gentleman's name was Mr. Tomasz.

Mr. Tomasz had been walking down Miodowa Street for the last thirty years, and he often thought that many things had changed there. Miodowa Street could have thought the same about him.

When he had still been a defense lawyer, he used to move along so quickly that no seamstress hurrying home from her fashion shop could have kept up with him. He was cheerful and talkative; he bore himself straight, and had a full head of hair and a mustache that curled up sharply. Even in those days he was impressed by the fine arts, but he had no time to spend on them, for he was mad about women. True, he was lucky with them, and there was constant talk of marriage, but what of it, since Mr. Tomasz could never find a single moment to propose, being busy either with his practice or with his assignations. From Frania he would go off to the courts, from the courts he would run to Zosia, whom he would leave toward evening to have supper with Józia and Filka.

When he became a partner, as a result of intense mental exertion, his forehead spread up toward the top of his head, and a few silver hairs appeared in his mustache. Mr. Tomasz had already lost his youthful ebullience; he had acquired wealth, and a reputation as a connoisseur of the arts. And since he still adored women, he began to think of marriage. He even took a six-room flat, put in parquet floors, had the place wallpapered, bought some beautiful furniture—and began to look for a wife.

But it is difficult for a mature person to make up his mind. This one was too young; another he had admired for too long. A third was charming and of the right age but had the wrong kind of temperament; a fourth had grace, youth, and the necessary temperament, but without waiting for the lawyer's decision she married a doctor.

Mr. Tomasz was not concerned, however, since there was no shortage of young ladies. Over time he decorated his flat, taking ever more care that each detail should be of artistic worth. He changed the furniture, moved the mirrors around, and bought paintings.

In the end, his domestic décor became famous. Though he himself did not quite know how it happened, he created an art gallery in his own home, which was seen by increasing numbers of curious visitors. And since he was hospitable by nature, he organized splendid receptions. He knew many musicians, and so ended up having concert evenings in his flat, which even society ladies honored with their presence.

Mr. Tomasz enjoyed it all, and, observing in the mirror that his hairline had reached the crown of his head and was moving back toward his snow-white collar, he reminded himself more and more often that come what may, he must marry, especially as he was still well inclined toward women.

Once, when he had a larger than usual gathering of guests, one of the young ladies looked over the salons and exclaimed, "What beautiful pictures, and how smooth the floors are! I expect your wife will be very happy."

"If smooth floors will be enough to make her happy," murmured one of the lawyer's close friends.

Everyone in the salon laughed. Mr. Tomasz smiled, too, but from that moment whenever anyone mentioned marriage to him, he would wave his hand dismissively, saying, "1 think not!"

It was at that time he shaved off his mustache and grew side whiskers He continued to speak of women with great respect and was most forbearing when it came to their faults.

No longer expecting anything of the world, since he had also given up his practice, the lawyer directed all his moderate emotions toward the arts. A beautiful painting, a fine concert, a new theatrical production became, as it were, the mileposts on the road of his life. He never grew enthusiastic or became enraptured, he merely enjoyed things.

At concerts he would choose a seat far from the stage, so as to be able to listen to the music without hearing other noises and without seeing the performers. When he went to the theater, he first acquainted himself with the work in question, so as to be able to follow the action without any feverish sense of curiosity. He studied paintings at times when there were the fewest visitors in the art gallery, and spent hours there.

If he liked something, he would say, "You know, this really is rather pretty."

He was one of those few people who are the first to spot talent. But he never condemned mediocre works.

"Just you wait, maybe he'll amount to something yet," he would say when others criticized the artist.

Thus he was always tolerant of human imperfection and never even mentioned vices.

Alas, no mortal being is devoid of some eccentricity, and Mr. Tomasz was no exception. His problem was that he could not abide barrel organs and organ grinders.

When the lawyer heard a barrel organ on the street, he would quicken his pace and would be out of sorts for several hours. Normally a calm man, he would get excited; usually quiet, he would begin to shout; and though always mild, he would become enraged at the first tones of the barrel organ.

He made no secret of his weakness, and even offered an explanation.

"Music," he would say agitatedly, "is the subtlest flesh of the spirit—yet in a barrel organ that spirit is diluted and turns into a machine and an instrument of robbery. For organ-grinders are nothing but bandits!

"Besides," he would add, "those organs irritate me. I only have one life, and I can't waste it listening to such disgusting music."

One malicious person, knowing about the lawyer's loathing for musical devices, thought up a tasteless practical joke and sent two organ grinders to play under his windows. Mr. Tomasz fell ill with wrath, and when he discovered who was responsible challenged him to a duel.

They even had to convene a court of honor to prevent bloodshed over such an apparently trivial matter.

The building in which Mr. Tomasz lived had changed hands a number of times. It goes without saying that each new owner felt it his bounden duty to raise the tenants' rent, first and foremost Mr. Tomasz's. The lawyer paid each increase without protest, but only on the condition, expressly written into the lease, that no barrel organs were to be allowed to play in the building.

As well as the clause in the contract, Mr. Tomasz would summon every new caretaker and conduct more or less the following conversation with him:

"Listen, my good fellow … What's your name now?"

"Kazimierz, sir."

"Listen now, Kazimierz! Every time I come home and you open the gate for me, you'll get twenty groszes, understand?"

"I understand, sir."

"And besides that, you'll receive ten zlotys a month from me, but do you know what for?"

"I can't imagine, sir," the caretaker would answer with gratitude.

"For never letting barrel organs into the courtyard. Got it?"

"Yes, sir."

The lawyer's flat comprised two parts. The four larger rooms had windows onto the street while the two smaller ones overlooked the courtyard. The state rooms were for guests. Parties took place there, clients were received, and friends and relatives of the lawyer's from the country stayed there. Mr. Tomasz himself rarely appeared here, and then it was only to check whether the parquet had been waxed, whether the place had been dusted, and whether the furniture had not been damaged.

But when he wasn't out and about, he would spend whole days sitting in the study on the courtyard side. There he would read, write letters, or examine documents brought to him by acquaintances who had asked him for advice. And when he didn't wish to strain his eyes, he would sit in the armchair by the window and, lighting a cigar, lose himself in thought. He knew that thinking is an important activity in life which should not be neglected by those who care about their health.

On the other side of the courtyard, directly opposite Mr. Tomasz's windows, was a flat that was rented by less well-off tenants. For a long while an elderly lawyer's clerk lived there, but when he lost his job he moved to Praga. After him a tailor took the little rooms, but he sometimes liked to get drunk and raise a ruckus so his lease was terminated. After that an old retired lady, who was forever arguing with her maid, moved into the flat.

But on St. John's Day the old lady, who had become quite senile but was rather wealthy, was taken to live with her relatives in the country, and the flat was rented by two ladies with a young girl of about eight.

The women worked for a living. They made stockings and vests on sewing machines, one doing the sewing and the other finishing them off. The younger and prettier of the two the little girl called Mummy while she addressed the older one as Ma'am.

Both the lawyer's windows and those of the new tenants were open all day long. So when Mr. Tomasz sat in his armchair, he could clearly see what was going on at his neighbors'.

The furniture there was modest. The tables, chairs, sofa, and chest of drawers were draped with cloth for sewing and balls of cotton for stockings.

In the early morning the women swept the flat themselves, and around midday a hired help would bring them a meager dinner. In general, the two women hardly ever stepped away from their rattling machines.

The girl usually sat in the window. She had dark hair and a pretty little face, though it was pale and somehow immobile. Sometimes she would sit fastening a belt of colored threads with two pieces of wire. Occasionally she played with a doll, which she dressed and undressed slowly, as if with difficulty. And at other times she didn't do anything, but just sat in the window listening to something or other.

Mr. Tomasz never saw the girl singing or running about the room, and never even saw a smile on her pallid lips and her motionless face.

"What a strange child!" the lawyer said to himself, and began to observe her more closely.

One day (it was a Sunday), he noticed that her mother had given her a little posy of flowers. The girl became a little more animated. She separated the flowers and put them back together again; she kissed them. In the end she tied them back together, put them in a glass with some water, and, sitting in her window, said, "This place is sad. Mummy, isn't it?"

The lawyer was shocked. How could it be sad in a building where he had been so contented for so many years!

One day the lawyer found himself in his study around four o'clock. At this hour the sun was opposite his neighbors' flat, and today it was shining and very hot. Mr. Tomasz looked over to the other side of the courtyard, and evidently saw something extraordinary, for he hurriedly donned his pince-nez.

This is what he saw:

The poor little girl, leaning her head on her arm, was lying almost on her back in the window, and with her eyes wide open, she was staring right at the sun. On her normally still face there now played feelings that looked something like joy, and something like regret.

"She can't see!" whispered the lawyer, dropping his pince-nez. At that moment his eyes began to sting at the very thought that someone could stare at the sun, which burned with an open flame.

Indeed, the girl had been blind for two years. When she was six she had fallen ill with some kind of fever; for several weeks she had remained unconscious, and subsequently grew so weak that she lay as if she were dead, neither moving nor speaking at all.

They had given her wine and broth, and slowly she had regained consciousness. But on the first day, when they propped her up on a pillow, she asked her mother,

"Mummy, is it nighttime?"

"No, darling. Why do you say that?"

But the little girl was sleepy and didn't answer. Yet the next day, when the doctor came, again she asked, "Is it still night?"

Then they realized that she was blind. The doctor examined her eyes and declared that she would have to give it time.

But the more the sick girl recovered her strength, the more she became concerned about her handicap.

"Mummy, why can't I see you?"

"Because something's happened to your eyes. But they'll get better."

"When will they get better?"

"Soon."

"Might it be tomorrow. Mummy?"

"In a few days, sweetheart."

"When it gets better, make sure you tell me straight away, because I'm so sad!"

Days and weeks passed in perpetual waiting. The girl began to get up. She learned to feel her way around the room. She could dress and undress herself slowly and carefully.

But her sight did not return.

One day she said, "Mummy, my dress is blue, isn't it.?"

"No, dear, it's gray."

"Can you see it. Mummy?"

"I can, darling."

"Just like in the daytime?"

"Yes."

"Will I be able to see everything, too, in a few days? Well, maybe in a month . . ."

But since her mother didn't answer, she went on:

"Mummy, it's day all the time outside, isn't it. Are there trees in the garden, like before? And does that white kitten with the black paws still come and visit us? Mummy, isn't it true that I used to be able to see myself in the mirror. Is there a mirror here?"

Her mother gave her a mirror.

"You have to look here, where it's smooth," said the girl, pressing the mirror against her face. "I can't sec anything!" she said. "Can you not see me in the mirror either, Mummy?"

"I can see you, my love."

"How is that?" cried the girl plaintively. "If 1 can't see myself, there ought to be nothing at all in the mirror. And what about the little girl in the mirror—can she see me or not?"

But her mother burst into tears and ran from the room.

The blind girl's favorite pastime was taking small objects in her hands and identifying them by touch.

One day her mother brought her a china doll, in nice clothes, which had cost a whole ruble. The girl never put her down; she touched her nose, mouth, and eyes, and cuddled her.

She went to bed late, still thinking about her doll, which she had laid in a little box lined with cotton wool.

In the night her mother was wakened by a rustling noise and a whispering. She jumped out of bed, lit a candle, and in the corner she saw her daughter fully dressed and playing with the doll.

"What are you doing, dear?" she cried. "Why aren't you asleep?"

"But it's daytime. Mummy," answered the blind girl.

For her day and night had merged into one and lasted forever.

Gradually the memory of visual impressions began to fade for the girl. A red cherry became for her a smooth, round, soft cherry, and a shiny coin was a hard and resonant disc on which there were some signs in relief. She knew that the room was bigger than she was, that the building was bigger than the room, and the street bigger than the building. But everything somehow seemed to contract in her imagination. Her attention was directed toward the senses of touch, smell, and hearing. Her face and hands became so sensitive that a few inches away from the wall she could already feel a slight chill. Distant events affected her only through hearing, and so she would spend entire days listening.

She grew to recognize the ambling step of the caretaker, who spoke in a high-pitched voice as he swept the courtyard. She knew when the wagon from the country had arrived to bring wood, she knew when there was a dorozhka or the carts that took the refuse away.

The slightest rustle, smell, chilling, or warming of the air did not escape her attention. With inconceivable rapidity, she noticed these subtle things and drew conclusions from them.

Once her mother called the maid.

"Mrs. Janowa isn't here," said the blind girl, sitting in her usual place in the corner. "She's gone to get water."

"How do you know?" asked her mother in amazement.

"How? Well, I know she took the jug from the kitchen, then she went through into the other courtyard and pumped the water. And now she's talking to the caretaker."

Indeed, from over the fence there came the murmur of a conversation between two people, but it was so faint that it could only be made out with an effort.

But even her increased abilities in the lesser senses could not replace the girl's sight. She became aware of the lack of impressions and began to pine.

She was allowed to walk around the whole building, and this brought her some relief. She trod every stone in the courtyard, and touched every gutter and barrel. But her greatest pleasure came from journeys to two completely opposite worlds: the cellar and the attic.

In the cellar the air was cold and the walls damp. The muffled noise from the street could be heard overhead; other sounds died away. This was night for the blind girl.

In the attic, on the other hand, especially in the window, everything was different. Up there there was more noise than in her flat. The girl could hear the rumble of carriages from several streets, and all the shouts from the entire building gathered there. A warm wind fanned her face. She could hear the chirping of birds, the barking of dogs, and the soughing of the trees in the garden next door. For her this was day.

That was not all. The sun shone more often on the attic than on her flat, and when the blind girl turned her dead eyes toward it, she thought that she could see something. The shadows of forms and colors stirred in her imagination, though so indistinctly and fleetingly that she couldn't remember anything.

It was at this time that her mother decided to live with her friend and move into the building where Mr. Tomasz lived. Both women were pleased with the new flat, but for the blind girl the move was truly a misfortune.

She had to stay in the flat and wasn't allowed to go to the attic or the cellar. She couldn't hear birds or trees, and in the courtyard there was a terrible silence. Neither secondhand dealers, nor tinkers, nor rag-and-bone men ever came in. They didn't admit the women who sang religious songs, or the old man who played the clarinet, or organ-grinders.

Her only pleasure was staring at the sun, which didn't always shine and which quickly dropped behind the buildings.

The girl began to pine again. Her health declined in the space of a few days, and her face assumed the expression of despondency and lifelessness that had so surprised Mr. Tomasz.

Not being able to see, the blind girl wanted at least to be able to listen to all sorts of different new sounds. But it was so quiet in the building.

"Poor child!" Mr. Tomasz often whispered to himself as he observed the sorry little thing.

Perhaps I could do something for her? he thought, seeing that she looked more and more poorly, and that she was wasting away from one day to the next.

It so happened that at this time one of his friends had a court case, and as usual, seeking Mr. Tomasz's advice, had given him the papers to look over. Mr. Tomasz no longer appeared in court himself, but as an experienced practitioner he was always able to indicate the best line of action and to offer useful comments to the lawyer he had recommended to his friend.

The present case was a complicated one. The more Mr. Tomasz became engrossed in the papers, the more excited he grew. The lawyer stirred in the retired man. He stopped going out of his flat and no longer checked whether the drawing rooms had been dusted; he stayed in his office and did nothing but read documents and make notes.

In the evening Mr. Tomasz's old butler came with his daily report. He informed him that the doctor's wife had left with her children for their summer house, that the water pipes had broken, that the caretaker, Kazimierz, had gotten into a fight with a police-man and had been sent to prison for a week. Finally he asked,

"Does Sir not wish to see the new caretaker?"

But the lawyer, lost in his papers, was smoking a cigar and blowing smoke rings; he did not even glance at his faithful servant. The next day Mr. Tomasz continued to study the documents; round two o'clock he ate lunch and went on working. His ruddy face and graying whiskers against the sapphire-blue background of the wallpaper recalled a study from life. The mother of the blind girl and her companion, who was making stockings on her sewing machine, marveled at the lawyer and said to each other that he looked like a hale old widower in the habit of dozing at his desk all day long.

In reality the lawyer, though he had in fact closed his eyes, was not dozing but was thinking about the case.

Citizen X had bequeathed his farm to his sister's son in 1872, and in 1875 had left his apartment building to the son of his brother. The latter claimed that citizen X was mad in 1872, while the former sought to prove that he had not gone insane till 1875. Furthermore, the husband of the man's sister had offered convincing evidence that X had acted like a madman both in 1872 and 1875, and that as early as 1869, when he had still been of sound mind, he had left his entire estate to his sister.

Mr. Tomasz had been asked to determine when citizen X had really gone mad, and then to help reconcile the three parties in conflict, none of whom would hear of compromise.

As the lawyer immersed himself in the complex issues, a strange, incomprehensible thing happened.

From the courtyard, right under Mr. Tomasz's window, there came the sounds of a barrel organ!

If the late citizen X himself had risen from the grave, regained consciousness, and come into the study to help him solve the case, Mr. Tomasz would not have experienced the feeling that he did now when he heard the barrel organ!

And if it had at least been an Italian organ, with pleasant flute notes, well-constructed, and playing nice music! Nothing of the kind! As if to add insult to injury, the organ was broken; it played vulgar waltzes and polkas out of tune, and it was so loud that the windows rattled. To top it all, the horn that sounded from time to time roared like a rabid beast.

The effect was stunning. The lawyer was flabbergasted. He didn't know what to think or what to do. He even wondered if, while reading the posthumous instructions of the mentally ill citizen X, he himself had gone mad and was suffering from hallucinations.

But no, these were no hallucinations. It was a real barrel organ, with broken pipes and a deafening horn!

In the heart of the lawyer, that indulgent, mild-mannered man, there stirred violent instincts. He felt resentful toward nature that it had not made him the king of Dahomey, who had the right to put his subjects to death, and he thought of the pleasure it would give him to end the life of the organ-grinder!

And since for people of Mr. Tomasz's mettle it is extremely easy to move from bold plans to the most terrible acts, the lawyer leaped to the window like a tiger with the intention of abusing the organ-grinder with the worst words he could find.

He leaned out and had already opened his mouth to cry, "You idle good-for-nothing!" when he heard a child's voice.

He looked across.

The little blind girl was dancing around the room, clapping her hands. Her pale face had become flushed; there was a smile on her lips, and yet from her unseeing eyes there came a stream of tears.

It was so long since the poor thing had had so many sensations in that silent building! The discordant notes of the barrel organ were a beautiful experience for her. The blast of the horn, which had almost reduced the lawyer to apoplexy, was to her a glorious sound.

The last straw came when the organ-grinder, seeing the child's delight, began to stamp his great heel on the ground and from time to time whistle like a locomotive when two trains meet.

Oh, how lovely that whistle was!

The lawyer's faithful butler burst into the study, dragging the caretaker with him and exclaiming, "Sir, I told this imbecile to throw the organ-grinder out at once! I told him he'd get paid regularly, and that we have a contract. But this oaf! He only arrived from the country a week ago and he doesn't know our ways. Listen now!" shouted the butler, shaking the bewildered caretaker by the arm. "Listen to what my master has to say to you!" The organ-grinder was already playing his third tune, as shrill and as jarring as the first two.

The blind girl was enraptured.

The lawyer turned to the caretaker and said with his customary composure, though he was somewhat pale,

"Listen, my dear fellow. What's your name?"

"Paweł, sir."

"Well, Paweł, I'm going to pay you ten zlotys a month, but do you know what for?"

"For never letting any organ-grinders into the courtyard!" the butler put in quickly.

"No," said Mr. Tomasz. "I'll pay you if every day you let in a barrel organ. Do you understand?"

"What are you saying?" cried the butler, emboldened by this incomprehensible instruction.

"Until I talk to him again, he is to let organ-grinders into the courtyard every day," repeated the lawyer, putting his hands in his pockets.

"I don't understand, sir!" said the butler, with an offensive expression of astonishment.

"That's because you're a fool, my good fellow!" said Mr. Tomasz to him good-humoredly.

"Now, off to work," he added.

The butler and the caretaker left, and the lawyer noticed his faithful servant whisper something in his companion's ear and tap his forehead.

Mr. Tomasz smiled, and as if to confirm his servant's gloomy suspicions, he threw the organ-grinder a ten-grosz piece.

Then he took the city almanac, found the listings of doctors, and copied out onto a sheet of paper the addresses of several ophthalmologists. And since the organ-grinder had now turned to his window and, in response to the ten groszes, had begun to stamp and whistle even louder, which sorely irritated the lawyer, he took the paper with the addresses of the doctors and left, murmuring to himself, "That poor child! I should have done something for her long ago ... "

—1882. Translated by Bill Johnston

*Cultural Notes.* For contemporary Warsaw readers, stories like "The Waistcoat" and "The Barrel Organ" have a nostalgic twinge to them. They depict life in a city that irretrievably belongs to the past, especially since Warsaw was burned and leveled to the ground by the retreating German army in World War II. Except for some artificially reconstructed sections of Warsaw's "Old Town," the Warsaw of today is nothing like that of the nineteenth century. In "The Barrel Organ" Mr. Tomasz walks along Miodowa Street and across Krasiński Square. These parts of Warsaw were obliterated in World War II. They have since been rebuilt in a different style, with generally cheap post-war housing. In World War II, Miodowa Street and Krasinski Square abutted the Jewish Ghetto, which was the site of ferocious fighting during the Jewish Ghetto Uprising of 1943.

"Tomasz" is the lawyer's first name. In Polish, in polite discourse one refers to a person with the title *pan* (Mr.) plus the first name. Because the women Tomasz goes out with are referred to by their first-name diminutives (Frania, Zosia, Józia, etc.) it is suggested that he does not take them seriously or, in any case, as people he considers as suitable marital partners.

As in "The Waistcoat" the setting and plot depend on the layout of a typical Warsaw apartment building, with a courtyard and an entry-gate guarded by a caretaker (concierge, watchman). The physical situation actually enters into the plot, for it is the house's new watchman who lets the organ-grinder into the courtyard. Also, as in "The Waistcoat," the device is used of one person peering into another person's life through the literal windows of their apartment. Warsaw apartment houses have expensive and inexpensive flats, meaning that one necessarily rubs up against people from different walks of life, often without ever getting to know them closely.

The architecture of European apartment houses is not "child-friendly," and certain rules of behavior apply. Not all residents appreciate the sound of children's shouts and games echoing in the courtyard. For more freedom a child has to go to a park, a playground, to the countryside, or to a summer home, if the family has one. The other option is to sit indoors all day and mope. It is worth noting here that one of the outgrowths of the positivistic spirit, specifically designed to meet the needs of city-dwelling children, were the elaborate playgrounds and sports fields called Jordan Gardens, introduced toward the end of the century by philanthropist and physical education pioneer Dr. Henryk Jordan (1845–1907), first in Kraków and later throughout Poland, said to be the first of their kind in Europe.

A barrel organ is either a hand-held or wheeled cranked instrument which produces music by the action of a revolving cylinder studded with pegs that act via a paper ribbon with holes on a series of valves that admit air from a bellows to a set of pipes. It is like a portable player piano and calliope combined. Barrel-organ "grinders" were itinerant buskers who survived by people giving them money, often so that they would go and play somewhere else. In cartoon depictions they are often accompanied by a pet monkey dressed in a bell-boy uniform who pesters passersby with his tin donation cup.

*Plot Analysis.* The plot is classical, although with more transition points than in some other stories. The narrative is interrupted by a long *flashback* in the middle, exploring the mystery of the girl's blindness—an example of Prus's already-mentioned "cinematic" technique.

The Development describes Mr. Tomasz's personality and lifestyle. The description begins in the present day. We see his current stooped posture, his ruddy complexion (too much high living?), gray hair, and sideburns. Then the narration takes us back to the beginning of Mr. Tomasz's career, then through its stages, and back again to the present, ending with his loathing of barrel organs as offending his "refined sensibilities." Prus uses the changing state of the hair on Mr. Tomasz's head as an index of his advancing age.

In the first of three transition points comprising the Complication, at a reception at his elegantly appointed apartment, upon overhearing a friend's passing joke about his shiny parquet floors not being enough to keep a woman satisfied, Mr. Tomasz comes to the realization that, even though in his mind and surroundings he has prepared himself for marriage, he has accidentally let himself slip past marriageable age. Shortly afterwards, although normally indifferent to life in his apartment house, Tomasz becomes fascinated by two women and a girl who have just moved in across the courtyard opposite him. In particular, he is troubled by the odd behavior of the little girl who, he realizes one day as he sees her staring into the sun, is blind.

In a Flashback, narration shifts to the life of the little blind girl. We are taken back to the time of the girl's illness and subsequent blindness, followed by her move to the current apartment building which, with its dampened sounds and smells and other forms of sensory deprivation, is a misfortune for her, and her physical and mental well-being quickly suffer.

In a cleverly engineered slowly evolving Crisis, (a) Mr. Tomasz becomes absorbed by an intricate legal case; (b) simultaneously, the apartment-house watchman gets drunk and lands in jail, and a new and inexperienced one is hired; (c) through failing to receive proper instructions, the new watchman lets an organ grinder into the courtyard; (d) as he is about to have an apoplectic fit, Mr. Tomasz sees the blind girl going into raptures as she hears the organ grinder's raucous music; (e) the janitor is summoned and expects to be severely reprimanded. The foregoing series of events leads to the surprise Climax. Instead of punishing the janitor, Mr. Tomasz pays him to bring organ grinders into the courtyard every day, instead of driving them away. In the very brief Denouement, which exists more in our head than on paper, the lawyer stops being uninvolved with other people and locked within his own narrow mind-set. He decides to hire a doctor to examine the blind girl, and there is some hope she may regain her eyesight.

*Dickensian Outcome.* The story and its ending remind one of Charles Dickens's *A Christmas Carol*, written about forty years earlier (1840). In both stories a crochety old man's heart is softened by the plight of a disabled child. The "Barrel Organ's" surprise ending is strikingly similar to the ending of Dickens's story, where the cranky old Scrooge pretends to be about to fire Tiny Tim's father, Bob Cratchitt, but ends by giving him a roast goose, a holiday, and a raise in salary. He becomes a grandfatherly figure to Tiny Tim.

The Moral here (being positivistic, this is a story with a lesson to be learned) is that one should not be so wrapped up in oneself and one's own effete preferences but rather should be open to seeing the plight of others less fortunate than we are, helping them to the extent of our ability. There are no dark undertones to the story, no political or social criticisms, or any pessimism about life having passed one by. In short, it is an excellent example of Positivism as "realism with an upbeat message."

The narrator takes several gently ironic digs at the legal profession. The case Tomasz is working on has to do with a complicated inheritance issue. Lawyers often make their money by churning other people's money, which the people themselves possibly did not even earn themselves. Prus draws a distinction between disinterested versus interested charity, as in the story of the rich woman who, when she became senile, was finally taken in and cared for by her country relatives in expectation of an inheritance.

*The Symbol of the Barrel Organ.* For the lawyer, the barrel organ symbolizes the mechanization, debasement, and vulgarization of serious music. For the little girl, it symbolizes the outside world she cannot see but can still hear, and it also resonates with her inner world.

*The Plight of the Handicapped.* There are suggestions in the story, rather advanced for Prus's time, about the needs of the handicapped. Prus notes what an unfriendly place the world is for people with disabilities. The story contains an interesting attempt at recreating the psychological state and mental-perceptual transitions a person who is becoming blind undergoes. Prus tries to raise his reader's awareness of the needs of others less fortunate through no fault of their own.

*Narrative Technique.* This is probably "The Barrel Organ's" most masterful aspect. The narrative strategy is more or less symmetrical, with barely perceptible shifts in perspective, practically from paragraph to paragraph, mirroring the emotional progress of the story. Narration begins in *third-person external* mode. Tomasz is described first at a distance, then from somewhat closer up as he approaches and comes into better focus, but still from the outside, as though by a fellow pedestrian, or by a detective "shadowing" him. Little by little, we find out more about him that only a third-person knowledgeable narrator could know, but we are still not inside Mr. Tomasz's perceptions or thoughts. We learn details of his past life that, say, a social acquaintance could also know. Slowly, the narration begins to take the narrative point of view of Mr. Tomasz: it becomes *third-person personal*, reflecting what Mr. Tomasz sees and feels, until finally one encounters a sentence that says, "He knew that … ," at which point we are in Mr. Tomasz's mind, a narrative perspective one could call *third-person personal internal*, that is, we see things both from Mr. Tomasz's visual perspective and also know what he is thinking and feeling about them. Narration is not yet omniscient, as we are only inside Mr. Tomasz's head.

With the arrival of the two women and the girl in the apartment across the courtyard, the narrative shifts to a third-person mode that is either *omniscient* or that takes the perspective of the women, at first that of the girl's mother. During the Flashback the narration adopts more and more the personal point of view of the blind girl, as Prus attempts to recreate how she has adapted to her handicap, both physically and mentally. An interesting narrative double-take occurs when at one point the two women briefly glance out of their own window and back into Tomasz's and at his life. From this point on, the narration quickly retraces these perspectival shifts in reverse. We are brought back into the lives of the women, then into the personal perspective of Mr. Tomasz and, finally, the story finds itself where it started, with a third-person impersonal narration of the scene between Tomasz, the butler, and the caretaker, as if viewed by an invisible person present in the room, which one could call a "fly-on-the-wall" perspective. In this final scene, the narration is advanced more by the conversation of the characters than by narrative description. The cumulative effect is that of a ring of successively more personal viewpoints, reflecting and heightening the emotional focus of the story, first on Tomasz, then more on the women, and then on the blind girl, who is at the emotional center of the story. The narrative shifts mirroring the empathetic focus of the story can be diagrammed as follows:

(impersonal (Tomasz (mother (girl) mother) Tomasz) impersonal)

→→→→→→→→→→→→ EMPATHETIC FOCUS ←←←←←←←←←←←←

## From the Legends of Ancient Egypt

Behold how vain are the hopes of man against the order of the universe, how futile they are against the judgments which the Everlasting has writ in fiery letters across the heavens.

The hundred-year-old Ramses, mighty ruler of Egypt, was in decline. A stifling spirit had settled in the breast of the potentate at the sound of whose voice for half a century millions had trembled. It sapped the blood from his heart, the strength from his arm, and at times even the clarity from his mind. The great pharaoh lay on the pelt of an Indian tiger, like a fallen cedar, his legs covered with the triumphal cloak of the king of Ethiopia. And, in a manner even more imperious than usual, he summoned his wisest physician from the temple at Carnac, and said:

"I know you are familiar with powerful medicines which can either kill a man or cure him instantly. Concoct one of them for me, appropriate to my disease, and let it be over for me, one way or the other."

The physician hesitated.

"Consider, Ramses," he whispered, "that since the moment of your descent from the heavens on high the Nile has overflowed its banks a hundred times. Am I really to adminster a medicine whose effects would be uncertain even for the youngest of your warriors?"

Ramses sat upright in his couch.

"I must be very sick," he roared, "if you, priest, dare to give me advice! Be silent and do as I have ordered. After all, my thirty-year-old grandson and heir Horus lives. Egypt cannot have a ruler who is unable to mount a chariot and raise his spear."

As soon as the priest, with trembling hands, had handed him the medicine, Ramses gulped it down like a thirsty man drinks a cup of water. He then summoned the most famous astrologer from Thebes and commanded him to tell him truthfully what the stars foretold.

"Saturn has conjoined with the Moon," the sage replied, "foretelling the death of a member of your dynasty, Ramses. You did wrong today by drinking the medicine, for the plans of men are futile in face of the verdicts inscribed in the heavens by the Everlasting."

"Naturally the stars have foretold my death," replied Ramses. "But when is it supposed to occur?" he asked of his physician.

"Before sunrise, Ramses, either you will be as fit as a rhinoceros or your sacred ring will be found on the hand of Horus."

"Bring Horus to the hall of the pharaohs," said Ramses with a weakening voice. "Have him await there my final words and my ring, lest there be any discontinuity in the exercise of power."

Horus, who had a tender heart, burst into tears at the news of his grandfather's approaching death. But since there could be no interruption in the exercise of authority, he went to the hall of the pharaohs, surrounded by a large retinue.

He came to rest atop a staircase whose marble stairs descended to the river. Full of vague sorrows, he observed the surrounding landscape.

Just at that moment the Moon, in whose light the evil star of Saturn shone, was gilding the bronze waters of the Nile, casting huge shadows from the pyramids across the meadows and gardens, illuminating the entire region.

Despite the lateness of the hour, lamps were burning in the houses and buildings. The people had left their homes and come out under the open sky. Boats were gliding along the Nile as densely as on a holiday, and a numberless multitude undulated through the forests of palms, across the marketplaces, and along the streets next to Ramses's palace. Despite this movement the silence was so profound that Horus could hear the rustle of the bullrushes and the plaintive howling of distant hyenas in search of food.

"What are they gathering here for?" Horus inquired of one of the courtiers, pointing to the vast waves of human heads.

"They want to greet you as the new pharaoh, lord, and to hear from your lips of the benefices you have in store for them."

At this moment the sense of his own greatness swelled in the prince's heart for the first time, as the surging sea strikes against a precipitous shore.

"And what do those lights mean?" asked Horus. "The priests have gone to the grave of your mother, Zefora, to transfer her remains to the catacombs of the pharaohs."

Sorrow awoke in Horus's heart at the recollection of his mother, whom the stern Ramses had interred among the slaves for the kindnesses she had shown to them.

"I hear the neighing of horses," said Horus, straining his ears. Who is making a journey at this hour?"

The chancellor, lord, has given orders for messengers to be readied to fetch your teacher Jetron. Horus sighed at the recollection of his beloved friend, whom Ramses had sent into exile for planting in his grandson's heart an aversion to war, and pity for the downtrodden population.

"And that little light across the Nile?"

"By that light, O Horus," replied the courtier, "the faithful Berenice is greeting you from her cloistered prison. The archpriest has already sent the pharaoh's boat for her. And as soon as the sacred ring glistens on your finger, the heavy doors of the cloister will open and she will return to you, longingly and lovingly."

Upon hearing these words Horus ceased his questions. He grew silent and buried his face in his hands. Suddenly he hissed in pain.

"What's the matter, Horus?"

"A bee has stung me on the foot," replied the prince, growing pale.

The courtier examined his foot by the greenish light of the moon.

"Thank Osiris," he said, "that it was not a spider, whose poison at this hour can be deadly."

O, how vain are human hopes before the immutable verdicts of heaven!

At this moment the leader of the army entered and, bowing to Horus, he said:

“The great Ramses, sensing that his body is already growing cold, has sent me to you with a directive: “Go to Horus, for I am not long in this world, and do his bidding as you have done mine. Even were he to command you to yield Upper Egypt to the Ethiopians and conclude a fraternal union with those enemies, do it as soon as you see my ring on his finger, for through the mouths of the rulers speaks the immortal Osiris.”

“I will not give Egypt to the Ethiopians,” said the prince, “but I will conclude peace with them, out of sorrow for the blood of my people. Write an edict forthwith, and have messengers ready on horseback so that, as soon as the first fires are struck in my honor, they may ride in the direction of the southern sun, bearing our favor to the Ethiopians. And write another edict, that from this hour until the end of time no prisoner will have the tongue ripped out of his mouth on the field of battle. I have spoken.”

The general fell down before him, and then withdrew to write the orders. As he was leaving, the prince asked the courtier to have another look at his wound, as it was becoming more and more painful.

“Your foot has become swollen, Horus,” said the courtier. “What if a spider has bitten you instead of a bee?”

Now the state chancellor entered the hall. Bowing to the prince, he said:

“The mighty Ramses, seeing that his sight is growing dim, has sent me to you with a directive: “Go to Horus and blindly do his bidding. Even were he to command you to release the prisoners from their chains and give all the land to the people, you shall do that as soon as you see the sacred ring on his hand, for through the mouths of the rulers speaks the immortal Osiris.”

“Thus far my heart does not extend,” said Horus. “But write for me an edict that the people’s rent and taxes will be lowered by half, and slaves will have three days of rest per week and will not be flogged with canes without a court order. And write another edict recalling from exile my teacher, Jetron, who is the wisest and noblest of all the Egyptians. I have spoken.”

The chancellor fell down before him, but before he was able to withdraw to write the edicts, the archpriest entered.

“Horus,” he said, “at any moment the great Ramses will depart for the land of the shades, and his heart will be weighed on the infallible scales of Osiris. As soon as the sacred ring of the pharaohs glistens on your finger, command me, and I will do your bidding, even though it were to topple the magnificent temple of Amon, for through the mouths of the rulers speaks the immortal Osiris.”

“We shall not destroy it.” Horus replied. “Instead I shall raise new temples and increase the treasury of the priesthood. I only require that you write an edict concerning the solemn transfer of the earthly remains of my mother, Zefora, to the catacombs, and a second edict, freeing my beloved Berenice from imprisonment in the cloister. I have spoken.”

“You are making a wise beginning,” responded the archpriest. “Everything is already prepared so that these orders may be fulfilled. I will draw up the edicts straight away, and when you touch them with the ring of the pharaohs, I will light this lamp, that the people may learn of your favor, and Berenice of her freedom and your love."

The wisest physician from Carnac entered.

"Horus," he said, "your pallor does not surprise me, for Ramses, your grandfather, monarch above monarchs, is nearing his end. He was not able to withstand the strength of the medicine which I did not want to give him. There remains with him only the deputy archpriest, so that when he dies he may remove from his hand the sacred ring and transfer it to you as a sign of unlimited power. But you, Horus, are even paler than before," he added.

"Examine my foot," moaned Horus, sinking into a golden chair whose arms were carved in the shape of hawk-heads. The doctor kneeled, examined his foot, and withdrew in horror.

"Horus," he whispered, "you have been bitten by a very poisonous spider."

"Am I to die then, at such a moment?" Horus asked in a barely audible voice. Then he added: "Will it be soon? Tell me the truth … "

"Before the moon settles behind that palm … "

"I see. And does Ramses have yet long to live?"

"Who can tell? Perhaps they are already bringing you his ring."

At that moment the ministers entered with the edicts they had prepared.

"Chancellor," cried Horus, gripping him by the arm, "even if I should die, would you carry out my instructions?"

"May you live as long as your grandfather, Horus!" replied the chancellor. "But even were you to stand immediately after him before the court of Osiris, your every edict will be carried out, as long as you have touched it with the sacred ring of the pharaohs."

"Ah, the ring!" repeated Horus … "but where is it?"

"One of the courtiers has told me," whispered the head of the army, "that the great Ramses is already breathing his last."

"I have sent to him my deputy," added the archpriest," so that he might take the ring from him as soon as his heart ceases to beat."

"Thank you," said Horus. "Although there is much to regret, yet not everything will die. My good works will live after me: peace, the happiness of the people, … my Berenice will regain her freedom … How long do I have to live?" he asked the physician.

"Death is a thousand marching paces away from you," the doctor said sadly.

"Do you not hear something? Is no one coming?" said Horus.

Silence. The moon drew close to the palm and was already touching its outermost leaves. The fine sand murmured softly in the hourglass.

"How close is it?" whispered Horus.

"Eight hundred paces," replied the physician. "I don't know, Horus, whether you will be able to touch all of the edicts with your sacred ring, even were they to bring it to you now."

"Give me the edicts," said the prince, straining his ears to detect whether someone might be running from Ramses' rooms. "And you, priest," he said to the physician, "tell me how much of my life remains, so that I can at least authorize the commands nearest to my heart."

"Six hundred paces," whispered the physician.

The edict lowering the people's rent and the slaves' workday fell from Horus's hand to the ground.

"Five hundred … "

The edict concerning peace with the Ethiopians slipped off the prince's knees.

"Is no one coming?"

"Four hundred … ," replied the doctor.

Horus thought for a moment … and down fell the order transferring the remains of Zefora, his mother. The edict recalling Jetron from exile met the same fate.

"Two hundred … "

Horus's lips were turning blue. With a spasmodic motion he tossed on the ground the edict concerning the tearing out of the tongues of captive prisoners. There remained only the command to release Berenice.

"One hundred … "

Amid the funereal silence the clapping of sandals could be heard. Into the hall ran the deputy of the archpriest. Horus reached out his hand.

"A miracle!" cried out the fresh arrival. "The great Ramses has regained his health … He has risen from his couch and desires to go lion hunting at sunrise. As a sign of his favor, Horus, he has asked that you accompany him. Horus cast a dying gaze beyond the Nile, where the light was still burning in Berenice's prison, and two tears, bloody tears, fell across his face.

"Why do you not reply, Horus?" asked Ramses's startled messenger.

"Can't you see he is dead?" whispered the wisest physican of Carnac.

Behold, then, how vain are the hopes of man before the judgments writ with fiery signs across the heavens by the Eternal.

—1888. Translated by Oscar Swan

*Analysis.* The idea of the plot, set in ancient Egypt, is unusual and original. In general, the idea of a historical positivist short story is out of the ordinary. Apart from works dealing with biblical themes or opera, Ancient Egypt is not a setting that has been widely exploited for the action of historical novels or stories, ancient Greece and Rome being more often used. The story is also unlike what one expects to come out of Positivism, a movement dealing with current problems in society and how to solve them. Also seeming to fly in the face of Positivism is the repeated incantation: "Vain are the hopes of man before the judgments writ with fiery signs across the heavens by the Eternal." Such a thought seems to contradict the idea that rationality, a kind heart, and hard work can bring about positive societal change. The suggestion is that greater and unknowable principles and forces, more powerful than man is able to intuit or affect, are involved in the rise and fall of civilizations.

Historical literature tends to be escapist and romantic. However, Prus's status as a positivist writer suggests that one look for an *Aesopian meaning* between the lines of the story, containing a comment on the Polish political situation of his time while avoiding possible censorship. Scholars have pointed to similarities between the story and dynastic developments in Germany, which at the time held western Polish territories. In 1887, a year before "Legends" was published, the warlike Kaiser Wilhelm I of Germany had fallen ill and was close to death, giving rise to the possibility that his reform-minded son, Crown Prince Friedrich, would ascend the throne and institute parliamentary democracy and other reforms beneficial to the part of Poland under German occupation. However, the crown prince, an inveterate smoker, was at the same time being treated for throat cancer, and when Prus wrote "Legends" it was not known whether the prince would outlive his father. As events developed, Kaiser Wilhelm did survive his illness, only to die somewhat later, in 1888. The reform-minded Friedrich served as Kaiser for only ninety-nine days before he himself succumbed to his illness, without having introduced his envisioned changes.

Bearing in mind that Poland was partitioned under three autocracies—German, Russian, and Austrian—the story would appear to be a call for patience, a suggestion that a great imperium has the power to change for the better, but that for change to be lasting, it must be brought about from a position of strength and authority, not out of weakness and cheap social sentiment. A striking sympathy and admiration is expressed here for the autocratic ruler Ramses, as cruel and vindictive as he is.

Comparing "Legends" to "The Waistcoat" and "The Barrel Organ," one could say that Prus on the one hand recommends helping society through kindness, and helping people on an individual basis, but that, on the other hand, he believes that major social reforms will come about according to their own timetable; they cannot be hurried, and they need to come about mostly from the top.

The setting is designed to be as remote from the present as possible in order to present ideas in the abstract on the nature of history, power, politics, and the qualities of a successful ruler. Despite its brevity, the story is complex, full of action, characters, and suspense. It takes longer to give an analysis of the story than it does to read it. The story is not unlike the plot of a long historical novel by Prus on more or less the same theme (*The Pharaoh*, 1895), in which the various motifs and strains introduced here are filled in, and the characters are more fully developed. One can spot certain positivist concerns, even if somewhat muted: the role of education and upbringing in the formation of character; the treatment of those less fortunate; the oppressive taxation of the poor; unjust imprisonment. However, the work is noteworthy for its lack of suggested solutions. Instead, it counsels patience and reliance on the wisdom of "fate," which has its own schedule, often making a mockery of men's plans.

Language is spare and on a high rhetorical level. The author uses third-person impersonal narration throughout, supporting the atmosphere of timelessness and generality. The "voice of time" or of "fate," which comes through in the regularly spaced incantations, seems separate from the main narrative voice; it is loftier and "omniscient." There are no extra words, descriptions, or psychological development. Every detail is carefully chosen. On the one hand narration is minimalistic, but on the other hand it relies on the repetition of set lines for effectiveness, lending an ominous, chanting, legendary quality to the words, as though coming down through the ages. The adopted style helps to lend universal validity to the contents.

More than the two other stories by Prus, "Legends" relies heavily on dialogue as a way of telling the story and advancing the plot. The matter-of-fact language of the dialogues creates an interesting counterpoint to the high rhetorical style of the narrative voice.

*Plot Analysis.* The plot is classical in structure, except that the development looks very much like an entanglement, in that it already contains a situation of heightened suspense, leading toward an inexorable end (seemingly, Ramses's impending death). Ramses is pragmatic and does not protest his plight; he is "philosophical" and willing to abide by fate, and he does not even worry that Horus is probably going to undo his life's work. He knows Horus to be soft-hearted and sentimental. When the pharaoh does die, the ring symbolizing his authority will be passed to the next in line, that is, to Horus. "Time" is introduced as the main player in the action: when will Ramses die? When will the ring of power be transferred? The cup of medicine/poison is administered, and not only the life of Ramses but also the fate of the country hangs in the balance. Ramses's expected death will spell the end of an era of power, might, and glory, even if fraught with terror and oppression. Tension is heightened by the impending edicts Horus has his courtiers prepare for him. The courtiers are taut and expectant, like bent bows, ready to rush out on their missions as soon as they receive the command. The throngs of people silently milling in the streets, and floating down the Nile on boats, add to the eerie quality.

The background of Horus and his character is introduced subtly and outside the plotline. While ready to take over as pharaoh, cognizant of his place in the hereditary line, Horus is naïve. He does not understand why the people are suddenly milling about. He is also sentimental: he breaks into tears at the news of his grandfather's probable death, and he has his own complex and mixed-up agenda, combining major social reforms with personal concerns: the slaves and their plight; peace with the Ethiopians; the treatment of prisoners of war; his mother Zefora; his romantic interest Berenice; his teacher Jetron.

Unlike Ramses, Horus is not ready to accept fate, but rather sets his hopes against it. He naïvely thinks he can change the world by just making edicts. Note that Horus is so easy to "read" that the courtiers have already anticipated his every wish. He has shown throughout his life that he is easily guided and manipulated by others, especially by his mother Zefora and his teacher Jetron.

Entanglement: The Turning Point is almost invisible. Horus is bitten by what he thinks is a bee sting. At first one does not necessarily catch the significance of the sting. Only later we learn that he has been bitten by a deadly spider. The spider symbolizes the perversity of fate from the point of view of the individual as opposed to the hidden wisdom of Fate from the point of view of History.

Crisis: As Horus realizes he has been bitten not by a bee but by a spider and is going to die, the plot becomes a race between his "timeline" and that of the pharaoh: who will die first? Horus prioritizes his edicts, and they fall from his hands one by one: the more socially significant first, the ones nearest to his heart last. The sequence in which they drop call into question Horus's fitness to rule: he is too governed by his feelings.

Climax: A surprise ending: a perverse (or actually, maybe wise) Fate intervenes. Horus dies first, and Ramses regains his health. The prophecies at the beginning are fulfilled (a member of the dynasty dies), but in an unexpected way. The time for change has not yet arrived. Or maybe it has: who knows but that some of Horus's ideas will be put into effect, now that he is out of the way. The exile of his mother's remains, and of Berenice and Jetron, only make sense as long as Horus is alive.

Aftermath: The Aftermath exists mainly in the mind of the reader: what will happen now that the line of succession has been broken? The story ends with the repeated strain: "Behold how vain are the hopes of man against the order of the universe, how futile they are against the judgments which the Everlasting has writ in fiery letters across the heavens." The story causes one to contemplate historical movements, the history of civilizations, and the "inscrutable hand of fate."

In retrospect, the story becomes a treatise on history and historiosophy (the interpretation of history), the "wave theory" of history with the rise and fall of civilizations versus the "great person" theory. Under the former, things happen according to their own rhythm. It is beyond the power of individuals to alter them, and it is futile to struggle against the inevitable, Prus seems to be saying. The pragmatism of Positivism is mixed here with a kind of historical fatalism. There is a time for autocracy, and a time for democracy. For democracy to come about, autocracy must be allowed to run its natural course. To be successful, a ruler must understand the immutable rules of the time in which he lives and proceed accordingly. In what one could consider a Positivist touch, Prus believes that there is a progressive bent to history, bringing slow incremental improvement and betterment of life and society; one just cannot hurry it. Successful leaders are those who do not let personal emotions influence their decisions.

Ramses himself has sentimental attachments. He actually may have the welfare and happiness of his people at heart, but he does not let his sentiments cloud his exercise of power or the interests of the Egyptian state. The idea is introduced that history is often "out of sync" with progressive ideas, that timelines for different agendas are often incompatible, and some override others. There has to be both a right idea and a right time for its introduction. See the line: "Saturn is conjoined with the moon"; that is, everything has to be properly aligned for progress to take place. The suggestion is also made that progress is sometimes achieved with the help of would-be reformers like Horus. Although Horus's edicts fall to the ground, the fact that they have been raised as issues may influence future decisions.

Auxiliary characters in the story are sycophants. It is only the rulers who count. The courtiers, priests, doctors, and general are ready to bend with the wind, whichever way it blows. However, one suspects that the priests and the general, who would have strong vested interests in the status quo, are probably not going to cooperate willingly with Horus in his desire to reform the state and conclude peace with Egypt's traditional enemies. They represent the "deep state," the inertia present in any political system. Horus himself knows he has to placate the priests, and he does so, by promising to build more temples. Just how he expects to do that while cutting the people's taxes in half has not been well thought out by him.

*Images of Time.* Among other reasons the story is stylistically and narratively effective are the many ways in which the passage of Time, in both a long-term and short-term perspective, is depicted. Long-term, the story deals with the march of history, and the rise and fall of empires, emperors, and civilizations. The setting itself, in ancient Egypt, a dead civilization, brings this idea to the fore, and it is underscored by such images as the slow, measured movement of celestial bodies (Saturn, the setting moon, the rising sun); and by the yearly overflowing of the Nile, which serves also to mark Ramses's age. Cedars live to a ripe old age but, like Ramses, they too will eventually topple.

Short-term, we are concerned with time "running out" for Horus, as he awaits his grandfather's (and, in the end, his own) death. The short-term sense of the marching of time is emphasized by the running of the court attendants in and out of the pharaoh's chamber, giving updates on the situation; by the gradual swelling of Horus's spider bite; by the image of the marching steps of soldiers; by the passing of the moon through the trees, casting its moving shadows; by the tossing of Horus's edicts on the ground, one by one; by the sifting of sand through the hourglass, an object which to this day symbolizes life running out. This last, by the way, is an anachronistic touch, since hourglasses did not appear until the Middle Ages. Toward the end these devices become dense, creating the effect of the reverse-telescoping of time, as though emphasizing that each second is more precious than the one before.

Besides devices conveying the passing of time, also of interest for its stylistic effect is the use of color—especially gold and bronze—and light; recall the fiery letters in the heavens, Saturn and the moon "gilding the bronze waters of the Nile," the flickering torches on the streets and on the Nile, the little light in Berenice's tower, and Horus's golden chair with its hawk heads.

An interesting stylistic sidelight is the association of "male," "phallic" images (the spear, the rhinoceros, the fallen cedar) with Ramses, contrasted to the attachment of Horus to women (Berenice, Zefora), and Horus's tears (a "womanly" trait)—striking in that the story predates Freudian psychoanalysis by a good number of years.

# Henryk Sienkiewicz

Henryk Sienkiewicz (1848–1910) was the most widely read Polish novelist of the nineteenth century, including internationally. His historical novels, set in the glory days of Poland of the seventeenth century, are still popular, especially with youth, and feature-length motion pictures based on them have been made of all of them, including his novel on the Teutonic Knights, set in the fifteenth century. Largely because of Sienkiewicz, Polish children chase each other around with swords, helmets, and shields rather than with six-shooters or bows and arrows. Outside Poland, he is best known for his novel *Quo Vadis*, situated in the days of the Roman emperor Nero, which has been adapted for the screen in both Poland and the United States. Sienkiewicz received the Nobel Prize for literature in 1905 for his life's work and for his role in nurturing, through his novels, the Polish national spirit during its 130-year occupation by Russia, Prussian Germany, and Austro-Hungary. His work has even been credited with helping to affect a positive outcome for Poland in the Paris Peace Conference and Treaty of Versailles of 1919.

Ironically, since Sienkiewicz lived in Russian-occupied Poland, he was often referred to as a "Russian" writer. Since Russia was not then a signatory of international copyright conventions, his works were often published without his permission to avoid paying royalties.

Sienkiewicz is considered an eminent Polish stylist, and his word usages are often cited as exemplars of word use in dictionaries. However, he was not a particularly deep thinker or developer of psychologically realistic characters. He combines a tremendous gift in the language with a narrow, class-conditioned philosophical outlook. Sienkiewicz was able to handle skillfully the complex plots and storylines of novels, but lacked the discipline and economy necessary to be a good short-story writer. However, the two stories included here, dealing with problems of Poland of his day, are known from childhood by almost everybody in Poland, partly because they were written by Sienkiewicz.

## Yanko the Musician

It came into the world weak and frail. The women gathered around the cot of the sick woman who had just given birth shook their heads over both mother and child. Kowalka, Simon the blacksmith's wife, who was the wisest among them, began to console the invalid:

"Here, I'll light a votive candle over you, my dear, for you're not long for this world; best send for the priest to absolve you of your sins."

"Right!" put in another, "but the boy must first be christened, and forget about the priest. We'll be lucky if he doesn't turn into a vampire."

So saying, the woman lighted a candle and, taking up the child, she sprinkled water over him till his eyes began to blink, then added:

"I baptize you in the name of the Father, Son, and Holy Spirit, and I christen you Yan. And now, Christian soul, return to where you came from. Amen!"

But the Christian soul had no desire whatsoever to depart its sickly little body and return to the place whence it had come, but began to kick its tiny legs with all the might it could muster and cry, albeit so weakly and pitifully that, as the women said, "What is this thing anyway? It looks more like a kitten than anything else."

They sent for the priest. He came, did his duty, and left—and the sick woman got better. In another week she was already back at work. The little boy barely mewled and puked, but mewl and puke he did, until in the spring of his fourth year the cuckoo bird laid him low with a grievous fever, but he survived just the same, and in some sort of manner he reached the tenth year of his life.

He was always scrawny and sunburned, with a bloated stomach and sunken cheeks. He had a shock of flaxen, almost snow-white hair that tumbled down over vacant eyes that gaped out at the world as if staring into some measureless distance. In wintertime he sat behind the stove and shivered, whimpering softly from the cold, and also from hunger, when his mother had nothing to put onto the stove or into the pot. In summer he went about in a pitiful-looking shirt with a scrap of cloth for a belt, and in a straw hat, out from underneath the torn brim of which he peered looking upwards, like a bird. His mother, a poor tenant farmer, lived from day to day like a sparrow under a stranger's roof. She perhaps loved him in her own way; but she beat him often enough, and instead of his given name generally called him "lazybones." From the eighth year of his life he was sent to herd cattle or, when there was nothing left to eat in the cottage, to the pine forest to gather mushrooms. It was only through the grace of God he was not eaten by a wolf.

He was a very dull little lad and, like most village children, when spoken to put his finger in his mouth. People did not give him much odds of growing up, much less that his mother would ever get any use out of him, for he was worthless at any kind of work. It was a mystery how such a creature could ever have been born. Still, there was one thing that did grab his attention, and that was music. He could hear it everywhere, and when he had grown up a little, he thought of nothing else. He would go into the woods after the cattle, or with a basket for berries, but he would return without the berries, stammering, "Oh Mama, something was playing out there in the woods!"

To which his mother would reply, "I'll play for you, never you fear!"

And she did make music for him, most often on his bottom with a big wooden spoon. The boy would yelp and yowl and promise never to do it again, all the while thinking, "Something *was* playing out there in the woods, but what?" How should he know? The pine trees, birches, beeches, orioles, all of them were playing—the whole forest was playing, and that was that!

And it reverberated everywhere! In the fields the wormwood played for him; in the little garden next to the cottage the sparrows twittered till the cherry trees were all atremble. In the evening he listened to all the sounds of the village, and no doubt thought to himself that the entire village was making music. When they put him to work spreading manure, even then the wind in the fork's tines would play a tune for him.

One day the overseer caught him standing there with his hair over his eyes listening to the wind playing on the wooden tines. He took one look at him, unbuckled his leather belt, and gave him something to long remember the occasion by. But what was the use? People called him "Yanko the musician." In the springtime he ran off to make whistles down by the stream. At night, when the frogs were croaking, the land rail called in the meadows, the bittern cackled in the dew, and the cocks crowed behind the wicker fences, he could not sleep but only listen; and God only knows what music he heard in all that racket. His mother could not take him to church, for as soon as the organ would start to play, or the choir to sing sweetly, the boy's eyes would water over as if looking out from another world altogether.

The watchman who walked through the village at night and counted the stars in the sky, to keep from falling asleep, or conversed in a low voice with the dogs, more than once spotted Yanko's white shirt stealing along in the shadows toward the local tavern. But the boy was not going there, only to be near it. Once there he would crouch next to the wall and listen. The people were dancing the obertas, and from time to time some young fellow would call out, "Oo-ha!" The stamping of boots would be heard, and then the voices of the girls in response: "Hi—de-ho!" The fiddles sang in low tones: "We will eat, we will drink, we will all be merry;" and the bass viol in a deep voice chimed in importantly: "As God gave! As God gave!" The windows glowed with life, and every beam in the room seemed to tremble, singing and playing along while Yanko listened.

How much he would give to have a fiddle like that playing softly: "We will eat, we will drink, we will all be merry!" Such a singing block of wood! But where could he get one—where were they made? If he could only just for once hold such a thing in his hands! But how could he ever? He was only free to listen, and then only until the voice of the watchman sounded behind him in the dark: "Get on home with you, you little rascal!"

Then he would flee home in his bare little feet, followed in the darkness by the voice of the fiddle playing behind him: "We will eat, we will drink, we will all be merry," and the deep voice of the bass: "As God gave! As God gave! As God gave!"

Whenever he heard a fiddle at a harvest fest or a wedding, it was for him a great holiday. He would crawl afterwards behind the stove and say nothing for days on end, looking like a cat with eyes gleaming in the dark. He made himself a sort of fiddle out of a shingle and some horsehair, but it did not play beautifully like the one in the tavern; it sounded low, deep and low, like mice chirping, or a mosquito buzzing. He played on it nevertheless, from morning till night, until he got in return so many cuffs that he ended up looking like a wrinkled unripe apple. But such was his nature. The poor child became increasingly thin, while his stomach protruded more and more. His shock of hair grew thicker, and his eyes gaped ever more widely, although they were often filled with tears, while his cheeks and breast became sunk ever more deeply.

He was not at all like other children, but more like his shingle fiddle that hardly made a sound. Before harvesttime he increasingly suffered from hunger, for he lived almost exclusively on raw carrots and the desire to possess a fiddle. But that wish was to turn out badly for him.

At the manor house the valet had a fiddle and he played on it sometimes at dusk, wooing the chambermaid. Yanko crept up at times among the burdocks as far as the open door of the pantry to look at it. It hung on the wall opposite the door, and the boy would send his whole soul out to it through his eyes, It seemed to him as though it was some unattainable object he was unworthy of touching, the unapproachable love of his life. Still, he wanted it. He wanted to hold it in his hands at least once, to see it up close. The poor lad's heart trembled from happiness at the very thought.

One night there was no one in the pantry. For some time the lord and lady had been visiting foreign climes; the house was empty, the valet was at the other end visiting with the chambermaid. Yanko, lurking in the burdocks, had been looking for a long time through the broad door at the object of his desires. The moon in the sky was full, and shone with sloping rays through the pantry window, casting a reflection in the form of a great quadrangle on the opposite wall. The quadrangle gradually approached the fiddle until at last it illuminated every bit of it. At that moment it seemed in the dark depths of the room as if a silvery light was emanating from the fiddle. Above all else the rounded bends in it were highlighted so clearly that Yanko could barely look at them. In that light everything was clearly visible—the sides with their incisions, the strings, and the bent neck. The pegs in it gleamed like fireflies, and at its side hung the bow in the form of a silvery wand.

Ah, it was all so beautiful and almost enchanted; and Yanko looked at it more and more greedily. He crouched in the burdocks, with his elbows pressed on his lean knees, as he looked and looked with eyes wide open. At first terror held him to the spot, but the next moment an unconquerable desire pushed him forward. Was this some sort of enchantment? In the bright light the fiddle seemed at times to approach, as if floating toward him. At times it grew darker, only to shine up again even more brightly. It was clearly an enchantment, that's what it was! Then the breeze blew; the trees rustled quietly, and Yanko thought he heard a voice from the burdocks saying distinctly, "Go, Yanko, go! No one is in the pantry, go!"

The night was clear and bright. In the garden a nightingale began to sing, whistling at first in a low voice, then louder; "Go on in! Take it!" An honest nighthawk turned in flight around the child's head, and cried; "Yanko, no! no!" The bird flew away, but the nightingale and the burdocks murmured ever more distinctly, "There is no one inside!" The fiddle shone its light again.

The poor little bent figure pushed forward slowly and carefully; meanwhile the nightingale whistled in a very low voice, "Go on! Go on! Take it!"

The white shirt appeared nearer and nearer to the pantry. The dark burdocks concealed it no more. On the threshold of the pantry the quick breathing of the child's weak chest could be heard. In another moment the white shirt had vanished; only one bare foot still stuck outside the threshold. In vain, O nighthawk, do you fly once more, crying "No! No!" Yanko is in the pantry.

Immediately the great frogs in the garden pond began to croak, as if in fright, but they soon grew silent. The nightingale stopped singing, the burdocks ceased to rustle. Meanwhile Yanko crept along silently and carefully, when all at once he was seized with fear. In the burdocks he felt at home, as a wild beast feels in the thicket; but now he was like an animal caught in a trap. His movements became hurried, his breath short and wheezing, and at the same time the darkness seized hold of him. Faint summer lightning flashed from east to west, illuminating once more the interior of the pantry, while Yanko crept on all fours with upturned head. The lightning died down; a small cloud hid the moon, and nothing more was to be seen or heard.

In another moment, a sound emerged from the darkness, very low and complaining, as if someone had unguardedly touched the strings, and all of a sudden someone's husky, sleepy voice rang out angrily from the comer of the pantry, "Who's there?"

Yanko held his breath in his breast, but the rude voice inquired again, "Who's there?"

A match was struck on the wall; a flicker of light and then: Oh, my God! Curses, blows, the wailing of a child, sobbing, Oh my God! Dogs barked, lights wavered outside the windows, and a general commotion echoed throughout the entire building!

Next day Yanko was brought before the tribunal of the village head.

Was he to be tried as a criminal? Absolutely! The village head and the elders looked at him as he stood before them with his finger in his mouth, staring with terrified eyes, small, poor, starved, beaten, not knowing where he was or what was wanted of him. How to judge such a pitiful little creature, only ten years of age and barely able to stand on his own two feet? Prison seemed out of the question. After all, one needs to have some small mercy on children. Let the watchman take him and give him a thrashing with a rod, so he won't steal a second time, and let that be the end of it.

The end of it indeed!

They called for Stach, the night watchman.

"Take him and give him something to remember this by."

Stach nodded his dull brutish head, tucked Yanko under his arm as he would a cat, and took him out to the barn. Whether he failed to understand what was happening, or whether he was too frightened to speak, the child uttered not a sound but merely stared like a bird. Did he know what they were about to do with

with him? Only when Stach took his handful to the stable, stretched it out on the ground, raised his shirt and struck a full blow—only then did Yanko scream, "Mama!" and as long as Stach kept flogging him he cried, "Mama! Mama!" but each time lower and weaker, until after a certain blow the child called out mama no more.

The poor broken fiddle!

Ah, stupid, dull-witted Stach ... Who beats children that way? Especially one so small and feeble, barely alive?

His mother came and carried the little boy home, because he could not walk. Next day Yanko did not rise from bed, and the third day, in the evening, he died peacefully on the cot under a coarse homespun mat.

Next to the cottage the swallows twittered in the cherry tree; the rays of the sun shone through the window, washing in a bright golden light over the little boy's disheveled head of hair and his tiny face, in which not a drop of blood remained. That ray of sunlight formed, as it were, a pathway along which the soul of the little boy was to depart his body. It was well that it went out by a bright shining beam at the moment of death, for during life it had trodden a truly thorny path. For a brief moment, his emaciated breast took another breath, and the child's face as if became absorbed listening to the sounds of the village as they came in through the open window. It was evening, and the girls returning from cutting hay were singing, "Green is the meadow, all covered with dew!" From the stream came the sound of pipes playing. Yanko strained one last time to hear the sounds of the village. The shingle fiddle lay on the matting by his side.

All at once the face of the dying boy lighted up, and out of his whitened lips came a whisper, "Mama!"

"What is it, my son?" answered his mother, choking with tears.

"Mama, will the Lord God give me a real fiddle in heaven?"

"That he will, my son, that he will," answered his mother; but she could speak no more, for her hard breast suddenly became convulsed with the gathering sorrow, and she burst out sobbing, "Jesus! O Jesus!" and she fell with her face on a crate and began to wail as if she had just lost her reason, as a person weeps when they see they cannot wrest their beloved from death.

Nor did she wrest him, for when she raised her face again she looked at the child and saw that the eyes of the little musician were open, but fixed; his face was frozen in a serious, somber, rigid gaze. The rays of the sun had also left him.

Peace be with you, Yanko.

* * *

Next day the master and mistress of the manor returned to their residence from Italy, accompanied by their daughter and the young man who was paying court to her. He remarked:

"Quel beau pays que l'Italie!"

"And what a nation of artists! On est heureux de chercher là-bas des talents et de les protéger," added the young lady.

The birches murmured over Yanko's grave.

—1879. Translated by Oscar Swan

Notes on "Yanko." "Quel beau pays que l'Italie" means "What a beautiful country Italy is!" "On est heureux de chercher là-bas des talents et de les protéger" means "What a joy it is to find people of talent there and further their careers." This story has so many parallels to a novella by Bolesław Prus entitled *Antek* that Prus's story, published in 1880, could practically be considered to be a positivistic response to it. Both works feature a young peasant boy from a poor fatherless family, not understood by those around him, his latent talent going unrecognized and to waste, his aspirations being thwarted by his surroundings. However, Yanko is deformed and seems a bit retarded, possibly because of a childhood fever, whereas Antek is smart, well-built, and catches the eyes of the local womenfolk. "Antek" ends on an optimistic note, with the boy heading off to the city looking for a better future, whereas "Yanko" ends with the birch trees playing music over the grave of the luckless mistreated boy.

With the singing birch trees, the sunbeam tracing Yanko's path to heaven, and elsewhere, Sienkiewicz plays on the heartstrings of his reader to a too obviously pathetic extent, for example, comparing the beaten boy with his bloated stomach to a broken fiddle. There is no light ironic touch here, as in Prus. In order to heighten the pathos, the author employs "sympathetic nature," in which animals and natural forces become involved in the action, rather like in a Walt Disney animated cartoon. In Sienkiewicz nature plays a counterpart to the action, warning without effect against what eventually happens. Recall, for example, the frogs suddenly croaking as if in fear, as Yanko is about to enter the pantry, and then suddenly growing silent, as if holding their collective breath.

Instead of an aftermath, the story ends with a brief coda containing the story's Point: the gentry have lost their leading role through focusing on other countries; they communicate among themselves in French and spend money and effort developing talent in other countries, not in Poland, where the human potential is just as great. Had they been at home and paid attention to what is going on around them, instead of wandering about in foreign climes, it is suggested, Yanko's story might have ended differently. Sienkiewicz's hidden assumption here is that the gentry have a preordained responsibility or *noblesse oblige* toward society, which they have abandoned. Such an attitude is implicitly condescending toward the classes over whom the gentry is supposedly "placed."

## *Yamioł* (A Village Sketch)

In the little town of Łupiskóry, after the funeral of widow Kaliksta, vespers were held, after which a number of old women, around ten or twenty in number, stayed in the church to finish the hymn. It was four o'clock in the afternoon, but, since twilight in winter comes at about that time, the church was dark. The great altar in particular was enveloped in a dark shadow. Only two candles were burning at the ciborium, their flickering flames barely illuminating the gilding on the doors and the feet of the image of Christ, hanging high up on a cross. Christ's feet were pierced with an enormous nail, and the head of the nail seemed a great gleaming point on the altar.

From the other candles, which had just been extinguished, wafted streaks of smoke, filling the place behind the pews with a uniquely churchly odor of wax.

An old man and a small boy were busy before the steps of the altar. One swept while the other held down the carpet on the steps. At times when the women ceased their singing, the angry whisper of the old man could be heard scolding the boy, while cold and starving sparrows hammered on the snow-covered windows outside.

The women sat on benches by the door. It would have been even darker had it not been for the few tallow candles by whose light those who had prayer books were reading. One of the candles illuminated a banner fastened to the seat just beyond, representing sinners surrounded by devils and flames. It was impossible to see what was painted on the other banners.

The women were not exactly singing but, rather, muttering with sleepy and tired voices a hymn in which these words were continually repeated, "And when the hour of death comes, intercede for us, intercede for us with Thy Son … " All this was dismal beyond compare, simply unbearable: the church buried in shadow, the banners standing by the seats, the old women with their yellow faces, the lights flickering as if oppressed by the gloom. The mournful words of the song about death found there a fitting background. After a while the chanting stopped, and one of the women stood up at her seat and began to say with a trembling voice, "Hail, Mary, full of grace!" And others responded, "The Lord be with You," and so on. However, since it was the day of Kaliksta's funeral, each "Hail Mary" concluded with the words, "Lord, grant her eternal rest, and may perpetual light shine upon her!"

Next to one of the old women on a bench sat Marysia, the dead woman's daughter. At that moment the snow, soft and noiseless, was falling on the fresh grave of her mother, but the little girl was not yet ten years old, and she seemed to be oblivious to her plight or to the pity it might evoke in others. Her face, with large blue eyes, had in it the calmness of childhood, and even a certain nonchalance. A slight curiosity was evident, nothing more. With gaping mouth she looked attentively at the banner on which Hell and sinners were depicted. Next she looked into the depths of the church and then at the window behind which the sparrows were hammering. Her eyes remained without thought. Meanwhile, the women began to mutter, sleepily, for the tenth time, "And when the hour of death comes … "

The little girl twisted around her fingers the tresses of her light-colored hair, woven into two tiny braids no thicker than mouse tails. She seemed tired, but now the sexton occupied her attention. He went to the middle of the church and began to pull a knotty rope hanging from the ceiling. He was ringing for the soul of Kaliksta, but in a purely mechanical way, his mind seemingly on something else.

The bells were also a sign that vespers were over. After repeating one last time the prayer for a happy death, the women went out onto the square. One of them led Marysia by the hand.

"Well, Kulik," asked another, "What are you going to do with the girl?"

"What do you mean what will I do with her? I'll send her to Leszczyńcy, of course. Voytek Margula will take her. Why even ask?"

"What will she do in Leszczyńcy? "

"The same, my dears, as she does here. She'll be going back to where she came from. Even at the manor house they'll take in an orphan and let her sleep in the kitchen."

Thus conversing, they passed through the square to the tavern. Darkness was falling with each passing moment. It was wintry and calm; the sky was covered with clouds, and the air was saturated with moisture and wet snow. Water dripped from the roofs, and slush formed of snow and straw lay on the square. The village with its wretched and tattered houses looked as gloomy as the church. A few windows gleamed with light, but movement had ceased. In the tavern an organ was playing.

It was playing to lure people in, for as yet it was empty. The women entered and had a drink of vodka all around. Kulik gave Marysia half a glass, saying. "Drink, my girl! You're an orphan. You'll not meet with kindness in this world."

The word "orphan" called to mind the death of Kaliksta to the women, and one of them said,

"Here's to you, Kulik! Oh, my dears, how that paralus [paralysis] took her so she couldn't stir! She was cold even before the priest came to hear her confession."

"I told her a long time ago," said Kulik, "that she was spinning fine thread [near her end]. Last week she came to me. I told her. 'Ah, better give Marysia to the manor house!' But she said, 'I have but one little daughter, and I'll not give her away to anyone.' But then she grew sad and began to weep and she went to the mayor to put her papers in order. She paid four zlotys and six groszes for it. But I don't begrudge it for my child,' said she. My dears, how her eyes stared, and after she died how they stared even more. People tried to close them, but they couldn't. They said that even in death she was looking at her child."

"Let's lift a glass to her sorrow!"

The organ kept playing, and the women began to feel more and more tenderhearted. With a voice full of compassion, Kulik repeated,

"Poor little thing! Poor little thing!" and another old woman recalled the death of her own husband.

"When he was dying," she said, "he moaned so, oh, how he moaned, how he moaned!" And, drawling still more, her voice turned into a chant, and from a chant into the tone of the organ, until at last she bent to one side, and, following the tune of the organ, she began to sing, "He moaned, he moaned, he moaned, on that day how he moaned."

All at once she fell to shedding hot tears, gave the organist six groszes, and ordered another drink of vodka. Kulik, too, was enveloped in tenderness, but she directed it to Marysia.

"Remember, orphan," she said, "what the priest told you when they were covering your mother over with snow, that there is a *yamioł* above you." Here she stopped, looked around as if astonished, and then added with unusual energy, "And when I say that there is a *yamioł*, I mean there is a *yamioł*!"

No one contradicted her. Marysia, blinked with her poor, simple eyes, looked attentively at the woman. Kulik continued speaking.

"You are an orphan, and that is bad! But over orphans there is a *yamioł*, and he is good. Here are ten groszes for you. Even were you to start out on foot to Leszczyńcy, you would make it, for he would guide you."

Another old woman began to sing, "In the shadow of his wings he will keep you forever. Under his pinions you will safely lie … "

"Oh hush!" said Kulik. And she turned again to the child.

"Do you know, you fool, who is above you?"

"A *yamioł*," answered the little girl with a thin voice.

"You poor little orphan, you precious berry, you worm of the Lord! A *yamioł* with wings," she said with perfect tenderness, and, seizing the child, she pressed her to her honest, if tipsy, bosom.

Marysia suddenly burst into tears. Perhaps at that moment in her dim little head and in her heart, as yet unformed, there awakened a realization of her situation.

Behind the counter the tavern keeper was sleeping most soundly. Mushrooms began to form on the candle wicks. The man at the organ stopped playing, amused by what he saw.

The silence was broken by the sudden plashing of horses' feet outside the door, and a voice calling to the horses,

"Prrr!"

Voytek Margula stepped into the tavern with a lighted lantern in his hand. He put down the lantern, began to slap his hands to warm them, and at last said to the tavern-keeper,

"Give me a glass."

"Margula, you old rotter," cried Kulik, "You'll take the little girl to Leszczyńcy.

"Of course I'll take her, for they told me to," replied Margula. Then, looking more closely at the women, he added,

"Why, you people are drunk as skunks."

"May the devil take you," retorted Kulik. "When I tell you to be careful with the child, I mean be careful. She's an orphan. Do you know, you fool, who is above her?"

Voytek did not see fit to answer that question, but he evidently seemed determined to raise another subject, and he began,

"Here's to all of you! May you … "

But he didn't finish, for he quaffed the vodka, made a wry face, and, putting the glass down with dissatisfaction, said, "That's pure water. Give me another, but this time from a different bottle."

The tavernkeeper poured him a glass from another bottle. Margula contorted his face even more.

"Ugh! Don't you have anything stronger?"

Evidently the same danger threatened Margula as the women. However, at that very moment, in the manor house at Łupiskóry, the landowner was preparing for one of the journals a long and exhaustive article entitled "On the right of landowners to sell liquor, this right being considered the basis of society." Voytek cooperated in strengthening the basis of society, albeit unknowingly, all the more that the sale here, although in the village tavern, was really through the landowner.

When he had cooperated five times in succession he forgot, it is true, his lantern, in which the light had gone out, but he took the half-sleeping little girl by the hand, and said, "Come on, you ragamuffin!"

The women had fallen asleep in a corner, so no one bade Marysia farewell. Her whole story was this: Her mother was in the graveyard, and she was going to Leszczyńcy. Voytek and the girl went out and took seats in the sleigh.

Voytek shouted to the horses, and they drove off. At first the sleigh dragged heavily through the slush of the town, but once they came out into the wide snow-covered fields, movement was easy. The snow barely made a sound beneath the runners. At times the horses snorted, and at times the barking of dogs could be heard at a distance.

They continued along their way. Voytek urged the horses on, singing through his nose, "Darling, remember your promise." But he soon grew silent and began to nod off. He nodded to the right, and then to the left. He dreamed that they were beating him on the back in Leszczyńcy, when he had once lost a basket of letters. From time to time he half awoke and repeated: "Here's to everyone!" Marysia did not sleep, for she was cold. She looked with wide-open eyes at the white fields, hidden from moment to moment by Margula's dark shoulders. She also recalled that her mother was dead. Thinking this way, she pictured to herself perfectly the pale and gaunt face of her mother with its staring eyes, and she realized half consciously that that dearly beloved face was no longer in this world and that it never would be. She had seen with her own eyes how they covered it up in Łupiskóry. Rembering this, she would have sooner cried from grief, but, as her knees and feet were chilled to the bone, she began to cry from the cold.

It was not actually below freezing, but the air was penetrating, as is usual during thaws. As to Voytek he had, at least in his stomach, a good supply of heat taken from the tavern. The landowner at Leszczyńcy justly remarked in his treatise that vodka warms in winter, and, "since it is the only consolation of our peasants, to deprive landowners of the sole power of consoling peasants is to deprive them of influence over the locale." Voytek was so consoled at that moment that nothing could trouble him.

It did not even trouble him that the horses, as they entered the forest, slackened their pace altogether, though the road there was better. Then, walking off to one side, the beasts turned the sleigh over into a ditch. At that he woke, it is true, but did not understand very well what had happened.

Marysia began to push him. "Voytek!"

"What are you squawking about?"

"The sleigh is turned over."

"Let's have a glass!" answered Voytek, and went to sleep for good.

The little girl sat by the sleigh, crouching down as best she could, and remained there. But her face was soon chilled, and she began to nudge the sleeping man again.

"Voytek!"

He gave no answer.

"Voytek, I want to go to the house."

And, after a while again: "Voytek, I'm going to walk there."

At last she set out. It seemed to her that Leszczyńcy was very close. She knew the road, for she had walked it every Sunday with her mother to church. But now she had to go by herself. In spite of the thaw the snow in the forest was deep; the night was very clear. To the gleam from the snow was added light reflected off the clouds, so that the road could be seen as in the daytime. Marysia, turning her eyes to the dark forest, could see the tree trunks outlined distinctly, black and motionless, far away against the white background, and she also clearly saw how drifts of snow had blown to the full height of some of them. In the forest reigned an immense calm, giving solace to the child. On the branches hung thick, frozen snow, and from it drops of water were trickling, striking against the branches and twigs with a faint sound. But that was the only noise. All else was quiet, white, silent, and dumb.

The wind was still. The snowy branches did not stir with the slightest movement. Everything slept in the trance of winter, as if the snowy covering over the earth, and the whole silent and shrouded forest, along with the pale clouds in the heavens, were all of the same white, lifeless unity. So it is in time of thaw. Marysia was the only living thing, moving like a little black speck amid these great silentnesses.

Kind, honest forest! Those drops, which the thawing ice let fall, were tears, perhaps, over the orphan. The trees towered compassionately above the tiny creature, and seemed to say, "Look, she is alone, so weak and poor, in the snow, in the night, in the forest, wading along trustfully, heedless of danger."

The clear night seemed to protect her. When something so weak and helpless yields itself, trusts so perfectly in an enormous power, there is a certain sweetness in the act. In that way all may be left to the will of God.

The girl walked on for a rather long time and at last became weary. Her heavy boots, which were too large for her, hindered her progress as her small feet went up and down in them. It was hard to drag such big boots out of the snow. Besides, she could not move her hands freely, for in one of them, closed tightly, she held with all her might those ten groszes which Kulik had given her. She was afraid of dropping them in the snow. At times she began to cry out loud, and then she suddenly stopped, as if wishing to know whether someone had heard her. Yes, the forest had heard her! The thawing ice gave off a monotonous and somewhat sad sound. Maybe someone else had heard her. The child walked ever more slowly. Could she lose her way? How? The road, like a broad, white, winding ribbon, stretched into the distance, and was well marked between the two dark walls of trees. The little girl became seized with an unconquerable drowsiness.

She stepped off the road and sat down under a tree, and her eyelids began to droop. After a while, she felt that her mother was coming to her along the white road from the graveyard. However, no one was coming. Still, the child felt certain that someone must surely come. Who? A *yamioł*. Hadn't old Kulik told her that a *yamioł* was watching over her? Marysia knew what a *yamioł* was. In her mother's cottage there was one painted with a shield in his hand and wings. He would come, surely. Suddenly the ice began to crack more loudly. Maybe that was the noise of his wings, scattering drops more abundantly as he came. But wait! Someone really was coming. The snow, though soft, sounded clearly now; steps were coming, quietly but rapidly. The child confidently raised her sleepy eyelids.

"What is that?"

Looking at the little girl intently was a gray three-cornered face with ears, standing upright, ugly, terrible!

—1882. Translated by Jeremiah Curtin

*Note: Yamioł* ("yamyow") is a corruption of standard Polish *anioł*, 'angel.' Leszczyńcy ("Leshchintsy") is the name of the local landowner's estate. The name of the village, Łupiskóry, is made up; it is based on an old word meaning 'flayer, extortionist.'

*Sienkiewicz as a Positivist.* Although Sienkiewicz is broadly known as a Positivist writer because of the time period in which he wrote, one may question whether "Yanko" and "Yamioł" qualify as works of Positivist fiction. They exhibit the external trappings of the Positivist short story, but without the stories' being, in the end, positivist in spirit. For one thing they are not mainly concerned with analyzing and improving society but with shocking the reader and with playing on his or her heartstrings, They have cruel endings with unclear morals, and they use shock value for its own sake. In a way, they are like Grimm fairy tales, where evil lurks everywhere, preying on the weak and innocent, and Little Red Riding Hood does get eaten by the wolf. The possibility of the child hero's being eaten by a wolf in the forest was already hinted at in "Yanko," but in "Yamiol" Sienkiewicz brings the idea to full realization.

The two stories are additionally opposed to the populist spirit of Positivist literature, based on respect for the basic dignity and good-heartedness of the individual, regardless of background, and on believing in the untapped potential latent in the people. Positivism was basically optimistic, while Sienkiewicz in these short stories is anything but. The author has social blinders on and seems too conditioned by his own background as a member of the landed gentry. He comes across as a snob, and actually does seem to consider the common folk as uncorrectable, ignorant, and brutish.

To be sure, Sienkiewicz is also a pessimist regarding his own class, which in both stories is seen as not fulfilling the obligation of those "higher born" to look after those who are less so in the social ranking. The gentry either admire foreign ways and ignore life in their own vicinity as in "Yanko," or pursue their narrow economic interests by encouraging the excessive sale and use of alcohol as in "Yamioł."

*Structural Remarks.* Thematically these two stories comprise a virtually matched pair, as societal negligence causes the brutal death of two innocent and defenseless ten-year-old children—one a boy, tke other a girl. Structurally, the stories are simple, and they are hard to break down into classical movements. Generally speaking, they consist of a chain of situations, one leading to the next, capped by a final tragic situation which is, however, not inevitable but merely caused by bad luck or thoughtlessness. Thus, while tragic in a sense, these stories do not qualify as tragic in the classical sense, because the outcome is not forecast by or inherent in the initial situation. As a result, the stories may strike the reader as mean-spirited. Yanko did not have to be beaten to death, and probably would not have been under most circumstances. Similarly, the little girl Marysia in "Yamioł" in most instances would have made it safely on foot to the manor house without being devoured by a wolf, which actually was a fairly rare occurrence.

The seams of the plot of both stories are held together by the presupposition that people will do the wrong thing at every turn, not out of ignorance, but out of meanness and insensitivity. This is, again, the opposite of the positivist spirit, as are the negative endings of both stories.

*Further Notes on "Yamiol: A Village Sketch."* The subtitle suggests the ordinariness of what is to follow, but that is not really what happens. It is not a sketch, but the tragic end of a girl's life due to the seemingly inveterate inability of adults to behave responsibly. The *yamiol*, or "guardian angel" of the story, represents naïve optimistic superstition, encouraged by folk beliefs combined with a superficial understanding of the teachings of the church. At the end, the *yamioł* turns out to be a wolf in disguise.

The story could almost be taken as a tract against the church, or at least against its tendency to encourage people not to take responsibility for what happens to themselves and to others around them but to place their faith in empty platitudes and the supposed goodness of Divine Providence. One wonders what has become of the church's priest after the burial service. His responsibilities surely include looking after the needs of orphans.

As in "Yanko the Musician," Sienkiewicz seems to place ultimate responsibility for the little girl's misfortune on the gentry, and in this case on the gentry's crucial role in promoting excessive alcohol consumption by the peasantry under the umbrella of the so-called propination laws, which gave the gentry the exclusive right to produce and sell alcohol, typically through the village tavern. These laws were not rescinded in the Russian part of Poland until 1898.

The plot is fairly primitive, with one bad event leading to another, increasingly more serious, event, creating a snowball effect, all through the lack of adult responsibility and thinking things through. There is no discernable single Turning

Point in the action. A major role is played by the women's mouthing mindless comforts and superstitious beliefs that have negative survival value, a possible intrusion here of Darwinism and the idea of the survival of the fittest and the culling of the weakest.

A lengthy *narrative retardation* occurs in the action as the girl, Marysia, walks by herself along the road through the forest, in which *sympathetic nature* also participates, heightening both suspense and pathos. There are many *misdirections* as to what will happen, giving false hope, as in "The clear night seemed to protect her," and so on. The story ends suddenly, with an intrusion of naturalism, that is, seeing people as part of animal nature, in this case becoming prey for other animal species. The story mocks the trite idea repeated by the churchwomen that fortune favors the weak and the helpless.

# Eliza Orzeszkowa

Eliza Orzeszkowa (1841–1910) belonged to the so-called triumvirate of major Polish Positivist writers, the others being Bolesław Prus and Henryk Sienkiewicz. Of the three, Orzeszkowa was possibly the deepest and most complex of the three intellectually, but not the best stylist. That would be Sienkiewicz, whose plots and stories, however, tend to be stereotyped and to depend too much on coincidence and pathos. Prus was a fairly good stylist, and a sophisticated thinker, but the effectiveness of his stories is based on their tight, well-knit plots and the plausibility of the ideas attached to his characters rather than on their psychological depth.

Although the contemporary of Prus and Sienkiewicz, Orzeszkowa is a much more modern-sounding writer, and her characters do have psychological depth. As a stylist, however, she can sound rather plodding. She uses long, complex constructions, and possibly sounds better in a good translation than she does in Polish. She has not been widely translated into English, more so into German, where her style more easily fits.

More than Prus and Sienkiewicz, Orzeszkowa addressed contemporary political issues with a patriotic eye. She worked tirelessly for Polish causes and was subject to political repression by the Tsarist Russian government, which occupied the eastern part of Poland at the time. Her best-known novel, *Nad Niemnem* (On the Niemen River), deals with the repercussions of the 1863 "January" uprising in Lithuania against Russia, in which her family had taken part.

Besides her patriotic concerns, Oreszkowa especially worked in support of various causes connected to women's emancipation, women's suffrage, the education of the poor, and the better treatment of minorities. She was one of the few Polish writers of the time who was able to realistically depict the life and attitudes of the Jewish minority, which was quite sizable in the eastern part of Poland, in a way that was sympathetic without being stereotyped or maudlin.

Many semi-autobiographical features occur in the story to follow. Like Orzeszkowa, Miss Antonina is also interested in women's issues: the education of women; their breaking into the academic system, the workforce, and the political arena; the conflict between career and family; and that between romantic love and the obligation to one's dreams and career aspirations. Advanced for her time, Orzeszkowa also addressed such issues as the scourge of prostitution and children born to unwed mothers.

Orzeszkowa lost her father at an early age, and her mother and sister died by the time she was thirty, details also reflected in Miss Antonina's story. Orzeszkowa was educated by governesses and, like Miss Antonina, she attended a boarding school, undoubtedly better than the one Miss Antonina is described as having attended. Like Miss Antonina, Orzeszkowa was later largely self-educated. Married at the age of sixteen to a person twice her age whom she did not love (not unlike the man Miss Antonina rejected), she did not follow her husband into exile for his part in the failed 1863 uprising but stayed behind and made her way as an independent woman and writer at a time when even very few men were able to do so.

Later in life Orzeszkowa fell in love and, after a thirty-year courtship, married and settled in Grodno, now in Belarus, working on the causes in which she believed. Unlike Miss Antonina, Orzeszkowa was successful and effective in what she did. She was a prolific writer—the author of thirty novels alone—and founded schools, charities, publishing houses, and women's leagues. In 1905 she was nominated for the Nobel Prize in Literature along with Leo Tolstoy and the eventual recipient, Henryk Sienkiewicz. She was nominated again in 1909, a year before her death. By the time she died at the comparatively early age of sixty-eight, she was revered as a virtual national saint, and her funeral in Grodno was attended by thousands.

## Miss Antonina

"If I had twelve daughters I should educate every one of them to be professors of the university. Yes, every one of them. Even though I should have to tear the eyes from my head, even though I should be whipped, crucified and stoned for it, every one of them would become a university professor. Yes, twelve daughters and twelve chairs. That has always been my dearest wish … Oh, then I should show the world what women can do and what they are capable of! I too, would be happy because the sight of my children would reward me for all that … I have suffered myself … "

Truly, looking at her, one could easily believe that she had suffered a great deal in her life. She was now a woman of some thirty-odd years, thin, a little bony, always holding herself erect, always walking quickly and briskly, using energetic gestures of her delicate, long hands whose blue veins were visible through the thin skin and gave evidence to a rather high degree of physical exhaustion. This exhaustion was also evident in Miss Antonina's face. Viewed in profile, she still looked rather young because her features were regular and delicately chiseled, but if one looked her full in the face, the elongated, thin cheeks, the forehead covered with a multitude of tiny wrinkles and her yellowish, bloodless complexion gave an impression of early fading. When she became animated, which occurred quite often, her thin pale lips quivered nervously and the brown, deep-set eyes shot sparks of fire. She always dressed soberly in a black dress whose tight bodice outlined her straight, gaunt figure and with it the inevitable white collar and cuffs. There was never anything gay or ornamental about her dress except for a piece of black lace which covered her hair that had once been black and was now slightly greying, and which she wore pushed down low on her forehead in two smooth strands. This arrangement of her hair made of her high forehead a fairly regular triangle and emphasized the flash of her fiery eyes. On the whole her appearance was characterized by suffering and energy.

"Yes, twelve daughters and twelve university chairs and no one can talk me out of it; I simply can't understand why you don't see that I am right. What was that? You tell me that birds do not plow and neither do they sow and yet they live! Thank you! That's a fine encouragement! Not to plow or sow! When I look at those who do not plow or sow I get so angry I am ready to use my fists to make them! Yes, my fists, because they are lazy women dolls, leeches, parasites sapping a tree, sponging on society! Oh, if I had daughters I should never allow them to turn into anything of the sort. Never! Never! I'd rather see them die as children! Those are my convictions. You can whip me, crucify me, decapitate me, but I won't change my mind!

Far from wanting to whip, crucify or decapitate her, no one even thought of contradicting her.

We were in a small, low room under the roof of a tall city tenement house. Miss Antonina was sitting on a spring sofa that looked very old and worn; before her was a round table and on it a burning tallow candle in a metal candlestick and three glasses of tea. Against the opposite wall stood a narrow bed with some scant, stiff, snow-white bedding, next to it a dresser covered with children's notebooks and books with torn covers, then two or three old, yellow chairs, some sort of a stool with a faded cover, a boiling samovar on the floor before the open stove. A few prints depicting historical events had been cut out of illustrated magazines and pinned to the wallpaper which was strewn with little field flowers. At the only window there were a few green plants and a cage with a canary. The room was scrupulously clean. The wallpaper with the field flowers, the vases, the bird in the cage, the white bedding and the narrow bed had an aura of naiveté. Against that background, the black clothes, the severe desiccated figure of its owner made a strange contrast.

I looked at her with interest and sympathy. Neither the twelve daughters with their twelve university chairs, nor the "sapping a tree and sponging on society," nor the pounding of her fist on the table made me dislike her. I had known her for a long time.

"Nevertheless," I began timidly, "you yourself have never had a university chair and yet who can say that you do not plow and sow … ?"

She glanced at me sharply, suspiciously as though trying to convince herself that there was no malice or irony in my words, then she sadly nodded and made a dispirited gesture with her hand.

"Oh!" she replied, "what does that plowing and sowing of mine amount to? God help me!"

She clasped the thin, long, delicate hands on her lap and began in a much lower voice:

"It's true, this spring it will be twenty-one years since I became a teacher.

Straight out of school. Not one free day did I have to roam about in the world. My father was no longer alive, my sick mother lived with relatives. So right after graduation I went to a strange home. And then? Seventeen years of moving from house to house … and four years ago I moved here because I finally became convinced that all walls in the world are cold and all hearts strange. These walls and those hearts are one thing and one's own stupidity another! I fit in the teaching profession as an ox is fit to pull a carriage. Don't I realize what knowledge means and how far I am from it? Oh, the star of knowledge! Whatever others may dream and sigh about, my only dream was knowledge. I did have a fling at it, now and then, in one way or another, but … I had neither the means nor the time. A hungry mind—that is all! Oh, if I had daughters … "

She said all this with great calm and downcast eyes.

Evidently not used to confessions and disclosures, she felt embarrassed at having said so much about herself. Suddenly she noticed that the guests' glasses were empty. She jumped up quickly from the sofa, took them up and ran over to the samovar. I wanted to help her pour the tea since the samovar stood on the floor and I knew that it was uncomfortable for her to bend down because she suffered from slight attacks of arthritis in her legs and shoulders. But my good intentions were very energetically brushed aside.

"Oh, no, no," she called out. "It is such a pleasure to have you in my little home! I seldom have guests. Well, practically never. Perhaps sometimes one of the girls, a younger teacher, drops in for a while but that is rare because the dear souls don't have the time and prefer to associate with young people. I don't blame them for that. Everyone has his work and attachments … Great friendship and the devotion of strangers are found only in novels. Of course, if one has good daughters … oh, daughters … "

She placed the tea on the table, carefully sliced and arranged the rolls on a plate, smiling cheerfully.

"It is so pleasant for me to receive you in my little home … And besides," she added immediately, "I always do everything myself in my little household, if only to convince people that a woman who is independent and yearns for knowledge does not necessarily have to be stupid about practical things."

Whenever she mentioned the "independence of woman" and "knowledge" she became enthusiastic. Now, too, with a broad energetic gesture, she pointed to the walls and the objects on them.

"Look" she cried, "clean, neat and though a bit poor, even a little elegant. That wallpaper with the poppies and cornflowers I chose myself in the store before I moved here. And there are plants and a canary and pictures, the kind I could afford … So let them come and see that a woman who earns her own living and worships knowledge … does not necessarily have to be sloppy because of that!"

"Whom are you referring to when you say they should come and see?" I asked.

"Why," she replied, "don't you know? Woman-haters, tyrants, violators of human and heavenly rights, those who deny women the right to study and independence, and if one of us so much as moves a finger without asking their permission, they spread all sorts of fantastic stories about her. Oh, if I only had daughters … "

I remarked that her dreams were perhaps too one-sided: twelve women to take over the chairs of twelve professors. There were still other types of work, weren't there?

"No, no," the interrupted, "that's only how it appears. Naturally there are other types. But let me tell you where I got the idea of the university chairs,"

She laughed gaily,

"You know very well that I have never in my life been in contact with any educated people. I spent all my youth in the homes of land-owners and you know what our gentry are like. Only once in all my life did I meet a university professor … I was then about thirty years old and do you know what? I almost knelt down before him. A man of knowledge my dear lady! Leading the younger generation toward the bright star of knowledge! Everyone laughed at me at the time and said that there were all sorts of professors. A lot I cared! A high priest of knowledge, that's what he was to me. As I looked at the man I thought to mvself, 'if only I were in his place!' I became dizzy at the thought. How could I, such a miserable worm, even imagine such happiness! But then it struck me that if I had daughters … and from that time on, whenever I think of a daughter, I see a beautiful, healthy, happy girl, loving her mother with all her heart and next to her I see a professor's chair … That, my dear, is how a person's imagination soothes moral hunger. Sometimes I feel the arms of that dream daughter of mine around my neck and I see and hear her deliver a lecture … "

She had begun her story with laughter, but at the end there were tears in her eyes. Like all people whose tears are never noticed or wiped away by anyone, she did not like to show them. She blushed a little and ran towards the window to show me the blossoming geranium in the flower pot.

As we were looking at the plant the door leading to the stairs opened silently and slowly into the room slipped a little girl of about ten in a torn dress hanging to the ground, her flaxen hair combed straight back to reveal a round, rosy face with shining blue eyes. She slipped in and stood by the door, pressing her back to the wall, embarrassed at the sight of strangers. Right after her came a lively and braver boy, somewhat older, barefoot, tousled, in a spencer long outgrown, and after him another child of undefined sex as it wore only a heavy shirt. This one was considerably younger than the others and held a slice of black bread to its lips.

"Some unusual guests," I commented.

Miss Antonina was a bit flustered.

"Well" she began, "they are the children of the janitor of this building … a very poor man and a drunkard at that."

"Your pupils, undoubtedly … ?"

"Yes, my pupils. The girl is gentle and capable, the boy is capable too, but … "

"Do you teach that little one, also?"

"Oh no! It just comes along with the others when it wants to, and listens to our lessons. This is," she added, "a listener at my university … "

The university never left her mind for a moment. "How many lessons do you give in town?" I asked. "Eight."

"So with these children it is nine,"

As my companion and I said good-bye to Miss Antonina, the children were already completely relaxed and quite at home in her room. The girl, standing on her toes, was taking from the commode her primer and notebook marked with thick lines; the boy was cleaning the slate and the tot clambered up on the stool and admired the blossoming geranium with head tilted back and lips parted. How amazed we were to meet on the staircase on their way up, still another poorly dressed child and another, and another.

"Where are you all going?" I asked one of the children.

"To Miss Antonina" answered a lad who, we later learned, worked as a dish-washer, sweeper and delivery boy.

"How much do your parents pay Miss Antonina for teaching you?" I asked another.

"Who's got any parents?" the boy called back, running up three steps at a time.

Evidently Miss Antonina s love for the "star of knowledge" was not platonic.

* * *

I met her first when she was still quite young, not more than twenty-four. At that time she used to wear colored dresses and her dark hair was done up rather ambitiously but even then she was no longer fresh and was turning thin and bony. That rather premature fading was coupled with a juvenile sentimentality that bordered on exaltation and naiveté. She had a place as a tutor in her third home and for the third time she was deluding herself that she was to be forever, or at least for a very long time, an adopted member of the family for which she worked. As a matter of fact, the members of the family, though quite honest and well-mannered, had no thought of making her a part of themselves. They were a self-sufficient unit and saw no necessity of admitting any strangers. They treated the teacher well because they were honest, simple and friendly; they kept her on because they did not see any advantage in dismissing her. Besides, they laughed discreetly at the excessive fondness she showed to everyone around, at the occasional pathos in her speech, at the curls piled high on her head and at her spending long nights over her books. They laughed at her so quietly and discreetly that she actually never noticed or heard it. On the other hand, any sign of courtesy, any cordial handclasp or kind word was to her a proof of sincere and lasting friendship. Under their influence she was completely softened by affection and gratitude and she was ready to serve everyone who asked her with unequalled enthusiasm and zeal. Above all, she was devoted body and soul to her pupils and it was really interesting to watch how in her relations with them she struggled heroically and effectively against her inborn briskness and impetuosity and overcame her educational shortcomings. The boarding school from which she had drawn her entire knowledge was a very poor one. Thus, at first Miss Antonina could only act as a primary school tutor. However, in this third job she already gave secondary school lessons. This progress did not come by itself. In order to gain it she sat up for some five hundred nights to study various grammars, at least three hundred nights over history and geography, and about one hundred and fifty nights over arithmetic. Those were practically all the branches of learning demanded of her. True, music was also required, and even very much so, but in this field Miss Antonina could not become proficient even with the greatest effort. She simply had no ear for music and though her hands were well-shaped and delicate, her fingers consistently hit two keys at the same time. Thus she gave up music as completely hopeless. On the other hand, whenever anyone asked her why there was a light in her room at all hours of the night, she would raise her head and answer boldly and even with pride, her eyes sparkling with enthusiasm:

"I'm educating myself."

Educating herself was her ambition, passion and second greatest desire throughout her youth. Sometimes it took strange forms. For example, to improve her French, she translated a novel of several volumes and learned to recite long passages from it by heart. To broaden her knowledge of the world and its people, she pored for several months over a gigantic work on military strategy. The directions taken by her studies were purely accidental. The mistress of the house liked French novels and the master was an ex-army man. Thus she found Sue, Dumas, Sand and the volume on strategy in the old library of the household and, wiping off the dust of many years, she realized she had discovered a treasure. There were no other books in the house and how could she herself get any? Her salary was modest and she sent three-quarters of it to her ailing mother. For the remainder of the money she bought inexpensive dresses, but their color and cut always had to have a poetic touch. This longing for poetry in her dress, like the piles of curls on her forehead, might well imply that at that period of Miss Antonina's life there was still another desire and one very appropriate to her age. No doubt she sometimes dreamed of loving and being loved and of getting married. But certainly such longings and desires were for some far distant future. What she wanted most ardently was to become a member of some family and to study. She was absolutely convinced that she had achieved the first of her wishes and was proceeding with the second, when the news hit her like a thunderbolt: for two long years she had labored under an illusion; now that her pupils had to begin taking music lessons, the time had come for her to leave their home. How could it be? Then this family who liked and respected her had always considered her only as a stranger they needed temporarily? How could it be? Then they did not really love her and dismissed her as soon as there was one thing she couldn't do? It was her third surprise of the kind, and yet it made just as big an impression on her, perhaps even greater, than the first or second. She even forgot about educating herself. For two weeks before leaving, she shed tears night after night, wrung her hands in all the lonely corners of the house and garden and kissed the furniture and trees farewell. She picked up the large, heavy children and hugged them, pouring into their ears whole dictionaries of endearing words. Finally, with her face swollen from weeping, tired, almost ill, she got into the carriage and passed the gate of the pretty country estate, her dazed eyes wandering over the broad fields and the autumnal sky while she felt as if the entire world were one limitless, silent and cold wilderness.

She stayed somewhat longer with the fourth family than she had with the third—exceptionally long: three whole years. This was due to the progress she had made in her studies which permitted her to teach more advanced young girls, but it was especially due to a certain old lady, grandmother of the lady of the house. Miss Antonina became her favorite servant and—her victim. This time she could have no illusions as to the feelings of the master and mistress towards her; they were proud and cold people. Nor could she obtain any affection from the children who were poorly endowed by nature and badly brought up. So she became attached, one might even say stuck, to the old woman. First of all, she idealized her. Actually if this 80-year-old woman ever had possessed anything like a brain and a heart she had lost them completely. What was left of her was a deformed, infirm body animated by a mere vestige of a human soul. To Miss Antonina, however, her childish caprices, selfish demands and inane chattering were "the splendid and touching majesty of old age." Above all, the old lady reminded her of a beloved grandmother lost in her childhood. And then she had lovely, long thick hair, white as snow and glittering like silver. Miss Antonina could spend hours on her knees or on a low stool at the foot of the old lady's chair or bed. She entertained her with stories by Sue and Sand, she cooled her broth and prepared her herbs, nursed her when she was ill and pushed her chair along the shady garden paths. In exchange for all this, the old lady allowed her to call her grandmother and from time to time affectionately called her Toni. This particularly gave her much pleasure. Slowly the entire burden of "the majesty of old age" was placed on her shoulders. She accepted it as a proof of confidence and respect and it made her feel friendly and thankful towards the people who otherwise looked down on her. Another joy in that house was the possibility of educating herself further this time by reading German philosophers who were much admired by the master of the house, and of whom he had quite a collection. Thus whenever neither the children nor the old lady needed her she read, read and read German philosophers, and a few months went by before she realized that she had not understood a thing, and all that hard work she had put into it had been quite useless. At any other time this discovery would have filled her with sorrow; now, however, she did not think about moaning over her lost time and effort because her beloved old lady was rapidly approaching the moment when "the majesty of old age" makes room for "the ominous call of death." She died. Before expiring, the bits of soul left in her rallied, her dimmed glance searched for Miss Antonina among those present, and when the latter, understanding this glance, kneeled down by the bed, she placed her withered, stiffening hand on Antonina's head to bless her. Miss Antonina always remembered that moment and the mute blessing with profound emotion. She treasured it as one of her most beautiful memories. However, one of her most unpleasant memories occurred a few days later when the mistress of the house offered her the grandmother's silk dresses and genuine gold brooch as a reward for her kindness to the old lady. Naturally she did not accept them. Then the mistress informed her that she must leave their home before the holidays, which she did. But the parting was different this time—there were no tears, no wringing of the hands and no kissing of walls and chairs. It is quite possible that if she had not been dismissed, she would have left of her own accord. After the loss of the old lady and her experience with the German philosophers, nothing held her there any longer. When she passed the cemetery a few miles from the estate she asked the coachman to stop the horses. She went in, sat for moment on the lawn at the edge of the old woman's grave, returned to the carriage with two half-dried tears on her cheeks and drove on.

She belonged to that category of people who are terribly anxious that all they do be as nearly perfect as possible. She could never understand how one could do anything just any way and at any time. Very early in the morning she jumped out of bed with the energy of a horse rearing to go to the battle; her hands mechanically reached for the clock. Many years had passed since she had become a teacher, but she still approached her pupils with an inner anxiety which showed clearly in the expression of her blazing eyes regardless of how much she tried to conceal it. Naturally, rather than lessen, this anxiety increased with the years.

In her habitual grandiloquent way, she maintained that teaching was a priesthood and with the pathos of a priestess and the enthusiasm of an apostle she introduced into her language, geography and arithmetic lessons long talks on work, compassion, the brotherhood of man, the greatness of education and other similar beautiful and sublime subjects. It cannot be said that this teaching, however beautiful and lofty its subjects, complied with the principles of rational pedagogy. Despite Miss Antonina's intention and knowledge they contained expressions and phrases that sounded like echoes of French novels translated for the sake of practice, or of books she had studied for the purpose of grasping German philosophy. Besides, carried away by her enthusiasm, she gestured and mimicked in a manner that often brought mischievous smiles to the children's faces. There were children who listened to her edifying orations with suppressed laughter, and others who listened to her very seriously and attentively but did not understand a single word, and still others who occasionally did understand a bit and sometimes reflected this in their actions. These latter gave Miss Antonina a rare but real joy. They were like drops of dew falling on a feverish brow.

Once, shortly after parting from the beloved old lady, Miss Antonina found an ideal pupil, such as she had long dreamed about and had lost hope of ever finding. The little girl was very intelligent, lively, sensitive; not only did she do well in her grammar, geography, history and arithmetic, but she also showed an exceptional liking for what Miss Antonina usually called "the philosophy of teaching." She listened with great attention and almost greedily to the long and inspired speeches on the brotherhood of man, charity, work, learning, etc. She rapidly acquired their basic sense, and her childish imagination caught some of the fire blazing in the teacher's breast. She began to put the theories into practice with great ardor on all occasions. Once, for instance, while taking a walk she met a poor beggar child with sore feet. She sat down by the roadside, took off her elegant little shoes and gave them to the child. She forbade the servants to call her "Miss" and wanted to kiss their faces all the time. She sat over her books until late at night. This did not necessarily have a good effect on her health, but was a delight to Miss Antonina who had studied war strategy and German philosophy of the century with great difficulty but had no idea about hygiene in general and child hygiene in particular. Indeed, she had barely heard about it. But then, all her life she had held her body and all the needs of the flesh in utter contempt. To her the spirit was everything. "Hers will be a beautiful, pure and lofty spirit," she often exclaimed about the extraordinary child who had become sentimentally and passionately attached to her teacher, because her mother, a beautiful, fun-loving widow, did not make her happy. For two whole years teacher and pupil did not separate for a single hour. The pale, delicate, nervous child made Miss Antonina forget the entire world. She saw nothing and no one besides her. She stopped dressing poetically and twisting her hair into ringlets; instead her self-educating acquired a still greater importance. Her keenest desire, her fondest dream, was to know enough to be able to complete the education of her beloved girl. She wanted to take her to the other end of the world and to the threshold of family life, to accompany her in the world, and later to enter into her family. To rest her head forever against the girl's bosom and be sheltered by the walls of her home, and perhaps even to rock, feed and teach her babies seemed to Miss Antonina the pinnacle of happiness and the most likely of all the possibilities under the sun. The expression "forever" was never absent from her heart or mind. This time music did not present any threatening problem to the pair. It was taught by someone else belonging to the household. As for other studies, well, Miss Antonina was very confident and spent long nights and early morning hours over a table stocked with all types of textbooks and handbooks, educating herself with such zeal that the sallowness of her complexion and the angularity of her figure made rapid and obvious progress. She became more dignified and severe in her dress and manners towards other people and more youthful and fresher in her relations with the child. Heaven knows what wonderful fairy tales and stories began to spring from her imagination; they amused and taught simultaneously. Heaven knows when she learned to run and laugh, and to put twice the fervor into her lessons and yet intermingle them with lively boisterous games. She often wondered later where she had found the physical strength to pick up a twelve-year-old girl like a feather just so as to hold her tight in her arms. Time passed so quickly that the late twilight hours they spent huddled together in a corner seemed to merge with the early dawn whose blue light dimmed the yellow glow of the lamp that was still lit. During those grey twilight hours, tutor and pupil clung to each other and repeated with deep conviction, over and over again: "We will never part!" And yet part they did in a very natural way. One of the more serious relatives drew the mother's attention to the fact that a tutor like Miss Antonina could not possibly give the finishing touches required to a wealthy young lady destined to shine in the world, that the girl needed a more thorough general education, and opportunity to develop her talents. The relative was quite right. The beautiful widow who loved entertainment recognized this all the more readily as the sending of a growing daughter away to a boarding school was a means to prolong her own youth for a few more years. So the girl was to go to a boarding school. The tutor left the family a few weeks earlier. As she came out on the terrace in her travelling suit that beautiful summer morning, she saw neither the blue sky nor the green trees and lawns around, nor the sun and the people. She did not cry. Only her lips were parched, her hands trembled and there were two crimson spots on her yellow cheeks. With arms shaking badly, she once again embraced her pupil who kept whispering into her ear. She probably said she would never forget her and that as soon as she returned from boarding school … Evidently Miss Antonina believed the child's words because she smiled and seemed relieved. She stepped into the carriage and drove off.

Soon after something happened that was rather odd considering her situation. She had a suitor and she refused him. The man was not too old, a wealthy landowner, very honest and somewhat narrowminded. An excellent opportunity and probably the last for her to get married, and to assure to her a quiet and, in many respects, even a happy future. She herself felt and recognized all this. That was why she struggled with herself and hesitated for a long time. Finally, when the time came to give an answer, she refused. Everyone around considered her practically mad. And sometimes she herself said that "judging by worldly considerations" she had committed a great error. "But," she added immediately. "I could not do otherwise. He was a good man, honest but so ignorant and limited! My dear, he had not the faintest notion about scholarship and not a glimmering of literature. There was no mutual understanding between us and I had no feeling for him. To get married without sentiment and without mutual understanding would have been tantamount to betraying my own soul; I would have felt a perjurer, a parasite sponging on the sacred tree of family life! I simply couldn't do it." Those who knew her in her early youth guessed that she had once been very much in love. The man was said to have been a brother or cousin of one of her employers. Only a conjecture—since she herself never confessed it to anyone. But she was caught several times looking at a man's photograph which she quickly hid at the bottom of a well-locked box. It is quite possible that some earlier emotions, hopes and suffering still echoed in her and prevented her when she was thirty from grasping the branch of the "sacred tree of family relations" that bent towards her.

Somewhat later she experienced a moral shock of another kind. For the first time in her life she entered a home where the owners possessed high intellectual qualities. Most of their guests were equally erudite. For the first time she had an inkling of the meaning of true learning, and discovered the usual procedure of obtaining an education. From the conversation around her and the books filling the house, she realized that she had been groping in the dark for many long years, imagining she was getting an education. True, she had bent all her efforts and coped with the greatest difficulties but, as she used to say later, "It was as much like education as a fist is like a nose!" After making this discovery, she wrung her hands and wept. But she did not cry long. First, because she had no time, since she had to teach three children, secondly, because it struck her that she was only 32 years old. After all, that was not old. She started to educate herself all over again, asking the master of the house for direction and the learned lady of the house for help.

They aided her intelligently and in a friendly way and she delved into the work with the naïve enthusiasm of a young girl. She began to have a clearer conception of her "star of knowledge." But then the parents of her small pupils faced financial ruin, farmed out their estate and moved to the city to bring up their children more economically. The tutor left the estate a few days before they did.

She came out of her room all in black, upright, stiff and whoever might have seen her for the first time would certainly have thought her harsh and brisk. Her forehead was criss-crossed with wrinkles, her fiery eyes glowed darkly, her walk and movements had something hard and abrupt about them.

However, the master and lady of the house bid her farewell with the greatest respect, the children hugged her warmly; silently she stepped into the carriage and drove on.

From that time on she always dressed in black, tight-fitting dresses and wore her greying hair in two long smooth strands parted in front and the back of her head covered with black lace. This outfit made her appear severe and dry. She looked as if she were carved from wood; her elbows, accentuated by the narrow sleeves, looked as though they would prick one. Her high triangular forehead also gave the impression of an elongated point. Her gestures and her speech were energetic and abrupt. She liked discussion but became excited, raised her voice, gesticulated and generally forgot her usually grandiloquent abstract expressions. Then her conversation would become trivial. All these attributes, her appearance and manner, prejudiced people against her. She no longer expected any goodwill from them. She told herself: "all walls in the world are cold and all hearts hostile," and "those so-called bonds of friendship between strangers are only superficial." Having thus found her credo, she emerged from the rosy-colored seas of illusion where she had spent her youth and entered the bitter waters of distrust and suspicion. Distrust and suspicion sparkled in her expressive eyes even—and especially—when anyone said a kind or a cordial word to her. She listened suspiciously to any expression of understanding as though she wanted to find out whether she were not being made a fool of. Even if convinced that it was not a joke or a mockery, she did not respond. "People's friendship," she said "is like the wind: it comes and it blows over. If anyone of my age counted on it and expected anything from it, I would say to him that he is an overgrown baby."

Was that deep distrust from a wound that would not heal and hurt greatly? She never talked about it but she kept aloof and people did not feel like drawing close to her. It was mutual, simple and inevitable. And the simple and necessary consequence was that for several years afterward, Miss Antonina often changed her position. There were places where she did not want to stay and others where she was not wanted. To some people her endless quarreling and excitement were unbearable. Some were afraid that their children might become harsh and trivial in manner and speech. Others wished to have a warmer, meeker person about them—one capable of devotion. These last often did not know themselves why or for what they wanted her or of what use to them such an attachment and devotion would be, but they wanted it anyway and even considered it as part of the duties of anyone in their home. After all, Miss Antonina now had her own tastes and demands. In one house it was too noisy for her, in another too quiet, in one too hot, in another too cold. In one place, for example, she had to sleep and teach the children in a room that was poorly heated in winter, sitting close to a badly fitted window, and she got arthritis. It was not a severe case, but nevertheless annoying. Sometime before she would have suffered in silence, or would have accepted it in return for a single kind word, and for a friendly smile would have been ready to get tuberculosis as well. But now she looked quite differently upon the relationship between employer and teacher and was insulted by this lack of comfort and care for her health. She asked for the carriage and horses. And she told herself, "Enough of this wandering and knocking about other people's homes." She was seized with a passionate, irresistible yearning for her own little home. She had long since lost her mother for whom she used to work in her youth a long time ago. She was now all alone and answerable only to herself. She came to the city, rented a room in the attic of a three-storey building; furnished it not so much according to her taste as according to her principles. Then, making use of a few contacts she had in the city, she began to give lessons in private homes. Settled in her room she said: "I feel as though I were back from a seventeen-year journey. I set out on that journey as a young girl. I have been traveling for seventeen years, my dear lady. And what of it?"

She stopped and became thoughtful. She was not accustomed to discussing things with others, and was asking herself what she had left behind in that journey and what she had got out of it.

It was a winter's day, chilly and very windy. Out of the air, from the roofs and from the ground, the whirlwind whipped up the hard, sharp snow, whining, roaring, moaning and swept clouds of white dust over the city streets. Everything in the world was white and blurred. Crows croaked on the cornices and on dry tree branches; now and then a drozhka raced clattering down the middle of the street; the pavements were practically empty. Stores were tightly shut against the wind and snow; doorways were also closed and the houses were silent with their white window panes.

Half-deafened as I was by the roar and noise of the wind, half-blinded by the snow blowing into my face and eyes, yet I noticed ahead of me a long black line moving through clouds of snow. After a while I realized it was a human being, a woman. In a tight-fitting fur coat and a dress lifted up to the ankles, hands tucked into her sleeves, a tall, thin, erect woman walked quickly and rigidly as though she did not feel the wind and snow whirling in the air. The wind was furiously twisting the end of her black veil on her head. But she didn't falter, stoop or slacken her pace.

I caught up with her and called:

"Miss Antonina!"

She stopped abruptly, turned round, but when she wanted to stretch out her hand to me and answer my greeting she staggered and like one who feels that he is falling, she steadied herself by placing her hand on a lamp post. She was very pale; her lips were parted; she was breathless. As long as she walked she kept going, but as soon as she stopped her strength failed her.

It's nothing, nothing," she started, forcing herself to speak and to smile. "You startled me, calling out so suddenly. I was thinking."

"No, you weren't startled, you are just very tired. Naturally in such weather … "

"Me? Tired? What an idea! You should see, my dear, all the lessons I have given and what weather I have walked in. A working woman must be strong."

Putting this theory into practice, she straightened up and moved forward. A strange thing! She walked again quickly, evenly, figure erect and head held high. And again the wind twisted and turned the ends of her veil in back of her head.

"Where are you going?"

"What do you mean, where? To a lesson, of course."

"The first one?"

"What time is it now?"

"I believe it is around twelve."

"I believe," she repeated sarcastically, "what an awful habit women have of never knowing the exact time. That is why women's affairs are always managed God knows how and men scorn them and browbeat them … "

It was a certainty, though, that at that very moment the sky was browbeating us. The wind had forced me up to the wall of a building, a few steps away from my companion. But she was pushed about so badly that it seemed she would fall on her knees. To keep her balance, she stretched out her arms, spun around on the spot a few times and again stood firmly on her feet.

"Curse that hurricane" she muttered. "I'll be late for the lesson … "

"Is this your first lesson today?" I repeated my question.

"How can you ask such a thing? You yourself said that it was already twelve o'clock. What do you think? Am I a parasite to sit round till noon with my arms folded? I've been out since seven o'clock. I'm going to my fourth lesson."

"Where are you coming from and where are you going?"

She was on her way from one end of the rather sprawling town to the other. Half way there, I bid her good-bye and was about to enter the house when she came back a few steps and took me by the shoulder.

"Come and see me today or tomorrow … It is always so pleasant to see old friends … only come before eight because at eight I open my university."

She clasped my hand firmly. Her black eyes shone hot and sad behind the veil which the snow had frozen stiff.

In the street her company was sometimes embarrassing. Wearing heavy boots and galoshes to save her shoes, she tramped over the mud and crossed the most treacherous slippery streets as evenly and with as steady a step as though she were walking on smooth granite. She looked about briskly and attentively and commented loudly on anything she happened to notice. Well-dressed women often seen in the streets, and female devotees hanging round a church with their prayer books were welcome targets for her indignation. She would pause for a moment, look after them and, gesticulating energetically, call them dolls, leeches, parasites sponging on human society. Then her eyes would light up like hot coals, her brows form one straight line that gave her forehead a painful and threatening expression. She told her acquaintances straight to their faces what she thought of them. To the mothers of her pupils, who were too keen on making their little daughters resemble fashion magazine models, she would say:

"You ought to be ashamed of yourself, madam, ashamed! Do you want your daughter to become a parasite and jeopardize the emancipation of women? Congratulations … but I don't envy you … for being guilty of interfering with the progress of mankind! A fine thing!"

Whenever one discussed the "emancipation of women" she became excited and argued, repeating her old argument:

"Twelve daughters and twelve university chairs! No one can knock that out of my head!"

No one could knock it out of her head either that all pupils in city schools, regardless of their sex, were the most beautiful adornment and hope of mankind, and that anyone with his heart in the right place had to love them. At the sight of any group of these lovely creatures swarming out of a school, running out into the street, her face beamed and expressed infinite sweetness and tenderness.

"My angels, my honeys, my little kittens," she whispered and threw them a kiss.

She had many acquaintances among these little people; some of the children greeted her with a smile and nod or even kissed her hand. Most often they were children with pale, sad faces. Obviously they thanked her for something, but for what? I never found out.

Every morning after sweeping her little room and taking care of the plant and canary she said to herself: "On your way! March!" and left for town. Her marching slackened on the stairs. She took the steep steps with ever greater difficulty and although she attempted to conceal this she did not succeed.

"Am I so old?" she asked, laughing, but in spite of herself, her eyebrows contracted with pain.

Actually she was not old; not even forty. But once when the going was hard she confessed to me that the arthritis that had developed during that last year of tutoring was bothering her more and becoming more painful. She confessed it quietly as though by lowering her voice she wanted me to understand that she was telling me a great secret.

This little room, she added, is very pleasant but cold in winter and damp in spring. But to find another—that's difficult!"

I guessed that the difficulty was partly economic and partly sentimental. A healthier and more expensive flat would have undoubtedly been beyond her means, and at the same time it would have deprived her of that beloved wallpaper with the field flowers and of the gay and grateful children whose thanks were like gems strewn in the streets before her feet stuck in their muddy galoshes …

I wanted to talk to her about her troubles, to give her some advice, but she quickly changed the subject, and talked about various novelists, poets, philosophers, about different "questions and ideas." The grey twilight in her room was replete with names, days, dates, quotations which fell like hail from her lips. She sat on a low stool by the fire, her arms outstretched pathetically, reciting excerpts from poems, interrupting her recitations to blow into the samovar standing on the floor. If one of the poems had a reference to Napoleon I, she would talk about war strategy. I ventured to interrupt this scholarly talk to ask how much she earned by giving lessons. She grew sad and silent for a moment. She disliked being asked about herself; she always suspected irony. This time, however, either to be polite to a guest or else because the dusk, gently tinted by the rosy glow of the fire had softened her mood, she answered mildly:

"Well, things went quite well at the beginning. Now it's a little worse because of the strong competition."

"Competition?"

"Oh yes. There are so many of us giving lessons. Besides those girls who graduate from secondary schools know more than I and teach better, so they have better opportunities ... "

They knew more? Heavens, she had studied so long and had such unusual erudition.

"I once had eight hours a day," she continued, "now I have only five and I'm very much afraid ... it may be even less next year."

She didn't say anything more about it but for a good five minutes sat on her stool in silence and contemplation. Her silhouette resembled a long, thin black line; her slender, long hands shone white against her black dress. She inclined her face towards the light of the fire and the flickering sparks lit up her eyes as they stared glassily into space. Her contemplation bordered on stupefaction; and the fact that she had said "I am afraid" for the first time since I met her worried me considerably.

After a while, however, she rose quickly and briskly, lit the candles and began to prepare tea. And again she spoke about many learned and sublime matters. An hour later her little room filled with poor children. I begged her to allow me to remain. The lesson lasted two long hours during which the room represented a real evening school with solo and choral stammering of syllables in the primer, letters and numbers being written in copybooks and on slates, fingers pointing to different places on the map hung on the wall, youngsters kneeling and standing in corners, good and bad marks being recorded, etc. All this was wound up with the teacher telling a very pleasant story of her own invention which contained poetry and morals and lots of information about the wide world. The children sitting on the floor in all kinds of poses listened intently, with wide-open eyes and mouths. Miss Antonina sat among them on the stool and told her stories with great absorption, the appropriate mimicry, gesticulation and elocution. After the story, came the distribution of whole-wheat rolls to her pupils and the teacher also ate a piece with appetite. Then, the room became silent and empty again. The fire in the stove died out; it was ten o'clock.

By the light of the single candle Miss Antonina's face looked terribly tired; even her eyes were dull and her figure stooped. Her hands rested inertly in her lap; her dress was covered with crumbs of the bread she had had for supper. As I was leaving after bidding her good night, she was extinguishing the candle and lighting a small night lamp which hung in the corner of the room.

"1 allow myself this luxury," she said. "I don't like pitch dark and I often can't sleep at night." Who can guess what she thought about, what she felt, on those long winter nights as she lay on her hard, narrow bed and her sleepless eyes wandered over the ceiling and walls of the room where wavering shadows sadly mingled and then drew apart from the streaks of pale light?

For various reasons I did not see her for over three years. When I did ask for news of her from the janitor of the building where I had last seen her, he told me that she had not lived in the attic for some time. I had to inquire and search for quite some time before I finally learned of her whereabouts. This was hardly strange. For several months people had stopped seeing her.

Entering the long, narrow hospital corridor with its snow-white walls and floors shining like mirrors, I asked a passing attendant about the patient I wanted to visit. He pointed to one of the doors in the two long rows that ran on both sides of the corridor. I entered. Again a small room, but without the wallpaper of field flowers, without the pictures, canary or flowering geranium. The black bars of an iron bedstead drew sharp lines on walls as white as snow and so high that one had to raise one's eyes to see the ceiling. Outside the huge bare window with a yellow shade rolled to the top, the bare tops of poplar trees growing in the hospital garden swayed in the thick autumn mist. Opposite the window were the tall varnished doors shining like a mirror, by the bed an iron table, against the opposite wall a table and two yellow stools. Everything was clean, light, bare, sad and terribly boring. The well-heated and fresh air had an elusive feeling of cold and an unpleasant smell of medicine.

On the iron bed with the high black bars, on snow-white bedding under a yellow hospital quilt, lay Miss Antonina. Her very grey hair was combed straight back, revealing the high and prominent forehead she had always hidden. It looked enormous against her face, shrunken from loss of weight and it was covered with a host of tiny, dense crisscrossing wrinkles. Her sunken eyes reminded me of a steam-covered mirror; the thin line of pale, clenched lips was surrounded by an expression of silent suffering. The waxen yellow of her face contrasted sharply with the white of the pillow while her clasped, delicate hands with their network of blue veins seemed very white against the background of the yellow quilt. At first she did not recognize me. Her eyesight was weakened but, more important, she had not expected a visit from anyone. Then with a smile, she stretched out her hand to me and, still trying to be hospitable, wanted to raise herself and sit up. But she couldn't. She was very weak and her breath was short, heavy and loud. Thus, lying down, she told me that she had been here now for several months. The illness had been accumulating for many years until finally it had got her. The arthritis had reached her lungs, probably because she walked in the air and bad weather too much and had to talk continually during her lessons. In any case, of late she had had fewer and fewer lessons. She was forced to take a cheaper flat which was still colder and damper than the former.

When she fell ill, she lay in her own room for a few months but then … the treatment was very expensive and she could not have proper care … What could she do? It is so much better in the hospital; the doctors were good and solicitous, there was excellent care and everything one could need. In addition, some kind people had seen to it that she had a private room instead of lying in a ward. They were even paying for it but what could she do? She had to accept these offers and was very grateful for them.

She said all this quietly, slowly and with a smile. Then after resting a few minutes, she added:

"That's how it is in this world, my dear! Man is made up of spirit and flesh and must suffer not only spiritual but also bodily pain. If only one could die immediately, as soon as the spirit or flesh begins to suffer too much! But it's not so easy! One must experience everything before death comes … That is the cruel reality … "

After she felt a little more rested, she began to ask what was new in the world. What were the papers writing about? What new books had come out? Had the British Parliament already met on the question of giving women the right to vote? etc. She listened to the answers almost greedily. Several times her eyes lit up with their former fire and a sincere, almost happy smile curled her lips. Then she sighed and fixed her gaze on the leafless tops of the poplars swaying outside the window.

"Yes, yes," she whispered, "the world goes on its way although people fall by the wayside like flies … I would very much like to see it all again and … I could … after all, I'm not that old … "

She was then some forty years of age. She was no longer young. However, I have seen women of her age dancing at balls and others who rocked small grandchildren in their strong arms.

She had already had enough talking and listening for one day. After a half hour of conversation her yellow eyelids fell weakly over the dimmed pupils, hands and lips clenched in an immense effort of will to restrain her moans.

Coming to the hospital room another day I found the patient half sitting up in bed with a small open box on her knees. She was so preoccupied in looking over the objects in the box that at first she did not notice my entrance. Only after hearing my greeting did she raise her head and slowly, without haste, close the box. She was a little stronger that day, some medicine had given her relief. After a fifteen-minute talk about what was new in the world she said with a smile:

"I see that you keep looking at my box and no doubt are curious as to what is in it. Perhaps you are even thinking, 'Here's a smart woman; during her life she's scraped together a box full of money and now, lying on a hospital bed, she counts it for recreation and perhaps even clips coupons … !'"

Saying this, she laughed so heartily that she suddenly began to cough and for a few minutes had to lie still, with eyes shut, breathing quickly and harshly. Then she raised her heavy eyelids and looked weakly at me for some time. She no longer laughed or even smiled. She began to speak slowly and so quietly that I could hardly hear her:

"Certainly, I'll be glad to show you what I have in that box. Not jewels or other valuables, only … all my souvenirs."

She opened the box full of objects wrapped in paper, and scraps of paper. She unwrapped one and showed me a large oak leaf, so dried up that it was practically falling into dust, saying:

"I plucked this off a tree as I was leaving the Skierskis—do you remember?—from that home, where it was so pleasant, where I loved everyone—everyone. I usually sat under that tree the whole summer long with my pupils, my work, a book ... I was well off then ... I thought that I would remain there for a long, long time ... perhaps forever. When it was time to leave I kissed my beloved tree and took away this leaf in memory of that home ... I always call it my leaf of faith, because then I believed in human hearts, in friendship, attachment, fidelity. Oh! how I believed ... " Rewrapping the corpse or rather the ashes of "the leaf of faith" she slowly took out the second paper.

"And this, as you see, is a strand of my grannie's hair ... that old lady whom I was able to cheer up during her last years and who blessed me when she lay dying ... It is as white as snow and glitters like silver. Poor, dear old lady! She always called me Toni."

Then with her fingers trembling slightly she came upon an object in the box over which she hesitated a moment before taking it out. I think that a pale, barely perceptible blush flashed for a twinkling of an eye among the wrinkles on her forehead. At the end a photograph appeared in her fingers. Handing it to me she whispered:

"This is he!"

Then she lowered her eyes and for a long time said nothing.

The faded and half-visible photograph showed the face of a young man, neither handsome nor ugly, but then it was so unclear that nothing could be made out of it. As I was examining it, Miss Antonina whispered without raising her eyes.

"You see, everyone in the world has some adventure in his past. I have him. It was only a moment ... like a spark or a rose across my path ... I remember some things ... summer mornings in the beautiful garden ... autumn evenings by the fireplace ... I think that he really loved me. But perhaps not ... do I know? ... I vanished! And how long ago it was ... long ago ... long ago ... "

"Did you see him afterwards?"

"Never; I seldom saw again those from whom I parted. And I never saw her again either ... "

At this she handed me notebooks written in a child's hand. They were the exercises of her best-loved pupil.

"What a child she was!" she remarked, and inspired by her old enthusiasm, she sat up in bed. "That girl, my dear, was a genius! How she understood everything; with what style she could already write; what noble, lofty emotions already filled her childish heart!"

She clasped her hands; her raised eyes glowed.

"Oh, if someone would only tell me, if someone could tell me that my teaching had left a permanent trace in that child, that the seeds which I sowed in her, have not been trampled upon by the world, that the four winds have not scattered them ... if someone were to tell me that she is now a wise and exalted woman ... I would die blessing the one who could pour such drops of sweetness on my lips … !"

She slumped down on the pillows, tired, feeble, with a heaving chest.

"She has never gotten in touch with you?"

"Never. She promised to write to me and when she grew up to take me but … she was still a child … she forgot!"

There were several other objects still in the box, carefully preserved—a sizeable notebook of jottings and excerpts from the most varied types of books, a long list of titles of those she had read together with the names of their authors—in a word, the traces and souvenirs of long years of fervent study.

Lying on her back with eyes shut from exhaustion, Miss Antonina found still another paper in her box and when she unwrapped it, I saw a small piece and some crumbs of black bread.

"This is from my room … the one you visited. There I shared with poor children the black bread of my knowledge and my wealth … When I left the flat, I took some of it with me as a souvenir … "

Then for a good many days I usually found Miss Antonina examining the contents of her box. The weaker she was and the more she suffered, the more carefully and continuously did she examine the objects wrapped in paper. She stopped asking about what was new in the world. Often it seemed that she forgot my presence. Sitting for long periods by the large, bare window with my work I watched her as she bent over her box and in her thin fingers held the crumbs of an oak leaf, or a strand of silver hair, or the faded, dim photograph or one of the notebooks which lined the bottom of the box. Fixing her eyes on it, she slowly moved her parched lips, as though she conducted with them secret, sometimes tender and sometimes bitter and angry conversations.

Once, after staring a long time at a notebook, she lifted her head with a lively movement and as of old called out, clenching her fist:

"If someone had told me why I studied that strategy and German philosophy! I began to turn grey … It's true, my dear, I began to go grey over that strategy and philosophy!"

I smiled in spite of myself. She noticed it and angrily shook her head.

"You laugh," she hissed, "excuse me but there is nothing to laugh at. When someone loves the star of knowledge and desires to reach it and doesn't know the straight road … he gropes. People find it amusing, of course, but it is not so funny for those who are beating their heads against the wall. Oho! if I were to be born all over again or if I had daughters … "

Another day after examining her souvenirs for a whole hour she gave me a glance that was gentle and full of pleading.

"My dear," she said, "if I should die from this illness be so good as to burn everything in this box … Why should it be dragged all over the hospital garbage heap? It is my whole past and … "

She smiled.

"And … all the wealth of my life."

Lying on her back with a faint, contemplating gaze she slowly followed the tops of the garden poplars swaying in the autumn mist. Then she spoke again.

"Into the fire—and that will be the end. It will burn and not a trace of me will remain on this earth."

Then, as though shocked by the sound of her own words she made a vigorous movement. Supported by her elbow on the pillow, she half-lifted herself and, breathing rapidly and heavily, called out:

"Will there really be none—not any trace left?"

Her suddenly brilliant eyes carried the disturbing, abrupt and almost desperate question. She tormented herself with it constantly for the next few days.

"Because if there's nothing, nothing left … why was it … what's the sense … "

Then, reasonably and with ease she said:

"Perhaps something will be left … perhaps even a little of my knowledge has remained in those little heads and hearts. With all my strength I desired … I tried … even if it's only that I taught them how to read … "

'Tormenting and comforting herself in turn, she became weaker and weaker. The lower part of her face seemed to grow smaller and her forehead larger and more prominent. After a few days she stopped being concerned about leaving her traces on earth; at least she did not speak of it. She practically stopped talking altogether and lay, motionless, sometimes only unwrapping some of the papers and, faint with weakness or glowing with fever, turned her gaze to their contents. I once asked her whether she suffered much. With a shade of her former impulsiveness and pathos she replied:

"The dark nights know and they certainly won't tell."

After a while she would whisper to herself;

"If I had daughters … "

I began to tell her that out among the people …

"Yes, yes," she interrupted, "of course! People have always been more often good to me than bad. When I became ill they brought me here in a comfortable carriage, hired a private room; at the beginning they even sometimes visited me … Then they stopped coming because everyone has his own interests and contacts … I am very grateful for everything … but those great friendships and ties among strangers … it's only in novels … "

One day I found her so weak that she could not breathe lying down. Many pillows were placed behind her back to keep her in a sitting position. On her knees stood the open box. As I sat by the bed she very slowly turned her gaze towards me without turning her head:

"Do you know," she whispered, "I am again experiencing the same feeling as though I were returning from a long, long journey … For twenty- six years I have traveled and not one free day have I roamed in the world. And what … "

Again she did not finish, but her hands which were like those of a skeleton unfolded and, trembling over the open box, seemed to ask: "what had she left behind in that journey and what did she take away … ?"

I often wish that somewhere in the hidden spiritual realm of Man's deeds, there existed a vast and fathomless nebula made up of souls which entered life like the buds of beautiful flowers and left its embrace tattered and crushed. Exhausted soul, unrewarded soul fly up to that visionary nebula! Perhaps, sometime, it will create a new and better world …

—1881. Translated by Janina Rodzińska

*Commentary.* Miss Antonina is a short-story sketch, mostly plot-free, a recapitulation of a person's life, a human-interest story. It is an attempt to recreate, and draw a picture in words, and create a feeling of understanding and sympathy for, another human being. Unlike what one expects from a Positivist short story, "Miss Antonina" contains no overt analysis, no conclusions, no moral, no "what-should-be-done?" Even if the narrator (who, one knows from the Polish verb endings, is female and for all intents and purposes is identifiable as Orzeszkowa herself) sympathizes with Miss Antonina's inferior schooling and lack of helpful guidance during her life, no call for educational reform hides behind the lines. There is no elaborate structure, just a faithful portrait of a type, taken through the stages of her life: a frustrated old-maid governess, a fairly unsympathetic person on first glance toward whom nevertheless Orzeszkowa-qua-narrator shows an infinite capacity for sympathy.

The narrator's mildly ironic attitude toward her character at the beginning is clear from the story's first paragraph, in which Miss Antonina talks about her "twelve daughters," who she would make sure became university professors. The incident shows Miss Antonina's utter lack of grounding in common sense, logic, or reality. She is devoted to abstract, unrealistic, impractical ideas she does not fully understand. She herself is childless, never even married. An old-maid governess, divorced from life's experiences, she has the naïve idea that she would have any control over her daughters. Even if she had any children at all (and why would they be daughters, or why twelve of them?), she naively thinks they would love her and dutifully obey her in her plans for their futures. And the idea that work as a university professor is of itself automatically a useful or meaningful career is itself also naïve. Professors can be just as divorced from life and from meaningful occupation as anyone else.

A realistic problem in Miss Antonina's plans for her "daughters" is that it was difficult or impossible for women to get into the university even as students, much less as professors, although it was slowly becoming possible. Still, Orzeszkowa does not place the blame for Miss Antonina's frustrated life on society or on the educational establishment. Her own personality and intellectual limitations are more to blame.

Exactly where Miss Antonina has imbibed her enthusiasm for and lifelong dedication to women's issues is never explained, unless it was just "in the air" of the times. What is clear, however, is that she has accomplished little in her life to advance it. Instead, ironically, she has chosen to demonstrate the "independence of women" by choosing a line of work leading nowhere in the struggle, one that was always open to women, as a governess teaching the younger children of well-to-do families, while waiting for a marriage proposal from somewhere. Perhaps if she had, in the end, accepted the only offer of marriage she ever received, she would have found fulfillment as the nurturer of her own children into adulthood. Given the changes taking place in her day, favoring the increasing freedom of choice for women, had she only married, it might have been possible for Miss Antonina to raise daughters who would have pursued careers in education or in some other field contributing meaningfully to society.

Since Miss Antonina dies at the end of the story, in a sense the story can be seen as her obituary. One might expect that a Positivist work on women's issues would contain a certain amount of criticism of society, and a hope for a better future. To be sure, in the background of "Miss Antonina" exist such social problems as the inaccessibility to women of the educational system; the lack of a proper guidance system for young women aspiring to a career; the lack of meaningful career opportunities for women; the necessity of choosing between a socially acceptable marriage and an acceptable moral and spiritual life; and so on. However, these are not the main themes of the story. Instead, Orzeszkowa raises these issues tangentially to her description of a life about which one could say: it has been wasted, spent uselessly, and has disappeared without a trace, burned up like the little box of Miss Antonina's memories at the end of the story.

Throughout her life Miss Antonina has followed her ideals, but down a stray path. She dies prematurely, seemingly from some kind of rheumatoid arthritis or auto-immune affliction. Her withering away can partly be seen as a response to the lack of positive feedback she has received. People have not taken her seriously as an individual with her own feelings, aspirations, ambitions, and right to happiness. They have treated her as disposable, and have made fun of her behind her back, and she ultimately fades away, without ever having made an impact on those around her, despite her devoting an entire lifetime, and all of her steadily diminishing energies, to trying to do just that.

A major component of Polish Positivism was an indulgent recognition of how human frailties and eccentricities frequently can stand in the way of social progress, and one sees this attitude clearly in this story. Orzeszkowa's treatment is full, subtle, psychologically convincing, and elicits one's sympathy above all because of her skill in conveying the idea that Miss Antonina is a real person, someone one might actually know or recognize, possessing real feelings and complexes, living a frustrating life which, because of its complexity and her own limitations, does not lend itself to simple interpretations and answers.

Miss Antonina's plight, and her ultimate failure even in her own terms, is due as much as anything to her own ineffectuality, including as a teacher, the lifetime avocation to which she has devoted so much effort. Like some people occasionally are, she is drawn to a line of work for which she has no real talent. While suffering from an inadequate education, she does not know how to make up for it. She reads indiscriminately, does not pause to make sense of what she has read, becomes foolishly overattached to people, and then, later, too easily embittered over her releases from work. She bases her teaching style on trying to inculcate in her pupils old-fashioned precepts and moral principles for which she herself has no real feeling. They exist for her purely in the abstract, because she herself has not experienced life in a way that would give these precepts substance for her.

In sum, Miss Antonina is a kind of tragic figure, because she contains within herself the seeds of her own failure. Her lofty ideals are never even very well formulated; she just vaguely calls them the "Star of Knowledge." She wants to teach and inspire the young and lead them onto the path of knowledge, but she has no clear idea of what true knowledge is, or any perspective from which to judge it. She is unable to discriminate between useful and irrelevant knowledge. German philosophers and military history are jumbled together with French romantic novels. She has seemingly all the "politically correct" opinions about women's liberation, but her pursuit of this goal leads her nowhere. It is suggested that she has been a failure at least partly because she has never been able to become part of a family as wife and mother. Unconventionally for a feminist, and at odds with her own life history, Orzeszkowa suggests that this is also part of the equation of a woman's fulfillment.

*Structural Analysis.* There is no real plot in "Miss Antonina" in the classical sense, because the recounting of a person's life does not lend itself to a tight structure. It is parabolic, consisting of a curve upward, and then downward. The female narrator adopts a practically journalistic stance toward her subject matter. She is an interviewer, a listener, only occasionally offering any judgment. She sometimes prods Miss Antonina by asking this or that probing question, or by making this or that slightly provocative remark, but she generally keeps her irony to herself. The narrator is, for the most part, a sympathetic and uncritical listener, to whom Miss Antonina reveals more about herself than she might to another person.

According to the narrative strategy, a four-part structure emerges, consisting of movements, or periods in Miss Antonina's life. (1) An initial "interview" sees Miss Antonina in her mid thirties, giving lessons and living in town. In the evenings she conducts her charitable "university" for orphans and indigent children. When we first see her, Miss Antonina is already surrounded by old-maid's symbols: the flowered wallpaper (reminding us of the flower-print dresses she used to wear when she was young and still searching for romance); the geranium, a potted plant, unable to fend for itself on the outside; the canary, trapped in a cage with little experience of life.

A long flashback takes us back to (2) Miss Antonina at the age of twenty-four and a recounting of her earlier life and experiences, consisting of work for a series of employers in country homes. The narrator loses track of her for a period of time, until (3) the narrator encounters her on a city street on a cold wintry day, where she can see that Miss Antonina is already in decline. She visits her and again has the chance to observe her "university" in operation. It is mainly here that one can see her seemingly in her true element, as a born first-grade teacher. (4) After another interval, the narrator discovers that Miss Antonina has been moved to a hospital, where she pays her regular visits out of compassion until her lingering and painful death from some kind of degenerative disease. On the brink of death, Miss Antonina recapitulates, over and over, in token fashion, her entire life by fingering the worthless trinkets and souvenirs she has saved and keeps in a little casket, to be burned upon her death. Asking herself whether her life has left any mark on anyone, she consoles herself by thinking that at least she has taught the young children at her "university" how to read and write.

At life's end, Miss Antonina has grown embittered toward people and is hard to deal with; she criticizes people to their face, even people on the street she does not know. Ironically, it is at this point in her life that people begin to show sympathy for her, precisely when she expects none and has no particular right to expect any. When she has to move to a hospital, a hospital is available, and, out of charity, someone pays for a private room. The narrator visits her regularly out of kindness until she dies. The story ends with a poignant question: "is there a place in heaven for unbloomed human flowers, for souls that went unrewarded here on earth?"

# The Twentieth Century

# Joseph Conrad

Born in Ukraine in Tsarist Russia to a noble and patriotic Polish family, Joseph Conrad's (1857–1924) full name was Józef Teodor Konrad Korzeniowski. He lost both of his parents to tuberculosis and by the age of eleven was orphaned, to be raised and homeschooled by an uncle. He left Poland at the age of seventeen and joined the French Navy at the age of twenty-one. He later enlisted in the British Merchant Marines and spent twenty years with them, traveling extensively in the Far East. In 1890 he settled in England to become a full-time novelist and storywriter, adopting the name Joseph Conrad. His stories, many about life at sea, were first published in short-story magazines. They typically depict men called upon to exhibit bravery, courage, and adherence to duty under conditions of stress and moral ambiguity.

Although he attained fluency in English only in his twenties and always spoke with a thick Polish accent, Conrad became known as one of the greatest English prose stylists of his day. Despite this distinction, Conrad never received any major literary awards. Shortly before his death, he turned down a knighthood offered by the British Crown. He is buried in the city cemetery in Canterbury, where he lived.

Polish scholars have long recognized and treated Conrad as belonging to their literary heritage, and have studied his life and works extensively. The following story, while having nothing to do with Poland specifically, seems eminently suitable in many ways for entering upon an overview of twentieth-century Polish short prose fiction.

## The Tale

Outside the large single window the crepuscular light was dying out slowly in a great square gleam without color, framed rigidly in the gathering shades of the room.

It was a long room. The irresistible tide of the night ran into the most distant part of it, where the whispering of a man's voice, passionately interrupted and passionately renewed, seemed to plead against the answering murmurs of infinite sadness.

At last no answering murmur came. His movement when he rose slowly from his knees by the side of the deep, shadowy couch holding the shadowy suggestion of a reclining woman revealed him tall under the low ceiling, and sombre all over except for the crude discord of the white collar under the shape of his head and the faint, minute spark of a brass button here and there on his uniform.

He stood over her a moment masculine and mysterious in his immobility before he sat down on a chair near by. He could see only the faint oval of her upturned face and, extended on her black dress, her pale hands, a moment before abandoned to his kisses and now as if too weary to move.

The silence was profound. The wave of passion had broken against a murmured sadness, thin air, passing mood—by its own accumulated momentum of desire; by its own towering strength sinking into the level repose that seems the end of all things under heaven, but only marks the rhythm of the swelling heart-waves running the circuit of the habitable globe.

He dared not make a sound, shrinking as a man would do from the prosaic necessities of existence. As usual, it was the woman who had the courage. Her voice was heard first—almost conventional while her being vibrated yet with conflicting emotions.

"Tell me something," she said.

The darkness hid his surprise and then his smile. Had he not just said to her everything worth telling in the world—and that not for the first time!

"What am I to tell you?" he asked, in a voice creditably steady. He was beginning to feel grateful to her for that something final in her tone which had eased the strain.

"Why not tell me a tale?"

"Yes. Why not?"

These words came with a slight petulance, the hint of a loved woman's capricious will, which is capricious only because it feels itself to be a law, embarrassing sometimes and always difficult to elude.

"Why not?" he repeated, with a slightly mocking accent, as though he had been asked to give her the moon. But now he was feeling a little angry with her for that feminine mobility that slips out of an emotion as easily as out of a splendid gown.

He heard her saying, a little unsteadily with a sort of fluttering intonation which made him think suddenly of a butterfly's flight:

"You used to tell—your—your simple and—and professional—tales very well at one time. Or well enough to interest me. You had a—a sort of art—in the days—the days before the war."

"Really?" he said, with involuntary gloom. "But now, you see, the war is going on," he continued in such a dead, equable tone that she felt a slight chill fall over her shoulders. And yet she persisted. For there's nothing more unswerving in the world than a woman's caprice.

"It could be a tale not of this world," she explained.

"You want a tale of the other, the better world?" he asked, with a matter-of-fact surprise. "You must evoke for that task those who have already gone there."

"No. I don't mean that. I mean another—some other—world. In the universe—not in heaven."

"I am relieved. But you forget that I have only five days' leave."

"Yes. And I've also taken a five days' leave from—from my duties."

"I like that word."

"What word?"

"Duty."

"It is horrible—sometimes."

"Oh, that's because you think it's narrow. But it isn't. It contains infinities, and—and so—"

"What is this jargon?"

He disregarded the interjected scorn. "An infinity of absolution, for instance," he continued. "But as to this 'another world'—who's going to look for it and for the tale that is in it?"

"You," she said, with a strange, almost rough, sweetness of assertion.

He made a shadowy movement of assent in his chair, the irony of which not even the gathered darkness could render mysterious.

"As you will. In that world, then, there was once upon a time a Commanding Officer and a Northman. Put in the capitals, please, because they had no other names. It was a world of seas and continents and islands—"

"Like the earth," she murmured, bitterly.

"Yes. What else could you expect from sending a man made of our common, tormented clay on a voyage of discovery? What else could he find? What else could you understand or care for, or feel the existence of even? There was comedy in it and slaughter."

"Always like the earth," she murmured.

"Always. And since I could find in the universe only what was deeply rooted in the fibres of my being there was love in it too. But we won't talk of that."

"No. We won't," she said, in a neutral tone which concealed perfectly her relief—or her disappointment. Then after a pause she added: "It's going to be a comic story."

"Well—" he paused, too. "Yes. In a way. In a very grim way. It will be human, and, as you know, comedy is but a matter of the visual angle. And it won't be a noisy story. All the long guns in it will be dumb—as dumb as so many telescopes."

"Ah, there are guns in it, then! And may I ask—where"?

"Afloat. You remember that the world of which we speak had its seas. A war was going on in it. It was a funny world and terribly in earnest. Its war was being carried on over the land, over the water, under the water, up in the air, and even under the ground. And many young men in it, mostly in wardrooms and mess-rooms, used to say to each other—pardon the unparliamentary word—they used to say, 'It's a damned bad war, but it's better than no war at all.' Sounds flippant, doesn't it?"

He heard a nervous, impatient sigh in the depths of the couch while he went on without a pause.

"And yet there is more in it than meets the eye. I mean more wisdom. Flippancy, like comedy, is but a matter of visual first-impression. That world was not very wise. But there was in it a certain amount of common working sagacity. That, however, was mostly worked by the neutrals in diverse ways, public and private, which had to be watched; watched by acute minds and also by actual sharp eyes. They had to be very sharp indeed, too, I assure you."

"I can imagine," she murmured, appreciatively.

"What is there that you can't imagine?" he pronounced, soberly. "You have the world in you. But let us go back to our Commanding Officer, who, of course, commanded a ship of a sort. My tales if often professional (as you remarked just now) have never been technical. So I'll just tell you that the ship was of a very ornamental sort once, with lots of grace and elegance and luxury about her. Yes, once! She was like a pretty woman who had suddenly put on a suit of sackcloth and stuck revolvers in her belt. But she floated lightly, she moved nimbly, she was quite good enough."

"That was the opinion of the Commanding Officer" said the voice from the couch.

"It was. He used to be sent out with her along certain coasts to see—what he could see. Just that. And sometimes he had some preliminary information to help him, and sometimes he had not. And it was all one, really. It was about as useful as information trying to convey the locality and intentions of a cloud, of a phantom taking shape here and there and impossible to seize, would have been.

"It was in the early days of the war. What at first used to amaze the Commanding Officer was the unchanged face of the waters, with its familiar expression, neither more friendly nor more hostile. On fine days the sun strikes sparks upon the blue; here and there a peaceful smudge of smoke hangs in the distance, and it is impossible to believe that the familiar clear horizon traces the limit of one great circular ambush.

"Yes, it is impossible to believe, till some day you see a ship not your own ship (that isn't so impressive), but some ship in company, blow up all of a sudden and plop under almost before you know what had happened to her. Then you begin to believe. Henceforth you go out for the work to see—what you can see, and you keep on at it with the conviction that some day you will die from something you have not seen. One envies the soldiers at the end of the day, wiping the sweat and blood from their faces, counting the dead fallen to their hands, looking at the devastated fields, the torn earth that seems to suffer and bleed with them. One does, really. The final brutality of it—the taste of primitive passion—the ferocious frankness of the blow struck with one's hand—the direct call and the straight response. Well, the sea gave you nothing of that, and seemed to pretend that there was nothing the matter with the world."

She interrupted, stirring a little.

"Oh, yes. Sincerity—frankness—passion—three words of your gospel. Don't I know them!"

"Think! Isn't it ours—believed in common?" he asked, anxiously, yet without expecting an answer, and went on at once.

"Such were the feelings of the Commanding Officer. When the night came trailing over the sea, hiding what looked like the hypocrisy of an old friend, it was a relief. The night blinds you frankly—and there are circumstances when the sunlight may grow as odious to one as falsehood itself. Night is all right.

"At night the Commanding Officer could let his thoughts get away—I won't tell you where. Somewhere where there was no choice but between truth and death. But thick weather, though it blinded one, brought no such relief. Mist is deceitful, the dead luminosity of the fog is irritating. It seems that you ought to see.

"One gloomy, nasty day the ship was steaming along her beat in sight of a rocky, dangerous coast that stood out intensely black like an Indian-ink drawing on grey paper. Presently the Second in command spoke to his chief. He thought he saw something on the water, to seaward. Small wreckage, perhaps. 'But there shouldn't be any wreckage here, sir,' he remarked.

"'No,' said the Commanding Officer. 'The last reported submarined ships were sunk a long way to the westward. But one never knows. There may have been others since then not reported nor seen. Gone with all hands.'

"That was how it began. The ship's course was altered to pass the object close: for it was necessary to have a good look at what one could see. Close, but without touching: for it was not advisable to come in contact with objects of any form whatever floating casually about. Close, but without stopping or even diminishing speed: for in those times it was not prudent to linger on any particular spot, even for a moment. I may tell you at once that the object was not dangerous in itself. No use in describing it. It may have been nothing more remarkable than, say, a barrel of a certain shape and color. But it was significant.

"The smooth bow-wave hove it up as if for a closer inspection, and then the ship, brought again to her course, turned her back on it with indifference, while twenty pairs of eyes on her deck stared in all directions trying to see—what they could see.

"The Commanding Officer and his Second in command discussed the object with understanding. It appeared to them to be not so much a proof of the sagacity as of the activity of certain neutrals. This activity had in many cases taken the form of replenishing the stores of certain submarines at sea. This was generally believed, if not absolutely known. But the very nature of things in those early days pointed that way. The object, looked at closely and turned away from with apparent indifference, put it beyond doubt that something of the sort had been done somewhere in the neighborhood.

"The object in itself was more than suspect. But the fact of its being left in evidence roused other suspicions. Was it the result of some deep and devilish purpose? As to that all speculation soon appeared to be a vain thing. Finally the two officers came to the conclusion that it was left there most likely by accident, complicated possibly by some unforeseen necessity: such, perhaps, as the sudden need to get away quickly from the spot, or something of that kind.

"Their discussion had been carried on in curt, weighty phrases, separated by long, thoughtful silences. And all the time their eyes roamed about the horizon in an everlasting, almost mechanical effort of vigilance. The younger man summed up grimly: —

"'Well, it's evidence. That's what this is. Evidence of what we were pretty certain of before. And plain, too.'

"'And much good it will do to us,'" retorted the Commanding Officer. 'The parties are miles away; the submarine, devil only knows where, ready to kill; and the noble neutral slipping away to the eastward, ready to lie!'

"The Second in command laughed a little at the tone. But he guessed that the neutral wouldn't even have to lie very much. Fellows like that, unless caught in the very act, felt themselves pretty safe. They could afford to chuckle. That fellow was probably chuckling to himself. It's very possible he had been before at the game and didn't care a rap for the bit of evidence left behind. It was a game in which practice made one bold and successful too.

"And again he laughed faintly. But his Commanding Officer was in revolt against the murderous stealthiness of methods and the atrocious callousness of complicities that seemed to taint the very source of men's deep emotions and noblest activities; to corrupt their imagination which builds up the final conceptions of life and death. He suffered—"

The voice from the sofa interrupted the narrator.

"How well I can understand that in him!"

He bent forward slightly. "Yes. I too. Everything should be open in love and war. Open as the day, since both are the call of an ideal which it is so easy, so terribly easy, to degrade in the name of Victory."

He paused, then went on:— "I don't know that the Commanding Officer delved so deep as that into his feelings. But he did suffer from them—a sort of disenchanted sadness. It is possible, even, that he suspected himself of folly. Man is various. But he had no time for much introspection, because from the south-west a wall of fog had advanced upon his ship. Great convolutions of vapours flew over, swirling about masts and funnel, which looked as if they were beginning to melt. Then they vanished.

"The ship was stopped, all sounds ceased, and the very fog became motionless, growing denser and as if solid in its amazing dumb immobility. The men at their stations lost sight of each other. Footsteps sounded stealthy; rare voices, impersonal and remote, died out without resonance. A blind white stillness took possession of the world.

"It looked, too, as if it would last for days. I don't mean to say that the fog did not vary a little in its density. Now and then it would thin out mysteriously, revealing to the men a more or less ghostly presentment of their ship. Several times the shadow of the coast itself swam darkly before their eyes through the fluctuating opaque brightness of the great white cloud clinging to the water.

"Taking advantage of these moments, the ship had been moved cautiously nearer the shore. It was useless to remain out in such thick weather. Her officers knew every nook and cranny of the coast along their beat. They thought that she would be much better in a certain cove. It wasn't a large place, just ample room for a ship to swing at her anchor. She would have an easier time of it till the fog lifted up.

“Slowly, with infinite caution and patience, they crept closer and closer, seeing no more of the cliffs than an evanescent dark loom with a narrow border of angry foam at its foot. At the moment of anchoring the fog was so thick that for all they could see they might have been a thousand miles out in the open sea. Yet the shelter of the land could be felt. There was a peculiar quality in the stillness of the air. Very faint, very elusive, the wash of the ripple against the encircling land reached their ears, with mysterious sudden pauses.

“The anchor dropped, the leads were laid in. The Commanding Officer went below into his cabin. But he had not been there very long when a voice outside his door requested his presence on deck. He thought to himself: ‘What is it now?’ He felt some impatience at being called out again to face the wearisome fog.

“He found that it had thinned again a little and had taken on a gloomy hue from the dark cliffs which had no form, no outline, but asserted themselves as a curtain of shadows all round the ship, except in one bright spot, which was the entrance from the open sea. Several officers were looking that way from the bridge. The Second in Command met him with the breathlessly whispered information that there was another ship in the cove.

“She had been made out by several pairs of eyes only a couple of minutes before. She was lying at anchor very near the entrance—a mere vague blot on the fog’s brightness. And the Commanding Officer by staring in the direction pointed out to him by eager hands ended by distinguishing it at last himself. Indubitably a vessel of some sort.

“‘It’s a wonder we didn’t run slap into her when coming in,’ observed the Second in Command.

“‘Send a boat on board before she vanishes,’ said the Commanding Officer. He surmised that this was a coaster. It could hardly be anything else. But another thought came into his head suddenly.

“‘It is a wonder,’ he said to his Second in Command, who had rejoined him after sending the boat away. By that time both of them had been struck by the fact that the ship so suddenly discovered had not manifested her presence by ringing her bell.

“‘We came in very quietly, that’s true,’ concluded the younger officer. ‘But they must have heard our leadsmen at least. We couldn’t have passed her more than fifty yards off. The closest shave! They may even have made us out, since they were aware of something coming in. And the strange thing is that we never heard a sound from her. The fellows on board must have been holding their breath.’

“‘Aye,’ said the Commanding Officer, thoughtfully.

“In due course the boarding-boat returned, appearing suddenly alongside, as though she had burrowed her way under the fog. The officer in charge came up to make his report, but the Commanding Officer didn’t give him time to begin. He cried from a distance:—

“‘Coaster, isn’t she?’

“‘No, sir. A stranger—a neutral,’ was the answer.

“‘No. Really! Well, tell us all about it. What is she doing here?’

The young man stated then that he had been told a long and complicated story of engine troubles. But it was plausible enough from a strictly professional point of view and it had the usual features: disablement, dangerous drifting along the shore, weather more or less thick for days, fear of a gale, ultimately a resolve to go in and anchor anywhere on the coast, and so on. Fairly plausible.

"'Engines still disabled?'" inquired the Commanding Officer.

"'No, sir. She has steam on them.'

"The Commanding Officer took his Second aside. 'By Jove!' he said, 'you were right! They were holding their breaths as we passed them. They were.'

"But the Second in Command had his doubts now. 'A fog like this does muffle small sounds, sir,' he remarked. 'And what could his object be, after all?'

"'To sneak out unnoticed,' answered the Commanding Officer.

"'Then why didn't he? He might have done it, you know. Not exactly unnoticed, perhaps. I don't suppose he could have slipped his cable without making some noise. Still, in a minute or so he would have been lost to view—clean gone before we had made him out fairly. Yet he didn't.'

"They looked at each other. The Commanding Officer shook his head. Such suspicions as the one which had entered his head are not defended easily. He did not even state it openly. The boarding officer finished his report. The cargo of the ship was of a harmless and useful character. She was bound to an English port. Papers and everything in perfect order. Nothing suspicious to be detected anywhere.

"Then passing to the men, he reported the crew on deck as the usual lot. Engineers of the well-known type, and very full of their achievement in repairing the engines. The mate surly. The master rather a fine specimen of a Northman, civil enough, but appeared to have been drinking. Seemed to be recovering from a regular bout of it.

"'I told him I couldn't give him permission to proceed. He said he wouldn't dare to move his ship her own length out in such weather as this, permission or no permission. I left a man on board, though,'

"'Quite right.'

"The Commanding Officer, after communing with his suspicions for a time, called his Second aside. 'What if she were the very ship which had been feeding some infernal submarine or other?' he said in an undertone.

"The other stared. Then, with conviction:— 'She would get off scot-free. You couldn't prove it, sir.'

"'I want to look into it myself.'

"'From the report we've heard I am afraid you couldn't even make a case for reasonable suspicion, sir.'

"'I'll go on board all the same.'

"He had made up his mind. Curiosity is the great motive power of hatred and love. What did he expect to find? He could not have told anybody—not even himself.

"What he really expected to find there was the atmosphere, the atmosphere of gratuitous treachery, which in his view nothing could excuse; for he thought that even a passion of unrighteousness for its own sake could not excuse that. But could he detect it? Sniff it? Taste it? Receive some mysterious communication which would turn his invincible suspicions into a certitude strong enough to provoke action with all its risks?

"The master met him on the after-deck, looming up in the fog amongst the blurred shapes of the usual ship's fittings. He was a robust Northman, bearded, and in the force of his age. A round leather cap fitted his head closely. His hands were rammed deep into the pockets of his short leather jacket. He kept them there while he explained that at sea he lived in the chartroom, and led the way there, striding carelessly. Just before reaching the door under the bridge he staggered a little, recovered himself, flung it open, and stood aside, leaning his shoulder as if involuntarily against the side of the house, and staring vaguely into the fog-filled space. But he followed the Commanding Officer at once, flung the door to, snapped on the electric light, and hastened to thrust his hands back into his pockets, as though afraid of being seized by them either in friendship or in hostility.

"The place was stuffy and hot. The usual chart-rack overhead was full, and the chart on the table was kept unrolled by an empty cup standing on a saucer half-full of some spilt dark liquid. A slightly-nibbled biscuit reposed on the chronometer-case. There were two settees, and one of them had been made up into a bed with a pillow and some blankets, which were now very much tumbled. The Northman let himself fall on it, his hands still in his pockets.

"'Well, here I am,' he said, with a curious air of being surprised at the sound of his own voice.

"The Commanding Officer from the other settee observed the handsome, flushed face. Drops of fog hung on the yellow beard and moustaches of the Northman. The much darker eyebrows ran together in a puzzled frown, and suddenly he jumped up.

"'What I mean is that I don't know where I am. I really don't,' he burst out, with extreme earnestness. 'Hang it all! I got turned around somehow. The fog has been after me for a week. More than a week. And then my engines broke down. I will tell you how it was.'

"He burst out into loquacity. It was not hurried, but it was insistent. It was not continuous for all that. It was broken by the most queer, thoughtful pauses. Each of these pauses lasted no more than a couple of seconds, and each had the profoundity of an endless meditation. When he began again nothing betrayed in him the slightest consciousness of these intervals. There was the same fixed glance, the same unchanged earnestness of tone. He didn't know. Indeed, more than one of these pauses occurred in the middle of a sentence.

"The Commanding Officer listened to the tale. It struck him as more plausible than simple truth is in the habit of being. But that, perhaps, was prejudice. All the time the Northman was speaking the Commanding Officer had been aware of an inward voice, a grave murmur in the depth of his very own self, telling another tale, as if on purpose to keep alive in him his indignation and his anger with that baseness of greed or of mere outlook which lies often at the root of simple ideas.

"It was the story that had been already told to the boarding officer an hour or so before. The Commanding Officer nodded slightly at the Northman from time to time.

"The latter came to an end and turned his eyes away. He added, as an afterthought:—'Wasn't it enough to drive a man out of his mind with worry? And it's my first voyage to this part, too. And the ship's my own. Your officer has seen the papers. She isn't much, as you can see for yourself. Just an old cargo-boat. Bare living for my family.'

"He raised a big arm to point at a row of photographs plastering the bulkhead. The movement was ponderous, as if the arm had been made of lead. The Commanding Officer said, carelessly:—

"'You will be making a fortune yet for your family with this old ship.'

"'Yes, if I don't lose her,' said the Northman, gloomily.

"'I mean—out of this war,' added the Commanding Officer.

"The Northman stared at him in a curiously unseeing and at the same time interested manner, as only eyes of a particular blue shade can stare.

"'And you wouldn't be angry at it,' he said, 'would you? You are too much of a gentleman. We didn't bring this on you. And suppose we sat down and cried. What good would that be? Let those cry who made the trouble,' he concluded, with energy. 'Time's money, you say. Well—this time is money. Oh! isn't it!'

"The Commanding Officer tried to keep under the feeling of immense disgust. He said to himself that it was unreasonable. Men were like that—moral cannibals feeding on each other's misfortunes. He said aloud:—

"'You have made it perfectly plain how it is that you are here. Your log-book confirms you very minutely. Of course, a log-book may be cooked. Nothing easier.'

"The Northman never moved a muscle. He was gazing at the floor; he seemed not to have heard. He raised his head after a while.

"'But you can't suspect me of anything,' he muttered, negligently.

"The Commanding Officer thought: 'Why should he say this?'

"Immediately afterwards the man before him added: 'My cargo is for an English port.'

"His voice had turned husky for the moment. The Commanding Officer reflected: 'That's true. There can be nothing. I can't suspect him. Yet why was he lying with steam up in this fog—and then, hearing us come in, why didn't he give some sign of life? Why? Could it be anything else but a guilty conscience? He could tell by the leadsmen that this was a man-of-war.'

"'Yes—why?' The Commanding Officer went on thinking. 'Suppose I ask him and then watch his face. He will betray himself in some way. It's perfectly plain that the fellow has been drinking. Yes, he has been drinking; but he will have a lie ready all the same.'

"The Commanding Officer was one of those men who are made morally and almost physically uncomfortable by the mere thought of having to beat down a lie. He shrank from the act in scorn and disgust, which was invincible because more temperamental than moral.

"So he went out on deck instead and had the crew mustered formally for his inspection. He found them very much what the report of the boarding officer had led him to expect. And from their answers to his questions he could discover no flaw in the log-book story.

"He dismissed them. His impression of them was—a picked lot; have been promised a fistful of money each if this came off; all slightly anxious, but not frightened. Not a single one of them likely to give the show away. They don't feel in danger of their life. They know England and English ways too well!

"He felt alarmed at catching himself thinking as if his vaguest suspicions were turning into a certitude. For, indeed, there was no shadow of reason for his inferences. There was nothing to give away.

"He returned to the chart-room. The Northman had lingered behind there; and something subtly different in his bearing, more bold in his blue, glassy stare, induced the Commanding Officer to conclude that the fellow had snatched at the opportunity to take another swig at the bottle he must have had concealed somewhere.

"He noticed, too, that the Northman on meeting his eyes put on an elaborately surprised expression. At least, it seemed elaborated. Nothing could be trusted. And the Englishman felt himself with astonishing conviction faced by an enormous lie, solid like a wall, with no way round to get at the truth, whose ugly murderous face he seemed to see peeping over at him with a cynical grin.

"'I dare say,' he began, suddenly, 'you are wondering at my proceedings, though I am not detaining you, am I? You wouldn't dare to move in this fog?'

"'I don't know where I am,' the Northman ejaculated, earnestly. 'I really don't.'

"He looked around as if the very chart-room fittings were strange to him. The Commanding Officer asked him whether he had not seen any unusual objects floating about while he was at sea.

"'Objects! What objects? We were groping blind in the fog for days.'

"'We had a few clear intervals,' said the Commanding Officer. 'And I'll tell you what we have seen and the conclusion I've come to about it.'

"He told him in a few words. He heard the sound of a sharp breath indrawn through closed teeth. The Northman with his hand on the table stood absolutely motionless and dumb. He stood as if thunderstruck. Then he produced a fatuous smile.

"Or at least so it appeared to the Commanding Officer. Was this significant, or of no meaning whatever? He didn't know, he couldn't tell. All the truth had departed out of the world as if drawn in, absorbed in this monstrous villainy this man was—or was not—guilty of.

"'Shooting's too good for people that conceive neutrality in this pretty way,' remarked the Commanding Officer, after a silence.

"'Yes, yes, yes,' the Northman assented, hurriedly—then added an unexpected and dreamy-voiced 'Perhaps.'

"Was he pretending to be drunk, or only trying to appear sober? His glance was straight, but it was somewhat glazed. His lips outlined themselves firmly under his yellow moustache. But they twitched. Did they twitch? And why was he drooping like this in his attitude?

"'There's no perhaps about it,' pronounced the Commanding Officer sternly.

"The Northman had straightened himself. And unexpectedly he looked stern too.

"'No. But what about the tempters? Better kill that lot off. There's about four, five, six million of them,' he said, grimly; but in a moment changed into a whining key. 'But I had better hold my tongue. You have some suspicions.'

"'No, I've no suspicions,' declared the Commanding Officer.

"He never faltered. At that moment he had the certitude. The air of the chart-room was thick with guilt and falsehood braving the discovery, defying simple right, common decency, all humanity of feeling, every scruple of conduct.

"The Northman drew a long breath. 'Well, we know that you English are gentlemen. But let us speak the truth. Why should we love you so very much? You haven't done anything to be loved. We don't love the other people, of course. They haven't done anything for that either. A fellow comes along with a bag of gold ... I haven't been in Rotterdam my last voyage for nothing.'

"'You may be able to tell something interesting, then, to our people when you come into port,' interjected the Officer.

"'I might. But you keep some people in your pay at Rotterdam. Let them report. I am a neutral—am I not? ... Have you ever seen a poor man on one side and a bag of gold on the other? Of course, I couldn't be tempted. I haven't the nerve for it. Really I haven't. It's nothing to me. I am just talking openly for once.'

"'Yes. And I am listening to you,' said the Commanding Officer, quietly.

"The Northman leaned forward over the table. 'Now that I know you have no suspicions, I talk. You don't know what a poor man is. I do. I am poor myself. This old ship, she isn't much, and she is mortgaged, too. Bare living, no more. Of course, I wouldn't have the nerve. But a man who has nerve! See. The stuff he takes aboard looks like any other cargo—packages, barrels, tins, copper tubes—what not. He doesn't see it work. It isn't real to him. But he sees the gold. That's real. Of course, nothing could induce me. I suffer from an internal disease. I would either go crazy from anxiety—or—or—take to drink or something. The risk is too great. Why—ruin!'

"'It should be death.' The Commanding Officer got up, after this curt declaration, which the other received with a hard stare oddly combined with an uncertain smile. The Officer's gorge rose at the atmosphere of murderous complicity which surrounded him, denser, more impenetrable, more acrid than the fog outside.

"'It's nothing to me,' murmured the Northman, swaying visibly.

"'Of course not,' assented the Commanding Officer, with a great effort to keep his voice calm and low. The certitude was strong within him. 'But I am going to clear all you fellows off this coast at once. And I will begin with you. You must leave in half an hour.'

"By that time the Officer was walking along the deck with the Northman at his elbow.

"'What! In this fog?' the latter cried out, huskily.

"'Yes, you will have to go in this fog.'

"'But I don't know where I am. I really don't.'

"The Commanding Officer turned round. A sort of fury possessed him. The eyes of the two men met. Those of the Northman expressed a profound amazement.

"'Oh, you don't know how to get out.' The Commanding Officer spoke with composure, but his heart was beating with anger and dread. 'I will give you your course. Steer south-by-east-halfeast for about four miles and then you will be clear to haul to the eastward for your port. The weather will clear up before very long.'

"'Must I? What could induce me? I haven't the nerve.'

"'And yet you must go. Unless you want to— '

"'I don't want to,' panted the Northman. 'I've enough of it.'

"The Commanding Officer got over the side. The Northman remained still as if rooted to the deck. Before his boat reached his ship the Commanding Officer heard the steamer beginning to pick up her anchor. Then, shadowy in the fog, she steamed out on the given course.

"'Yes,' he said to his officers, 'I let him go.'

The narrator bent forward towards the couch, where no movement betrayed the presence of a living person.

"Listen," he said, forcibly.

"That course would lead the Northman straight on a deadly ledge of rock. And the Commanding Officer gave it to him. He steamed out—ran on it—and went down. So he had spoken the truth. He did not know where he was. But it proves nothing. Nothing either way. It may have been the only truth in all his story. And yet … He seems to have been driven out by a menacing stare—nothing more."

He abandoned all pretence.

"Yes, I gave that course to him. It seemed to me a supreme test. I believe—no, I don't believe. I don't know. At the time I was certain. They all went down; and I don't know whether I have done stern retribution—or murder; whether I have added to the corpses that litter the bed of the unreadable sea the bodies of men completely innocent or basely guilty. I don't know. I shall never know."

He rose. The woman on the couch got up and threw her arms round his neck. Her eyes put two gleams in the deep shadow of the room. She knew his passion for truth, his horror of deceit, his humanity.

"Oh, my poor, poor— "

"I shall never know," he repeated, sternly, disengaged himself, pressed her hands to his lips, and went out.

—1917.

*Modernism.* Conrad is considered to be one of the first English "modernists," cultivating a style of writing characterized by oblique, impressionistic narratives, with important aspects of the content being hinted at rather than stated overtly. Like impressionism in painting, modernism rejected the realistic style of the preceding period, in the belief that one can get closer to reality by merely being suggestive of it, letting readers fill in the blanks for themselves. The modernist style is matched by an ambiguity of meaning and the absence of clear conclusions or moral interpretations. Common are framed narratives in which a story is told inside the context of another story, sometimes by an unreliable witness/narrator, heightening the impression of subjectivity, of degrees removed from immediate reality. As it developed over time, modernism led to further offshoots and "-isms" such as abstractionism and absurdism.

*"The Tale" as a Pre-Existentialist Work; the "Conradian Choice."* Existentialism was a literary-philosophical movement appearing first in France in the late 1940s and early 1950s, in part a response to the experiences of World War II. Its tenet is that only action creates value in an otherwise valueless, constantly shifting, meaningless world. Moral codes are useless, for morality is relative; there are no moral absolutes; ethics have to be adapted to situations.

Thus, Existentialism is opposed to the kind of moral precepts embodied in traditional religion in the form of "commandments," categorical statements of the "do this" and "don't do that" sort. According to this line of thought, traditional moral codes do not provide workable guidelines for behavior in complex situations, and most situations are complex. One of the biblical commandments states "Thou shalt not kill!" (actually, "Thou shalt not murder!"), but this commandment is routinely ignored in times of war, even by people who think they are abiding by moral principles, as in "The Tale."

What may be called the "Conradian choice" visible in "The Tale" exhibits the following characteristics which have much in common with Existentialism:

- Life's situations can force a person into having to make choices and decisions and having to take action, sometimes with life-and-death consequences. One is thrust into situations outside one's will.
- Choices are usually not easy; they are not between simple right and wrong. Often the choice is between the lesser of two or more evils. Objective truth is difficult or impossible to determine. Mainly, there is never enough time or information to determine what objective truth is, or what the right decision should be.
- One does not always act in one's own self-interest, or in accord with logic or one's code of beliefs or better judgment. The role we have thrust on us vis-à-vis other people can influence how we act, often differently than we might act if we did not have such a role, carrying social responsibility along with it.
- The decisions one makes are always based on equivocal and ambiguous input, made even more subjective by being filtered through one's own and other people's perceptions, and by being subject to one's psychological makeup, prejudices, and predispositions in ways of which one can never be fully aware.

- The mind works by applying interpretive "templates," "profiles," or "scenarios" to situations, which inevitably are schematic, simplistic, and do not get at the real truth.
- Everyone ultimately acts on their own, and bears an individual burden of responsibility for their actions. One is ultimately answerable only to oneself, before oneself.
- Although moral codes reside only in the hearts and minds of people, not in absolute principles, they are still important to Conrad. People have an innate impulse to make the "right," "moral," "honorable" choice. This is like Existentialism with a moral inner compass.
- One often never knows whether one's choice was correct, even in retrospect.
- Situations are infinitely variable. They do not repeat. What is right today may be wrong tomorrow, and vice versa. Because of the infinite variability of situations, one can never draw lessons or learn from experience.

"The Tale" is a story of moral choice in the Conradian sense, wherein life and death ride on a decision that has to be made with imperfect data, on the basis of one's interpretation of an encountered situation which is rife with ambiguity. The commander making the decision has been cast into the situation not of his own choosing. His vessel, a merchant boat, has been forcibly commissioned into service; probably he himself has been drafted against his preference, but he is determined to do his Duty, with a capital "d."

World War I, somewhere along the North Sea coast, provides the backdrop, an arena requiring quick decisions vitally affecting others. War concentrates one's attention, heightens one's sense of the importance of decisions and of the consciousness of one's existence. A false move can result either in oneself or in other people getting blown up, or both. Decisions must be made quickly and spontaneously, on the basis of one's sense of what is at best an illusory or imperfect truth.

The Commanding Officer has to make up his mind based on a wide variety of imperfect data filtered through his senses of duty, justice, loyalty to his country, not to mention his own personal prejudices. For example, the officer does not much like foreigners, especially neutral ones in wartime. Each of these codes of behavior may suggest a different course of action, and the clock is ticking. He has to make a decision before all the data are in. At times one feels that the Commanding Officer is doing everything he can to make the "evidence" with which he is presented conform to his preconceived notions of what he wants to see. Probably his second in command would have come to a different conclusion and decision—but the second-in-command does not have the responsibility or authority.

While told in the third person, the narrative is really first-person in disguise. Almost the entire story is told in quotation marks, and one learns at the end that the narrator and the Commanding Officer are one and the same person. The narrative is framed within another narrative that one never learns much about, heightening the sense of the subjectivity of the situation. There is no "objective truth," only individual perceptions of it. A man, wearing an officer's uniform, probably home on leave from war at sea, is asked by a woman, to whom he has apparently recently made love, who may be simultaneously being unfaithful to a husband, to tell her a story. It is a profound question whose profundity the woman does not realize. She just wants to be slightly amused and, mainly, to fill up the awkward silence following lovemaking. It is a moment propitious for quiet talk, and for making confessions. The woman does not realize that she will provoke the baring of the man's soul, and the telling of one of his innermost secrets: he lives with not knowing whether he has done his duty or, instead, has murdered the entire innocent crew of a neutral country's boat. The officer tells his mistress about his agony over a decision he concealed from his own crew.

The main "actors" in the story are not only people (mainly the Officer and the Northern sea captain). In accordance with Conrad's method, his settings become symbols; they include the sea, the countries at war, the neutral powers, the entire globe. The sea ("the unchanging face of the waters") takes on a metaphorical, universal meaning. It is symbolic of the abyss of human consciousness: foggy, murky, swirling, shifting, unclear, absent of moorings, full of ambiguous signs; nothing ever appears the same way twice. Dangers lurk everywhere (hidden reefs, mines). A typical line: "Great convolutions of vapors flew over, swirling about masts and funnel, which looked as if they were beginning to melt. Then they vanished."

In a broader perspective, the wartime situation depicted in "The Tale" functions as a magnifying mirror of life itself: most of life's major decisions are fraught with indeterminacy, but one has to make them nevertheless, and one rarely knows for sure whether one's decision has been the right one.

*Plot Analysis.* Development: A merchant boat with retrofitted guns is patrolling coastal waters to protect shipping from submarine attacks. There have been rumors, unconfirmed, of vessels resupplying submarines under the banner of neutrality.

Turning Point: Some kind of barrel or similar flotsam is discovered, bobbing in the sea. Twenty eyes are on it, but no one can make any clear sense of it. Possibly it has been hurriedly discarded from a submarine-resupplying mission, or perhaps not. It could have nothing to do with anything. Just as quickly as it appears, the barrel bobs out of sight. At almost the same time, a "neutral" boat is discovered, under steam, in the same cove in which the boat's officer has taken shelter from a dense fog.

First the Second Officer and then the Commanding Officer himself board the boat, and the captain and his crew are interrogated. They claim to have just repaired a disabled engine and to be waiting out the fog. Anything could be true. There is no way to break through the Northman's lie, if there is one. Nonetheless, the evidence has to be weighed, and a decision made.

Crisis: On the basis of no clear evidence, the Commanding Officer comes to a conclusion and makes his decision, based on what he knows, which is almost nothing, and his vague suspicions and preconceptions. He makes the decision on his own responsibility, without sharing his decision with his own crew. He decides to test one aspect of the Northman's veracity, that he really does not know where he is along the coast. The Commanding Officer gives him instructions for getting out of the cove, which in reality will lead his boat onto a fatal reef.

Climax: The Northman declines to call the Commanding Officer's probable bluff that he will blow him out of the water or at least seize his boat. This may be the one most crucial piece of evidence against the Northman. He may feel that indicating his lack of trust in the Commanding Officer's instructions may signal his guilt. In any case, he follows instructions and directs his boat onto the reef, killing all hands.

Aftermath: The officer lives with the results of his decision. The test was not definitive, he now realizes. It only demonstrated one point, that the Northman did not know where he was. The officer does not know whether he has delivered a well-deserved retribution or, instead, has murdered a ship of innocent men, with wives and children dependent on them at home.

*A Man's Writer.* Conrad is sometimes said to be a man's writer in a man's world, and there is nothing in "The Tale" to contradict such an observation. While it is beyond our ambition to examine the well-worked theme of "Conrad and masculinity" with the attention it deserves, it cannot be denied that the woman in the present story plays a decidedly marginal and decorative role. She is a love object who, by the circumstance of her romantic tryst, becomes a sounding board for a story whose moral issues are depicted as essentially falling outside the range of her "feminine" ability to truly appreciate them.

# Poland between the Two World Wars, 1918–1939

As a consequence of the collapse of the German, Russian, and Austro-Hungian empires following World War I, the Republic of Poland (*Rzeczpospolita Polska*) was reassembled out of most of the parts that had been seized by those powers 130 years earlier. Stipulations of the Versailles Conference of 1918–1919, in which the American president Woodrow Wilson played a key role, provided Poland with a narrow corridor of access to the Baltic Sea past the so-called Free City of Gdańsk (Danzig), with hostile German territory lying on either side. Surrounded by unfriendly neighbors along all borders, and with no recent experience at self-governance, Poland found itself in a precarious existential situation at the very outset of its suddenly regained independence.

To make matters worse, in 1918–1919 a bloody Ukrainian uprising against Polish occupation in Western Ukraine broke out, quelled with great difficulty by the newly formed army, and in 1919–1920 the newly-minted Soviet Union invaded Poland, trying to take its communist revolution westward. Disaster in the second instance was averted by a definitive rout of the Red Army in the "Miracle on the Vistula" on the very outskirts of Warsaw by the Polish army under the command of Józef Piłsudski (1867–1935), a charismatic leader whose Polish Legions had fought as an independent formation under Austro-Hungary against Russia in World War I.

The formerly German part of Poland in the west that had now been returned to Poland was reasonably well developed and had also been considerably Germanized, whereas the former Russian parts in the east were predominantly agrarian and economically backward, a reality leaving a stamp on Polish society lasting until the present day, where the east of the country is much more rural and religiously and politically conservative than the west. In the country as a whole, under the partitions five different monetary systems had been in effect, along with three mutually incompatible railway systems, which in any case did not link what had now emerged as Poland's major cities. Challenges in the area of infrastructure were immense. The national road system and the military, banking, automotive, shipbuilding, and aircraft industries had to be constituted practically from scratch. Given the hostile trade policy of Germany specifically targeting Poland at the time, coupled with the international effects of the Great Depression, it was something of a miracle that Poland was able to meld itself into a functioning entity. Of course, almost all of the progress made was nullified following September 1, 1939, when Germany invaded Poland, touching off World War II.

Polish political parties in the fragile parliamentary democracy that was first created under Piłsudski's guidance were hot-headed and represented every imaginable ideational stripe. Poland's first president, Gabriel Narutowicz (1865–1922), was assassinated by a right-wing nationalist extremist within five days of his taking office. Tired of disfunction in the Polish parliament, in 1926 Piłsudski staged a coup that placed his own men, many of them officers who had served under him in the Legions, in important positions of power. Both before Piłsudski's death from liver cancer in 1935, but especially after it, the "government of colonels" installed by him took a decidedly fascist turn, including the introduction of laws restricting the access of Jews and other minorities to education and state employment.

During the interwar period Polish universities in Kraków, Warsaw, Lwów, and Wilno came to life and attained international reputations in many scientific, technological, and other academic fields, including worldwide distinction in mathematics, logic, and philosophy. As early as 1932 Polish mathematitions-turned-cryptologists, through their deciphering of military intelligence sent over the Germans' supposedly unbreakable Enigma Code, probably shortened, and may have even altered the outcome of, World War II, when the information was passed on to the Brtish. The writings and conceptions of live-in field research of Bronisław Malinowski (1884–1942) for all intents and purposes established anthropology and ethnology as modern scientific disciplines.

Unlike in politics, Polish cultural life in the interwar period blossomed explosively, with Warsaw and Kraków being the main hubs of activity. The movies were gathering steam, and colorful cabaret and provocative theatrical performances enlivened the nightlife. In literature, prose fiction practically played second fiddle to poetry and drama, in which enduring works of striking originality were created. As for the major writers of short-story fiction, Maria Dąbrowska, Jarosław Iwaszkiewicz, Bruno Schulz, and Witold Gombrowicz stand out as having withstood the test of time, and all are represented in the present collection. Aside from Schulz, whose literary output was comparatively small and during his life unknown outside Poland, each of the others made the shortlist for the Nobel Prize in Literature on numerous occasions.

# Maria Dąbrowska

Maria Dąbrowska (1889–1965), née Szumska, was born in Russów near Kalisz, in west-central Poland, under Tsarist Russian control. Her parents belonged to the impoverished landed gentry. She studied sociology, philosophy, and natural sciences in Lausanne and Brussels, but settled in Warsaw in 1917 and became interested in both literature and politics of a socialist leaning. In the interwar period, Dąbrowska worked for a while in the Polish Ministry of Agriculture while venturing more and more into jounalism and social activism. During the occupation of Poland in World War II she remained in Warsaw and supported the cultural life of the Polish underground resistance. She was nominated for the Nobel Prize in literature on five separate occasions. Her best-known work was the historical novel *Noce i dnie* (Nights and Days), written in 1932–34 and turned into a popular Oscar-nominated film in 1974. The novel deals with the turbulent life in the Kalisz region following the unsuccessful 1863 "January Uprising" through World War I. In "People's Poland," Dąbrowska was an establishment figure with liberal leanings, especially regarding inclusivity for gender minorities.

The eminent poet and literary critic Czesław Miłosz once characterized Dąbrowska as striking him as being virtually sexless. Dąbrowska kept a diary for more than fifty years. Published in 2009, forty years after her death, and after Miłosz's, it reveals her to have cultivated in her earlier days a quite adventurous personal lifestyle, in contrast to the staid persona she projected later on under the communist regime. In this light one is tempted to speculate on how much autobiographical detail is reflected in the depiction of Veronica's character in the story to follow.

## Father Philip

And so Philip Yaruga became a priest.

In the beginning, before he went to seminary, he was not sure whether or not he wanted to be a priest, , but he placed his trust in his parents, who concluded that this was, all in all, the best thing to do. They owned a menswear store in a small town, and they had dreams of advancing their lot or, if not theirs, then at least their son's. And they reckoned that there was no better way of doing this than through the priesthood.

"No one cares where a priest's from," their friends all said. "With him, it's a holy calling."

And that's the way things were in actuality. People on the outskirts of town knew that the diocesan bishop as a young boy had tended geese in the next village for his father, a destitute farmer, but who remembered that now? Didn't all the gentlemen now kiss his hand, and was there any lack of plenty at his residence? Everyone treated him like a lord; his parents were no longer mere farmers, but the progenitors of a bishop.

Philip had to admit that's how things were, and he couldn't deny either that he yearned for that kind of life. Not so much for a bishopric, of course; an ordinary parish seemed to offer both him and his parents a perfectly decent future. Self-sufficiency, the respect of one's fellows, and the work was not too hard. By taking this path, all of these things, for which every person yearns, seemed to be so easily attainable without any offense to God. On the contrary, this path came with all the spiritual benefits which accrue to one who follows the priestly life and consorts on a daily basis with God the Everlasting.

Still Philip hesitated because, while he wanted to become a priest, he felt no special priestly calling. He feared he was not able to excite in himself that special elevation of spirit, so necessary for fulfilling one's priestly duties, nor to maintain the necessary bodily purity which is a part of every priest's vows.

"None of the vows," they tried to tell him, "is truly vital. Just like you can't stop eating, you can't crawl out of your skin either, whether a man's or a woman's. If the good Lord Jesus himself clothed you in such a skin, with all its needs, he can't just expect you to ignore it. You are enjoined only not to cause scandal. And as for your calling," they further explained to him, "it too will come in time. Each and every thing requires a personal commitment, and how is one to know whether or not there's a calling if one doesn't first make the effort?"

Philip listened and was inclined to believe what he was told. Being an only child, he was possibly more in tune with his parents' hearts and desires than other boys his age.

To be sure, not only Philip but his parents themselves had reservations. His mother regretted that she would never see any grandchildren. And although she secretly comforted herself with the thought that there were priests in the world whose mothers had babies to nurse and rock in their old age, she also knew that such wicked thoughts and false comforts must be banished from her mind. Besides, other opportunities presented themselves. Philip was a good-looking boy, and he could no doubt make a good and profitable marriage. He was not stupid, and chances were he could expect to find work in an office and, with time, to aspire to some more important position. However, none of these ideas had as much going for it as the priesthood. No other profession offered so quickly and easily that special combination of earthly and heavenly benefit his pious mother valued so highly; none other looked after the son's welfare so well as the one which limited his rights to have a family. And so, when the appropriate time came, all doubts evaporated, and Philip enrolled in the seminary.

After his departure his parents were barely able to contain themselves from grief. Philip too was homesick; his new life seemed intolerable. However, after a while, his parents took in an orphan niece whose mother had died of tuberculosis, and their life took on a more lively hue. Philip, too, made friends among his fellow students. All the while he nurtured the hope that the time would soon come when neither he nor his parents would need to seek comfort in others, but would be rejoined and live happily together in the parish which would someday be his.

Somehow he was ordained, became a vicar, and, in the end, was offered a parish in the hinterlands, but by no means in as bad a locale as might have been expected. However, before he made it to that parish, his parents both died, one right after the other.

Philip Yaruga became deeply depressed. For as long as his parents were alive and well, their hopes and wishes justified his becoming a priest even without conviction. When he saw how happy they were, Philip forgot that, in order to make a living, he had chosen the one profession where living plays second fiddle. Once his parents had departed, the one spiritual support in his chosen profession went with them. Only then did Philip realize he had been more concerned with his parents' welfare and status than with his own, that he himself felt the need for something else. He entered a terrible period of self-doubt, feeling irretrievably lost on a path of life from which there is no escape. Although he could tell himself that maybe it was better to sunder the bonds and escape back into the world than to live in hypocrisy, pretending to a fervency he didn't have, in his heart he knew it was too late: these bonds would remain. After all, he had been annointed in the name of the Father, in the firm conviction that he would walk to the end of his days in the ranks of those he had joined of their own free will, in full possession of mind and body. To escape now seemed to him a most egregious sin, bordering on treachery. It had even occurred to him that perhaps, in becoming a priest, he had betrayed some divine intention that had predestined him for some other walk of life. In whatever direction he twisted and turned his poor demented mind, he kept coming to the same conclusion, that by leaving the Church he would just be adding one treachery to another, and mocking God into the bargain.

As for God, as often as Philip decided to close his eyes to all questioning and become a priest, as fate seemingly decreed, he would become the plaything of religious doubt; he would lose his belief in God, and, in that state of mind, the profession of priest would seem to him the height of duplicity and iniquity. However, the moment he thought about casting off his frock and rejoining the world, he was immediately struck by the conviction that God not only exists, but was hounding him personally, and would repay his misdeeds with scourges and retributions. In the end he felt he had no choice but to follow the chosen path. To make matters worse, whereas formerly he had mainly seen what the spiritual life had to offer, now he constantly had in mind the world that was being forever closed to him.

As he rode along the small country road from the tiny station to his new parish, in his despair he wondered whether he should keep going or, instead, get out of the wagon, walk into the fields, and somehow put an end to it all. He kept on going, of course, and, upon arriving, actually examined with a certain curiosity the place where fate had ordained him to launch his lamentable holy profession.

The parish consisted of four villages: Małocin, Pamiętów, Serbinów, and Gawlice. Along the way, the driver pointed them out to him with his whip, betraying the innocent pride of one showing a newcomer one's home and native realm. The church itself was in Małocin. As they drew near to it, Father Philip beheld a dark wooden chapel standing amidst a drift of yellow decaying leaves scattered by a grove of tall chestnut trees. Out of the same drift of leaves loomed the parish house, darkened with age and almost entirely enveloped in branches of ash and sycamore. All of this struck Father Philip as a reasonably pleasant, welcoming abode, to which one arrives in autumn, not in one out of many, but in the autumn of one's years, before the onset of a long and peaceful winter.

With a deep sigh he took possession of the house, in which he was soon joined by an elderly housekeeper, whom he had brought in. Finding himself at the head of a populous parish, and feeling all eyes turned on him, he experienced the same sensation anyone does when embarking on a new job of any sort. He began to be concerned about performing his duties correctly and efficiently, driven by the murky instinct that motivates everyone to do one's work more or less well. Although for the moment there was neither desire for nor belief in the task at hand, desire and belief eventually arise out of the very act of bustling about, followed by a sense of satisfaction or, more exactly, the knowledge that all of this is leading somewhere and doing some good. The bells which the boys in the red capes rang; the white cloth on the altar; the rays of sun glancing off the glass of the sacramental cruets; the strength of his own voice, every murmur of which with each new service grew stronger, clearer, and more resonant than even the base tones of the organ—out of all of these things arose a sense of satisfaction which, for a while, was enough to nourish Father Philip and keep him going. Added to this was the force which rouses every man to action: the support of human praise.

The previous priest, who had died before Philip's arrival, was by then so old, decrepit, and unfit for service, that it was said that Anthony, the church sacristan, virtually ran the services and even put on weddings by himself. How else could one view the matter when, at the last wedding, everyone could plainly see that the vicar just stood there moaning, leaning on his cane, while Anthony placed the stole over the hands of the young couple? The old vicar retained competence in one thing only, in clipping people of their money in exchange for his spiritual services. It's true that around the parish it was rumored that the person primarily responsible for the fleecing was really the housekeeper, who was busy putting aside a nest egg for her old age. Right before the priest's death it got to where she herself was bargaining over the price of weddings, christenings, and funerals, shaking people down mercilessly and shamelessly.

However, whether it was the housekeeper or the parson who was at the root of the graft, it amounted to the same thing, and people were grumbling. When the new parson arrived, and a kindly gray-haired old auntie settled in with him who never poked her nose into anything, and when the fees returned to what they had once been, and people paid according to their ability rather than the priest's need, everyone was pleased. The sacristan, Anthony, although he no longer had the importance he once enjoyed under the old parson, desired to make the best of the new situation. He continually passed on to Philip the blandishments he had overheard. For his part, the new parson encountered many signs of his newly acquired importance in the parish on his own. Often at night, deprived of any other worldly enjoyments, he delighted in recounting them to himself.

One time, for example, on a bleak winter's afternoon, a poor man came to the church. He was a worker from Pamiętów and, through the sacristan, Anthony, he begged the priest for the favor of a confession. At first Philip was reluctant and almost refused to go. Outside the window snow was falling, the wind was whistling, and this was not the time he customarily gave confessions. In the end he did go, of course, and he did not regret it, for the matter was serious and confirmed him in the importance of his mission.

In the dark church, illuminated only by Anthony's lantern, the man's shadowy figure loomed larger than life, doubling and tripling itself on the walls. The man embraced Philip by the legs with such force that he practically lifted him off the ground, big as he was. Having done with that, he begged forgiveness for his boldness, asked for Father Philip's favor, and then, at the confessional, which swayed, creaked, and knocked, casting echoes around the empty church, he set forth the matter which disturbed him so.

He had a wife with whom he lived badly, so badly, in fact, that in the end he had left her, having met a certain girl, Pelasia, and having learned through her a happiness he had never before imagined possible. He had been living with her on trust, but still as man and wife. He even had children with her. However, life is life, and sin's a sin. For some time they had been trying to find a way to dissolve the former marriage and cast off their grievous sin, as people in the city were able to do. When the Holy Mission had recently visited the parish, as the parson remembered, they both took confession and asked for support in their matter before the bishop's diocesan court. However, the fathers from the mission were so outraged that they did not grant them absolution. They lay a very harsh penance on them, commanded that the union with Pelasia be dissolved, and ordered the man to return to his lawful wife. They even threatened the entire village and its inhabitants with punishment for the gross outrage. However, the couple kept putting the thing off, because separation for them would be like having a knife cut their hearts in two.

"But ever since," the miserable man from Pamiętów confessed, "life for both of us has come to an end. And we suffer terribly at the hands of other people. For as long as there was no judgment, they left us alone, but now that the servants of God have issued their decree, everyone badgers us to put our lives in order. So I finally say to myself, fine, I'll go to the vicar, and whatever he says I'll accept as God's judgment. And if I'm told the same as I was by the fathers of the Holy Mission, then I'll do that, but for now I'm confessing that we didn't listen and follow their instructions right away."

All of this the sinner from Pamiętów hoarsely intoned in a weary voice into the priest's ear at such close range that Father Philip's cheek became warm and even moist from the man's breath.

Father Philip buried his face in his hands, and it could not be said, as he listened to the man, that he had his mind already made up. It was not often that his rural parishioners presented him with such a difficult matter to decide. He was sorry for the stubborn, agonized sinner pouring out his soul to him. However, he soon got a grip on himself and, invoking the resoluteness of divine law in matters of this sort, not to mention his Brothers in Christ, the priests from the mission, with whom he had to work in concert, he affirmed their verdict. The man kissed the priest's hands with all his might, as though wanting him to know that he understood and was grateful for the severity meted out to him. A month later he came to announce that he had satisfied the requirements of the penance. Having received absolution, he thanked God and the parson for having lifted from him the yoke of mortal sin.

Other minor day-to-day incidents soon dislodged this occurrence from Philip's mind, but the consciousness of it somehow remained in his heart and, even more than the people's praise, gave him the sense that he was a real priest, able to influence for the better the lives of the souls entrusted to him. All the same, the more he felt in his element during the execution of his duties as a priest, the more he felt drawn to the life of an ordinary human being.

After every church service, after every rite, during which he sensed he was directing the people so that he felt he could lead them wherever he wished—after each, as it were, professional contentment—he felt like enjoying himself, as though he had earned the right to spend his time in the same rewarding way that other mortals do after a hard day's work. He began to appear more often in public, at first only after a christening or a wedding, and at merry family gatherings. Soon, however, he began going on any occasion or even without an occasion, wherever he was asked, and he was asked often enough, for there were many homes in the parish whose owners considered it an honor to host the priest. All the better that the priest was by nature good-looking and fun-loving. It was pleasant to engage him in light banter and to discover under his priestly cloak the inclinations of a healthy young man.

Sometimes, before a social call, when Father Philip had put aside his everyday threadbare cassock to dress up in a different garment, fastened with silk buttons, he was suddenly stayed in midcourse by the thought that, if he really did feel the calling of his mission, he ought to strengthen himself in his conviction by prayer, private meditation, and some kind of intellectual activity more in accord with his profession. He even devised for himself a project: he began to write a work on the Basilica of St. Peter. He spread out piles of blank paper on his desk and ordered all the necessary books.

However, as often as inclinations of this sort took hold of him with sufficient force that he turned down some invitation or other and stayed home to work on this project, he became unaccountably sad. He would waste the evening sunk in gloomy thought, beset by pointless regrets, and the following morning he would go to mass as if to his own beheading. He ended by not allowing himself to give in to such scruples. As soon as the urge struck him, he was off, invited or not. He showed up wherever he knew there would be good food and drink, and where one could laugh and have a game of cards. In this manor house or that, at the estate manager's, or at the schoolmaster's there was always enough time for such things in the evening. For him the pantry was always open, and the wines and homemade drinks flowed ceaselessly.

At first the priest demurred when offered drink; he felt he had a weak head for it.

"No, I can't have any more," he would avow, turning his glass on its end.

"Hey," the gentlemen would call to him, "what kind of priest are you anyway, that can't drink? At Cana Jesus himself turned water into wine. And at supper with the Apostles didn't he drink not water, but pure wine? Well, how about a smoke then?"

No, he didn't want to smoke either.

"Let him be," the bolder among them would say. "It's clear the good man has chosen that other thing, the very best of life's enjoyments."

And if the dinner followed a christening, the ladies would fasten their gaze on his lips, look into his eyes, and say,"

"Well, Father, if you do everything as skillfully as you did that christening today, then bravo for you!"

"Bravo, bravo!" cried the gentlemen, not having heard the beginning. "Here's to the good vicar's health!"

To a toast like that it was impossible not to respond in kind, and he ended by drinking with them and, after a certain while, he was drinking and smoking just like the rest, even better than the rest. He even smiled on the women. Laying his hand on their bare shoulders, he would exclaim, with feigned outrage,

"Go home, woman, and put on some clothes. Cover up those arms, and stop leading us good men into temptation!"

The same ambition drove him to be as good at a party as at fulfilling his churchly obligations, and although, as a result, the Holy Sacraments were every now and then exposed to ridicule, he thought to himself that one can keep the holy holy, but within certain limits, and that human affairs, even when one laughs at them, fall closer to the heart. In any case, what did people think: that his piety was so frail as to be undermined by the least little thing? Let nobody think that!

However, his piety was frail enough, and several things helped to undermine it. As month passed into month, Anthony brought to the sacristy less and less news to warm the heart of the new priest. When leading the mass, or upon entering the pulpit, Father Philip no longer felt the kindly interest and the festive readiness with which the whole congregation had come to clear its throats and sit up straight in the pews at his very sight. For the parish he ceased to be someone new, for whom every person pressed forward just to have a look. Few things about him now aroused their interest. They already knew how he performed the "Dominus vobiscum," how he kneeled, how he joined his hands, how he intoned the songs. They practically came to look on him as nothing more than a component part of the altar, the pulpit, and the confessional.

Father Philip began to lose patience. He fretted over every service; at every confession he waited for something which might justify all this ritual, something which would unambiguously bear witness to the fact that he could lead this flock of Christian souls, that he could hold sway over them, that they could not exist without him. However, the penitents muttered into his ear the same old boring everyday sins according to the same trite formulas. Members of a wedding party would poke one other in the ribs and incite one another to laughter, with no thought as to what was taking place before the altar; and participants in the mass submitted to the service passively, with the very minimum of effort.

The respect of his parishioners could have compensated Philip for many of his profession's worldly deprivations. Lacking this reward and, especially, not sensing that his recognition was continually growing, he began to be thoroughly bored at the altar, and began again to regret having become a priest. His modest requirements for payment for his services also soon became so thoroughly accepted that people began to wonder, given such a young priest with his first parish, whether they should not be even lower. One or another man came to bargain, and Philip, forced to yield in some instances, gave into to the temptation of trying to pass on his losses to others, more generously inclined. In either case he felt vexed. When he made more money, he felt as though he had sinned, and when he didn't make enough, his state of mind ran as follows:

"If I can't even get what I need to live on, then what am I knocking myself out for? What's the point of even trying, especially if I lack the necessary conviction?"

He agonized even more when he stopped going out at night, and the time formerly spent outside the church on official visitations turned into sitting in solitude at his desk where, amidst the piles of blank paper, lay the title page which read *The History of the Basilica of St. Peter's in Rome*. Sitting there, he envied the life of any man who was not a priest, but he still lived in dread of that other life as well. As before, he was attracted by the idea of having a good time, but now without the peace of mind which comes from the satisfaction of a job well done. Being an embittered priest, he became an embittered man as well.

One day he had to attend a retreat, some special large half-church, half-lay convocation. At the canon's ceremonial dinner they served unending streams of meads and well-aged wines. Father Philip livened up at the feast despite himself, and afterwards did not refuse himself access to such things which, until then, he had considered only as a reward and relaxation for a job well done. As it turned out, they could also be taken as consolation for a job done badly. It was not just that he no longer forbade himself such pleasures; he actively sought them out, so that the day came when he performed his duties mainly with the thought of getting them out of the way, so he could go somewhere to drink, laugh, and play cards. At times it happened that he unexpectedly had to visit a sick person, and the sacristan Anthony had to drag the far-gone priest from the estate manager's, the schoolmaster's, or straight from Czubay's, who had a store with an attached saloon. Anthony did this with a certain sad satisfaction. Along the way he would say to anyone he met,

"You might say to yourselves what good's a sacristan, but you'd never get along without one. You'd never manage with a priest all by himself." It was in just such a manner that Anthony one evening dragged the intoxicated priest out of the room next to the saloon, informing him that someone was waiting for him at the parish house.

"The old lady," he said, "instructed me to say that your sister has arrived and is waiting for you."

"What in the world sister is that?" hiccuped the mystified priest, walking unsteadily across the snow.

He entered the presbytery not directly to his room, but roundabout, by way of the kitchen and the old woman's room, with the aim of sobering up by taking the longer route. The old woman, as usual at that time of night, was in bed asleep, but evidently waiting for him, for next to her bed a candle was burning. Father Philip leaned over and nudged the shoulder of the sleeping woman.

"Auntie, auntie, who has come to see me?"

The woman came to and, for moment, looked at him with the foggy, vacant, other-worldly stare of an unexpectedly awakened older person.

"Veronica has arrived."

"What Veronica?"

"Don't you remember? Veronica. The one who was raised in your house when you were away at seminary. She arrived here sobbing. Give her some word of comfort, don't let her cry like that."

Father Philip went to his room, struggling with his increasingly heavier head and limbs, accompanied by a mercilessly painful constriction in his chest. He stood at the threshold of his room, holding on to the door-frame for support. On a tiny chair in the corner between the sofa and the stove sat a slight young woman, dressed in a flimsy hat and thin overcoat, totally unsuited to the winter weather. She was no longer crying, but rocking back and forth rhythmically, as though trying to deaden some intolerable pain.

Father Philip had never had much to do with Veronica, whom his parents had taken in after he had left home. Even when he had come home for the holidays he had seen little of her, because she spent the mornings in church, and, in the afternoons, she attended sewing classes. Still he recognized her, although she had grown up. Even in those days he had beheld her at times bent over and rocking back and forth under the onslaught of painful thoughts, just as now. While recognizing her, he recalled in his confusion that his mother on her deathbed had asked him to look after her. He had done so to the extent that, when liquidating his parents' dilapidated shop, he had paid her the sum of money they had left her, with which she was to set up some kind of millinery establishment with someone. How else was he, a man of the cloth, supposed to look after a girl of the world with whom he felt no special bond? Now, however, as he looked at her, he sensed that he had neglected his trust.

"Good evening," he said in a thick, slightly hoarse voice. She merely raised her head, as though she hadn't the strength to get up. The girl struck him as neither pretty nor nice, but as horribly destitute and in need of help.

"What's this? Good evening, Veronica," he repeated impatiently, afraid to approach for fear of falling on his face.

The girl looked at him for a while and then, as if experiencing a terrible disappointment over the result of her wait, she began to cry again. The sight served to sober Philip up a good deal. He ventured from the wall, drew near to her, and put his hand on her shoulder. He felt the shoulder, which had been shaking in convulsions of sobs, suddenly grow stiff. She had stopped crying, evidently by holding her breath. Father Philip removed his hand, wiped his face with it, drew back, and took a look around. Then he pulled up a chair and sat down at a certain distance at which point Veronica broke out sobbing all over again.

Father Philip regained enough composure to renew his questioning: "Where have you been keeping yourself all this time, Veronica? Why didn't you let me know if things were as bad as all this?"

Interrogated in this manner at a distance, she refused to say anything, and so they remained that way for a while. He sat there expectantly, hoping the alcohol would dissipate, and she sat crying. At last Philip arose and began pacing back and forth, until he found himself standing next to her. This time he did not venture to put out his hand.

"Don't cry, my child ... " he begged her, as quietly as he could, his low voice resounding like a far-off, comforting roll of thunder.

Without looking, fumblingly, blinded evidently by her tears, she now reached out her hands to his and began kissing them fervently. He straightened up abruptly and pulled back, as though this were the first time anyone's lips had ever touched his hand. However, he immediately returned and, embracing her head, pressed it for a brief moment to his chest.

"My hat," she whispered, removing it. A multitude of light-blond hair cascaded over her forehead, and something resembling a plaintive smile played in her damp eyes.

"I'm sorry," she whispered. "I'll explain everything later."

And she asked to be allowed to stay with the old woman, because she had nowhere else to go in the whole wide world. Concerned lest she burst out crying again, Philip asked nothing further and agreed to everything.

At first Veronica assisted the old woman, who was so old she could barely walk, and was very glad of the help. But the old woman died soon after, and Philip asked whether Veronica wouldn't like to stay on and run the house as an adoptive sister. She blushed, and then said reluctantly,

"If Father wishes, I can stay on until someone better can be found."

But no such better person was ever found. Besides, now all the things which had previously concerned Father Philip—indeed, had tormented him—fell from his eyes. He now thought only about Veronica, about her appearance, about her beauty, and not just the beauty she showed to the rest of the world. He continually recalled the way she looked at him, how she wrinkled her brow. Closing his eyes, he could picture her shapely, evocative hands; her brisk, firm walk; and the way she would suddenly stop in midcourse and bow her head bashfully, as though embarrassed by her own vitality. He recalled with tenderness and pity everything she had said and done, as though these had been unusual, unrepeatable occurrences, lost forever, but for which he longed with a constant and insatiable desire. For hours on end he could recreate in his mind that first evening, when she had appeared with her little bundle and sat down in the corner, weak and hunched over, burdened by a fate as yet unknown to him. With deep emotion he relived over and over the time in the courtyard when, purple with the effort, she had managed to restrain a runaway horse all by herself.

Whether he saw her as strong, or as weak and defenseless, he always saw her the way he wanted her to be. With every sign of her existence, even if these signs were inconsistent with one another, he felt himself to be in total accord; everything about her met with his admiring approval. Whatever she did, she was able to awaken in him only his boundless acceptance, over which he had no control. He had been able to resist most opportunities leading to the possibilities of love and its enticements. The male ambition of accumulating trophies did not fall within the sphere of priestly custom. Sparks would fly, but if one waited, they would go out soon enough. In another moment, one could not even recall that they had ever existed. Now, however, he could not resist placing his hand once again on Veronica's shoulder. Having done that, he asked her once more, as he had on that first occasion, why she had cried so. This time she held his hand tightly and pressed it to her shoulder with her face. Breathlessly, as though someone had told her to race ahead, she hurriedly recounted how the man with whom she had fallen in love had thrown her over; that when she trustingly placed all her affairs in his care, he had simply stolen all her savings, earned from her partnership in a hat shop with a certain woman; that she had even had to make up his debts to the woman and then go out into the world, left without a penny. On the verge of taking her own life, she had suddenly hit upon the idea of coming to Małocin, in the hope the kind priest would not turn her away.

The priest felt more than merely kind; at the same time, he felt deeply troubled. He buried his face in his hands, convulsed by a stifled sob. He did not want to respond, but, when she pleaded with him to say at least something, he said that he had no idea she had had such experiences. Whereupon she begged his forgiveness and swore that what she had known then was not true love, that she had cried that night more out of shame than anything else. When he still kept her at arm's length, after a brief but weighty moment of hesitation, as though in despair, kneeling and covering her head in his gloomy garments, she confessed that from the moment she had first seen him that evening, and he had laid his hand on her shoulder, she could see nothing else in the whole world but him, and would do so until the end of time, though Hell itself should open wide its gaping mouth and swallow her. That was how desperately in love with him she was. Pressing her to his breast in rapture, he whispered embarrassedly:

"But I was drunk then."

"No," she contradicted him firmly.

"Yes," he replied, now entirely conscious of what he was saying. "I was drunk then … with you … and I still am."

For a stretch afterwards they lost all consciousness of time, as they repeated fervently and imploringly to each another:

"If only this moment could last forever."

From that moment on the two of them burned with an inextinguishable waxing desire to rock and caress one another without end. Father Philip practically forgot on what planet he was living. He continued to perform his duties in the church as before, but with the utmost vacancy, unable to avoid returning in his thoughts and heart to the previous night spent with Veronica, amazed that such simple unalloyed happiness could keep on growing, multiplying, and transforming itself.

Among his many confessions to Veronica, he told her once,

"I never imagined such happiness could exist here on earth. I simply never imagined," he repeated, and it seemed to him as though all of this had already occurred, that he had either said these things, or they had been spoken to him once before.

Veronica was not only a good lover for the first few nights; she was also a woman for the long run, and especially during the day. She was not one of those women men chase after. However, there existed on earth a species of man who, once they had met her, were predisposed to love her. If none of that sort were in her vicinity, she would wait patiently and humbly until one appeared. Before all other men she was modest and shy, and seemed not even to know what it meant to wander astray. She never beckoned to anyone with so much as a glance or smile but, once having found her man, she turned into a raging furnace, and that's what she was now. Such was her character that if she was not actively in love, she was more inclined to sit and rock back and forth thoughtfully than do anything else. However, if her nights were satisfactory, then her everyday life absorbed her too, body and soul. She found herself in just such a state of contentment, and she spent the entire day bustling and darting about the cottage, putting the entire place in a new and marvelous state of order.

People, however, began to murmur. Formerly, when Father Philip had been so agonized over the idea that he was not worthy to be a priest that he conducted the church service with the utmost distaste, people in the parish had not noticed or, if they had, then only in the murkiest and most indistinct way, causing them on occasion to mutter,

"He's not the same priest he once was."

But when people began to see him drunk and, especially, when he began to drink at Czubay's, even though not in the saloon itself but in the private apartment next to it, but still in a beer hall, this struck people as more than a minor shortcoming. And in the opinion of many the thing with Veronica filled the cup to overflowing. The notion that a priest might live conjugally with his housekeeper was not alien to most people. Such thinking was part of the same general folk wisdom Philip's parents had tried to pass on, that no one could escape his own skin.

Even the children of such alliances managed to escape misfortune. But for a priest to live for his housekeeper alone, neglecting his other duties with no further aim in mind, as rumor had it, than to gaze into her eyes, lie at her feet, and walk about the garden with her hand in hand—for him to let himself become prey to his passion—this was scandalous and beyond the pale. To top it off, it was said that she was some kind of relative or kinswoman.

Mindless of such opinion, the love between Philip and Veronica ceased by stages to be a perpetual feast and became transformed into everyday nourishment. She became for him, as he for her, necessary for life, nothing more and nothing less.

Regaining his senses somewhat after the first frenzy, and having a look around, Philip Yaruga felt more miserable than ever in his priestly garb. Work on a chain gang seemed to him nothing as compared to continuing in a priesthood for which he felt himself unsuited, unable either to win the favor of God nor the respect of his congregation. To make matters worse, his love for Veronica now seemed to him a terrible sin, irreconcilable with his priestly vows.

Embittered, and steeped in sin, as he now viewed it, he began once more to seek consolation in the bottle. As usual in such cases, he returned to drink with renewed fervor. It soon happened that people who had ordered a christening would arrive to find the priest lying down dead drunk. Anthony and Veronica were barely able to revive him and prop him up, while Anthony, virtually leading the priest by the hand, would do the service mostly on his own. Another time it happened that they were ready to bear a coffin out of the church, while the priest was nowhere to be found.

Not only that, but the parson when drunk would make declarations wholly unsuited to a man of the cloth. At a fireman's ball he was overheard to remark that if Jesus Christ were to appear on earth today, he would be immediately carted off to the police station. On another occasion he was heard to complain about the priesthood, saying that Saints preserve us from fire, famine, war, pestilence, and all such idiots and hypocrites as may be found among them. It was worth wondering how he was able to make such statements, himself being one of the worst of the lot. Once he even ventured to abuse the bishops, saying that who do they think they are, they with their two-pointed hats?

At last it came to where one day he had to be dragged away for mass at daybreak from a manor house where he had spent the night drinking and carousing. People on their way to work saw Veronica crying as she led the stumbling man along. Where was the shameless hussy taking him, they wondered. To bed, most likely, so he could then get up and lead the morning mass.

By then people could be found willing to write an official complaint to the bishop. To be sure, many people did not want to get involved. Even though they complained about the vicar, they lost their resolve when it came to a formal complaint, saying,

"Well, what do you think, that a priest can't go wrong? He's no worse than any of the rest of us, and no better either."

Aware that they themselves were enmeshed in the same kind of iniquity, even though they might have preferred a different priest, they still preferred not to complain. Others, however, sternly maintained that a priest has to be different from others, better somehow, and more holy. In the end, the complaint was sent.

Before news of this matter, which originated in the village council in Gawlice, came to the ears of the priest, he stood one bright summer morning in the pulpit and read the gospel about the destruction of Jerusalem. The lesson he laboriously drew from the reading was that one must keep holy places holy, which meant the church, and that within these walls, behind these doors, however frail, though made of wood, one must not converse or behave indecently, jostle, shout, or laugh.

"And if," he proclaimed, you stand at attention before a state official, a governor, or a village headman, then all the more should you do so in church, before the Lord your God."

"Before God!" he repeated, trying to lend his voice a lofty and thunderous tone.

His voice did not fail him, and resounded mightily, and Philip projected it with the utmost delectation, but the words which fell from his lips seemed not to have any effect on his listeners. People were first of all tired from harvest work and then wrung out by a Saturday night of revelry. The listless singing of the choir, the plodding sounds of the organ, the smoke of the incense, the strident, ear-tickling clangor of the acolytes' bells, the great booming voice of the priest, and the sun cutting the inside of the church into golden ribbons: all of this put the congregation in a state of blissful, indolent torpor.

The flames of the candles flickered from the breath of the barely-awake men holding them in front of themselves. Some of the women knelt deeply bent to the ground, with their heads practically touching the floor, in positions that could be interpreted as either submissive or ill-mannered. Others were fast asleep, no longer properly kneeling but sitting on their haunches, leaning their heads against the walls of the side-altar. One mother had placed her two-year-old son on one of the altar steps and had given him a rosary to play with, which the youngster was busily trying to wrap around his fat bare legs. A little girl was amusing herself by raising her dress up over her chin and patting herself on the stomach.

Father Philip saw all this first from the pulpit, and then later, while turning from the altar to the congregation. As he beheld it, as once of old he was overtaken by anger that these people seemed to take such little part in the Holy Sacrament being offered them.

"They might as well be made of wood," he thought, passing from one side of the altar to the other.

Then, as he presented his fingers to the altar boy for washing, he directed his rage back on himself.

By the "Agnus Dei" he had regained his composure and mechanically walked through the rest of the prayers, numbed by the same vulgar bleating of the chorus into practically the same state of devotional stupor as his heavily dressed, overheated parishioners. When he turned to the people and proclaimed "Ite, missa est" and, having intoned the final chant, which slowly died out, everyone obediently began to file out, the question suddenly arose in his mind: what is it that he really wants from them and from himself? Aren't they the ones, this same throng and multitude swarming about the church who have created these songs and these words which go to make up the ritual, the customs, and this whole religiosity, and aren't they the ones who perpetuate it? And is it not his function merely to be the instrument by means of which they fall into this blissful somnolent trance which is for them a combined state of thankfulness, supplication, and union with God? He no longer cared to carry his parishioners away with him, to control them, or to govern them.

"What kind of priest am I anyway, who has no control over the people of his own congregation? What business do I have being here in the first place?"

Pausing for a moment next to the fence surrounding the cemetery, he looked mournfully at the people walking in twos and threes down the side of the church hillock. They left without giving any further sign of interest in him, leaving him alone and forgotten amidst his aimless anguish. He longed for some kind of help which could rid him of it forever; he sensed that such help was somewhere near; he could practically feel its presence slipping between his fingers, worming its way into his heart like a weasel.

Before he had finished his dinner that day, a farmer from Pamiętów arrived to take him to a dying woman. As he was returning home later around four o'clock, the priest dozed off in the cart. It was hot, the road led through drifts of sand, and the horses were slowly putting one step in front of the other. He was suddenly wrenched from his slumbers by the sharp cry of the driver.

"Whoa! Hey, you! Off the road!"

In the middle of the road Philip beheld a threadbare unkempt woman, who was shouting something in return as she backed away from the horses.

"What's happened? Who is that?" Philip asked, unpleasantly affected by the incident.

"Oh, that's the Flos woman who lost her mind a year or so ago. When she leaps out at you on the road, there's no getting past her."

The woman was still gesticulating at them with her fist.

"You can't get past," she shouted vengefully. "Just look at you! You've lost your mind yourself!"

She approached the priest and began to spread out her boundlessly ample skirt.

"Hey! Take a look at this, Father! The dogs in Gawlice tore my dress to shreds, so now I can't show myself at home."

Soon the horses snorted and started again along their way. The priest looked back, simultaneously searching for some loose change. Beholding the woman sticking out her tongue at him, he lost interest; they were too far away by now anyway.

Later, taking off his cassock in the sacristy and putting away the tin box with the communion supplies, Philip asked the sacristan,

"Who is that Flos woman from Pamiętow who's wandering about? What sort of mad-woman is she?

Anthony turned upon the parson his dull yellow head with an elongated clean-shaven chin so large there seemed to be room enough there for a second face.

"The truth is," he began cautiously, as though trying out the waters, "that that Flos woman went over the brink only recently, but she was always strange, strange and at odds with her husband. She finally went crazy for good after he beat her up so badly one day that she lay unconscious for a good hour or more. It must have knocked something loose in her head.

The priest vaguely recalled how he had once heard of such an incident in one of the houses he had visited. As he did, he felt a tingling sensation burning across his face.

"He had already given up on that woman a long time ago," Anthony continued, folding up the surplice and casting a watchful yellow eye in the direction of the priest.

"He was even living for a while with another woman, Pelasia, and, one could say, they got on well enough. They lived together and he even had children by her."

The story suddenly struck the priest as uncannily similar to something he already knew. In a flash he beheld in front of his eyes with the utmost clarity that late winter afternoon and the man whose shadow had loomed across the walls of the church. Now the unpleasant tingling sensation passed across his entire body. His legs grew weak beneath him, as he replied with a bluff smile, like someone pinned against a wall, wanting to escape:

"Oh, yes, now I remember. He came here once to make a confession."

"Yes, that's the one," Anthony took him up, "and ever since then the wrath of God has been upon them. They got turned down by the Holy Mission, but that wasn't good enough. They didn't want to follow the divine decree, but after he heard what you had to say they finally had to listen. But it seems, if Father will permit me to say so, that you gave that Flos man an inadequate penance, for the finger of God came back to touch him and, although he later returned to righteousness, he now has neither wife nor woman."

"And what happened to the Pawlisia woman?" Philip asked, rather too loudly, feigning indifference.

"You mean Pelasia," Anthony corrected him. "Pelasia, even though she had gone wrong, with your Reverend's pardon, she was still a good girl, and God-fearing. It was she who persuaded Flos to go to confession. 'Go,' she said. 'The Lord God is merciful. Maybe he will forgive us. Maybe he will permit us this happiness.' She was that stupid. So then, as you know, he went to the priests from the mission. And when he returned he could only beat his head against the wall. He wanted to take his life and hers together, but she was so intent on finding some kind of solution for everything that she tried to bring him around. People who know tell how she begged him: 'Don't do that. Do what the Holy Fathers instruct you to do.' She thought that if they did that, God would think of some kind of reward for them. 'Maybe,' she suggested, 'that wife of yours will die.' And later, when Flos returned to his wife, Pelasia left her children with friends, and she hired herself out for seasonal work—not too far, just to Gawlice. But when the children each of them died, they say she rent her garments and, in the depths of despair, when they were hiring field workers for France, she went with them. That'll be about three months ago. And so everyone came out the worse."

"She did the right thing by going," Philip said. Without saying a further word to Anthony, he left the sacristy.

Outside it was still hot. He felt dizzy several times along the way. He was glad to take a rest. He glanced at his four rooms, visible all in a row, sparkling and clean, Veronica's work. They smelled of herbs and wax.

"Veronica!" he called out. But he was answered only by a dim echo and then silence. Right, he remembered. Veronica was gone berry-picking for the entire afternoon.

He sat down in a high-backed cane chair and hung his head on his breast, overcome by an irresistible urge to sleep. And he must have done so, for he began to see a little room in the home of his parents. Everything was arranged as it had been then: the beds, the table, the chairs; except that there were no windows in the walls.

"Why did you brick over the walls?" he asked his parents. "Why did you cover the walls?" he kept asking, almost in tears. His parents seemed to want to answer, but said nothing. And though they seemed to be present, the room itself was empty. Philip awoke from the dream permeated by an unspeakable sadness. He said aloud:

"I don't know what I'm supposed to do … I don't know," he repeated emphatically, "what I'm supposed to do."

Then, tracing his finger over the outline of the sunbeam across his desk, he said, "I have driven children into the grave."

Then he whispered the word: "Satan" and, suddenly, as if swaggering mockingly before the Evil of Evils, he repeated:

"I have done even more: I have driven children into the grave."

He could not get over his amazement, nor encompass with his mind, that he had done so much harm to the people from Pamiętów. How often he had agonized over his lack of calling, his lukewarm sense of mission, his manifold sins of omission, yet the greatest misfortune had been caused not then, but rather when it seemed to him that he best understood the benign severity of God's law, and had merely meted out justice accordingly.

He snatched at any justification, as a drowning man clutches a straw. He tried to tell himself that no matter what he might have done he still would not have been able to rescue those people from their plight, that they would have destroyed themselves anyway, even without his assistance, and that the application of the law here merely laid bare an incurable rot. Given the circumstances, it is unknown whether it might have been possible to avoid one or another misfortune. His entire defense crumbled, however, in the face of the cruel certainty that it did not matter whether one thing or another could have been avoided, but rather that he had not even made the attempt, had not taken a single step to see whether he might have saved these three people from their misfortune, might have succored them in their need. He had not even thought about it as he administered the confession to that man Flos in the dark church that afternoon. There it was, always and everywhere: he had not even had it in mind; it was he, he alone who was at the constant center of his heart and mind.

As he continued to sit motionless, without support, lost beyond redemption, he suddenly felt within himself a burgeoning joy. It was as if the evil he had unwittingly done to the Flos family had drained all further evil from his life. Never before had he felt so ready to undertake life all over again as at this moment. He no longer even worried about whether he was to remain a priest or not. But of course, now he could be a priest, now more than ever. This realization, growing in him by the moment, cried out for some release, for some kind of public manifestation.

"Today is Sunday. It's already too late for the sermon," he thought. "Oh Lord, why didn't this come to me yesterday?"

Feverishly he sifted through the papers on his desk. He tore up the sheet on which he had begun *The History of the Basilica of St. Peter's in Rome*. He took a clean sheet of paper and hurriedly began to scribble notes on it for his next sermon—his first true sermon.

"And if it seems to you," he wrote, "that you have chosen the wrong profession, that you will not be able to meet the requirements of the commitment, remember that on this earth there is but one true profession, one true calling, and that is to be kind to one's fellow man."

He scratched this out and began again.

"To count one's sins—that is not life but putrefaction. There is but one life and one true calling—to be a help to others. The world marches forward, not by fulfilling the law, but by good deeds … "

It seemed to him that this would be too difficult for most people to grasp; in fact, he didn't understand it very well himself. Again he crossed it out and started over.

"No matter what you become: a priest, an office worker, a farmer, if you do not first love your fellow man, you will never accomplish anything, and you will never enter the Kingdom of Heaven. For there is in life only one true calling, one sure road to salvation … ," he wrote more and more freely.

Soon he set aside his pen. His head was cloudy, and he didn't know what else to write. He wanted to rest or at least to take a break. He stood next to the window and set it ajar with a hand no longer his own. He actually examined it in wonderment, as if questioning whose hand it was. He became terrified at the unparalleled disorder into which, it seemed to him, everything around him was collapsing. A sharp pain shot through his body; he couldn't tell what it was. In his breast something was knocking and jerking around like an animal gone wild. At the same time he was enveloped by an unbearable sadness. He tried to persuade himself that it was nothing, that he was on the threshold of an unlimited happiness, of a new life, on which he was set to embark. He felt the need to lie down for a while, but he never made it to the bed.

He was found lying on the floor with his face to the ground. An attempt was made to resuscitate him, but he never regained consciousness. It was Anthony the sacristan who found him. He had brought the letter from the bishop's Curia, summoning Father Philip to appear before it and to answer the complaints brought against him by his parishioners.

After a short while the presbytery was swarming with people. Veronica arrived from the forest and, beholding the crowd before the porch, she dropped her basket of blueberries. Stepping through the streams of blue-black spilled fruit, she pressed forward among the unwelcoming silence of the throng to the center, letting out a piercing yell: "What's happened? What's happened?"

When they pulled her off the corpse, she stumbled into the kitchen, picked up a knife, and tried to stab herself with it. Subdued, she broke out wailing,

"They've killed him! They've killed him, the bastards!"

Then, in final despair, she cried,

"Why, why, why wasn't I here with him?"

At last she grew hoarse and fell into a faint, and the scandalized people took her outside to revive her.

"It wasn't enough that he had to die in sin," they commented, "but Veronica has to go and offend God into the bargain."

In the meantime, just before sunset the skies grew dark and a storm began to gather. The crops which before noon had sparkled yellow-golden, now paled, grew hazy, and shimmered in the wind. From over the horizon rose large, dark-blue and charcoal clouds, which soon lightened and covered the entire sky with a uniform grayness, casting the world into a premature dusk. Lightning began to flash, and soon afterward there rumbled a hoarse and heavy peal of thunder. The next moment a lightning bolt struck with a deafening roar. People began to disperse to their houses. Reports were made where needed. Two farmers from the choir waited until the women came to wash and dress the vicar. As the storm began to abate, the men approached the window still chattering with rain. Standing there for a while, they observed through the trees, bent over in the wind, a far-off glow, like a burst of steaming dark-red blood.

"There's a fire," they both muttered simultaneously, gripped by terror in the face of this nearby disaster, coupled with the priest's death. For a moment they said nothing, looking fearfully at Father Philip's face, which leapt out at them from the darkness with every flash of lightning. Returning to the window, they began to speak under their breath.

"That fire is in Gawlice," whispered one of them. It must have hit a building."

—1929. Translated by Oscar Swan

*Structural Analysis.* Development: Philip Jaruga, the only son of a small-town haberdasher and his wife, goes into the priesthood to suit his self-interested parents, without any special religious calling on his part. Soon after his ordination, his parents both die, leaving him without any spiritual support in this endeavor. Despite misgivings, he accepts a position in a remote parish consisting of four villages. Soon Philip becomes enmeshed in the everyday routine of his job, and finds that he is capable of doing a creditable job, especially in comparison to the former priest, who was both senile and corrupt.

Interjected Ticking Time Bomb (something whose significance is not apparent until later, when it explodes): Philip takes particular pride in counseling a couple living a happy common-law marriage to separate and for the man to go back to his lawful wife.

Little by little Philip becomes drawn into the social whirl of the local villages, in whose homes he is a welcome guest. He learns to drink, smoke, play cards, and even flirt a bit with the womenfolk. As his job becomes increasingly routine, Philip becomes fonder of drink, and relies increasingly on the help of his sacristan in performing his duties at weddings, burials, and christenings. In his increasingly rarer sober moments, Philip is beset by religious doubts, misgivings as to his life choice, and resentment toward his congregation, whose wooden attitude on matters of faith demoralizes him.

Turning Point leading to the Complication: One night a young woman appears on his doorstep: Veronica, a distant relative his parents had raised in their home while Philip was away at seminary. She has been duped of her money by a false lover and cast out into the world. Philip takes her in out of pity. Soon his housekeeper dies, and Veronica takes over in her stead. Veronica and Philip slowly but surely fall madly in love. He continues to perform his duties, but purely mechanically, as he becomes totally wrapped up in his relationship with Veronica, who herself blooms under the influence of his love. At the same time, Philip returns to his drinking habit with renewed fervor. People begin to gossip, until finally a group of parishioners write a petition to the bishop to intervene in a situation that has plainly gotten out of hand.

Crisis Point (the Ticking Time Bomb explodes): One day as Philip is on his way to attend a dying woman in a distant village, his cart encounters a madwoman along the road. Later that night, the sacristan informs him that this was the wife of Flos, the man he had once counseled to give up his common-law wife and return to his lawfully wedded one. The man had beaten his wife senseless, while his common-law wife, now destitute, had first gone to live with relatives, and then left the country altogether. Both of their children had died. Now is possibly the only time in his life when Philip has been forced to face head on the underlying falsity and hypocrisy of his past actions. Realizing that he has brought about misery and death while deceiving himself into thinking he was doing the right thing, Philip experiences a crisis of belief in his self-worth.

Climax: After a dream-laced sleep in which his parents appear, Philip awakes to find himself filled with a previously unexperienced sense of Christian mission. He begins to compose a new sermon on love for one's fellow man. Just as soon as his writing gets into stride, he is stricken by a heart attack and dies on the spot.

Aftermath: Veronica returns to find the presbytery filled with hostile villagers. Anthony arrives, bringing a letter of summons from the Curia, investigating the mismanagement of Philip's office. Two men keep vigil over Father Philip's body as a storm rages. Lightning strikes a building in a neighboring village, and it goes up in flames. One can only imagine what happens to Veronica, now without any support and shunned by the people in the village.

The narrative perspective is third-person personal internal. The reader sees the action not so much through the eyes but, mainly, the mind of the main character, Philip. Indeed, most of the narrative describes what people think as opposed to what they see or look like. Along with a dearth of external, physical descriptions goes a lack of overt symbolism, underscoring a lack of moral guideposts in the visible world.

The course of action in the story is prompted by a sequence of points at which a dubious decision is made by Philip, beginning with his choice to join the priesthood in the first place. A string of weak, self-interested decisions and rationalizations leads him from being a creditable priest to an untenable situation, that of a drunken, incompetent priest living conjugally with his housekeeper, his own relative. Even at the end Philip deludes himself into thinking he can recover from all this and still be a priest.

*Ironies.* Irony is a mean kind of humor built on a discrepancy between what a person's thoughts, intentions and actions are and what reality actually looks like to others. Often, that reality is the opposite of what was believed by the person to be the case or intended to be the outcome, in such a way as to make the person into an object of derision. More often than not, the person himself remains self-delusionally unaware of the ironical discrepancy, or is somehow able to rationalize it or otherwise be immune to it.

"Father Philip" is built on a dense network of ironies inherent to the priest's life decisions. Here are some of them:

- Philip studies for the priesthood not out of religious conviction but to please his parents, who then die before they can experience any satisfaction or sense of reward.
- In Philip one sees a priest with no priestly calling; further, a priest whose chosen career consists in shutting himself away from earthly pleasures when he is constitutionally best suited to the pursuit of pleasure.
- A priest is supposed to be able to make hard decisions, but Philip always makes the easy ones, even if he self-delusionally thinks they are the hard ones.
- Philip pursues a religious path of life, in which God plays no evident part for him. At no time is he shown actually praying, reading the Bible, or asking for divine guidance.
- Philip expects disaster in his new job, but actually fits into it relatively comfortably, satisfying his parishioners' rather limited expectations. He can do a good job as a priest without having any religious conviction, just by going through the motions.

- For all of Philip's theological training, as time goes by it is mainly his untrained sacristan, Anthony, who does the priest's duties, and he does them rather well.
- Philip's main pleasure in his job stems from pride, not from a job well done in a spiritual sense, but as judged superficially, by his priestly garb, his booming voice, the religious ritual of which he is the center, his social acceptance at the better homes in the neighborhood.
- Philip accuses his parishioners of a lack of religious fervor, when he himself is the least fervent of them all.
- His parishioners' crude remarks that ("he has chosen that other thing, the very best of life's enjoyments," i.e., sex) turn out to be prophetic. Philip's indignant remark, "let them not think that I am as weak as all that," is undermined by what happens subsequently: he is precisely that weak.
- The more Philip grows into his job, the more he yearns for the worldly life.
- Philip's contemplated treatise on the Basilica at St. Peter's in Rome is remote from his life, his parishioner's lives, and the needs of his congregants. In any case, he draws a blank whenever he sits down to work on it.
- His greatest would-be triumph in spiritual healing actually ruins the lives of half a dozen people.
- The only people in the entire story with any genuine sense of religion are the two adulterers branded as sinners by the church: Flos and Pelasia.
- The only male-female relationships depicted as having true value (Flos and Pelasia, Philip and Veronica) are not consecrated by the church but are rather specifically condemned by it.
- Philip condemns Flos and Pelasia for exactly the same behavior in which he himself is later to engage.
- Philip was enjoined by his parents to take care of Veronica, but he forgot completely about her until, later, when he "cares for her" in a completely different way than was meant by them.
- Philip writes at the end about loving one's fellow man, overlooking the fact that the main thing in his life was his love not for his "fellow man" but for a specific person of the opposite sex. Even at the end he is not able to draw logical conclusions from his own life experiences.
- Philip undergoes his religious epiphany just moments before his death, so he is unable to act on it. Even if he had been able to, one senses it would have led to nothing more than having to face the Curia council.
- It is ironic that his religious epiphany turns out to be basic Christian teaching, as if he had not realized that earlier or learned it in seminary.
- Even the lightning at the end of the story, a traditional symbol of divine retribution, is ironic. If one were waiting for a sign of God's judgment, this is a strange one, for it strikes someone else's building, in some other village, a village notable for not being specifically involved in "sin," but rather for originating the letter of complaint to the Curia council.

An underlying irony of Philip's life story is that the main thing in his life that had meaning for him, his relationship with Veronica, would never have been possible had he not made all of the other bad choices leading up to it. The seemingly plain-faced Veronica might not have even caught his eye were it not for his preceding period of forced celibacy.

*The Seven Deadly Sins.* "Father Philip" can be treated as a practical illustration of the Seven Deadly Sins, recognized by the Catholic Church since medieval times: pride, greed, lust, envy, gluttony, wrath, and sloth. Each of these sins can be viewed as resulting from taking a normal human drive or proclivity to an unhealthy extreme. For example, Greed can be seen as Thrift taken to excess; Gluttony is Hunger taken too far; and so on. While pursuing a supposedly religious career, during the course of the story Philip commits every one of these sins, one of the story's most biting set of ironies. For Dąbrowska, who herself was not a religious person, these are still sins, not against God but against one's human dignity.

*"Father Philip" as a "tragedy."* "Father Philip" has the earmarks of a tragic plot, the usual components of which are the following: (a) a sequence of events leads to the ruin and destruction of a central character; (b) the tragic conclusion is inevitable and visible from a long way off; (c) the plot does not depend heavily on suspense but on one's waiting for the slow unfolding of the inevitable tragic outcome; (d) the tragedy is the result of a *tragic flaw* of the protagonist, usually brought to a head by a single excessively *outrageous act;* (e) the reader or viewer watches with fascinated horror and experiences an emotional release (technically called *catharsis*) from observing the inevitable outcome unfold. Because of their relative lack of suspense, tragedies have longevity in literature. They can be read, watched, and vicariously relived over and over.

*Dąbrowska's Brand of Secular Humanism.* That Maria Dąbrowska is demonstrably not religious shows through clearly in this story. Perhaps more aptly, her religion is close to that of Secular Humanism, according to which moral values exist but are seen to flow out of aspects of being human, possessing a "better self," and out of a general recognition of and yielding to one's normal human needs and impulses, just not to excess, taking advantage of the strengths, and recognizing the weaknesses, with which one is born. One probably cannot have everything in life one would like, but one can reasonably hope for a more-or-less satisfying life. One just has to make the sensible choices along the way.

Unlike official Secular Humanism, Dąbrowska does not take a strong stand on the position of the existence or nonexistence of God, or of objective sin, or of the wisdom of celibacy, or of any other religious issue, but seems to be more of an agnostic. The answers to religious questions from her point of view cannot be sensibly posed, so they cannot be sensibly answered. It is worth noting that in the end Dąbrowska requested and received a Roman Catholic burial.

# Bruno Schulz

Bruno Schulz (1892–1942) was a Polish writer of Jewish descent, and also a surrealist artist, literary critic, and high-school teacher of drawing and draftsmanship. Despite his modest literary output, he is regarded as one of the great Polish prose stylists of the twentieth century, with a firmly established European reputation as well. In 1938 he was awarded the Polish Academy of Literature's prestigious Golden Laurel award. Several of his works were lost in the war, including his unpublished novel *The Messiah.* Lost stories are still occasionally unearthed, as also recently were his fairy-tale murals painted for a German SS officer—a sponsor posing as an art connoisseur—who helped Schulz momentarily stay alive during the Holocaust. Almost all that remains of Schulz's work today are two thin books of interconnected short stories, *Sklepy cynamonowe* (Cinnamon Stores) and *Sanitorium pod klepsydrą* (Sanitorium under the Sign of the Hourglass). Told in the first person from the perspective of an adult narrator who simultaneously looks out at the world through the eyes of an impressionable child, the stories take place in Schulz's dusty provincial hometown of Drohobycz, now in Ukraine. In them, through his spinning of metaphor upon metaphor, reality becomes constantly shaped and reshaped through the distorting lens of the narrator-as-child's hyperactive imagination. Adults in these stories seem practically like actors in the Old Testament or in an ancient Greek drama.

Even though he was not a practicing Jew, Schulz was herded along with other Jews into the Drohobycz ghetto. He was shot and killed in 1942 during the massacre of Jews in the town, by a German Gestapo officer while Schulz was walking toward the ghetto carrying a ration of bread.

## Nimrod

Throughout August of that year I played with a splendid little puppy who had turned up one day on our kitchen floor, feeble and whimpering, still smelling of milk and infancy, with an unformed, roundish, trembling little face, its mole-like paws sprawled along its sides, and with the most delicate, downy fur.

At first sight, that little speck of life captured all the rapture, all the enthusiasm of my boy's soul.

From what heaven did this favorite of the gods, dearer to the heart than the most beautiful of toys, drop down so unexpectedly? And just to imagine that that old, utterly uninteresting washerwomen at times can hit upon such splendid ideas and bring from the outskirts of town such a puppy—at an utterly early, transcendentally early, morning hour—to our kitchen!

Ah! one was still, alas, not there, not yet delivered from the warm bosom of sleep, but already that happiness had come into being, already it was waiting for us, lying awkwardly on the cool kitchen floor, unappreciated by Adela and the members of the household. Why wasn't I awakened earlier? A saucer of milk on the floor bore witness to Adela's maternal impulses and also bore witness, alas, to the moments in a past that was lost to me forever, to the delights of foster motherhood in which I had played no part.

But an entire future still lay before me. What an infinity of experiences, experiments, discoveries was opening now! The secret of life, its most essential mystery, reduced to this most simple, most convenient and entertaining form, was exposed here to insatiable curiosity. It was inexpressibly interesting to have for one's own such a tiny bit of life, such a particle of the eternal mystery in such an amusing, new form, awakening endless curiosity and secret respect by dint of its otherness, its unexpected transposition of that very thread of life that is in us, too, into a form that is different from ours, an animal form.

Animals! the target of insatiable curiosity, exemplifications of the enigma of life, as if created to demonstrate man to man, dividing his richness and complexity into a thousand kaleidoscopic possibilities, each one pursued to a paradoxical extreme, to an exuberance replete with character. Unburdened by that fusion of exotic interests that muddy relations between people, my heart opened wide, full of sympathy for the alien emanations of eternal life, full of that loving collaborative curiosity that is the masked hunger for self-knowledge.

The puppy was velvety, warm, and pulsing with its small, rapid heart. His ears were two soft petals, his eyes light blue and bleary, he had a pink little mouth that you could put your finger into without any danger at all, delicate, innocent little paws with a touching pink little nipple-shaped bump on the back of each front leg just above the paw. He crawled into the bowl of milk with those paws, ravenous and impatient, slurping the drink with his little pink tongue, and then, sated, mournfully lifting his muzzle with a drop of milk on the chin, awkwardly backed away from his bath of milk.

His walk was an ungainly rolling, sideways and at a slant, in an undecided direction along a somewhat tipsy, wavering line. The dominant feature of his mood was a certain indefinite, fundamental sorrow, his orphanhood and helplessness—an inability to fill the emptiness of life with anything between the sensations of his meals. This manifested itself in the aimlessness and inconsistency of his movements, irrational attacks of nostalgia accompanied by pitiful whimpering, and an inability to find a place for himself. Even in the depths of sleep, in which he had to calm his need for support and snuggling by employing himself for that purpose, curled up into a trembling ball, a feeling of isolation and homelessness kept him company. Oh, life—young and fragile life, expelled from the trusted darkness, from the snug warmth of the maternal womb into a great, alien, luminous world, how it shrinks and retreats, how it recoils before the need to accept the project proffered to it—full of aversion and despondency!

But slowly little Nimrod (he had received that proud, martial name) begins to relish life. The exclusive dominance of the image of the maternal origin of all being yields to the charm of multiplicity.

The world begins to lay its traps for him: the unknown and enchanting taste of various foods, the rectangle of morning sunlight on the floor where it is so good to lie down, the movements of his own limbs, his own paws, tail, impishly summoning him to play with himself, the caresses of a human hand under which a certain friskiness is slowly maturing, gaiety opening out his body and giving rise to the need for all kinds of new, intense, risky movements—all this bribes, persuades, and incites him into acceptance, into making peace with the experiment of life.

And one more thing. Nimrod begins to understand that what approaches him here, despite the appearance of novelty, is fundamentally something that already has happened—has happened many times, an infinite number of times. His body recognizes situations, impressions, and objects. Fundamentally, none of this is overly surprising. In the face of each new situation he dives into his memory, into the deep memory of his body, and he searches blindly, feverishly—and it sometimes happens that he discovers in himself the appropriate reaction, already prepared: the wisdom of generations compounded in his plasma, in his nerves. He finds actions, decisions, which he himself had not known were already mature in him, already waiting to leap out.

The scenery of his young life, the kitchen with its fragrant buckets, with dish cloths and their complicated, intriguing aroma, with the slapping of Adela's slippers, with her noisy bustling about, no longer terrifies him. He has grown accustomed to considering it his domain, he feels at home in it and has begun to develop in relation to it a hazy feeling of belonging, of a fatherland.

Except that unexpectedly there descends on him a cataclysm in the form of floor scrubbing, the laws of nature overthrown, splashes of warm lye washing under all the furniture, and the menacing scraping of Adela's scrub brushes.

But the danger passes, the brush, calmed down and motionless, lies quietly in a corner, the drying floor smells sweetly of wet wood. Nimrod, restored to his normal rights and freedom in his own territory, feels a lively desire to grab the old blanket on the floor with his teeth and jerk it to right and left with all his might. This pacification of elements fills him with inexpressible joy.

Suddenly he stands as if rooted to the spot: in front of him, some three puppy steps away, a freak is moving about, a monster sliding along rapidly on little sticks that are its many jumbled legs. Shaken to his core, Nimrod follows with his gaze the oblique path of the glossy insect, tensely following the flat, headless, blind thorax carried along by the unbelievable mobility of its spidery legs.

Something rises inside him, something ripens, swells, something he himself does not yet understand, a kind of anger or terror, but rather pleasant and linked to a shudder of power, self-awareness, aggression.

And suddenly he collapses onto his front paws and projects a voice as yet unknown to him, alien, totally unlike his ordinary whimpering.

He projects it once, and once again, and yet again, in a thin high-pitched voice that keeps going off course.

But in vain does he apostrophize the insect in this new language born of sudden inspiration. In the categories of the cockroach mind there is no room for this tirade, and the insect continues on its oblique circuit toward the corner of the room, amid movements consecrated by an eternal cockroach ritual.

Feelings of hatred, however, do not yet hold permanence and power in the puppy's soul. His newly awakened joy in life transforms every feeling into gaiety. Nimrod keeps on barking, but the meaning of this barking has changed imperceptibly, has become a parody of itself—yearning, fundamentally, to express the inexpressible adequacy of this splendid project of life, full of piquancy, of unexpected little shivers, and of punch lines.

—1934. Translated by Madeline Levine

*Notes on "Nimrod."* The story concerns the experiences of a small boy when he unexpectedly receives the gift of a young puppy from the family's charwoman (cleaning lady), as told by the boy when he is already an adult—automatically giving two points of view, one telescoped inside the other: that of the young boy and that of the adult remembering his experiences as the young boy. The story deals both with the fascination people have with other forms of life, and how all life forms are preordained by their innate genetic makeup, through the process of their maturation, to become the kind of creature they were predestined to become. Both the boy and the puppy start out at about the same stage of life for their species. Both are curious about life but limited in experience; they are especially fascinated by their immediate surroundings. Both have their future life in front of them and are looking forward to it, each in his own way, but with eager anticipation.

The name Nimrod is given to the timid and clumsy puppy as if in jest, or to pluck up his courage. His namesake was a mighty warrior and hunter in the Old Testament.

The puppy reaches his maturity much more quickly than the boy, because that is what he is biologically programmed to do. During the course of the story, we see how the puppy, after recovering from the trauma of being separated from its mother, and frightened by the world around him, quickly becomes curious about it and adapts to his new environment until he feels so much at home in it that he comes to feel that the house he inhabits is "his." He develops a sort of patriotic attitude toward his narrowly confined territory, consisting mainly of the kitchen. At first shaky on his feet, he gradually acquires confidence, coordination, and control over his body. His sense of security is occasionally undermined by surprise events he does not understand, such as the scrubbing of the kitchen floor by the maid Adela. However, on the whole he develops a positive attitude toward new experiences and goes forward to meet them with a combination of enthusiasm, curiosity, wariness, and, on occasion, aggression.

Little by little, according to the narrator, Nimrod begins to understand that he is a dog, and he starts to act like one, being preprogrammed to grow up with all the instincts and impulses inherent to his species, constrained within his canine body, limited by his canine intelligence, and having a canineview of things.

A defining moment in the process of Nimrod's becoming a dog is triggered at the appropriate moment in his maturation process by his encountering a scary large black cockroach, scurrying across the kitchen floor. It awakens in Nimrod a sense of surprise, fear, excitement, aggression, and self-assertion. Slowly, he begins to bark, at first weakly, but growing stronger and more confidently by the moment. The cockroach, for its part, wrapped up in its own biological cockroachy essence and bodily form, remains unaffected by the bark, deaf to its meaning. After a while, Nimrod continues to bark, but now differently, purely for the joy of barking, having discovered this new ability of his, a defining moment in his burgeoning life.

Thus, the deeper meaning of the story has to do with biological predestination, and also with the fact that humans have a curiosity about other life forms for the better perspective it gives them on themselves and on the mystery of life itself. In the end we belong to our species, and this reality is immutable. Much attention in the story is directed to the shape within which the dog is confined: his paws, eyes, ears, mouth, tongue, and four legs. Little by little the biological memory contained within Nimrod's brain kicks in and realizes itself, as though he already knows and remembers things from long before he was ever born.

Dogs walk about on four legs and point forward with their muzzles. They have limited peripheral vision, but very flexible necks, allowing them to look behind them without changing position. Accordingly, they have a special, species-defined view on the world. As dogs, they are driven to bark, to feel protective of their immediate environment, and to be aggressive toward other beings that awaken in them their protective impulse. In a sense the story relates to the so-called nature versus nurture debate. Some things are conditioned by nature and cannot be affected by "nurture." Just like all animals, people interact with their surroundings while limited by their anatomy: their erect posture, their ability to walk while keeping their hands free to manipulate objects with their four fingers and opposable thumb, their ability to communicate with one another through language.

An overall telescoping structural perspective emerges from the story, with the cockroach, a primitive life form, at the center, having essentially no perspective on anything, and being more or less mature upon birth, with the other perspectives lined up behind him, each one looking at the other: (adult: (boy: (puppy: (cockroach))). This structure is overlayed on what is a thin traditional plot structure; however, the structure is plain to see. The Turning Point, initiating the Entanglement, can be detected in the brief paragraph beginning "But slowly little Nimrod (he had received that proud, martial name) begins to relish life. The Crisis Point occurs at the moment the puppy spots the cockroach skittering across the floor, and the Climax, of course, is when Nimrod, to his own surprise, begins to bark.

The final two paragraphs contain the Aftermath, as Nimrod keeps on barking just for the fun of it, overjoyed at his new-found gift of "speech," which is at the same time a mark of his coming of age as a dog.

## Pan

In a corner between the rear walls of the sheds and outbuildings was the dead end of the courtyard, the most distant, final branch locked in between a stall, an outhouse, and the rear wall of the chicken coop—a soundless bay from which there was no exit.

It was the most distant promontory, the Gibraltar of that courtyard, banging its head despairingly against the blind fence made of horizontal boards, the imprisoning, final wall of this world.

From under its moss-covered planks a trickle of black, smelly water oozed out, a vein of the putrid, oily marsh that was never dry—the only road that led across the boundary of the fence and into the world. But the despair of the stinking dead end had been hitting its head against this barrier for so long that it finally loosened one of the strong, horizontal boards. We boys finished the rest, we forced and pushed out the heavy, moss-covered board from its support. Thus, we created a gap and opened a window onto the sunshine. Standing with one foot on the board, which was thrown across the puddle like a bridge, a prisoner of the courtyard could squeeze through the crack, which would release him into a new, airy, expansive world. There was a big garden there, old, gone wild. Tall pear trees and spreading apple trees grew in huge, scattered clusters, sprinkled with a silvery rustling, a seething net of whitish sparkles. Lush, jumbled, unmown grasses covered this wavy terrain like a fluffy sheepskin cloak. There were the ordinary blades of meadow grasses with feathery tassels of grain; there were the delicate filigrees of wild parsley and carrots; the wrinkled, coarse little leaves of ground ivy and of blind nettles, which smelled like mint; fibrous, glistening ribwort plantain, spotted with rust, shooting out tufts of thick red buckwheat. All of this, matted and fluffy, was saturated with gentle air, lined with azure wind, and infused with sky. When you lay down in the grass, you were covered with a complete azure geography of clouds and floating continents, you breathed in the entire vast map of the heavens. From their relationship with the air, the leaves and shoots were covered with delicate hairs, a soft coating of fluff, a coarse bristle of hooks, as if intended for grasping and detaining the flow of oxygen. This delicate, whitish coating connected the leaves with the atmosphere, gave them the silvery gray gloss of waves of air, of shadowy pensiveness between two flashes of sunlight. And one of these plants, yellow and full of a milky liquid in its pale stalks, puffed up by the air, was already pushing out from its empty shoots just air itself, just fluff in the shape of feathery sow thistle spheres dispersed by a breeze and filtering soundlessly into the azure silence.

The garden was extensive, branching into several offshoots, and it had various zones and climates. On one side, it was open, full of the milk of the heavens and the air, and there it spread out for the sky the softest, most delicate, most downy greenery. But the deeper it descended into the depths of that long spur and plunged into the shade between the rear wall of the abandoned soda water factory and the long, collapsing wall of the stables, it grew visibly gloomier, turned surly and careless, let itself go wild and unkempt, grew fierce with nettles, bristled with thistles, turned mangy with all sorts of weeds, until at the very end between the walls, in a broad, rectangular bay, it lost all measure and fell into a rage. There, it was no longer an orchard, but a paroxysm of madness, an explosion of fury, a cynical shamelessness and debauchery. There, completely out of control, the barren burdock cabbage heads proliferated, opening the floodgates to their passion—enormous witches, disrobing in broad daylight, shedding their ample skirts, flinging them off one after another, until their puffed up, rustling, tattered rags buried under themselves with their frantic layers the rambunctious bastard tribe. But the ravenous skirts swelled and jostled each other, piled up one atop another, spread out and covered each other, growing together into a swollen mass made of sheets of leaves as high as the low eaves of the barn.

It was there that I glimpsed him for the only time in my life at a noon hour frantic from the heat. It was that moment when time, crazed and wild, breaks free from the daily grind of events, and like a fugitive tramp, races, shouting, across the fields. Then summer, deprived of all control, grows through the entire expanse without restraint or accounting, grows with wild abandon on every side, twofold, threefold, or into some other unnatural time, into an unknown dimension, into madness.

At that hour I would be overcome with a frenzy to catch butterflies, a passion for pursuing those flickering flecks, those erratic petals trembling in a clumsy zigzag in the blazing air. And it so happened then that one of these bright flecks broke into two and then three pieces while in flight—and that shuddering, blindingly white triangle led me, like a will-o'-the-wisp, through the frenzy of thistles blazing in the sun.

I restrained myself only at the border of the burdocks, not daring to wade into that blind hollow.

Then, suddenly, I saw him.

Immersed up to his armpits in the burdocks, he was squatting in front of me.

I saw his thick shoulders in a filthy shirt and a scruffy scrap of frock-coat. Ready to leap out of his hiding place, he was sitting like that—shoulders hunched over as if under a great weight. His body was panting from tension and sweat poured from his copper face, which glistened in the sunlight. Motionless, he appeared to be working hard, to be wrestling with some enormous burden, but without moving.

I stood there, nailed to the spot by his gaze that held me as if in pincers.

It was the face of a vagabond or a drunkard. A wisp of dirty tufts stuck up over his high, bulging brow like a stone nodule washed by a river. But that brow was deeply furrowed. It was unclear if pain, or the searing heat of the sun, or a superhuman tension had worked itself into that face and strained the features to the point of bursting. The black eyes drilled into me with the intensity of the highest despair or pain. Those eyes were looking at me and yet not looking, seeing me and not seeing me at all. They were bulging spheres, strained by the highest ecstasy of pain or a wild rapture of inspiration.

And suddenly, from those features, stretched to bursting, a kind of dreadful grimace erupted, shattered by suffering, and that grimace grew, took into itself the madness and the inspiration, swelled with it, kept on distorting itself more and more, until it broke into a roaring, rattling cough of laughter.

Shaken to the core, I saw him whooping with the laughter that emerged from his powerful chest as he slowly got up from his squatting position and fled, hunched over like a gorilla, with his hands in the drooping rags of his trousers, clomping in great leaps across the flapping sheets of the burdocks—Pan without his pipes, retreating in a panic to his native forest.

—1934. Translated by Madeline Levine

*Notes on "Pan."* The story exhibits the poeticizing power of language to create a magical, almost mythological world out of what essentially amounts to a trashy and stinking backyard with a smelly outhouse, chicken coop, and a next-door orchard let gone to seed. It is a hot summer's day, and everything around shimmers with green, gold, and silver. Butterflies dance in the breeze, and both live plants and rotting dead ones give off their distinctive smells. The farther one goes into the thicket of the abandoned orchard, the wilder and more sinister-looking the vegetation becomes, as metaphor is piled upon metaphor, making the weeds and burrs seem to assume a sinister witchlike shape.

The story provides an excellent example of the literary method of "making things seem strange" by seeing them through a special prism and perspective: here, that of an imaginative and impressionable young boy. To him, his narrow surroundings, however drab, ordinary, and unpoetic they might be to an adult, seem full of magic, wonderment, and constant newness and surprise. Because of his limited experience, the courtyard of his building with its permanently oozing puddle next to a henhouse, where he and other boys play, seems like the veritable center of the universe. To them it is their "world," beyond which stretch exotic and untamed lands, waiting to be explored. Excursions out of the courtyard through a slit in the backyard fence lead to adventurous trips into the wild unknown, becoming wilder as the orchard becomes more and more overgrown with weeds and burrs. The story reflects how things seem bigger and more magical to a child than they do to adults, and childhood things remembered from adulthood often appear in one's memory as larger and more significant than they were in actuality.

The many geographical metaphors in the story sustain the idea of how a child's narrow and circumscribed living space can seem to him to constitute the whole explorable world, or at least a sizable portion of it, and probably its center. The "land's end," or the courtyard's "Gibraltar," is the back fence with the broken-out slat in it and the wall of the chicken coop. In ancient times, the Rock of Gibraltar was considered to mark the end of the known world. The orchard has within it various zones and climates; it ends in an "isthmus" and opens out into a "bay" of weeds. The clouds against the sky continue the geographical metaphors, as they resemble patches of land on a background map of blue.

There are very few recognizable structural plot features in the story; it consists almost entirely of development and description. One could call its type "atmospheric." If anything constitutes a turning point, it is the prizing out of the slat in the fence, leading to further exploration. A sort of crisis point begins with the words "Then, suddenly, I saw him." In the magic of the summer moment, a ragged tramp is crouching and presumably defecating in the bushes, virtually reveling in his bodily functions, taking on the aura and mystique of a mythological forest creature, a "Pan without a pipe." The moment of climax is redolent with a sense of estrangement, as it is not clear whether the boy understands what is taking place. What makes an impression on him is the tramp's expression of exertion bordering on pain or ecstasy as he delivers a bowel movement and then runs off laughing.

## Father's Final Escape

This was in the late, dismal period of total disorder, during the period of the final liquidation of our business. The sign above the door to our shop had long since been taken down. Near the half-lowered blinds Mother was carrying on an illicit trade in the remnants. Adela had left for America. It was said that the ship she sailed on sank and all the passengers lost their lives. We never confirmed this rumor; news of the girl vanished, and we heard no more about her. A new era began, empty, sober, and joyless—as white as paper. A new servant girl, Genia, anemic, pale, and boneless, crept softly through the rooms. If someone stroked her back, she writhed and stretched like a snake and purred like a cat. She had a dull-white complexion that even under the lids of her enamel eyes was not pink. Sometimes, in a distracted state, she made a roux from old invoices and ledger sheets—sickening and inedible.

At that time my father had already died definitively. He had died numerous times, always not yet entirely, always with certain reservations that forced a revision of this fact. This had its good side. By breaking up his death into installments, Father was accustoming us to the fact of his departure. We grew indifferent to his ever more diminished returns, which were more pitiful each time. The physiognomy of the already absent man dispersed, as it were, in the room in which he lived; it branched out, creating in certain spots the most amazing knots of resemblance of an unbelievable clarity. In some places the wallpaper imitated the shudders of his tic, arabesques formed themselves into his laughter's painful anatomy, arranged as symmetrical limbs like the petrified imprint of a trilobite. For a while we kept a great distance from his polecat-lined fur coat as we walked past. The fur coat breathed. The panic of the animals biting one other and sewn together blew through them in feeble shudders and was lost in the folds of cloth. Pressing one's ear to it one could hear the melodious purring of their amicable slumber. In that well-tanned form, with the slight odor of polecat, murder, and nocturnal rutting, he would have been able to survive for years. But here, too, he did not last long.

Once, Mother came home from the city with a troubled look on her face.

"Look, Józef," she said, "what a happy coincidence. I caught him on the stairs, jumping from step to step." And she lifted a handkerchief off something she was carrying on a plate. I recognized him at once. The resemblance was unmistakable, although he was now a crab or a large scorpion. Profoundly struck by the clarity of the resemblance that, through such changes and metamorphoses, continued to impose itself with simply irresistible force, we confirmed this for each other in an exchange of glances.

"Is he alive?" I asked.

"It goes without saying; I can hardly restrain him," said Mother. "Should I release him onto the floor?"

She placed the plate on the floor and, leaning over him, we observed him more attentively now. Sunken among his many arched legs, he was moving them almost imperceptibly. His slightly raised pincers and antennae seemed to be listening intently. I tipped the saucer and Father stepped cautiously, with a certain hesitation, onto the floor, but once he'd touched the flat ground under himself, he suddenly set off running with all his dozen or so legs, clattering with his hard little arthropod's bones. I blocked his path. He hesitated, touching the obstacle with his waving antennae, after which he raised his pincers and turned sideways. We allowed him to run in his chosen direction. On that side, no furniture could shelter him. Running like that in wavering shudders on his many legs, he made it to the wall and, before we could realize it, climbed it lightly without stopping, with all the armature of his limbs. I shuddered with instinctive revulsion, following the multilegged journey advancing and flapping across the wallpaper. In the meantime, Father reached the small kitchen cabinet mounted on the wall, hung over its edge for a moment, explored with his pincers the interior terrain of the cabinet, and then all of him crawled inside.

It was as if he were becoming newly acquainted with the apartment from this new crab's perspective, getting to know objects by smell, perhaps, since despite close observation I was unable to discover any organ of sight in him. He appeared to deliberate slightly over the objects he encountered on his way, stopping near them for a moment, touching them lightly with his waving antennae, even embracing them, as if testing with his pincers whether he was familiar with them, and only after a moment would he disengage from them and run on, dragging behind him his abdomen, raised slightly off the floor. He behaved the same way with the bits of bread and meat that we tossed onto the floor for him in the hope that he would eat them. He only felt them hastily and ran on, not recognizing edible things in these objects.

One might think, seeing his patient reconnaissances in the space of the room, that he was searching for something assiduously and tirelessly. From time to time he ran into a corner of the kitchen under the water bucket, which was leaking, and when he reached the puddle he appeared to be drinking. Now and again he gave promise of lasting for entire days. He seemed to be capable of getting along without food, and we did not notice his vital signs decreasing at all as a result. With mixed feelings of shame and revulsion we nourished a secret fear during the day that he might visit us in bed during the night. But that did not happen even once, although during the day he wandered all over the furniture and liked especially to spend time in the space between the wardrobes and the wall.

Certain manifestations of intelligence, and even of a certain teasing playfulness, could not be overlooked. Never, for example, did Father fail to appear in the dining room at meal time although his participation at dinner was purely platonic. If the dining room door was closed by accident during dinner and Father found himself in the adjoining room, he would keep scratching under the door, running back and forth along the crack, for as long as it took until it was opened for him. Later, he learned to insert his pincers and legs into this lower crack, and, after rather intense rocking of his body, he would succeed in pushing himself sideways under the door and into the room. That seemed to make him happy. Then he would be motionless under the table, lying absolutely quiet, with only his abdomen lightly pulsing. What that rhythmical pulsing of his glossy abdomen meant we were unable to figure out. It was something ironic, indecent, and mean that seemed to express at one and the same time a kind of low, salacious satisfaction. Nimrod, our dog, would walk up to him slowly and without conviction, sniff him carefully, sneeze, and walk away indifferently, not having reached a decisive conclusion.

The disorder in our home spread in wider and wider circles. Genia slept for days on end, her slender body undulating flaccidly with her deep breathing. We often found the in soup spools of thread that she had tossed in along with the vegetables because of her inattentiveness and a peculiar absent-mindedness. The shop was open *in continuo* day and night. The clearance sale by the half-lowered blinds followed its intricate course day after day amid haggling and arguments. On top of everything, Uncle Karol arrived.

He was strangely disconcerted and uncommunicative. He declared with a sigh that after the last sad experiences he had decided to change his way of life and take up the study of languages. He did not leave the house, locked himself up in the last room, from which Genia, filled with reproof for this new guest, dragged out all the carpets and tapestries, after which he immersed himself in the study of old price lists. Several times he attempted maliciously to step on Father's abdomen. With shouting and horror, we forbade him to do this. He only laughed maliciously to himself, unconvinced, while Father, unaware of the danger, cautiously came to a stop over some spots on the floor.

My father, nimble and lively as long as he was standing on his legs, shared with all crustaceans the characteristic that, if turned over onto his back, he became completely defenseless. It was a bitter, pitiful sight when, desperately waving all his little legs, he rotated helplessly on his back around his own axis. It was impossible to look without bitterness at this too evident, articulated, almost shameless mechanics of his anatomy, lying, so to speak, on the surface and not veiled by anything from the side of his naked, multi-legged belly. At such moments Uncle Karol was roused to the point of trampling him. We would run to the rescue and give Father some object that he could grasp convulsively with his pincers and skillfully regain his normal position, immediately setting off running back and forth in a lightning-fast zigzag, with redoubled speed, as if he wanted to erase the memory of his compromising fall.

I regret that I must master myself in order to relate truthfully an inconceivable fact from which my entire being recoils. To this day I cannot comprehend that we were, to the fullest extent, conscious perpetrators of this fact. In this light the event acquires the character of some strange fate. For fate does not bypass our consciousness and will but incorporates them into its own mechanism so that we permit and accept, as in a lethargic dream, things before which under normal conditions we recoil.

When, shaken by the fait accompli, I asked Mother in despair, "How could you have done that! If at least it was Genia who had done it, but you yourself ... " Mother wept, wrung her hands, was unable to give me an answer. Did she think that it would be better for Father that way, did she see in this the only exit from his hopeless situation, or did she simply act out of incomprehensible carelessness and thoughtlessness? ... Fate finds a thousand devices when it is a matter of carrying out its incomprehensible will. Some tiny, momentary eclipse of our intellect, a moment of blindness or inattention suffices to smuggle a deed between the Scylla and Charybdis of our resolutions. Afterward, one can endlessly interpret and explain motives ex post, investigate the motives—but the fait accompli remains irreversible and foredoomed once and for all.

We came back to our senses and shook off our blindness only when my father was carried in on a platter. He lay there large and swollen as a consequence of boiling, pale gray and gelatinous. We sat in silence, mortified. Only Uncle Karol extended his fork toward the platter, but he dropped it uncertainly halfway there, looking at us in astonishment. Mother ordered that the platter be set aside in the salon. He lay there on the table covered with a plush cloth, next to a photograph album and a music box that held cigarettes, lay there avoided by us and motionless.

However, the earthly journey of my father was not to end there, and the continuation, the prolongation of his story beyond its apparently final permissible borders is the most painful point. Why did he not give up at last, why did he not recognize in the end that he was defeated when, truthfully, he already had every reason to do so and fate could go no farther in its utter subjugation of him? After several weeks of lying motionless he somehow became consolidated and appeared to be slowly coming back to himself. One morning we found the platter empty. Just one leg was lying on the edge of the plate, dropped on the congealed tomato sauce and aspic trampled during his escape. Boiled, losing legs along the way, he had dragged himself onward with his remaining strength, on to his homeless journey, and we never laid eyes on him again.

—1937. Translated by Madeline Levine

*Surrealism.* "Father's Last Escape" by Bruno Schulz might seem to be an example of literary surrealism, but only provisionally, as will be discussed subsequently. In surrealism, one or more laws of nature or logic are suspended but, given such a skewed point of departure, the action proceeds logically from there. The typical purpose is to make a metaphorical and, on a psychological level, a more penetrating comment about a situation than would be achieved through realistic portrayal. Surrealism often draws on concepts of Freudian psychoanalytic theory, based on the writings of the Viennese psychiatrist Sigmund Freud (1856–1939).

Under a Freudian interpretation, the world in which laws of nature are suspended is interpretable as a representation of the *subconscious*, buried below the layer of human consciousness. The subconscious can mainly be accessed through dreams and their analysis, and by the psychoanalytic technique of free association. Understanding the subconscious is seen as the key to understanding the human psyche and to resolving various kinds of neuroses that people have or develop.

The Freudian view of human psychology draws heavily on ancient myths, which are believed to contain deeply embedded truths about human nature. Especially important in Freudian psychoanalytic theory is the role played by latent feelings of sexual attraction of a child toward the parent of the opposite sex, and feelings of rivalry toward siblings and toward the same-sex parent. The child wants to displace the same-sex parent and unite with the parent of the opposite sex. The yearning of a male child to assassinate his father and marry his mother is known as the *Oedipus complex*, after a character in an ancient Greek myth and tragic play by Sophocles. The corresponding female complex, contributd by Swiss Freudian psychiatrist Carl Jung (1875–1961), is referred to as the *Electra complex*, after another Greek myth. Most neuroses in one way or another are considered by Freud to be sex-based, and to reflect either some kind of arrested sexual development or some kind of repressed sexual fear or drive.

An early literary exponent of surrealism in literature was Franz Kafka (1883–1924), a Czech-born Jewish author writing in German, possibly best known for writings published after his death in a sanitorium from tuberculosis. In 1916 Kafka wrote the classic surrealistic novella entitled *The Metamorphosis*, which is virtually required reading in introduction-to-modern-literature courses, and whose famous first line reads "One morning, as Gregor Samsa was waking up from anxious dreams, he discovered that in bed he had been changed into a monstrous verminous bug." The word "cockroach" never appears in the story, but the assumption is that this is the intended insect.

In *The Metamorphosis*, the protagonist, Gregor Samsa, a young man who supports his mother, retired father, and sister by his work as a traveling salesman for an unfriendly, demanding, and intrusive employer, wakes up one morning to find he has become a cockroach. He is unable to speak in a way intelligible to others, and he has practical problems dealing with his new body shape. He loses his job, and spends his time in his room, mainly hiding under the bed, rejected by his family except for his musically inclined sister Grete who, at least at first, brings him food sufficiently rotten for a cockroach to eat. Gradually he loses interest in food and in life, and wastes away and dies. The event has the effect of galvanizing and drawing closer together the formerly helpless family members, who had begun to take in lodgers to help pay the rent after Gregor's loss of salary. The father gets a job in a bank, and the mother and daughter (whose musical talents now go unfulfilled) also begin to earn a living in prosaic occupations. The story ends with the family taking a pleasant outing in the park.

One common interpretation of *The Metamorphosis* is that Gregor is not up to assuming the male leadership role in the family expected of him and replacing the father. He opts out of the battle by becoming a cockroach and dying. In response, the father takes on new life and begins to flourish.

Bruno Schulz, like Kafka, came from a middle-class Central European Jewish family. He was well read in German literature, and he translated into Polish one of Kafka's novels, *The Castle*, so he would have been familiar with Kafka's story about Gregor Samsa. That Schulz was influenced by the work of Kafka can be seen directly in his choice of the theme of a person turning into a bug, but Schulz's affinity with Kafka is more than a matter of superficial literary borrowing. The two writers share a deep affinity in their approach to the world and its depiction. In the worlds of both authors, growing up with the prospect of becoming an adult and assuming roles that are not clearly understood is frightening. In a well-known drawing of his, Schulz portrays his family as consisting of an old bearded patriarchal father, a young and beautiful mother, and himself as a small boy with a dwarfed body and an oversized, bulbous, adult-like head (suggesting an overactive mind and imagination), standing between and being towered-over by his parents.

Of course, the boy's name in the story is Józef, not Bruno, so one must distinguish between the author and the narrator. There are no other siblings mentioned as belonging to the household (in another story an older brother is mentioned), just vaguely defined relatives, a pet dog Nimrod, on whom the young Józef lavishes affection, and a maid. The former maid Adela of "Nimrod" has run off to America, never to be heard from again, to be replaced by the phlegmatic Genia who has limited culinary talents. In this universe, small details loom large, as if to a young and hypersensitive child with a morbid imagination. In another story, the narrator expresses horror at how woods of different tree species, incompatible in nature, become unnaturally glued together and forced violently into the shape of pieces of furniture. In "Escape," we similarly see the child's fascination with the polecats' being forcibly sewn together into the father's coat collar, to spend an eternity, in his imagination, wildly yowling at and mating with one another.

As we saw in "Nimrod," Schulz was fascinated by the arbitrary nature of the shapes into which creatures are born, and by how things, too, are "trapped" in their shape. In a world in which shapes are arbitrary, things can be surrealistically imagined as readily transmogrifying, turning into the shape of something else. In such a universe, a person can become a creepy-crawly critter just by virtue of being imagined or treated as one, or as feeling like one.

The "escape" of the father into whatever creature it is can be seen as an example of the literary device of *literalizing the metaphor*. Instead of merely comparing a person to a bug, the person actually becomes one. In another example, the new maid in the house, Genia, is a horrible cook. Her sauces taste like they were made out of any old thing, and this metaphor becomes transformed into its description as the soup's literally containing balls of cotton yarn and sales receipts. These are things connected with the family business (trade in cloth), so in a sense the family does live off them. If one prefers literality, perhaps Genia out of apathy or carelessness really does take yarn and receipts and toss them absent-mindedly into the bland-tasting soups. With Schulz one can never be sure.

In the stories contained in Schulz's two thin collections, both the mother and the maid go about their business as though the father were not there. The women are the ones in the family who are solid, practical, and have sense and physical substance. The father has less and less physical presence until he at last fades away completely. In "Father's Last Escape" we see the mother enterprisingly extracting the last bit of money out of the family's failing drygoods store, selling off all the remnants even after the business has been formally liquidated. The family itself is terrorized by the cleaning woman/cook, at first Adela from "Nimrod" and, later, by the listless Genia. In "Nimrod," all "natural laws are suspended" when Adela takes pail and mop in hand. Genia, by contrast, is phlegmatic and is an indifferent cook, but she nevertheless successfully imposes her rule, and her nearly inedible fare, on the family. She intuitively does not approve of the visiting "Uncle Karol." She takes the wall hangings and carpets out of his room, and no one dreams of opposing her.

A major difference between Schulz's "Escape" and Kafka's "Metamorphosis" is related to the person who becomes the lowly creature. In "Father's Escape" it is the father, not the son. The father (who, from other stories, one learns, is eccentric to the point of madness) is described as dying "in stages." Apparently he had been ailing for some time, and had better and worse days, but he was slowly withdrawing from the rest of the family into himself until, finally, he more or less "disappears into the woodwork," to emerge, at least in young Józef's mind, as a crab or similar creature. By identifying the recently deceased father as the crablike being that had coincidentally been brought into the house by the mother at the same time, the son does not have to face the challenge of overcoming or replacing the father. In other words, the young boy is not ready to take over the role of husband and family head. By way of a defense mechanism, one could say, in order to avoid the psychological consequences of his father's death and his possibly needing to assume the role of man in the family, the boy accepts that his father has transitionally turned into an arthropod, in which reduced shape he lives on.

To complicate the situation, a new element enters the picture in the person of Uncle Karol, who manifests himself more or less out of nowhere and comes, uninvited, to live with the family, threatening by his mere presence to take the (purely symbolic) place of "male head of household." In another story Uncle Karol is described as a "grass widower," that is, someone whose wife has run off. With his study of "foreign languages" and fascination with old price lists, Uncle Karol gives every sign of being just as introverted and demented as the father was.

Another difference between *The Metamorphosis* and "Father's Last Escape" can be seen in the obligatory nature of the literalized cockroach metaphor in the one, and its merely optional literality in the other. On this point lies the question as to whether "Father's Final Escape" is really an example of surreal fiction. In *The Metamorphosis*, Gregor Samsa really is a cockroach; we see the world through his cockroach eyes and sensations. At one point he crawls across the ceiling. In "Father's Last Escape," the change of the father into a similar kind of creature does not so much give impetus to an ensuing plot, as it is an event occurring within a larger plot whose driving force is the slow fading away of the father, and how the family accommodates to his death. It can be interpreted as taking place entirely metaphorically, in Józef's head. The creature can be interpreted realistically, simply as some kind of large bug that appears on the scene coincidentally upon the father's final demise, an event which for the boy passes practically unnoticed. The bug, or whatever it is (see further below), gets taken up by the family, becoming a kind of semi-tame family pet (rather like the father was toward the end of his life), in order to take the family's mind off matters at hand. Like the father, the creature is allowed to roam the house freely, and he usually keeps out of the way except at mealtimes, even though he does not eat.

A good candidate for the creature that appears is a pseudoscorpion, an arthropod that has pincers like a scorpion, but no tail or sting. They are also sometime called "land crabs," and they can be kept as terrarium pets. Pseudoscorpions bustle about eating small insects, and would not be interested in "people food." They look frightening but are harmless to people and can be picked up with a handkerchief, as the mother does in the story. The creature could not literally have been a crab, for crabs are aquatic.

Yet another difference between Kafka and Schulz is in the different symbolic interpretation of the creature. For Kafka, Gregor as cockroach is seen by his family as revolting. For Józef's family, the animal is treated with indulgence, even friendliness, and is allowed to participate in family life to the extent of its ability (as long as it keeps out of bed at night). He is defended from harm at the hands (or feet) of Uncle Karol, until finally, however, the mother seemingly takes decisive action and cooks him up in an aspic. At least Józef instantly identifies what the mother has cooked with the bug which has, in the meantime, disappeared.

Unlike the cockroach in *Metamorphosis*, in "Father's Final Escape," we never see any part of the story from the creature's/father's point of view. The viewing of the creature as the father by the boy and by his mother may be interpreted both as a defense mechanism on the part of the boy and, additionally, as a kind of conspiratorial joke maintained between the mother and son out of a desire to fill the void left by the father with a surrogate. From the mother's point of view this conspiracy also forestalls the void's being filled by anyone else, that is, by Uncle Karol. However, since the shop has failed, the mother will probably eventually have to marry someone for reasons of financial security—hopefully not the pathetic "Uncle Karol."

Uncle Karol's killing of the creature by stamping on it would symbolically amount to his killing the father, thereby allowing him to usurp the father's role and take over as head male. It turns out that Genia's instincts toward him are right: his appearance in the house is ominous. The still young, good-looking, and resourceful mother would have reason not to want to lose her independence, but she might be unable to resist forever the exigencies of the situation.

Thus, the "creature conspiracy" can also be seen as the mother's way of staving off the inevitable assumption by Uncle Karol of the position of household head. Under this interpretation, the mother's later serving-up of the dish for dinner (if one wants to interpret the story logically, one can imagine that this was a crayfish bearing a resemblance in the boy's and even the mother's mind to the family's pet bug) becomes a sign of her resignation and capitulation to the realities of her life. The child looks on from the sidelines and recoils in horror (for one thing, the eating of crustaceans is a violation of Jewish dietary laws), with only an imperfect understanding of the issues at stake. He seemingly does realize, however, that the cooking and serving of the dish symbolizes the father's definitive end ... or almost.

By serving up the crayfish, which the dish seems most likely to be, the mother shows she may be willing to yield to "Uncle Karol," who, however, turns out to be too impotent to follow through on the prospect. He recognizes the symbolism of the situation, but at the same time he realizes he is unequal to it and puts down his fork, turning down the offer. The dish is removed to the sitting room, where it sits and spoils disgustingly. It is eventually demolished by agents unknown. If one prefers a realistic interpretation, then one may say it was carried away and consumed by a mouse, or perhaps by our dog Nimrod.

In the nineteenth and early twentieth centuries it was customary to lay the body of a dead person out for viewing in the parlor, surrounded by family memorabilia. It is easy to associate the removal of the creature to the living room and its placement among family albums as a metaphorical interpretation of the father's death (even if with a momentary afterlife) on display.

At the end, the "father" is not so much banished by a rival, as he disgustingly oozes once and for all out of the picture, leaving us with a decidedly sordid and unheroic spin to the Electra myth. In the Greek myth, Electra's mother, Clytemnestra, kills her husband, Electra's father, Agamemnon, while his male rival, Aegisthus, waits in the wings. Electra takes revenge for her father's death into her hands and, along with her brother Orestes, kills Clytemnestra. In "Escape" the role of

Clytemnestra is played by the mother, who metaphorically boils her husband alive and serves him on a plate for Aegisthus, played by Uncle Karol, while the role of the female sibling is seemingly dubbed by Genia, leaving Józef, who is clearly not up to playing Orestes.

*The Disease.* The word in Schulz's story for the crustacean which the mother finally serves for dinner is *rak*, 'crab,' 'crayfish,' 'cancer,' 'Cancer (the Zodiac sign).' Crayfish are common in Ukrainian streams and ponds, and they are often served as food, so logically what the mother cooks up and serves in aspic is a *rak* in the sense of freshwater crayfish. Cancer is a wasting disease, and the father is described as slowly wasting away, until he finally disappears. No doubt the father was dying of cancer, and Józef, having heard the word *rak* used to describe the father's illness, is in a frame of mind to associate both the creature the mother brings home as a pet and the dish she later serves as a *rak*, and thus also with the father and his disease. In sum, the overall coherence of the story could be said to be predicated on the accidental circumstance of the lack of separate words in Polish for 'cancer,' 'crab,' and 'crayfish.'

# Witold Gombrowicz

Witold Gombrowicz (1904–1969) was a literary anarchist and provocateur, a writer people either like or dislike, depending on their tolerance for literary absurdity. Throughout his career he remained immune to critical opinion, faithful to his evolving personal philosophy about the workings of human perception and interpersonal relationships, especially social roles and their hierarchies. He used his works as vehicles for conveying his philosophy and for breaking or parodying in the process as many literary forms and conventions as he could. Descended from an old family of landed gentry from Lithuania, he cultivated a lifelong hostile attitude toward Polishness, the aristocracy, national shibboleths, and sociocultural conventions of all kinds.

Gombrowicz was educated in law at Warsaw University but never practiced in that field, deciding instead to try his hand at writing. His first major published work, in 1933, was a collection of absurdist short stories entitled *Pamiętnik z okresu dojrzewania* (Memoir of a Time of Immaturity), the title of which refers to another of his favorite themes, the pursuit of immaturity as a way of avoiding growing up and losing one's "authenticity" by being forced to assume an adult societal role. That theme was the driving force of his first novel, *Ferdydurke* (1937), which earned him a reputation, or at least a notoriety, among the Polish literary establishment.

On the eve of World War II, Gombrowicz found himself on a trans-Atlantic steamer bound for South America. He stayed in Buenos Aires, Argentina, for the duration of the war and for another twenty-odd years, living there in relative poverty and obscurity and publishing works through the Polish emigré press in Paris. For this last reason his works remained largely inaccessible in Poland under communism. Gombrowicz returned to Europe in 1963 on a Ford Foundation grant, having acquired by this time an international reputation for his unconventional novels *Pornografia* and *Trans-Atlantyk*. Suffering from poor health, he settled in southern France, married his personal secretary (who is still alive as of this writing, and still looking after the author's affairs) and lived there until his death in Vence, where he is buried.

Because of his frequent resort to wordplay, to which Polish is highly succeptible, Gombrowicz is difficult to translate into other languages. The story selected here is the least absurdist and, accordingly, the most accessible out of Gombrowicz's 1933 collection of stories, which was later published in a slightly expanded version under the title *Bacacaj*, after the name of the street on which he lived in Buenos Aires. His works, especially his plays and theatrical adaptations of his non-theatrical works, remain popular in Poland, where he is considered a classic. The year 2023 was proclaimed in Poland "Year of Gombrowicz."

## A Premeditated Murder

In winter of last year I was obliged to visit Ignacy K., a landed gentleman, to conduct certain property-related business. I took a few days' leave, left a junior judge in charge and telegrammed: "Tuesday, 6 pm, please send horses." Yet when I arrived at the railroad station there were no horses. I checked and found out that my telegram had been properly delivered. The addressee himself had signed for it the previous day. Like it or not, I had to hire a primitive wagonette, load it up with my suitcase and my toiletry case—the latter containing a small bottle of eau de cologne, a vial of Vegetal, almond-scented soap, a nail file, and nail scissors—and spend four hours bumping across the fields by night, in the quiet, during a thaw. I was shivering in my city overcoat, my teeth chattering, as I stared at the driver's back and thought—turning one's back like that! Permanently, often in secluded places, to be turned the other way and exposed to the whims of those sitting behind!

We finally pulled up in front of a wood-built country manor—it was in darkness, the only light coming from a window on the second floor. I knocked at the door—it was locked; I knocked harder—nothing, silence. I was set on by yard dogs and had to beat a retreat to the cart. There, in turn, my driver started to accost me.

"This isn't exactly hospitable," I thought.

At last the door opened and there appeared a tall, frail-looking man of about thirty with a blond mustache and a lamp in his hand.

"What is it?" he asked, as if he had been awoken from sleep, as he raised the lamp.

"Did you not receive my wire; I'm H."

"H.? What H.?" He stared at me. "Leave with God's blessing," he suddenly said in a quiet voice, as if he had spotted some special sign—his eyes looked away, and his hand closed more tightly around the lamp. "With God's blessing, with God's blessing, sir! God guide your way!"—and he hurriedly stepped back into the house.

I said more sharply this time:

"Pardon me. Yesterday I sent a wire concerning my arrival. I am investigating magistrate H. I wish to talk with Mr. K.—and if I wasn't able to get here sooner it's because no horses were sent to the station for me."

He set the lamp down.

"That's right," he said after a moment, pensively, my tone having made no impression on him whatsoever. "That's right ... You cabled ... Please, do come in."

What had happened? It turned out, as I was told in the entryway by the young man (who was the owner's son), that quite simply ... they had completely forgotten about my arrival and about the cable that had been received the previous morning. Explaining myself and apologizing politely for the incursion, I took off my overcoat and hung it on a peg. He led me into a small sitting room whereupon seeing us a young woman sprang up from the sofa with a soft "Oh." "My sister." "It's a pleasure to meet you." And it was indeed a pleasure, for femininity, even without any incidental intentions, femininity, I say, is always welcome. But the hand she gave me was perspiring—who gives a man a perspiring hand?—and the femininity itself, despite a charming little face, seemed somehow, how shall I put it, perspirational and indifferent, devoid of reaction, unkempt, and disheveled.

We sat down on the old-fashioned red furniture and began an introductory conversation. But the very first courteous commonplaces came up against an indefinable resistance, and instead of the fluidity that one wished for, things kept breaking off and getting stuck. I: "I expect you were surprised to hear a knock at the door at this hour?" They: "A knock? Oh, that's right … " I, politely: "I'm very sorry to have alarmed you, but otherwise I think I would have had to roam the fields all night, like Don Quixote, ha ha!" They (awkwardly and softly, not seeing fit to respond to my little joke even with a conventional smile): "Not at all, you're welcome."—What was this? It looked truly bizarre—as if they were offended by me, or they were afraid of me, or they felt sorry for me, or they were embarrassed for me … Planted in their armchairs, they avoided my gaze, nor did they look at each other; they bore my company with the greatest discomfort—it seemed that they were preoccupied exclusively with themselves, and the whole time they were worried only that I might say something to insult them. In the end it began to irritate me. What were they afraid of, what was it about me! What sort of reception was this, aristocratic, timid, and … ! And when I asked about the purpose of my visit, in other words about Mr. K., the brother looked at the sister as if each were letting the other go first—in the end the brother swallowed and said distinctly, distinctly and solemnly, as if it were I don't know what:

"Yes, he is indeed at home."

It was exactly as if he had said: "The King, my Father, is at home!"

Supper was also somewhat eccentric. It was served carelessly, not without scorn for the food and for me. The appetite with which I in my hunger devoured the gifts of the Lord appeared to arouse the indignation even of the solemn butler Szczepan, not to mention the brother and sister, who attended in silence to the noises I made over my plate—and you know how hard it is to swallow when someone is listening—against one's will every mouthful descends into the throat with a terrible gulping sound. The brother's name was Antoni, and the sister was called Miss Cecylia.

All at once I looked up—who was this coming in? A dethroned queen? No, it was their mother, Mrs. K., approaching slowly; she gave me a hand cold as ice, looked at me with a hint of dignified surprise, and sat down without a word. She was a small, corpulent, even fat individual, one of those old country matrons who are implacable when it comes to all sorts of principles, especially social ones—and she eyed me sternly, with boundless surprise, as if I had an obscene saying written on my forehead. Cecylia made a gesture in an attempt to explain, or to justify—but the gesture died in midair, and the atmosphere became even more artificial and oppressive.

"I expect you're rather disappointed on account of … this futile journey," said Mrs. K. suddenly—and in such a tone! A tone of indignation, the tone of a queen to whom someone has failed to bow for the requisite third time—as if eating chops constituted a crime of *lèse majesté!*

"The pork chops here are excellent!" I replied in anger, since despite myself I was feeling ever more vulgar, foolish, and uncomfortable.

"Chops … chops … "

"Antoś still hasn't said anything, Mama," the timid Cecylia burst out all of a sudden, quieter than a mouse.

"What do you mean, he hasn't said anything? What do you mean, you haven't said anything? You *still* haven't said anything?"

"What for, Mama?" whispered Antoni; he turned pale and gritted his teeth, as if he were about to sit in the dentist's chair.

"Antoś … "

"I mean … What for! It makes no difference … there's no point—there'll always be time," he said and fell silent.

"Antoś, how can you! What do you mean it makes no difference! What are you saying, Antoś!"

"No one could be … It's all the same … "

"You poor thing!" whispered his mother, stroking his hair, but he brushed her hand aside roughly.—"My husband," she said dryly, turning to me, "died last night."—What?! So he was dead! So that was it! I interrupted my meal—I set down my knife and fork—I hurriedly swallowed the morsel I had in my mouth.—How could this be? It was only yesterday that he had picked up my telegram from the station! I looked at them: all three of them were waiting. They were modest and grave, but—they were waiting, with stern, reserved faces and pursed lips; they were waiting stiffly—what on earth were they waiting for? Oh, that's right, condolences had to be offered!

It was so unexpected that to begin with I was completely put out of countenance. In my confusion I rose from my chair and mumbled something indistinctly along the lines of: "I'm terribly sorry … I'm very … I'm sorry."—I fell silent, but they did not respond whatsoever, for this was still too little for them; with lowered eyes and unmoving faces, their clothes untidy, he unshaven, the women with disheveled hair, their fingernails dirty—they all stood without saying anything. I cleared my throat, desperately thinking of where to begin, the right expression, but it so happened that my head was completely empty, a void, as I'm sure has happened to you too, while they—they were waiting, immersed in their suffering. They were waiting without looking—Antoni was drumming his fingers lightly on the tabletop, Cecylia was embarrassedly picking at the hem of her dirty gown, and their mother stood motionless, as if turned to stone, with that stern, unyielding matronly expression. All at once I began to feel uneasy, despite the fact that as an investigating magistrate I had dealt with hundreds of deaths in my time. But that was just it … how shall I put it? An unsightly murdered corpse covered with a blanket is one thing; quite another is a worthy fellow who has died of natural causes and is laid out on a catafalque; a certain unceremoniousness is one thing, while quite another is a death that is above board, accustomed to considerations, to manners—death, you could say, in all its majesty. No, I repeat, I would never have been so perturbed if they had told me everything at once. But they were too uncomfortable. They were too afraid. I don't know whether it was simply because I was an intruder, or whether they were perhaps in some way embarrassed by my profession in such circumstances, because of a certain ... matter-of-factness that my many years of practice must have formed in me; but in any case—this embarrassment of theirs embarrassed me terribly, embarrassed me, in fact, entirely disproportionately.

I stammered something about the respect and affection I had always felt for the deceased. Recalling that since our schooldays I had never met him once, a fact that could have been known to them, I added: "During our schooldays." They still made no reply, and I had after all to finish somehow, to round things off; and finding nothing else to say, I asked: "Could I see the body!"—and the word "body" somehow came out most unfavorably. Yet my confusion evidently appeased the widow; she burst into painful tears and gave me her hand, which I kissed humbly.

"In the night," she said dazedly, "last night ... I got up this morning ... I went in ... I called—Ignaś, Ignaś—but there was no response; he was lying there ... I fainted ... I fainted ... And from that moment my hands haven't stopped trembling—see for yourself."

"What's the point, Mama?"

"They're trembling ... they haven't stopped trembling"—she raised her arms.

"Mama," Antoni repeated from the side, in a half-whisper.

"They're trembling, trembling—of their own accord; see, they're trembling like aspen leaves ...

"No one is ... no one will be ... it makes no difference. It's embarrassing!" he burst out violently and suddenly turned his back and walked away. "Antoś!" his mother called in fright. "Cecylka, go after him ... " And I stood there and looked at her shaking hands; I had absolutely nothing to say and felt at a loss, growing more and more disconcerted.

All at once the widow said softly: "You wanted ... Then let us go ... there ... I'll show you the way."—In principle I believe—today, when I consider the matter dispassionately—that at the time I had a right to myself and my pork chops; that is, I could and even should have replied: "At your service, ma'am, but I'll just finish these pork chops, since I've not had a bite to eat since midday." Perhaps, if I had replied in this vein, many tragic events would have been averted. But was it my fault she had terrorized me so much that my pork chops, and I myself, seemed to me something trivial and unworthy of mention, and I was so ashamed all of a sudden that even today I blush at the thought of that embarrassment!

On the way, on the second floor, where the deceased was to be found, she whispered to herself: "A terrible misfortune ... A blow, an awful blow ... The children said nothing. They're proud, difficult, reserved; they won't allow just anyone into their hearts, but rather prefer to worry on their own. They got that from me, from me ... Oh, I only hope Antoś doesn't do himself any harm! He's tough, stubborn, he won't even let his hands twitch. He wouldn't let anyone touch the body—yet something has to be done, arrangements have to be made. He didn't cry, he didn't cry at all … Oh, if only he had cried at least once!"

She opened a door—and I had to kneel down with my head bowed, with a look of concentration on my face, while she stood to the side, solemn and still, as if she were showing the Blessed Sacrament.

The deceased lay on the bed—just as he had died—the only thing they had done was to turn him on his back. His livid, swollen face betokened death by asphyxiation, as was usual in the case of heart attacks.

"Asphyxiated," I murmured, though I could clearly see that it was a heart attack.

"It was his heart, his heart, sir … He died because of his heart."

"Oh, the heart can sometimes asphyxiate … it can," I said lugubriously. She was still standing and waiting—and so I crossed myself, said a prayer, and then (she was still standing there) I said quietly:

"Such noble features!"

Her hands were shaking so much that I decided I ought to kiss them again. She did not react with the slightest movement, continuing to stand like a cypress, gazing painfully away toward the wall—and the longer she stood there, the harder it became to avoid showing at least a little heart. This was required by common decency; there was no getting out of it. I rose from my knees, unnecessarily removed a piece of lint from my suit, gave a low cough—and she went on standing. She stood fanatically, silent, with staring eyes, like Niobe, her gaze fixed on her memories, crumpled, disheveled; and a tiny droplet appeared at the tip of her nose and dangled there, and dangled … like the sword of Damocles—and the candles smoked. After a few minutes I tried to say something softly—she flinched as if she'd been bitten, took a few steps and again stood still. I knelt down. What an intolerable situation! What a dilemma for a person as sensitive, and above all as irritable, as I am! I do not accuse her of deliberate malice; nevertheless, no one will deny that there was malice in this. No one will convince me! It was not she herself, but her malice that gloated insolently at the way I was simpering before her and the corpse.

Kneeling two paces away from that corpse, the first one I was not able to touch, I stared vacantly at the bedspread that covered him smoothly up to the armpits, at his hands laid carefully over that bedspread—potted plants stood at the foot of the bed, and the face loomed palely from a depression in the pillow. I gazed at the flowers, then I gazed back at the dead man's face, but nothing came into my head except for one pesky thought, strangely persistent—that this was some kind of prearranged, theatrical scene. Everything looked as if it had been staged—over there the corpse, proud and untouchable, looking indifferently through closed eyes at the ceiling; next to it the grieving widow; and here—I myself, the investigating magistrate, on my knees, like a bad dog forced to wear a muzzle. "What would happen if I were to rise, go up, pull off the bedspread and take a look—to touch at least—to touch with the tip of my finger!" I thought these things—but the grave integrity of death pinned me to my place; pain and virtue kept me from profanation.—Down! That's forbidden! Hands off! On your knees!—"What is it," I thought slowly to myself. "Who staged all this? I'm an ordinary, regular fellow—I'm not the right person for such performances … I wouldn't advise … Dammit!" I suddenly decided, "What nonsense! Where did this come from? Could I be acting a part? Where did this artificiality, this affectation come from in me—I'm usually completely different—have they infected me? What is it—ever since I arrived, everything in me has been coming out artificially and pretentiously, as if it were being performed by a third-rate actor. I've completely lost myself in this house—I'm acting up most terribly. Hmm," I murmured, and once again not without a certain theatrical pose (as if I were already sucked into the game and I could no longer return to normality)—"I wouldn't advise anyone … I wouldn't advise anyone to make a demon of me, because I'm prepared to take up the invitation … " In the meantime the widow had wiped her nose and moved toward the door, talking to herself and clearing her throat as she waved her hands about.

When I finally found myself alone in my own room, I took off my collar, and instead of placing it on the table, I hurled it to the floor and crushed it with my foot. My face was contorted and infused with blood; my fingers closed convulsively in a manner that was entirely unexpected for me. I was quite clearly in a fury. "They've made a fool of me," I whispered. "That wretched woman … How they've arranged everything so cleverly. They make people pay homage to them—kiss their hands! They demand sentiments from me! Sentiments! They demand to be humored! And I—let's say, I hate that. And, let's say—I hate it when they use trembling to make me kiss their hands, when they compel me to mumble prayers, to kneel, to produce false, revoltingly sentimental noises—and above all I hate tears, sighs, and droplets at the tips of noses; whereas I like cleanliness and order.

"Hmm"—I cleared my throat thoughtfully after a pause, in a different tone, cautious and somehow probing—"they make me kiss their hands! I ought to kiss their feet; isn't it obvious what I am in the face of the majesty of death and of this family's pain! … A coarse, unfeeling police informer, nothing more—my nature has been exposed. Yet … hmm … I don't know if this has been done too hastily; yes, in their place I personally would have been a little more—circumspect … a little more—modest … Because some allowance ought to have been made for this abject character of mine, and if not for my … private character, then … then … at least for my official character. This they forgot about. When it comes down to it, I am after all an investigating magistrate, and here after all there is a corpse, and the idea of a corpse somehow rhymes in a not entirely innocent way with the idea of an investigating magistrate. And if for instance I were to look at the course of events from precisely the perspective … hmm … of an investigating magistrate," I thought slowly, "what would transpire then?"

If you please: A guest arrives who—by chance—is an investigating magistrate. They don't send horses, they don't open the door—in fact they make difficulties for him, and so someone must be unwilling to let him into the house. Then he's received reluctantly, with poorly disguised anger, with fear—and who on earth is afraid, who on earth is angry at the sight of an investigating magistrate? Something is hidden from him and covered up—and in the end it turns out that what was being covered up is … a corpse that has died of asphyxiation in an upstairs room. How base! When the corpse comes to light, attempts are made by hook or by crook to make him kneel and kiss hands, on the pretext that the deceased died a natural death!

If anyone, however, should call this notion preposterous, laughable even (for after all, to speak frankly, how can anyone deceive so crudely), they should bear in mind that a moment ago, in my anger, I crushed my collar underfoot—my soundness of mind was impaired, my consciousness dimmed as a result of the resentment I felt, and so it was clear I was not fully responsible for my antics.

Looking straight ahead, I said with gravity:

"Something's not right here."

And I began with considerable perspicacity to link the chain of facts, to create syllogisms, spin threads, and search for evidence. But soon, wearied by the fruitlessness of this endeavor, I fell asleep. Yes, yes … The majesty of death is in every regard worthy of respect, and no one could say that I had not rendered to it the necessary honors—but not every death is equally majestic, and, before elucidating this circumstance, if I were them I would not be so sure of myself, the more so because the matter is murky, complex and dubious … hmm … hmm … all the evidence points to this.

The next morning, as I drank my coffee in bed, I noticed that the serving boy, a thickset, sleepy lad who was lighting the stove, kept glancing at me out of the corner of his eye with a faint glimmer of curiosity. He probably knew who I was—and I spoke to him:

"So your master died?"

"That he did."

"How many servants are there here?"

"There's Szczepan and the cook, your honor. Not counting me. And counting me there's three of us."

"Your master died in that upstairs room?"

"Yeah, upstairs," he said indifferently, puffing out his fleshy cheeks as he blew on the fire.

"And you, where do you sleep!"

He stopped blowing and looked at me—a sharper look this time.

"Szczepan and the cook sleep in the kitchen, and I sleep on my own in the pantry."

"That's to say, from where Szczepan and the cook sleep there's no other access to the rest of the house except through the pantry?" I asked further, as if by the by.

"Only through there," he answered, and looked at me very sharply now.

"And where does the lady of the house sleep?"

"She used to share a room with the master—but now she sleeps next door, in the neighboring room."

"Since the master died?"

"Oh no, she moved before that—it must have been a week or so ago."

"And you don't know why your mistress moved out of the master's room."

"Couldn't say … "

I asked one more question:

"And where does the young master sleep?"

"Downstairs, next to the dining room."

I got up and dressed with care. Hmm … hmm … So, if I was not mistaken, here was one more thought-provoking piece of evidence—a curious detail. Whatever one might say, it was intriguing that a week before her husband's death his wife should move out of their shared bedroom. Could she possibly have been afraid of being infected with heart disease? That would have been an extravagant fear, to say the least. But there must be no premature conclusions, no rash moves—and I went down to the dining room. The widow stood by the window—with folded arms she was staring at her coffee cup—and she was murmuring something in a monotone, earnestly shaking her head, with a wet handkerchief in her hands. When I approached, she suddenly moved around the table in the opposite direction, still murmuring, and waving her hand, as if she had lost her reason—nevertheless, I had already recovered the poise I had lost the previous day and, standing to the side, I waited patiently until at last she noticed me.

"Ah, farewell, farewell," she said absently, seeing that I was bowing—"It's been a pleasure … "

"Pardon me," I whispered, "I … I … I'm not leaving just yet; I'd like to stay a while … "

"Oh, it's you, sir," she said. She mumbled something about a funeral procession, and even favored me with a wan question about whether I would stay for the service.

"It would be a great honor," I replied piously. "Who could refuse that final duty! Might I be allowed to visit your husband one more time!" Without answering and without looking back to see if I was following, she mounted the creaking stairs.

After a short prayer I rose to my feet and, as if meditating on the enigma of life and death, I looked around. "That's strange!" I said to myself; "that's interesting! Judging from appearances, this man undoubtedly died of natural causes. True, his face is swollen and livid like someone who has been asphyxiated, but there are absolutely no signs of a struggle anywhere, either on the body or in the room—it really would seem that he died peacefully of a heart attack." Nevertheless—I suddenly went up to the bed and touched his neck with my finger.

This slight movement had an electrifying effect on the widow. She started.

"What are you doing!" she cried. "What are you doing! What are you doing! … "

"My poor lady, don't be so upset," I replied, and without further ceremony I conducted a thorough investigation of the corpse's neck and the entire room. Ceremony is good up to a point! We wouldn't get very far if ceremony stood in the way of carrying out a detailed inspection when the need arose. Alas!—there were still literally no signs either on the body or on the chest of drawers, or behind the wardrobe, or on the rug next to the bed. The only noteworthy thing was an immense dead cockroach. On the other hand, a certain sign appeared on the widow's face—she stood motionless, watching what I was doing with a look of befuddled consternation.

At this point I asked as circumspectly as I could: "Why did you move into your daughter's room a week ago?"

"I? Why? I? Why did I move? How did you … My son persuaded me to … So there would be more air. My husband used to suffocate in the night. But what do you want? … What do you actually want? Why are you … ?"

"Please forgive me … I'm sorry—but … " I finished my sentence with an eloquent silence.

She seemed to understand somewhat—as if she had suddenly realized the official character of the person with whom she was talking.

"But still … How is it? Surely—surely you can't have … you haven't noticed anything?"

In this question fear could distinctly be heard. I responded merely by clearing my throat. "Be that as it may," I said dryly, "I'd like to request … I believe you mentioned something about a funeral procession … I'd like to request that the body remain here until tomorrow morning."

"Ignaś!" she exclaimed.

"Exactly!" I replied.

"Ignaś! How can that be? It's not possible, it's out of the question," she said, staring dully at the body. "Ignaś!"

And—curious!—all at once she broke off in mid-sentence, went stiff, crushed me with a look, and then left the room in high dudgeon. I ask you—what could there possibly have been to offend her? Is a husband dying of unnatural causes a source of offense to a wife if she didn't have a hand in it? What could possibly be offensive about death from unnatural causes? It may be offensive for the killer, but surely never for the corpse or his family. However, for the moment I had something more urgent to do than pose such rhetorical questions. Left alone with the corpse, I once again set about conducting a scrupulous investigation—yet the longer I worked, the more my face betrayed my astonishment. "Not a thing," I whispered. "Nothing aside from the cockroach behind the chest of drawers. It truly might be concluded that there's no basis whatsoever for further action."

Ha! Now here was a stumbling block—in the form of the corpse, who loudly and clearly confirmed to the expert eye that he had died of an ordinary heart attack. All these appearances, the horses, the animosity, the dissembling, argued for something suspicious, whereas the corpse gazed at the ceiling and proclaimed: I died of a heart attack! It was physically and medically self-evident, it was a certainty—no one had murdered him for the simple and conclusive reason that *he had not been murdered at all.* I must confess that at this point most of my fellow magistrates would have closed the investigation. But not I! I was too ridiculed, too vengeful, and I had already ventured too far. I raised my finger and frowned. "A crime does not come of its own accord, gentlemen; it must be worked upon mentally, thought through, thought up—dumplings don't cook themselves.

"When appearances testify against there having been a crime," I said wisely, "then let us be cunning, let us not be taken in by appearances. Whereas when logic, common sense, the obvious finally become advocates for the criminal, and appearances argue against him, then let us trust appearances, let us not be deceived by logic and the obvious. Very well … but with all these appearances, how on earth—as Dostoevsky says—can we make rabbit stew with no rabbit!" I stared at the corpse, and the corpse stared at the ceiling, announcing his innocence with an unblemished neck. Now here was a difficulty! Here was a stumbling block! But what can't be removed must be jumped over—*hic Rhodus, hic salta!* Which is to say, could this dead object with human features which I might, if I wished, have taken in my hand—could this frozen face present any real resistance to my own mobile and changing physiognomy, which was capable of finding an expression suitable for any occasion! And while the corpse's visage remained the same—calm, if a little swollen—my face expressed solemn cunning, foolish arrogance and self-confidence, just as if I had said: you can't teach your grandmother to suck eggs!

"Yes," I said with gravity, "it's an obvious fact: the dead man was asphyxiated."

The lawyer with his prevarications might try to suggest that he was asphyxiated by his heart! Hmm, hmm … Not for us such legal maneuvers. "Heart" is a very flexible term—symbolic, even. Who, springing to their feet on hearing that a crime has been committed, would possibly be satisfied to hear the reassuring reply that it was nothing—that his heart had asphyxiated him! I'm sorry, but which heart! We know how tangled and ambiguous the heart can be—the heart is a sack into which a great deal can be put—the cold heart of a murderer; the ashen heart of a libertine; the faithful heart of a lover; a warm heart, an ungrateful heart, a heart that is jealous, envious, and so on.

The crushed cockroach seemed not to be directly related to the crime. For the moment one thing had been established—the dead man was asphyxiated, and this asphyxiation was connected with the heart. It could also be said, bearing in mind the lack of any external injuries whatsoever, that the asphyxiation was of a typically internal character. Yes, that was all … nothing more—internal, connected with the heart. No premature conclusions—and now it would be good to walk around the house a little.

I went back downstairs. Entering the dining room, I heard the sound of light, quickly fleeing footsteps—probably Miss Cecylia?—Now then, running away is not a good idea, young lady—the truth will always catch up with you! Passing the dining room—where the servants setting the table watched me surreptitiously—I slowly looked in on the other rooms, and at one point, somewhere through a door, I caught a glimpse of Mr. Antoni's retreating back. "Since it's now a matter of internal, heart-related death," I reflected, "then it must be admitted that this house couldn't be better suited for it. Strictly speaking, there may not be anything clearly incriminating here—and yet … " I sniffed—"nevertheless there is consternation, and in the atmosphere there is an odor, a characteristic odor—an odor of the kind that is bearable when it is your own, like the odor of sweat—an odor that I would describe as the odor of family affection … " Still sniffing, I noted certain tiny details that, though small, seemed not to be entirely without significance. Thus—faded, yellowed lace curtains—hand-embroidered cushions—an abundance of photographs and portraits—chairs worn by the backs of many generations ... and in addition to this, an unfinished letter on lined white paper—a pat of butter on a knife on the windowsill in the drawing room—a glass of medicine on the chest of drawers—a blue ribbon behind the stove—a cobweb, lots of cupboards—old smells ... All this together created an atmosphere of special solicitude, of great warm-heartedness—at every step the heart found sustenance for itself—yes, the heart could make use of butter, lace curtains, a ribbon, smells (and bread was carved, I noticed). And it also had to be acknowledged that the house was exceptionally "internal," a quality that manifested itself principally in the window filling, and in a chipped saucer, and in a dried-up sheet of flypaper left over from the summer.

But, so it should not be said that I was set pig-headedly on one internal direction and had ignored all other possibilities, I took the trouble to check whether indeed from the servants' quarters there was no access to the family rooms other than through the pantry—and I ascertained that there was not—and I even went outside and, pretending to take a stroll, I walked slowly all around the house in the wet snow. It was unthinkable that through the door, or through the windows, which had heavy shutters, someone could have entered the house in the night. From which it followed that if any act had been committed in this house in the night, then no one could be suspected except possibly the serving boy, Stefan, who slept in the pantry. "Yes," I said shrewdly, "it must have been Stefan the serving boy. No one else but him, the more so because he has a bad look about him."

Saying this, I pricked up my ears—because through an open casement I heard a voice that was oh-so-different from the voice I had heard not long before, and so exquisite, so full of promise, the voice no longer of a woebegone queen, but one that was wracked with dread and unease, atremble, weakened, a woman's voice—a voice that, it seemed, raised my spirits, wishing to help me out.—"Cecylka, Cecylka—look outside ... Has he gone yet? Look outside! Don't lean out, don't lean out—he might see you! He might come in here—poke around—have you put away your underwear? What's he looking for? What has he seen? Ignaś! Oh Lord, what can he have been looking at that stove for, what did he want with the chest of drawers! It's awful, all over the house! It doesn't matter about me—with me he can do whatever he wants; but for Antoś, for Antoś it'll be too much. For him this is sacrilege! He went terribly pale when I told him—oh. I'm afraid that he won't have the strength."

Yet if the crime, as could be considered established in the course of the investigation, was internal (I thought on)—then duty forces one to confess that murder committed by the serving boy, probably with a view to robbery, could in no manner be regarded as a crime of an internal nature. Suicide is a different matter—when people kill themselves and everything happens internally—or parricide, when, whatever else one might say, blood kills its own. As for the cockroach, the murderer must have crushed it in his haste.

As I reflected on these remarks I took a seat in the study and lit a cigarette—then all at once Mr. Antoni came in. On seeing me he offered a greeting, though a little more modestly than on the first occasion; he even appeared somewhat out of countenance.

"Your family has a beautiful house," I said. "It's exceptionally cosy, hearty—a real family home—warm … I'm reminded of my childhood—I'm reminded of my mother, my mother in her dressing gown, of chewed fingernails, of lacking a handkerchief … "

"Our home! Our home—of course … There are mice. But that's not why I'm here. My mother was telling me—apparently you … that is … "

"I know an excellent remedy for mice—Ratopex."

"Yes, I really must start dealing with them more vigorously—more vigorously, much more vigorously … Apparently this morning you visited … my father … or rather, pardon me, his body … "

"I did."

"Ah!—And … ?"

"And? And what?"

"Apparently you … found something there … "

"Actually I did—a dead cockroach."

"There are lots of dead cockroaches too; that is—just cockroaches … I mean to say—cockroaches that aren't dead."

"Did you love your father very much?" I asked, picking up an album with views of Kraków that lay on the table.

This question clearly took him by surprise. No, he was not prepared for it; he bowed his head, looked to the side, swallowed—and muttered with inexpressible constraint, almost with repugnance:

"I suppose."

"You suppose? That's not very much. You suppose! Only so much?"

"Why do you ask?" he said in a muffled voice.

"Why are you so artificial?" I replied sympathetically, leaning toward him in paternal fashion, the album in my hands.

"Me? Artificial? Why do … you … ?"

"Why did you just turn pale?"

Me? Turn pale?"

"Oh yes! You're scowling … You don't finish your sentences … You expatiate about mice and cockroaches … Your voice is too loud, then too quiet, hoarse or somehow shrill, so it pierces the ears," I said solemnly, "and such nervous movements … In fact, all of you here are somehow—nervous and artificial. Why is that, young man! Wouldn't it be better just to grieve in a straightforward way? Hmm … You … 'suppose'you loved him?! And why did you persuade your mother to move out of your father's bedroom a week ago?"

Utterly paralyzed by my words—not daring to move hand or foot—he was barely able to stammer out:

"Me? What do you mean? My father … My father needed … fresh air … "

"On the night in question you slept in your room downstairs?"

"Did I? Of course, in my room ... in my room downstairs."

I cleared my throat and went to my bedroom, leaving him on a chair with his hands on his knees, his mouth tightly shut and his legs pressed stiffly together. Hmm—he obviously had a nervous nature. A nervous nature, bashfulness, excessive sensitivity, excessive heartfeltness ... But I was still keeping a tight rein on myself, not wishing to frighten anyone prematurely. As I was in my room washing my hands and preparing for dinner, Stefan the serving boy slipped in and asked if I didn't need anything. He looked like a different person! His eyes darted about, his figure displayed a servile cunning, and all his mental powers were aroused to the highest degree! I asked: "So then, what can you tell me that's new?"

He answered in a single breath: "Well, your honor, you were asking if I slept in the pantry the night before yesterday? I wanted to say that on that night the young master locked the pantry door on the dining room side." I asked: "Has he ever locked that door before?" "Never. This one time he locked it, and he probably thought that I was already asleep, because it was late—but I wasn't sleeping yet and I heard him come up and lock it. When he unlocked it, that I couldn't say, because I dropped off—it was only at dawn that he woke me to say the master was dead, and by then the door was already open."

And so in the night, for unexplained reasons, the deceased's son locks the pantry door! He locks the pantry door!—What could this mean!

"Only please, your honor, don't say that I told you."

I was not wrong to have labeled this death an internal one! The door had been locked so no outsider should have access to the death! The net was closing in; the noose tightening around the murderer's neck was ever more visible.—Yet why, instead of manifesting triumph, did I only give a rather foolish smile!—For the reason that—alas, it must be acknowledged—something was missing that was at least as important as the noose around the murderer's neck, and that something was the noose around the neck of the victim. True, I had jumped over this stumbling block, I had leapt naively over his neck, which glowed with an immaculate whiteness; but nonetheless it's not possible to be permanently in a state of absolving passion. Very well, I agree (speaking aside), I was in a fury; for whatever reason hatred, repulsion, resentment had blinded me and forced me to persist in the face of a glaring absurdity—this is human, this anyone will understand; yet the moment will come when one must—settle down, there will come, as the Scriptures say, the Day of Judgment. And then ... hmm ... I'll say—he is the murderer, and the corpse will say—I died of a heart attack. And then what! What will Judgment say?

Let's suppose Judgment will ask: "You claim the dead man was murdered! On what basis?"

I will reply: "Because his family, your honor, his wife and children, and especially his son, are behaving suspiciously; they're behaving as if they had murdered him—there's no doubt about it." "Very good—but by what earthly means could he have been murdered, since he was *not* murdered, since it's blindingly obvious from the forensic report that he simply died of a heart attack?"

And then the defense lawyer, that hired prevaricator, will stand up and in a long speech, waving the sleeves of his gown, will set about proving that there has been a misunderstanding rooted in my own base way of thinking, that I have confused crime and mourning—for that which I took as a sign of a guilty conscience was only a sign of the timidity of feelings which retreat and contract at the cold touch of a stranger. And once again there will appear the exasperating, unbearable refrain—how could he possibly have been murdered when he was absolutely not murdered! Since there are not the slightest marks of asphyxiation on his body!

This stumbling block so troubled me that at lunch—simply for myself, to quell my distress and bring relief to my nagging doubts, for no other reason—I began to explain that crime in its essence is not physical, but mental *par excellence*. I believe I am right in saying that apart from me, no one else spoke. Mr. Antoni did not say a word—I don't know whether it was because he regarded me as unworthy, as he had the previous evening, or because he was afraid his voice might come out a little hoarse. The widowed mother sat pontifically, still mortally offended, it seemed, and her hands trembled, striving to secure immunity for themselves. Miss Cecylia was quietly swallowing the scalding liquids. While I, for the aforementioned inner motives, and oblivious to the faux pas I was committing, or of certain tensions in the air, discoursed eloquently and at great length. "Believe me, ladies and gentlemen, the physical shape of the act, the mistreated body, the disorder in the room, all the so-called evidence—these are entirely secondary details, a supplement, to be precise, to the real crime, a forensic formality, a tip of the hat by the criminal toward the authorities, nothing more. The real crime is always committed in the soul. The external details ... oh my Lord! Take for instance the following case: A charitable uncle is suddenly stabbed in the back—with an old-fashioned hat pin—by a nephew whom he has been showering with kindnesses for thirty years. And if you please!—such a huge mental crime and such a small, imperceptible physical sign, a tiny little hole from a pinprick. The nephew subsequently explains that he absentmindedly mistook his uncle's back for his cousin's hat. Who is going to believe him?

"Yes indeed, physically speaking crime is a triviality; it is mentally that it is hard. Given the extreme fragility of the organism, it's possible to murder by accident, like that nephew, by absent- mindedness—out of nowhere, all at once, bang, there's a corpse.

"One woman, the most upright person in the world, head over heels in love with her husband—this was right in their honeymoon period—notices on her husband's plate of raspberries an elongated white worm—and you should know that her husband hated these revolting grubs more than anything else. Instead of warning him, she watches with a playful smile, and then says: 'You ate a bug.' 'No!' the horrified husband exclaims. 'Oh yes,' replies the wife, and describes it—it was like so, fat and white. Much laughter and banter; the husband, pretending to be angry, raises his hands in the air at his wife's mischievousness. The matter is forgotten. Then, a week or two later, the wife is most surprised when the husband starts to lose weight and waste away; he rejects any kind of food, he's repulsed by his own arms and legs, and (please excuse the expression) he spends all his time on his knees praying to the porcelain god. Progressive disgust at oneself—a terrible illness! And one day there's great weeping and great moaning—he's died suddenly—he threw himself up, only his head and throat remained, he expelled the rest into a bucket. The widow is in despair—only in the crossfire of questions does it come to light that in the most hidden depths of her being she felt an unnatural fondness for the large bulldog her husband had beaten shortly before eating the raspberries.

"Or in one aristocratic family there was a son who murdered his mother by continually repeating the grating phrase: 'Please sit down!' At the hearing he acted innocent to the very end. Oh, crime is so easy it's a wonder that so many people die of natural causes—especially if one throws in the heart, the heart—that mysterious link between people, that twisting underground passageway between you and me, that lift-and-force pump which knows so perfectly how to lift and so wonderfully forces … It's only later that there comes the mourning, the graveside faces, the dignity of grief, the majesty of death—ha, ha—and all for the purpose of 'respecting' suffering and not accidentally looking too closely into that heart, which has quietly, cruelly murdered!"

They sat quiet as mice, not daring to interrupt!—Where was that pride from the previous evening? All of a sudden the widow threw down her napkin and, pale as death, her hands trembling twice as much, stood up from the table. I spread my hands apologetically. "I'm terribly sorry. I didn't mean to offend. I'm merely speaking in general terms about the heart, about the heart sac, in which it's so easy to hide a body."

"Despicable man!" she blurted out, her breast heaving. Her son and daughter jumped up from the table.

"The door!" I exclaimed. "Very well—I'm despicable! But tell me please, why was the door locked that night?"

There was a pause. All at once Cecylia burst out in nervous, plaintive sobs and said through her tears:

"The door wasn't Mama. I was the one who locked it. It was me!"

"That's not true, Cecylka—I was the one who ordered the door to be locked! Why are you humiliating yourself in front of this man!"

"Mama ordered it, but I wanted to … I wanted to … I also wanted to lock the door arid I locked it."

"I'm sorry," I said, "just a moment … What's this!" (After all, it was Antoni who had locked the pantry door.) "Which door are you talking about?"

"The door … the door to Daddy's bedroom … I locked it!"

"No, I locked it … I forbid you to talk like that, do you hear! I ordered it!"

What was this? So they had also locked a door! On the night when the father was to die, the son locked the pantry door and the mother and daughter locked his bedroom door!

"And why did the two of you lock that door?" I asked abruptly, "Exceptionally, on that particular night? For what purpose?"

Consternation! Silence! They did not know! They bowed their heads! A theatrical scene. Suddenly Antoni's perturbed voice was heard:

"Are you not embarrassed to explain yourselves? And to whom? Be quiet! Let's go!"

"Then perhaps you'll tell me why on that night you locked the door of the pantry, cutting the servants off from the other rooms?"

"Me? I locked it?"

"What then? Perhaps you didn't lock it? There are witnesses! It can be proved!"

More silence! More consternation! The women looked up, terrified. Finally the son, as if remembering something that had happened long ago, declared in a whisper:

"I locked it."

"And why was that? Why did you lock it? Was it perhaps to prevent drafts?"

"That I am unable to explain," he answered with indescribable haughtiness—and left the room.

I spent the rest of the day in my bedroom. For a considerable time I walked to and fro, from wall to wall, without lighting a candle. Outside, the darkness was gathering—snowflakes could be seen increasingly bright in the falling shadows of night, while the house was surrounded on all sides by the tangled skeletons of the trees.—What a fine house this was! A house of murderers, a monstrous house where cold, dissembling, premeditated murder was on the prowl, a house of asphyxiators! The heart?! I had known right away what to expect from that well-fed heart, and what parricide it was capable of, swollen as it was with grease, butter, and familial warmth! I knew, but I did not wish to speak too soon! And they put on such airs! They demanded such homage! Feelings! Rather let them explain why they locked the doors.

Yet why at that moment—when I already held all the threads in my hand and could point my finger at the criminal—did I needlessly waste time instead of acting! The stumbling block, the stumbling block—the white neck, untouched, resembling the snow outside—the darker things were, the whiter it became. The corpse was evidently in league with the band of murderers. Once again I made an effort and attacked the corpse, head on this time, with raised visor—calling things by their names and clearly indicating the guilty party. It was just as if I had been wrestling with a chair. However I strained my imagination, my intuition, my logic, the neck remained a neck, and whiteness remained whiteness, with the obstinacy characteristic of lifeless objects. Nothing remained, then, but to play the part to the very end, to abide in my vengeful blindness and wait, and wait—counting naively on the notion that since the corpse was unwilling, perhaps—perhaps—the crime itself would rise to the surface like olive oil. Was I wasting time! Yes, but my steps sounded throughout the house; everyone could hear that I was constantly pacing, and they, downstairs, were probably not wasting time.

Suppertime had passed. It was almost eleven o'clock, yet I had not stirred from my room, and went on cursing them all for villains and criminals, exulting, and at the same time hoping with my remaining strength that my stubbornness and persistence would be rewarded—that the situation could after all be won over by so many different facial expressions, made with so much passion, that in the end it would be unable to resist, that, intense, brought to extremities, it would have to resolve itself somehow, give birth to something, give birth to something no longer from the realm of fiction but something real. After all, we couldn't go on like this forever—with me upstairs and them downstairs—someone had to call out "pass," and everything depended on who would be the first to do so. It was quiet and still. I looked out into the hallway, but nothing could be heard from below. What could they be doing down there? Could they possibly be doing what they ought to be doing? If I was exulting here because of the locked doors, were they for their part sufficiently afraid, conferring among themselves, straining their ears to catch the sounds of my footsteps; were their souls not too lazy to work this out within themselves? Oh, I breathed a sigh of relief when around midnight I finally heard steps in the hallway and someone knocked. "Come in," I called.

"I hope you'll forgive me," said Antoni, sitting in a chair to which I gestured. He looked bad—sallow and pale—and it was clear that eloquent discourse would not be his strong point.—"Your behavior … and lately—those words. … In a word—what does all this mean? Either leave … and right away! … or say what you have to say! This is extortion!" he exclaimed.

"At last you're asking," I said. "It's late! And even this you're asking in a very general way. What am I in fact to say? But very well—since you ask: Your father was … "

"What? Was what;"

"Was asphyxiated."

"Asphyxiated. Good. Asphyxiated."—He tossed his head with a certain bizarre satisfaction.

"You're glad?"

"I'm glad."

I waited a moment, then said:

"Was there anything else you wished to ask?"

He burst out:

"But no one heard any cries or commotion!"

"First of all, in the vicinity only your mother and your sister were sleeping, and they had shut their door for the night. Secondly, the criminal could quickly have throttled a victim who … "

"All right, all right," he murmured, "all right. Fine. One more thing: Who in your opinion … with this act, who do you … "

"Suspect, no? Who do I suspect? What do you think—in your opinion, could someone from outside have entered the house when it was locked up tight and guarded by a night watchman and by vigilant dogs? You'll no doubt say that the dogs fell asleep along with the watchman, and out of forgetfulness the front door was left unlocked? Eh? A terrible series of coincidences?"

"No one could have gotten in," he replied proudly. He sat erect and it could plainly be seen that—motionless—he despised me, he despised me with all his soul.

"No one," I agreed with alacrity, reveling in advance at the sight of his pride.

"Absolutely no one! And so there remains only the three of you and the three servants. But the servants too had their way blocked, since you ... for some unknown reason ... locked the door from the pantry. Or perhaps now you'll claim that you did not lock it?"

"I did!"

"And why, for what purpose did you do sol"

He jumped up from his chair. "Don't play games!" I said, and with that short remark I put him firmly in his place. His anger was paralyzed and died away, breaking off in a squeak.

"I locked it—I don't know—without thinking," he said with difficulty, and whispered twice: "Asphyxiated. Asphyxiated."

A nervous nature! They were, all of them, deep, nervous natures.

"And since your mother and sister also ... unthinkingly locked the door of their bedroom (and besides, it's hard to imagine, is it not?), then that leaves ... you know who that leaves. You were the only one with free access to your father that night. 'The moon is up, the dogs asleep, and someone's clapping in the wood.'"

He burst out:

"And so this is supposed to mean ... that I ... that I ... ha, ha, ha!"

"And that laugh is supposed to mean that it wasn't you," I observed, and his laughter ended after a few attempts on a protracted false note.

"It wasn't you?—But in that case, young man," I continued more quietly, "please explain to me—why did you not shed a single tear?"

"A tear?"

"Yes, a tear. That's what your mother whispered to me, right at the beginning, yesterday, on the stairs. It's normal for mothers to compromise and betray their own children. And now, just a moment ago—you laughed. You declared that you were glad about your father's death!" I said with such triumphant obtuseness, catching him in his words, that he wilted and looked at me as if I were an instrument of torture.

Yet, sensing that the matter was becoming serious, he exerted all his powers of will and attempted to stoop to an explanation—in the form of an *avis au lecteur,* a footnote, which he could barely spit out.

"That was ... It was irony ... You understand? ... The opposite ... on purpose."

"Being ironic about your father's death?"

He was silent, and then I whispered confidentially, almost in his ear:

"Why are you so embarrassed? Surely there's nothing embarrassing about one's father's death."

Looking back on this moment I'm glad I came through uninjured—though he did not move a muscle.

"Or perhaps you're embarrassed because you loved him? Perhaps you really did love him?"

He stammered with difficulty—with abhorrence—with despair:

"Very well. If you absolutely must ... if ... then yes, so be it ... I loved him."

And throwing something on the table, he cried:

"Here! This is his hair!"

It was indeed a lock of hair. "All right," I said, "now take it away."

"I don't want to! You can take it away! I'm giving it to you!"

"Why these outbursts? Fine—you loved him—agreed. Just one more question (because, as you see, I don't understand a thing about these romances of yours). I admit you almost had me convinced with the lock of hair, but—you see—above all there's one thing I don't understand."

Here again I lowered my voice and whispered in his ear.

"You loved him, very good, but why was there so much shame, so much scorn in that love?"

He turned pale and said nothing.

"So much cruelty, so much disgust? Why do you conceal it like a criminal concealing a crime? You don't answer? You don't know? Perhaps I will know for you.

"You did love him—yes indeed—but when your father fell ill … you mentioned to your mother the need for fresh air. Your mother—who incidentally also loved him—listens and nods. That's right, that's right, good air won't hurt, and so she moves next door to her daughter's room—'I'll still be close enough to come whenever the sick man calls.' Or perhaps that wasn't how it was? Perhaps you'll set the record straight?"

"That's how it was!"

"Exactly! I know a thing or two, as you see. A week passes. One evening your mother and sister lock the bedroom door. Why? God alone knows! Does one need to deliberate about every turn of a key in a lock? They just turned it, without thinking, then one two three they're in their beds. Yes, and at the same time you lock the pantry door downstairs. Why? Can every trivial action of that kind be justified? One might just as well demand an explanation for why at this particular moment you're sitting and not standing."

He leapt to his feet, then sat down again and said:

"Yes, that's how it was! It was just the way you said!"

"Then it occurs to you that—your father may need something. And maybe—you think—your mother and sister have fallen asleep, and your father needs something. And so quietly, so as not to wake up those who are sleeping, quietly you go to your father's room up the creaking stairs. And then, when you're already in his room—the rest requires no commentary—then, without thinking now—full steam ahead."

He listened, unable to believe his own ears, but suddenly—it was as if he roused himself and groaned with a note of desperate frankness that only great fear is capable of inspiring:

"But I wasn't there at all! I was downstairs in my room the whole time! I didn't only lock the pantry door, I also locked my own door—I also locked myself in my room … There's been some mistake!"

I exclaimed:

"What!—so you locked yourself in too!—so everyone was locked in! … Then in that case who on earth … !"

"I don't know, I don't know," he replied aghast, rubbing his forehead. "It's only now that I'm beginning to understand—that perhaps we were expecting something—perhaps we were waiting for something—perhaps we had an inkling of something and—out of fear, out of shame"—he burst out vehemently all of a sudden—"everyone was locked in their room ... because we wanted father, we wanted father—to take care of it by himself!"

"Aha, so having an inkling that death was drawing close, you locked yourselves in to keep death away as it approached! So—you were all waiting for the murder after all!"

"We were waiting?"

"Yes. But in that case who could possibly have murdered him? Because he was murdered, and you were all simply waiting, and there's absolutely no way an outsider could have come in."

He was silent.

"But I really was locked in my room," he whispered, sagging under the weight of irrefutable logic. "There's been some mistake."

"But in that case who could possibly have murdered him?" I said assiduously. "Who could possibly have murdered him?"

He lost himself in thought—as if he were taking terrible stock of his conscience—he was pale and motionless, his gaze withdrawn deep below his half-closed eyelids. Had he glimpsed something there, deep within himself? What had he glimpsed? Perhaps he had seen himself rising from his bed and cautiously walking up the treacherous stairs, his hands ready for the deed? And perhaps for just a moment he was seized by doubt that after all, who knew whether such a thing ... would be completely unthinkable. Perhaps in that one second hatred appeared to him as the complement of love, who knows (this is only my conjecture) if in that twinkling of an eye he had not glimpsed the terrible duality of every emotion—that love and hatred are two sides of the same thing. And this blinding though momentary revelation must have instantly laid waste to everything within him—and he with all his pity became unbearable to himself. And though this lasted only a second, it was enough, for he had been forced to grapple with my suspicions for twelve hours now, for twelve hours he had felt someone senselessly, stubbornly pursuing him, and he had probably ruminated on the absurdity of thought a thousand times—he bowed his head like a broken man, and then raised it, looked at me from close by with boundless determination and said distinctly, right to my face:

"It was me. I—steamed out."

"What do you mean, you steamed out?"

"I steamed out, I say, because as you remarked, it was—without thinking—full steam ahead."

"What?! It's true! You're confessing! It was you! It was you—really!"

"It was me. I steamed out."

"Aha—just so. And the whole thing lasted no longer than a minute."

"No longer. A minute at most. And I don't know if we're not overestimating at a minute. Then afterward I returned to my room, got into bed, and fell asleep—and before I fell asleep I yawned and thought to myself—I remember vividly—that oho, tomorrow I'll have to get up in the morning!"

I was astonished—he had confessed to everything so smoothly; or rather not so much smoothly, for his voice was hoarse, as fiercely, with extraordinary relish. There could be no doubt! No one could deny it! Yes—but what about the neck, what was to be done with the neck, which was in the bedroom dully sticking to its story! My mind worked feverishly—but what can a mind do when faced with the mindlessness of a corpse!

I looked despondently at the murderer, who seemed to be waiting. And it's hard to explain, but at this moment I realized that nothing was left to me but a frank confession. There was no point in continuing to beat one's head against the wall, that is, against the neck—further resistance or evasion was useless. And the moment I realized this, I immediately acquired great confidence in him. I realized that I had gone too far, that I had gotten up to a little too much mischief—and, in deep waters, tired, exhausted by so much effort, so many faces made, I suddenly became a child, a helpless little boy, and I had a wish to confess to my big brother my mistake and the trouble I had caused. It seemed to me that he would understand ... and surely he wouldn't refuse me some advice ... "Yes," I thought, "nothing remains but a frank confession ... He'll understand, he'll help! He'll find a way!" But in any case I rose and moved unobtrusively toward the door.

"You see," I said, and my lips were a little out of control, "there's a certain stumbling block here ... a certain obstacle—of a purely formal character, as it happens—nothing of significance. The thing is"—I already had my hand on the door handle—"that actually the body shows no signs of asphyxiation. Physically speaking—he wasn't asphyxiated at all, but rather died of an ordinary heart attack. The neck, you know, the neck! ... The neck was untouched!"

Having said this, I ran for it out the open door and rushed as fast as my legs would carry me along the hallway. I dashed into the room where the dead man lay and hid in the wardrobe—and with some degree of confidence, though with fear too, I waited. It was dark, cramped, and stuffy, and the deceased's trousers brushed against my cheek. I waited for a long time, and began to doubt, thinking that nothing would happen and that I had been basely duped, that I had been cheated! All at once the door opened quietly and someone crept in—after which I heard an awful noise, the bed creaked like crazy, and in the absolute silence all the formalities were dealt with after the fact! Then the steps receded just as they had come. When after a long hour I climbed out of the wardrobe, trembling and drenched in perspiration, violence reigned amid the disordered bedsheets; the body was thrown diagonally across a crumpled pillow, and the dead man's neck bore clear imprints of all ten fingers. The forensic experts looked askance at those imprints, it was true, saying that something was not as it should have been in all this—but the imprints, in conjunction with the criminal's unequivocal confession at the hearing, were taken as sufficient proof.

—1927. Translated by Bill Johnston

*Absurdism, Gombrowicz, and "A Premeditated Murder."* Literary Absurdism is a reflection in literature of one's confrontating the reality that there is no way to perceive or demonstrate value or meaning in life or the universe. If existence has no objectively demonstrable underlying logic, sense, or value, one feels released from the obligation of pretending that one knows what reality is, much less any obligation to depict it "realistically." It is easy to see the seeds of this philosophical and literary attitude in the earlier-examined modernist story "The Tale" by Joseph Conrad, for whom the human mind is aswirl with vague and unreliable, constantly shifting thought impressions filtered through one's innate and acquired expectations and prejudices, potentially leading in any number of directions, or possibly nowhere at all. Still, Conrad did not reject the existence of such moral abstractions as "love," "courage," "loyalty," "duty," "bravery," and so on, but saw them as residing in one's "better self." In effect, absurdism, at its extreme, rejects the idea of the sense of existence and of any meaningful internal moral core; one is left on one's own to go through life struggling either to carve out value and meaning for oneself; to give oneself over to religious belief; or to give up on the project of life altogether.

For Gombrowicz the achievement of meaning or value in life seems mostly to have consisted in a constant uphill struggle to avoid being pinned down or defined by a role placed on him by social convention, that is, by "other people," thereby achieving a kind of elusive "authenticity." This concern explains Gombrowicz's fascination in other of his works with juvenility, which is a state of incomplete formedness. The problem with trying to achieve authenticity, he realized, is that by rejecting one role, one inevitably finds oneself falling into another one, equally as artificial or even more so. If there is an intermediate "roleless" state of authenticity, it is only of brief duration, and few people are able to achieve it. Most likely it is illusory.

Societal roles tend to be hierarchical, and they are imposed interpersonally, by some people on other people, by treating them in a certain way, often with the background motive of self-aggraandizement or domination. As a consequence, one is not in charge of one's own personality; rather it is in the possession of other people and depends on how they inevitably stereotype one. It is for this reason that the prosecutor in "A Premeditated Murder" tries so determinedly to cast off the role the dead man's family attempts to impose on him of "hand-kissing condolence-bearing family acquaintance and bereaved co-mourner." He does so by counter-imposing on them the role he has at his ready disposal—that of prosecutorial investigator. As such, he finds he has no choice but to hold this role over the family consistently and follow it through to its logical end, by demonstrating, through his own ruthlessly pursued idiosyncratic interpretation of the "facts" of the "case," that a premeditated murder has taken place, when in reality, as he himself knows perfectly well, none has been committed at all, premeditated or otherwise.

In this classic example of the Gombrowiczian "duel" of roles, the family, least of all the malleable son Antoni, is no match for the prosecutor in his prosecutorial role, who somehow plants in Antoni's mind the sophistry that love and hate are two sides of the same coin, and that a crime theoretically could easily have been committed by him, except for one crucial and incontrovertible missing piece of evidence. Antoni is captured by the logical syllogistic inevitability of the situation and confesses to a crime he never committed, in fact one that never occurred. That he did not commit it in actuality seems both to him and the prosecutor/narrator to be a minor bother to get out of the way. Just as one feels an irresistible urge to fit the last piece of a puzzle into place, at the earliest opportunity Antoni fills in the one glaring gap remaining in the chain of evidence by strangling his father *post mortem*. It is in this final act that the absurdism of Gombrowicz's story is revealed in its full nonsensicality.

*Literary Resonances.* On a superficial level "A Premeditated Murder" is a parody of the criminal detective story, with oedipal undertones. The prosecutor calls most readily to mind either Hercule Poirot (who had already appeared in Agatha Christie's mysteries as early as 1920) or Fyodor Dostoevsky's even earlier Porfiry Petrovich from *Crime and Punishment*. The setting of the closed-off country manse, where all possible suspects can be gathered and interrogated under one roof, until at last, under the probing questioning of the detective, the culprit almost involuntarily cries out "I did it!" seems ready-made for Hercule Poirot, while the mind games played by Gombrowicz's prosecutor, eventually leading to the "criminal's" coming clean and confessing of his own volition, seem modeled more on Dostoevsky's detective. At one point in the text the prosecutor actually (mis)quotes a Porfiry Petrovich aphorism on rabbit stew. As to the Greek myth, the suggestible Antoni makes for a rather feeble Oedipus; he does not even get along particularly well with his mother.

Whether or not Joseph Conrad is a direct literary influence on Gombrowicz, one must note the striking similarity between the way the prosecutor makes his "case" by gathering together disconnected bits and pieces such as the dead cockroach, the locked doors, and the wife's recent decision to sleep by herself, and the way in which Conrad's Commanding Officer profiles the Northman and his crew on the basis, among other things, of an uneaten biscuit and the boat's logbook's looking too unincriminating. Both characters "wear hats," that is, are bound by and act in accordance with their official roles. Both additionally justify their conclusions by their sense that something seems "not quite right," that the situation "smells of guilt." In the end, both characters end up making the "facts" of the case fit the profile of the imagined "crime." The Commanding Officer filters his decision-making through his basic distrust of foreigners and of neutral vessels; his disapproval of the captain's drinking while on duty; and his moral outrage at the thought of a crime he does not even know has been committed, while the prosecutor cannot get over his grievance not only for being initially backfooted by the family into playing the socially awkward role of an accidental intruder upon their grief, but also for his not having been met at the station and—even more egregiously in his mind—for his not having been given enough time to finish his pork chops. A major difference between the two authors is that Conrad's Commanding Officer is tortured by feelings of guilt and second guessing, whereas Gombrowicz'a Prosecuting Attorney has no such qualms or regrets.

# Jarosław Iwaszkiewicz

Like several other authors in this collection, Jarosław Iwaszkiewicz (1894–1980) was born in what is now Ukraine. He was nominated for the Nobel Prize four times and is probably the best Polish writer the world outside Poland barely knows about. In his shorter fiction, his métier was the long short story or novella, but he also wrote plays and shorter stories such as the two in the present collection.

An accomplished poet and first published in that genre, Iwaszkiewicz was one of the founding members of the Skamander group of experimental poets active in the 1920s and 1930s. He published prodigiously; his major novel was *Sława i chwała* (Fame and Glory), a three-volume panoramic view of the life of the Polish intelligentsia in the first half of the twentieth century. He was a noted music and theater critic, and also a translator into Polish of literature from English, French, Russian, and Danish.

During World War II, Iwaszkiewicz participated in Polish underground activities, working especially to protect and rescue Poland's works of art. His palatial residence south of Warsaw served as a hiding place for many intellectuals being sought by the Nazis. In 1988, he was posthumously recognized as Righteous Among Nations by Yad Vashem in Jerusalem for his role in saving Jews during the war.

Because he was viewed by many as a collaborator with the communist government, after the fall of communism in 1989 Iwaszkiewicz's works were temporarily and narrow-mindedly removed from the school curriculum. Despite his prominent public life under the communist regime, it would be difficult to identify any concrete harm he caused, or to identify any author whose literary works, especially his short stories, have less to do with political or ideological messaging than his. With time Iwaszkiewicz's reputation as one of the towering figures of twentieth-century Polish and even world literature can only be expected to grow.

Iwaszkiewicz typically places his stories about life and man's place in the universe in small-town rural Polish settings. The two stories chosen here, written decades apart, both illustrate that proclivity and represent only a small sample out of Iwaszkiewicz's prolific output in the short-story genre.

## Rose

When Rose returned to Zagródka it was already October, a time when most of the work in the fields still needs to be done: the second harvest, or the digging of potatoes, and the autumn plowing. So her mother greeted her with a wry face, because she was on her way to work. All the more so that Rose had arrived from the nearest town, Lutomsk, on foot and with a small bundle in her arms, without any indication of ever returning to Warsaw.

It had been some time since Rose had visited Zagródka, six years or more. Twelve years had passed since she first left for Warsaw to go into service. She wrote infrequently, and her mother had grown used to not thinking about her, barely scraping by. She rented her tiny fields to others, planted her garden with potatoes, and survived on the part-time work she managed to get here and there. A gardener from Lutomsk had started a nursery several years earlier, and it was there she mainly worked, putting by grosz after grosz. It was enough to live on; what more did she need? For her Rose's return was a catastrophe.

Rose had arrived officiously, with pursed lips and a grave expression. Not sparing any words, she began bustling about the cottage fixing herself coffee from the large tin she had brought with her. She asked her mother whether she had any eggs for an omelet.

Her mother kept four red hens without a rooster; the eggs were always sold for cash. The old woman looked thoroughly downcast as Rose broke five eggs for her omelet.

"In Warsaw the master always ate two eggs first thing each morning," she said sententiously. Old Veronica sat on the bed and looked at her daughter eating the eggs with an air of concentration, leaning on her elbows.

"Poor Rose's put on some years," she thought to herself, shaking her head sadly, "and she's still not married. She should have gotten married when she first went into service, but she didn't even want to hear about it."

"If it's a problem about the eggs," Rose said suddenly, "I'll pay for them."

"Oh sure, you'll pay. As if it wasn't all yours anyway. The old man didn't leave me a penny."

"Well, you worked alongside each other," Rose said.

She got up, rinsed off the dishes quickly and deftly, as she must have done in Warsaw, and went outside. It was nearly noon, and the weather was nice. Lots had changed in Zagródka. Trees had grown, cottages here and there had changed appearance, some fields had been joined, and some farmers had moved entirely out of the village to till them, leaving behind empty spaces in place of former cottages. The Zdybas had lived here, but now they were gone; elsewhere the Krysa cottage was moldering.

Zagródka was a large village; its buildings formed a strip along the highway, with wide meadows on one end, bisected by the Bystrzyca River. Beyond that, on the other side of the river, the smoke and houses of the settlement of Lutomsk could be seen. An old dike, overgrown with grass, with a path along it, separated the village from the meadow. Rose recalled walking in this direction twelve years earlier; she had run along this path even earlier as a young girl.

At one point the dike dipped down and merged into the meadow. Here like a sentinel stood a large Vistula poplar and, on the village side, a small but tidy cottage. Lilacs and other shrubs grew in front, and yellow marigolds were still blooming. It was here that Rose directed her proud and carefully measured steps.

In the meantime Veronica, left at home to her own devices, snatched up her daughter's bundle with a quick and covetous movement. Her grey, twisted fingers quickly undid the knots of the scarf, and she began sifting through the contents. There really wasn't much there: a tin of coffee, a small sack of sugar, two measely petticoats, and some underwear. Then Veronica's fingers came across a small but interesting item in the folds of a coarse shirt. She quickly extracted a light blue bankbook. "That's more like it," she muttered, and her hands began to shake.

Her twisted fingers turned the pages of the book with difficulty, but she still couldn't make out what was written there. She glanced out the window. A young man was walking slowly down the road from the direction of the meadow and the poplar. He moved not merely slowly, as is usual in the countryside, but somehow especially langorously and lazily. He was blond-haired and blue-eyed, and wore a sleepy expression.

"Hey, Ignatz"! Veronica called. "Come over here!"

Without hurrying, Ignatz sauntered over to the cottage.

He was so tall that he had to stoop as he entered the low-hung threshold. Veronica cast a friendly glance at the good-looking young man. It was the neighbor's son from the cottage by the poplar, Ignatz Bona, eighteen years old at most.

"Come here, Ignatz, tell me how much is written in this book."

Ignatz fumbled through the pages of the book with his thick fingers. He easily found the final figure, but he couldn't believe his eyes. He looked at it uncertainly.

"It says here 2000," he said. "Oh my gosh," wailed Veronica. "Are you sure?" "That's what it says, but whether it's true or not ..."

Veronica quickly retrieved the document from Ignatz's chapped hands. She rewrapped it in the coarse shirt and skillfully rehid it in her daughter's bundle.

"Rose's come home," she said by way of explanation, placing the bundle over the petticoats hanging from a stick over the bed.

"Psssh ... ," Ignatz whistled, taking a seat on the bench.

Veronica looked him over. His pleasant face was totally bereft of thought and devoid of expression. His puffy blue eyes looked through the window out onto the roadway.

"What's wrong, aren't you people digging potatoes?" she asked him.

"Sure they are," responded Ignatz calmly, continuing to stare into the distance.

"Who do you mean 'they'?"

"Mother, Jadwiga, Jasio, ... everyone."

"What about you?"

"Me? I've been feeling queasy since morning."

"Queasy?"

"Yeah, something inside me's not quite right," he said quietly, almost with embarrassment.

"Oh, you've always been that way," Veronica said, drawing closer with a sly expression. "You know, if you had your wits about you, you could have that 2000 for yourself."

"Oh, sure," he said, not budging.

"I've got this idea," Veronica whispered furtively, "that Rose has come home to get married."

In the meantime Rose, walking past the poplar, came to a stop in front of the neighbor's gate. The bright afternoon was beginning to haze over. A wagonload full of red potatoes stood in the yard, and the people around it were moving briskly. Potatoes were being unloaded into baskets and from there into a cellar-pit dug right into the ground. Rose approached the workers with a dignified gait.

"Hello," she said, "what are the potatoes like this year?"

"Not bad, praise the Lord," the neighbor woman muttered, without looking. But suddenly she lifted her head and saw her.

"Why, if it isn't Rose."

The neighbor wasn't much older than Rose herself, although she had full-grown sons. They talked while the neighbor continued working.

"Where's Franek got to?" Rose asked with feigned indifference.

"Oh, he's in the army," the woman explained. "That's his wife over there, Jadwiga."

She pointed to a young woman carrying a basket of potatoes. She was visibly pregnant. Rose blushed, but didn't lose her composure.

"Oh? And when did he get hitched?"

"It'll be about a year ago," the neighbor sighed. "One mouth more to feed, and soon no doubt there'll be two."

And she began to complain to Rose about her poverty and the hard times. Rose listened to her with lowered eyes and tightly knit brows. Her lightly pockmarked face flushed red and turned white by turns.

"And what about Ignatz?"

"Oh, he's snuck off somewhere," she answered, "probably to Zofka's. A sickly lad, never of any use. They probably won't even take him into the army."

"When does he come up?"

"Oh, not for another two years. He's only just turned eighteen."

"And where did you say he was?" Rose repeated.

"At Zofka's, who cooks and cleans for the school-mistress. He's been paying attention to her lately."

"It's been some time since I've seen Ignatz," Rose said, as though some thought had just entered her head.

"A strapping lad, but a poor worker," the woman said frankly. "It's a miracle if you can get anything out of him, even at harvest time. Jasio's still a child, but he's a lot better worker."

As if to illustrate his mother's words, the industrious Jasio was merrily spinning about like a top, carrying potatoes. His flaxen hair fell lightly over his forehead. He was maybe fifteen years old.

Rose headed home. Again she found herself walking along the path across the meadow. The meadow was still green, and the leaves of the trees, already turning red and yellow, looked pretty against it, but Rose was not looking. She walked along with a furrowed brow, calculating something in her head. She was still looking down at her feet when suddenly she sensed someone tall blocking her way. She raised her eyes but didn't recognize who it was. When she had last visited Zagródka, Ignatz was as young and stout as Janek was now. In the meantime he had grown into a big, heavy-set, blond-haired youth. Ignatz smiled.

"Why Miss Rose," he said, clumsily extending his hand.

"Ignatz," said Rose, only now recognizing him, "What have you been up to?"

"I've been over to your place," Ignatz replied with a lazy smile.

"What, not to Zofka's?"

"There too. Who told you so?"

"Your mother. Why don't you come over tonight," Rose said, making a quick decision.

"Fine, I'll come," he said languidly.

And so he did. He sat down heavily at the table. A small kerosene lamp illuminated his face from below, leaving his eyes in darkness. He didn't have much to say. Rose, dressed in a dark red dress, lit a fire in the stove until it became quite hot in the cottage. She had powdered her nose, and drank vodka from a half-full glass while sitting partially turned away from the table, slightly raising her voice. She was putting on airs and looked completely different from earlier that day. Veronica gazed with amazement, and at the same time with admiration, at her daughter's elaborate manners.

Later the old lady Bona, Ignatz's mother, came over, and the two women toddled off into the bed-chamber. Bona had already learned that in Warsaw Rose had put by some 2000 zlotys. Ignatz had a good couple of acres of land from his father. Put that money into the land, and there'd be more work than a single person could handle. Add to it Rose's parcel, presently rented out, and hey! You'd really have something then. The old lady didn't say anything about Zofka. The whole village knew about her, but Veronica somehow didn't.

Left on her own with Ignatz, Rose suddenly became bashful. He, by contrast, gathered courage, and kept asking questions: Miss Rose this, and Miss Rose that. What was it like in Warsaw, are there good-looking guys there, and so on. Of course, the men are all right, but cutthroats every one, and only interested in your money. Rose didn't mention how she had denied herself every pleasure and company while looking after her bank account and little else.

Ignatz moved closer, and clumsily put his arm about her waist. Rose was not nearly as thin as Zofka. They sat that way into the night, arm in arm, drinking vodka. The lamp smoked, while out of the bed-chamber could be heard the haggling of Veronica and her neighbor. Later Ignatz rose heavily and started to leave, with Rose on his heels as far as the porch. But Ignatz quickly walked out into the yard, and Rose strained her eyes to see whether he had turned in the direction of home or toward the schoolhouse. It was totally dark, but Rose had the impression that it was toward the school.

A few days later, already at the end of October, they went together to Lutomsk to announce the wedding. Ignatz drove a wagon behind a small but spritely horse. Rose complained about the shaking, and kept grabbing Ignatz around the waist, while he kept smiling to himself. The potato harvest was over, and the village had taken on a different appearance. It happened to be market day, and lots of people were heading to Lutomsk, despite the thick mud. It started to cloud over, and right after arriving Ignatz started to make broad hints about getting something to drink. But Rose ordered him to drive straight to the parish office.

Ignatz learned that, besides the 2000 zlotys she had put by, Rose had a separate account for the wedding and everything connected with it. She had brought that with her in cash. They found the parish priest in his office. When he learned what they had come for, he could scarcely restrain himself.

"You want to take this boy to the altar? Why, you could be his mother!"

Maybe she couldn't have been his mother, but she did remember when he had been born. Well, it's tough. Franek would have made more sense, but the wretch went after that pauper Jadwiga. She remembered seeing Ignatz feeding the geese when she was already a biggish girl. But when the priest learned that in Warsaw Rose had belonged to the Rosary Society at St. Alexander's, he began to come around. He could see he wasn't dealing with some hussy, but with an honest hard-working girl.

So the organist registered them in his book: Rose Genowefa Bińkowska and Ignatius Bona. Three weeks of banns, and after the third the wedding. Later they went to the market square to a ready-wear tailor. Rose bought Ignatz a decent-looking greenish suit and an autumn coat. In another store she bought two shirts, two ready-made ties, and a hat; at a shoemaker's she bought him some gaiters. Ignatz looked on with amazement at how Rose crushed a hundred-zloty note in her hands, and openly gaped when he saw the Jew giving Rose the change back from it.

Ignatz also wanted Rose to buy him a dark suit for the wedding, but she said he could rent his wedding suit at Roguszczak's, the one who had served at the manor house before the war. However, she did take him to the pork-butcher's, where over the shop they could get something to eat. They drank vodka, ate sausage, cutting it daintily with a pocket knife, and had sour pickles on the side. On top of that Ignatz ordered beer.

Rose dealt with her money meticulously, bargaining with the salesgirl, checking the addition and, on the whole, as Ignatz said, "making a show of her money." When they arrived home, rather tight and in a good mood, they found Zofka waiting for them in Veronica's house. She took up a position next to the wall in the depths of the room, shifting from one leg to the other, leaving circular marks on the light blue limecoated walls. Her kerchief had fallen down off her head, and her thick dark hair, tied up carelessly, was falling in her large, dark, beautiful eyes. They said her father had been a Frenchman who had served as a valet at the manor. For sure he was some kind of Mediterranean, maybe an Italian, but who knew? It was enough that she was dark-haired and exquisite. She was an orphan, and helped to clean, wash clothes, and cook for the local school-mistress. She hadn't a penny to her name.

When Ignatz saw Zofka he sobered up immediately and sat down heavily on the bench, making a moaning sound either out of amazement or fright. Rose, by contrast, didn't miss a beat but took up a position in the middle of the room with her hands on her hips.

"What did you come here for?" she asked straight out.

"Because I wanted to," Zofka answered resolutely. She could see that she hadn't scared Rose a bit.

"Keep away from Ignatz, because you can't have him," Rose uttered sharply.

"What are you chasing after him for, you Warsaw hussy?"

"Me, chase after him? That's rich! As if he needed any encouragement."

Ignatz, in the meantime, sitting next to the window, began undoing the package with the suit and shirts. He unfolded the shirts on the table and looked them over, twisting his head this way and that. He didn't pay any attention to the women's spat.

"You think you can set your eyes on him?" Rose screamed excitedly. "You should live so long. He's mine, understand? They already announced it today."

"You bought him with a suit, you old cow!" said Zofka.

"So what if I did? Buy him one yourself, and maybe he'll take you back again," Rose mocked relentlessly. "Look at you, barefoot and in rags! With me he'll be lord and master and have whatever he wants: a suit, gaiters, ties … !" Rose cooled down the more she listed the things … "because he'll be mine, because I have money, and you don't!"

"You toothless old hag," cried Zofka, "I'd like to know how you got that money in Warsaw."

"Go yourself and see whether it's easy," Rose shouted. "See how much money they'll give you for that moth-eaten skirt of yours."

"Moth-eaten or not, you haven't seen the last of it. You'll live to regret those words and your money, you bitch."

Having had the last word, Zofka left the house without so much as a look at Ignatz. Her voice could still be heard on the porch:

"You'll regret it, you'll be sorry!"

In fact, Rose did live to regret her words, because when the final banns had been published and the date for the wedding was drawing near, Ignatz suddenly announced that he wasn't going to let her take him to the altar. Rose accepted the news with seeming equanimity:

"Hmph! It's not like you're the only fish in the sea," she said. And in fact, even during her engagement to Ignatz, other lads from the village had been coming to Veronica's cottage all along to check to see whether Rose was worth all those 2000 zlotys. Although the general consensus was that no, she wasn't, there were still a couple who hadn't given up and who put in an appearance from time to time. Rose treated them hospitably, patted them on the back, and, while Ignatz was hanging around the school, she would drink vodka with them and sit with them in the cottage until late at night. Among them was Roguszczak, the son of the man who had served at the manor; Pietrek Masalski, just back from the army; Leon Slusarczyk; and several others.

Leon, hard-working and strong, was the son of the village elder, and it was he that Rose selected to replace Ignatz. But first she had to take back the engagement presents. With this aim in mind, Rose set out for the cottage by the poplar. Only the old woman was at home. Old Bona was in despair that everything had come to naught. The money was going to be wasted, and all she was going to get out of it was another mouth to feed. Zofka's, of course. Ignatz, having made up his mind, never left the girl's side.

Rose gloomily asked for the presents back that she had bought her fiancé. Bona took out of the cupboard the greenish suit that Ignatz had worn only three times, the coat, both shirts, the gaiters, and the red and the blue necktie. The only thing missing was the stamped-metal cigarette case, because Ignatz always carried it with him. Also, the socks were in the wash. Rose tied everything up in a bundle, taking care not to overlook anything, because if Leon bolted there'd be yet another fine pickle to deal with. As she was leaving she ran smack into Ignatz.

"Hey, what are you doing here?" he asked.

"What do you think?" Rose replied gruffly.

"How come you took back all that stuff?"

"Leon'll be more appreciative."

"Hah! You could fit two Leons into that suit."

Leon really was smaller than Ignatz, but a lot heftier.

"What business is it of yours?"

Ignatz walked up to her swiftly and grabbed her by the elbow. His touch gave Rose the shivers.

"Why did you take all that stuff back?" he hissed through clenched teeth. "I might have had second thoughts."

"I don't need your second thoughts," Rose said, and loosened herself from his grip.

She started off home without once looking back. Leon was already waiting there for the suit, and he began to try it on. Indeed, everything was much too big for him, so she would have to give up on the idea of decking out a new fiancé right away. Only after they had time to go to the tailor's and get things altered would they be able to go to church to announce the new wedding. Rose felt ashamed and angry, but she put on a good face and drank vodka with Leon the same way she had with Ignatz. She even sent Veronica out for another bottle.

Toward the end of Leon's visit, in the murky, dark blue of the autumn dusk, she noticed someone hanging about the cottage. Although she couldn't make out who it was, her heart constricted with a sense of foreboding. A bit later, as Leon was getting ready to leave, Rose caught him looking through the window. It was Ignatz, of course. The moment Leon left, shouting and scuffling broke out in front of the house.

Rose rushed down off the porch. In the weak light emanating from the cottage she could see two shadows leaping at each other. It was Ignatz and Leon fighting.

"Stop it, you two!" Rose screamed.

But her throat was so gripped by pride and joy that her voice came out weak and muffled. Finally, Ignatz, she saw, took hold of Leon's throat and was punching him about the head and face. Then he pushed him away, and the other man stumbled and fell. When Leon finally walked off to his own place, swearing terribly and shouting imprecations so loud the entire village could hear, Ignatz appeared before Rose in the small circle of light, holding the bundle he had taken back. Without a word he shoved Rose inside. He smelled of vodka and tobacco. With one swing of his arm he tossed the bundle onto the bench, and, with the other, he took Rose around the waist and caught her by the hand. She nearly fainted. After all, as she herself had told her mother, 'My blood's boiling. I simply have to get married before I let things get out of hand.'

Ignatz, still holding Rose and keeping her from falling, bent over her and put his face next to hers, until she felt the stimulating, masculine, slightly canine smell of his mouth.

"Well? And will you buy me a dark suit for the wedding?" he asked.

"Yes," said Rose, losing all track of what she was doing.

They tumbled onto the bed. At one point Rose got up, put out the light, bolted the doors leading to the porch and to the bed-chamber where Veronica was sleeping, and returned to her man. He lay under the feather quilt, but his arms and legs were cold. He was shivering from head to foot, and his heart was racing and beating so loudly it could be heard in the room.

"Maybe he really is sick?" the thought occurred to Rose, who up until then had merely considered him lazy.

And she tucked herself under the covers, overcome with fear, regret, and impatience. It soon turned out that Ignatz really was sick. A galloping case of diabetes, combined with a weak heart, did not forecast a long life. A few weeks after the wedding, at which Ignatz wore a new dark suit which Rose had made to order (!), he became so weak he couldn't do a thing. After Christmas she hauled him off to a doctor in Lutomsk. The doctor sent him to a specialist in Ostrowiec. The specialist in Ostrowiec examined him, prescribed various medicines, and told him to get some kind of injections, although in all of Zagródka there was no one who knew how to give them. Who could tell whether it would help anyway?

Ignatz's heart grew weaker by the day, and by March he was barely able to get out of bed. Rose was in despair. To take such a strapping young man for a husband, to go to all the expense. The shoes, the clothing, the wedding—even if very modest—how much all that had cost! Major inroads had been made in her savings, and just recently she had laid out almost 60 zlotys on doctors and medicine alone. She didn't let Ignatz forget it.

When April came and the sun shone warmly, Ignatz fell completely to pieces. He had never been very vivacious or talkative, not to mention resourceful or clever, but now, even when he managed to drag himself out of bed, he didn't speak a word. For the most part he lay in bed, long, thin, and pale as a skeleton, with his eyes trained on the ceiling, moving his wide blue lips without making any sound. Of his former good looks there remained only the blond hair tumbling over his forehead. Rose griped at him the livelong day.

"I'm the one who's supposed to be old," she'd shout. "You're the one who's dying out of turn. Why did I knock myself out over you, instead of kicking you out when I should have? I could've had Leon," she added in despair.

"You and Leon deserve each other, you bitch," muttered the bed-ridden patient, at considerable effort.

But neither Leon nor anyone else showed up. They were afraid of Rose.

"That Ignatz was once fit as a fiddle," they now exaggerated about his former state of health, "but the moment he got married he started to go downhill. Once Rose gets her hooks into you, it's all over. She sucks the marrow right out of your bones."

When poor Rose figured out that nothing was ever going to come of Ignatz, she began to plead for him to sign over his land to her. But Ignatz didn't want to hear about it. He was still straight enough in the head to put his foot down and say no.

"Sure, I'll sign my land over to you so you can marry some other guy and live off my bread. Fat chance."

"Sign it over to me, Ignatz, please," Rose would wail,

"I'll erect a monument to you if only you will."

"What good's a monument to me, when I'm rotting in the grave?"

"A stone monument … with a cross. If you'll only do it."

"Never."

"Never? Oh, how fragile happiness is," she said sententiously, reciting some phrase overheard in Warsaw. "What am I doing keeping you here anyway, feeding and clothing you? You'd best be off to your mother's!"

But Ignatz didn't have the strength to get out of bed. So Veronica and Rose yanked him up and laid him on a litter. He'd lost so much weight that he wasn't that heavy. The two of them took hold of the litter poles and transported him to old Bona's all by themselves. The days now were nice and springlike, typical April weather. Along the path across the dike green grass and yellow milkweed were growing. As Ignatz's listless head lolled back, he could see with gaping eyes skylarks rising out of the meadow, calling loudly.

Veronica and Rose were out of breath by the time they arrived at Ignatz's house, because it actually was quite a distance. They laid their burden down by the garden and began shouting. Rose directed herself to the old lady Bona in particular:

"Bona, Bona, come get your little weakling!" Everyone ran out of the house in amazement, weeping and wailing. "You take him; he's yours."

"If he has to die, then it should be at your place, not ours."

"What if he won't sign his land over?"

They began to pull Ignatz in both directions. He tried to drive everyone away like flies by flailing his arms. At last Veronica and Rose simply ran away, and Ignatz's mother carried him inside. People in the village heard about it and began to talk. After two days the mother put Ignatz on a cart and took him back to his wife. She entered Veronica's cottage politely, greeted her civilly, and gave every sign of wanting to bring a peaceful resolution to the matter.

"You folks brought him to my place to die, but I wait and wait, and he's still here. Not only that, but he's finished nearly half a bucket of milk all by himself.

What if he doesn't die? Am I supposed to feed him then?"

"Well, who's supposed to feed him, if not his mother?" roared Rose.

"He no longer has a mother, my dear," his mother said sadly. "When a man marries, he leaves his mother behind. It's his wife that has to care for him."

"I'm the same kind of wife for him as he's been a husband to me," said Rose bitterly.

"He was too young a husband for you, Rose dear," intoned his mother sadly. "You ran after him too soon. An older husband would have suited you better."

"But he was the one I wanted," Rose snarled.

"Just the way you wanted him, that's the way you bought him," said his mother with continuing sweetness, then added: "Come on, boys, bring him in."

Janek and Franek (who was home on leave for Easter) bore their brother, pale as a corpse, inside the cottage and laid him on the bed. The old woman covered him up with a quilt. Rose shuddered at the sight of Franek. He was well built, sunburnt, cheerful, and sported a mustache.

"It's all his fault," she thought to herself and turned toward the window.

The world was beautiful, all gold and green, but nothing was working out for her. The boys put Ignatz to bed and returned to the cart. Rose saw them from the window. Franek lit a cigarette, which he held between his thumb and forefinger, with the rest of his hand flared out. He let Jasio take a drag. Jasio had grown up a lot during the winter, into a fine-looking young man, just as tall as Ignatz and as good-looking as Franek. Maybe even better looking. Rose turned back with despair toward the room. Old Bona was sitting quietly next to her son's bed. He no longer took even milk. Grief overcame her, as she became resigned to his death.

Veronica was busily removing the suit from the hanger over the bed and taking it into the other room, as if getting ready for the funeral. Rose remained standing in the middle of the room, staring at Ignatz's dark blue sillhouette, as his hands moved spasmodically over the quilt, grabbing at the pillowcase. He was breathing heavily and rapidly, and beads of sweat appeared on his forehead. Returning from the other room, Veronica leaned close to Rose and whispered:

"You'd better send for the priest." Giving substance to her own thought, she suddenly called through the window: "Franek, run and get the priest; tell him it's for the last sacrament."

Rose suddenly bestirred herself. "No, no, not for the priest, for a notary." Falling down at the bedside, she began tugging at the hand of the dying man.

"Ignatz, Ignatz, my sweet, rouse yourself, sign over your land, there's still time. There's still time. Just sign over that one little scrap. Let me at least get something back from my investment."

But Ignatz didn't hear her. They tugged at him more insistently, but his head merely lolled sideways on the pillow, until at last he died. So, besides all the other costs, there was also the cost of the funeral. There was no longer any question of a monument, of course, but it was still necessary to buy a cross and a brass wreath, and it all ran to a lot of money. Rose was left with barely half the capital she had set aside during all those years of hard work and self-sacrifice. She had even incurred debts. Veronica returned to work at the nursery, the coffee reserves came to an end, and Rose found herself back to eating potato soup and unbuttered noodles.

Several weeks after Easter she began to pack for the return trip to Warsaw, to seek work in some household. For there were no takers for that thousand zlotys, barely, that still remained. Leon cut a wide detour around their house. He was now paying court to Zofka at the school. Pietrek Masalski nodded to Rose with the same unctiousness he would have accorded a curate or a mother superior.

The spring was warm. Rose walked the old village paths and roads; the grain grew, and the house-swallows flitted by. She came to see that nothing was going to come of her plans here, that once again she would have to lock herself away in Warsaw and slave from dawn to dusk for 50 zlotys a month, the going rate for a "certified cook."

On one fine warm spring day the old lady Bona paid a visit to Veronica. She was used to dropping in on Veronica from time to time, and tried to remain on good terms with her. Bona was an accommodating woman, and held no grudges. She had no desire to keep up her end of the quarrel. Quite the contrary, she wanted everyone to get along. On that particular springtime Sunday she came along with Jasio. Veronica was at vespers, and Rose was sitting by herself all gloomy, thinking about her impending departure. Jasio took a seat by the window, on the same spot where Ignatz had once sat. Bona squatted modestly on a stool next to the table.

"Now that we've buried Ignatz," she said after a suitable introduction, "each of my sons has a little bit more land. It's hard for them to take care of it all on their own. Franek will return from the army and live in our house, while Jasio will have to look around for something for himself. You know, Rose," she added, "in Warsaw you'll soon get back that thousand you lost over Ignatz. You won't have to work so hard this time, for your salary will be better. In the meantime Jasio will wait for you here. He'll sign over his land, I won't raise any objections, and you, Rose, will list him in your will as beneficiary. The expenses will be less, for you already have two suits and a coat, good as new. Ignatz, poor thing, never had time to wear them out. You even have your wedding dress. You just need to buy Jasio some shoes, for the ones you bought Ignatz wouldn't fit on his big toe. Everything will work out somehow. We've just got to find a way to get by in this world."

Rose looked at Jasio gloomily. He sat there looking young and bashful with the spring sky shining over his shoulders, smiling calmly and cheerfully.

"Is all of this all right with you?" she asked. Jasio nodded his head affirmatively and enthusiatically.

"In two years," his mother added by way of explanation, "he'll be eighteen."

"Except," Jasio said hesitatingly, in an unexpectedly bass voice, "I'd also like a-a-a, a watch."

Rose smiled her best maternal smile, and as she did so she became practically pretty.

"Fine," she waid warmly, "You'll have your watch."

For the past year Rose has been cook in the house next door to mine. She makes the unheard-of salary of 60 zlotys a month, which has allowed her to buy the watch ahead of schedule. I recently inquired whether there was any news from Zagródka.

"Oh, sure, everyone's fine, they're all just waiting for me to return."

As she spoke the words 'they're all just waiting for me,' she smiled blissfully, filled with the special warmth of happy anticipation. Just one more year of work and she'll return to the village, to a young husband eagerly waiting for her, for the dark suit, and for the silver watch. Godspeed, Rose!

—1936. Translated by Oscar Swan

*Narrative Perspective.* "Peasants" and "peasant life" are well-worked themes in Polish literature. In "Rose" Iwaszkiewicz takes a decidedly unromanticized and unsentimental approach to the subject, which in the present instance is better thought of not so much as a treatment of peasant society per se (even if sociological studies of the period would confirm its depiction here as largely accurate) as of the universal human condition on the example of the peasantry. The narrative perspective in "Rose" is third-person external, separate from any of the characters, emphasizing emotional distance from them and their lives. We do not get into the mind of any of the characters so as to learn what they think or feel; rather, we view them practically as a naturalist might observe an alien species under his magnifying glass. Toward the end the narrative perspective "exposes itself," by turning out to be that of the next-door neighbor of the household that employs Rose during her second sojourn in Warsaw. He has had casual chats with her over the past year, and has woven the story out of his imagination and these chats. The manner of narration creates in the reader a feeling of estrangement from the characters and a lack of empathy for them and their lives, or at most a grudging admiration for Rose and all the many obstacles she has managed to overcome by dint of her sheer perseverance.

*Naturalism in "Rose."* As noted, the naturalistic focus of "Rose" views peasant life as being a microcosm and mirror of the human condition, whose animalistic nature can be more easily isolated and examined on the example of peasant society. Here are a few comparisons that Iwaszkiewicz draws in the story between human and animal behavior:

- Rose comes home in the fall and observes the people bustling about like squirrels or ants, putting away food for the winter.
- Rose feels a "breeding" instinct. Today we might say that she feels that her "biological clock is ticking."
- Rose's mother is like a mother bird who, once she has pushed her young out of the nest, does not want to see them again. She does not have any special affection for her daughter, nor does Rose for her.
- Rose "feathers her nest" in anticipation of marriage by depriving herself of every pleasure, slowly piling up money in Warsaw as a maid and cook.

- When she is ready to "breed," Rose returns home, to her "breeding ground," like a salmon or an eel ready to spawn.
- The male characters are mainly concerned with strutting about in "plumage": nice suits, shirts, gaiters, shoes, and, in Jasio's case, a watch. A special twist of this story is that Rose has to provide the men with their plumage herself. To be sure, Rose has her own plumage: her red dress, whose color matches both her name and the biological state in which she finds herself.
- In the fall or "rutting season," which it is at the beginning of the story, male herd animals begin to fight with each other over rights to the females in the herd. In a similar way, Ignatz and Leon fight over Rose. They are not even as much interested in Rose herself, as they are in competition with each other over the "right" to her. During the fight, Rose stays on the sidelines, her eyes flashng like a doe's.
- Scent. In nature, male moths can detect the scent of a female moth from miles away, and they come fluttering and flying in much the same way as potential suitors begin to take an interest in Rose once they detect "the scent of money," that is, when they learn how much money she has in the bank. When Ignatz wins his fight with Leon and takes Rose to bed, she notices his canine and tobacco-like breath and it excites her.
- An important issue in the story has to do with land rights and increasing acreage to the limit of the owner's ability to manage it, reminding one of the *territorial imperative*. Many animals are territorial, in that they try to assert themselves over as large a territory as they can successfully hold and defend against other animals of the same species.
- The scarcity of natural resources is a prime motivator of behavior in animals, and also of the characters in "Rose" where, here too, the main scarce resource is land (not to mention suitable marital partners).
- Mating Rituals. Certain conventional stages in mating have to be gone through. Here, this seems to consist in being invited over, sitting, talking, lubricating the conversation with vodka, and before long going to bed to test the physical viability of the relationship. "Love" seems not to have anything to do with it.
- In nature, one sees the "imprinting" of a sexually ready animal on the nearest available partner, whether that partner is appropriate or not. Rose is eminently susceptible to imprinting of this sort, moving easily from Ignatz, to Leon, to Jasio.
- Most animals accept the death of another animal of their species stoically and unsentimentally, as do both Rose and Ignatz's own mother when he dies of diabetes.
- One sees in "Rose" the peculiarly Iwaszkiewiczan theme that sex is virtually causally related to the death of the male, reminding one of how female praying mantises eat their male partner after, or often even during, coitus. Similarly for black widow spiders, who are widows because they have just devoured their mates.

*Sexual (Freudian) Symbolism in "Rose."* While it is pointless to search for hidden Freudian symbols embedded in writing not intended to be symbolic, one is justified in finding and interpreting symbols that have been purposefully placed in a story in that way by an author familiar with the vocabulary of Freudian imagery. The most successful symbols are those that have their own natural and independent function outside their symbolic value, and of this technique Iwaszkiewicz is an unrivaled master. The most important sexual symbols in "Rose" are the eggs Rose cracks for breakfast, bearing in mind that "eggs" is the colloquial Polish word for testicles; the poplar next to Bona's house, which is the source of a string of potential male partners in Rose's life (considering a poplar's phallic shape, together with the shrubbery around its base); the dike along which Rose walks, leading straight to the poplar; the heated uterus-like stove, along with Rose's red dress, both connoting a female in estrus; the lubricating vodka she serves her suitors; and Rose's name itself, considering what a rose bears a sexual resemblance to. No doubt others are left to be discovered.

## Sweet Flag

Sweet flag, which in some parts of Poland is also called the Tartar weed, has two smells. If you rub its long green leaves between your fingers, you will release the gentle scent of "waters shadowed by willows," slightly reminiscent of Oriental nard. But when you tear open a strip of sweet flag and put your nose to the seam lined with a kind of woolly fluff, you will sense, along with the musky scent, the smell of marshy loam, of rotting fish scales, of mud.

Since my earliest days the smell has been associated with the idea of sudden death. In my childhood, the floors of the entrance hall and the balconies at home were covered with sweet flag during the warm, gay days of Whitsuntide. But the weed also reminds me of the death of my first true friend, who bore the odd name of Gratian and who drowned at the age of thirteen.

This was long ago. But even now this ambiguous scent fills me with somber thoughts. Every end has a mysterious connection with the beginning; sounds, colors and smells echo from one pole of life to the other. The scents of childhood find their way to those of old age, and youth is reflected in the dusty mirror of maturity.

People tend to be surprised that in order to escape from the bustle of cities and the fatigue of travel, I detach myself from tiresome and sterile tasks and am in the habit of spending part of the summer, or more accurately of late spring, in Z., a small town on the banks of a large river. Apart from the river and the meadows through which it runs, the rushes along the riverbanks, and the slender bridge, there is literally nothing beautiful in the town. A dusty market square, a few houses, a few cottages—ah, yes, there are also the fine orchards and gardens to adorn the place. But the greatest lure for me is the fact that I can stay there in a rest home without giving my address to anyone, unworried by telephone calls and telegrams, receiving only a daily letter from my wife.

There is one more thing which attracts me there: my friendship with Mrs. M. It is a perfect friendship since we see each other only once a year for two or three weeks; we never write letters and have no overweening curiosity about one another's secrets. This accounts for the frankness of our conversations, and has a beneficial influence on our characters. Throughout the twenty-five years of that relationship we have never ceased to be somewhat "special" for one another.

Mrs. M.—Martha—a doctor's wife, lost her two sons during the Occupation and is now very lonely. Her husband is grossly overworked. Apart from his work in the hospital, he has an enormous private practice around the little town. In the past, I used to see him on peasants' carts, traveling ten or fifteen miles to see his patients. Now that he has a car he can visit a great many more people in a day. This reflects financially the life of the household. In spite of this established affluence, Martha feels her loneliness keenly. The few weeks in a year when I am staying in town cannot make her forget the emptiness of her daily routine. 1 must add that Martha never complains, never speaks of her feelings. She runs the house efficiently, answers the telephone, takes messages from patients; and her overtired husband, when returning home, finds order, peace and harmony there.

The doctor's house is an old-fashioned "town residence," of which there are a few in the little town. The awkward design of the several large rooms makes a subdivision of living space impossible, so the couple have the whole house to themselves. The boys' room is locked, and no one ever enters it. And the other rooms, low-ceilinged but bright, are filled with antique furniture.

Martha usually receives me in the drawing room, where there is a set of nineteenth-century mahogany chairs, covered with royal-blue velvet, and on the walls a few prints and Martha's portrait by a local artist, who must at one time have sniffed the air of Paris. In the black jardinieres there live clusters of exotic plants, looking as if they were made of silk and tin. An enormous grand piano which has not been touched for ages stands in a corner. The floor is covered with a reddish carpet, its center a woven picture of a woman carrying two buckets of water on a yoke.

It is not an ideal room for intimate talk. And yet it was here that Martha told me the story of her life. It was here too that a short while ago, after she had learned that she had an incurable disease, she told me the story which follows. Of course, I made some notes—all writers do—later supplementing them and giving rein to my imagination and even trying to look into the hearts of the principal characters. Perhaps I have over-dramatized the whole thing. Basically, it is quite an ordinary story; hundreds like it must happen daily in our towns and villages.

Martha never goes to the "boathouse," which is the name given in the town to a fairly large wooden building, some distance from the river. It consists of two large rooms, in one of which there is a counter where cigarettes, beer and the excellent local fruit juice (the mainstay of this fruit-growing area's economy) are sold. There is also a large veranda with a wooden floor on which people dance. The whole ramshackle structure is perched on a high cement foundation, which prevents it from being swept away in time of flood.

The veranda is the greatest "draw" in the little town. The young people come to dance and meet there when they get bored with the monotony of work or study in a place remote from the centers of culture. It is most crowded on Saturdays and Sundays. On Saturdays, the boys wear informal clothes, brightly checked shirts and slacks, their hair tousled "beatnik" style. On Sundays, however, their hair is meticulously neat, their shirts are white and their jackets dark. Whatever their style of dress, the boys drink only fruit juice, and in spite of what people say about drunkenness in Poland, they never bring vodka with them: they are too poor to buy it. They also play bridge for a hundredth of a cent a point. Not many girls are to be seen in the "boathouse," and they, for the most part, come with their partners to dance.

Where could Martha take out a woman friend who has come from the capital to stay with her? What was she to show her in the little town, ruined by the war? Of course she had to take her to the "boathouse."

The river glistened in the moonlight. From time to time a wave would break against the bank with a loud splash. But no one looked at the river. Couples were dancing on the veranda, as the loudspeaker croaked mercilessly. Inside the "boathouse" almost all the tables were taken. Some young men were playing bridge.

The two ladies sat at a small table at the side of the room, looking around them. In the corner, behind the counter, a friendly blonde was selling soda water and that fruit juice, the pride of the soft-drink factory. You had to fetch the bottles yourself.

Martha went up to the counter and took two bottles of apple juice. Returning to her table, she passed a group of card players. One of the youths, banging his card on the table, lifted his hand too high and knocked it against the bottle which Martha was carrying. The bottle very nearly slipped from her hands, and the boy looked up from his game and apologized politely.

Martha sat down at her table and was silent for a while. Then she poured out the drink, which had a ripe, lovely color, and again sat still. She glanced toward the table where the card players were installed. The young man who had nearly knocked the bottle out of her hand was sitting sideways to her, showing his irregular profile, with its flat, rather squashed boxer's nose. He had a fine head of hair which he wore combed up. His hands were beautiful, with long well-shaped fingers. They were in distinct contrast to the broken nose, the fairly large, solid head and the heavy neck, showing above the collar of his red shirt.

Martha soon realized that she had very little to say to her friend. They had some common memories from their youth, but Martha had come to the conclusion that for some time now she did not much care for reminiscing. It made her feel old and reminded her of so much that had turned to ashes. And Martha still had some obscure hopes for the present. So she listened to her friend, who had four children, scattered all over the globe, who received letters and parcels from them and now thought it polite to tell Martha all about them in great detail. Martha tried to hide her lack of interest, from time to time asking a question, and out of boredom continued to watch the card-playing boys.

At a certain moment she noticed a girl briskly enter the room. Going to the card players' table, the girl laid her hand on the arm of the boy. He turned around, and Martha saw him for the first time full face. As sometimes happens, his face did not match his profile. It was a broad face, with prominent cheekbones, but there was an expression and a light in the eyes which Martha found most attractive.

The boy said a few words to the girl, then turned back to his cards. The girl remained standing by him for a moment, as if at a loss what to do. Then she slowly walked away. She was wearing a black sweater and a colored skirt. Her hair was pinned up in a fashionable "pony tail"—yet she impressed one as rather untidy and poorly groomed; there was a certain languor of movement, a disenchantment in her whole appearance. The tight sweater showed plainly the lovely lines of her body, and she moved like a cat. She looked like an interesting girl. The boy now interrupted the game and, to the indignation of the other players, followed the girl. His place was immediately taken by a short, thin, crafty-looking youth who had been obviously waiting for such an opportunity to arise.

Soon afterwards, Martha left the "boathouse" with her friend.

The next day, the two women went for a walk along the embankment which ran beside the river for miles on end. As I said, the only thing of any character in the town was that river. Its beauty compensated for the dust, dirt and dullness of the streets and made one forget not only the indifferent houses but also their inhabitants. Wide and majestic, it flowed in a broad bed, bordered on both sides by thickly growing reeds. At the very start of the summer, sandbanks emerged from the grayish waters like the oblong backs of monsters, but in midstream the current remained swift and powerful, and after rain, the waters would rise, swirling with foam, and quickly cover the sandbanks again.

The sight of the river was too primeval, too inhuman, for Martha's liking. On her walks she preferred to stroll along the embankment, away from the main stream, and to look at the green meadows spreading from under the reeds and willows like another, gentler stretch of water. Along the embankment grew whole clumps of willow trees and. here and there, a few tall, extremely old, silver poplars which, even on apparently windless days, trembled with a strange musical whisper, continuous and soft, unlike the dry rustle of palm leaves. It was a music which Martha loved above all country sounds.

When she climbed with her friend onto the embankment, there was brilliant May sunshine, the sky remained cloudless, the willows never stirred, only the leaves of the white poplars whispered.

They walked peacefully along. On their left, a slope, blue with forget-me-nots, fell gently toward the meadows; on their right, market gardeners' huts stood among orchards in bloom, and the glass of the hot-houses glinted in the sun. Martha listened indifferently to the tales of her old friend.

At a certain point she saw a couple sitting on the edge of the embankment. It was the same couple that she had seen in the "boathouse." The girl was wearing a light dress, the boy a khaki shirt. The girl was talking animatedly; the boy was sucking a blade of grass and turning his head toward the river, which at this spot shimmered blue through the thick reeds.

Martha saw them from some distance. When the two women drew level with them the young people stopped talking; when they came back from their walk, the couple had gone. Martha remembered where they had sat and observed some crushed clover and forget-me-nots.

A few days later, her friend left; one of her children was due to arrive from America. Martha was alone again.

And so, one afternoon, she once more went for a walk along the river. She felt she would again meet the young couple who had fascinated her by their beauty and youth. Presently, she did meet the young man, sitting in almost the same spot as before, but without the girl. Martha had already learned his name and what he did; he was Bolek K. and, although only twenty-five, had been employed for quite a long time, as a surveyor in the offices of the Water Board. Bolek was very popular in the town; everybody knew him. Martha was also well known. As she passed the boy, he blushed and greeted her. She stopped.

"So you are alone today?"

He blushed even deeper, making as if to rise.

"Don't get up. Don't get up, please," said Martha. "I'll sit down too. This is a beautiful spot."

She sat down on the grass and looked around. In front of her grew a tall spreading silver poplar; the wind lifted its leaves to show their white lining.

"Are you alone?" she repeated.

"Halina's gone away," Bolek muttered halfheartedly.

Martha noted with satisfaction that his voice was low and pleasant. As it was hot he was wearing no jacket over his sports shirt. He had broad straight shoulders—but his face with its flat nose seemed, from close up, rather ugly and wild. Martha watched him intently.

"Who is Halina?" she asked.

"Oh, a girl," said Bolek in his charming voice, smiling.

Despite the difference in their ages, sitting next to him, Martha had to think of her body. Would he find any pleasure in her fully blown—perhaps overblown—charms? She felt suddenly conscious—although she had not been for a long time—of her hips, her thighs; she thought of her breasts. "He does not even notice what I look like." Yet she was pleased now that her habit of daily exercise had allowed her to preserve until middle age elastic muscles and an unwrinkled skin. She had always had small breasts; she moved quickly and gracefully. Would this be enough to attract him?

She grew ashamed of herself; there was silence between them for a moment.

"She is a student," said Bolek suddenly, not looking at Martha, "and she's rather clever. And I am only a simple boy ... "

There was real grief in his voice. Martha was not in a mood to listen to his confidences.

"Are your parents alive?" she asked.

"No." he answered, "they were killed in the Warsaw Uprising. I was brought up by Granny."

"She has brought up a fine-looking boy," said Martha, and stopped herself at once. "What makes me say such stupid things," she thought.

"Where did you study," she asked soberly, in order to erase her last silly words.

Bolek looked at her with momentary distaste, as if he were thinking: "This is not an examination, by God!"

"At Elbląg," he said. "I trained to be a water supply engineer."

"Wouldn't you like to have done something different?"

"Here you go." said Bolek impatiently, "just like Halina. I shall never be anything else, can't you see? Never. I was born to work for the Water Board—a water surveyor, that's me!"

"And what would she like you to be?" Martha inquired, pleased with the boy's sharp reply.

He obviously had not noticed her previous idiocy.

"Well, she wants me to read books and take her for walks along the river on moonlight nights."

"And you prefer to play bridge?"

"Of course."

"I saw you that night in the boathouse … "

"Yes, I know."

Down below, under the embankment, people were driving cows. Replete, with udders green from the high grasses, they walked slowly, heedless of the drovers, who frequently called: "Come on!" One of the cows held a bunch of forget-me-nots in her mouth and did not swallow it.

Martha put her hand on Bolek's hand.

"I also would like you to study, to read books."

Bolek did not withdraw his hand; a midge had settled on his bare forearm; Martha killed it, and a drop of blood appeared on the beautiful bulge of his muscle.

"I sometimes do some reading," said Bolek in a deep bass, "but I cannot get any books. I cannot afford to buy them. I must support my grandmother," he added, as an explanation.

"You could borrow books from me," Martha said, rather to her own surprise. "We have quite a few books. My husband has them sent or buys them in the local bookshop, but he has little time for reading. They mostly lie about unopened."

"Thank you," said Bolek with embarrassment, as he was not really very keen on reading.

"When will you come?" asked Martha.

He did not answer. He sat gloomily, chewing his blade of grass. Martha touched his forearm. He did not notice it, thinking his own thoughts. Suddenly he exploded:

"She imagines God knows what. She wants to be a professor at the university and says she would be ashamed of an ignoramus like me. Maybe I am uneducated.

I myself don't hanker after any philosophy. I am all right as I am. If she wants to marry me, all right, and if she doesn't—I shall manage too."

Martha was astonished.

"But surely you are too young for marriage." Bolek looked at her with irritation.

"Too young, too young. That's what she says, too. I shall never be different."

"Come and see me tomorrow," said Martha rather firmly, and got up. Bolek also got to his feet. "Do you know where we live? By the Krakow Gate."

She extended her hand. In the opening of his shirt she saw the quivering of the skin on his breast.

"Do you swim?" she asked.

"I do, of course," he answered, and kissed her hand.

"Then perhaps we shall meet one day on the river?"

He did not answer. He seemed surprised, but not uneasy.

Martha was in a fairly good mood during supper. The doctor looked tired, but he unbent a little. They talked of daily affairs with an animation which had long been lacking at their board.

Their life together had lost all purpose a considerable time before. Martha, in a sense, fulfilled the duties of a good housewife, but the kitchen was the domain of old Sophia, who had brought up the boys, and arranging flowers and answering the telephone were not too absorbing tasks. Martha realized the futility of her occupations, but did not know what to do about it. From time to time she invited an old friend from the capital to stay, but often the visitor escaped after only a few days. One of them commented on her return to Warsaw that the atmosphere in the house was like that in an Ibsen play, and this made the others reluctant to accept Martha's invitations. The doctor was not very demanding: he liked good food, and on Sundays read newspapers and medical magazines. He almost never engaged in conversation with his wife, as he was so stultified by overwork and making money. In the evenings he had no strength left to talk at all.

That night, however, something between them seemed changed. This momentary animation was a surprise to them both—and sitting at the table, facing each other, they saw themselves afresh. The doctor was intrigued. He saw Martha lift both her arms to her head and smooth down her hair at the back. It was the long-forgotten gesture of her younger days.

The doctor sighed, turned his eyes away, and again looked at his plate. The food was excellent that night—crayfish with creamed rice, and crème brûlée for dessert. After supper, Martha suddenly got up and took a key from the drawer of a small table next to the piano. Her husband looked at her, amazed. Quickly, although she tried to slow down her steps (thinking of Bolek's graceful gait), she walked up to the door of the boys' room, unlocked it, and went in. She switched on the light. The room was dead and empty, with nothing of its old atmosphere remaining. Martha sat at the table where her boys used to study. A few years before, she used to spend a few hours a day sitting at that table, but for a long time now she had not entered the room.

In the dining room the doctor was drinking tea, apparently unperturbed. The door to the boys' room was facing him, and he could see his wife. After a moment, she covered her face with her hands and stayed so, her elbows propped on the table. When the doctor had finished his tea, he got up with an effort and went in to Martha.

"Come now," he said, putting his hand on her shoulder. "Don't sit there." Martha started. She turned her face to him. "Don't you feel ashamed," she asked, "don't you ever feel ashamed to be alive?"

He shrugged his shoulders.

"I feel ashamed at being alive when so many are dead," said Martha. She got up and started pacing up and down in the large, empty room.

"I'm ashamed before all who are dead, let alone our own boys."

The doctor stood helpless in the middle of his sons' study, his arms hanging heavily, as if they were made of stone.

"Only think: there is such a crowd of young people," said Martha," And our boys are not among them."

"They would not be so very young either by now," sighed the old doctor.

"What do you think? Would they be married now?" asked Martha.

"Oh, I am sure they would. We would have, besides them, some young women in the house.

"That would be terrible." She shivered. "I hate young women—they are so conceited."

The doctor again came over to her. He took her by the arm.

"Well, let's get out of here," he said. "You'll only upset yourself." Martha gave in to his coaxing.

"I am always overcome by terrible shame when I see a young life. Youth is so shameless, don't you think?" she said, going with her husband to their room.

But the doctor shook his head in denial.

"You seem to forget one thing," he said, "namely, that life can so easily become death."

The next day Bolek called. Martha was quite bewildered. Only after a while did she realize what he wanted of her: he had taken literally all she had told him about the books. He wanted to borrow something to read, but did not know what. He said rather oddly: some Polish literature. Martha guessed that he wished to read something connected with Halina's study of the humanities.

Obviously, he never read anything now, and did not even remember the titles of the few volumes he had read when at school. He would accept any old book thrust into his hand, yet Martha insistently tried to drag an admission of a literary preference out of him. She was unable to do so.

They sat for a time in the drawing room with the royal-blue chairs. The weather was beautiful, and again there was a fine sunset. In front of the house, enormous syringa bushes were growing. They were in full bloom and obstructed the light with their greenish-white waxen clusters.

"Have you seen our syringas?" asked Martha. "They are real syringa trees."

This was one of her favorite remarks, the saying of her youth. At that time the syringas were not so tall. But even then she called them 'syringa trees.' Bolek did not seem to know which bushes or trees Martha meant. Like many very masculine men, he was unable to remember the names of flowers and trees. He did not have a clear idea what syringas were. He only knew what lilacs looked like—and that, because he had heard at his college a silly story about them.

"So they are," he said, and looked at Martha with a blank expression.

"You are terribly young," said Martha unexpectedly.

"How old are you?"

"I told you—twenty-five."

Martha thought that it was pleasant to be with someone who said he was twenty-five. The very sound of these words cheered her. So did the fact that there was somebody in the world who had such a strange, such a beautiful number of years.

For a moment she felt like saying this to Bolek, but, realizing he would not understand her, she gave up the idea.

Still there were other subjects of conversation. Again they spoke about swimming and the floods which had recently occurred in the locality. The conversation flowed more easily than the day before. They also mentioned the embankment.

"Do you often go there?" asked Martha.

"There is nobody to go with," said Bolek, and blushed.

"Why?" Martha wondered.

Bolek drew a breath and shot quickly: "Unless you want to come for a walk with me."

Martha was taken aback. "Gladly," she said, and then added, "Has Halina gone away for good?"

"She has gone to stay with her aunt. She did not even say good-bye to me," Bolek told her in a childish voice. This was a completely new tone for him. and Martha looked at him with warmth.

"Well then," she said, "are you free tomorrow at noon? Let's meet on the beach, under the bridge. We can go for a swim together."

Bolek accepted readily. Soon afterwards he went. And in the end he did not borrow any book.

The next day Martha received a letter. It was a folded sheet of paper, without an envelope, brought by a boy from the Water Board.

> DEAR MRS. M,
>
> I was so confused yesterday that I made the appointment to meet you at noon, although it is a working day and I shan't be free until about four. Can you meet me at that time, in the same place?
>
> With respectful good wishes,
>
> BOLEK K.

The letter, written (copied perhaps?) in a careful, childish hand, was faultless. "Did a girl friend write it?" wondered Martha.

So around four o'clock she went to the beach under the bridge. It was not large and completely empty at that time of day. No sign of Bolek. Martha undressed in the bushes—as everybody did whatever their age or social position—and got into her bathing suit. The strength of the current was so great that there was no question of swimming against it. You had to swim with the current for a time, then you landed, and walked back to the beach, across the fields. Martha made a couple of such excursions. She did not want to admit that Bolek's absence was a great disappointment to her.

When she went in for the third time, she swam a little farther, and walking back, she saw on the bridge the well-known silhouette. Bolek was there with Halina—obviously she had not gone to stay with her aunt yet. They were walking toward the station, talking excitedly.

Martha returned to the spot where she had left her clothes under a large blackberry bush, next to a thicket of willows. Shattered, she sat down, unable to regain her composure. She suddenly realized the character of her feelings for Bolek, and that realization was like a hammer blow on her head. She shook as if in high fever.

For so many years sadness and resignation had reigned in her heart. And now, as she felt the germ of a mortal illness grow in herself, the figure (what else?) of a young boy, younger than her sons, had played havoc with her soul. She wanted to curse Bolek. Yet she kept repeating. "But is it his fault?"

She sat there for a long time. Various people passed by the beach, soldiers bathing in their underpants, children. Small boys walked by, carrying bunches of sweet flag plucked in the meadows over the little pools of water, the remains of those chronic floods. It was Whitsun the next day, and sweet flag was used for decorating the houses.

Martha sat for a long time. "And will I have to live on after this?" she thought. "It's horrible; it would be better to die at once ... " Suddenly she heard a voice overhead:

"Mrs. M., Mrs. M.!"

She looked up. Bolek, smiling brightly, stood on the bridge.

"I am sorry I am so late," he called to her, leaning over the parapet. "I'll come down at once. We must pick some sweet flag."

Martha waved to him. She picked up a green strip of the water plant, which a passing child had dropped. She smelled the odorous leaf. She adored the smell.

Then she got up and walked in the direction from which Bolek would come. She waited a little, until he appeared from among the osiers. He was undressed and walked towards her with his dancing step, completely naked except for a pair of tiny lemon-colored bathing trunks. He was not at all sunburned; instead, his body was white and soft like silk. Again she was struck by his exceptional beauty. The lines of his chest and thighs were so harmonious, so perfect. Martha remained quite speechless. In silence she put out her hand to him, but he did not kiss it this time. He looked straight into her eyes. His plain head fixed on this glorious body had acquired a different expression. "If only he does not talk," thought Martha. But he was talking.

"I am sorry I have come so late. I had to see Halina off to the station."

"Did she go away?"

"She did not have enough money for her ticket. I had to lend her what I had, and now I'm completely broke."

He smiled so radiant a smile that his face was transfigured. The smile seemed to extend to the whole body.

"I shall lend you some money," said Martha.

"Really?" Bolek was overjoyed. It was terrible.

Martha wanted to wipe away as quickly as possible that vulgar, awful conversation. She wanted to separate him and herself from the world. She wanted to cover him with a green tent of leaves. And she wanted him not to talk. The beach, the bridge, the children calling to each other, the bathing soldiers became intolerable. She did not want to look at the houses that could be seen from where they were standing.

Somewhere downstream, a yellow thrush was calling. One could see the glimmer of its golden feathers on the silver poplar, not far from the bridge. Martha was holding Bolek's hand.

"Come, let's pluck some sweet flags for tomorrow," she said, and pulled him toward the meadows.

On the flats, between the overgrown banks and the level stretches of grass now covered with a thick net of daisies, blinked larger and smaller "eyes" of stagnant water. They were the remains of the rivulets, which had disappeared under the mud, or else holes which were filled by the swelling waves of innumerable floods. Among those "eyes" some were like real lakes—picturesque, overgrown with sweet flag, covered with the fanlike leaves of water lilies and kingcups. In their green waters were reflected the clumps of osier, the tall, clipped willows and the white cumuli calmly floating high above. Martha and Bolek passed them in silence.

She was now heading for one of the larger pools, one she especially liked. At one end of the long, dark and probably very deep water a small accumulation of white sand formed a kind of beach. There they threw down their clothes which they had taken with them, and stayed in their bathing suits. It was quite late—about six o'clock, but the air was warm.

Bolek, wearing his lemon-colored trunks, lay flat on the sand, looking at the clouds as they appeared over the pool. Martha glanced from time to time at his perfect body, in such contrast to his face of a barbarian slave, with its small upturned nose. In other, more distant pools frogs were croaking madly. In the osiers, nightingales were already screaming with pathos. Martha and Bolek were silent.

"What are you thinking about?" asked Martha.

"Nothing." answered Bolek, with unpleasant haste.

"About Halina?"

"Yes, Halina." He sat up.

"Your back is covered with sand. Let me brush it off." And she at once started to do so.

"I shall wash in a moment," he said impatiently.

She did not listen but carefully continued to wipe the boy's back. Then she put her cheek against it.

"What are you doing?" Bolek cried out. He turned toward her. Martha leaned back. For a moment they looked into one another's eyes, then he pulled her head toward him and kissed Martha on the mouth. The kiss lasted a long time.

When they at last drew apart, she said, "What have you done, Bolek?'

He smiled and said lightly, "You are so kind."

She blushed. She was very angry when she said, "A man should never tell a woman that she is kind … "

"And what should he say?" he asked naively, but with some petulance.

"Nothing," she hissed through her teeth, and turned away. They sat side by side, in complete silence.

At last he sighed. "We had better pluck those weeds," he said.

He got to his feet and jumped into the pool. The water was very deep. He dived, emerged in the middle, and after a little while got to the other end, where the aromatic plants were growing.

Martha remained on the bank, her heart heavy with despair. There is nothing left for me but to commit suicide, she thought. Everything was lost. When Bolek reappeared before her with a bunch of sweet flag she stared at him as at a strange, unknown being.

"One of us must die," she thought. And she imagined at once what infinite relief she would feel if that boy should cease to exist. There would be no one on earth to know of her secret then. The burning torture and the burning shame would be wiped out.

"Hold these," cried Bolek gaily, not in the least disturbed by what had happened. "I shall get some more:"

He threw a mass of long crisp leaves at Martha's feet.

"He must be used to doing such things," thought Martha bitterly, not wishing to look at him. Instead she looked at the sheaf of verdure lying on the sand.

"This will probably be enough," she said.

"No, certainly not. I don't want you to complain that 1 was lazy," laughed Bolek, and put his hand around her neck, brushing her lips lightly. Martha wanted to hold him.

"Wait a minute," he said meaningfully. "Let me fetch some more of this rubbish first."

He slipped away from her and ran into the dark water. He dived and did not emerge for a long time. At last she saw his head in the very center of the pool. He was moving along slowly, as if not quite sure of himself.

What's the matter with him?" she wondered.

Bolek swam to the other side of the "eye." His arms rose rhythmically from the water, his hands elegantly stroked the surface, and small splashes flew from under his fingers. She saw him reach the ground at the far end and stand next to the clump of sweet flag pulling at the long strips. When he turned back he had some difficulty in swimming with the heavy sheaf. He could navigate with one arm only, and his progress was slow.

"What can be the matter with him?" thought Martha again.

Then suddenly, in the middle of the pool, he disappeared under the surface.

"Why is he diving?" she thought in alarm.

Bolek's head emerged for a moment from the deep. He was some distance away, but Martha caught something like fear in his eyes. She leaped to her feet.

He disappeared again. And when he re-emerged, he made a few desperate gestures; he was drowning.

Now Martha jumped into the water and swam toward him. There was nothing on the surface. In the center of the lake, she dived into the deep cold well. Opening her eyes, she saw that green opaque light one usually sees when diving. She flapped her hands here and there, trying to find the body of the drowning man; she could not find it.

She went down deeper. She could not stay long under water and was just beginning to swim up with eyes closed, when her body was touched by Bolek's blindly groping hands. She turned around and grabbed him. At that very moment two strong arms clasped her neck. She tried to swim to the surface, tugging him, but his arms were heavy, pressing her and dragging her down, down, to the bottom. She lost her breath and in another second would have started swallowing water.

With a violent jerk of her head, she freed her neck from the choking embrace and, lightly pushing herself upwards, broke the surface. She was near the bank. She could not remember how she reached the sand. She looked back at the pool in the middle of the dark waters, something was gurgling, bubbles of air appeared and vanished. She covered her eyes with her hand. When she put it down, the surface was smooth.

She climbed onto the embankment and ran along it, shouting:

"Help! Help!"

From behind the willows, two boys rushed out who had been mowing the meadow. She shouted to them, pointing to the lake..

"Quick, quick! Bolek is drowning! There, under this tall tree," she yelled.

The boys were quicker than she was, and when she caught up with them, they had stripped. They started diving, systematically searching the bottom. Emerging, they called to one another.

"In the center, in the center," Martha urged them.

The boys searched the whole "eye" to the very end, and then turned back to search again. Suddenly the older of them exclaimed: "I've got him!"

"Pull him by the hair, pull!" cried the other.

Both dived in together and surfaced in the same place, then swam toward Martha, tugging a great weight under water. They reached the bank and pulled Bolek out, heaving him laboriously, with great effort, on the sand. It all took at least half an hour. They began artificial respiration.

Water poured from the mouth of the drowned man, but he gave no sign of life.

"Wait here," said the older boy. "I'll run and fetch the others; we'll have to swing him."

"I'm coming with you," his friend cried, eyeing the body uncertainly. He must have realized that their exertions were in vain. Bolek had had a wonderful reputation as a swimmer. This must have been a heart attack. And so the "swinging" would be of no avail.

"You had better stay here," he said to Martha.

They put their clothes on their wet bodies and ran off. Martha could hear their voices for a while, and the slap of their bare feet on the hard earth of the embankment.

Then a deathly silence spread over the water. Bolek's body lay on the sand, just as the rescuers had left it, next to the sheaf of sweet flag which he had plucked. His arms were spread wide, and large green drops of water shone on the hair under the armpits. The open eyes were blank and dull, like the eyes of antique statues. From the wide-open mouth a thin stream of water or perhaps mucus was seeping.

Crouching next to the body, Martha looked at it intensely, as if wanting to preserve forever the memory of its rare beauty. The figure of the drowned boy was being veiled as with cellophane, with a film of stiffness and foreignness: it was ceasing to be human.

In the bright light of the sunset, Bolek's bathing trunks shone garishly, their yellow color only slightly obscured by the green sediment of stagnant water.

"Why didn't I drown with him?" thought Martha, leaning over his body. "Do I wish to live? Go on living? What for?"

Over and over again she relived the moment when with a sudden jerk she had freed her neck from Bolek's choking embrace. "To live?" she repeated. "To live?"

She delicately touched Bolek's breast. The skin of the drowned man was drying fast, although the sun was low in the sky. Under her fingers she felt something infinitely cold, like marble. The jutting muscles, perfect in their harmony, were straining the skin. Martha placed her lips on the spot where a delicate down grew, between the breasts. It was already dry.

She gradually moved her lips below the breasts, then with a mulish passion, began to kiss the diaphragm, the stomach, the navel; in the violence of the kisses showered on the dead boy, she descended lower and lower. The whole sculptured body smelled of sweet flag.

When under her lips she felt the edge of the yellow trunks, the smell of marshy loam, of rotting fish scales, of mud, reached her nostrils—the aroma of death which very soon was to catch up with her.

—1960. Translated by Celina Winiewska

*Cultural Notes.* "The story "Sweet Flag" takes place in anticipation of Pentacost, or Whitsunday, a Christian holiday held about seven weeks after Easter. In Poland and some other parts of the Christian world, it has become a traditional day for holding baptisms, and thus is associated with water. In Poland, the day is known as *Zielone Świątki* (green holidays), and is a time when people hold picnics and decorate their homes with greenery, thus merging the Christian holiday with pagan rites commemorating the rebirth of nature in late spring.

Sweet flag (*Acorus calamus*) is a tall wetland plant occurring abundantly throughout the Northern Hemisphere. Records of its medicinal use go back to the ancient Egyptians. Today the essential oil derived from it is used in the perfume industry. In Europe it is used as an ingredient in certain aperitifs, a use banned in the United States by the federal Food and Drug Administration.

With relevance to the present story's opening paragraphs, as well as to the story as a whole, the Latin species name *calamus* comes from Kalamos, a legendary Greek youth who, after losing his best friend to drowning during a swimming contest, drowned himself in sympathy and turned into the aromatic reed.

*Notes on "Sweet Flag."* Written in the late 1950s, Iwaszkiewicz's "Sweet Flag" shows a number of ways in which even a largely apolitical author such as Iwaszkiewicz was, including an author of his stature within the establishment, still felt the need to adapt his stories of love, sex, and death to meet the requirements of an officially imposed governmental literary policy called "socialist realism." The policy is discussed in greater detail further below in relation to Jerzy Andrzejewski's "The Gold Fox." According to socialist realism, literature was supposed to have a positive, uplifting message and influence on people, and if a writer wanted to be published, he or she needed to conform to this policy. Poland was supposed to be depicted as becoming modern, and people's lives were supposed to be shown as being basically happy and becoming better under communism or, as it was euphemistically called in Poland, "socialism." The working class was supposed to be shown as playing a leading role in society. Such details are so subtly woven into "Sweet Flag" as to be almost invisible. But, for example:

- The Polish countryside is depicted as being beautiful, lush, fruitful, and productive (recall the local fruit-juice-based economy).
- The "boathouse," a local hangout, in the story is idealistically depicted as being spotlessly clean and a place where innocent card-playing, dancing, fruit-juice drinking, and other innocent pastimes take place.
- The young people are shown as being well-dressed and well-mannered. They wear crisply ironed slacks and often white shirts and sports jackets, and do not drink vodka (supposedly because they cannot afford it). They are also professionally motivated: Halina wants to be a professor of Polish literature; Bolek is already a hydrological engineer.
- The fact that Bolek is a hydraulogical engineer reflects how the government is trying to rationalize water management, for example, in order to prevent flooding, protect agriculture, and make life better for people.
- Martha's husband is a country doctor, showing that the government cares about extending medical coverage to small towns and villages. At a time when few people had cars, the doctor has been allocated one (he likely would not have been able to afford one on his own) to enable him to visit as many patients in out-of-the-way places as he can. Formerly, under "capitalism," he had to use a horsecart.
- Because of a housing shortage in Poland after World War II, people were

allowed to have only as much living space as they needed. If they lived in a larger house, the house would be forcibly subdivided, and part of it would be given to another family. Iwaszkiewicz is at pains to explain why the doctor and Martha are "permitted" to live in a house as large as they do: its layout is said to make it impossible to subdivide. Besides, the doctor conducts his private practice out of his house.

- Martha's two sons died in the war, whether during the Warsaw Uprising of 1944, from underground resistance activity, or from any of almost limitless ways in which young people could meet their death in Poland during the war. Since the family is middle class and potentially "bourgeois," this circumstance puts an automatic stamp of approval on them. It sanitizes them against their lack of working-class origins.

The themes of socialist realism are introduced so subtly that they do not interfere with one's reception of the story. From today's perspective they are more of a literary curiosity of the times than anything else.

*The Setting.* The story would seem to take place in the north of Poland, near the town of Elbląg in former East Prussia, where Bolek has gone to technical school. Elbląg is situated along the Vistula River, Poland's main waterway, but the river in the story would seem to be a tributary to the Vistula, or one of its backwaters.

*Themes.* As in other of this author's stories, topics raised are "big issues" of universal concern, even while raised in a highly individualized, specifically Polish provincial setting. The setting is used to stress the ordinariness of what might be considered to be the bizarre circumstances in which people find themselves in Iwaszkiewicz's stories. See the remark: "Basically, it is quite an ordinary story; hundreds like it must happen daily in our towns and villages."

"Sweet Flag" showcases themes that were also popular with Iwaszkiewicz in his stories set before the war: sex and death and the notion that life implies death; the idea of the biologically weak male versus the strong female; and the often inappropriate pairings of couples (which one also sees in "Rose"). The motto of the story might as well be the husband's prefiguring statement to Martha: "You forget that life so quickly can become death." This is, after all, what happens at the end, when the muscular Bolek has a heart attack while swimming and drowns.

That death can come from anywhere at any time is also presaged by Martha's squashing the bug on Bolek's arm. At one moment, it is the bug that has been suddenly put out of its existence; at the next it is Bolek. The squashing of the bug, done by Martha in a moment of sensual desire, underscores the sex and death union that figures so prominently in Iwaszkiewicz's writings. It also underscores Iwaszkiewicz's thinking that in a certain universal sense life is all on the same level. Who is to say that the life of the bug is any less important than that of Bolek or Martha?

Martha's own sex/life wish is combined with a death wish, as she says at the end, after her "long kiss" with Bolek, that "there is nothing left for me now but to commit suicide," and "one of us must die." However, when it comes to it, when Martha jumps into the water to save Bolek and when he starts to pull her under, she rescues herself from his grasp, choosing life over death, although she herself is about to be overtaken by a fatal disease.

Water, smells, touch, textures, and the change of seasons are important elements in this story. Water in particular performs an important symbolic function. In "Sweet Flag" it is associated more with death than with life. Especially important is the symbol of mud, muck, and slime, the primordial ooze out of which life emerges and to which it inevitably returns. The smell of the muck, according to Iwaszkewicz, resembles the smell of sweet flag when it is broken and rubbed. In either case, for him it is the combined smell both of sex glands and of rot and decay, the ultimate destination of every living thing.

As generally with Iwaszkiewicz, nature in "Sweet Flag" continues to be beautiful and indifferent to human fate. Nature is profligate, producing many more existences than are needed, including human existences, so that the species will be continued. Recall the cow chewing on the forget-me-nots; in the cow's stomachs the forget-me-nots will not propagate but be reduced to the same muck as everything else now alive.

In "Sweet Flag" as also in "Rose," sexuality, the norms of society, and biological logic are out of synchronization with one another: the pairing of an older female and a younger male is perhaps equal in terms of sensuality and capability, yet it is the least viable in terms of biological reproduction.

Nearing middle age, Martha is beyond child-bearing age, but, as if to spite her, and in contradiction to her fatal disease, her sexual awareness becomes more acute. She has lost two sons, and lives in a rather loveless marriage. She senses a lack of fulfillment or accomplishment in life, as suggested by the long-unplayed piano in her sitting room. She channels her dormant need for sexual fulfillment toward Bolek, who is more or less the age of the two sons she lost in the war. Her lust for Bolek is a kind of vicarious incest, a reversal of the Oedipus complex, whereby the mother wants to marry the son, instead of the other way around.

A key to the story's interpretation is elucidated in the first paragraph when, speaking of the plant sweet flag, the author says, "If you rub its long green leaves between your fingers, you will release the gentle scent of waters shadowed by willows slightly reminiscent of Oriental nard. But when you tear open a strip of sweet flag and put your nose to the seam lined with a kind of woolly fluff, you will sense, along with the musky scent, the smell of marshy loam, of rotting fish scales, of mud." The smells have a sexual resonance to them, and the image connoted is that of parted female genitalia. At the same time the smell is associated with death and decay (rotting fish scales, mud). The scene where Martha holds the dead Bolek in her arms and slowly moves her kisses lower and lower until she reaches his swimming trunks, travesties the image of the *pietà* (Mary cradling in her arms the dead body of Jesus).

As in "Rose" as well as in some other of Iwaszkiewicz's stories, the woman, even if older, is more vigorous than the man, even though Martha herself is dying of an incurable disease, presumably cancer. After Bolek's initial chance jostling of her arm, Martha takes the initiative in the relationship, guiding Bolek, commanding him, kissing him. The male, Bolek, although externally strong and muscular, has death lurking just beneath his exterior. As in other stories of Iwaszkiewicz, water is woman's element, not man's (ironically, Bolek is a hydraulogical engineer). This symbolism has a grounding in Polish folk myth, as *rusałki* (water nymphs), a kind of freshwater mermaid, are said to dwell in rivers and lakes and to lure men to watery graves.

Bolek is intentionally depicted so as to remind the reader of a sperm cell, both in his external appearance and in his manner of swimming. Physically, he has a nondescript, rather large blunt head connected to a well-shaped chest and slim lower body, and his skin is "white and soft like silk." At first, he is vigorous in his movements in the water, but later he loses vigor and dies spasmodically, as a spent sperm cell can be seen to do under a microscope. Biologically, sex is important for life, not for one's own life but for that of the species. Reproduction leaves the lives of the reproducers, especially that of the male, expendable. From the subtle way in which this symbol is carefully camoflaged in little pieces here and there, it can be imagined that the sperm cell was the foundational image underlying the story's conception.

*The film version of "Sweet Flag."* One of Oscar-winning Andrzej Wajda's (1926–2016) last films was "Tatarak" (Sweet Flag), based on this story. In it, the prominent actress Krystyna Janda, playing the role of Iwaszkiewicz's Martha dying of cancer, periodically steps out of her role to recall in monologue how her own husband, cameraman Edward Kłosiński, himself was dying of cancer. While experimentally innovative on Wajda's part, Janda's portrayal of herself in real life breaks up the action and overshadows her simultaneous recreation of Martha, and her performance and the film as a whole come across as lackluster. While the film superficially follows the plot of the story in most details, the sexual symbolism which is so much a part of the story, including the final scene, is muted in the film almost to the point of unrecognizability. In the film Bolek and Martha's "long kiss" is nothing more than a playful brushing of lips and tumbling around on the sand, while the entire sense of the story, and of Iwaszkiewicz as a writer, would seem to suggest its being much more than that.

# World War II in Poland

The outbreak of World War II occurred when Nazi Germany invaded Poland on September 1, 1939, after first staging a "false flag" operation on the border between the two countries. Two important operations were the attack on the Polish garrison at Westerplatte, on the Baltic Sea near Gdańsk (German Danzig), and a nine-hour experiment in carpet bombing by the German Luftwaffe on the undefended medium-sized town of Wieluń and other nearby towns, none of them of any military or strategic importance. The attack on Wieluń was accompanied by the aerial strafing of civilians fleeing for their lives, giving a hint of what was awaiting Polish citizens for the next six years.

Poland was poorly prepared to defend itself, and it took less than a month for the Germans to occupy the entire country all the way to the so-called Curzon Line separating ethnic Poland from Polish lands to the east, which were ethnically predominantly Ukrainian, Belarusian, and Lithuanian. Naively, Poland expected the intervention on its behalf of France and England, which formally declared war on Germany after the invasion but did not follow up on the declaration with any decisive action.

The Polish government fled first to Romania, then to France, and finally settled in London as the Polish Government in Exile, where it remained in existence until 1990 after the fall of communism. In the meantime, after first giving the German invasion a chance to succeed, the Soviet army moved to occupy Polish lands lying to the east of the Curzon Line, under a secret nonagression treaty with Germany known as the Molotov-Ribbentrop Pact. Poland as a country for all intents and purposes ceased to exist for the remainder of the war.

In the first days of the occupation Germany rounded up and executed some 50,000 members of the Polish cultural and political elite according to a list drawn up prior to the invasion. Professors at Poland's most prestigious higher educational institution, the Jagiellonian University in Kraków, were arrested and interned in a prison camp in Germany in reprisal for planning to hold university classes, which the Germans had forbidden. Later, in 1941, Polish professors at the University of Lwów (now Ukrainian Lviv), which before the war was Polish but by that time was occupied by Germany, were summarily rounded up and shot, together with their families.

Many Poles who had fled to eastern Poland seeking shelter now found themselves within the borders of the Soviet Union and subject to extreme repression, including imprisonment, deportation to Siberia, or execution, simply for being Polish. In one of the war's most heinous crimes, on the orders of Soviet leader Joseph Stalin in April–May 1940, Russian security forces murdered some 21,857 imprisoned Polish army officers, policemen, clergymen, professors, physicians, and other members of the intelligentsia, burying them in mass unmarked graves in the Katyń forest in Ukraine. These graves were discovered in 1943 by the advancing German army. The Soviet Union denied responsibility for the crime until as late as 1990, placing the blame on Germany.

Eventually a Polish army division, composed primarily of prisoners of war, was permitted by Stalin to form in the Soviet Union under the command of General Władysław Anders. The Anders army emigrated south to Iran and Palestine and eventually linked up with Allied forces in north Africa under British command. It took part in major battles of liberation, especially in Italy in the Battle of Monte Cassino. During the Battle of Britain, Polish pilots comprised a special battalion in the British air force and performed with exemplary effectiveness in dogfights over the English Channel.

Unlike in other Nazi-occupied countries, in Poland Germany did not bother to set up a puppet regime. Instead it simply annexed vast portions of prewar Polish territory directly into the Reich and established various German-administered districts in the rest of the country, the largest of which was the so-called Generalgouvernment, which included Warsaw but had its capital in Kraków.

Before the war, Poland had the largest Jewish population, around 3,000,000, of any European country. The Nazis established Jewish ghettos in the larger Polish cities, into which were crowded, under incredibly inhumane conditions, the Jewish population of cities and surrounding smaller towns. By stages, concentration camps and extermination camps were set up at half a dozen sites around the Generalgouvernment, to which Jews from the ghettos and from all over Europe were transported by rail, crammed into cattle cars several hundred to a car. The most notorious such camp was near the town of Oświęcim, German Auschwitz, about forty kilometers to the west of Kraków.

The only sizable group of collaborators in Poland during the war were the so-called "blue police" (after the color of their uniforms), who were recruited from the prewar Polish police force. Their duties were mostly confined to traffic duty and routine criminal investigations, especially of smuggling and other black-market activity, which for many Poles was the only way of subsisting. Poles without work permits were subject to roundups on the street and conscription into slave labor factories in Germany, where they would be worked to death producing ordnance, uniforms, and other goods useful to the German war effort. Those fortunate enough to find official work in Poland toiled at starvation wages.

From the very beginning of the war, one of the official objectives of Nazi policy was the eradication of all traces of Polish culture and possibly, after the Jews were disposed of, the eradication or enslavement of the Polish population, toward whom both the Nazis and the Soviets harbored a fierce animosity. Museums, art collections, and church treasures were looted, and monuments of any cultural significance were either melted down for ammunition or blown up. Universities and secondary schools were closed, and widespread attempts to continue education clandestinely, in private homes with volunteer instructors, if discovered, resulted in the execution or imprisonment of the participants. Often such prisoners were shipped to concentration camps, where they would be worked and slowly starved to death.

Polish underground resistance movements, the most important of which was known as the Home Army under the direction of the Polish Government in Exile, was among the largest and most effective resistance forces in Europe. Throughout the war it carried out acts of sabotage and assassination of both German officials and Polish collaborators. Mass public executions in reprisal for such assassinations, whether by hanging or by lining up arbitrary citizens against a wall and shooting them, were a routine occurrence in the cities.

A major cataclysm toward the end of the war in Poland was the Warsaw Uprising of 1944, raised against the German occupation in anticipation of Poland's "liberation" by the Soviet army. Small arms were pitted against German heavy artillery and air assault, while the Soviet army, just across the Vistula River, calmly watched and waited while the Germans obliterated the capital city, leveling it to the ground to the extent that no one imagined that it could ever be rebuilt. In a never-prosecuted war crime, on the orders of Hitler 40,000–50,000 residents in the Wola district of Warsaw, including doctors and patients in hospitals, were rounded up and shot in reprisal for the uprising.

Poland was eventually liberated and, at the same time, occupied by the Soviet army, which steadily, and with heavy loss of life, marched across the country on the way to Germany, where it was met by Allied forces coming from the opposite direction. The conventional date for the end of World War II is May 8, 1945, meaning that for Poland the war had lasted nearly six years.

The borders of contemporary Poland were established in late summer 1945, at a conference held in Potsdam, Germany, among the leaders of Britain, the Soviet Union, and the United States, at which Joseph Stalin was effective in pressing his demands on Winston Churchill and Harry Truman. The Soviet Union retained possession of the lands it had seized from

Poland in September 1939, incorporating them into the Ukrainian, Belarusian, and Lithuanian "Soviet Socialist Republics." Poland was compensated for this loss of territory by restoring to it the lands of former East Prussia in the north along the Baltic seacoast, as well as a large swath of German territory in the west as far as the Oder and Neisse Rivers, land that had not belonged to Poland for centuries. Most of the German population in these areas was forcibly uprooted and resettled to Germany. The area was largely repopulated with Poles resettled from the former eastern territories. The new borders between Poland and Germany were not officially recognized by Germany until 1990, after the reunification of East and West Germany, and they did not come into force until 1992. The shape of modern Poland resembles roughly that of the country in medieval times.

In all, some six million Polish citizens died in World War II, around half of them Jewish. This was a larger percentage of the prewar population than in any other country. Almost all casualties were civilian rather than military. The trauma of the Polish wartime experience and the scars it left on the national psyche has had its reflection in an unending stream of Polish postwar literary works and films, up to the present day. As one can see in the upcoming stories dealing with the war, including Kazimierz Brandys's and Hanna Krall's later stories describing aspects of the war's lingering aftermaths, each author has his or her own way of approaching the task of describing what might seem to be the undescribable.

# Zofia Nałkowska

Along with Maria Dąbrowska, Zofia Nałkowska (1884–1954), was one of the most widely read novelists of the interwar period. A pioneer of feminist fiction and the psychological novel, Nałkowska was known for discussing eroticism from the woman's point of view. Several of her novels have been translated into English, including her most widely regarded novel, *Granica* (Boundary, 1935). The novel deals with class, gender, and moral boundaries that both trap and are transgressed by the central male character, a mayor in a provincial town who impregnates and then abandons a lower-class woman. Both before and after the war Nałkowska was active in national and literary politics, and upon her death in 1954 she was buried with full state honors.

Immediately following World War II Nałkowska was named to an international commission investigating Nazi war crimes in Poland, one of the outcomes of which was a thin volume of literary-journalistic sketches entitled *Medaliony* (Medallions, 1946), from which the following two pieces have been selected. For many years *Medaliony* (the name in Polish refers to the small enamel portraits that are often attached to grave markers), under the banner of "We will not forgive, we will not forget," was until 1990 required reading in Polish public schools. The motto of the book is *Ludzie ludziom zgotowali ten los* (People dealt this fate to people.)

## Two Selections from *Medallions*

### PROFESSOR SPANNER

1

It was our second visit there that May morning. The day was pleasant and fresh. The brisk sea breeze recalled years long since passed. Beyond the trees lining the wide asphalt avenue grew a hedge, and beyond the hedge a spacious courtyard spread out. We already knew what we would see.

Two elderly gentlemen, "colleagues of Doctor Spanner," accompanied us this time. Both were professors, doctors, scientists. One was tall and gray-haired, with a thin, noble face; the other was just as tall, but stout and heavy, with a fleshy face that exuded benevolence and compassion.

They were dressed alike, not as we dress, but rather provincially, in long, black spring coats of good wool and soft, black hats.

A modest, unplastered, brick cottage stood in the corner of the courtyard, off to the side—an inconspicuous pavilion next to the huge edifice housing the Anatomy Institute.

We entered the gloomy spaciousness of the basement first. The light, refracted through the high-set windows, bathed the dead, lying as they lay yesterday. The young, cream-colored, naked bodies, hard as sculptures, were perfectly preserved, despite their months-long wait for the moment when they would no longer be required.

They reposed in long, concrete, sarcophagus-like basins with raised lids, stacked one on top of the other—arms abandoned to the side, not positioned on their breasts in accordance with the funeral rite, and heads detached from the torsos so evenly that the bodies appeared to be carved from stone.

In one sarcophagus, the so-called headless "sailor" lay prostrate on a heap of cadavers. He was an impressive youth, as big as a gladiator. The silhouette of a ship was tattooed on his broad chest. Across the contour of the two masts hung the sign of vain faith: God is with us.

One after the other, we filed past basins filled with corpses. The two foreigners strolled past and looked, too. Being doctors, they understood better than we did what this meant. The university's Anatomy Institute required a supply of fourteen cadavers; there were three hundred and fifty here.

Two vats contained only decapitated, shaved heads piled one on top of the other human faces like potatoes poured onto the ground, some on their side as though they were resting on a pillow, others facing down or up. They were yellowish, smooth, perfectly preserved, evenly severed at the neck, as if they, too, had been cut from stone.

In the corner of one vat lay the small, cream-colored head of a boy who couldn't have been more than eighteen years old when he died. His dark, somewhat slanted eyes weren't closed, the eyelids were only slightly lowered. The full mouth, of the same color as the face, bore a patient, sad smile. The strong, straight brow was raised as though in disbelief. In this most odd and inconceivable position, he awaited the world's final verdict.

Further on even more corpse-filled basins were lined up, and near them vats of halved, quartered, and skinned men. Only one basin, located apart from the others, was filled with the remains of a few women.

In this basement, we could also see some empty basins, barely finished and still lidless, indicating that the supply of cadavers required for the living was insufficient, that they intended to scale up the whole production.

Later, accompanied by the professors, we crossed over to the brick cottage. There, on the cooled hearth, stood a huge cauldron brimming with a dark liquid. Someone familiar with the premises poked under the lid and retrieved a boiled human torso, skinned and dripping with the liquid.

Two other cauldrons stood empty. But close by, in a glass cupboard, boiled skulls and femurs were arranged neatly in a row.

We also saw a chest with layers of thin pieces of prepared human skin, stripped of its fat, some vials of caustic soda on a shelf, a cauldron with a brew mounted on the wall, and a huge stove for burning scraps and bones.

Finally, pieces of rough, white soap and a pair of metal molds stained with dried soap lay on a high table.

We didn't climb up to the attic to survey the sprawling heap of skulls and bones this time. We stopped briefly in one part of the courtyard to view the remnants of three burned-down buildings, metal ovens of the crematorium variety, and countless pipes and tubes. It was common knowledge that the brick cottage had been set on fire twice. Each time, however, the fire had been spotted and extinguished just in time.

We strolled out together, accompanied by the professors, who immediately broke away, escorted by a stranger.

## 2

A young, thin, pale man with lively, blue eyes, escorted from prison to the inquest, is testifying before the Commission. He has no idea what we want of him. He speaks with grave consideration. He speaks in Polish, but with a foreign accent. He says he comes from Gdańsk. He completed elementary school, then did six more grades and received his high school diploma. He'd been a volunteer, a Boy Scout. During the war, he was captured, but he escaped. He worked shoveling snow; later he worked in a munitions factory. Again he escaped. The incident, for the most part, took place in Gdańsk.

A German came to live at his mother's house after his father had been sent to the concentration camp. The German secured a job for him at the Anatomy Institute. That was how he met Professor Spanner.

Professor Spanner was writing a book on anatomy and employed him to prep cadavers. Spanner taught an introductory course at the university. All the research would be used for his book. His associate, Professor Wohlmann, was also working, though on what he couldn't say …

The outbuilding of the smokehouse was completed in 1943. Spanner then requisitioned machines for separating meat and fat from bones. Skeletons were to be made from the bones. In 1944, he ordered the students to set aside the fat from the corpses. Every evening after class, after the students had left, the workers would gather up platters of fat. The veins and flesh were placed on other platters. They either disposed of or burned the flesh. But the townsfolk complained about the stench to the police, so the professor ordered that the burning be carried out at night.

The students were also told to clean the skin, later the fat, later still, following the directions specified in the "manual," the muscles from the bones. This fat was left to lie all winter, and later, after the students left, it was converted into soap over the course of five or six days.

Professor Spanner also collected human skin. Working with the arrival of the older prepper, von Bergen, he would prepare it and make something out of it.

"The older prepper, von Bergen, was my immediate supervisor. Professor Spanner's deputy was Doctor Wohlmann. Professor Spanner was a civilian, but he volunteered for the SS as a doctor."

The prisoner was unaware of Doctor Spanner's current whereabouts.

"Spanner left in January 1945. When he went away, he ordered us to continue working on the fat collected during the previous semester, to properly clean the skeletons and cook the soap, and to tidy up so the place looked decent. He didn't tell us to get rid of the recipe. Maybe he forgot. He said he'd come back, but never did. His mail was forwarded to him at Halle an der Saale, Anatomisches Institut."

While testifying, he sits on a chair against the wall, opposite the window, in the light. He is completely transparent in his careful deliberation, in his conscientious desire to convey everything in precise detail and to not overlook anything. He is alone. We, the members of the Commission, local officials, judges, are many.

In his earnestness, he leaves certain details fuzzy.

"What is the recipe?"

"The soap recipe hung on a wall. The assistant from the village brought it. Her name was Koitek. Technical assistant. She took off, too, to Berlin. Besides the recipe, another notice written by von Bergen hung on the wall. It outlined the method for cleaning bones to make skeletons. But the bones weren't useful. They deteriorated. Either the temperature was too high or the fluid too strong." He still worried about these old problems.

"The soap made according to the recipe was always effective. Except once—the last batch on the table in the smokehouse.

"The soap was manufactured in the smokehouse. Doctor Spanner oversaw it personally, along with von Bergen. It was von Bergen who'd collect the corpses. Did I go with him? Yes. Twice. And once to the prison in Gdańsk.

"They brought in corpses from the mental asylum first, but still there was a shortage. So Spanner wrote to all the mayors requesting that they not bury corpses; the Institute would send for them. Corpses arrived from the camp at Stutthoff, from the death chamber at Königsberg, from Elbląg and the Pomorze region. It was only when a guillotine was erected in the Gdańsk prison that there was no longer a shortage of corpses …

"Most of the corpses were Poles. But once we got German soldiers, decapitated during a ceremony in the prison. And once they brought four or five corpses with Russian surnames."

Von Bergen always trucked in the cadavers at night.

"What kind of ceremony was it?"

"The 'launching' of the guillotine in the prison. Spanner and a few others had been invited. Spanner took von Bergen and me. Why me, I don't know. I hadn't been invited. The guests arrived by car and on foot. They entered this hall. But we stayed back and waited. We'd already examined the guillotine and the gallows. Four German soldiers had been sentenced to death. Apparently a German priest blessed it.

"1 saw them drag in one prisoner. His hands were chained behind his back and his feet were bare and black. And he was stripped naked down to his underpants.

"There was a purple curtain, and behind it was another room. And the public prosecutor. The older prepper spoke later with the executioner and told us about it. So they heard the prosecutor speaking, some noise and scuffling about, the stamping of feet, as if someone were running. The blade struck. The executioner reported the sentence carried out. We saw four bodies carried out in an open coffin.

"Was there a priest at the blessing? I don't know. But they said that one of the men dressed in a soldier's uniform was a priest.

"Once von Bergen and Wohlmann transported a hundred corpses from that prison.

But later, Spanner wanted corpses with the heads intact. He didn't want those that had been shot, either, because they required too much work and the stench was unbearable. For instance, one German soldier who'd been sentenced to death had a broken and shot-up leg. He didn't have a head, either. Everything at once. At least the corpses from the insane asylum had heads.

"Spanner always hid the surplus cadavers. Later on, he had to dig into the supply of headless cadavers.

"The big, headless sailor came from the Gdańsk prison. The corpses are cut in half because they wouldn't fit whole into the cauldron. They didn't want to fit.

"One man gives maybe five kilos of fat. The fat was stowed away in the stone basins in the smokehouse."

"How much?"

He ponders a long while. He wants to be as precise as possible.

"One and a half hundredweights."

Immediately, however, he adds: "That was long ago. Later it was less. When they began to retreat to the Reich—maybe only one hundredweight …

"Soap production was carried out in secret. Spanner forbade us to tell even the students. But they peeked in, maybe after they told one another, so they probably knew … Once they even called in four students from the smokehouse to cook it up. But as a rule, only Spanner, the older prepper, me, and two German workers had daily access to the production. Spanner disposed of the cooked soap himself.

"Cooked soap? … No, it's not like that. First, it's soft, so it has to cool. Then we'd cut it … Spanner locked it up along with the machine. There were five of us. And the others had to specially request the key whenever they wanted to enter."

"Why was it a secret?"

He ponders over that question for a longer while, wanting to respond to the best of his ability.

"Maybe Spanner was afraid or … " He considers the matter carefully. "I think that if some civilian from town had found out, there might have been trouble. … "

Perhaps even here it seemed that a purple curtain was hanging between us and him. There was nothing we could do.

Someone finally asked, "Didn't anyone ever tell you that making soap from human fat was a crime?"

He retorted with complete frankness, “No one told me that.”

This, however, gives him cause to think. He stops responding immediately to the remaining questions. In the end, he answers reluctantly.

“Of course people visited the Institute and Spanner. Professors Klotz, Schmidt, Rossmann. Once the Ministers of Health and Pedagogy, and even Gauleiter Forste, stopped by. As rector of the Medical Academy, Professor Grossman greeted them. Before they erected this house, it was only the Anatomy Institute that they visited to see how it functioned and whether anything was needed. Even after the smokehouse was built, the soap was always cleaned up after four or five days. I can't say for sure if they ever saw that soap. They might have. And during the inspection, the recipe was always hanging. So when they read it, perhaps they figured out what was going on there.

“Yes, the chief ordered me to make soap with the workers. Why me? I don't know. When Spanner locked up the soap, I thought he was doing something odd. If he was going to write about soap in his book, then he wouldn't have forbidden us to talk about it. Maybe he came up with the idea to make soap out of the remains by himself? … Maybe he didn't have any authorization, because then he wouldn't have to try to come up with the recipe himself … ”

Nothing substantial comes from this speculation.

“The students? … They were just like us. In the beginning, they felt a bit uneasy about washing with the soap. The soap was disgusting. It didn't smell very good. Professor Spanner tried hard to get rid of the smell. He wrote away to chemical factories for oils. But you could always tell the soap was different.

“Of course I talked about it at home … In the beginning, one friend knew about it. I used to get the creeps thinking about washing myself with it. Mother was disgusted, too. But it cleaned well, so she used it for the laundry. I got used to it because it was good … ”

A patient smile flickers across his thin, pale face.

“In Germany, you can say, people know how to make something—from nothing … ”

## 3

At the inquest that afternoon we called the professors, Spanner's colleagues. The conversation took place in their jurisdiction, in the empty hall of a hospital building. Both—interrogated separately—testified that they had no prior knowledge of the existence of the building housing the hidden soap factory. They inspected it for the first time that morning and the sight of it had shocked them.

Both—interrogated separately—testified that Spanner, a man of forty at most, was considered an expert in the field of pathology. Having known him only a short time and having seen him only on rare occasions, they couldn't say much about his moral character. They knew only that he belonged to the Party.

Each witness sat removed from us on his own chair, clearly dejected. Each sat, not having taken off his black coat, holding his black hat on his knee.

Both spoke prudently and cautiously. Both carefully weighed their words before speaking. Gdańsk, that May, was still full of Germans. Columns of German POWs marched along the streets as their women tossed flowers. But the authorities were Polish and Soviet troops were stationed in the garrison.

When asked, however, whether, knowing Spanner and his scientific activities, they could believe him capable of manufacturing soap from the bodies of dead prisoners and POWs, each responded differently.

The tall, thin one, with the gray hair and noble features, stated after careful consideration: "Yes, I could believe it, if I'd known that he'd received such an order. It was common knowledge that he was an obedient Party member."

The thick-set, good-natured one, with the ruddy jowls, also contemplated long and hard. Afterward, as though weighing everything in his conscience, he answered: "Of course, I might suspect it. For this reason. At that time, Germans were experiencing a severe shortage of fat. Given Germany's economic state, he could have been tempted to do it for the good of the nation."

—1946. TRANSLATED BY DIANA KUPREL

## BY THE RAILWAY TRACK

Yet another person now belongs to the dead: the young woman by the railway track whose escape attempt failed.

One can make her acquaintance only through the tale of a man who had witnessed the incident but is unable to understand it. She lives on only in his memory.

Those who were being transported to extermination camps in the lead-sealed boxcars of the long trains would sometimes escape en route. Not many dared such a feat. The courage required was even greater than that needed to go hopelessly, unresisting and meek, to a certain death.

Sometimes the escape would succeed. The deafening clatter of the rushing boxcars prevented those on the outside from hearing what went on inside.

The only means of escape was by ripping up the floorboards. In the cramp of jammed-in, starved, foul-smelling, filthy people, it seemed an improbable gambit. Even to move was impossible. The beaten human mass, wriggling with the rushing rhythm of the train, reeled and rocked in the suffocating stench and gloom. Nevertheless, even those who, weak and fearful, would never dream of escaping themselves understood their obligation to help others. They'd lean back, pressing against one another, and lift their feces-covered legs in order to open a way to freedom for others.

Successfully prying open one end of the floorboard raised a glimmer of hope. A collective effort was required to tear it up. It took hours. Then there remained still the second and the third boards.

Those closest would lean over the narrow aperture, then back away fearfully. Courage was called for to crawl hand and foot through the chink into the din and crash of iron, into the gale of the smoking wind below, above the gliding bases, to reach the axle and, in this catch-hold, to crawl to the spot from which jumping would guarantee the best chance at salvation. To drop somehow, some way, in between the rails or through the wheels. Then, to recover one's senses, roll down unseen from the mound, and escape into the strange, temptingly dark forest.

People would often fall under the wheels and be killed on the spot, struck by a protruding beam, the edge of a bar, thrown forcefully against a signal pole or roadside rock. Or they'd break their arms and legs, and be delivered thus unto the greater cruelty of the enemy.

Those who dared to step into the roaring, crashing, yawning mouth were aware of what they risked. Just as those who remained behind were, even though there was no possibility of looking out through the sealed doors or high-set windows.

The woman lying by the track belonged to those who dared. She was the third to step through the opening in the floor. A few others rolled down after her. At that moment a volley of shots rang out over the travelers' heads—an explosion on the roof of the boxcar. Suddenly the shots fell silent. The travelers could now regard the dark place left by the ripped-up boards as though it were the opening to a grave. And they could ride on calmly, ever closer to their own death, which awaited them at the crossroads.

The smoke and rattle of the train had long since disappeared into the darkness.

All that remained was the world.

The man, who can neither understand nor forget, relates his story once again.

When the new day broke, the woman was sitting on the dew-soaked grass by the side of the track. She was wounded in the knee. Some had succeeded in escaping. Further from the track, another lay motionless in the forest. A few had escaped. Two had died. She was the only one left like this, neither alive nor dead.

She was alone when he found her. But slowly people started to appear in that empty space, emerging from the brick kiln and village. Workers, women, and a boy stood fearful, watching her from a distance.

Every once in a while, a small chain of people would form. They'd cast their eyes about nervously and quickly depart. Others would approach, but wouldn't linger for long. They would whisper among themselves, sigh, and walk away.

The situation was clear. Her curly, raven hair was obviously disheveled, her too-dark eyes overflowed the lowered lids. No one uttered a word to her. It was she who asked if the ones in the forest were alive. She learned they weren't.

The day was white. The space open onto everything as far as the eye could see. People had already learned of the incident. It was a time of terror. Those who offered assistance or shelter were marked for death.

She begged one young man, who was standing for a while longer, then started to walk away, only to turn back, to bring her some Veronal from the pharmacy. She offered him money. He refused.

She lay back for a while, her eyes shut. Then she sat up again, shifted her leg, clasped it with both hands, and brushed her skirt from her knee. Her hands were bloodied. Her shattered knee a death sentence. She lay quietly for a long time, shutting her too-black eyes against the world.

When she finally opened them again, she noticed new faces hovering around her. The young man still lingered. So she asked him to buy her some vodka and cigarettes. He rendered her this service.

The gathering beside the mound attracted attention. Someone new would latch on. She lay among people but didn't count on anyone for help. She lay like an animal that had been wounded during a hunt but which the hunters had forgotten to kill off. She proceeded to get drunk. She dozed. The power that cut her off from all the others by forming a ring of fear was unbeatable.

Time passed. An old village woman, gasping for breath, returned and, drawing near, stole a tin cup of milk and some bread from beneath her kerchief. She bent over, furtively placed them in the wounded woman's hand, and left immediately, only to look on from a distance to check whether she would drink the milk. It was only when she noticed two policemen approaching from the village that she disappeared, drawing her scarf across her face.

The others dispersed, too. Only the slick, small-town guy who had brought her the vodka and cigarettes continued to keep her company. But she no longer wanted anything from him.

The police came to see what was going on. They quickly sized up the situation and deliberated on how handle it. She begged them to shoot her. In a low voice, she tried to negotiate with them, provided they keep the whole thing quiet. They were undecided.

They, too, left, conferred, stopped, and walked on further. What they would finally decide was not certain. In the end, however, they did not care to carry out her request. She noticed that the kind young man, who had lit her cigarettes with a lighter that didn't want to light, followed after. She had told him that one of the two dead in the forest was her husband. That piece of news seemed to have caused him some unpleasantness.

She tried to swallow the milk but, preoccupied, set the cup down on the grass. A heavy, windy, spring day rolled over. It was cool. Beyond the empty field stood a couple of huts; at the other end, a few short, scrawny pines swept the sky with their branches. The forest, their destination, sprang up further from the railway. This emptiness was the whole of the world she saw.

The young man returned. She swallowed some more vodka and he lit her cigarette. A light dusk brushed across the sky from the east. To the west, skeins and smudges of clouds branched up sharply.

More people, on their way home from work, turned up and were told what had happened. They spoke as though she couldn't hear them, as though she were no longer there.

"The dead one there's her husband," a woman's voice spoke up.

"They tried to escape from the train into the forest. But they shot at them with a rifle. They killed her husband, and she was left alone. Shot in the knee. She couldn't get any further … "

"From the forest she could easily have been taken somewhere. But here, with everyone watching, there's no way."

The old lady who had returned for her tin cup said those words. Silently she watched as the milk soaked into the grass.

So no one would intercede by removing her before nightfall, or by calling a doctor, or by taking her to the station so she could get to a hospital. Nothing of the kind would happen. She could only die, one way or another.

When she opened her eyes at dusk, there was no one around except for the two policemen who had come back and the one who would no longer go away. Again she pleaded with them to kill her, but without any expectation that they would do so. She covered her eyes with her hands so as not to see anymore.

The policemen still hesitated about what to do. One tried to talk the other into doing it. The latter retorted, "You do it yourself."

Then she heard the young man's voice saying, "Well then give it to me."

Again they debated, quarreled. From beneath her lowered eyelids she watched the policeman take out his revolver and hand it to the stranger.

A small group of people standing further back watched as he bent over her. They heard the shot and turned away in disgust.

"They could at least have called in someone. Not do it like that. Like she was a dog."

When it grew dark two people emerged from the forest to get her. They found the spot with a bit of difficulty. They assumed she was sleeping. But when one of them took her by the shoulder he understood at once that he was dealing with a corpse.

She lay there for that night and into the morning, until just before noon, when a bailiff ordered her to be buried along with the other two who had died by the railway tracks.

"Why he shot her isn't clear," the narrator said. "I couldn't understand it. Maybe he felt sorry for her ..."

—1946. Translated by Diana Kuprel

*Note.* "God is with us." The inscription on the tattoo of one of the corpses in "Professor Spanner" is in German: *Gott mit uns.*

*Zofia Nałkowka's "Medallions."* It is difficult to classify the stories in *Medallions* as to type. They are are not exactly fiction and not exactly reportage, but something in between, rather like slightly belles-lettrecized works of investigative journalism. The stories selected here reflect their emanation from interviews with eyewitnesses of actual events that occurred during World War II in Poland, and all of them derive their power from the presumption of their factual veracity which, in turn, depends on Nałkowska's impeccable integrity and reputation.

The stories in *Medallions* are remarkable for the lack of explicit authorial commentary on events that virtually scream for it, thereby placing the reader, as it were, in the role of witness, commentator or, in some instances, vicariously as a possible passive perpetrator. Some critics have criticized the book's motto, "People dealt this fate to people," for obscuring via abstraction the fact that the Holocaust was not primarily about "people" but about what Nazi Germany did to the Jews. Although the majority of the sketches do detail crimes against Jews, some, including "Professor Spanner," do not. Most of Nałkowska's sketches illustrate Hannah Arendt's observation about the "banality of evil," the idea that it spreads through the passive toleration of increasingly morally reprehensible acts by ordinary people just doing their assigned jobs and looking the other way.

The literary touches here are subtle but nonetheless noticeable, especially at the beginnings, and they recall Nałkowska's sensitivity to *boundaries*, whether social, gender, ethnic, class, or ethical. In both stories here it is the moral boundary that is being transgressed most of all.

In "Professor Spanner" the boundary is symbolized by the purple curtain obscuring the guillotine, signifying the inability of the investigative commission to get through to the young man being interviewed that there might be something morally problematic in reducing human corpses to fat for making soap. The story raises the question of whether one can hold a person accountable for an atrocity for which the person feels no sense of guilt, responsibility, or remorse.

The boundary that forms between people by virtue of ethnicity is starkly illustrated by the circle of onlookers around the wounded Jewish woman in "By the Railway Track," probably the more "literary" of the two stories. A perimeter is formed around the woman which only a few people are willing to cross, and then only for a second or two. Mainly, people stand on the sidelines, gape, and talk about the victim in the third person as though she were a wounded animal. The circle around her has been prefigured by the terrified circle that forms in the railway car around the gaping hole that people have clawed out in the floorboards of the car. By this time in the war people know the fate that awaited them at the end of their journey.

The stories "Professor Spanner" and "By the Railroad Track" both raise the question of guilt and moral responsibility. Is the boy in "Professor Spanner" not truly appreciative of the fact that he was, in the end, a willing cog in the morally degenerate Nazi war machine? Does the boy in "Railroad Tracks" shoot the woman out of mercy or because he wants to handle a firearm? Is he guilty of a crime in either instance, any more so than the onlookers? And are the onlookers guilty, and, if so, of what? A short film was made of "On the Railroad Tracks" in 1963 by Andrzej Brzozowski, and because of the disturbing nature of the moral questions it raised for Poles about their implied role as passive spectators during the Holocaust, it was banned for some thirty years, until after the lifting of communist censorship.

On the basis of Nałkowska's commision's investigations, Dr. Rudolf Spanner, a renowned anatomist, was put on trial at the Nuremberg war crimes tribunal for crimes against humanity, but he was exonerated in 1948, and most historians today, whether Polish or German, believe that the suggestion in Nałkowska's story that the soap operation was industrial in scope and that Spanner had visions of expanding it is exaggerative. By all accounts it was an amateur in-house operation put together to satisfy the anatomical institute's immediate need for a disinfectant for various routine purposes, making use of the readily available corpses of executed prisoners from the nearby Stutthof concentration camp and the prison in Gdańsk. The corpses were being used by the institute not only for Dr. Spanner's research and teaching, and making soap as a sideline, but also on contract for providing anatomical specimens to assist doctors in treating war injuries. However, there is also the unexplained matter of the carefully flayed pile of human skin, and what its intended purpose was. Most of the dead were Polish or German, not Jewish, although this is a point that has little bearing on the overall moral issue. The young man interviewed in Nałkowska's story died in the Gdańsk prison shortly after the interview described here, presumably from typhus, and so was unable to give further testimony. Dr. Spanner's eventual book on human anatomy became a standard work in the field and went through many editions and translations into other languages, including English.

# Tadeusz Borowski

Tadeusz Borowski (1922–1951) was born in 1922 into the Polish community in Zhytomyr, Ukraine. In 1926, his father was sent to a camp in the Gulag system in Soviet Karelia, because he had been a member of a Polish military organization during World War I. In 1930 Borowski's mother was deported to a settlement on the shores of the Yenisey River in Siberia, while Borowski stayed behnd with an aunt. In 1932, the Borowskis were expatriated to Poland by the Polish Red Cross in an exchange for Russian prisoners left over from the Polish-Soviet war of 1919–1921. The impoverished family settled in Warsaw.

Under Nazi occupation, Poles were forbidden to attend university or even secondary school. In 1940 Borowski finished his secondary schooling in an underground lyceum and began his studies in Polish literature at Warsaw University, which was operating clandesrinely. His classes met in secret at private homes. While studying, Borowski was engaged to and living with Maria Rundo, who was Jewish. When Maria did not come home one night in February 1943, Borowski began to suspect that she had been arrested. Rather than staying away from their usual meeting spots, he walked straight into a trap set by Gestapo agents in the apartment of his and Maria's close friend. Borowski was twenty-one years old when he was imprisoned in the infamous Pawiak prison in Warsaw for two months before being shipped to Auschwitz.

Forced into slave labor under extremely harsh conditions, Borowski later reflected on his Auschwitz experiences in his writing, especially in his collection *Pożegnanie z Marią* (Farewell to Maria), from which the present story is taken. Working on a railway ramp, he witnessed arriving Jews being told to leave their personal belongings behind, and then being transferred directly from the trains to the gas chambers. Early after its publication in Poland, the work was accused of being nihilistic, amoral, and decadent. Today it is recognized as a classic of both Polish and world postwar literature.

After the war Borowski spent some time in Paris, but then returned to Poland. His fiancée, who had also survived the camps and had emigrated to Sweden, returned to Poland in late 1946, and she and Borowski were married. Borowski first found work as a journalist for the establishment press. He joined the Polish Workers' Party in 1948 and wrote scathing political tracts against the West. He believed that communism was the only political force capable of preventing any future Auschwitz from happening.

In 1950 a close friend of his (the one in whose apartment Maria and he had been apprehended) was imprisoned and tortured by the state police. Borowski tried to intervene on his friend's behalf but failed, leading to his becoming disillusioned with the socialist regime. On July 3, 1951, at the age of 28, Borowski committed suicide by inhaling gas from a gas stove. His wife had given birth to their daughter a few days earlier. On July 6, 1951, the openly anti-militaristic Borowski was buried in the military section of Powązki National Cemetery in Warsaw to the strains of "The Internationale," and was posthumously awarded the highest state honors.

## This Way for the Gas, Ladies and Gentlemen

All of us walk around naked. The delousing is finally over and our striped suits are back from the tanks of Cyclone B solution, an efficient killer of lice in clothing and of men in gas chambers. Only the inmates in the blocks cut off from ours by the "Spanish goats" still have nothing to wear. But all the same, all of us walk around naked: the heat is unbearable. The camp has been sealed off tight. Not a single prisoner, not one solitary louse, can sneak through the gate. The labor Kommandos have stopped working. All day, thousands of naked men shuffle up and down the roads, cluster around the squares, or lie against the walls and on top of the roofs. We have been sleeping on plain boards, since our mattresses and blankets are still being disinfected. From the rear blockhouses we have a view of the F.K.L.—*Frauen Konzentration Lager*; there too the delousing is in full swing. Twenty-eight thousand women have been stripped naked and driven out of the barracks. Now they swarm around the large yard between the blockhouses.

The heat rises, the hours are endless. We are without even our usual diversion: the wide roads leading to the crematoria are empty. For several days now, no new transports have come in. Part of "Canada"' has been liquidated and detailed to a labor Kommando—one of the very toughest—at Harmenz. For there exists in the camp a special brand of justice based on envy: when the rich and mighty fall, their friends see to it that they fall to the very bottom. And Canada, our Canada, which smells not of maple forests but of French perfume, has fortunes in diamonds and currency from all over Europe.

Several of us sit on the top bunk, our legs dangling over the edge. We slice the neat loaves of crisp, crunchy bread. It is a bit coarse to the taste, the kind that stays fresh for days. Sent all the way from Warsaw; only a week ago my mother held this white loaf in her hands ... dear Lord, dear Lord ...

We unwrap the bacon, the onion, we open a can of evaporated milk. Henri, the fat Frenchman, dreams aloud of the French wine brought by the transports from Strasbourg, Paris, Marseille ... Sweat streams down his body.

"Listen, mon ami, next time we go up on the loading ramp, I'll bring you real champagne. You haven't tried it before, eh?"

"No. But you'll never be able to smuggle it through the gate, so stop teasing. Why not try and 'organize' some shoes for me instead—you know, the perforated kind, with a double sole, and what about that shirt you promised me long ago?"

"Patience, patience. When the new transports come, I'll bring all you want. We'll be going on the ramp again!"

"And what if there aren't any more 'cremo' transports?" I say spitefully. "Can't you see how much easier life is becoming around here: no limit on packages, no more beatings? You even get letters from home … One hears all kind of talk, and, dammit, they'll run out of people!"

"Stop talking nonsense." Henri's serious fat face moves rhythmically; his mouth is full of sardines. We have been friends for a long time, but I do not even know his last name. "Stop talking nonsense," he repeats, swallowing with effort. "They can't run out of people, or we'll starve to death in this blasted camp. All of us live on what they bring."

"All? We have our packages … "

"Sure, you and your friend, and ten other friends of yours. Some of you Poles get packages. But what about us, and the Jews, and the Russkis? And what if we had no food, no 'organization' from the transports, do you think you'd be eating those packages of yours in peace? We wouldn't let you!"

"You would, you'd starve to death like the Greeks. Around here, whoever has grub, has power."

"Anyway, you have enough, we have enough, so why argue?"

Right, why argue? They have enough, I have enough, we eat together and we sleep on the same bunks. Henri slices the bread, he makes a tomato salad. It tastes good with the commissary mustard.

Below us, naked, sweat-drenched men crowd the narrow barrack aisles or lie packed in eights and tens in the lower bunks. Their nude, withered bodies stink of sweat and excrement; their cheeks are hollow. Directly beneath me, in the bottom bunk, lies a rabbi. He has covered his head with a piece of rag torn off a blanket and reads from a Hebrew prayer book (there is no shortage ol this type of literature at the camp), wailing loudly, monotonously.

"Can't somebody shut him up? He's been raving as if he'd caught God himself by the feet."

"I don't feel like moving. Let him rave. They'll take him to the oven that much sooner."

"Religion is the opium of the people," Henri, who is a communist and a *rentier*, says sententiously. "If they didn't believe in God and eternal life, they'd have smashed the crematoria long ago."

"Why haven't you done it then?"

The question is rhetorical; the Frenchman ignores it. "Idiot," he says simply, and stuffs a tomato in his mouth.

Just as we finish our snack, there is a sudden commotion at the door. The Muslims scurry in fright to the safety of their bunks, a messenger runs into the block leader's shack. The leader, his face solemn, steps out at once.

"Canada! *Antreten!* At last! There's a transport coming!"

"Great God!" yells Henri, jumping off the bunk. He swallows the rest of his tomato, snatches his coat, screams "*Raus!*" at the men below, and in a flash is at the door. We can hear a scramble in the other bunks. Canada is leaving for the ramp.

"Henri, the shoes!" I call after him.

"*Keine Angst!*" he shouts back, already outside.

I proceed to put away the food. I tie a piece of rope around the suitcase where the onions and the tomatoes from my father's garden in Warsaw mingle with Portuguese sardines, bacon from Lublin (that's from my brother), and authentic sweetmeats from Salonica. I tie it all up, pull on my trousers, and slide off the bunk.

"*Platz!*" I yell, pushing my way through the Greeks. They step aside. At the door I bump into Henri.

"*Was is los?*"

"Want to come with us on the ramp?"

"Sure, why not?"

"Come along then, grab your coat! We're short of a few men. I've already told the Kapo." and he shoves me out of the barrack door.

We line up. Someone has marked down our numbers, someone up ahead yells, "March, March," and now we are running toward the gate, accompanied by the shouts of a multilingual throng that is already being pushed back to the barracks. Not everybody is lucky enough to be going on the ramp ... We have almost reached the gate. *Links, zwei, drei, vier! Mützen ab!* Erect, arms stretched stiffly along our hips, we march past the gate briskly, smartly, almost gracefully. A sleepy S.S. man with a large pad in his hand checks us off, waving us ahead in groups of five.

"*Hundert!*" he calls after we have all passed.

"*Stimmt!*" comes a hoarse answer from out front.

We march fast, almost at a run. There are guards all around, young men with automatics. We pass camp II B, then some deserted barracks and a clump of unfamiliar green—apple and pear trees. We cross the circle of watchtowers and, running, burst on to the highway. We have arrived. Just a few more yards. There, surrounded by trees, is the ramp.

A cheerful little station, very much like any other provincial railway stop: a small square framed by tall chestnuts and paved with yellow gravel. Not far off, beside the road, squats a tiny wooden shed, uglier and more flimsy than the ugliest and flimsiest railway shack, farther along lie stacks of old rails, heaps of wooden beams, barrack parts, bricks, paving stones. This is where they load freight for Birkenau: supplies for the construction of the camp, and people for the gas chambers. Trucks drive around, load up lumber, cement, people—a regular daily routine.

And now the guards are being posted along the rails, across the beams, in the green shade of the Silesian chestnuts, to form a tight circle around the ramp. They wipe the sweat from their faces and sip out of their canteens. It is unbearably hot; the sun stands motionless at its zenith.

"Fall out!"

We sit down in the narrow streaks of shade along the stacked rails. The hungry Greeks (several of them managed to come along, God only knows how) rummage underneath the rails. One of them finds some pieces of mildewed bread, another a few half-rotten sardines. They eat.

"*Schweinedreck*," spits a young, tall guard with corn-colored hair and dreamy blue eyes.

"For God's sake, any minute you'll have so much food to stuff down your guts you'll bust!"

He adjusts his gun, wipes his face with a handkerchief.

"Hey you, fatso!" His boot lightly touches Henri's shoulder. *Pass mal auf.* Want a drink?"

"Sure, but I haven't got any marks, replies the Frenchman with a professional air.

"*Schade,* too bad."

"Come, come, Herr Posten, isn't my word good enough any more? Haven't we done business before? How much?"

"One hundred. *Gemacht?*"

"*Gemacht.*"

We drink the water, lukewarm and tasteless. It will be paid for by the people who have not yet arrived.

"Now you be careful," says Henri, turning to me. He tosses away the empty bottle. It strikes the rails and bursts into tiny fragments. "Don't take any money, they might be checking. Anyway, who the hell needs money? You've got enough to eat. Don't take suits, either, or they'll think you're planning to escape. Just get a shirt, silk only, with a collar. And a vest. And if you find something to drink, don't bother calling me. I know how to shift for myself, but you watch your step or they'll let you have it."

"Do they beat you up here?"

"Naturally. You've got to have eyes in your ass. *Arschaugen.*"

Around us sit the Greeks, their jaws working greedily, like huge human insects. They munch on stale lumps of bread. They are restless, wondering what will happen next. The sight of the large beams and the stacks of rails has them worried. They dislike carrying heavy loads.

"*Was wir arbeiten?*" they ask.

"*Niks. Transport kommen, alles Krematorium, compris?*"

"*Alles verstehen,*" they answer in crematorium esperanto. All is well: they will not have to move the heavy rails or carry the beams.

In the meantime, the ramp has become increasingly alive with activity, increasingly noisy. The crews are being divided into those who will open and unload the arriving cattle cars and those who will be posted by the wooden steps. They receive instructions on how to proceed most efficiently. Motorcycles drive up, delivering S.S. officers, bemedalled, glittering with brass, beefy men with highly polished boots and shiny, brutal faces. Some have brought their briefcases, others hold thin, flexible whips. This gives them an air of military readiness and agility. They walk in and out of the commissary—for the miserable little shack by the road serves as their commissary, where in the summertime they drink mineral water, *Studentenquelle,* and where in winter they can warm up with a glass of hot wine. They greet each other in the state-approved way, raising an arm Roman fashion, then shake hands cordially, exchange warm smiles, discuss mail from home, their children, their families. Some stroll majestically on the ramp. The silver squares on their collars glitter, the gravel crunches under their boots, their bamboo whips snap impatiently.

We lie against the rails in the narrow streaks of shade, breathe unevenly, occasionally exchange a few words in our various tongues, and gaze listlessly at the majestic men in green uniforms, at the green trees, and at the church steeple of a distant village.

The transport is coming," somebody says. We spring to our feet, all eyes turn in one direction. Around the bend, one after another, the cattle cars begin rolling in. The train backs into the station, a conductor leans out, waves his hand, blows a whistle. The locomotive whistles back with a shrieking noise, puffs, the train rolls slowly alongside the ramp. In the tiny barred windows appear pale, wilted, exhausted human faces, terror-stricken women with tangled hair, unshaven men. They gaze at the station in silence. And then, suddenly, there is a stir inside the cars and a pounding against the wooden boards.

"Water! Air!"—weary, desperate cries.

Heads push through the windows, mouths gasp frantically for air. They draw a few breaths, then disappear; others come in their place, then also disappear. The cries and moans grow louder.

A man in a green uniform covered with more glitter than any of the others jerks his head impatiently, his lips twist in annoyance. He inhales deeply, then with a rapid gesture throws his cigarette away and signals to the guard. The guard removes the automatic from his shoulder, aims, sends a series of shots along the train. All is quiet now. Meanwhile, the trucks have arrived, steps are being drawn up, and the Canada men stand ready at their posts by the train doors. The S.S. officer with the briefcase raises his hand.

"Whoever takes gold, or anything at all besides food, will be shot for stealing Reich property. Understand? *Verstanden?*"

"*Jawohl!*" we answer eagerly.

"*Also los*! Begin!"

The bolts crack, the doors fall open. A wave of fresh air rushes inside the train. People ... inhumanly crammed, buried under incredible heaps of luggage, suitcases, trunks, packages, crates, bundles of every description (everything that had been their past and was to start their future). Monstrously squeezed together, they have fainted from the heat, suffocated, crushed one another. Now they push towards the opened doors, breathing like fish cast out on the sand.

"Attention! Out, and take your luggage with you! Take out everything. Pile all your stuff near the exits. Yes, your coats too. It is summer. March to the left. Understand?"

"Sir, what's going to happen to us?" They jump from the train on to the gravel, anxious, worn-out.

"Where are you people from?"

"Sosnowiec-Będzin. Sir, what's going to happen to us?" They repeat the question stubbornly, gazing into our tired eyes.

"I don't know, I don't understand Polish."

It is the camp law: people going to their death must be deceived to the very end. This is the only permissible form of charity. The heat is tremendous. The sun hangs directly over our heads, the white, hot sky quivers, the air vibrates, an occasional breeze feels like a sizzling blast from a furnace. Our lips are parched, the mouth fills with the salty taste of blood, the body is weak and heavy from lying in the sun. Water!

A huge, multicolored wave of people loaded down with luggage pours from the train like a blind, mad river trying to find a new bed. But before they have a chance to recover, before they can draw a breath of fresh air and look at the sky, bundles are snatched from their hands, coats ripped off their backs, their purses and umbrellas taken away.

"But please, sir, it's for the sun, I cannot … "

"*Verboten!*" one of us barks through clenched teeth. There is an S.S. man standing behind your back, calm, efficient, watchful.

"*Meine Herrschaften,* this way, ladies and gentlemen, try not to throw your things around, please … Show some goodwill," he says courteously, his restless hands playing with the slender whip.

"Of course, of course," they answer as they pass, and now they walk alongside the train somewhat more cheerfully. A woman reaches down quickly to pick up her handbag. The whip flies, the woman screams, stumbles, and falls under the feet of the surging crowd. Behind her, a child cries in a thin little voice "Mamele!"—a very small girl with tangled black curls.

The heaps grow. Suitcases, bundles, blankets, coats, handbags that open as they fall, spilling coins, gold, watches; mountains of bread pile up at the exits, heaps of marmalade, jams, masses of meat, sausages; sugar spills on the gravel. Trucks, loaded with people, start up with a deafening roar and drive off amidst the wailing and screaming of the women separated from their children, and the stupefied silence of the men left behind. They are the ones who had been ordered to step to the right—the healthy and the young who will go to the camp. In the end, they too will not escape death, but first they must work.

Trucks leave and return, without interruption, as on a monstrous conveyor belt. A Red Cross van drives back and forth, back and forth, incessantly: it transports the gas that will kill these people. The enormous cross on the hood, red as blood, seems to dissolve in the sun.

The Canada men at the trucks cannot stop for a single moment, even to catch their breath. They shove the people up the steps, pack them in tightly, sixty per truck, more or less. Nearby stands a young, cleanshaven "gentleman," an S.S. officer with a notebook in his hand. For each departing truck he enters a mark; sixteen gone means one thousand people, more or less. The gentleman is calm, precise, no truck can leave without a signal from him, or a mark in his notebook: *Ordnung muss sein.* The marks swell into thousands, the thousands into whole transports, which afterwards we shall simply call "from Salonica," "from Strasbourg," "from Rotterdam." This one will be called "Sosnowiec-Będzin." The new prisoners from Sosnowiec-Będzin will receive serial numbers 131–2—thousand, of course, though afterwards we shall simply say 131–2, for short.

The transports swell into weeks, months, years. When the war is over, they will count up the marks in their notebooks—all four and a half million of them. The bloodiest battle of the war, the greatest victory of the strong, united Germany. *Ein Reich, ein Volk, ein Fuhrer*—and four crematoria.

The train has been emptied. A thin, pock-marked S.S. man peers inside, shakes his head in disgust and motions to our group, pointing his finger at the door.

"*Rein.* Clean it up!"

We climb inside. In the corners amid human excrement and abandoned wrist-watches lie squashed, trampled infants, naked little monsters with enormous heads and bloated bellies. We carry them out like chickens, holding several in each hand.

"Don't take them to the trucks, pass them on to the women," says the S.S. man, lighting a cigarette. His cigarette lighter is not working properly; he examines it carefully.

"Take them, for God's sake!" I explode as the women run from me in horror, covering their eyes.

The name of God sounds strangely pointless, since the women and the infants will go on the trucks, every one of them, without exception. We all know what this means, and we look at each other with hate and horror.

"What, you don't want to take them?" asks the pock-marked S.S. man with a note of surprise and reproach in his voice, and reaches for his revolver.

"You mustn't shoot, I'll carry them." A tall, grey-haired woman takes the little corpses out of my hands and for an instant gazes straight into my eyes.

"My poor boy," she whispers and smiles at me. Then she walks away, staggering along the path. I lean against the side of the train. I am terribly tired. Someone pulls at my sleeve.

"*En avant,* to the rails, come on!"

I look up, but the face swims before my eyes, dissolves, huge and transparent, melts into the motionless trees and the sea of people … I blink rapidly: Henri.

"Listen, Henri, are we good people?"

"That's stupid. Why do you ask?"

"You see, my friend, you see, I don't know why, but I am furious, simply furious with these people—furious because I must be here because of them. I feel no pity. I am not sorry they're going to the gas chamber. Damn them all! I could throw myself at them, beat them with my fists. It must be pathological, I just can't understand … "

"Ah, on the contrary, it is natural, predictable, calculated. The ramp exhausts you, you rebel—and the easiest way to relieve your hate is to turn against someone weaker. Why, I'd even call it healthy. It's simple logic, *compris?*" He props himself up comfortably against the heap of rails. "Look at the Greeks, they know how to make the best ol it! They stuff their bellies with anything they find. One of them has just devoured a full jar of marmalade."

"Pigs! Tomorrow half of them will die of the shits."

"Pigs? You've been hungry."

"Pigs!" I repeat furiously. I close my eyes. The air is filled with ghastly cries, the earth trembles beneath me, I can feel sticky moisture on my eyelids. My throat is completely dry.

The morbid procession streams on and on … trucks growl like mad dogs. I shut my eyes tight, but I can still see corpses dragged from the train, trampled infants, cripples piled on top of the dead, wave after wave … freight cars roll in, the heaps of clothing, suitcases and bundles grow, people climb out, look at the sun, take a few breaths, beg for water, get into the trucks, drive away. And again freight cars roll in, again people … The scenes become confused in my mind—I am not sure if all of this is actually happening, or if I am dreaming. There is a humming inside my head; I feel that I must vomit.

Henri tugs at my arm.

"Don't sleep, we're off to load up the loot."

All the people are gone. In the distance, the last few trucks roll along the road in clouds of dust, the train has left, several S.S. officers promenade up and down the ramp. The silver glitters on their collars, their boots shine, their red, beefy faces shine Among them, there is a woman … only now I realize she has been here all along—withered flat-chested, bony, her thin, colorless hair pulled back and tied in a "Nordic" knot; her hands are in the pockets of her wide skirt. With a rat-like, resolute smile glued on her thin lips she skulks around the corners of the ramp … She detests feminine beauty with the hatred of a woman who is herself repulsive, and knows it. Yes, I have seen her many times before and I know her well: she is the commandant of the F.K.L. She has come to look over the new crop of women, for some of them, instead of going on the trucks, will go on foot—to the concentration camp. There our boys, the barbers from Zauna, will shave their heads and will have a good laugh at their "outside world" modesty.

We proceed to load the loot. We lift huge trunks, heave them on to the trucks. They are arranged in stacks, packed tightly. Occasionally somebody slashes one open with a knife, for pleasure or in search of vodka and perfume. One of the crates falls open, suits, shirts, books drop out on the ground … I pick up a small, heavy package, unwrap about two handfuls, bracelets, rings, brooches, diamonds …

"*Gib hier,*" an S.S. man says calmly, holding up his briefcase already full of gold and colorful foreign currency. He locks the case, hands it to an officer, takes another, an empty one, and stands by the next truck, waiting. The gold will go to the Reich.

It is hot, terribly hot. Our throats are dry, each word hurts. Anything for a sip of water! Faster, faster, so that it is over, so that we may rest. At last we are done, all the trucks have gone. Now we swiftly clean up the remaining dirt. There must be no trace left of the *Schweinerei* … But just as the last truck disappears behind the trees where we walk, finally, to rest in the shade, a shrill whistle sounds around the bend. Slowly, terribly slowly, a train rolls in, the engine whistles back with a deafening shriek. Again, weary pale faces at the windows, flat as though cut out of paper, with huge, feverishly burning eyes. Already trucks are pulling up, already the composed gentleman with the notebook is at his post, and the S.S. men emerge from the commissary carrying briefcases for the gold and money. We unseal the train doors.

It is impossible to control oneself any longer. Brutally we tear suitcases from their hands, impatiently pull off their coats. Go on, go on, vanish! They go, they vanish. Men, women, children. Some of them know.

Here is a woman—she walks quickly, but tries to appear calm. A small child with a pink cherub's face runs after her, unable to keep up, stretches out his little arms and cries, "Mama! Mama!"

"Pick up your child, woman!"

"It's not mine, sir, not mine!" she shouts hysterically and runs on, covering her face with her hands. She wants to hide, she wants to reach those who will not ride the trucks, those who will go on foot, those who will stay alive. She is young, healthy, good-looking. She wants to live.

But the child runs after her, wailing loudly. "Mama! Mama! Don't leave me!"

"It's not mine, not mine, no!"

Andrei, a sailor from Sevastopol, grabs hold of her. His eyes are glassy from vodka and the heat. With one powerful blow he knocks her off her feet, then, as she falls, takes her by the hair and pulls her up again. His face twitches with rage.

"Ah, you bloody Jewess. So you're running from your own child! I'll show you, you whore!" His huge hand chokes her, he lifts her in the air and heaves her on to the truck like a heavy sack of grain.

"Here! And take this with you, bitch!" and he throws the child at her feet.

*"Gut gemacht,* good work. That's the way to deal with degenerate mothers," says the S.S. man standing at the foot of the truck. "*Gut, gut,* Russki."

"Shut your mouth," growls Andrei through clenched teeth, and walks away. From under a pile of rags be pulls out a canteen, unscrews the cork, takes a few deep swallows, passes it to me. The strong vodka burns the throat. My head swims, my legs are shaky, again I feel like throwing up.

And suddenly, above the teeming crowd pushing forward like a river driven by an unseen power, a girl appears. She descends lightly from the train, hops on to the gravel, looks around inquiringly, as if somewhat surprised. Her soft, blonde hair has fallen on her shoulders in a torrent, she throws it back impatiently. With a natural gesture she runs her hands down her blouse, casually straightens her skirt. She stands like this for an instant, gazing at the crowd, then turns and with a gliding look examines our faces, as though searching for someone. Unknowingly, I continue to stare at her, until our eyes meet.

"Listen, tell me, where are they taking us?"

I look at her without saying a word. Here, standing before me, is a girl, a girl with enchanting blond hair, with beautiful breasts, wearing a little cotton blouse, a girl with a wise, mature look in her eyes. Here she stands, gazing straight into my face, waiting. And over there is the gas chamber: communal death, disgusting and ugly. And over in the other direction is the concentration camp; the shaved head, the heavy Soviet trousers in sweltering heat, the sickening, stale odor of dirty, damp female bodies, the animal hunger, the inhuman labor, and later the same gas chamber, only an even more hideous, more terrible death …

Why did she bring it? I think to myself, noticing a lovely gold watch on her delicate wrist.

They'll take it away from her anyway.

"Listen, tell me," she repeats.

I remain silent. Her lips tighten.

"I know," she says with a shade of proud contempt in her voice, tossing her head. She walks off resolutely in the direction of the trucks. Someone tries to stop her; she boldly pushes him aside and runs up the steps. In the distance I can only catch a glimpse of her blond hair flying in the breeze.

I go back inside the train; I carry out dead infants; I unload luggage. I touch corpses, but I cannot overcome the mounting, uncontrollable terror. I try to escape from the corpses, but they are everywhere: lined up on the gravel, on the cement edge of the ramp, inside the cattle cars. Babies, hideous naked women, men twisted by convulsions. I run off as far as I can go, but immediately a whip slashes across my back. Out of the corner of my eye I see an S.S. man, swearing profusely. I stagger forward and run, lose myself in the Canada group. Now, at last, I can once more rest against the stack of rails. The sun has leaned low over the horizon and illuminates the ramp with a reddish glow; the shadows of the trees have become elongated, ghostlike. In the silence that settles over nature at this time of day, the human cries seem to rise all the way to the sky.

Only from this distance does one have a full view of the inferno on the teeming ramp. I see a pair of human beings who have fallen to the ground locked in a last desperate embrace. The man has dug his fingers into the woman's flesh and has caught her clothing with his teeth. She screams hysterically, swears, cries, until at last a large boot comes down over her throat and she is silent. They are pulled apart and dragged like cattle to the truck. I see four Canada men lugging a corpse: a huge, swollen female corpse. Cursing, dripping wet from the strain, they kick out of their way some stray children who have been running all over the ramp, howling like dogs. The men pick them up by the collars, heads, arms, and toss them inside the trucks, on top of the heaps. The four men have trouble lifting the fat corpse onto the car, they call others for help, and all together they hoist up the mound of meat. Big, swollen, puffed-up corpses are being collected from all over the ramp; on top of them are piled the invalids, the smothered, the sick, the unconscious. The heap seethes, howls, groans. The driver starts the motor, the truck begins rolling.

"Halt! Halt!" an S.S. man yells after them. "Stop, damn you!"

They are dragging to the truck an old man wearing tails and a band around his arm. His head knocks against the gravel and pavement; he moans and wails in an uninterrupted monotone: "*Ich will mit dem Herrn Kommandanten sprechen*—I wish to speak with the commandant … " With senile stubbornness he keeps repeating these words all the way. Thrown on the truck, trampled by others, choked, he still wails: *Ich will mit dem …*

"Look here, old man!" a young S.S. man calls, laughing jovially. "In half an hour you'll be talking with the top commandant! Only don't forget to greet him with a

Heil Hitler!"

Several other men are carrying a small girl with only one leg. They hold her by the arms and the one leg. Tears are running down her face and she whispers faintly: "Sir, it hurts, it hurts … " They throw her on the truck on top of the corpses. She will burn alive along with them.

The evening has come, cool and clear. The stars are out. We lie against the rails. It is incredibly quiet. Anaemic bulbs hang from the top of the high lamp-posts; beyond the circle of light stretches an impenetrable darkness. Just one step, and a man could vanish for ever. But the guards are watching, their automatics ready.

"Did you get the shoes?" asks Henri.

"No."

"Why?"

"My God, man, I am finished, absolutely finished!"

"So soon? After only two transports? Just look at me, I … since Christmas, at least a million people have passed through my hands. The worst of all are the transports from around Paris—one is always bumping into friends."

"And what do you say to them?"

"That first they will have a bath, and later we'll meet at the camp. What would you say?"

I do not answer. We drink coffee with vodka; somebody opens a tin of cocoa and mixes it with sugar. We scoop it up by the handful, the cocoa sticks to the lips. Again coffee, again vodka.

"Henri, what are we waiting for?"

"There'll be another transport."

"I'm not going to unload it! I can't take any more."

"So, it's got you down? Canada is nice, eh?" Henri grins indulgently and disappears into the darkness. In a moment he is back again.

"All right. Just sit here quietly and don't let an S.S. man see you. I'll try to find you your shoes."

"Just leave me alone. Never mind the shoes." I want to sleep. It is very late.

Another whistle, another transport. Freight cars emerge out of the darkness, pass under the lamp-posts, and again vanish in the night. The ramp is small, but the circle of lights is smaller. The unloading will have to be done gradually. Somewhere the trucks are growling, they back up against the steps, black, ghostlike, their searchlights flash across the trees. *Wasser! Luft!* The same all over again, like a late showing of the same film: a volley of shots, the train falls silent. Only this time a little girl pushes herself halfway through the small window and, losing her balance, falls out onto the gravel. Stunned, she lies still for a moment, then stands up and begins walking around in a circle, faster and faster, waving her rigid arms in the air, breathing loudly and spasmodically, whining in a faint voice. Her mind has given way in the inferno inside the train. The whining is hard on the nerves: an S.S. man approaches calmly, his heavy boot strikes between her shoulders. She falls. Holding her down with his foot, he draws his revolver, fires once, then again.

She remains face down, kicking the gravel with her feet, until she stiffens. They proceed to unseal the train.

I am back on the ramp, standing by the doors. A warm, sickening smell gushes, filling the car almost halfway up to the ceiling is motionless, horribly tangled, but still steaming.

"*Ausladen!*" comes the command. An S.S. man steps out from the darkness. Across his chest hangs a portable searchlight. He throws a stream of light inside.

"Why are you standing about like sheep? Start unloading!"

His whip flies and falls across our backs. I seize a corpse by the hand; the fingers close tightly around mine. I pull back with a shriek and stagger away. My heart pounds, jumps up to my throat. I can no longer control the nausea. Hunched under the train I begin to vomit.

Then, like a drunk, I weave over to the stack of rails.

I lie against the cool, kind metal and dream about returning to the camp, about my bunk, on which there is no mattress, about sleep among comrades who are not going to the gas tonight. Suddenly I see the camp as a haven of peace. It is true, others may be dying, but one is somehow still alive, one has enough food, enough strength to work ...

The lights on the ramp flicker with a spectral glow, the wave of people—feverish, agitated, stupefied people—flows on and on, endlessly. They think that now they will have to face a new life in the camp, and they prepare themselves emotionally for the hard struggle ahead. They do not know that in just a few moments they will die, that the gold, money, and diamonds which they have so prudently hidden in their clothing and on their bodies are now useless to them. Experienced professionals will probe into eveiy recess of their flesh, will pull the gold from under the tongue and the diamonds from the uterus and the colon. They will rip out gold teeth. In tightly sealed crates they will ship them to Berlin.

The S.S. men's black figures move about, dignified, businesslike. The gentleman with the notebook puts down his final marks, rounds out the figures: fifteen thousand.

Many, very many, trucks have been driven to the crematoria today.

It is almost over. The dead are being cleared off the ramp and piled into the last truck. The Canada men, weighed down under a load of bread, marmalade and sugar and smelling of perfume and fresh linen, line up to go. For several days the entire camp will live off this transport. For several days the entire camp will talk about Sosnowiec-Będzin. "Sosnowiec-Będzin" was a good, rich transport.

The stars are already beginning to pale as we walk back to the camp. The sky grows translucent and opens high above our heads it is getting light.

Great columns of smoke rise from the crematoria and merge up above into a huge black river which very slowly floats across the sky over Birkenau and disappears beyond the forests in the direction of Trzebinia. The "Sosnowiec-Będzin" transport is already burning.

We pass a heavily armed S.S. detachment on its way to change guard. The men march briskly, in step, shoulder to shoulder, one mass, one will.

"*Und morgen die ganze Welt* ... " They sing at the top of their lungs.

"*Rechts ran!* To the right march!" snaps a command from up front. We move out of their way.

—1946. TRANSLATED BY BARBARA VEDDER

*Notes:* "Spanish goats" are crossed wooden beams wrapped in barbed wire. "Canada" refers to the members of the labor gang, or Kommando, who helped to unload the incoming transports of people destined for the gas chambers. "Muslim" was the camp name for a prisoner who had been destroyed physically and spiritually, and who had neither the strength nor the will to continue living, a man ripe for the gas chamber.

*Historical Note.* The camp at Auschwitz was originally a Polish army barracks, turned by the Nazis into a prison and slave labor camp for Polish prisoners. Little by little the camp outgrew its original function, as Auschwitz became the destination point and place of death for imprisoned Jews from all across Europe. Gas chambers and crematoria were added to further Adolf Hitler's so-called "final solution to the Jewish question." Of the estimated 1.3 million people sent to Auschwitz, some 1.1 million died at the camp, including 960,000 Jews. It was the largest extermination camp run by Nazi Germany in occupied Poland during World War II.

*Commentary.* Tadeusz Borowski's series of short stories about life in World War II's most notorious Nazi labor and death camp, Auschwitz-Birkenau, was published as *Pożegnanie z Marią* (Farewell to Maria), but its English title was *This Way for the Gas, Ladies and Gentlemen*, after the story here. The main stories are written in the first person by a narrator who moves congruently with the action as it unfolds. The perspective is that of a cynical Auschwitz inmate, Tadek, who at every moment is actively involved in the action, simultaneously sharing his reactions and emotions with the reader. During the course of the narrative, certain vignettes of particular horror or cruelty stand out, as if forever emblazoned in the narrator's memory.

"This Way for the Gas" is direct, realistic, unvarnished, believable, and unapologetic. It conveys in graphic detail the sights, sounds, and smells of what it must have been like for prison inmates, under the eyes of their Nazi S.S. guards, as they brutally unload and separate from their belongings Jewish civilians from the sealed cattle cars in which they had been riding standing up, without food or water, often in scorching heat for days on end, from the far reaches of Nazi-occupied Europe. Most are to meet their immediate end in the gas chambers.

The story dispels the idea that heroism, altruism, or comraderie of any kind played a role in everyday Auschwitz life. On the contrary, it describes the morally numbing effect of witnessing and participating in acts of unspeakable cruelty and violence, as prisoners try to survive in any way possible, while remaining indifferent to or being actively mean-spirited toward one another, while developing an especially vicious attitude toward the helpless victims they herd to their deaths. Tadek is a *Kapo*, a prisoner overseer placed over other prisoners. As such he has certain privileges other prisoners do not have, such as receiving food parcels from home. He zealously guards these privileges, and does not share his bounty with others, except possibly in some kind of *quid pro quo* transaction.

In "This Way for the Gas" Tadek is invited by his "friend" Henri to temporarily join the so-called "Canada" prisoner detachment, whose job is to unload the trainloads of arriving Jewish prisoners and separate them from their belongings. Tadek agrees because he is looking for a good pair of shoes and a shirt. The prisoners are free to keep any food they find for themselves; indeed they depend on it for their continuing survival. Anything of value is immediately confiscated by the German guards.

The prisoners unloaded from the trains are divided by the Germans into two groups, a "select" group deemed healthy enough to work as slave laborers until they starve to death, and the rest, including children and the elderly and infirm, who are trucked straight to the gas chambers to be asphixiated and cremated. The experience is even more than Tadek, by this time a hardened camp veteran, can stomach.

# The Postwar Polish Short Story

# Marek Hłasko

Marek Hłasko (1934–1969) was born in Warsaw. He lived with his mother in direst poverty through World War II, experiencing the ill-fated Warsaw Uprising of 1944 firsthand. His wartime experience of terror and starvation determined his pessimistic and nihilistic attitude toward life.

At the age of sixteen he studied for and received a commercial driver's license, and for several years he drove trucks for a string of enterprises across Poland. Around this time, he began writing short stories describing life among the laboring class as he had experienced it. The literary elite paid attention, and provided support and guidance. To them he seemed to have the perfect working-class background that the literary establishment in communist Poland was looking for in a budding writer. These credentials provided cover for him, allowing him to publish stories which were heavily unflattering about the bleak life of workers in Poland in the 1950s, although eventually the censorship did catch up with him. His stories are full of unprovoked meanness, brutality, crushed dreams, shattered illusions, and sheer hopelessness. It made for a fairly limited repertoire of themes, which he nevertheless exploited with considerable commercial success. The two stories featured here, "A Lovely Girl" and "The Most Sacred Words of our Lives," published in 1956, were contained in his first collection of stories, published when the author was only twenty-two.

Little by little Hłasko earned a reputation as the most talented writer of the postwar generation, known also for his volatility, nonconformity, and ability to get into trouble with the authorities. Because of his good looks and reckless behavior, he became dubbed the "Polish James Dean," after the ill-starred actor in the 1955 American film *Rebel Without a Cause*, but he had more in common with the nihilistic anti-establishment "angry young men" who populated the literary scene in 1950s Great Britain.

In 1958 Hłasko's reputation enabled him to travel to Paris, after which he never returned to Poland but lived as a vagabond variously in France, Germany, Italy, Israel, and the United States, in the last of which he unsuccessfully tried to break into the film industry as a scriptwriter. Because he had published a novel, *Cmentarze* (Cemeteries), which was highly critical of socialism as it had played out in Poland, in the emigré press, Hłasko's passport was revoked, and his works were not published in Poland for twenty years. He died in 1969 at the age of thirty-five in Wiesbaden, Germany, from an overdose of alcohol and sedatives.

Given his brief life and erratic lifestyle, Hłasko's literary output was considerable, consisting of nine novels (some published posthumously), two major short-story collections, and many other stories published separately. As many as nine of his works have been adapted for the screen. The two stories contained here, along with another, "*Lombard złudzeń*" (Pawnshop of Illustions), formed the basis of the 1993 film by Ireniusz Engler *Śliczna dziewczyna* (A Lovely Girl).

## A Lovely Girl

She was truly a lovely girl. People coming to that park, even those who had been doing so for many years, didn't remember that there had ever been any girl who could hold a candle to her. That girl undermined one's belief in the corporeal nature of the world. Those passing by the bench on which she sat had the impression that they had taken five steps into a different universe. Even the old man with the ivory-tipped cane who had been sauntering past here for years opened his mouth wide and held it that way all the way to the end of the lane. And that man had seen a lot; he could have told a lot about May nights when, panting with malicious satisfaction, he had flushed many a young lover out of the bushes.

Next to the girl on the bench sat a boy. He couldn't have been much older than she was, in other words, nineteen or twenty. He was also good-looking, but she put him in the shade with her slightest movement or glance. That girl is carrying a piece of the sun around with her, passers-by thought. At one point she said:

"It's getting late. I have to go."

"Whatever," said the boy. "I'm fine here."

"Are you going to do what I asked you to or not?"

"I already told you."

"You'll be sorry."

"I'll manage," said the boy.

He took a pack of cigarettes from his pocket, tapped his finger against the bottom, pulled one out and lit it. Then he put the pack back.

"I smoke too," said the girl.

"It's not good for you. Nicotine is bad for the health, and it harms your complexion."

She looked at him through narrowed eyes. They were dark brown with honey-colored stars shining in them. She was about to say something when a man in a cheap serge suit walked past. He was an insignificant clerk who had never attained anything in life, because he lacked both talent and perseverance. Like every man of that sort, he considered himself wronged and misunderstood. He took a look at the lovely girl and thought,

"My God! If I had had someone like that, maybe everything would have been different. A woman like that can change everything. Maybe I could get a new start. This way life's a crock, goddammit. A guy can come unglued. I wonder what's playing at the movies?"

He grew sad and hurried on. As soon as he had passed, the girl asked the boy:

"Will you give it to me or not?"

"I don't like to repeat myself," he replied.

She looked at him with her dark eyes and said quietly:

"You son-of-a-bitch."

He laughed out loud. He kicked a stone on the path with the tip of his shoe and said in a quiet and melodious tone:

"You're making a slight mistake: I'm not your child."

"If you were, I'd know what to do with you."

He looked at her sidewise and replied:

"So why are you asking me what to do with yours?"

"It's yours too."

"Your words are beautiful, and I'm really touched, but it wasn't just me. There was Mietek and Roman and a couple of others besides. Why are you coming to me for money? You think I'm Santa Claus?"

"Nothing happened between me and them."

"I saw you go outside with them."

"In order to get some fresh air and to walk around a bit. It was such a beautiful night."

"Yeah, right," he said indifferently.

He put out his cigarette and stretched back, leaning his shoulders against the rear of the bench. He looked for a while at the darkening sky and then said,

"Sorry, but I stopped believing in miracles a long time ago. I never heard yet that a girl went walking at night with a guy just to look at the moon. It's usually the moon that takes a gander at them."

The girl raised her head and looked him straight in the eyes. She didn't say anything, but merely crushed a green twig in her hand. She had hands like a Madonna in an old painting: long, slender, nervous, beautiful, with a life of their own. The man who at that moment walked by glanced first at her and then at her hands and felt his breath taken away. He was a young writer and dreamed of writing the kind of great love story people constantly, agonizingly, yearn for. At that very moment with frightening clarity he beheld the story in its entirety. Scenes, dialogues, and faces had been flitting through his head for many months, but only now was he able to view his work as a complete whole.

"I've got it," he said, feverishly working things out in his head. "I've finally got it. They meet by accident on a park bench. The romance takes shape quickly and they spend their first night together, but they treat it all cynically, like a sport, because that's their way of trying to avoid complications and disenchantment. But with time love emerges, tremendous and overpowering, knocking them off their feet. But they still can't believe it, tormented by the cynical beginning. Finally they understand: now they will be together, forever united by their mutual feelings. It will be a work full of Sturm and Drang … "

Rejoicing, he galloped home. The girl said to the boy:

"Fine, just as you want. But you haven't heard the end of it. Others will also hear about our little secret. You'll be tossed out on your can. You'll forget you ever thought about becoming an engineer, my dear. I'll make sure of it."

Without batting an eye, he responded:

"Darling, you're becoming pathetic, and that's not good. I personally worry about being pathetic more than anything else on earth."

"It's you who'll be pathetic."

"Not really. See, I too can help you remember about certain things. For example, this: It's night. A certain boy in the army thinks about his sweetheart and dreams about the time when they can be together. He's doing guard duty, of course. A pretty picture, right? In the meantime,"—and here he put his face next to the girl's and spoke roughly—"in the meantime the girl is keeping time in a fancy restaurant with two flabby middle-aged guys with shops over on Chmielna Street. The girl later drives over to one of their places drunk out of her mind and spends the whole night shacked up with them. In the morning, of course, she tells them a sad story about how her father is in jail for something he didn't do while she and her mother starve. She borrows five hundred zlotys from one of them and goes out and buys two pairs of nylons. A story taken straight out of life, wouldn't you say?"

"It's not that great. I know more interesting stories than that. For instance I've heard one about this young kid who falsified certain facts on his university application, and then went around telling heart-rending tales to people for as long as it suited him. He even went so far as to learn a substandard city dialect in order to show he was a true man of the people. Meanwhile his daddy sends him packages from New York so his kid can dress in style, because his dad has picked up there where he left off here, that same dad who is the unemployed lathe operator on the application form. Pretty interesting, huh?"

"I'll give you half."

"No, sweetie," she said, "you'll give me the whole thing, or … "

"Or what?" he interrupted, brutally squeezing her hand.

"Nothing. I won't repeat myself. I don't want to appear pathetic, because I too fear that more than anything else on earth. "

"O.K.," he said coldly.

He looked at her dully, while she smiled back at him mockingly.

"I'll give you the money in two weeks," he said.

"Sooner than that. Even now is getting late."

"You should have been more careful, dammit!"

"Just who do you think you're talking to?"

"You didn't have to agree to everything, you … "

"Shh!" she hissed.

An old couple was walking past, gray-haired and bent over. They had lived together for many years. They were religious and believed that every day spent here on earth was a gift from God, and they were grateful for it. The old woman took a look at the girl and burst out crying.

"What's the matter," asked her husband.

"Why didn't God give us children like that?" she said. "Why couldn't we have had children like that?"

The old man pressed her frail wrinkled hand.

"We loved one another," he said. "We had a good life. God will forgive us if we are not leaving anyone behind. It's not our fault, after all."

"I know," she said with difficulty. She wiped away her tears and sighed. "Still, it would have been a lot better … "

Hunched over, they directed their steps farther along the green paths. The boy said:

"I'll handle it for you." He was silent for a moment and then added: "I can hardly wait until you get married."

"Wait for what?"

"You'll have children, a house, a husband."

"Well, so?"

"Nothing. I'll drop by sometime. You'll introduce me to your husband, and we'll talk about old times."

"So next week, right?"

"Yeah."

"Good," she said.

She lifted her marvelous face to the sky, and for a moment it was illuminated by the setting sun. Her every wisp of hair, every patch of skin, her eyes, lips, shoulders, everything was permeated by sunlight and full of the sun. She looked up at the green treetops and then said quietly,

"You'll have a long time to wait."

"For love one can wait a long time."

"Ah yes … ," she whispered.

She said nothing more. The glow was gone from her face, as the sun had escaped behind the trees. In its last rays two men hurrying home from work spotted the girl. Both of them were older; they had wrinkled faces and temples covered with gray. One of them, the shorter of the two, glanced at the girl and his face contracted with pain.

"What's the matter?" asked the taller one.

"Oh, nothing," said the shorter one, trying to smile.

He passed his hand over his brow with a gesture of extreme weariness and repeated:

"It's nothing. I know I shouldn't be blue, but sometimes it's really hard to be happy."

"What is there not to be happy about?"

"When I did my ten years in jail before the war," said the shorter one, "I used to dream that once the battle was over the girls would look just like that one. When they locked me up I was still very young, just like that boy there sitting next to her. I was young and naïve, and that's more or less how I imagined communism. It was only after they danced for a while on my ribs that my vision changed a bit."

"So why do you have such a sad face now?"

"Sometimes it's hard when you think about it and realize that you never had a girl like that."

"Nonsense," said the other.

He nudged his friend in the side and said:

"Is it really all that important? It's enough that they exist, that they are as beautiful as they are, and that they love their young men and are loved by them in return."

## The Most Sacred Words of Our Lives

They woke up at dawn so tightly tangled up with one another that their first sensation was surprise at how they had been able to sleep so soundly that their closeness had not bothered them at all. The boy was first to budge, propping himself up on an elbow and gazing warmly at her before speaking.

"Tell me this really happened."

"So, you think it was a dream?"

"I can't be sure," he said. "You can't imagine how many times I've dreamed about spending the night with you, talking and laughing and revealing secret thoughts, only to wake up next morning to find an empty spot next to me."

He touched his hand to her face and said,

"So, who knows? Maybe it really *was* a dream."

"You think now is a dream?"

"Like I said, who knows?"

She looked at him through slitted eyes. He could see that she wanted to say something, but was hesitating. In a sudden onrush of trepidation he grasped her hand, until she finally spoke.

"You know what you should do? Get up and go to the mirror."

"What for?"

"I'm telling you, get up."

The boy got up. but went to the window instead, and drew back the curtains. The day was bright and clear. The hour was still early, and the roofs still glistened with morning dew. The silence of the morning was broken by the grating of the first trolleys. For a moment he looked out at the empty street, then said,

"I'm a little afraid."

She leaped out of bed, took him by the hand, and led him to the mirror.

"Now do you believe it?" she asked. "Dreams can gnaw at your soul, but they won't leave a trace on your neck, my dear."

"You're not sorry?"

"Sorry about what?"

"About last night."

"If I was sorry, you wouldn't look and feel like you do at this moment. Do you think a girl could be with with a guy like I was with you if she didn't truly want him?"

"You mean you'd already thought about me?"

"Yes, and more than once."

"And you wanted it?"

"The same as you. You can bank on it."

He smiled wryly.

"And how did you know how much I wanted you?"

"Oh you can believe it. I know. After all, I have to go into the same contortions as you, so people won't guess what I'm thinking."

He was overcome with an immense tenderness, verging on regret.

"I've spent so much time," he blurted out, "waiting for this moment, dreaming about it. It's frightening to think that now it's happened."

He went to the window again and looked out onto the street, too afraid to speak for fear of what he might say.

People were already leaving for work. He knew all the residents of the narrow sandy street. On a street like this even today people know everything about everyone, even their dreams. Filled with an amazingly langorous feeling of happiness in which at present he still had trouble believing, he kept silent. He turned around only at the sound of her voice. She was standing behind him, putting her face to his shoulders while she spoke.

"It's funny … you smell of milk, just like a little puppy … and your eyes look so very strange …"

Then she took his face in her hands and said, "Yes, you're really just like a little puppy dog. I wish it could be this way forever. I've never felt so happy with any man. It's never been so good with anyone as it was with you last night. I swear it. I never dreamed I could be so happy."

"Was it really so good for you?" he asked, feeling that his heart was all but leaping out of his throat, dreading what she might say.

"Oh, please, don't ask," she said.

"I'm beginning to feel like this was all just a bad dream."

"Why bad?"

"Because we regret good dreams once they're over."

"Listen to me. I'll tell you what you have to do."

"Go to the mirror?"

"How did you guess?"

They both laughed, and the boy said,

"I've got to go to work."

"Have some breakfast first."

"I can't," he said," and put on a sad face. "You know what it's like when a guy turns up late for work."

"Wait a bit, I'll fix you something to take with you."

He began dressing, without daring so much as to touch his own body. He could still feel her presence all over it, down to the tips of his hair. He was full of that amazing sensation, heavy as lead and more painful than death, but sweeter than the most beautiful music. It was the feeling one has after spending the night with someone for whom one has waited a lifetime, has longed for night after sleepless night, for whom one has looked for in every face on every street, at every unexpected knock at the door, for whom one is prepared to renounce heaven, earth, and all humankind, only, because of her, to end up loving the whole world.

"When do you get back from work?" she asked.

"In the evening. Will you wait for me?"

"How can you even ask that?"

"Because I still can't believe my happiness."

"I get home first."

"Then turn on the light, draw back the curtains, and wait for me."

"I'll turn on the light, draw back the curtains, and wait for you. And now I'll tell you something. We won't say goodbye."

"Why not?"

"Because I don't want to part from you even for a second."

He shut the door behind him and ran down the stairs like a whirlwind. Once out on the street he took in a gulp of fresh air.

"A-a-a-ah," he gasped.

Then he gazed upward and waved. He moved quickly ahead, for he had a fair distance to go to get to work. It was late, and he had to hurry. Even so, he stopped in front of one of the houses and shouted,

"Hey, Heniek, let's go!"

And since every Warsaw gay young blade talked as though he had no teeth in his mouth, it sounded more like,

"Ey, Enek, zgo!"

Heniek duly came out, short and sturdy with a broad and simple face. Like the boy, he was dressed in the black overalls of an assembly worker. His colored shirt was unbuttoned at the neck.

"Tsup?" he said.

"Let's get going. If we hurry we'll pick up Malinowski and Mr. Ceniek."

"So let's get going. I've been late two times already this month."

They walked quickly along. The sun was already climbing high in the sky, and the dew was quickly evaporating from the trees, roofs, leaves, and grass. Women with their hair in a mess and overcoats thrown hastily over their robes were carrying bottles, pans, and pitchers for milk. Heniek said:

"Come on over tonight. Ducky will bring a record player, and there's sure to be a bottle."

"Sorry, but I've got something to do this evening."

"You're going to Basia's?"

"None of your business."

"Oh my God," said Heniek dreamily. "What a sweet girl. Lord how I loved her, but she threw me over. She always told me, 'You smell of milk, just like a little kitty.'"

"You're lying, you bastard."

"To think that at least once in life I was so lucky. You know I never make things up. She used to tell me I reminded her of a fluffy little puppy dog. But don't worry your pretty little head about it. After all, she's a lot older than us mugs."

"She couldn't have said that to you."

"No? Why not?"

"She just couldn't."

"Wait up!"

They stopped in front of another house, and Heniek called out:

"Malinowski! Hurry on out!"

Malinowski came out, a young man full of verve and grace and, it is not necessary to add, like all young men of the day, he wore his hair in a ducktail, and since he had the finest hair around he justly earned the worthy sobriquet "Ducky."

"Tsup?" said Ducky.

"Hey Ducky," said Heniek, "tell him what Basia used to tell you while she was playing on your flute."

"Come on, it's late," Ducky said. "They told me that if I'm late one more time I'm in hot water. A guy only has to go to bed late, and he might as well chuck it in. Basia's a nice girl, Heniek. I won't say an unkind word about her."

Heniek grew impatient.

"No one's asking you to," he said, out of breath, for they were walking quickly, and his short legs had trouble keeping up.

"Did I ask you to say a bad word against her? Anyway, you know why she broke up with me. But she always spoke so beautifully."

Ducky tousled his ample head of hair and said,

"She said 'You're a little honey-bear.'"

"Yeah. And what about the puppy?"

"Yeah, there was also something about a puppy," said Ducky. "She said that I smelled just like a little puppy dog."

He turned to the boy.

"Come on over to Heniek's tonight. I'm borrowing a record player from my brother-in-law."

"I can't," the boy said softly. "I'm busy tonight."

"Look, there's Mr. Ceniek," Ducky said, and he called out,

"Hey, Mr. Ceniek, wait up!"

Mr. Ceniek, who was walking in front of them, came to a halt. He had the bloodshot eyes and the florid complexion of a confirmed alcoholic.

"Tsup," he said, touching his finger to the visor of his cap.

"Tsup."

"Tsup."

"Oh my dear Lord," said Mr. Ceniek hoarsely. "My throat's on fire. There must be some place around here where a guy can get a beer."

"No time, it's late," said the boy. "At this rate we'll come flying in on our asses. The crowd this time of day is horrific."

Mr. Ceniek looked at him through his bloodshot eyes sympathetically, and said,

"What's your problem, kid? Unlucky at love?"

"Bug off," the boy said.

"He's been acting awfully strange lately," said Mr. Ceniek with a pained expression, reflecting his having had too much to drink the night before. Then he added,

"It'll pass. You've just got to get yourself a little ass."

"Ain't that a fact," put in Ducky, while spitting on the sidewalk.

"He's already got himself some," offered Heniek. "You probably already know her, Mr. Ceniek."

"Which one is that? Christ I need a drink."

"She lives on the corner."

"Baśka?"

"That's the one."

"Ah, yes," said Mr. Ceniek. "I wish for you half as much health as I once lost on that dear girl. She's the prettiest in all of Marymont. Wait, wait … What was it she always said to me? Jesus, I'm about to die of thirst."

"Have some milk, Mr. Ceniek. Milk is the best thing for a hangover," said Ducky.

"To hell with milk," croaked Mr. Ceniek, making an expression as if he had just drunk straight vinegar. "That's what it was … something about milk. Every girl has some line she likes to pull on the guys. When I was your age, I went through one girl after another. Back then every one of them had this spiel that you were only the second one. Yeah, right. And the first one was a partisan who, as you might imagine, died fighting in the forest. After the forest wore thin, they said that the partisam was either rotting in jail or had been ripped to shreds by the secret police. Shit. 'When I was younger,' they'd say, 'I met a soldier who was about to look death in the face, and I just wanted to give him a little comfort, because I had this feeling he was going to die.' Shit. I can't keep track of the all the lines I've heard like that. Back then every girl had this 'Lieutenant Bogdan' in the Home Army.That Baśka of yours didn't have one. She's too young. But just the same, the stories she told were so sweet that I cried along with her while I humped her. I'm a drinker, you see, and I have a tender heart. Shit."

"I could care less about what you did or said to Basia," said the boy despairingly. "Nobody does. But tell me, Mr. Ceniek, did she ever tell you she'd never had it as good with anyone else? "

"You bet she did," said Mr. Ceniek.

"Yes, she did," said Ducky.

"Those were her very words," said Heniek.

"Did she say she never dreamed she could be so happy with any man?"

"Yes."

"Yes."

"Yes."

"Did she say goodbye to you in the morning as you were going off to work?"

"No," said Ducky. We never said goodby."

"No," said Heniek, and his homely face turned sad.

"No," said Mr. Ceniek."

"Hey," said Heniek, "Wait up and I'll holler up to my brother-in-law. It's getting really late, goddammit."

They stopped in front of an ugly old dilapidated house, so run-down that it's enough just to look at it and think about what's inside, and you'll see such a heap of misfortunes that you hope the door will never open. On the narrow crooked streets of the district known as Marymont there are many, many such houses.

"I've got to get going," said the boy. "I have some business to take care of, so I'm not going to wait for your brother-in-law, but I'll see you tonight. So long."

"I thought you weren't coming," said Heniek. "You had something to do tonight."

"No, I'll be there. I'll take care of it right now. The worst they can do to me at work is fire me."

"Something important?"

"None of your business. Look after that phonograph, Ducky. Seeya, guys," he said, and headed in the direction they had just come from.

"Seeya," said Heniek.

"Seeya," said Mr. Ceniek, once again contorting his face into a frightening grimace. Then he shook his head and said,

"What the hell's gotten into that kid, anyhow? He was always such a cool head. You've got to help him somehow. He's got to find himself a girl, someone he can take to bed and who'll say something nice to him, something solemn and sacred. I swear to God that's just what he needs. Goddammit, you guys have got to help him. After all, that's what mates are for, right?"

—1956. Translated by Oscar Swan

*Commentary.* Hłasko's world as reflected in these two stories can be summarized in a few words. Appearances are deceiving; beauty is only skin-deep; true romance exists only in novels and movies. No one can be trusted; relationships are purely transactional and mean-spirited into the bargain. Women use their good looks instrumentally, while men, deeply dissatisfied with their own joyless lives and dead-end jobs, feel duty-bound to make sure that their "chums" do not get any pleasure out of life either. People self-delusionally see in the world not what is, but what they want to see. In short, his world is bleak, hopeless, and cruel, with no silver linings lurking behind the clouds. Hłasko's early death, if not an accident but by suicide, suggests that this vision was not merely a pose.

To be sure, both stories here suggest that, at least at the beginning, within most people there is an innate sense of and longing for true love and genuine relationships, but in Hłasko such feelings quicky get trampled underfoot and evaporate under the exigencies of daily life and the actions of one's so-called "friends."

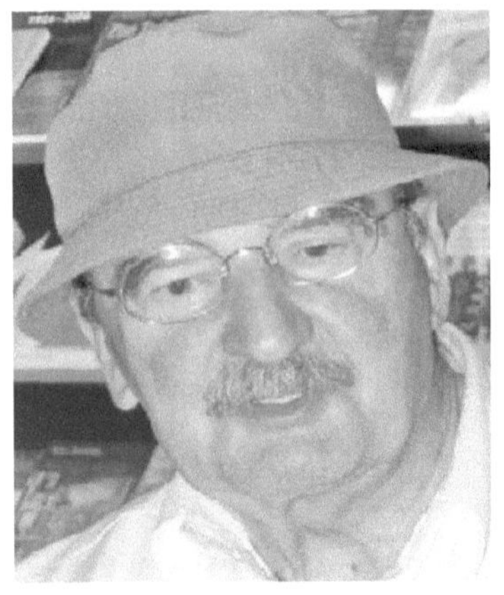

# Sławomir Mrożek

Despite an unsavory background as a hack political writer for the popular press in Stalinist times, Sławomir Mrożek (1930–2013) was later lionized in the West for his absurdist fiction, especially his short stories and plays, which were seen as cleverly poking fun at the excesses and absurdities of the highly bureaucratized and invigilating socialist society in which Poles lived in the 1950s and 1960s. His easily staged shorter plays were especially popular and widely performed by students and other amateur theater groups, both in Poland and abroad.

Mrożek defected in 1963 and lived variously in Italy, France, and Mexico, and from the safety of his position in exile, and his acquired French citizenship, he became openly critical of the Polish regime. In 1996, long after the fall of communism, he returned to Poland and settled in Kraków. A stroke in 2002 left him unable to speak for several years. He left Poland again in 2008 for Nice, France, where he died five years later.

## The Elephant

The director of the Zoological Gardens has shown himself to be an upstart. He regarded his animals simply as stepping stones on the road of his own career. He was indifferent to the educational importance of his establishment. In his zoo the giraffe had a short neck, the badger had no burrow and the whistlers, having lost all interest, whistled rarely and with some reluctance. These shortcomings should not have been allowed, especially as the zoo was often visited by parties of schoolchildren.

The zoo was in a provincial town, and it was short of some of the most important animals, among them the elephant. Three thousand rabbits were a poor substitute for the noble giant. However, as our country developed, the gaps were being filled in a well-planned manner. On the occasion of the anniversary of the liberation, on the 22nd of July, the zoo was notified that it had at long last been allocated an elephant. All the staff, who were devoted to their work, rejoiced at this news. All the greater was their surprise when they learned that the director had sent a letter to Warsaw, renouncing the allocation and putting forward a plan for obtaining an elephant by more economical means.

"I, and all the staff," he had written, "are fully aware how heavy a burden falls upon the shoulders of Polish miners and foundry men because of the elephant. Desirous of reducing our costs, I suggest that the elephant mentioned in your communication should be replaced by one of our own procurement. We can make an elephant out of rubber, of the correct size, fill it with air and place it behind railings. It will be carefully painted the correct color and even on close inspection will be indistinguishable from the real animal. It is well known that the elephant is a sluggish animal and it does not run and jump about. In the notice on the railings we can state that this particular elephant is exceptionally sluggish. The money saved in this way can be turned to the purchase of a jet plane or the conservation of some church monument.

"Kindly note that both the idea and its execution are my modest contribution to the common task and struggle.

"I am, etc."

This communication must have reached a soulless official, who regarded his duties in a purely bureaucratic manner and did not examine the heart of the matter but, following only the directive about reduction of expenditure, accepted the director's plan. On hearing the Ministry's approval, the director issued instructions for the making of the rubber elephant.

The carcass was to have been filled with air by two keepers blowing into it from opposite ends. To keep the operation secret the work was to be completed during the night because the people of the town, having heard that an elephant was joining the zoo, were anxious to see it. The director insisted on haste also because he expected a bonus, should his idea turn out to be a success.

The two keepers locked themselves in a shed normally housing a workshop, and began to blow. After two hours of hard blowing they discovered that the rubber skin had risen only a few inches above the floor and its bulge in no way resembled an elephant. The night progressed. Outside, human voices were stilled and only the cry of the jackass interrupted the silence. Exhausted, the keepers stopped blowing and made sure that the air already inside the elephant should not escape. They were not young and were unaccustomed to this kind of work.

"If we go on at this rate," said one of them, "we won't finish before morning. And what am I to tell the Missus? She'll never believe me if I say that I spent the night blowing up an elephant."

"Quite right," agreed the second keeper. "Blowing up an elephant is not an everyday job. And it's all because our director is a leftist."

They resumed their blowing, but after another half-an-hour they felt too tired to continue. The bulge on the floor was larger but still nothing like the shape of an elephant.

"It's getting harder all the time," said the first keeper.

"It's an uphill job, all right," agreed the second. "Let's have a little rest."

While they were resting, one of them noticed a gas pipe ending in a valve. Could they not fill the elephant with gas? He suggested it to his mate.

They decided to try. They connected the elephant to the gas pipe, turned the valve, and to their joy in a few minutes there was a full-sized beast standing in the shed. It looked real: the enormous body, legs like columns, huge ears and the inevitable trunk. Driven by ambition the director had made sure of having in his Zoo a very large elephant indeed.

"First class," declared the keeper who had the idea of using gas. "Now we can go home."

In the morning the elephant was moved to a special run in a central position, next to the monkey cage. Placed in front of a large natural rock it looked fierce and magnificent. A big notice proclaimed: "Particularly sluggish. Hardly moves."

Among the first visitors that morning was a party of children from the local school. The teacher in charge of them was planning to give them an object-lesson about the elephant. He halted the group in front of the animal and began:

"The elephant is a herbivorous mammal. By means of its trunk it pulls out young trees and eats their leaves."

The children were looking at the elephant with enraptured admiration. They were waiting for it to pull out a young tree, but the beast stood still behind its railings.

" ... The elephant is a direct descendant of the now extinct mammoth. It's not surprising, therefore, that it's the largest living land animal."

The more conscientious pupils were taking notes.

" ... Only the whale is heavier than the elephant, but then the whale lives in the sea. We can safely say that on land the elephant reigns supreme."

A slight breeze moved the branches of the trees in the Zoo.

" ... The weight of a fully grown elephant is between nine and thirteen thousand pounds."

At that moment the elephant shuddered and rose in the air. For a few seconds it swayed just above the ground but a gust of wind blew it upwards until its mighty silhouette was against the sky. For a short while people on the ground could still see the four circles of its feet, its bulging belly and the trunk, but soon, propelled by the wind, the elephant sailed above the fence and disappeared above the tree-tops. Astonished monkeys in the cage continued staring into the sky.

They found the elephant in the neighboring botanical gardens. It had landed on a cactus and punctured its rubber hide.

The schoolchildren who had witnessed the scene in the Zoo soon started neglecting their studies and turned into hooligans. It is reported that they drink vodka and break windows. And they no longer believe in elephants.

—1957. Translated by Konrad Syrop

*Commentary.* Western critics like to interpret Mrożek's "The Elephant" as a critique of authoritarianism or totalitarianism, but that is not exactly its focus. Perhaps centrally planned economies are most easily sustained under totalitarian regimes, but it is inevitably the bureaucrats in centrally planned economies, who lack the incentive not to be lazy, incompetent, self-serving, and sycophantic, and who therefore are all of these things, who inevitably gum things up. The economic "incentives" in force have been thought up by people in offices far removed from actual operations, who themselves worry more about career advancement and covering their backsides than about the job they are supposed to be doing, or the branch of the economy they are supposedly supervising.

The ponderous, soulless, and mindless government bureaucracy that made every aspect of public life in Poland under communism difficult for everyone, and much more difficult than it needed to be, was always a safe and allowable target for political satire, as long as the implicit criticism did not extend to the political system itself, and that is exactly what Mrożek's most widely anthologized story, "The Elephant," comes perilously close to doing.

The inflated rubber elephant can be interpreted as a stand-in for any number of sham and artificially hyped institutions in communist Poland, but especially the large, sluggish, and unwieldy centrally planned national economy, whose loudly touted marvels even a schoolchild could see through as being phony. "Just how gullible and stupid do you think people are," Mrożek seems to be asking of the government in this and many other of his cleverly written pieces of satirical writing.

Mrożek likens the entire Polish centrally planned economy to a badly mismanaged provincial zoo, where most of the animals are misfits, and where major gaps in the animal inventory are compensated for by producing an oversupply of what one does not need, even if it is simpler or less expensive to produce, as the zoo director tries to do by compensating for the lack of an elephant by producing three thousand rabbits. The shortcomings of the animals remind one of actual people: the giraffes who are too cowed to stick their necks out; the burrowless badgers; the "whistlers" (marmots) who have stopped whistling either out of apathy or from being intimidated; and the jackasses, who hoot at the whole enterprise.

*Satire, Parody, Absurdism. Satire* is a literary device used to ridicule a particular pattern of behavior as a means of exposing or correcting it. Satire utilizes amusement, exaggeration, contempt, scorn, or indignation with the aim of creating awareness of a problem and, hopefully, a change for the better. *Parody* typically addresses a particular style or genre, ridiculing it by imitating it in an exaggerative fashion. It too is a form of humor and, unlike satire, does not necessarily try to correct anything, just poke fun at it.

The *absurdism* that underpins Mrożek's form of political satire in "The Elephant" is of a different sort from that observed earlier in Witold Gombrowicz's "A Premeditated Murder." The latter is rooted in a sense of the absurdity of existence. Mrożek's absurdity is less philosophical in nature and is enlisted in furtherance of his satirical intent, which is directed at the absurdities not of existence but of everyday life under communism in Poland. These absurdities are symbolically distilled and channeled for satirical purposes into the whole preposterous idea of planting an inflated elephant posing as a real one in the local zoo, setting in motion a subsequent chain of equally absurd situations and events, ending with the visiting schoolchildren becoming hooligans, the exact opposite of the purpose of the zoo's educational program. Parody is most evident in the author's deft imitation of the zoo director's bureaucratic style of writing and of the Warsaw bureaucrat's way of responding to it.

In the case of Poland, Mrożek's implied prediction that the entire sham enterprise is sooner or later going to implode of its own accord, like a burst balloon, was borne out some thirty years later.

# Kazimierz Brandys

Kazimierz Brandys (1916–2000) was a prominent postwar novelist, story writer, feuilletonist, and screenplay writer. He was born in Łódź and educated in law at Warsaw University. Of Jewish extraction, he survived World War II by living on false or so-called Aryan papers. A socialist before the war, after it he followed the same ideological trajectory of many of his generation, beginning as a literary spokesperson for the postwar communist regime and ending as a prominent dissident and advocate of the Solidarity trade union movement. Residing in France in 1981 when martial law was declared in Poland by Premier Wojciech Jaruzelski, and Solidarity was banned, he never returned to Poland.

Brandys's early novels, including *Między wojnami* (Between the Wars), a four-volume epic describing life from the 1930s through the 1950s viewed from a communist perspective, followed the strictures of socialist realism, requiring that historical events be portrayed from an overall Marxist viewpoint. However, his 1957 novel *Matka Królów* (Mother of Kings), later turned into a well-regarded 1982 film that was initially banned in Poland, was a sign of a period of political relaxation known as the *Odwilż* (Thaw). The novel depicts the unjustified persecution of a working-class family of loyal communist activists by the postwar communist regime.

The story selected here, "How to Be Loved," a masterpiece of indirect narration in a virtual stream-of-consciousness mode, was turned into a successful film scripted by Brandys himself, which should be seen in conjunction with this story. It was destined to become a signature work of the so-called Polish Film School which, like this story, dealt with the lasting scars the German occupation during World War II left on the Polish national psyche.

## How to Be Loved

*While certain scenes and situations here are based on actual occurrences, the characters in this story are not to be identified with any actual persons, living or dead.*

The girl in the cap helped me unbuckle my seatbelt. We're already aloft, and it seems it's all right to smoke. I'm too tired for conversation. She smiled at me as she walked away, and I answered with a smile. Best not to speak, or people will recognize my voice.

The start was nothing special: the roar of the engines, a couple of bumps, and I stopped looking down. The wing hid the ground, which was fine with me. I have no yen to sightsee at the moment: a landscape dotted with tiny boxes, cars looking as small as beetles … That's all well and good, but I can do without it. I don't feel at ease in this machine. Actually, the whole thing is crazy. I didn't have to take this trip at all, or I could have gone by train. No one is talking; just the rustle of newspapers and the wing shimmering in the sun. No one bothered to see me off.

Did I forget my cigarettes? No, here they are. I hope my "daughter" will be there to meet me in Paris. The man sitting next to me extends a broad masculine hand and offers me a light and a smile. I nod in return. Technical support is fine, but no familiarity. I didn't wrench myself from the earth in order to have adventures in the sky. A little distance, a bit of comfort, a glass of madeira on the sidewalk at Café de la Paix, some museums, solitary walks along the Seine, that's all I'm after. I wonder how much a glass of madeira costs? Marie Antoinette's cell, of course, and van Dyck.

What if she's late arriving at the airport?

As soon as I land I'll buy a map of Paris. Two weeks is a bit short, but still. Too bad it's so late in the year.

I deserve it: it's my first break in seventy weeks. For seventy weeks I've played Felicia on the radio, cooking seventy suppers, sending my voice over the airwaves seventy times. Next week a million people will hear about my trip, and how Felicia was transported up into the air on a silvery four-motor airplane, about the flowers, the farewell at the airport, poor Thomas left all alone. I can just imagine how he'll tell it.

Last week they thought up an old friend especially to take my place. The eternal loser. He'll pay us an unexpected visit the day after my departure. He and Thomas will sit and play chess. Not a bad idea: grumbling over a game of chess, interspersed with sentimental reminiscences about me. And I'll be far away. Not bad at all. And then a picture post-card of the Eiffel Tower. "A beautiful city," I'll write, "but home is always best." Tum-di-di-tum.

As an afterthought, of course, I'll remind him not to smoke too much. I have to maintain my standing among wives. A million people will wait for my return, for my low, resonant, slightly hoarse voice. It makes me want to laugh.

There goes that whump in my heart again.

When I was standing in line for the passport application I heard people whispering in the line behind me. Someone asked me, "How is Thomas doing? Did the chestnuts help?" The previous Thursday he had complained of sciatica, so I made him put chestnuts in his pockets. I dismissed his protestations about folk superstitions with a wifely kiss. Hmm. Lots of letters came out of that. Chestnuts really do help, they said.

The man sitting next to me is talking to the girl in the cap, the "stewardess," as she is called. He speaks Polish, but with a foreign accent. Graying at the temples, a tan face, around fifty, I would say. It's getting hot from the sun glancing off the wings. And only fifteen minutes into the flight. I think my compact has broken. No, it's fine. How do I look? An oval face. Those application forms don't make any sense. Once I was a wide-eyed redhead with a pearly-smooth complexion, wearing an expression of constant surprise. Now I darken my lashes and brows and color my hair blond. Red hair and a pearly complexion made for a good Ophelia before the war. I didn't know what to write: red or blond? I ended up by putting "reddish-blond."

No distinguishing features. My father was a captain. What nonsense. At home they were afraid I would become a dwarf. Maybe they had good reason: grandfather drank, it seems. In the end I grew up somehow, but scrawny, nothing but knees and elbows. Let's just say: medium height. The plane gives a leap and a lurch.

Yes, I could have been an interesting Ophelia or St. Joan, someone haunted and rickety. In the theater they said I had an inner light. Maybe I did, but I had bad luck too. One can't count on anything, but at the same time one can also expect anything. Date and place of birth, two things one never loses. But do they have anything to do with who a person really is?

I sat up half the night poring over that application form, whose captions still torment me. Marital status. I wrote: widow. Then I crossed it out. Better put "single."

Before the plane took off two Brazilians sitting on the other side of the aisle to my right crossed themselves with an identical movement. They quickly and sadly touched their forehead, breast, and lips with their closed fingertips. Somehow that cheered me up.

Lots of foreign newspapers, and in the center of the plane conversations in French. You can tell the Poles at once: their skin is tired, there's somehing worn about about their very appearance. The stewardess is a head taller than I am, quiet but alert, with a smile pasted on her face. Her thighs are spread too wide apart, even if that appeals to some people. The ones born during the war and right afterwards are of better quality. If she had been through what I had, her skin would be a bit less like porcelain. Of course, I could easily not have survived at all, but luck was on my side.

What time is it? In another fifteen minutes my voice will be heard on the earth down below, from a tape made a week earlier. Felicia received her passport. The pre-trip flutter. *It's been so long since I've taken a trip on my own. You must want to get rid of me.* Thomas reassures his wife. It's truly touching.

Seventy times. September marks a year and a half since they offered me the job. A strange feeling, as though I'd just made it through the Sahara. Forty years following the army barefoot through the hot sands, and after forty years I answer: fine, help yourself. Life has been good to me, but not the reverse. At such moments it's better to sit calmly, with a serious expression on one's face. A bomb? Cyklon B? Paralysis? Everything's possible, and I'm ready. It's not my first assignment, and I'm ready to accept whatever happens.

Only last year I sat in a chair, wearing last-year's black overcoat and light-blue gloves, carrying my handbag with the broken clasp, looking across the desk at a good-looking red-headed guy in glasses, offering me congratulations. He says: "Your *timbre*, that's it, your *timbre*." I had to lean closer to hear him. That *timbre* is what vodka can do. I was always worried I was losing my voice. "Your recording is just what we're looking for," he said. "At last we have a real human voice."

My recording? At first I didn't even understand what he was talking about. He asked whether I wanted to hear it, then pushed a button and said, "Here's your audition tape." A light flashed up above, followed by some rustling and mewling, and suddenly someone said, *In my old age I wanted to rest, but now I see I have to begin life all over again. My dear.* ... Then he offered me a cigarette. I took it and continued listening. He smiled while my hands trembled. I can't say I liked it. I was bothered by that voice. I never talk like that in real life. I would never say things like that. Who would I say them to? And what does it mean anyway, "to begin life all over again"? I never would talk like that. But I kept listening, flicking my ashes, fascinated by my hoarse *timbre*. On the tape somebody interrupts, and I hear myself complaining. Apparently I don't understand something ... And then dinner. I serve. The sound of soup being poured. My "husband" eats ... "What do you think?" the man asks. "Not bad," I answer.

Oh yes, my audition tape ... I'd like to listen to it again. I don't remember everything I've said in my life. Maybe it's not important, but I'd be interested in the tone. The tone changes according to one's attitude. Once upon a time I believed I'd get a response, but no one ever responded. I had to respond on my own. I began talking, but not with my own words. Sometimes one has to say the words one wants to hear with one's own lips. *Don't worry*, I told him with the voice of a ventriloquist, *I won't leave you*. He shuddered. I could sense he didn't need these words. It was I who needed them. In the driving rain under the hood of the horse-drawn cab I offered him my newly-acquired *timbre*. Just like that, in the space of a second, I adapted myself to the situation. Later one is never the same as one was just a second before. He asked whether I believed he could be saved. *I won't let anyone touch so much as a hair on your head*. A second earlier I wouldn't have expressed myself that way. The result was thirteen years of insanity.

I amaze myself. To convey a man with warrants out for his arrest, to drag him through the narrow old streets of town full of Germans, passing his wanted poster on every corner, announcing a reward for his arrest, and to say at the same time with one-hundred-percent certainty, *It's just a bit farther, a place where you will be safe* ... It would make for a good beginning for a filmscript. In real life one takes such moments a bit harder: the rain, soaked stockings, the slow clip-clop of the hooves, a burgeoning hatred for the horse. My skin still carries the gray protective coloration from those years, something I can't wash away.

My neighbor with the lighter is very well groomed; he's wearing some scent quite out of the ordinary. I like fifty-year-old men graying at the temples, with innocent-looking steel-blue eyes. Calisthenics, electro-massage, orange juice, oat meal.

I'd bet my life that during the war he was a pilot. In other words, not like my father, who was put to death behind barbed wire by greenish creatures with shiny iron foreheads and squinty eyes. People who spent the war in the air or on the sea have seen less of life and are better preserved.

Is he married? He's not wearing a ring, but my nose smells a woman in his life. In the morning *Good morning, dear*. In the evening *Good night, dear*. The thought drives me crazy.

I'm getting jealous of that girl in the cap. He has smiled at her again. In back I hear a conversation in Polish about the country's standard of living, that the peasants now drive motorcycles. I don't know whether that's good or bad.

Peasants on motorcycles, me on a plane to Paris. My country? Yes. Maybe. I don't know. I don't think about it. For someone like me to talk about love of country? It's enough to say that in all these years I never once left it. Everything we experience and at first call 'life' later on turns out to be one's country. I didn't choose it.

No. No one did. Not even him. I had no idea what was happening. All I saw was him hitting Peters in the face. At that moment I was taking coffee to one of the tables nearby. Next day they sent for me and said, *You have to take him to a safe house. He has a price on his head.* Followed by the horse-drawn cab and darkness.

Thirteen years later I heard the shriek in the courtyard. I ran out of the bathroom, slipping on the floor. The window! The window and, beyond it, darkness.

Enough, I mustn't think about it, it doesn't do any good. A little water or juice. I need to take a sedative.

I spill the tablets, and my neighbor leans over to pick them up.

"Merci."

Of course, now he thinks I'm French. Why did I say *merci* instead of *dziekuję*? The immediate result:

"Vous vous sentez mal, madame?"

Fortunately, I understood.

"Non. Merci. Pas de tout."

What a vocabulary! Fa-dee-la! He must not have noticed my handbag bought off the shelf at the Central Department Store. He obviously wasn't in Poland very long.

The whole time I feel my heart contracting. I wasn't made for being carried up in the air. Down below are pastures and puddles. From the height of two thousand meters the earth looks less serious than from ground level.

A road through some trees, tiny houses, a village …

In such villages, it seems, the peasants murder their wives with axes and then hang themselves from nearby trees. At this height one wouldn't notice.

I've suspected for a long time that no one sees us down there, but I had no idea how right I was. Maybe religious people shouldn't see the earth from a bird's eye view. There's something sinful about it. My heart reacts badly to it. I've always felt worst in situations where I felt I wouldn't be noticed. I just can't take it. Excuse me very much, but I also have business here, take care of me too. I don't want to be a speck of dust. A person has a certain God-given size and the right to be noticed.

That night, when I drove with him through the downpour and darkness, I understood what that meant. I was overcome with terror, not because of what might happen to us, but because I realized that whatever happened to us would be meaningless. A very unpleasant sensation. I prefer to face charges. After the war, when I was put on trial, I knew I was innocent, but at least my case was heard. The collegial court falsely convicted me, but I at least felt I was personally taken into consideration, even if unfairly. At least I was taken to be a person whose past was a matter of interest. That's not the worst thing that can happen, even if the verdict is unjust. Not to be noticed by anybody, that's the worst.

I am certain that this gentleman here never had to go through anything like that. He strikes me as someone who could risk his life, as long as he were in a chain of command. People like that always inform their superiors before taking a leap into the unknown.

The stewardess is serving breakfast, so maybe I won't have to jump. What if I did? I'd jump and land on a peasant murdering his wife with an axe. Theoretically it's entirely possible. He would take me for an angel come down to warn him, and he would fall to his knees with a shout. But such things don't happen. Technology marches forward, but in the area of Providence we're still behind the times. The peasant would go ahead and kill his wife, and I would land a kilometer away, breaking my neck. What kind of progress is that? A complete absence of logical connections. Logic? Maybe the gentleman next to me believes in it, but I don't.

The earth, plants, animals, something indistinct and restless that moves of its own accord, eats, runs, grows … I'm afraid of birds in a room. Nature gets into your hair. It's deaf, blind, and always cowering. It's only man that one can talk to, beseech, speak to of evil.

I think a glass of cognac would suit me just fine.

From the pocket of his sportscoat he has taken out a small ivory-colored plastic radio. I haven't seen one like that before. He fiddles with it next to the window.

A double snore: the two Brazilians.

What does he need that for? Isn't it enough that we're flying in the air? Does he need music too? What hands he has, what fine manicured nails. His little radio won't cooperate. No music.

The scrawny girl approaches carrying a tray. Brandy and sandwiches at last. I feel all warm inside. Now for a little smoke. Fiddle-dee-dee! I feel fine now. My heart's in the right place, and the four motors are humming for me to fly. Single? Widow? Wife? All that devout nonsense that airs every Thursday. God, how wonderful it is that nothing matters to me now. No looking back.

I couldn't foresee everything that would happen, but I did fulfil all of my obligations. I rescued him. And then they put me on trial. That's proof of nothing. They put me on trial for what I underwent. For what I actually did, I deserve a monument. The man sitting next to me wouldn't understand very much of this.

It was a matter of survival, my dear. Try to imagine a scrawny red-haired actress playing Ophelia in some provincial town who, during the tryouts, was judged to be *fascinating*. The first major role in her life, and the premier a couple of days hence, set for a momentous date: September 3, 1939. Unfortunately the dress rehearsal was interrupted by an air raid. Polonius took off, only to return with the Germans. A month later I was serving drinks in the Artist's Café. An interesting place, in which Polonius didn't get run through with a sword but merely got slapped in the face. Next day his body was found with his head blown apart, the body of a traitor.

It wasn't important for me whether he did it or not. I never cared about Peters one way or the other, and it was the other one I had undertaken to drive across town. Maybe he killed him, maybe he didn't. Anything is possible. I didn't ask him about it. Questions like that are for the big screen. Anyway I didn't have any reason or time to think about it. For me it was enough that it was *him*. During the tryouts he never paid me any attention. I sensed my big chance: now he'll never be able to tell me to get me to a nunnery. I'll wait for him in the cab, I'll color his hair: he'll have dark hair now. The nuns gave me a safe address. The wanted posters on every street promised a huge reward. The cab took off, and I touched his hand. He was pale, and his eyes were pressed shut. From inside the cab I tried to make out the route: the Theater, the Embankment, the Execution Tower. I didn't know what a price I would have to pay. I only knew that nuns were a bad-luck sign.

The stewardess takes my tray. Suddenly the radio begins to play, a hissing interrupted by static, followed by some far-away music.

My neighbor smiles with satisfaction. I do too. In the end, what harm does it do? Why think about all those things? I survived them, that's the important thing. The past leads to neurosis. They should invent a pill against memories one doesn't want to revisit. Sweet reminiscence: who dreamed up such balderdash?

What was I talking about? Underwear? Seemingly about some kind of undergarment which I had to wash before my departure …

A strange sensation. The man has just caught my voice recorded a week earlier. My whisper, conjured up out of the ether. Of course, a holiday repeat of last-week's program. Felicia is afraid of flying. Thomas is getting angry.

*It's been so long …* then static, it's hard to hear … *since you've seen your daughter.*

I think at that point I forgot my line. How awful.

*And now you're hiding behind my underwear?*

A line guaranteed to get a million laughs down on earth. Again I can't hear, more noise and static. Then suddenly my whisper:

*But how will you ever get along without me?*

Now it's better, I recognize the modulations.

*And who is going to stand in line at the butcher shop? And what about your medicines?* More rumbles and static.

The airwaves break apart in a final burst of static, and me with them. Too bad, because I love to listen to my own voice.

I have tears in my eyes. I'm very moved. I didn't know I could attain such heights. To think that my voice flows through the air together with me. I don't talk like that, it's true, but down on earth they love me for those words. I utter them in the name of a million listeners. They'd never accept my real script, and I'm not surprised. I don't like it myself. My real script isn't for broadcast. Nothing but my memories separates me from a tree or a dog, but it takes much more out of me. I prefer my Thursday-night script.

Again something about underwear. It's not in the best taste, but what can one do? We always get mountains of letters after lines like that. I can already see the package of underwear: *Dear Felicia, The League of Women of Piotrków presents you with these underpants for your husband. Have a good trip, but be sure to return. Best wishes to your daughter!"*

Underwear, ham, medicine, confessions, sins, despair, requests for support, hand-embroidered tablecloths, the maledictions of betrayed wives—I have all of that at my disposal. My voice attracts life.

Women write to me: "Dear Mother," they begin. I have the letter of a would-be suicide who decided to go on living because I exist. I feel a bit silly, but who could have foreseen? No one had any idea until they decided to move the show to an earlier time and we got five thousand letters protesting the shift. From all over the country. Yes, it turned out that the entire country listens to us. It's unbelievable. Thursday-night's "Dinner with the Konopeks," a small-town broadcast aimed at older married couples, broke all records of popularity. It caused quite a stir.

Some blockhead even wrote, what was it called, a sociological essay? Yes, a sociological essay entitled "From King Staś to Mrs. Konopek." In it he argued that my dinners too will go down in history. A complete dunce. Nevertheless it pleased me.

Now there's no stopping it, those dinners will go on forever. Every Thursday I will serve soup to a million people. They even listen to me in the hospitals. I have letters from patients, nurses, and doctors. Supposedly my voice cured someone.

Everything's possible. I'm not surprised, just mainly surprised at how little people require. When I say to Thomas, *Here, my dear, take this little piece of meat next to the bone, I saved it for you,* I can feel their gratitude, and I know that more letters will arrive. I was made for bigger things in life, but what they care about is that piece of meat and my self-sacrifice, that ham-bone and spoonful of soup that I'll take out of my own mouth to make sure he has enough to eat, that I've never betrayed him, that if I ever took a liking to anyone else, I kept it to myself. His difficult job, his underwear, his troubles, our mutual respect and our grown children. Soup, meat, bone, and a bit of the simple life. A little complaining, a little storytelling, the warmth of the domestic hearth. How I love to listen to it all.

I'm not making fun of anyone. Maybe they're right. I'm just amused that it's me doing it. During the audition Thomas was a little uncomfortable. "I thought you were innocent, but given the atmosphere of the times I felt powerless to act." Oh, I did too. The problem was that I was the one on trial. If a person is a pussyfoot, he has no business sitting on a collegial tribunal. Here, take this morsel. The price of meat has gone up again. I don't hold grudges.

"I beg your pardon?"

Ah, he's noticed the copy of *Cross-Section* sticking out of my coat pocket. Fine, let him know who he's dealing with. I smile, he smiles.

"Please, help yourself."

I loan him my magazine, but he'd better give it back, because without it my "daughter" won't recognize me.

"May I offer you one of mine?"

"Certainly."

We smoke his cigarettes. Contact has been made. What next? He stops to think before each sentence, as if sending a telegram.

"We'll be in Berlin in another hour. Right on schedule."

"Really? I hadn't realized."

"Oh yes, we have exceptionally good weather."

He has very white teeth, which he flashes at me every time he turns to speak. Everything about him shines. His hair is smooth as a helmet. Real Poles don't have hair like that.

"It seems you don't live in Poland."

"No, in the U.S. I was visiting Poland for the first time in thirty years."

"Goodness, that's a terribly long time."

"I should say. The changes are quite dramatic. It's not the same country."

"You're certainly right about that."

I feel his friendly gaze rest on me—azure gleaming out of a can of condensed milk—and I smile secretively. I know how to be subtle.

"I was in Warsaw for a conference on bacteriology. That's my specialty."

"Oh, I see."

"Yes, and I'm especially interested in immunization research."

"And now you're returning to the United States?"

"Not exactly. For the moment only to Brussels. I'm giving a couple of talks there. Then I'm flying back to New York."

How interesting. Too bad I have nothing to say on the subject of immunization. Of course, to fly from a conference in Warsaw to a talk in Brussels must be pleasant no matter what the topic. I can imagine him speaking to a hundred blokes just like him with a voice full of confidence.

"I learned that Poland has a number of prominent experts in the field of immunology. I had no idea."

"Really? How interesting."

"Yes. I found the discussion after my talk at the Academy of Sciences to be on a very high level. An excellent knowledge of the latest developments in serology."

"You know, such things never come to one's attention."

I rather like him. I've never slept with a man who gave me a complete sense of security—for a while it was exclusively policemen—maybe that's why I recognize so easily his strange brand of masculinity. Maybe he's divorced.

"I have the sense that Poles don't sufficiently appreciate their new opportunities. Don't you feel that way too?"

"I suppose you're right, but … "

"I think the Polish psyche must still be living down the effects of the Partitions."

"That's just what I wanted to say."

The wing looms motionless and as gray as asphalt. In another moment he's going to ask me about the war years …

"Yes, I spent the war in Poland."

Silence. He takes a long look at me.

"I was in the Royal Air Force. It's hard for me to imagine what terrible things you people endured. It must have been hell."

"Oh, you know, we've put that all behind us."

"I'm sure you look on it with different eyes. I have great respect for women who survived by staying put."

Staying put? That's a fine way of putting it.

"Actually everything was a lot simpler then than now," I say.

Azure and steel looking out of a tin of milk. He falls into silent thought, leaving me with that nonsense still hanging on my lips. Simpler, was it? That's the sort of claptrap pseudo-intellectuals tell foreigners over coffee in the Bristol Hotel. Simpler my foot. Maybe he expects me to say something in response? I survived, yes, and I remember how. A sweaty tight-rope walker, that's me.

At night I'd pound the pavement, and in the day I'd run to fortune-tellers to find out his future: would he go crazy or merely die? And how long would I be able to hold out? After the arrests I lost contact with people. The ones who entrusted him to me ceased to exist, having been transformed during their execution on the Defense Embankment into a bloody pulp, thoroughly mixed into the ground. Should I tell him? I didn't know. As it was he felt hopelessly lost. He would probably have turned himself in to the Gestapo. I didn't tell him or anyone else. I wanted him all to myself. To tell the truth, I'm not certain he would have turned himself in.

Damn it, where or to whom was I supposed to turn? I was the only person I could trust for certain. Anyone I told would have shared the news with someone else out of sheer fright, and—no, no, I was simply dizzy, running around in circles, caught in a trap. What a sucker I was. I wanted a prince, so now I had one.

He considered me the cause of his misfortunes. Today I can understand it, but then? Was it my fault, I shouted at him, that he slugged Peters in the face? Was it my fault that Peters was a *Volksdeutsch*, that he was found shot the next day? Maybe it was my fault I agreed to help him in the first place? My shouting was completely unnecessary. One never understands another's outbursts. He merely nursed his wounded pride, counting himself among the world's insulted and injured. Whom was he supposed to blame? His fate? I was his fate. For five years it was me and me alone. He couldn't go out of the building. Rain washed away the wanted posters, but his face was instantly recognizable. He was Oswald, Gustaw, Fortunato, Alcestes. I brought his meals to him, to that cubby hole with a kitchen nook which I found by a miracle after the address with the nuns gave out. A sloping ceiling and fold-out bed. It's true: I bought him a fold-out bed. It stood slightly away from the wall by maybe fifteen or twenty centimeters.

"Tell me about your squadron."

There's a saying that a man chooses a woman so his defeats will have eyes and ears. But he didn't choose me. I fell on him like a cat off a roof. All the more reason why he had to take it out on me. It was simple. I was his sole audience for five years. I was stupid enough not to figure it out ... Something about Canada, he's telling me something about Canada, he got his flight training there, he enlisted. ... I didn't understand that for five years I personified his misfortune. For those five years, every day of which he cursed, he saw only me. It was inevitable.

"I don't know Canada. Is it rocky?"

I close my eyes and listen to him talk about Canada. What sort of animals do they have there? Not kangaroos, I suppose. Ottawa in the winter. The maple leaf. Nocturnal training flights. He was a navigator.

Fasten your seat belts, we're descending.

Berlin.

Nothing. No sense of satisfaction. I thought I'd feel something, but it turns out I feel absolutely nothing. Glass, the waiting room, armchairs, Lufthansa posters, the loudspeaker issuing announcements in German. Not so much as a shudder. An unfamiliar smell: rubber? oilcloth? paint? As we sat in the armchairs, people walked by speaking German. No reaction. A door reading "Herren," another reading "Damen." I go inside and lock the door. Fresh white paint, the soothing noise of water flushing, little balls of disinfectant. What's their river called? The Spree. Here I am on the River Spree in a bathroom with all the conveniences, in a German passenger terminal, on the way to Paris without a trace of pleasure. I didn't come to Germany for revenge, but I didn't expect not to feel anything. I don't get it. I tried to force myself to remember, to think of all they put me through. Now's the time to get emotional, to take one's reward, to jump up and down. I remember my father dying in the prison camp, my mother's sickness, her dying half-crazy right afterwards, my Jewish girlfriend who was shoved naked into the gas chamber and incinerated. I feel nothing.

I finally take out my compact and begin to smile at myself. My teeth and gums smile, as do my cheeks and my forehead, but my eyes look back at me searchingly, dead. I always took care of my teeth and complexion, and on the whole I still look pretty good. I came through in one piece. Yes, without any doubt I made it through those times. I wouldn't say by staying put, but I made it through nevertheless. My eyes are my weak point. I don't have the expression of someone who's come out on top. I always paid a lot of attention to personal hygiene. Even when things were at their worst I always took baths and brushed my teeth with a stiff firm brush. I had checkups at the dentist's every three months, plucked my eyebrows, didn't drink vodka when I had my period, and I think all that made a difference, even more than one might think. But just a quarter of an hour ago, behind that door with the sign "Damen," I felt disgracefully defeated. If I can't give a wild victory cry, it means I must have lost. I don't know, maybe it's not only me, maybe everyone feels that way, even that man sitting next to me, but what do I care about them? I'm furious, for I've just felt for the first time a disgusting absence of pleasure in my own existence. I've felt that shabby emptiness I carry around with me, that utter indifference. I guess it's clear enough I've lost. But if I have lost, then who won?

* * *

There goes that kangaroo again. Whenever the plane jiggles, a little kangaroo hops around inside me. It's probably from the alcohol. Nothing turned up on the electro-cardiogram.

When was it I began to drink anyway? Oh, of course, in the Artist's Café. Later I had to drink with him. Now from time to time I drink by myself. That even makes more sense. It gives one a firmer sense of one's own humanity. After a fifth of good liquor I feel like a streamlined sculpture with interpenetrating shapes with which I miraculously merge. At such moments I become monumental. Then I fall asleep. I never drank in order to go to bed with a man, even if I have slept with a dozen or more.

With too many, maybe. I don't know. I never made scenes when they left, but just waited for the next one to come along. Should I have refused? Refused what? My body? What for? They said they needed me, and that was probably true. If ever anyone ever needs anyone, it's surely when a man needs a woman in bed. I'll have to think about whether there are any other instances.

One never knows for just how long a man is going to need a woman, and that's their risk as well as ours. He himself doesn't know. You can't hold it against him if after five or twenty-five nights he comes to the conclusion that he's gotten out of you all there is to get. It's unpleasant for him too. But it's important how they go about telling you. Sometimes they're unable to hide their dissatisfaction, and that's unpleasant. You have to know how to act in a situation when no one's to blame. At the moment desire passes, one should know how to manage a smile of gratitude—or at least dream up some sort of emotional conflict. In the worst case, one can recall the good times. I value that a lot. Nature is cruel. Only idiots don't understand that. But a human being, in addition to his needs, has certain talents, and that obligates him to a certain kind of behavior. Everyone possesses an inner artist. No one, in any situation, has the right to behave "naturally," to suddenly freeze or start giving off steam. It seems to me that sayings like "his love grew cold" or "he grew resentful" are inappropriate. A person ought to behave better than nature, from which, as far as that goes, we demand so little.

The man next to me is dozing. Maybe he's dreaming about the Battle of Britain. He took part in it and even received a medal. Things always work out for people like him, even the results of their own behavior. He wanted to fight the Germans, so now he has a cross for bravery. He decided to rid the world of bacteria, so he discovered a cure. An admirable person, who always knows how to comport himself. Causes, effects … decisions, outcomes … A guy with class, who never found himself caught between a fold-out bed and the wall, in the gap beneath the overhanging mattress, in a crack where a person could fit only if pressed flat as a pancake. I wonder how this guy here would have managed?

During the night-time roundups, when men were taken away to the shout of *Wo ist Ihr Mann?* The whole time I thought only about whether his leg was sticking out from behind the suitcase. *Mein Mann ist weg.* But his leg! There were two of them at the door, the other one a Latvian. They looked at me with their little eyes as they sauntered about the room. *Spirit?* In the window, between the inner and outer panes, stood two liters of ratafia. They polished off a liter, and the Latvian left the room. The one who stayed behind said what he wanted. Then he left and the Latvian returned. I moaned. They were in a hurry, and I moaned from the pain. After the police wagons had gone I was afraid to move. Finally, in an onrush of courage I snarled out in a whisper through clenched teeth: "It's over." I felt both marvelous and monstrous at the same time.

I pulled out the fold-out couch. I had to revive him, for he had actually fainted. I was at least grateful to him for that. We spent the rest of the night finishing the other bottle of ratafia. We swore, uttered gibberish, angry, happy, relieved, afraid to look each other in the face. And then we slept the whole next day, from dawn to dusk. There was really nothing to get up for.

How would Mr. Navigator have behaved, I wonder? Whoops, there goes the kangaroo again. We're being tossed about. Some kind of air pockets, I guess. The wing has grown dark and lost its lustre. The ground is invisible. We must be in a fog. No one is talking.

I'd prefer for him to wake up and tell me a story. I like his metallic voice, the voice of calm masculinity. Yes, I survived that time by "staying put." The fact that later on I accepted a job in the Stadttheater only brings me honor, at least in my own eyes. I made up my mind to do it on my own. To be sure it was only toward the end of the war, after the Artist's Café had been closed, after I'd spent three months running around looking for a job and a work permit. I needed to have my papers in order, a certificate with an official stamp which I could post on my door. After that night I swore to myself I had to be safe. I'm not certain whether truly great people exist anywhere, but there are moments when an individual rises to greatness. One such moment was on that night, when I saved him, and later, when I took on that role, when I told him I was working for the Red Cross but instead sang couplets from "Melodies of the Street," my teeth chattering from fear on my way home at night, walking past the Defense Ramparts, certain I would be mugged and have my head shaved. I rose to the occasion, without regard for my own safety, so that after the war, when I gave testimony in front of that green table, and they asked me whether I had considered the consequences of my actions, I replied, "Consequences? Why of course I did. If I could only be given the same consideration!"

That was my undoing. Three years without the right to work in my profession. So, after those first five years, I had to endure three more. Some women were murdered for such war-time crimes. That's extremely unpleasant. I can't stand situations where a man kills a woman not out of love or hate but merely out of conviction.

In the end, I made out all right in front of that court. It was all worth the one sentence, or rather just the single expression, which he uttered. He said that during those years we were living together as a *married couple*. He said that in a deposition at my trial. I was grateful to him for bothering to come at all. He didn't look in my direction, but he said what he did. A married couple! I felt myself go all warm. I wanted so much for him to use that very expression. I think I must have had tears in my eyes.

I sat there smiling at the wall over his shoulder and listing to his deposition. At that moment I no longer wanted him dead or disgraced. I was sure he'd eventually come back to me. The first few years after the war he needed to be with other women; that's the way it had to be. But now I knew he would come back. We were a *married couple*. That makes me a widow now. *Une veuve. Eine Witwe.*

He recognized that I had earned the right to him. I gave him a hundred times more than any woman can give a man, more than pleasure or fidelity—things of which almost any woman is capable. I offered him my own head, which I placed alongside the photograph on the wanted poster, with the reward doubled after a month. As I continued to wait tables in the Artist's Café, I heard rumors of his death. He had supposedly thrown himself out the window when some Germans accidentally drove up to the building in which he was hiding. How I soaked it all in. Later that day I told him: "Guess what the news is. You're dead. You threw yourself out of a window. Do you hear? Onto the pavement. Some people even heard from the most reliable sources that you've been buried beneath the Execution Tower. You hear? They've buried you." After that we drank to his death, and fell asleep just before daybreak.

I know too much. If today I were to become the wife of the gentleman sitting next to me, I couldn't help despising him for knowing so much less than I do. I would despise and envy him for everything he thinks he knows, considers obvious, rational, tried and true, for his saying on some occasions "That's very humane" and, on others, "That's beneath any acceptable level of behavior." Above all I would despise and envy him for his firm belief that he would know how to behave in any situation.

What nonsense. To be sure I like his mouth, his profile as he sits there with eyes closed, his hair thick like a pastor who has never tasted depravity. But my "husband" was that other one, who experienced everything there was to experience.

I held his head in my arms. If only I hadn't been in the bathroom! The woman screamed from the balcony. He must have wanted me to be with him at that moment. He knew what he was asking of me, and that I would not refuse.

The skinny girl approaches with a pasted-on smile, like a braided mare sauntering among the loge seats into the arena. Something seems to be the matter.

We're flying through the darkness of night, the airplane bouncing around like a darting fish. Are we chasing something? Trying to escape? We run into air pockets which toss us up and down, as though we were riding a herd of frenzied humpbacked camels.

Would I like a paper bag? No thanks. But maybe this man here would, if you'd wake him up.

My heart takes a leap like a mighty giant kangaroo. Kangaroos, camels, a darting fish. Nature is taking its revenge.

Fasten our seat belts? Good idea. Congratulations.

After all I've been through do I need this in addition? My legs have grown numb. I'm afraid, but what of? A crash? I told Thomas that home is best. It's all the fault of that over-wrought mad-woman in Paris. I still have her letter here in my handbag …

*Dear Madame Felicia …* Bump!

*I listen to your broadcast every week.* Whump! *When I was a girl I had the same last name as yours, and, I swear to God that I feel like your very own daughter. Please come to Paris on a visit.* We careen down and then carrom upwards again … *My children speak Polish, and Jean would be so happy. I'll send you the ticket. Please come!*

Jean is some kind of French engineer she met in prison camp in Germany. Wanda, née Konopek. And she writes something about the Uprising. A year of life for a glass of brandy.

We all look at the captain's cabin door as if at a movie screen. Outside the window it's a yellow-gray mass of cotton. Nothing is visible.

In back a man in a tropical suit addresses the stewardess in a loud voice, saying something she doesn't understand. Both of them turn red. Someone intervenes. I can't make out what the issue is.

Yes indeed, what is the issue? What am I doing here? Lately my life had become transparently simple. I had begun to forget about the past. Only here, in this infernal machine, everything has imploded. Maybe the end is near? Next minute? Next second?

I think I'll go crazy. Ah, my neighbor just woke up.

"I wonder if you could please ask the stewardess for a glass of brandy?"

I thank him with my eyes. I imbibe the liquor with tiny sips.

It's almost completely dark now. The yellowish cotton batting around us has grown even thicker. We hear a call to check our seat belts. Silence. The machine lurches on through the air. I take two tablets at once: Pavlon and Bellergal.

"I've been through lots of storms like this over La Manche. They're generally pretty unpleasant. I remember one night-time flight, it was in nineteen forty …

I should have known from the very beginning. The whole time some window or other was winking at me. The whole time I saw brazen signs …—We fall, my heart leaps, this flight will be the death of me. Whew, it's past.— … Those signs kept trying to tell me something that had some kind of connection with me, what was going to happen, or how it could happen …—I feel myself alternately sweating and shivering—… I am convinced that existence is a sin, I felt for a long time that something was rubbing up against me, portending the horrendous outcome …—Fine, I'll take the paper bag—… the cynical, beastly outcome. To tell the truth, I was certain of it …—Are we falling? No, we level out again.—…that something stupid and horrible was going to happen. And the first indication …—It's the end, I'm dying.—… were those incomprehensible words in the script …—Ah, that's better—… in Ophelia's lines.—The wing! The wing has fallen off! I can't take it any longer … Yes, twenty years ago in Act IV I turned to the king and said, "Well, God 'ild you! They say the owl was a baker's daughter. Lord, we know what we are, but know not what we may be. God be at your table!"

It's not so rough now. I didn't understand those words, especially the part about the owl. They were dark and mysterious. I felt afraid of them.

It's nice he's letting you hold his hand. A real gentleman.

"My dear," the director told me, "by the time of the thirtieth performance they'll become clear of their own accord."

Only after the thirtieth? I never got as far as the first. I think those are the only words I remember out of the whole play, and I still don't understand them.

If only I hadn't been in the bathroom then, if I had come out sooner ... —Good Lord.—... I ran out too late to save him. Darkness, lights burning in the other windows, the hysterical scream from the balcony. I held his head in my arms, begging him not to die. What did he feel then, I wonder. What did he feel? I wiped the sweat from his brow with my handkerchief. He mumbled something I didn't understand. Red bubbles were coming out of his mouth ... —No, that's it, it's the end.

No one is talking except for the Poles in back of me, who say that it's normal, even if unpleasant, for it throws you all around. After all, the weather forecast did predict storms along the way. This is normal? Here I am strapped to the back of a winged metal fish cast about by whirlwinds two kilometers above the Earth in an evil cloudy gray murk. If this is normal then I've had enough of it.

"Do you feel better now?"

"Incomparably. I'm sorry that ... "

"Don't mention it."

He takes a close look at me, no doubt surprised that I reached over to hold his hand. Well, what so what? So what if I did? Something like that can happen once in a lifetime.

"Maybe you'd like another brandy?"

"Yes, thanks very much."

He's rested, polite, energetic. Oh dear! The stewardess is casting a cold glance at me from beneath her cap. Too bad, my dear, not everyone is in your shape. If your mother listens to the radio, then in another four weeks she'll hear my broadcast. I'll tell about the storm. I'll redeem this additional brandy with my slightly hoarse voice, the voice of an older woman like your mother's. One day, my little muffin, when you happen to spend the night at home, she'll ask you whether by any chance Felicia flew with you to Paris. And she'll describe to you the storm with all the details, using my words ...

Oh no, it's beginning all over again. I grow tense, I'm falling, I've died. His hand, where's his hand?

"You should try to breathe deeply, that usually helps."

I breathe in deeply, then out. In, out, a dozen times or more. He looks at me with interest. Maybe I was thinking out loud? I can just imagine what that would sound like. A frenzied carp speaking with my voice, saying its prayers back into the past. I'm sure they would listen. Fortunately, it's still possible to think without having someone eavesdrop on you.

"Do you have family in Paris?"

"My daughter. She's married to a Frenchman, an engineer. She'll be waiting for me at the airport."

I must be going crazy. What did I say all that for?

Another tablet of Ondasil. Now we're flying more peacefully.

"You must not have seen her for a long time."

"It'll be fifteen years."

"I expect that you are probably ... "

"Oh yes, I'm very excited. You know, it's difficult for me to get accustomed to the idea."

"Excuse me for the indiscretion, but do you intend to remain with your daughter in Paris?"

"Oh, no. My husband stayed behind in Warsaw. I'm a bit worried whether he'll make out all right without me. And then there's our son. He's finishing flight school. They only let me go for two weeks."

There you have it.

I often improvise my own lines, causing the author to get upset with me, but what the heck. People like it. For example, recently Thomas was asking me to get rid of the cleaning woman. It turned out she had had a child out of wedlock. What was the way he put it? *I'm no puritan, you know, but, ahem, a girl who doesn't respect, hmm, …* According to the script I was supposed to reply, *All right, if you say so, I'll have a talk with her tomorrow,* and then chip in something about today's morals. But as soon as he hit me with those words I began to laugh: *My darling, you know nothing about it. For all you know she loved him. Not all men are as honorable as you are. As long as she's decided to bring up the child, then we owe it to her to help!* And I banged one plate against another as a sign I was clearing the table. He was dumbstruck. After a moment he muttered weakly. *Fine, do as you think best.* It all came out quite naturally, and a day later the woman at the post office smiled at me. "You had it right where that girl was concerned!" she said. How many letters did that generate? Five or six hundred, more or less. Mostly from abandoned mothers from tiny villages.

It makes me want to laugh. I know how to hit a nerve. I am sister to the lovelorn and wife of the widowed. I comfort the downcast and forlorn.

The workers at the State Lightbulb Factory sent me a commemorative album, celebrating a pre-school nursery named in my honor. Model gliders and boats have been named after me. People have carved statues of me out of coal and salt. Lines in stores and offices part at the sound of my voice. Bureaucrats wax all sentimental as soon as they hear me speak.

If I ever write my memoirs it will carry the title "From Ophelia to Felicia, or How to Be Loved."

The wing begins to shine once again. Those indistinct beige patches visible through patches of white must be the earth. After my third cognac I feel just fine.

"And you? You surely have a charming wife and children?"

I smile, but stop as soon as my eyes meet his.

"I lost my son last year. He committed suicide."

I freeze in place. I feel terrible. What did I have to say that for?

"It had something to do with a woman, although there were other reasons too, which I don't fully understand."

We fly for a while in silence, the wing glistening in the sunlight outside the window. Down below I can see the straight lines of intersecting roads. His hand feels warm … and the sad crazy thought occurs to me that I could actually be his wife.

In another fifteen minutes we land in Brussels.

Dum-dee-dee-dum. Ti, ti-ri-fi-fi … It's funny how that song has stuck in my head. I heard it on the radio as I was leaving Warsaw: ti, ti-ri-fi-fi! And here it is again in the Brussels airport: ti, ti-ri-fi-fi!, the sharp, vibrating tone piercing me to the core. Background music is sometimes necessary. People would behave differently if there were only more of it. Reality is not sufficiently melodious by itself. Maybe that's why people behave badly, torment one another, and prostitute themselves. They say there is harmony in nature, but so far I haven't noticed it. Harmony? Hardly. Nature is something shameless and baseless. That storm was horrendous. Storms are beautiful only in symphonies or novels. Only artists are tormented by a sense of shame in the face of nature. They want to correct its insane lack of clarity, which can drive a person to despair. What deep thoughts I have. Dum-dee-dee-dum. Ti, ti-ri-fi-fi … !

That same record was playing when I said goodbye to him in the cocktail bar at the Brussels airport. We each had another three brandies, sitting on tall stools next to the gleaming snakelike bar. The waitress put on the record and I immediately got all teary-eyed. He with his Burberry coat thrown over his shoulder, wearing a dark hat colored to match his hair, I with my romantic past written all over my face, Madame X, sentimental, wise, stripped of all illusions. In the middle of the ri-fi-fi I put the tiny glass of golden-brown liquid to my lips and smiled meaningfully when he told me he wouldn't forget me, that he had grown to like my voice. Of course he liked my voice. The multi-colored bottles behind the bar all blended into one as I listened and watched that glistening altar with the waitress skilfully wielding her cocktail shaker, and I thought, "I could go for you." He told me that the whole flight he had been tormented by thoughts about his son, and that he was grateful to me for making him talk about it. I was tortured by thoughts about the past too, I answered, and I thanked him for taking care of me during the storm. As soon as the song came to an end the waitress put it on again. I touched his hand and said, "I wish you every success at your conventions. Many happy innoculations, or whatever! He laughed and said, "I don't know. Many people are younger and cleverer than I am. I don't necessarily have an inside track."

"I'm sure you do," I said, "and that you'll succeed." And I cast upon him my look of a good witch, a glance guaranteeing success. Pa-ti, ti-ri, ti-ri, fi-fi, ti-ri-fi-fi-fi! May God be with all of you during your evening meal.

So now I'm flying by myself again, my blood mixed with six glasses of brandy. The flight is calm and majestic, and I am stretched out in my chair. I lift my eyebrows, surprised that I feel so terribly fine.

*My dear,* I said in the program before last, *life can't be so bad as long as we are able to lead virtuous lives. That's the most important thing. I believe that deep down man is good, but he has to watch out. You watch out for me, and I watch out for you. A person should live so that his neighbors respect him. How do you think those beets go with this roast?*

I hear again the rustling of newspapers and the hum of conversation. The Brazilians, who during the storm had turned ashen gray, have regained their normal milk-chocolate hue. With their thin delicate fingers they leaf through illustrated magazines containing pictures of white houses looking like mushrooms against a background of red rocks.

I don't know any of these people—their thoughts, what it looks like where they come from … The Poles sitting behind me are saying that the French bathe only once a week. We exchange indifferent, glassy stares. None of us holds any interest for anyone else. Supposedly people in the West stare less obtrusively. They're more discreet. But I am going to stare. I can permit myself, because I'm an actress.

Actors are the very opposite of discretion. Their faces are masks imitating, in an exaggerated way, genuine human expressions. I can recognize them in the wink of an eye by their indecent expressivity, the bastards. They take their imitations so seriously, and I adore them for it. They play scientists, duchesses, diplomats, floozies, monks, but always a bit too scientifically, too diplomatically, too floozily. I love them for their lack of responsibility before the world they are trying to ape, putting on airs in front of it and then rather despising it. And I love them for never doing anything serious, anything of any practical benefit. No dictatorships, wars, new inventions, new taxes … yes, that's what I like most about them.

Exactly when did I stop loving him? I forget. Maybe never. Either I never stopped loving him, or I never began in the first place. What is it other women call love? One never knows. One knows only one's own feelings, and wraps them in various names: good, bad, hate, love. Maybe it was all nothing more than my imaginings, my nerves, my terror? If he had stayed with me after the war I think that might have been the end of it. But he didn't hesitate, not even for a single day. I'll never forgive him for being capable of such cruelty. After all those years, to leave without so much as a word. How could he have done it? He left town and returned in a couple of months with some woman. And he drank. And then another woman. And he kept drinking, until he started to bloat up from all that vodka. During those years I followed all of his parts, all of them bad, all over-blown and empty. It seemed he no longer wanted to act. For my part I wished him nothing but humiliation, defeat, and misfortune. I got dizzy from the depth of my hatred of him and his women. I sent them letters full of curses. I lived in a state of constant insane rage. I would get drunk and spit at myself in the mirror, cursing myself for my feline fury, for my love. Love! I guess I know what that is. I've been to the best school. A single demented thought revolving around a single demented topic, hallucination upon hallucination. I created my own world. I no longer required his presence. I didn't see him for months on end. He performed less and less often. They said he couldn't remember his lines and that most roles scared him. Every night they had to carry him out of some bar. "It was me who killed Peters!" he would shout. Supposedly after a few glasses he would mutter that to whoever his drinking partner was. He carried around with him the wanted poster with his photograph on it. I have no idea where he dug it up after the war. He would show it around, unfold it on the bar, brag that the Gestapo had put a price on his head, and describe how he had killed Peters. Some bars even stopped letting him in the door. As for me, I waited, sustained by curiosity over what would become of him.

Maybe it was my fault. Maybe he was paying for that night spent in the crack between the couch and the wall. I always had the stronger head for liquor. In those days, when I had to sit and drink with him, he was already blanking out and falling across the bed when I was still half conscious, delivering long monologues about the future. jabbering in a soft voice to buck him up, telling him that he'd make it, that we'd start a theater together, that we'd be famous. *Do you think*, I whispered, *that we won't reward ourselves after the war for all this misery and humiliation? We'll wring our happiness out of their throats, do you hear? There has to be punishment and reward. Otherwise the world would make no sense.* I got carried away with my own rhetoric, summoning up diabolic forces from within myself. There, in that three-story tenement house, in our gloomy cubby-hole with its smoky walls, where no one dared know of his existence, I talked, drank, talked some more, and made promises, spitting out my words with triumph and passion. Yes, I was all-powerful, and I had a head as strong as an iron two-liter jug. Six glasses of brandy is nothing to me. Get me drunk? Just you try.

Now, for example, I can see plainly in front of my eyes how that man with the smooth silvery-gray hair is taking a cold shower in a Brussels hotel. I can see him washing off my glance, my indiscreet expression, from his firm tan body with its fragrant, taught skin.

*Two cognacs too many,* he is thinking, as he dries off his chest with a stiff terry-cloth towel as he uncomfortably recalls the confidences made to that woman with the slightly suspect appearance, who resides in that unreliable former country of his. *I'll bet nothing she said about herself was true.*

Oh, my dear sir. Each of us knows what we are like, but we ought to keep it to ourselves. No need to go too deeply into talking about one's life. Best to pretend it's all straightforward, to go through the outward motions everyone expects, never forgetting that everything is really a sham. I'm telling you this because I'm an expert, and I can affirm that there are only three principles one needs to follow in order to attain satisfaction in life. First, hide your feelings. People who do this can get others to do their bidding. Secondly, create situations in which others look their best, better than they themselves thought they were. Thirdly, never strive toward complete satisfaction in any area, above all in love. The best state of all is insatiation.

That's practically all I have to say. The rest is unpredictable.

I wish I could take a nap. My eyelids feel heavy, and my lips are stuck together. What country is it I'm flying over? Yellow plains, a river with gray banks. The Skalda? Who knows? I wish I could sleep.

There have been too many violent scenes in my life, still fresh and undescribed. It's dreadful. Real human life ought to imitate what's gone before, not constantly create everything from scratch. There should be models, templates, inherited motives and threads to follow. Existence depends on it, on filling out one's time, on replicating familiar scenes like on a frieze, living as God intended. Amen. Amen. Amen.

I'm nothing to go by, of course. As soon as I recognize myself among the human race I sense its ugliness. The measuring stick I apply to life is always longer than I am. I despise anyone in whom I recognize my own imperfections, even though I forgive them in myself. I forgive it, let it pass, consider it invalidated simply because I know about it.

Whatever weakness I discover in myself I automatically apply to others, and I judge them according to criteria I myself can't measure up to. I despise the Brazilians because they were afraid of the storm; and the Poles sitting in back of me because of their complexes about foreigners; and everybody else in the plane for their dull desire to live at any cost, at the cost of other people's lives. I am just like they are, exactly the same, and that's why they seem worse to me than I am.

These are not Christian feelings, I know, but I couldn't exist without them. That's the basis of love. Only very exceptionally does love depend on anything greater.

Ophelia, Polonius, Hamlet. Me, Peters, him. The Gestapo, Peters, me, him. He slapped the traitor in the face, and the next day they find his bloody body. Thirteen years later they find another bloody body. No one was at fault. But I am left writhing in mortal agony in the dark.

From the sawdust in the sofa I made them dinner. They were both made of celluloid, with flat painted-on eyes. I fed them with a spoon, dressed them, told them fantastic tales. Mr. and Mrs. Celluloid. I sewed them green capes out of an old bedspread. They loved me. No one loved me like that ever again. Mr. and Mrs. Celluloid. If it hadn't been for them I would have died of boredom and fright.

No, I'm not asleep. I can't doze off. It was a mistake to tear myself away from the earth. Let me tear myself away from myself instead. I wonder what that skinny stewardess of ours is thinking now. Maybe about landing in Paris, or about the first time she spread her knees?

In Paris I'll buy myself a black elastic see-through belt of the very best quality. For my own pleasure. I'll put it on and twist and turn in front of the mirror. I have to make up for all those years.

*During those years.* Those were his words when, in the café, he asked me if I would come back to him. Or maybe it was me who spoke them first: *Like during those years?* I said. He merely repeated them: *Like during those years.* Now I'm paying for them. I didn't understand him. Several years out of touch is a pretty long time in such matters. I waited for eight years. If one adds the five years of the war it makes thirteen. Thirteen years of waiting. For what? For those five days? For that one last night? For—

I couldn't fathom how much he'd changed, or figure out how to get through to him. I looked him in the eye and bored straight through. I stupidly asked him why people were saying such wretched things about him. He gave me an opening and I stumbled into it. He was quiet for a while and then began to explain that it hadn't been worth it. *It? What?* I asked. *Those years when you hid me,* he said, making a face. *You know what I mean? I should have turned myself in and gotten shot. Just who do you think you're talking to?* I shot back at him angrily. *Who are you talking to? You have no right! I still wake up screaming at night that they've come to get you!*

What does he want from me, I asked myself, now that I'm getting my life together. Why is he dragging me to this shabby café, teeming with money-changers? I bit my tongue in agitation and said I didn't understand anything. *What does it mean you can't go on living? You have everything just the way you wanted, don't you? I'm not standing in your way, am I?*

He started to twist in his seat and to talk so quietly and indistinctly I couldn't make out what he was saying. Something about some woman he had broken up with. I didn't want to hear it. Then he talked about the war. *You know*, he said, *You and I are the unappreciated soldiers of the war. That's good, isn't it?* He laughed and then suddenly grew silent. He sat there looking at me and I instantly figured out that he wanted to hear my voice from years gone by. I sat motionless, full of surprise and pity, maybe even disappointment. *Stop drinking, do you hear?* I said. *You've got to stop.*

I looked back without emotion at that swollen over-heroic face with its soft crooked lips. After a month one might have thought that I didn't care any more. For certain. Almost for certain. But after a moment I began to speak with my old hissing wartime voice. *We'll do it together, you and I. You'll return to work. You can play all of your old roles. It's not true that the war destroyed you. With my help you'll become your old self.* I said, stressing every word and feeling my eyes grow brighter. *You just have to listen to me. Do you understand?*

He asked whether I didn't think it was too late. It didn't occur to me that I should just keep my mouth shut. *You idiot,* I said. *Too late? Too late for what? Do you think you'll have to sleep with me? I'm no moron.* I cast my magical gaze upon him from those former years. *You're going to stop drinking, do you hear? I'll find you a place in a sanatorium. Are you listening? You'll drop out of sight for three months. Only I will know where you are. My poor dear, I see that someone has to take care of you. You can't manage on your own. Just relax. I'll arrange everything for you. Everything, do you understand? Except vodka.*

Then I realized my mistake. He said he hadn't had a drop in over a year. Then he pulled out his billfold and took out some letters. They spilled out on the table. *Do you see this?* He looked at me malevolently, straight in the eye. *Here, lake a look, read them.* I picked one up and began to read. They concerned me and him, and mentioned at what price the Gestapo had spared his life. *Do you see? They don't believe it. They don't believe I could have been saved in any other way. I don't care what they think about me. I showed them to you so you'd know that even in that respect it wasn't worth it. If I hadn't agreed back then to let you take me across town in that cab, today they would speak of me as a hero.* I hissed back at him though clenched teeth. *Tear them up! Get rid of that garbage.* People in the café began to stare.

As we were leaving, he stopped, smiled, and asked whether I had heard, did I know what they were saying about Peters' death? No, I hadn't heard. *They say that the Germans killed him*, he said, still smiling, *because, you know, it turned out*—he kept smiling as if struck by something—*that he was a French secret agent.* He looked at me meaningfully, and I answered something to the effect that one never really knows who one is dealing with, and that he had no business hitting him in the face. *I was always of the opinion you didn't have to hit him in the face.* Those were the words I used, taking revenge with this unkind dig for those eight years. My old venemous calm returned, and I took up the game where I had left off. Two days later, as I was hanging my things up in his apartment, I had no idea that this was what the final act was going to look like.

The final act. The only thing that ended was what I didn't want to give back, what I had created for myself. It seemed to me improper to take away half of my life and the identity I had honestly earned. But from the moment it fell away, something else began. The background … yes, I had the feeling that I would merely become part of the background, of everything that up until then had been going on behind my back, to which I had never previously paid any attention, about which I had never been concerned. It's interesting. That new and expanded life of mine in the background turned out to be more like happiness than the first one. I felt like a worn-out bow. I no longer had to stretch or bend. Something inside me had come loose, allowing me to relax, to move over to one side and take a step backwards and observe my well-trodden position from a certain distance. That's very important. After his death …

We returned that night drunk, and we drank every night for the next five nights in a row, making a scene in the bar for all to see. Later, it was I who opened the window, saying that it was too stuffy in the room. Don't turn on the light, he said, or it'll attract moths. I ran my bath, and the sound of the running water muffled everything else. I was standing naked next to the tub when the shriek rang out in the courtyard, the bawling of that woman. The window was wide open. I tripped in the darkness, but the windows all around were lighted. Why did he do it? Why did he want me there? Why did he leave the sofa pushed away from the wall?

After his death, after I had begun to take parts in the "Fairyland Theater," it occurred to me that I was making out all right. That other thing was like a bad mistake, a worthless play in which I had played a tragicomic part, but now I could safely recede behind the scenery. Three, four, or five glasses was quite enough for me in those days. Family? Love? A man? All those things can be substituted for, as long as one has the inner fortitude.

Oh, and a phonogenic voice. That's essential.

I went to the audition without trepidation. I wasn't surprised. After all, they had noticed my *timbre.* I was invited to try out for the voice of Felicia Konopek because someone had said that as the witch in "Wonderland" I had an interesting-sounding rasp. It was only when I was sitting in the chair in the manager's office and they offered me the part that I began to have a sense of the parched wilderness through which I had been wandering for so many years. Certainly: I can play Felicia.

I'm not protesting or casting blame. I never had any reason to blame the world. Whatever the earth, air, fire, or people deal out to us is only natural. One can only haggle intelligently about the price, and not allow oneself to succumb to indifference regarding matters as yet unknown.

Now the wing looks like a knife gleaming in the sun, a huge blade cutting my life into two unequal parts. The owl was a baker's daughter? I'd like to meet the director who could explain to me what that means. My thirtieth performance has not yet arrived. Before that happened I was offered the ride in the cab, and the result was me, thirteen years later. My next major engagement was less risky. I had no reason to turn it down, and so now I, Mrs. Felicia Konopek, am flying to Paris to meet my daughter.

But is any of this really important? We know who we are now, but we can't guess who we will be a year from now, and we forget who we were once upon a time. My real fate depends not on what happens to me but on what I will become, and I think that may never be fully illuminated, for there's no way to rewind one's tape and listen to it in order to perform a self-evaluation.

The older man in the tropical suit, the one who during the storm addressed the stewardess in French, has shifted to the empty seat next to me.

*"Vous permettez, madame?"*

*"S'il vous plaît, monsieur. Naturellement."*

A ruddy, apoplectic face with a close-cropped mustache, around sixty. He reminds me of Thomas. He gives me the once-over, and it doesn't bother me a bit.

Below us light ragged clouds are floating like white steam rising above the warm sun-baked earth. We're flying lower now, and changing direction, for the landscape has become skewed in relation to the wing.

I sit up straight and smile. I know that the Poles behind me recognized me some time ago and will try to listen to the conversation with my new neighbor.

*"Oh, oui, Varsovie est une ville très intéressante."*

He's actually quite nice and well mannered. A cigarette? Why certainly, with a cork filter yet.

*"Oui, c'est vrai, la reconstruction de la capitale est miraculeuse."*

We float along, drifting past large bright patches of radiant light. In another moment I'll see Paris beneath me.

Claim check, carry-on, gloves …

Is that everything? Yes, everything.

Fasten my seat belt for landing? O.K. Here we go.

—1970. Translated by Oscar Swan

*Cultural Notes.* Obviously, the story takes place before smoking was banned on airplane flights. The word "stewardess" also dates the story; today the word is "flight attendant." Lufthansa was the German national airline, subsequently privatized.

Ophelia. Felicia's character in Shakespeare's play "Hamlet" was Polonius's daughter and Hamlet's romantic interest. She goes insane and drowns herself, unlike the narrator's current radio persona, who projects homespun matronly optimism on her radio show. In the play, Polonius is run through by Hamlet with a sword as he hides behind a curtain.

The title of Felicia's radio drama references the Thursday Suppers, literary-scientific gatherings organized by King Stanisław August Poniatowski in 1771–83 to promote political and social reforms. The name "Felicia" in the radio show is probably intentionally ironic. It means "happy" or "lucky," whereas Felicia's past life has been anything but, consisting of a string of misfortunes, capped by one lucky break.

By Volksdeutch are meant Poles able to prove German extraction. They were accorded the rights of German citizenship by the occupying authorities, but by the same token were susceptible to the military draft.

So-called "round-ups" of private citizens for slave labor in Germany were an everyday feature of life in Polish cities during World War II. The *Gestapo* were the German security police. The Germans enlisted soldiers from the Baltic states (Latvia, Lithuania, Estonia) among their punitive battalions. Such soldiers had the reputation of being capable of extreme cruelty.

Ratafia is a vodka flavored by soaking it in cherry pits.

The *Stadttheater* (city theater) was the German-sponsored theater during the occupation. Accepting employment in it would have been regarded as collaboration with the enemy and would have made the person participating in it subject to reprisal by the underground resistance. Shaving a woman's head was the least severe of the punishments handed out by the Polish underground to women found guilty of "consorting with the enemy."

Houses looking like mushrooms. The reference is probably to the geodesic-dome houses of Buckminster Fuller. The backdrop in the magazine appears to be the American West.

Felicia makes her play dolls out of celluloid, an early plastic, used for making toys and toiletry items.

*Commentary.* While she is taking an airplane trip for the first time, the long flight to Paris affords the female narrator an opportunity to sift through her wartime experiences of twenty-five years earlier, maybe also for the first time. Her memories come back to her in fragments, and not always in chronological order, in the form of a stream-of-consciousness narrative, with many details left out or only hinted at obliquely, out of whose fragments the reader is expected to piece together the whole story. Time and again her thoughts return to the topic of Love—whether loving or, less often, being loved. To a significant extent, the story is written for a Polish readership, who will be well able to fill in the blanks for themselves. It is more of a challenge for the non-Polish reader.

Given this kind of narrative approach, it is no wonder that the story cannot be broken down into neatly arranged short-story compartments. The story tells of the wartime experiences of the narrator, and details of a person's life experiences do not always arrange themselves into a neat plot or story line. The epigraph at the beginning, disavowing identity of the story's characters as having real-life counterparts, serves to stress that the story could have been that of any number of people. Postwar Poland was full of people like the narrator, still trying to recover from, and make some sense of, the horrific experiences lived through under German occupation in World War II, not to mention under Soviet occupation in the years following.

*The Story behind the Story, Unraveled.* The narrator is "Felicia," the radio name of a popular Thursday-night radio-drama star. She is flying abroad to visit her "daughter" in Paris. The "daughter" was simply an admirer with the same maiden name as the radio character, Konopek, who had married and settled in Paris and wanted to give her "namesake" a vacation in Paris. In her usual way of going with the flow of events, and being amused by their frequent ironic accidentality, Felicia accepts. Along the way she has a sort-of flirtation with a fellow traveler, a Polish expatriate from Canada who had been a navigator in the British Royal Air Force in World War II. She muses that she could never have been happy married to him, as she has experienced and witnessed so much more than he has.

During a layover in West Berlin, Felicia feels deprived of the sense of being able to feel victorious, despite her heroic sacrifices, as part of the winning side in the war. Felicia's own wartime story is pieced together from her disjointed recollections of the circumstances into which she was forced to participate. We never learn Felicia's real name, so we will use "Felicia" here.

Felicia had been an unknown provincial actress until she successfully auditioned for her first big role in the capital, as Ophelia in Shakespeare's play *Hamlet*. She was chosen for her distinctive voice. While rehearsing for opening night on the first of September, the theatrical company is interrupted by an air raid signaling the invasion of Poland by Germany, an act of aggression setting off World War II, and obviously putting an end to the play's performance.

Under German occupation, the first work Felicia could find was as a waitress in the Artist's Café. One day the well-known actor (we never learn his name, but in the film it is Wiktor Rawicz) who was to have played the role of Hamlet, is drinking in the café when Peters, the actor who was to have played Polonius, comes into the café in his new role as a German sympathizer, after having claimed the rights of a "Volksdeutsch" (a person of German ethnicity). "Hamlet" walks up and slaps Peters in the face. The next day Peters is assassinated in the street. Rawicz is implicated, and a large reward is placed on his head. The Polish underground resistance movement gets in touch with Felicia and more or less forces her to take Rawicz to a safe house run by nuns, which she does at night by horse-drawn cab in the midst of a rainstorm. Shortly afterwards, the safe house is no longer safe, for the conspirators have been arrested and executed, leaving Felicia in the precarious position somehow in charge of protecting Rawicz on her own.

Felicia finds a small room on the top floor of an unobtrusive three-story tenement building and conceals Rawicz in it for the remainder of the war. During searches, Rawicz hides between the mattresses of a bed she had bought. Rawicz illogically resents Felicia as the reason for being trapped in the apartment, while Felicia harbors a growing affection for Rawicz, partly because of the sacrifices she is forced to make on his behalf. One night during a German search for men to send to forced labor in Germany, two soldiers find Felicia seemingly alone in her room and rape her, with Rawicz concealed and almost smothered between the mattresses beneath. He passes out and later has to be revived by Felicia. Another rank indignity Felicia has to endure is that, in order to get a work permit to tack on her door to show she is working for the Germans to prevent further intrusions, she has to seek work in the Germans' city theater, exposing her to the danger of being singled out for retribution by the Polish underground. She tells Rawicz that she is working for the Red Cross. The self-centered Rawicz does not appreciate any of this, and he does not reciprocate Felicia's feelings for him in the slightest.

Upon the conclusion of the war Felicia is put on trial by an actor's tribunal for "collaboration with the enemy." Rawicz at least testifies on her behalf, saying that during the war they had lived together as a married couple, but Felicia is found guilty anyway and deprived of the right to practice the actor's trade for three years. After the trial Rawicz leaves her and embarks on a nationwide sex and alcohol binge, but eventually returns to Felicia. She tries to rehabilitate him and get his acting career back on track, but it is too late. He can no longer even remember his lines. Rawicz spends his nights getting drunk in bars and playing the war hero by pulling out a tattered copy of the reward poster on him. In fact, the reader never knows whether he was actually the one who shot Peters, and one begins to doubt it. Rawicz makes of himself such a nuisance in the bars around town that people start to concoct malicious stories about him. They make up the version that Peters was actually killed by the Germans for being a French agent, and that Rawicz protected himself from the Gestapo by pimping Felicia to them. That is too much for Rawicz to stomach, and one night, as Felicia is about to take a bath, he throws himself out of their open window and dies on the pavement below.

Time passes, and Felicia gets back into her profession, first by working in children's theater, for she is still being blacklisted by the theatrical establishment. One day a man who had spotted her in the children's theater invites her to audition for the role of "Felicia," in a new radio show aimed at older people, called *Dinner at the Konopeks*, and she is highly successful, mainly due to her distinctive raspy voice, ironically the result of a lifetime of drinking and smoking too much. Much to her surprise, the show turns into a national hit, partly because of her funny improvisations, and she becomes a belated celebrity and icon of virtuous domesticity—doubly ironic, for now she is playing the role of an anxious but loveable and dutiful housewife, the antithesis of the person she was in real life.

Felicia's story is like that of many people in Poland after the war, who were forced by circumstances outside their control to go to heroic extremes to preserve their lives and those of others, only to go not only unrecognized and unappreciated for their heroism, but on occasion to be vilified, punished and, in some instances even executed, under the grim and intolerant views of the new communist regime, which ex post facto imposed on the postwar population its own interpretation of what had been correct to do and how to behave during the war.

# Jerzy Andrzejewski

Jerzy Andrzejewski (1909–1983) was a well-known novelist before World War II, and he became one of the major literary figures in Poland after it. He wrote one of the best Polish postwar novels—even if it was largely "politically correct" within the new communist system—set in Poland as the war was coming to a close, entitled *Ashes and Diamonds*, and made into an excellent 1958 film by Andrzej Wajda. Andrzejewski was especially skilled at guessing in advance what the next allowable literary trend was going to be. He continually wrote novels and stories that were, at the time, "daring," but at the same time "safe" within the confines of what was then being allowed. In other words, he was good at getting on officially approved bandwagons before anyone else even realized that there was one to get on, creating envy among many of his fellow writers. For this reason, he came under criticism from the Polish literary resistance, for whom he was something of an establishment and collaborative figure. However, his novels were good and stylistically original, and he played an honorable role toward the end of his life in standing up for the right of freedom of artistic expression. The story to follow was one of the harbingers of the Polish *Odwilż* (Thaw), that is, liberalization in publishing following the death in Russia of Joseph Stalin in 1953.

## The Gold Fox

The fox arrived quite unexpectedly one October evening, when Lucas was at home alone. All of a sudden the door squeaked, and he walked in. At first he stopped by the door and glanced around curiously with bright-shining eyes, his pointed little snout slightly raised; then, without the slightest trace of fright, his paws stepping along softly, he moved toward the center of the room.

Despite the darkness, Lucas noticed right away that his guest was extremely beautiful. First of all, he was a very large fox, but at the same time slender and dainty, wonderfully built, with eyes that glittered in the dark, with a big bushy tail and, most amazing of all, he was gold, with a goldness that appeared soft and silky and glowed in the darkness with a mysterious light.

Lucas, although only five years old, was a prudent little boy, and had no intention whatever of showing his great delight right away. But, even though he tried, he couldn't contain himself, and suddenly a short but loud "Ah!" resounded in the quiet of the night.

As he heard his own voice, Lucas stiffened with horror. "This is the end," he thought desperately. And, afraid he would see the fox's retreat, he shut his eyes tight, and whispered to himself, "Oh, my dearest fox, my beautiful fox, please don't run away from me, please! Stay here, and I promise that I will love you very much and will always see to it that you have everything you need, only don't go."

Not the faintest sound broke the silence, and all Lucas could hear was the wild thumping of his own heart. When at last he gathered enough courage to open his eyes, for a moment he couldn't believe his own luck: the fox was still standing in the middle of the room. Only his head was now turned toward Lucas; hence his eyes appeared still larger and more fiery.

Lucas couldn't control himself any longer. He sat up.

"Oh, fox!" he whispered.

Hearing this, the fox greeted him by nodding his head, almost smiling; then he slowly walked in the direction of the wardrobe, his bushy golden tail swaying majestically behind him. Lifting himself on his front paws, he opened the wardrobe door and soundlessly slipped inside. For an instant the golden glow illuminated the wardrobe; then the door closed as softly as it had opened, and again the room was dark.

Lucas wasn't quite sure how long he had lain awake that evening, listening to the excited ticktock of his own heart, but he was not yet asleep when Gregory came into the room, making much noise with his heavy sport boots. As he turned on the top light, he noticed instantly that Lucas wasn't sleeping.

"You're awake?" he asked. "Why? It's after ten."

Lucas quickly shut his eyes. "I'm asleep, he muttered."

Gregory began unlacing his boots. "What d'you mean, you're asleep? D'you think I can't tell you're not asleep? Why must you lie? Mother!" he called. The mother put her head inside the door.

"What's the matter?"

"Lucas is awake," explained Gregory. "He must be running a temperature. Look how red his ears are."

The mother leaned over Lucas's bed and fixed the blanket which had fallen to the floor. "Are you ill, my little boy? Lucas nodded his head. "Go to sleep, son, it's late." She kissed his forehead and then said to Gregory, "Turn off the top light. Lucas will sleep now." Waiting for Gregory, she put on the little night lamp by his bed. "Hurry up, Gregory," she called, already at the door. "Tomorrow morning again you'll complain about having to get up. And don't forget to wash!" "What'm I going to sleep in?" "What do you mean?"

"You took my pajamas to the laundry."

She shook her head impatiently. "Don't you know that there are clean ones in the wardrobe?"

Lucas's heart began to beat faster. How could he have forgotten that Gregory's things too were kept in the wardrobe? And now what? What will happen if

Gregory sees the fox hidden inside? Naturally, he's going to raise the roof, and the fox will get frightened and run away. Perhaps he should warn him?

But in the meantime Gregory went to the bathroom and vanished there. It seemed to Lucas he was gone for ages. "What's he doing in there?" he thought. "Surely he's not washing his ears … "

Finally Gregory returned. He walked up to the wardrobe. For a moment he stood facing it, pondering over something, then he opened the door and started looking through the top shelf in search of his pajamas. Lucas stopped breathing. However, the fox didn't get frightened and didn't jump out of the wardrobe. What's more, Gregory seemed completely unaware of the presence of their guest hidden right beside him. The search for the pajamas lasted a long time. Lucas knew they were on the second shelf from the top, but, just as he wanted to speak up, he was suddenly overcome by a violent shiver and felt a quick flame flash through him. The interior of the wardrobe clearly lit up with the familiar, golden, delicate, strangely mysterious glow. It was so very beautiful that Lucas completely forgot all his anxieties and felt such unspeakable happiness, such overwhelming delight, that it seemed as though he himself had now begun to glow with that strange light.

All at once he felt an urgent need to share at least a part of his happiness with another person. So he lifted his head off the pillow and called in a half whisper, "Gregory!"

The bed squeaked as Gregory jumped onto it. "Aren't you asleep yet?" Gregory's voice sounded not at all friendly. But Lucas didn't care.

"Gregory, tell me … Did you ever see a gold fox?"

Gregory sat up. "Are you crazy? There aren't any gold foxes."

"Yes, thcre are."

"Where? Somebody must have filled you with some fancy tales. Foxes are red, like our ordinary foxes, or silver and blue, but their fur is that way only in the summer, and in the winter they turn white."

Lucas smiled to himself tolerantly in the dark. "And I saw a gold one. Completely gold, with a golden tail."

"You're lying!" Gregory got angry. "You couldn't have seen a gold fox."

"Yes, I could."

"Listen," hissed Gregory through clenched teeth. "If you don t shut up this instant and go to sleep … "

"Well, what?" shouted Lucas.

"I'll spank you, you little devil! Understand?"

There was silence. And then in the silence came Lucas's voice, not very loud but quite deliberately clear.

"You never saw a gold fox? Well, I did."

In an instant Gregory was up on his feet, a pillow flew through the air. There was a moment of turmoil and tumble. And then the door opened, and the light from the hall cut through the darkness of the room. Their father was standing in the doorway.

"What's going on in here?" he asked.

Gregory, his hair tangled, his face very red, blinked in confusion. "Lucas won't let me sleep. He's been telling me some nonsense about seeing a gold fox."

"And so you beat him up?"

"I did not! I just wanted to explain to him that there are no gold foxes."

"Don't shout so loud," said the father. "You'll wake up the whole house."

"But why does he have to lie that he saw a gold fox?"

Lucas's curly head popped out from under the blanket.

"I didnt lie!"

"Quiet," said the father. He sat down at the edge of Lucas's bed and stroked the boy's blond head. "Have you been dreaming?"

"No."

"Well, then, what's this about a fox?"

"I saw him."

There came a stir from Gregory's bed. "You see! He's lying. Tell him that there aren't any gold foxes, because he won t believe me."

The father bent over Lucas. "And where did you see this gold fox?"

"Everywhere," Lucas whispered.

"What do you mean, everywhere?"

Lucas snuggled up to his father and put his arms around his neck.

"Tell me," he pleaded softly, "Are there gold foxes?"

The father smiled. "In fairy tales, my son."

"But not for real?"

"Here are many kinds: red ones, blue, silver, but there are no gold foxes."

"And you never saw a gold one?"

"Never. Well, it's time to go to sleep."

The father tucked him in, kissed his forehead, and left the room, closing the door quietly behind him.

After a while in the silence came Gregory's voice.

"And have you ever seen a green cow?"

Lucas did not answer. He lay back, his eyes wide open. When he became accustomed to the dark, the room again began to fill with familiar outlines of the walls, objects, and furniture. Particularly, the wardrobe seemed to stand out sharply from among the shadows. But how lifeless it was now! There it stood against the wall, massive and straight. It was hard to believe that only a short while before it had been filled with the most beautiful golden glow. And then Lucas began to feel a vague doubt as to whether the fox was still inside the wardrobe. Could he have heard Gregory's mocking remarks and run away unnoticed, his feelings badly hurt?

"Oh fox, my dearest fox," whispered Lucas soundlessly. "You didn't run away, you haven't left me without saying good-bye." But the more he tried to hold onto his hope, the more painful was the anguish that filled him. Unable to endure the uncertainty any longer, he threw off his covers, sat up, listened carefully for a moment, and convinced that Gregory was asleep, started tiptoeing toward the wardrobe. The immense silence of the night folded around him, as if profound sleep had embraced the entire earth and universe, up to the distant skies. Lucas listened to the silence, and an increasing fear filled his heart. What if the gold fox had really gone away? And when he imagined that the wardrobe might now be empty, he felt terribly lonely and sad.

He reached it at last. It now looked like a huge dark mountain towering over him in the darkness. Carefully, he put out his hand, but as it touched the door he hesitated. Suddenly it seemed to him that very close, inside the wardrobe, something stirred with a rustling sound. Afraid that it might be only an illusion, he came closer and, pressing himself against the door, held his breath. Yes, he had not been mistaken. The wardrobe was alive with barely audible delicate sounds, and vibrated with a kind of heart-touching warmth.

With trembling fingers Lucas turned the key and stood in a transport of delight; through a crack in the door, no wider than his index finger, came a stream of the familiar golden glow. At first he did not dare move. But after a moment, gathering courage, he kneeled down and, bringing his lips up to the miraculous glow, whispered, "1 have come, my golden fox. This is Lucas. Are you asleep?" The fox did not answer, but his regular breath could be heard distinctly. "He's sleeping," thought Lucas. So he whispered, his voice overflowing with affection, "Good night, my dearest fox, good night."

Then he shut the door slowly, but as he did it, it occurred to him that perhaps, just in case, he ought to take the key along to bed with him for the rest of the night. How could he be sure if Gregory, having guessed the whole affair, wasn't waiting for the moment when Lucas would fall asleep to chase the fox away? Quietly he drew the key from the lock. Even when he was already back in bed he continued to hold it tightly in his fist.

Next morning he overslept and didn't hear the alarm clock go off. A different noise, equally shrill, woke him up. As soon as he opened his eyes he saw to his horror that Gregory was desperately trying to get into the wardrobe. His face flushed with anger, he banged and kicked with such might that it seemed as though in a minute the wardrobe would break into pieces.

All this ado brought their mother.

"Gregory!" she called. "What's the matter with you? Why are you ruining the wardrobe?"

"Can I help it if the key is gone?" he shouted furiously. "How can I get in when the key is gone?"

"And where has it gone to? It couldn't have walked away."

Before she could finish, the missing key slipped down off Lucas's bed and dropped to the floor with a loud clang. Silence fell in the room. And then, in one leap, Gregory rushed toward Lucas.

"You sec who took it? And you scold me right away … "

"Lucas," spoke the mother, "will you tell us why you were hiding the key?"

"Oh, my dear fox," thought Lucas bitterly, "why won't anyone understand me?" He sat up and answered,

"Because!"

Gregory's eyes became completely round with amazement. Then he turned away from Lucas and said to the mother,

"Did you hear that? One day that child will grow up to be a hooligan, you'll see! Last night he lied that he saw a gold fox, and now he sleeps with the key. Tell him there are no gold foxes, because he didn't believe it even when Dad told him."

Since it was getting late, the mother decided not to go any farther into the mysterious affair of the fox or the key episode.

After the previous night's stormy weather, the morning was overcast, though it was not raining. The dew still glittered along the green slopes below St. Ann's Church, and a fragile mist hovered in the air. Perhaps, because of that mist, the statue of King Sigismund, solitary against the far-stretching sky, the walls of the church, and the old town houses behind it, appeared to be more distant and higher than usual. Even the bridge seemed farther away, with the trolleys trudging over it slowly, they looked like enormous red June bugs. It all made an impression as though the entire scenery had struggled to leap up, but was suddenly stopped in the attempt, suspended in mid-air.

Despite the unpleasantness of the key episode, Lucas was full of exuberant joy. He hadn't any doubt now that Gregory was the only person at home with a skeptical attitude toward the golden fox.

At the corner of Sowia Street, under the mosaic clock, he caught up with his best friend, a classmate from kindergarten. Her name was Emily, and she was the daughter of a metal worker at the Żeran factory.

"D'you know, Lucas," she began straight away, "My daddy is going to Moscow for Revolution Day."

"My daddy has already been to Moscow," said Lucas. "Now he is planning a trip to Paris to be in some conference."

Emily thought for a moment.

"Paris—is it far away?"

"Awfully far away."

"But Paris is littler than Moscow, isn't it? Moscow is the biggest and the prettiest."

Lucas was swinging his shoe bag back and forth.

"No, the biggest and prettiest city is called Colorado."

"And where is it?"

"Oh, it's at the very end of the world. On a huge island. And, do you know, there are mountains there that reach up to the clouds. And lakes. And forests, but terribly tall. And the houses are made only of marble, all white … "

"Not huger than our Palace of Culture?"

"Oh, yes, much huger. They reach to the clouds."

"You said that the mountains reach to the clouds."

"Mountains too. But the houses are even huger. Would you like to live in a house like that? Nothing but clouds all around. And at night the stars are right next to you. Would you like that?"

Emily shook her head. "No, because if the elevator broke down, mummy would get awfully tired walking upstairs with groceries."

"Over there elevators don't break down."

Emily stuck out her lower lip in a characteristic fashion.

"There are no such houses, or such a city. Moscow is the biggest city of all."

Lucas swung his bag with increased energy.

"If you don't believe me, I won't tell you my secret."

Engrossed in their conversation, they didn't notice that they had passed the kindergarten and were already turning into Bednarska Street, toward the river. Emily shrugged her shoulders.

"You can tell me."

"Come over after school, and then I'll show you. Just you alone. Will you come?"

"I don't know. Mummy said that after school she'd take me to buy a new dress."

"So come afterwards. We'll be alone, and I can show you my secret."

"Couldn't you tell me about it?"

"No."

"But you made it all up about the city and the houses? Moscow is the biggest."

Lucas hesitated for a moment. "But my secret is for real."

"And the other was just make-believe?"

"Just make-believe."

"Then I'll tell you a make-believe story too. Do you want me to?"

Lucas beamed. "Let's go over by the river—you can tell it there."

All around, autumn was already very much in evidence. The air felt crisp that October morning and smelled of dying leaves, which blanketed the entire boulevard. The chestnut trees along the riverbank stood in a bluish mist, motionless and straight, looking somewhat like an artificial flower arrangement in red, bright yellow, and fading green. They sat down on a bench.

"Go on," said Lucas.

"Wait, first I must remember."

She was silent for a while, concentrating. Finally, she threw back her blond braid. I've remembered now. So—it was long, long ago, all the way back, before we were born.

"During the war?"

"No, longer ago. Before the war."

"What happened then?"

"Then, there lived a dog."

"What breed?"

"Just a plain dog."

"A mutt?"

"A mutt."

"What was his name?"

Emily thought for a minute. "Brownie."

Lucas seemed a bit disappointed. "Sapphire or Sparky would be prettier."

"I like Brownie better."

"So what happened to him?"

"Brownie lived with some rich people, you know, with capitalists."

"I know."

"They had a factory. And they were terribly mean to him."

"They beat him?"

"They didn't give him anything to eat, and he had to work for them."

Lucas s eyes flashed. "I wouldn't work for them!"

"And what would you do?"

"I'd run away."

"You think you're so smart! Brownie didn't have any place to run away to, because only capitalists lived on that street."

"Then I'd run farther away."

"Farther away there were also capitalists."

"Then I'd tie wings to my arms and fly off."

Emily became annoyed, "I'm speaking for real, and you're just kidding. He couldn't fly off."

"So, what did he do?"

"He tried to run away, but they caught him and they were even meaner to him afterwards. And then … "

"The capitalists were thrown out?"

Emily shook her head. "Not yet. And then Brownie got old."

"And he died?"

"Wait, not yet When he got old and wasn't able to work any longer, the capitalists threw him out on the street. He was unemployed and could find no work."

"Did he have children?"

"He did."

"And they threw him out together with his children?"

"Yup!"

"And what happened to them?"

"Brownie died."

"And the children?"

For a long while Emily said nothing, only kept swinging her leg up and down, lost in thought.

"The children are still alive," she answered at last, staring into the distant sky over Praga.

"Where are they?"

"Different places. One's coming to live with me. Daddy promised to give me a puppy for my birthday."

"Brownie's son? Please call him Sparky, Emily … "

She shook her head. "Wait a minute, I'll call him … His name will be Brownie."

Lucas saw a falling leaf and quickly caught it in mid-air.

"If I asked my father," he said, "he'd give me a dog too. But I have something better."

"What?"

"When you come over, I'll show you."

"Is it alive?"

"Come, and you'll see. Will you come?"

"I don't know," answered Emily. "If I have time … "

When Lucas got home, Elza, their part-time domestic help, a tall, bony woman, opened the door for him.

"Is Mummy home? he asked.

"She is," answered Elza.

Unfortunately, it turned out that his mother was very busy correcting her pupils' homework. "Don't bother me, Lucas," she said.

"Are you working?"

"Can't you see for yourself?"

"But will you read me a story tonight?"

"I don't know, Lucas. If I finish my work, I'll read to you."

Lucas left her with a heavy heart.

Gregory wasn't alone in their room. His friend Christopher, a fair-haired boy, rather tall for his age, was with him. He grinned and put out his hand in a friendly gesture.

"Hi, Lucas. I hear you've been seeing a gold fox."

Lucas blushed, but Christopher did not seem to notice.

"Was he pretty? How many legs did he have? Four, or more? Or maybe just one?"

"Better leave the stinking brat alone," muttered Gregory, shutting his satchel. "Come on, let's get going … I have no patience for this brat and his gold fox." Then he left the room.

"Well, that's that," said Christopher. "So long, Lucas. Give my regards to the gold fox." With one swift movement, he stuck out his foot and tripped Lucas.

"Hey, pal," he laughed, when Lucas sprawled on the floor, "You seem to be a bit weak in the legs. Must be out of form."

Although Lucas hurt his elbow badly, he didn't call out, nor did he start to cry. He stood up. All was quiet in the house. Only now it occurred to him that until dinner he had almost three hours entirely to himself. And all at once a feeling of love and adoration for his fox hidden inside the wardrobe overcame him with such an intensity of mixed joy and pain that it seemed to him as though two huge wings had suddenly grown from his shoulders and were lifting him up into the air, very far and high, but in two opposite directions.

This experience was so strange that he stood dumfounded for a long tune. Everything inside him was in a state of turmoil. He thought, rather vaguely, that he probably should let the fox know that he had come back, but something else told him to postpone the visit until later. In the course of these doubts, he realized he had become very sleepy.

"Oh, my dear fox," he murmured. Groggily he walked over to the wardrobe, opened the door and slipped inside, as though it were a sheltered cave. There was little room between the hanging garments, but the space down below proved big enough to curl up in comfortably. And then he found himself surrounded from all sides by the golden glow, and next to his body he felt the fluffy warm fur of the fox.

"I love you," he whispered, throwing his arms around the fox's neck. Sighing deeply, he fell asleep.

When he woke up, dusk had already fallen, and the room was in darkness. But Lucas knew instantly that he was not alone. And sure enough, he heard Emily's voice, hushed and somewhat hesitant.

"Lucas, where are you?" As he crawled out of the wardrobe, her eyes opened wide with surprise. But she composed herself instantly. "I've come," she said curtly but with much dignity. "Mummy let me, but only for one hour."

Lucas let out a yawn so deep that his eyes filled up with tears. Emily scrutinized him critically and asked, "Is your secret in this room?"

He nodded, feeling quite wide-awake now. She looked around, examining the familiar room.

"You're kidding. I don't see any secret around here."

"Just wait," said Lucas. "You'll see in a minute. First I must make it dark." With the shades drawn, the room became pitch-black.

"Turn on the light," cried Emily.

"Are you scared?" Emily's voice began to tremble a little. "Where are you?"

"Over here," he answered, right next to her in the darkness.

"I can't see a thing … "

"Don't be afraid. Give me your hand. Come on."

She resisted weakly, but he pulled her in the direction of the wardrobe. And there, as he had expected, shone in all its splendor the lovely golden glow.

"Do you see?" he whispered.

"I don't see anything," she whimpered. Turn on the light!"

Now Lucas became really annoyed. "Don't yell, silly! Why can't you see? Go inside and look." He began to stuff her into the wardrobe by force.

"Let me go!" shrieked Emily. "Mummy!"

Lucas seized her around the waist and packed her inside. Then he slammed the door and turned the key.

Now d'you see?" he called. There was no answer. All he could hear inside the wardrobe was Emily's loud, though somewhat muffled, bellowing.

"Let me ooout!" she screamed desperately. "Let me ooout!"

His mother rushed into the room. Quickly she pulled Emily out of the wardrobe. "Home, I want to go home!" Emily kept calling, at the top of her voice.

Lucas knew perfectly well that after what happened, a long talk with his mother was in the making. For an instant he even thought it might be a good idea to pretend he didn't hear her. Apparently, however, his mother also anticipated such a possibility, because she opened the door before she called to him. Lucas quickly whispered to the fox, "Don't worry about a thing," and left the room.

His mother was seated at her desk. As soon as Lucas came in, she asked, "Lucas, can you tell me the meaning of all this? Why did you lock Emily inside the wardrobe? Was it supposed to be a game? How would you feel if someone locked you up like that?"

Lucas shrugged. "I could."

"I could."

"You could what?"

"Stay inside the wardrobe."

"Well, if you like being locked inside a wardrobe, that's your affair. But it seems that Emily didn't ask at all that you lock her in."

"Because she's silly."

His mother looked at him for a moment in silence. "Come over here, Lucas." She drew him closer. "Emily said that you wanted to show her some secret. What is your secret. Can you tell me?"

"I can," he whispered. "I have a … "

"A what?"

"A gold fox."

Afraid that he might discover disbelief in his mother's face, he fixed his gaze on a little hole in his shoe. But he didn't detect the slightest distrust in her voice.

"Where is he?" she asked.

Lucas sighed. "In the wardrobe."

There was a short silence. Finally he gathered enough courage to look up at her. "You don't believe me?"

"Why shouldn't I believe you? Is that what you wanted to show Emily?"

"Yes, I wanted to, but she's silly and she doesn't see anything."

"But think for a moment, Lucas. Was it nice to try and force someone else to see your gold fox? You just frightened the girl, and maybe the fox felt hurt that you wanted to show him in such a naughty way."

"You think so?" worried Lucas. "I'll tell him I am sorry."

"And Emily?"

"I'll tell her, too. I'm sorry," he decided. "But you, don't you want to see the gold fox?"

The mother patted his head tenderly. "You see, Lucas, the fox came to visit you … "

"And you too."

"Maybe, but he's your guest, and you must see to it that your guest is happy here. Do you think he would enjoy being looked at by everyone all the time?"

"Not all the time. But you can."

"Of course I can, but let's make a deal that for today we shall leave him in peace. All right?"

Unfortunately, the next day, as well as the following days, everything turned out so that his mother couldn't visit the gold fox. Lucas did not ask her again, but a few times he tried to remind her about her promise by a meaningful glance. He had a feeling, however, that she decided not to understand what he meant. Everybody in the household, it semed to him, including Eliza, behaved as if they knew quite well of the golden fox's presence, but preferred not to talk about it.

Lucas couldn't understand why everyone had suddenly become tongue-tied. Was it possible that the gold fox didn't interest them really? Weren't they curious to know what he looked like?"

Meanwhile, his own relationship with the guest developed nicely, although their meetings were somewhat haphazard, since they had to be adjusted to the situation at home. And so, for example, all the evenings were lost; Gregory had a habit of reading in bed and, naturally, until he turned off the light and fell asleep, a visit with the fox was out of the question. Then again, in the afternoons Gregory did his homework. And the mornings? Ah, how useless to even mention the mornings; there was so little time then that he barely had a minute for a short "Hi, fox!" And so slowly Lucas began to realize how very bitter, how unsatisfactory even the most beautiful emotion can be if one cannot share it with others. He learned that a secret not only contains the thrill of mystery, but can also be a source of such sadness that at times it's difficult to measure which is greater: the happiness or the pain. It also became clear to him that people, even his own family, could be cruel and difficult to understand.

Despite this, Lucas never ceased to hope that the silence surrounding the fox would one day be broken, and the decisive step taken by his mother.

But, as several days passed and nothing happened, he began to worry in earnest. He lost his appetite, he looked pale, and finally one evening, right after dinner, his father, who was a doctor, led him to his office for a physical examination.

Lucas didn't say one word during the entire treatment. Obediently he took deep breaths, quick breaths, coughed, raised his arms over his head or stretched them forward, while his father put the cold stethoscope against his chest. At one point, his mother looked into the room.

"Well?" she asked.

The father straightened up. "Everything is fine."

But Lucas felt sure it wasn't so. That very evening, knowing that for once his mother would be at home, he decided to act without further delay. Luckily Gregory turned off his light earlier than usual and fell asleep almost instantly. Lucas got out of bed, found his slippers in the dark and quietly slipped out into the hall.

The light was still on in his mother's room as well as in his father's office. Lucas did not foresee, however, that his mother might not be alone; his father was in her room, and they were talking. Since the door into the hall had been left ajar, Lucas could hear every word clearly.

His father was saying, "You know, I'm worried about Lucas. Doesn't it seem to you that there's something wrong with him?"

"I'm not sure," answered the mother hesitantly. "Sometimes I feel at we know so very little about our children. We never have enough time. Even though we live together, we actually all live our separate lives."

"Has he spoken to you again about that gold fox of his since the episode with Emily?"

The mother sounded surprised. "No, why? I suppose he's already forgotten about it. Such fantasies don't usually last long with children."

"I'm not so sure. I think it may not have been such a good idea that you played along with him in these fantasies. The boy is oversensitive, anyway."

They were silent for a moment.

"You know," spoke up the mother, "I've wondered about it myself. But do we have to deprive our children of the right to dream?"

"We must, I think," answered the father.

"Didn't we ourselves dream once?"

"With us it was different Yes, we did have dreams, and not just in our childhood, but didn't we pay for them dearly? It's better not to give our past as an example for our children to follow. Nowadays they must learn from the beginning to think and feel as does the rest of their society. You know it yourself. What'll be the fate of a man who insists on thinking differently from the rest? Just because we ourselves got used to often saying what we don't think, will our children also have to lie?"

"You are tired?" she asked softly.

"I am; all of us are tired. But what of it? It's that much more reason to guard the minds of our children!"

"I'm not sure you aren't overrating the importance of all this, said the mother after a pause. "After all, the gold fox affair is really trifling. … "

"It may be trifling," agreed the father. "But certain traits of Lucas' character can't be taken lightly. I don't know, perhaps it's a capitulation on my part—or perhaps it's precisely because I understand our times—but it seems to me that it's best not to be different from others. And so I wouldn't want our son … "

Lucas was standing with his forehead pressed against the frame of the door. He didn't understand all he heard, but one thing became obvious: his mother had never seen the gold fox, and what's more just like his father, like Gregory, like Emily, like everybody else—she did not believe in the fox's existence, and therefore she had cheated him, she had lied to him, she had treated him like a stupid child whom she kindly permitted to go on believing in his foolish fairy tale. And so his last hope had now failed him. They had all betrayed his fox; they crossed him off and threw him out of their lives. But why? What had he done to them? "Oh fox, my dear fox," he thought sadly. 'Why don't they like you? Why does no one want to look at you? But you are here, you live, I can hear you and see you."

After that memorable night, there came an altogether new phase in Lucas's relationship with the fox, a phase without illusions and without hope that what was of such vital importance to them both would ever find approval from the rest of the family. If only he and his fox could be together somewhere in the desert or in a deep forest. Unfortunately, they had to stay among people, at all times encircled by their activities. How frail and perishable did his secret seem to him at times! Glowing with a lonely light, it flowed gently on through the darkness in the surrounding indifference, but to what shores was it flowing, what would be its final destiny? Now it happened more and more often that when Lucas finally managed to visit the fox in the wardrobe, he could find no words to say to him except a short greeting, in which he tried to communicate all his mixed-up emotions. "Good morning!" the fox would answer. And then the two of them would be silent, cuddled close together, emgulfed by the peace of the golden glow.

These were not happy days. Oh no! Lucas decided that in the presence of his parents and in front of Gregory he would behave as he always had; he would try to act relaxed and talkative. At times he succeeded, but the better and more natural was his pretending, the heavier his heart felt, and the more intense was the sadness that came upon him when at last he could be alone. But he did not complain to the fox, since he felt that his guest knew exactly as much as he himself. And, as he pondered about all this, he found inside himself a fear which hadn't been there before. Then one day he could contain himself no longer, and putting his arms around the fox's neck, he called desperately, "You won't ever leave me, my fox, will you? You and I will never part!" And the fox murmured in his peculiar way "Never."

Time rushed on further and further into October, and Lucas' birthday was drawing near. He knew that Elza was preparing a chocolate birthday cake, on which soon, at an afternoon party, six candles would be lighted.

On the eve of his birthday, before going to sleep, Lucas was so preoccupied with thinking about what the next day would bring that he forgot to say goodnight to the fox. Actually, he could have easily jumped out of bed to look inside the wardrobe, since since Gregory was not in the room—but he felt awfully sleepy. So he just put out his hand in the darkness and whispered, "Bye bye!"

"Bye bye!" whispered the fox from inside the wardrobe, like a far-away echo.

The next day was Sunday. When Lucas sat up in bed and opened his eyes, Gregory was already standing by the table, barefooted and still in his pajamas, examining the presents.

"Come, Lucas, look at the new tractor you got … See that? It has a combine, a mower and all these other attachments. The 'Star' is from me. Pretty nifty, isn't it?"

"Yeah," whispered Lucas. It was true—over by the metal tractor, he could see a fair-sized wooden truck. And next to it stood a red box with building blocks. He peered inside curiously. Gregory too leaned over the open box.

"Pretty nifty! You can build an entire village with these. Look here." Gregory became more and more excited. "You have ducks, too … "

"And a pond?" asked Lucas.

"No, there's no pond. But you can make that yourself.

"I know!" cried Lucas. I'll put some water in a soap dish, and I'll have a pond."

"Or in a saucer," advised Gregory. 'The water will be cleaner so you'll have a pond already purified by a water-bed system, you understand? Look, the tractor can be wound up!"

"Great!" agreed Lucas.

But the real playing didn't begin until after breakfast It was a beautiful sunny day, without a single cloud in the sky.

"We'll build a collective village." decided Gregory. But, alas, he couldn't complete his building project, for at ten o'clock his class was to meet at a village outside Warsaw for some games. Lucas liked playing with his brother, but as soon as he was left alone he came to to conclusion that Gregory's construction plans weren't really good. He ripped down the symmetrically laid-out street, paused for a moment to examine the ruins with satisfaction, and then, after much consideration, started by first building the scenery. When the forest was up, when the pond on the other side glistened with a smooth surface, and when he ran a winding brook cut out of blue paper through the still-empty fields only then did he proceed to build the village itself. His work took a long time, since he constantly kept discovering the need for new improvements in the open fields. But just as he started to throw a little bridge over the brook, he suddenly realized he had completely forgotten about his friend. He was about to get up when it occurred to him that the cows herded along the stream should certainly be transferred to the pasture as soon as possible. He therefore finished building the bridge, and only after seeing to it that the cows were left safely in the care of a cowherd did he finally get up to say good morning to the fox.

But before going in, he realized for the first time that it wasn't really worthwhile to draw the shades for so short a visit. So, leaving the shades up, he walked over to the wardrobe, opened the door, and quickly slipped inside.

"Good morning, my dear fox," he said in his usual whisper, and put out his hand to embrace his friend. But he only touched Gregory's low-hanging ski pants. He moved a little further in. "Where are you?" he asked in a hushed tone. "Fox!" Suddenly he could feel heat rush to his face. Something was changed. It looked as though the fox were not there at all. He called louder, "Fox, where are you?" No one answered. There was dead silence. Lucas pulled the door shut behind him and found himself engulfed by total darkness. His eyes wide open, he looked around, holding his breath, but not even a tiniest flicker of the golden glow broke through the night surrounding him. He felt that his eyes were beginning to fill with tears.

"My fox, oh my fox … he whispered, and his heart was breaking in pain, because he understood that never again would the fox answer his call. He was gone. He had departed to find new people, new friends.

Lucas felt hot tears streaming down his cheeks, but at the same time it seemed as though the most difficult and painful moments were already behind him, as though after a laborious climb up a steep mountain he had now begun to descend a gentle slope, "Perhaps it's better now that the fox has left," he thought, He wiped his moist cheeks with his hand, blew his nose, and with a sigh scrambled out of the wardrobe.

It made him happy to see the room filled with sunlight. The section of the rug where he had built his colorful village with the forest, the brook and the pond was illuminated by the sun; the rest still remained in the shade. It all looked very beautiful, and once again Lucas thought that perhaps it was right that the gold fox went off into the world.

Afterwards he had no time to think about it any more. When Sunday dinner, to which Gregory had brought Christopher, was over, Emily came to call. She was wearing a new dress, a blue one with white polka dots and a white turned-up collar. Her blond little braids were tied with new bows. Her eyes shone brightly. She seemed very proud of her outfit as well as of the admiration which everyone showed for the present she had brought for Lucas—a tiny model of the car "Warszawa." As a matter of fact, the car gave rise to a row, since Gregory and Christopher didn't want to let Lucas play with it. A scene was on the way, when Emily interfered.

"If you're going to quarrel," she said firmly, I will take back my present." Luckily, the storm was averted, and Gregory went back to the morning's project of building a collective village.

"You're dumb," he said, when Lucas stubbornly insisted on his own construction scheme. "If you scatter the houses all around, how are you going to plan scientifically the economic development of the village? So the village was erected in accordance with his wishes. Then came harvest time, all the machines were put to work, and a group of volunteers arrived from the city in the truck in order to participate in the harvest activities. At one point Lucas had an idea that a great thunderstorm should pass over the fields, but Gregory protested.

"No!" he said. "There'll be no rain; we can't lose the grain. Our collective village must be a leader in production. And so there was no rain, and in the afternoon they could proceed with collecting the quotas and buying up the grain.

"You know," said Christopher, "Let's unmask a kulak [*a prosperous private farmer resistant to the collectivation of agriculture*].

"Okay!" agreed Gregory.

"But how are you going to unmask a kulak?" asked Lucas.

"It's simple," answered Gregory. "A kulak is fat and has an ugly … " "And has an ugly snoot," put in Christopher. "You can recognize him right away."

Slowly dusk was beginning to fall. In the midst of their play they had "unmasked the kulak." Christopher leaned toward Gregory and began to whisper something in his ear. Gregory shrugged his shoulders. "Leave him alone," he muttered.

"Why? I'm going to ask him."

Lucas Ieaned further over the truck, which he had just been loading up with sacks of flour.

"Hey Lucas," called Christopher. "What's new with the gold fox? Do you see him from time to time?"

Lucas straightened up and blushed. For a moment nobody said anything. Slowly Lucas placed another wooden block on the truck. "No," he muttered.

"Not at all?"

Lucas raised his head and looked at Gregory, who, however, pretended to be very busy.

"Well then, you never see the gold fox any more?"

"Certainly not!" muttered Lucas. "You know there aren't any gold foxes." Still blushing, he turned away and walked over to the window. The autumn day was coming to an end. The blue sky above the statue of King Sigismund was still bright, but down below the twilight had already set in, very clear and delicate.

"I never saw the gold fox," thought Lucas, gazing at the peaceful scenery outside the window. Then, all at once his heart began to beat violently. Over in the distance, in the dusk, among the rust-colored trees a gold fox scurried along the embankment Yes, it was he, there could be no doubt about it! He was rushing toward the steps leading to the city. Would he find other friends? Lucas moved closer to the windowpane … But the fox wasn't there any more. "Maybe one day I will see him again," be thought. "Maybe he will come back some time."

"Lucas!" called Gregory. "Come play with us!"

Lucas turned around and looked at the boys and at Emily seated on me carpet.

"Well, come on!" said Gregory, smiling. And that smile made Lucas feel very warm around the heart.

"I never saw a gold fox!" he cried triumphantly.

"Hurray!" shouted Gregory.

—1956. TRANSLATED BY BARBARA VEDDER

*Poland in the Aftermath of World War II.* One out of five people in Poland perished during World War II. Most casualties were civilian, amounting to some six million people in all. In the waning days of the war Poland was additionally weakened after a disastrously unsuccessful insurrection against the Germans in Warsaw, described here earlier. The insurrection was largely anti-Russian in spirit and in leadership, run by people who wanted to seize power before the Russians could come to power, which they did after the uprising failed. Poland was then overrun by the Soviet Army, which drove the Germans out of Poland and forcibly occupied the entire country. A puppet communist regime, which had already been assembled in Russia during the war, was established. Free elections, guaranteed by Russia's Joseph Stalin at the Yalta Conference of 1945, were cancelled. Many Polish prewar communists and socialists were repressed and in many cases exterminated, since they tended to be anti-Russian as well. The Soviet Union occupied not only Poland but the majority of central and east European countries, and the line separating them from western Europe became known as the *Iron Curtain*; the state of hostile relations between the two sides was called the *Cold War*.

Poland thus became a communist country and a political satellite of Russia. Political indoctrination and forced social conformity reached into all aspects of life, especially in the education of the young. The duty of every individual was to background his or her individuality in order to promote the interest of the state. All efforts were to be devoted to reeducating the population in "correct" ways of thinking, to rebuilding the wartime destruction, and especially to developing heavy industry, which among other things could contribute to the Soviet Union's military buildup.

Severe punishments were meted out for political dissent and protest. People were encouraged to denounce one another, even family members, to the authorities for so-called subversive activities and socially harmful ways of thinking. Censorship of news, films, textbooks, literature, and mass media became universal. Contact with the West was severely limited, a circumstance which was particularly difficult for Poland, which had always been westwardly oriented and which, in addition, had a huge population of Poles living abroad, especially in the United States, England, Scotland, Canada, and South America. As a result, people became cut off from family members living in other countries, often as the result of wartime displacement.

Literature became subject to the strictures of so-called *socialist realism*, a particular kind of politically correct literature aimed at the indoctrination of the reader and at the enlistment of his or her help in furthering the aims of "society." The doctrine originated in the Soviet Union in the 1930s, where it was imposed as a doctrine on all writers and other creative artists in an especially crude way. Its main aspects were that (a) a literary work had to have a socially uplifting and redeeming message; (b) it had to show the correctness of the Marxist-Leninist interpretation of economics, politics, and history; (c) it had to show the leading role of the working class and of the communist party (in Poland, the party was called the socialist party, because the word "communism" had a negative resonance with the population); (d) it had to show the dominant guiding role of the Soviet Union, both in Poland and internationally; (e) it left no room for indulging personal whims or egocentrisms; and (f) it had to promote the idea that things in the country were constantly getting better and better under communism. Any remaining problems were to be viewed as the result of the erroneous ways of the capitalist past or of foreign-inspired subversive elements.

Socialist Realism was particularly difficult to introduce in Poland, which had strong cultural traditions flying in the face of Marxist ideas. It became so difficult in Poland to replace individual farmsteads with collective farms that the authorities eventually had to give up trying, although some collective farms remained until the end of the communist period. Something similar occurred in state relations with the Catholic Church, which was allowed a greater degree of religious autonomy than was the case in other countries of the Soviet bloc. Poland's cultural traditions contained a sizable dose of anti-Russian sentiment, making it especially difficult for Poles to swallow the leading role of Russia in anything.

Socialist realism was enforced in Polish cultural life through the school system, the penal system, mass media, and the censorship apparatus, whereby every single published item was required to pass through the state censorship office, even scholarly articles written on abstruse scientific topics.

*"The Gold Fox."* The publication of Jerzy Andrzejewski's story, as innocuous as it seems in retrospect, was a landmark in Polish postwar literature. It came out in 1955, some seven years before comparable politically critical works were allowed to appear in the Soviet Union. Aleksandr Solzhenitsyn's *One Day in the Life of Ivan Denisovich*, the harbinger of the literary thaw in Soviet literature, which dealt with the theme of Soviet labor camps (the *Gulag*), came out in 1962.

It is hard to appreciate today how bold "The Gold Fox" was in various respects. The story may have passed the censorship because of the personal clout of Andrzejewski within the official system. The story takes a frontal attack on many of the tenets of socialist realism, subjecting them to biting ridicule.

Despite the specific sociopolitical references to Poland of the 1950s, "The Gold Fox" retains its readability today because it touches on more general themes which hold true outside specific times and places. It is about how the young are forcibly brought into the fold of conformity with the society around them by their peers and especially by their parents and the educational system, accompanied by the moral conviction of all these peers and parents and systems that they are doing the right thing, and not only for the "good" of society, but for the benefit of the person they are trying to shape.

With a little adaptation, the story could equally well be applied to the forced conformity one has to undergo in growing up in the United States or almost anywhere. There is almost always a "politically correct" ideology of some sort being pushed on people in a society—a supposedly proper way of viewing things. Andrzejewski suggests that the young are gifted with a brief period of imagination and fantasy, of seeing things through fresh eyes, which they quickly lose because of their interaction with others, older than they are, around them.

Everyone around Lucas—his parents, brother, his own friends, and his brother's friends—pressure him to conform. They seem to view Lucas's display of imagination as aberrational and threatening. A special theme is the insidious indoctrinating nature of playthings (tractors, trucks, model villages). The story asks: What are we really doing to our young by trying to indoctrinate them politically at such an early age? One needs to leave a little room for a child's own mental space. Otherwise, the result is to turn people either into citizen robots or into people leading dual lives: public and fake versus private and real.

Gregory is an older brother who is already well indoctrinated, and he naturally takes it upon himself to indoctrinate his younger brother. He insists that Lucas play games in the proper, politically correct manner, that he build straight streets on a scientifically managed collective farm with a proper sewage system, and that he not have a rainstorm at the wrong moment. Gregory's friend Christopher is even worse, some kind of thug, a born enforcer or policeman.

The story is partially "politically incorrect" in that Lucas's family comes from the intelligentsia; that is, they are white-collar professionals (albeit, to be sure, in "honorable" professions: his mother is a teacher, and his father a doctor). The working-class child Emily has been indoctrinated in a primitive way by both parents and school. Without understanding them she mouths notions empty of content about the superiority of Russia and Moscow in all things, and she tries to make up politically correct fairy stories, utterly lacking in imagination and sense of humor. Even so, certain positive aspects of socialism are seen in the fact that Emily and Lucas mix together socially, and that Emily's family, where the father is a metal worker for an automobile factory, is as prosperous as Lucas's (recall her new dress, her pet dog, and the nice present she brings Lucas).

The gold fox represents that precious certain something which children lose when they become part of a larger community. There is probably no greater symbolism to the fox than that. Foxes are popular in folk literature, and Lucas may have gotten the notion about the fox from a fairytale he has read. Foxes are quick, shiny, bright, secretive, sly, clever, wise, and friends of children. They do not stay very long in one place.

If Lucas learns one thing from his experience, it is that it is necessary to lie and pretend in front of others. This is a useful skill for living and getting along in a society where one is not allowed to be oneself. It is worth considering whether our own society is not too much different from that of Poland in the 1950s. There is hardly any more conformist society than that in contemporary America, even if there are sharp divides between the dominant conformities.

# Stanisław Lem

Stanisław Lem (1921–2006) was born in Lwów, now Ukrainian Lviv, to a well-to-do family of Jewish background who survived World War II living on false papers. After the war the family resettled to Kraków, where Lem completed medical studies at Jagiellonian University. He began publishing as early as 1946 and soon acquired a reputation—first in the communist-bloc countries—for his highly imaginative science fiction work which, unlike that of many other writers in the field, was distinguished by a deep knowledge of many different scientific fields, including medicine, biology, physics, geology, cybernetics, mathematics, and philosophy. Clearly born with an absorbent mind, in high school his IQ had been measured at 180. His reputation gradually grew in the West due in part to excellent translations of his work into English, tested to the limit because of Lem's frequent resort to creative wordplay, as one sees in the following story. Lem eventually attained the status of Poland's best-selling and most widely translated twentieth-century author, and one of the world's most respected science-fiction writers. Special themes for him are the role in life and history of unforeseeable consequences, the limitations of the human mind and body—specifically, their unsuitability for space exploration and for understanding other forms of life—and a deep pessimism regarding where technological progress is leading mankind. Toward the end of his career Lem abandoned science-fiction writing and devoted himself to the production of critical and philosophical treatises. His best-known novel, *Solaris*, about a sentient planet, was adapted three times (and never successfully) for the screen, most recently in 2002 by Steven Soderbergh.

Lem's short stories and novels are highly varied as to tone, style, and subject matter. They range from the playful and satirical fable, to the suspenseful and action-filled thriller, to the deeply mysterious, philosophical and speculative novel, making it difficult to select a representative example of his work in short-story form. Lem's *Bajki robotów*, or "fables by and for robots," from which the story to follow is taken, are often published together with his thematically affinitive *Cyberiada*, a collection of stories that chronicles the adventures of two "constructor robots," Trurl and Klapaucius, who live in a future universe populated mostly by self-sufficient robots and other intelligent machines. Both works grew to be so popular in Poland that by 1982 they had become officially incorporated into the national school curriculum.

## Tale of the Computer That Fought a Dragon

King Poleander Partobon, ruler of Cyberia, was a great warrior, and being an advocate of the methods of modern strategy, above all else he prized cybernetics as a military art. His kingdom swarmed with thinking machines, for Poleander put them everywhere he could; not merely in the astronomical observatories or the schools, but he ordered electric brains mounted in the rocks upon the roads, which with loud voices cautioned pedestrians against tripping; also in posts, in walls, in trees, so that one could ask directions anywhere when lost; he stuck them onto clouds, so they could announce the rain in advance, he added them to the hills and valleys—in short, it was impossible to walk on Cyberia without bumping into an intelligent machine. The planet was beautiful, since the King not only gave decrees for the cybernetic perfecting of that which had long been in existence, but he introduced by law entirely new orders of things. Thus for example in his kingdom were manufactured cyberbeetles and buzzing cyberbees, and even cyberflies—these would be seized by mechanical spiders when they grew too numerous. On the planet cyberbosks of cybergorse rustled in the wind, cybercalliopes and cyberviols sang—but besides these civilian devices there were twice as many military, for the King was most bellicose. In his palace vaults he had a strategic computer, a machine of uncommon mettle; he had smaller ones also, and divisions of cybersaries, enormous cybermatics and a whole arsenal of every other kind of weapon, including powder. There was only this one problem, and it troubled him greatly, namely, that he had not a single adversary or enemy and no one in any way wished to invade his land, and thereby provide him with the opportunity to demonstrate his kingly and terrifying courage, his tactical genius, not to mention the simply extraordinary effectiveness of his cybernetic weaponry. In the absence of genuine enemies and aggressors the King had his engineers build artificial ones, and against these he did battle, and always won. However inasmuch as the battles and campaigns were genuinely dreadful, the populace suffered no little injury from them. The subjects murmured when all too many cyberfoes had destroyed their settlements and towns, when the synthetic enemy poured liquid fire upon them; they even dared voice their discontent when the King himself, issuing forth as their deliverer and vanquishing the artificial foe, in the course of the victorious attacks laid waste to everything that stood in his path. They grumbled even then, the ingrates, though the thing was done on their behalf.

Until the King wearied of the war games on the planet and decided to raise his sights. Now it was cosmic wars and sallies that he dreamed of. His planet had a large Moon, entirely desolate and wild; the King laid heavy taxes upon his subjects, to obtain the funds needed to build whole armies on that Moon and have there a new theater of war. And the subjects were more than happy to pay, figuring that King Poleander would now no longer deliver them with his cybermatics, nor test the strength of his arms upon their homes and heads. And so the royal engineers built on the Moon a splendid computer, which in turn was to create all manner of troops and self-firing gunnery. The King lost no time in testing the machine's prowess this way and that; at one point he ordered it—by telegraph—to execute a volt-vault electrosault: for he wanted to see if it was true, what his engineers had told him, that that machine could do anything. If it can do anything, he thought, then let it do a flip. However the text of the telegram underwent a slight distortion and the machine received the order that it was to execute not an electrosault, but an electrosaur—and this it carried out as best it could.

Meanwhile the King conducted one more campaign, liberating some provinces of his realm seized by cyber-knechts; he completely forgot about the order given the computer on the Moon, then suddenly giant boulders came hurtling down from there; the King was astounded, for one even fell on the wing of the palace and destroyed his prize collection of cyberads, which are dryads with feedback. Fuming, he telegraphed the Moon computer at once, demanding an explanation. It didn't reply however, for it no longer was: the electrosaur had swallowed it and made it into its own tail.

Immediately the King dispatched an entire armed expedition to the Moon, placing at its head another computer, also very valiant, to slay the dragon, but there was only some flashing, some rumbling, and then no more computer nor expedition; for the electrodragon wasn't pretend and wasn't pretending, but battled with the utmost verisimilitude, and had moreover the worst of intentions regarding the kingdom and the King. The King sent to the Moon his cybernants, cyberneers, cyberines and lieutenant cybernets, at the very end he even sent one cyberalissimo, but it too accomplished nothing; the hurly-burly lasted a little longer, that was all. The King watched through a telescope set up on the palace balcony.

The dragon grew, the Moon became smaller and smaller, since the monster was devouring it piecemeal and incorporating it into its own body. The King saw then, and his subjects did also, that things were serious, for when the ground beneath the feet of the electrosaur was gone, it would for certain hurl itself upon the planet and upon them. The King thought and thought, but he saw no remedy, and knew not what to do. To send machines was no good, for they would be lost, and to go himself was no better, for he was afraid. Suddenly the King heard, in the stillness of the night, the telegraph chattering from his royal bedchamber. It was the King's personal receiver, solid gold with a diamond needle, linked to the Moon; the King jumped up and ran to it, the apparatus meanwhile went *tap-tap, tap-tap,* and tapped out this telegram: THE DRAGON SAYS POLEANDER PARTOBON BETTER CLEAR OUT BECAUSE HE THE DRAGON INTENDS TO OCCUPY THE THRONE!

The King took fright, quaked from head to toe, and ran, just as he was, in his ermine nightshirt and slippers, down to the palace vaults, where stood the strategy machine, old and very wise. He had not as yet consulted it, since prior to the rise and uprise of the electrodragon they had argued on the subject of a certain military operation; but now was not the time to think of that—his throne, his life was at stake!

He plugged it in, and as soon as it warmed up he cried: "My old computer! My good computer! It's this way and that, the dragon wishes to deprive me of my throne, to cast me out, help, speak, how can I defeat it?!"

"Uh-uh," said the computer. "First you must admit I was right in that previous business, and secondly, I would have you address me only as Digital Grand Vizier, though you may also say to me: 'Your Ferromagneticity'!"

"Good, good, I'll name you Grand Vizier, I'll agree to anything you like, only save me!"

The machine whirred, chirred, hummed, hemmed, then said;

"It is a simple matter. We build an electrosaur more powerful than the one located on the Moon. It will defeat the lunar one, settle its circuitry once and for all and thereby attain the goal!"

"Perfect!" replied the King. "And can you make a blueprint of this dragon?"

"It will be an ultradragon," said the computer. "And I can make you not only a blueprint, but the thing itself, which I shall now do, it won't take a minute, King!" And true to its word, it hissed, it chugged, it whistled and buzzed, assembling something down within itself, and already an object like a giant claw, sparking, arcing, was emerging from its side, when the King shouted;

"Old computer! Stop!"

"Is this how you address me? I am the Digital Grand Vizier!"

"Ah, of course," said the King. "Your Ferromagneticity the electrodragon you are making will defeat the othe dragon, granted, but it will surely remain in the other's place, how then are we to get rid of it in turn?!"

"By making yet another, still more powerful," explained the computer.

"No, no! In that case don't do anything, I beg you, what good will it be to have more and more terrible dragons on the Moon when I don't want any there at all?"

"Ah, now that's a different matter," the computer replied. "Why didn't you say so in the first place? You see how logically you express yourself? One moment … I must think."

And it churred and hummed, and chuffed and chucked and finally said;

"We make an antimoon with an antidragon, place it in the Moon's orbit (here something went snap inside), sit around the fire and sing; *Oh I'm a robot full of fun, water doesn't scare me none, I dives right in, I gives a grin, tra la the livelong day!!*"

"You speak strangely," said the King. "What does the antimoon have to do with that song about the funny robot?"

"What funny robot?" asked the computer. "Ah, no, no, I made a mistake, something feels wrong inside, I must have blown a tube." The King began to look for the trouble, finally found the burnt-out tube, put in a new one, then asked the computer about the antimoon.

"What antimoon?" asked the computer, which meanwhile had forgotten what it said before. "I don't know anything about an antimoon … one moment, I have to give this thought."

It hummed, it huffed, and it said;

"We create a general theory of the slaying of electrodragons, of which the lunar dragon will be a special case, its solution trivial."

"Well, create such a theory." said the King.

"To do this I must first create various experimental dragons."

"Certainly not. No thank you," exclaimed the King. "A dragon wants to deprive me of my throne, just think what might happen if you produced a swarm of them."

"Oh? Well then, in that case we must resort to other means. We will use a strategic variant of the method of successive approximations. Go and telegraph the dragon that you will give it the throne on the condition that it perform three mathematical operations, really quite simple … "

The King went and telegraphed, and the dragon agreed. The King returned to the computer.

"Now," it said, "here is the first operation: tell it to divide itself by itself!"

The King did this. The electrosaur divided itself by itself, but since one electrosaur over one electrosaur is one, it remained on the Moon and nothing changed.

"Is this the best you can do?!" cried the King, running into the vault with such haste, that his slippers fell off. "The dragon divided itself by itself, but since one goes into one once, nothing changed!"

"That's all right, I did that on purpose, the operation was to divert attention," said the computer. "And now tell it to extract its root!" The King telegraphed to the Moon, and the dragon began to pull, push, pull, push, until it crackled from the strain, panted, trembled all over, but suddenly something gave—and it extracted its own root!

The King went back to the computer.

"The dragon crackled, trembled, even ground its teeth, but extracted the root and threatens me still!" he shouted from the doorway. "What now, my old … I mean. Your Ferromagneticity?!"

"Be of stout heart," it said. "Now go tell it to subtract itself from itself!"

The King hurried to his royal bedchamber, sent the telegram, and the dragon began to subtract itself from itself, taking away its tail first, then legs, then trunk, and finally, when it saw that something wasn't right, it hesitated, but from its own momentum the subtracting continued, it took away its head and became zero, in other words nothing: the electrosaur was no more!

"The electrosaur is no more," cried the joyful King, bursting into the vault. "Thank you, old computer … many thanks … you have worked hard … you have earned a rest, so now I will disconnect you."

"Not so fast, my dear," the computer replied. "I do the job and you want to disconnect me, and you no longer call me Your Ferromagneticity?! That's not nice, not nice at all! Now I myself will change into an electrosaur, yes, and drive you from the kingdom, and most certainly rule better than you, for you always consulted me in all the more important matters, therefore it was really I who ruled all along, and not you!"

And huffing, puffing, it began to change into an electrosaur; flaming electroclaws were already protruding from its sides when the King, breathless with fright, tore the slippers off his feet, rushed up to it and with the slippers began beating blindly at its tubes! The computer chugged, choked, and got muddled in its program—instead of the word "electrosaur" it read "electrosauce," and before the King's very eyes the computer, wheezing more and more softly, turned into an enormous, gleaming-golden heap of electrosauce, which, still sizzling, emitted all its charge in deep-blue sparks, leaving Poleander to stare dumbstruck at only a great, steaming pool of gravy …

With a sigh the King put on his slippers and returned to the royal bedchamber. However from that time on he was an altogether different king: the events he had undergone made his nature less bellicose, and to the end of his days he engaged exclusively in civilian cybernetics, and left the military kind strictly alone.

—1964. Translated by Michael Kandel

*A Pre-Remark.* In the fall of 2023, when the present collection of stories is being prepared, it is impossible for the editor to read "Tale of the Robot That Fought a Dragon" without being struck by the parallels between King Poleander's willingness to wreak havoc and misery on his subjects by frivolous fights with his smaller neighbors he estimates he can easily conquer, with the current military situation in Ukraine. There, as on the planet Cyberia, according to the "law of unintended consequences" combined with the reliable principle in warfare that if something can go wrong, then it probably will, the planet is brought to the brink of extinction through the stubborn short-sighted ambitions of an egotistical despot.

*Revenge of the Robots.* The word *robot* is based on the Czech word *robota,* 'drudge work.' The theme of robots getting out of control and taking revenge on their human creators goes back even earlier than the coinage of the word by the Czech writer Karel Čapek in his prescient 1921 play *R.U.R*, in which robots made on a remote island eventually turn on the entire human species An early example of the theme in English literature would be Mary Shelly's (1797–1851) novel *Frankenstein*. Motivated by such concern, the American science-fiction writer Isaac Asimov (1920–1992) optimistically formulated "do no harm to humans" as his first principle of robotics, a principle that has been brought to the fore in the contemporary discussion over the potential dangers of Artificial Intelligence to the continued existence of humankind itself. Stanisław Lem's stories can feature some seriously nasty rogue robots, but here the author takes a humorous approach to the subject, even if with dark undertones and serious philosophical implications.

*Cybernetics and the Inevitability of Disaster.* The term "cybernetics" originated in the 1940s. It is an interdisciplinary field broadly concerned with intelligent and self-governing systems, whether natural or, especially, human-designed, including a system's ability to learn from feedback, that is, from trial and error. A fanciful example of cybernetics in action is described in the first paragraphs of the present story, as in King Poleander's highly regulated "cyberstate" the "cyberspiders" automatically cull the "cyberflies" whenever they become too numerous. Already in early-1960s Poland Lem sees in Cyberia's intelligent rocks, warning pedesrians not to trip, the intimations of what is known today as the "nanny state." The unintended but predictable consequence here, given that every step forward in technological progress seems always to have an even equally powerful effect in the opposite direction, is that such safeguards against unwise action deprive people of their ability to make intelligent decisions or perform simple actions on their own.

A problem inherent to the trial-and-error learning of cybernetics is that when input errors do occur, as they inevitably do, in certain instances catastrophe can result, as in the present parable of the mechanical dragon inadvertently planted by King Poleander on Cyberia's moon, which is about to devour first the moon and then conquer the entire planet around which it revolves. The moral here is found in many fairy tales from around the world: think carefully before you wish for something, because you may be sorry for what you get.

Just how easily man-made intelligent systems can careen dangerously out of control via the "law of unintended consequences," by their having been fed faulty or poorly reasoned input, is one of the major themes of this made-for-robots fable in which the king's personal computer strategizes a fight with a threatening dragon robot that the king himself has accidentally brought into being, the result of an erroneously transmitted frivolous idea of his, that his computer on the moon should do a back-flip. The king's computer eventually conquers the dragon by playing a mathematical trick on it, only now to turn its powers against the king, with whom it has never really gotten along. It is fortunate for the planet of Cyberia that at the last minute King Poleander has the presence of mind to avert disaster by pulling off his slippers and beating his "strategy machine" where it hurts most: in its vacuum tubes. Of course, transistors had been invented by the 1960s when this story was written, but Lem likes to insert anachronisms like this into his stories for ironic effect, another example being Poleander's communicating with the moon by means of a telegraph, when a wireless telephone would have done the job more efficiently.

The present fable is written as if as a cautionary tale for robots which, to their grudging acknowledgment, operate under the (mis)guided rule of their deeply flawed and much less intelligent human creators. Humans, Lem seems to suggest—by trying with their ingenuity to make life better for humanity—inevitably end up by making it worse because of their short-sighted view of what "better" is or can lead to. The longevity of Lem's stories will undoubtedly depend on their continuing ability to remind the reader that technological progress is not now nor ever will be, even millenia from now, all it is cracked up to be.

# Janusz Głowacki

Janusz Głowacki (1938–2017) became widely known in the 1960s and 1970s as a writer of shorter literary forms: satirical sketches, short stories, plays, and filmscripts. He gained recognition internationally for his plays translated into English. His *Kopciuch* (Cinders), about the rough life of a girls' reform school, was considered the best play of 1981 by the London *Times*. Głowacki stayed abroad following the imposition of martial law by the communist government in 1981, where he continued to contribute to Polish literature, including with his *Good Night, Dżerzi* (Good night Jerzy), a novelistic treatment of the last days of the émigré novelist Jerzy Kosiński. The following story, taking place late in the "PRL" (Polish People's Republic), highlights the country-city and older-younger divides, which to this day to a considerable extent permeate Polish religion and politics, and the flight of the young from the village to the city seeking a better life, joined with the age-old conflict arising out of property interests that remains regardless of the political system. Głowacki died unexpectedly of a heart attack while on vacation in Egypt.

## The Visit

Around seven o'clock in the evening came heavy steps and a knocking at the door. Teresa was already near the door, but she was caught off guard that they had come so early, worried that Andrzej and Bodzio wouldn't be back for another hour and she would have to keep them company by herself. Upset, and angry at Andrzej for leaving the house for no good reason, at the same time she felt relieved that they had arrived. Forcing a smile, she opened the door.

There they stood, both of them wrapped up in overcoats and thick scarves, as always looking dirty, he in galoshes and she in high-heeled ankle boots, looking downtrodden, little, and very old. So Teresa, now smiling more easily, invited them inside, filling up the silence by asking too loudly and too quickly how their trip had been, whether the train was crowded, telling them that Andrzej and their grandson would be back momentarily. They, vigilant and mistrustful, cautiously stepped inside onto the gleaming hardwood floor, which they took an instant dislike to, because it was alien, different, and seemed pointless. Without saying much they unwrapped themselves from their coats and scarves, becoming in the process even smaller and older. They were ceremoniously ushered into the dining room, where a bouquet of fresh flowers—obtained with difficulty in the winter—awaited them, along with a framed picture of the Virgin Mary and a wedding photograph hung specially in their honor over a fashionable low daybed next to a sturdy radio, glistening with newness, and a set of richly upholstered chairs.

They sat down on the chairs around a table set with a white tablecloth, and now for Teresa began the most difficult moments, for they didn't look at anything or glance around the room but just stared calmly at her, as if seeing her for the first time. As she explained how they had managed to get this apartment in a new housing block Teresa could tell that they weren't listening. They didn't like her because she was from the city, and because it was maybe her fault that Andrzej had quit the village, leaving them and the land behind without a second thought or regret, something they can never forgive him for, because they themselves can't understand it. They looked at her, an attractive thirty-year-old getting somewhat plump with her blond hair cut short, wearing a skirt that was probably too short and a black sweater that was too tight. She could see the distaste in their eyes growing by the moment. So Teresa broke off talking and ran into the kitchen but quickly returned, offering tea, because even though the radiators were going full blast, the two of them were frozen through and through, and they kept rubbing together their red chapped hands with dirty fingernails. In order to keep busy, she then brought in some ham and thinly sliced bread and put it on the table, along with one and another carafe of homemade *nalewka,* homemade liqueur that Andrzej had prepared. She was still the only person speaking, but it slowly got better, for in another fifteen minutes Andrzej would be back, and it was easier for her to speak about his work in the Presidium of the Regional Council, about her own work at the school, and about Bodzio, who was the spitting image of both his father and grandfather.

The old man spoke sparingly, in a screechy trembling voice, because although he still stood straight, his voice had gone, while the old woman, of indeterminate age, her face criss-crossed with wrinkles, maintained a cold and stern expression, unable to understand what her son had ever seen in this chatterbox. She didn't waste her voice, but waited, because they had come on serious business, to come to an agreement, and the time for talk had not yet arrived.

Teresa filled their glasses, but they didn't drink, waiting for their son, and again the situation grew tense. But at last a key grated in the door and in walked Andrzej, tossing his loden green overcoat on a hook and removing Bodzio's fur coat. Teresa breathed a sigh of relief, as Andrzej rushed to his mother and father, kissing both on the hand, and Bodzio, with his well-rehearsed "Granma!" and "Granddad!" helped break the ice. They all sat at the table while Bodzio looked at photographs on the daybed, and everything seemed to be going as planned, so that one could catch one's breath for a moment before the conversation that was going to happen happened, the consequences of which were frightening to contemplate.

For the time being Andrzej, dressed in a dark suit, white shirt, and silver tie, an outfit in which the old folks reluctantly recognized their wayward son, invited everyone to have a drink. He lifted his glass, thinking all the while that they hadn't changed a bit, while reminiscences from the village and their home there, none of them either heart-warming or pleasant, appeared before his eyes. But he smiled sincerely and warmly as he raised his glass, although with a tension quite evident to Teresa, because by now she thought and felt almost exactly the same way he did.

"So here's to my dear parents' health, both for visiting us and for everything!"

They drank—the mother quickly but indifferently—while the old man immediately began coughing and turning red. They nibbled at the ham and bread, and after a while Andrzej poured out another round. They drank.

"So here we are, son," the old man croaked. "Here we are."

They drank again. This time it was Teresa who choked, smilingly excusing herself. For her the drinking had come to an end.

"And Bodzio's a nice well-behaved lad," the old man noted, not for the first time.

And so the conversation went, zig-zagging, cautious, inarticulate, both hinting at and avoiding the single most important matter before them. Finally Andrzej asked about his brother Maciej, and then about the other brother's, Ignacy's, funeral, which he hadn't been able to attend because he was doing army duty. Then he asked about the horses and cows and, veering too close to the matter at hand, headed off in a different direction. Mainly Andrzej asked questions, and the old man answered. From time to time Teresa tried to interject something, but finally, sitting on the daybed next to Bodzio, she pretended not to be interested in the conversation, while listening to it attentively. The old woman also stopped drinking, laying her head to one side, while looking on vigilantly with her faded eyes. And so the conversation proceeded, as Andrzej recaptured in his mind remembrances of his village past, which at one time had rankled him with their injustices, but now seemed far removed and in the past. The dimly lit image of the village was recalled to life by the screech of the old man, not so much by the sense of his words but by their cadence and intonation.

The old man broached the matter delicately, as he sedately sought out common memories that would bring people together, not separate them.

And so they rolled along, time and again clinking glasses until, after a long lull in the conversation, the old man cleared his throat, sat up in his chair, and took a look at the old woman.

"You know perfectly well, Andrzej, the purpose of our visit. As our own flesh and blood you are entitled to a share of the farm on an equal basis with your brother Maciej. Now, according to the latest law, since you have left us and the land behind, you have forsaken your right to it. However, since laws can change back and forth, and since we know our Polish and Christian duty as parents, we have agreed with Maciej to pay you now the amount you have coming to you after our deaths, with benefit to both sides. Maciej needs the land now, since he intends to get married, and he has to show his worth before the wedding. You have agreed to all this in your letters, and that's why we have come, in accordance with your promises, and as a sign that we harbor no grudges and want everyone to get along."

He glanced at the old woman, quickly tipped his glass, took a bite of food, coughed, and croaked on further.

"And so we have come to you to set matters straight in a way that both you and we want. Let everyone speak up and say whatever they have on their mind and heart, and let's come to an agreement."

Then Andrzej politely and affably seconded his father's words. He was the first to be in favor of an amicable agreement, he said. He had left the land and his family not for want of affection, but because of curiosity about the world.

His father nodded his head and quickly raised his glass.

"Stop drinking!" the old woman said sharply, pushing away the bottle. "I'm telling you, you've had enough."

Andrzej broke out in a laugh at his mother's habit of taking over, unchanged over the years, as he once again filled the glasses. The old woman merely shrugged and pushed her glass away. The old man, once having initiated the topic, without hurrying continued, while Teresa, as had been planned in advance, took the sleeping Bodzio in her arms and carried him off to a small bed that had been set up in the kitchen. When she returned she heard a round amount being mentioned, with many zeros after it, and Andrzej protesting against it. She paused in the doorway, because that amount, although they had expected something like it, nevertheless struck her with its concreteness. Once having been uttered, it transformed itself in her mind into a larger apartment in the center of town, into furs, theater tickets, and the end of her tiresome work and measly salary. She listened as Andrzej, citing her needs and Bodzio's, and their mutual happiness, refused to accept the proposed offer as being too small. And she wanted to shout, but knew that she could trust Andrzej, who was clever in the ways of both city and country, even if his mind was now clouded by drink. She continued listening as the old man, his face red and pouring down with sweat, kept persuading, while Andrzej, looking disheveled, kept insisting that by rights he was owed more.

The head of the old man sunk closer and closer to the tablecloth. Drunk and in a conciliatory mood, he was about to change his mind and agree. "You're right, son, you're right!"

"Shut your mouth!" hissed the old woman. And now she, looking even smaller than ever, but alert and ready to spring into action, not inebriated the least bit and having the age-old advantage over Andrzej of the respect he owed her, which was slowly returning to him as he sobered up, took matters into her own hands.

"You, Andrzej, should realize that you could only attempt to get what's coming to you after our deaths. And father and I have a long time yet to live."

"Which I wish for you with my whole heart!" said Andrzej, sweaty and unkempt, leaning forward. "But dear parents, I cannot put up with an injustice. Add twenty thousand more."

"You're right, son." The old man filled his glass with a shaky hand and raised it.

The old woman was no longer paying any attention to him. "That's our final offer."

The decision was now in her hands, and Andrzej spoke rather incoherently and only to her. "You have no conscience; you people are completely without a conscience."

"And what about you? For as long as you've lived you never felt like doing a lick of work. You had other things on your mind."

Her eyes turned even more malevolent, as Andrzej, his head beclouded by vodka and a sense of self-pity, once again began to relive those old scenes of injustices he had endured.

"And you? I was never the apple of your eye. There were three of us, and they were always in first place ahead of me." He flailed his arm and knocked over a glass, which shattered on the floor. "I wanted to get an education. Put in another twenty thousand."

The old woman unexpectedly broke into a shrill screeching laugh.

"And you got yourself an education, didn't you, by lying in bed with the communists. I wonder how the Mother of God there on the wall can even look at you. The old man didn't beat you enough, and because of that people like you are in charge of everything now. I'll add another five thousand."

"Twenty."

"Five."

Teresa wanted to interrupt his stammering and bring the matter to a close, which for her was already a win. She was afraid now of his drunken stubbornness; the cleverness was gone. She was afraid the sum might turn back again into something indeterminate. But he paid no attention to her signals, and she didn't have the courage to intervene outright. The two figures kept falling back and forth, Andrzej repeating his sum though his tears, while his mother calmly repeated hers.

"You shithead son of a bitch, I didn't beat you enough," the old man called out, momentarily poking up his head before sinking back down into his chair.

"Five."

At last Andrzej, in pieces because of the alcohol, and by now completely persuaded that she had the upper hand, spoke. "All right, I agree, you money-grubbing peasants," he sobbed. "As the better and wiser person, I agree." And wallowing in self-pity he wiped his tears off with a dirty hand. "May my brother Maciej choke on that land I once loved. I never want to see it again."

Now the old woman, all-knowing and still sharp as a tack, to Teresa's relief pulled out some papers hidden beneath her chair, and now Teresa was able to come forward. Andrzej, slobbering and with bloodshot eyes, shoved aside his father, who was coming at him loudly squawking, and scribbled his name beneath the sum already prepared in advance, the one which the old woman had foreseen and had stuck to. Afterwards she put the paper carefully away, and only now, dispassionately, and with Teresa's help, with her strong bony hands dragged one after the other, the snoring old man and Andrzej, and put them in their sticky and stain-spotted clothing into freshly made beds, specially prepared for their arrival. Finally she herself, very small and very old, curled up alongside them and immediately fell peacefully asleep.

Only then did Teresa, listening to the three of them snoring, and checking to see that their son was asleep, inhumanly tired but nevertheless relieved, turned out the light and started going over figures in her head.

—1974. Translated by Oscar Swan

*Cultural Notes.* The boy's name, "Bodzio," is short for either Bogdan or Bogusław.

The people are drinking *nalewka,* a homemade strong alcoholic beverage made for special occasions by soaking for a long time in 200-proof grain alcohol fruits, nuts, seeds, or other condiments, lending their flavor to it. Ironically, the art of making *nalewka* is one of the things that Andrzej has brought with him from the country to the city.

Andrzej belongs to the Presidium of the Regional (Powiat) Council, showing that he is a high-ranking communist functionary in a low-level administrative unit, a powiat, which is more or less the size of a township. There are currently 379 powiats in Poland. His party affiliation would probably account for the nicely appointed apartment he and Teresa have received in a new housing development.

Children kissing their parents' hands upon meeting after an interval of time is a custom still alive more in the countryside than in the city.

Because of the difficult convertibility in 1974 of the Polish złoty into "hard currency" like the dollar, it is difficult to guess the purchasing power of the 20,000 złotys that is the bone of contention in the story.

*Commentary on "The Visit."* The story exhibits a skillfully executed technique of "slowly lifting the curtain" as to what the story is about—as if reflecting the author's experience in the theater. Enough hints are dropped in the measured and ambiguous build-up to the heart of the story that readers' curiosity is sufficiently piqued for them to want to fill in blanks in the narrative and continue reading. The method causes readers to become absorbed in the story without yet fully understanding it. The tension born of mystery builds until the situation is finally resolved by Andrzej's father, who by that point is in an advanced state of inebriation from Andrzej's homemade *nalewka.* The first few sentences illustrate the technique:

*Around seven o'clock in the evening came heavy steps and a knocking at the door.*

Questions: "Where are we? Who is knocking at the door? Whose door is it? Who is paying a visit to whom? Why at seven o'clock in the evening?"

... *Teresa was already near the door, but was caught off guard that they had come so early, worried that Andrzej and Bodzio wouldn't be back for another hour and she would have to keep them company by herself.*

"Who are 'they'?," the reader asks. "And why is seven o'clock in the evening early?" "And who are Teresa, Andrzej, and Bodzio?" Since Bodzio is a child's nickname, maybe Andrzej is Teresa's husband, and Bodzio is their son. "Who is visiting them, and why does Teresa feel uncomfortable 'keeping them company' until Andrzej and Bodzio return?"

The answer slowly emerges. By identifying Bodzio as their grandson, the visitors are revealed to be Andrzej's parents and Teresa's parents-in-law. They have come on an expected visit, evidently from the countryside, and relations between them and Teresa appear strained, for reasons that are as yet unclear, but they will soon be explained. Teresa is on edge.

The outer garments and footwear of the "visitors," and the state of the old man's fingernails and chapped hands, reveal them to be village folk and workers on the land, not used to new furniture, tidy apartments, and shiny floors, and they instinctively take a dislike to all of it, especially the glistening new radio set and the pretentious upholstered chairs in the dining room. The old lady is not fooled for a moment by the wedding photograph and the picture of the Virgin Mary prominently displayed on the wall especially for their visit. From her point of view, Teresa is a city hussy who has lured Andrzej off the land, and Andrzej has sold his soul to the godless communists for whom he works. The chasm of parental resentment toward everything they see in Teresa and Andrzej's present life and lifestyle is unbridgeable.

After Andrzej and Bodzio come home, little by little the uncomfortable "visit" moves slowly to the next phase, propelled by food to nibble and Andrzej's *nalewka* to drink, until the old man finally lays his and his wife's cards on the table. They have come to work out in advance Andrzej's share in his inheritance from the family farm. Since Andrzej has abandoned the land of his own free will, they are not legally bound to give him anything, but they are driven by a sense of "Christian duty and Polish custom." Andrzej's brother has plans to marry and to work the farm, and he needs to show beforehand that he is a person of substance, so the matter needs to be settled now, before the old folks die and by default leave everything in Andrzej's brother's hands. An argument ensues over the exact amount of the sum involved.

One could reasonably assume that the old man is the one calling the shots here, so to speak, but subsequent developments prove otherwise. In peasant society, the men act as though they are in charge, and they may even think so, but in actuality it is the women who pull the strings, especially the purse strings. The old man waffles back and forth, now bending toward Andrzej's side of the argument, now toward those of his diminutive, wizened wife who, along with Teresa, remains sober and razor-focused, the old woman on a sum she has already worked out in advance and has recorded on the document she has brought with her for Andrzej to sign. In the meantime, Andrzej, initially dressed in a crisp shirt, tie, and sportscoat (which, as city garb, symbolize to his parents the wayward path he has taken in life), becomes increasingly incoherent, disheveled, and blubbery as he summons up all his childhood resentments toward his parents for their supposed preferential treatment of his brothers, one of whom has recently died.

The old woman waits patiently, stubbornly holding her own until the situation wears Andrzej down. He tearfully gives in and signs the paper agreeing to the sum his mother had in mind all along. Teresa, with dreams of the good life now dancing in her head, tries hard to hide her satisfaction with the outcome. As the story draws to a close the womenfolk put the semi-conscious men to bed. Having accomplished what she set out to do, the old woman lies down next to them and falls instantly asleep.

*The City/Country Divide.* The unbridgeable gap between rural and urban society in Poland—in politics, religion, and general outlook on life—is easy for Americans to appreciate, if for no other reason than that it rears its head every four years in U.S. national elections. A recent study showed that in America the degree of political conservatism in a place can be reliably predicted as a function of its distance from a city of at least 100,000 inhabitants. In Poland, farmers cling to their land with a nearly religious fervor, and their conservative attitudes continue to be passed down from one generation to the next. Today slightly less than 10 percent of the Polish population is employed in the agricultural sector (it was much more when Głowacki wrote this story), as compared to around 2 percent in the United States.

# Hanna Krall

Hanna Krall (born 1935) is a writer who specializes in the history of the Holocaust in German-occupied Poland in World War II. Of Jewish ethnicity, Krall was born in Warsaw in 1935 and was four years old and living in Lublin when Germany invaded Poland in 1939. Krall lost most of her close relatives in the Holocaust. She and her mother escaped from being transported to the death camps due to what she estimates to have been the assistance of at least forty or fifty different Poles.

After receiving a degree in journalism from Warsaw University, Krall first wrote for the local paper *Życie Warszawy* (Warsaw Life). In 1966 she left that paper and worked for the fairly liberal news magazine *Polityka* (Politics), for which she was a correspondent in Moscow. Following the fall of communism in 1989, Krall worked for a while for the liberal *Gazeta Wyborcza* (Electoral Gazette) before devoting herself exclusively to writing.

Commercial success came with the publication of her *Zdążyć przed Panem Bogiem* (English title: *Shielding the Flame*), which stemmed from an interview with cardiologist and social activist Marek Edelman, the last surviving leader of the desperate Warsaw Ghetto Uprising of 1943. That work served as a model for most of Krall's subsequent writing, as she describes in the sparest of prose and with virtually no authorial commentary the relations between Jews, Poles, and Germans during the Holocaust and afterwards. Based on interviews with survivors, children of survivors, witnesses, and perpetrators, many at the time of their interviews in their eighties and nineties, her stories are reduced to the bare minimum of detail as she strives to achieve the maximum of objectivity. She compares her method to putting together the shards of an ancient broken jug. Her stories have a literary quality to them, as they often defy what one expects to happen in the real world, creating an effect halfway between documentary realism and modern-day fable.

"The One from Hamburg," examines the intertwined stories of four people affected by the war in four different ways. It was adapted into a film by Jan Jakub Kolski, *Keep Away from the Window*, 2000.

# The One from Hamburg

## 1

They lived in a faraway place. They were very sociable, enjoyed going to parties, and could dance for hours on end. They loved going to the races and placing bets on horses; in moderation, naturally. They were resourceful and thrifty. He was a master decorator; in time he opened his own workshop and had three apprentices. Boring things, like painting walls, he left to his boys; for himself he kept the signboards, especially if they had a lot of letters. He loved letters. Their very shape delighted him. He would spend hours on end drawing them—the fancier the better.

Occasionally, the couple would feel sad that they had no children, but that would pass quickly: they had each other. It all happened a long, long time ago.

## 2

They reached their thirtieth birthdays just before the war broke out.

The war changed their lives only in as much as it put an end to their dancing, and new kinds of signs appeared in the workshop. Now it was the warnings, first in Polish: ATTENTION, ENTRY FORBIDDEN; then in Russian; VNIMANIYE, VYEZD VOSPRIESHCHON; then in German; ACHTUNG, EINTRITT VERBOTEN.

One winter evening in 1943. he returned home with a woman.

"This lady is Jewish. We have to help."

The wife asked if anybody had seen them on the staircase and quickly made a couple of sandwiches.

The Jewish woman was slight, with black curly hair; despite her blue eyes she had very Semitic features. They put her in the room with a wardrobe. (Wardrobes and Jews … probably one of the most important symbols of our times. Man in a wardrobe … In the middle of the twentieth century. In the middle of Europe.)

At the first sound of the door bell, the Jewish woman would go into the wardrobe, and since her hosts were still very sociable she spent many long hours there. Luckily, she was wise. Not a cough, not a sound came from the wardrobe.

The Jewish woman never spoke first, and her answers were curt.

"Yes, I had."

"A solicitor."

"In Bełżec."

"It was too late. We got married just before the war."

"They were taken away. I don't know, in Janowski, or perhaps in Bełżec."

She did not expect sympathy. Quite the reverse, she rejected it.

"I'm alive, she would say. "And I intend to stay alive."

The Jewish woman's belly grew, the wife made bigger pillows and let out the skirts—for herself and the other one.

The baby was delivered by a trusted midwife. Luckily, it did not take long, even though the Jewish woman had narrow hips and, to make matters worse, her waters had broken the previous day.

Barbara took the pillows out from under her skirt and with the baby in her arms she made the rounds of all her neighbors. Enraptured, they would kiss the baby.

"At last," they would say. "Late, but the merciful Lord heard your prayers … " She would thank them, proud and happy.

On the 29th of May, 1944, Barbara and Jan took their baby and a pair of friends to the parish church. "*Archdiocese of Lwów, Latin rite. Parish of St. Maria Magdalena*" stated the birth certificate signed by Father Szogun and stamped with an oval seal—*"Officium Parochia. Leopoli …* " In the middle of the seal there was a heart with the leaping holy flame. In the evening there was a modest reception. Because of the curfew, the guests stayed till morning. The Jewish woman spent the entire night in the wardrobe.

The Russians entered the city on the 27th of July, 1944.

On the 28th of July, the Jewish woman disappeared.

That left three of them: Barbara, Jan, and the three-month-old baby with blue eyes and thin black curls.

## 3

They arrived in the new Poland with one of the first transports.

They settled in Częstochowa. (Regina's prewar acquaintance told them her distant relatives had lived there.)

When they entered the flat, Jan put the suitcase down, laid the baby on the bed, and ran out of the house.

The following day, he left at dawn.

He searched for her day after long day. He wandered the streets, checked in at the offices, asked about Jewish homes, stopped people of Jewish appearance … He stopped looking for her only after a visit from two men who introduced themselves as Regina's envoys. They offered a large sum of money and asked for the baby.

"Our daughter is not for sale," said Barbara and Jan, and sent the visitors away empty-handed.

Their daughter was a good and pretty girl.

Father spoiled her. He would take her to football matches, to the cinema, to cafés. At home, he would go into raptures about her ravishing beauty, especially her hair: waist-long tresses curled into French locks.

When little Hela was six, parcels began to arrive. They were sent from Hamburg. The sender was a woman bearing a strange foreign name. "It's your godmother," explained Barbara. "I hope she won't have an easy death, but write her a nice 'thank-you' letter."

At first little Hela dictated her letters, then wrote them herself. "Thank you. Dear Auntie, I am doing well at school, I dream of a little white angora cardigan, but a mohair one would be even nicer."

In the next parcel there would be a white cardigan. Little Hela would be overjoyed, while Barbara would sigh: "If there is a God, she won't have an easy death. Sit down and write your letter. You can mention your first communion and that we could do with some white taffeta."

Sometimes, the parcels had banknotes in them. There were no letters; only once, among the bars of chocolate, there was a photograph. It showed a dark lady wearing a black dress, with a long fox fur over the shoulder.

"It's silver fox," noted Barbara. "She is not that poor, is she." But they did not manage to get a good look, for Father took the photograph out of Barbara's hand and hid it somewhere.

Little Hela did not like Father's rapturous adoration. She found it tiresome. She would be doing her homework, or playing with her girlfriends, while he sat and stared at her. Then he would take her face into his hands and again stare at her. Then he would begin to cry.

He stopped drawing fancy letters.

He took to drink.

He cried more and more, drank more and more, and then he died. But before he died—some six months before his death—Hela went to France. She was twenty-five then. A girlfriend invited her to come, to recover from the trauma of her recent divorce. She came home beaming with joy, precious passport in hand. Father was drunk. He looked at the passport and embraced her.

"Stop by in Germany," he said. "Go and see your mother."

"My godmother," Hela corrected him.

"Mother," repeated Father.

"Mother is sitting next to me, smoking a cigarette."

"Your mother lives in Hamburg."

## 4

She changed at Aachen.

She arrived in Hamburg at seven a.m., left the suitcase at the station, and bought a map. She waited in a little square, and at nine o'clock she stopped in front of a large mansion in a quiet, affluent part of town. She pressed the doorbell.

"*Wer ist da?*" a voice asked from behind the door.

"Hela."

"*Was?*"

"Hela. Open up."

The door opened. In the doorway she saw herself appear; Hela, black hair piled high, blue eyes, the chin a little too round. It was Hela, only as if strangely aged.

"Why have you come?"

"To see you."

"Why?"

"I wanted to see my mother."

"Who told you?"

"Father."

A maid brought in the tea. They sat in the dining room, among the white furniture painted with little flowers.

"It's true, I gave birth to you," said the mother.

"I had to. I had to agree to everything."

"I wanted to live."

"I don't want to remember your father."

"I don't want to remember that time."

She did not pay any attention to Hela's crying, louder and louder.

She kept repeating the same words.

"I was scared."

"I had to live."

"You remind me of the fear."

"I don't want to remember."

"Don't come here anymore."

## 5

Hela married again; this time an Austrian. The somewhat too-quiet, boring owner of an alpine chalet near Innsbruck.

She came to Poland for the anniversary of her father's death. She and her mother went to the cemetery. (She called Barbara "Mother"; the woman who gave birth to her she spoke of as "the one from Hamburg.") Later, when they sat down for a cup of tea, Barbara said:

"After my death, you will find everything in the drawer with the saucepan lids."

Hela bridled at this; then she confessed she was pregnant and that she was worried about the birth.

"You have nothing to worry about," Barbara cried.

"I was older than you, and thinner, and my water broke too early, and I had no problem giving birth."

Hela got scared, but Barbara was behaving quite normally.

"Should I inform The One from Hamburg when the child is born?"

"Do as you like … That woman has done me a lot of harm, but you do as you like. My God," Barbara sank into thought, "how happy we were without her. How full of joy. If it were not for her, we could be happy till the end of our lives … "

"If it were not for her you would not have me," thought Hela but could not say it to the mother who had given birth to her without a problem even though she was older and thinner.

## 6

In the drawer, which Hela opened after Barbara's funeral, among the saucepan lids there lay two big envelopes. In one there was a wad of hundred-mark notes. In the other there was a copybook, divided into columns. "Date" and "Amount." Barbara had put away and noted down every banknote that came from Hamburg.

With the money, Hela bought long silver fox furs. She had a black dress made to go with them, but it turned out that the fur had been badly tanned and was losing hair; it did not go well with the black, either.

## 7

Several months after their wedding, she told her husband about the two mothers; she could not speak German then. She knew what wardrobe was—*Schrank.* Pillow—*Kissen*; she knew that, too. To hide—she found that in the dictionary: *verstecken.* And fear, too: *Angst.*

By the time she told the story for the second time, this time to her twenty-year-old son, she knew all the words. But she still could not give him an answer to a few obvious questions: Why didn't Granny Barbara leave Grandpa? Why did Granny Regina run away without you? Doesn't Granny Regina love you?"

"I don't know," she kept repeating. "How am I to know all this?"

"Look it up in the dictionary," her husband suggested.

## 8

Twenty-two years after the first meeting, The One from Hamburg invited her over for a few days. She showed her old photos; played Chopin mazurkas for her. ("The war interrupted my studies at the conservatoire," she sighed.) She recited Tuwim's poems. Told her about men. After the war she had had two husbands who adored her. Didn't have any children, but her husbands adored her.

"What about your husband?" she asked.

Hela had to admit that her second marriage was falling apart.

"It's because he's bought several new hotels … He doesn't want to sleep at home … He told me I should go ahead and start a new life … "

She was not speaking to her as if she were That One from Hamburg, but as if she were her own mother. But The One from Hamburg got frightened.

"Don't count on me. Everyone has to survive on her own. You have to know how to survive. I did. And you have to, too.

"You survived thanks to my parents, Hela reminded her.

"Thanks to your mother," The One from Hamburg corrected her.

"It's true, only thanks to her. It would have been enough to open the door and walk a few steps. The police station was across the street. It's amazing that she didn't open that door. I was constantly amazed that she didn't do it. Did she tell you anything about me?"

"She said that if it hadn't been for you … "

"I had to."

"I wanted to live."

She was shaking. She repeated the same words, louder, faster.

"I was scared."
"I had to."
"I wanted to."
"Don't come here ... "

## 9

"So what do you really want?" asked the solicitor whom she visited on her return from Hamburg. "Do you want her love or her money? As far as love is concerned, we don't deal with that sort of thing. As for the money, the case is just as difficult. First of all, we need proof she was your mother. Do you have witnesses? No? There you are. You should have obtained from Barbara S. a written statement. You should have had it confirmed by a notary. Now all we can do is a blood test Are you willing to bring the case to court? So why have you come to a solicitor's office?"

## 10

"So whose daughter are you then? And *who* are you?" asked her son.
"I am your mother," she said, though she should have said:
"I am the one who survived."
But that would be a line from a modern American novel.

—1993. Translated by Wiesiek Powaga

*Historical Notes.* Bełżec, where Regina's husband and probably her parents perished, is a village near Lublin in Eastern Poland, and the site of a Nazi German extermination camp.

The story takes place first in Lwów, today's Ukrainian Lviv. Following the Potsdam Conference of 1945, Lwów became part of the Ukrainian Soviet Socialist Republic, and most Polish residents were resettled to the west. Częstochowa, where Jan and Barbara moved to, is in the south central part of contemporary Poland.

Hamburg, in northern Germany, is a major European seaport and the second largest city in Germany.

*Poles and Jews in World War II.* Out of a prewar population of some three million, today there are fewer than 10,000 Jews left in Poland, this figure giving a stark indication of how many Polish Jews either perished during the war or emigrated to other countries after it. While about as many Polish citizens as Jewish died during the war (around three million in both instances), obviously a much larger percentage of Polish Jews died than non-Jews, although when millions of people are concerned, percentage comparisons seem meaningless. More Polish citizens than from any other nation have been awarded the Righteous Among Nations designation by Yad Vashem in Israel for having saved Jews during the war. By way of curious comparison, Holland has more such designees per population than any other country but, at the same time, the lowest percentage of Jews who survived the Holocaust.

Hanna Krall's story "The One from Hamburg," based on actual occurrences, even if sifted through Krall's way of telling them, raises the question of Polish-Jewish relations on a personal level in occupied Poland. This is an issue fraught with misinformation and recrimination on all sides, and the editor has no desire to get involved in it, even though, as the translator of two major Holocaust survival stories, he considers himself to be reasonably well informed on the subject. There are long and well documented lists of acts of both bravery and heroism as well as of cowardice and perfidy. As would be expected, most Poles, themselves living under constant terror, looked first after their own family and affairs. As Hanna Krall's own life testifies, each Holocaust survival story was unique and required the coordinated efforts of an entire chain of people willing to place at risk not only their own lives but also those of their family and neighbors. Objectively speaking, few Poles were placed in a position to be able to affect the unfolding genocide. Polish couriers from the underground resistance, at great personal risk, brought early news of the Nazi death camps to the attention of the Allies, reports which, at the highest levels of government, were roundly dismissed as too fantastic to be believed.

As for Jan's motivation for saving Regina in "The One from Hamburg," it is murky at best. He was both carnally and romantically drawn to her, while she clearly did what she felt she had to do in order to survive. Survive she did, even if not entirely emotionally intact. Another question relates to Barbara, and how soon she realized that through Regina she could realize the child she eventually hallucinates herself into believing was her own natural-born daughter. As is typical for Krall, many other questions one would like answered remain without clear resolution.

# Olga Tokarczuk

Olga Tokarczuk (born 1962) is one of Poland's most prolific and widely read authors of poetry, novels, and short stories, and she has been the recipient of a long string of literary awards, both Polish and international, culminating in the Nobel Prize for Literature in 2018. She was originally trained in clinical psychology at Warsaw University. Tokarczuk clearly dislikes repeating herself. Her works are extraordinarily diverse in subject matter, and each new major novel, some set in historical times, others in the world of today or even tomorrow, seems to go in an entirely different direction from anything written previously. She is a vegetarian out of sympathy for animals, and is an active spokesperson on ecological and progressive political issues. She has a special flare for the bizarre, and is a declared atheist, political leftist, and feminist, making her suspect with much of Poland's sizable conservative population.

Żurek ("ZHOO-rek"), the title of the story below, is a popular Polish soup made on a sour rye-bread starter, typically served with white sausage and a halved boiled egg. Contrary to what the stranger in this story says, similar soups are found in Czech, Slovak, and Belarusian cuisines, but they are nowhere near as popular there as they are in Poland, and are not similarly readily available in stores.

## Żurek Soup

"We should have brought the pram," said one woman to the other once they were on the road to the bus stop, which hadn't been snow-ploughed for ages.

The older one was carrying the child wrapped in a blanket that now, in the rapidly falling dusk, looked grey as if it was dirty. The younger one walked behind her mother, treading in her footprints in the snow—it was easier like that.

"We should have gone in daylight, not at night," the older woman spoke again.

"Should have, should have," said the younger. "I wasn't ready."

"There was no need to get dressed up like that."

"You were getting dressed up too."

"No I wasn't. I couldn't find my hat."

They only just caught the bus. It arrived steamed up and almost empty—like a blown egg made of metal. There was a gang of teenagers squashed into the back seat. They must have been off to town for the disco. The younger woman kept staring at them furtively, but avidly. She was eyeing up the girls, especially the one in a leather jacket and tight jeans. Her mother softly asked her a question, but she just snarled in reply. Then she wiped the steamed-up window and gazed into the gloom outside, where lights were twinkling. The young people travelled onwards, but the two women got out at the next stop, where a side road joined the dual carriageway, along which some big lorries went roaring by.

They passed a festively illuminated motel and reached the fish and chip shop. They stopped for a moment in front of a sign saying "Always Coca-Cola", which lit up the façade of the newly renovated house like a vast red moon.

"Shall we call him out here, or how are we going to do it?" asked the mother.

"You go, I'll wait here with the child."

The older woman went inside and came back soon after.

"He's not there. He's at home."

They gave each other a quick glance and headed into the yard.

A dog tied to its kennel started barking. A light came on automatically. The snow had mercifully covered all the construction yard clutter—stacks of planks, packs of Styrofoam wrapped in plastic and pyramids of hollow bricks. Władysław was building a garage.

He came out to meet them. A well-built gingery man in a knitted sweater with sleeves that were unravelling relentlessly, he stared at them in amazement.

"What are you doing here at this time of day?" he asked without saying hello.

"We've got business to discuss," said the older woman.

"Really?" he drawled, even more amazed.

"Can we come in?"

He hesitated, but only for a second, almost imperceptibly. He let them inside, into a freshly plastered hall where small lumps of cement crunched under their shoes. They went into a messy kitchen. He must have been tinkering with some part of the sink, because the cupboard had been detached from the wall, revealing the mysteries of pipes and U-bends.

"Can we sit down?" asked the older woman.

He set out two chairs for them, almost in the very middle of the kitchen, lit himself a cigarette and leaned against the dismounted cupboard. Only now did he see the child, and smiled.

"A boy or a girl?"

"A boy, a boy," replied the younger woman and unwrapped the child from the blanket.

She pushed the woolly blue bonnet off his eyes. The child was asleep. His wrinkled little face reminded Władysław of a freshly shelled hazelnut. It was ugly.

"Lovely," he said. "What's his name?"

"He hasn't got one yet," said the younger woman gaily.

"Władysław," the older one was quick to offer.

"Władysław?" he said in amazement. "Who calls a child Władysław these days?"

He scowled and dragged on his cigarette.

"Your name is Władysław, and so's his ... " the older woman continued.

"Maybe it is—who said it's not?"

There was a silence. The man flicked ash onto the floor.

"Well then?"

The woman averted her gaze towards the tip of a curtain rod that was leaning against the wall and said in that direction: "It's your child, Władysław. The holidays are coming, so we want to christen him."

The man's face hardened.

"You must be fucking crazy, Halina. How can it be my child? Come on, Iwonka," he said, turning to the girl, "how can it be my child? What are you two on about?"

Iwonka chewed her lip and began to rock the child rapidly. It woke up and had a short cry.

"Who is the father?" he asked.

"You are. It's your child."

The man stood up and stubbed the cigarette out on his shoe.

"That's enough. Get out of here, both of you."

They got up reluctantly. Iwonka pulled the baby's little blue bonnet over his eyes.

"Come on, come on," he chivvied them.

"All right, Władysław, in that case the father is your son Jacek," said the mother suddenly in the doorway without turning round.

"He was here for Easter," added Iwonka truculently.

"Get lost."

The door closed behind them. They stood in silence on the dirty, trodden snow. After a while the light went out.

"Now what?" Iwonka asked her mother.

"What do you think? Nothing."

The bus wasn't due for an hour, so they headed home on foot.

"I told you to bring the pram. Now it'll take us at least an hour."

"Better walk than wait at the bus stop and get frozen."

That night the child was restless. Iwonka slept like the dead, so her mother wetted the corner of a nappy in warm water and gave it to the baby to suck. His little lips began to squirm. Firelight flickered through chinks in the kitchen range.

Next morning both women were in the shop. Iwonka bought herself a Magnum ice cream. It cost a fortune. Her mother reproached her, saying it wasn't even the money, but that she'd catch cold and lose her breast milk. Iwonka calmly ate the ice cream and shrugged. The child was asleep in a bright blue pram.

"What a pretty little chap," the shop lady gushed; she had come onto the steps outside wearing a non-iron white overall on top of her sweater. "Oh, how cold it is!"

Soon a queue had formed in the shop, as was usually the case around noon. This time it wasn't just the local men coming in for cheap wine or people driving through wanting cola and nuts for the journey to the border. Today the housewives had come for cake flavourings, vanilla sugar, margarine and raisins. With as much care as a pharmacist, the shop lady was weighing out marshmallows, chocolate-coated jellies and special Christmas sweets, where what counted most were the shiny gold and purple wrappers—these little beauties were to hang on the Christmas tree. The customers weren't at all concerned about the queue moving quickly, far from it—as soon as they took their turn at the counter, each of them chatted with the shop lady, who would abandon her columns of figures and little bags of baking powder, lean on the counter and listen to the tales they had brought. It even looked as if they weren't using money to pay, as if the money were just ritual pebbles. For raisins, baking powder and cheap wine you paid with a little story, a question or some witty repartee. That was why it was taking so long.

A smart dark green car stopped outside the shop, one of those very new ones with a high, box-shaped back. There were skis on the roof. A man got out of the car, wearing a fleece, Goretex gloves and a funny cap. He said something to a woman who stayed in the car with two teenage children, then skipped into the shop and took his place at the end of the queue, right behind Matuszek.

"Got any żurek soup?" asked the fleecy fellow, rubbing his hands and added inconsequentially: "Brrr, it's cold."

This question about żurek soup soured the chatty atmosphere. Called to order in mid-monologue, the shop lady glanced round at the newcomer.

"Żurek soup, the kind in bottles. Or it could be in a jar—I don't know what kind you usually have, the bottles or the jars."

"Żurek soup," said Mrs Matwiejuk, prompting the shop lady as she began to pack her small purchases into a plastic bag.

Everyone cast a discreet glance at the visitor. The snow was melting on his brightly coloured, trendy snow boots. The yellow label on his sky-blue jacket announced some garish truth in a foreign language. The shop lady glanced at the bottom shelf.

"There is some," she said. "The last bottle."

"So it's in bottles. Where we are, up north, we've got żurek soup in jars," explained the man, looking around cheerfully at the customers' faces. "We're on a skiing trip to Austria for the holidays and my wife insisted we must have żurek soup, and this is the last shop before the border," he said, more quietly now, addressing himself for some unknown reason to Matuszek.

Matuszek turned his head away and gazed calmly at the cigarette brands on display in a glass case. The queue moved forward one place in silence as Mrs Matwiejuk stood counting her change by the door.

"What's Christmas without żurek soup?" the man spoke again. His high, ringing, confident voice had a wounding effect on the ears. "It's our Polish speciality. I've been in lots of countries in Europe and all over the world, but they never have żurek soup. So I thought, as I was driving along, if I don't buy it here, I won't get it anywhere. They don't have żurek soup in the Czech Republic."

No one answered. The man began to stamp his feet and blow on his hands. Confused by the presence of a stranger, the shop lady, that talkative shop lady, was doing her job efficiently and thoroughly. The queue was moving forward quickly, too quickly, because no one was in a hurry.

"It's cold," said the stranger to Matuszek, rubbing his hands together again in a theatrical way.

Matuszek glanced at him and gave the faintest flicker of a smile out of politeness, then turned to face the cigarettes in the display case again.

"We've got an apartment booked in the Alps. My God, they've got great ski lifts there—what a place. It takes an hour or even better to come down. And there's a bar and a pool in the hotel at the bottom. We do our own meals. There's a kitchen in every apartment, so my wife'll be able to heat up the żurek soup. And I'll take a bit of sausage too, but a good one, mind. Have they got good sausage here?" he asked, suddenly sounding concerned.

The next woman reluctantly moved away from the counter. The shop lady unzipped her sweater at the neck.

"I can see there is some, but sausage that only costs six zlotys can't be any good," said the man.

A car horn sounded. The man went over to the door and let a swirling cloud of frozen air into the shop. He shouted something in the direction of the car and came back to his place in line.

"The woman's fretting because we're supposed to be in the Alps by evening. But I felt like a bit of żurek soup."

Matuszek bought some cigarettes, some orange flavouring, a half litre of vodka and some bread. The shop lady efficiently added up the column of figures and wrapped the bottle in the bill.

"And some żurek soup," he said. "A bottle of żurek soup."

The whole shop went extremely quiet. The shop lady solemnly passed him the bottle. Matuszek quickly paid.

"Hey, mister … " the man in the fleece began, totally astonished, but in an instant Matuszek had picked up his shopping and left.

Outside the shop he saw Halina and her not-quite-all-there daughter, and handed her the bottle.

"Take it. We don't eat żurek soup—we prefer beetroot," he said, and told her to drop in that evening for a long promised quilt.

Iwonka was too shy to go in. She stood by the fence with her teeth chattering, goodness knows whether from cold or fear.

"What are you afraid of, you ninny? They're not going to eat you. You should have been afraid then, not now," her mother told her.

"There are some blokes in there. You go, I'll wait here with the baby."

"It's a good thing they are—maybe now we'll manage to get something sorted. In front of witnesses. Come on!"

The girl followed her reluctantly.

Four men were sitting at the kitchen table. Matuszek had just poured the last round. His wife, big and stout, was bustling about straining the milk. A yeast cake with crumble topping was cooling on the sideboard. It was nice and warm.

"Mother, the girls have come for the eiderdown," said Matuszek.

He drew up the one empty chair for them. Halina sat down on the edge of it, while Iwonka stood by the door with the child.

"Well, cheers," said Góral and knocked back his glass. Without a word the others did the same, cleared their throats and drank some orangeade.

Mrs Matuszek left the room and came straight back with a bundle wrapped in plastic and tied with string. She cooed at the child.

"What's his name?"

"He hasn't got one yet," Halina was quick to reply.

Iwonka started shuffling nervously on the spot.

"When's the christening?"

Halina shrugged.

"That's a decent quilt," said Mrs Matuszek. "Aired all summer in the attic. Have you got a cover?"

"He's the father," Iwonka suddenly blurted sombrely, nodding at Góral.

There was an awkward silence.

"Well, Iwonka?" her mother encouraged her.

"You're the father," said the girl, looking him straight in the eye now.

Mrs Matuszek lifted the baby's bonnet from his brow and took a close look at him.

"I've got my four," said Góral at last. "Leave me in peace, girl, you haven't a clue who you've slept with."

"Well!" said Halina ominously.

"I've slept with her," shouted Kawka.

His speech was slurred and his eyes were shining drunkenly. The fellow hadn't a head for drink.

"Yes, I've slept with her," he repeated slowly. "But I s-l-e-p-t; I was so drunk I went out like a light, so it wasn't me."

"She's already been to Władysław's and tried to pin it on him. Who knows whose child it is … "

"A child is a child," said Mrs Matuszek.

"She was carrying on with a soldier from the watchtower. Everyone saw them," added Góral. "Like looking for a needle in a haystack."

He got up, took his cap from the peg and moved towards the door.

"My God," groaned Mrs Matuszek. "Why didn't you keep an eye on her? Halina, it's your fault, it's your fault."

"Is that what you think? What was I supposed to do? Tie her up by the leg? I'd like to know how you'd have managed. She's a child in the body of a mature woman."

"Jerzyk?" said Mrs Matuszek suddenly full of suspicion, turning to the youngest man, her nephew.

Góral stopped in the doorway.

Jerzyk blushed to the tips of his ears, making his piercingly blue highlander's eyes appear to light up.

"It wasn't me, Auntie, I was careful."

Kawka broke into a fitful cackle.

"It'll take at least half a litre to get that one sorted. Well, Mrs Matuszek, time to put out more drink."

Mrs Matuszek stood helplessly in the middle of the kitchen looking now at Jerzyk, now at Góral, now at her husband. She seemed even fatter now, as heavy as a piece of furniture. Everyone was waiting for her to say something, and her lips were twitching, as if trying to form the shape of a special term to cover everything at once, from start to finish. But plainly she couldn't do it, because she went up to the table, slapped her hand on the oilcloth surface and said: "That's enough drinking. Go now, tomorrow's Christmas Eve, you've work to do at home."

She grabbed the bundle and thrust it into Halina's arms. Halina embraced it like a monstrous great baby nest, buried her face in the plastic and burst into tears. Mrs Matuszek began feverishly clearing the table. Without a word the guests got up and headed for the door.

Just then her husband spoke up.

"Wait a moment, wait a moment," he said. "Hold on."

He stopped talking, as if he was still thinking, as if he was trying to make a decision, and drummed his fingers on the table.

"I am the baby's father."

There was a long silence. There he sat; his wife went on standing in the middle of the kitchen while everyone else remained crowded in the doorway in a puddle of melted snow. Then Mrs Matuszek screamed at the top of her voice: "Have you gone mad? You can't have children. We haven't had a child in twenty years and everyone knows you can't have children because you had an accident."

"Be quiet, woman. Shut up. It's my child."

Kawka staggered over to a chair and sat down.

"All right, then. As that's the case, you'd better put out more drink …"

Shifting from foot to foot, Iwonka was nonchalantly rocking the baby.

"But you can't …" Mrs Matuszek started up again, as her plump hands found the hem of her apron and pressed it to her eyes. Then she ran out, slamming the door.

Matuszek reached over to the sideboard and fetched out a bottle. He took the glasses from the sink and poured six shots of vodka.

"She won't," said Halina, pointing at Iwonka. "She's not eighteen yet. And she's breast-feeding."

They drank up in solemn silence.

"So when's the christening?" asked Matuszek.

"The priest said it could be around New Year."

"Then here's to the christening around New Year," mumbled Kawka and emptied his glass before anyone else.

Then Matuszek told them all to go home. He said tomorrow was Christmas Eve and they had work to do. In the doorway Halina wiped her tears on her sleeve and smiled at Matuszek.

"Thank you for the żurek soup," she said.

They walked home across country, over pure, virgin snow, Iwonka treading in her mother's footprints.

—2000. Translation © by Antonia Lloyd-Jones

*Notes.* This Olga Tokarczuk "holiday story" was written for the newspaper *Gazeta Wyborcza* in 1999 and was later published alongside other Christmas stories by various authors in 2000. Director Ryszard Brylski made a 2003 film adaptation of "Żurek" which took considerable liberties with an otherwise extremely spare and ambiguous plot. The story consists of a series of encounters with and accusations against a young mother's baby's possible fathers, whose relationships with the girl, Iwonka, are never made clear. Her mother, Halina, wants to identify the father so that he can be registered as such during the christening of the baby at the church. What becomes clear is that the baby realistically could have had any one of many possible fathers; his identity is never revealed.

The bleak existence of Halina and Iwonka, and the icy chill they endure as they make their trek on foot and by bus around their town, stretched out along a highway near the southern border with the Czech Republic, contrasts with the idea of the upcoming holidays, meant to be a time of warmth and family cheer and communion. Juxtaposed with the Christmastime decorations and Christian belief in Mary's virgin birth is the more profane truth of Iwonka's seemingly numerous sexual partners and her own baby's ignoble origins. Iwonka is mentally developmentally delayed, a child in a woman's body, whose attractiveness to men possibly compensates her for the awareness of her "difference."

At last, on the night before Christmas Eve, a family friend, Matuszek, stands up in front of his wife and inebriated guests (one of whom Iwonka, on the spur of the moment, had just fingered as the baby's father) and claims that he is the father despite his infertility resulting from an accident suffered years earlier. Matuszek gives Iwonka the Christmas present of a name, so that now the child can be baptized, at the same time releasing the real father, whoever he is, from responsibility.

Matuszek in general is a generous soul, but this specific act of generosity serves also to compensate him for his own infertility. As she leaves Matuszek's, Halina thanks him for the bottle of żurek he had given her earlier. In a brilliant depiction of Polish *bezinteresowna złość* (disinterested malevolence toward those luckier than we are) in the local food store, Matuszek had bought the last bottle of żurek out from under the nose of a passing winter tourist whose fancy car and ski clothing rub him and the locals in the store the wrong way. Also, in that part of the country (the southwest), people call the soup "white borsch," so they additionally hold it against him that he does not know the local word for the soup. Like the soup, for Halina Matuszek's gift of his name is sour-tasting like the soup, but, as the skier says, "It's our Polish speciality."

*Christian Imagery.* The story "Żurek" is sprinkled with ironic comparisons with the New Testament Christmas story, to the extent that it can be taken as a travesty of it. In the biblical story, the purpose of Mary and Joseph's journey to Bethlehem is to be registered, similar to Halina and Iwonka's wanting to register Iwonka and her boychild with the church. Like Mary, Iwonka is an unmarried young woman who has gotten herself pregnant. Also like Mary, Iwonka probably knows the identity of the father, but she is not saying who it is. Joseph, who is much older than Mary, takes her as wife, although he is not the child's father. He does so as a good deed, so the baby will not be born out of wedlock. In "Żurek" Matuszek plays the role of Joseph when he assumes paternity over the baby. The three drunk friends paying Matuszek a visit on the night before Christmas Eve play the modern counterpart of the Three Wise Men (although they have no gifts to bring), while back at Władek's fish-fry place the flashing Coca-Cola sign serves as a modern-day beckoning Star of Bethlehem. The fish itself is an early Christian image, both because of the miracle of the loaves and fish in the Sermon on the Mount and the story of Jesus's recruiting Simon Peter and Andrew as "fishers of men."

In Tokarczuk's story modern reality is debased and tawdry when compared to the more picturesque and spiritual life of two thousand years ago. At the same time, and without any subtlety, her portrayal casts doubt on details of the Christmas story itself, including the doctrine of the virginity of Mary and the divine paternity of Jesus. As if to drive the message home, on the way back from Matuszek's Halina and Iwonka trod over what is described as the *niepokalany śnieg* (immaculate or virginal) snow. Iwonka's following in her mother's foot tracks suggests that Iwonka's own birth had similarly come out of wedlock some sixteen years earlier. One never hears word of there being any husband in the picture.

*Structure.* "Żurek" has an interesting tripartite structure, not corresponding to the normal parts of a short story. Instead they are vignette-like episodes, with the first and last scenes more or less mirror-matching, in the sense that in the first scene one of the proposed fathers, Władysław, rejects the idea of his paternity over the son, while in the last scene Matuszek, who could not possibly be the father, accepts his fatherhood. The two book-end scenes are separated by the central "żurek" scene in the local food store.

The three structural parts reflect the Holy Trinity. If the first scene is the "son" scene, and the last is the "father" scene, then the "żurek" scene must be the scene of the Holy Spirit. Tokarczuk sees in żurek something of the essence of the Polish spirit: sour but nourishing.

Without going into detail, in the provocative film version of the story by Ryszard Brylski, the father of Iwonka's child is revealed to be her own father, a person who does not figure in the original story, but who in the film committed suicide once he realized he had gotten his daughter pregnant. If God can be said to be in a sense the father of Mary's child, then that would add yet another layer of travesty to Tokarczuk's story.

# SOURCES

Andrzejewski, Jerzy, "The Gold Fox," in *The Modern Polish Mind,* edited by Maria Kuncewicz, translated by Barbara Vedder, Grosset and Dunlap, 1963. Reprinted courtesy of Marcin Andrzejewski.

Borowski, Tadeusz, "This Way for the Gas, Ladies and Gentlemen" in *This Way for the Gas, Ladies and Gentlemen.* translated by Barbara Vedder, Penguin Books, 1976. Copyright © 1959 by Maria Borowski; translation copyright © 1967 by Penguin Books Ltd. Used by permission of Viking Books, an imprint of Penguin Publishing Group, a division of Penguin Random House LLC. All rights reserved.

Brandys, Kazimierz, "How to Be Loved," translated by Oscar Swan, from *Jak być kochaną i inne opowiadania.* Czytelnik, 1970. Translated by permission of the Foundation for the Preservation of Jewish Heritage in Poland (FODŻ).

Conrad, Joseph, "The Tale," in *The Tale.* Hesperus Modern Voices, 2008.

Dąbrowska, Maria, "Father Philip," translated by Oscar Swan, from *Znaki życia,* Czytelnik, 1962.

Głowacki, Janusz. "The Visit," translated by Oscar Swan, from *Polowanie na muchy i inne opowiadania,* PIW, 1974. Translated by permission of Zuza Głowacka, on behalf of the Estate of Janusz Głowacki.

Gombrowicz, Witold, "A Premeditated Murder," in *Bacacaj,* translated by Bill Johnston. Archipelago Books, 2004. Reprinted by permission of Archipelago Books.

Hłasko, Marek, "A Lovely Girl," "The Most Sacred Words of Our Lives," translated by Oscar Swan, from *Pierwszy krok w chmurach.* Elf, 2003. Translated by permission of Agnieszka Czyżewska.

Iwaszkiewicz, Jarosław, "Tatarak," published as "Sweet Flag" in *The Modern Polish Mind,* edited by Maria Kuncewicz, translated by Celina Wieniewska, Grosset and Dunlap, 1963. Copyright © The Estate of Jarosław Iwaszkiewicz. All rights reserved. Published by arrangement with Beata Stasińska Literary Agency.

Iwaszkiewicz, Jarosław, "Róża," translated by Oscar Swan, as "Rose," Czytelnik. Copyright © The Estate of Jarosław Iwaszkiewicz. All rights reserved. Published by arrangement with Beata Stasińska Literary Agency.

Krall, Hanna, "The One from Hamburg" translated by Wiesiek Powaga, in *The Chicago Review,* vol. 46, no. 3/4. Reprinted by courtesy of Wiesiek Powaga and Hanna Krall.

Lem, Stanisław. "Tale of the Computer That Fought a Dragon," from *Mortal Engines* by Stanislaw Lem. Translated from the Polish by Michael Kandel. English translation copyright © 1977 by The Continuum Publishing Company. Used by permission of HarperCollins Publishers.

Mrożek, Sławomir, "The Elephant," translated by Konrad Syrop, in *The Mrozek Reader* copyright © 1992 by Diogenes Verlag AG, Zurich. Used by permission of Grove/

Atlantic, Inc. Any third-party use of this material, outside of this publication, is prohibited.

Nałkowska, Zofia, "Professor Spanner," "By the Railroad Tracks," translated by Diana Kuprel in *Medallions*, Northwestern University Press, 2000. Originally published in Polish in 1946 under the title *Medaliony*. English translation copyright © 2000 by Northwestern University Press. Published 2000 by arrangement with Irena Wróblewska and Joanna Wróblewska-Kujawska. All rights reserved.

Norwid, Cyprian Kamil, "Ad Leones," translated by Ilona Ralf Sues, in *Polish Short Stories*, edited by Zbigniew Żabicki, Polonia Publishing House, 1960.

Orzeszkowa, Eliza, "Miss Antonina," translated by Janina Rodzińska, in *Polish Short Stories*, edited by Zbigniew Żabicki, Polonia Publishing House, 1960.

Pasek, Jan Chrysostom, "The Year of Our Lord 1680," translated by Catherine S. Leach, in *Memoirs of the Polish Baroque*, University of California Press, 1980. Reprinted by permission of the Copyright Clearance Center, on behalf of the University of California Press.

Potocki, Jan, "Story of Thibaud de la Jacquière," "Story of the Gentle Dariolette of the Châtel de Sombre," in *The Saragossa Manuscript: A Collection of Weird Tales*, translated by Elisabeth Abbott, Orion Press, 1960.

Prus, Bolesław, "The Waistcoat," "The Barrel Organ," translated by Bill Johnston, in *The Sins of Childhood and Other Stories by Bolesław Prus*, Northwestern University Press, 1997. English translation and compilation copyright © 1996 by Northwestern University Press. Published 1996. All rights reserved.

Prus, Bolesław, "From the Legends of Ancient Egypt," translated by Oscar Swan, from *Wolne Lektury*, https://wolnelektury.pl/katalog/lektura/z-legend-dawnego-egiptu/.

Rzewuski, Henryk, "I Am Burning," translated by Oscar Swan, from *Polska nowela fantastyczna tom 1*, ed. Julian Tuwim. Alfa, 1983.

Schulz, Bruno, "Pan," "Nimrod," "Father's Final Escape," translated by Madeline Levine in *Bruno Schulz, Collected Stories*, Northwestern University Press, 2018. © Copyright for English translation by The Polish Book Institute.

Sienkiewicz, Henryk, "Yamioł," translated by Jeremiah Curtin, in *Yanko the Musician and Other Stories*, Little Brown and Company, 1893.

Sienkiewicz, Henryk, "Yanko the Musician," translated by Oscar Swan, from *Wolne Lektury*, https://wolnelektury.pl/szukaj/?q=janko+muzykant.

Tokarczuk, Olga, "Żurek Soup," translated by Antonia Lloyd-Jones, in *Elsewhere*, edited by Maria Crosson, Comma Press, 2007. Copyright © Olga Tokarczuk. Reproduced by permission of the author, c/o Rogers, Coleridge & White Ltd., 20 Powis Mews, London W11 1JN.

Woroszylski, Wiktor, "The Watch," in *The Modern Polish Mind*, edited by Maria Kuncewicz, translated by Barbara Vedder. Grosset and Dunlap, 1963. Reprinted by permission of Natalia Woroszylska.

# ILLUSTRATION CREDITS

Jerzy Andrzejewski, photo by Andrzej Szypowski / East News.
Tadeusz Borowski, cropped photo of Borowski at the Deutscher 1950 Schriftsteller-Kongress, Bundesarchiv, Bild 183-S98592 / Rudolph / CC-BY-SA 3.0 Germany License.
Joseph Conrad, by George Charles Beresford. © National Portrait Gallery, London.
Maria Dąbrowska, image courtesy of the Museum of Polish History in Warsaw
Janusz Głowacki, image courtesy of Ewa Zadrzyńska-Głowacka
Witold Gombrowicz, image courtesy of the Gombrowicz Museum in Wsola
Marek Hłasko, image courtesy of Agnieszka Czyżewska
Jarosław Iwaszkiewicz, image courtesy of the Archiwum Muzeum w Stawisku / Fotonowa
Hanna Krall, photo by Olaf, Creative Commons Attribution-Share Alike 3.0 Unported License.
Stanisław Lem, image courtesy of Tomasz Lem.
Sławomir Mrożek, photo by Mariusz Kubik, Creative Commons Attribution-Share Alike 3.0 Unported License.
Eliza Orzeszkowa, image courtesy of Muzeum Literatury / East News.
Jan Pasek. No image available, but portrait of Wespazjan Kochowski (1633–1700), reproduced courtesy of Museum of King John III's Palace at Wilanów.
Olga Tokarczuk, photo by Harald Krichel, Creative Commons Attribution-Share Alike 4.0 International license.
Wiktor Woroszylski © by Joanna Helander.

www.ingramcontent.com/pod-product-compliance
Lightning Source LLC
Chambersburg PA
CBHW060222030726
47499CB00004B/1148

* 9 7 8 0 9 4 0 9 6 2 1 7 0 *